BATTAGLIA MAFIA SERIES — BOOK 5

AMORE

SIENNA MYNX

Cover art by Reese Dante

Published by The Diva's Pen LLC
http://thedivaspen.com
diva@thedivaspen.com

First Edition March 2015
Printed in the United States of America

AMORE

PRELUDE

Villa Mare Blu - 1972, Mondello Beach / Palermo Sicily—

RAGE AND HURT SHOULD NEVER EXIST in a young boy at once. Blinded by tears, fifteen-year-old Giovanni Battaglia stormed down the stairs of his seaside home in search of sanctuary. The cellar welcomed him. It was a dark paneled, windowless cavity that only the men in the family frequented to smoke hand rolled cigars and guzzle homemade whiskey.

Hurt lashed his heart once more when he too recalled the room's prior personal use. Often he'd sneak Carmella inside through the cellar doors for a lover's kiss, and adventurous sex. The whore!

She was never his.

She betrayed him.

She was dead to him now.

Dead.

Dead.

Dead.

The chair flew from his hands and smashed into the wall. It splintered with two of its legs breaking. He threw everything within his reach. First went an oil lamp with a glass ball shade, and then a cedar box of cigars that had recently been delivered to his father. Bottles of aged whiskey flew from his hands. Each plucked out of the open crates and tossed as if they were bowling pins. Wet streaks of pungent liquor and kerosene splattered over the walls. Shattered glass shards littered the concrete floor.

It hurt to love.

That's what *amore* was—pain. He loved his mother and couldn't protect her. He loved his father and couldn't please him. He loved his girl and she betrayed him.

Giovanni Battaglia failed at love. He wanted to destroy something. He needed to destroy someone. He needed it more than he needed to breathe. Killing Armando Mancini was his intent. Even now he didn't know if he succeeded. Still he wished to do more harm. To himself and everyone that betrayed him.

"Hai una faccia tosta!" A voice boomed like a blast from a cannon behind him. Giovanni whirled on the intruder. He squinted in the shadowy darkness for clarity. Breathing was hard when angry. He exhaled deeply through flared nostrils. He stumbled backward and tried to remove any trace of tears from his face. But his actions were all the more revealing and the tears kept flowing. He heard *Patri* was in Palermo on business. No one expected him to return to Villa Mare Blu until the weekend.

He had been summoned.

"Answer me, boy! Who the fuck do you think you are?" Tomosino demanded. He descended the last stair and flipped the switch. Light flooded the room thanks to a single bulb hanging from the lowered ceiling. Giovanni squinted against the glare. He would have preferred the darkness.

Don Tomosino Battaglia was a lion amongst men. Not just in stature and build, but in ruthless intolerance. He wore a long tan trench coat splattered with wet spots from the rain, and a fedora that rested on his head. His father had just arrived and came in search of him. That meant he knew the truth—all of it.

Tomosino took off his hat and threw it. He shrugged off his coat and dropped it. Giovanni continued to step back. Tomosino rolled up one sleeve and then the other to the bend of his elbow. His hands curled into fists as large as boulders.

Giovanni glanced around at the destruction he'd done to his father's belongings, and shuddered inwardly over the expected consequences. Before he could explain the scene and his actions to his father, his left jaw caved in and the molar to the left side of his mouth loosened. The backhanded blow ripped through his face and rattled his skull. He was knocked into the shelf. Several bottles crashed on him and the floor.

"Disgraziato! Minchia fredda!" shouted his father. He was called a spineless pussy before his father delivered a swift kick to his stomach.

Giovanni nearly choked on his vomit.

"Get up, you worm!" his father growled, with spittle coating his lips. The savagery of the beating continued. "You're a man! Right? Right? *In piedi!*"

How was he to stand? He was being hit and kicked all over. His mind willed his body to obey, but he struggled to protect himself. Giovanni wept. He curled into a ball as his father's rage became unstoppable. Tears proved to be an unforgivable mistake. His father kicked him again! And again! This time he did spew his lunch. He tried to turn away from the kicks and suffered several to his back.

"*In piedi!* Be a man! You want to! You think you are! *In piedi!*"

"*Patri!*" he begged. "No more!"

How could Giovanni atone when nothing his father had shown him in his young life thus far prepared him for such gut churning emotion? His girlfriend and best friends betrayed him. He was the laughing stock of Mondello, Sicilia, hell the universe. He hated life. He hated his father. He hated everyone. He wept hard.

"You will answer for this. Do you hear me? Only *I* take a life! I alone decide who is punished! I will break your fucking neck for disgracing me!" His father grabbed him by the hair and brought Giovanni up to his feet. He delivered a bone-crushing blow to the center of his face, either with his fist or a weapon. Giovanni did not know. Darkness began to descend on his mind, and his vision rolled up in his head. He heard a woman scream. *Was it Carmella?* When Giovanni plunged the knife into Armando she had screamed, and her screams chased him all the way back to Villa Mare Blu.

No! No. It wasn't Carmella, the whore. It was his mother. She screamed so hysterically that the sound stopped his father's hands from crushing his throat. Giovanni sagged against the wall. His face was bloody, his nose dripped blood, he spit up a tooth and more blood from the back of his mouth. He blinked awake in time to see his pregnant mother charge at his father with her fists. Her long red hair whipped about as she fought with no consideration of the danger she put herself and her unborn child in.

"Don't you ever hit him!" she screamed. "Don't you ever touch him!" she wept. "Ever! Ever! Ever! Ever! Ever!"

Tomosino tried to calm his mistress, the mother of his only son. He took her by the arms to still her, but it was of no use. She fought him with the same madness his father used when he attacked Giovanni. The only defense left to Tomosino was to back away from them both. Evelyn came to her knees and pulled Giovanni over into her arms. She stroked his face. She kissed his brow.

She glared up at his father while cradling Giovanni to her breast. "You swore to me, Tomosino. On your life! You swore you'd never raise a hand to any of us. You swore it. But you are a monster who lies! A monster who could beat his own son with his own fists. THE DEVIL! I hate you for this! I hate you!"

"The boy's actions today, Eve. He has put this family in jeopardy. He knifed the son of Don Mancini—"

"You swore!" she shouted him down, and Tomosino silenced. "He is your blood! How much blood have I lost to give you your son? Whatever his crimes are, he's learned the sin from you!"

Tomosino looked down at his hands bruised and reddened by Giovanni's blood. He shook his head in disbelief over either his own actions or his mother's prophetic words. Giovanni wasn't sure. What he did see out of his bleary vision was his father's retreat. No one living or dead could make his father retreat other than his mother.

"I'm not a monster. *Perdonami per favore*," his father said before he was gone.

"Let me go, *Madre*." Giovanni tried to escape his mother's embrace. He tried to be a man and rise to his feet. He could not. When he broke free of her she grabbed his face and it hurt. He crumbled. He wept. He cried in pain and humiliation. She made him look into her eyes.

"Listen to me. I want you to go upstairs and pack a bag. You will go to *Zio* Vito's. I don't want you here or near your father now. I know what you've done," she wept. She shook her head and wept. She gathered her strength to continue, and it pained him to see her do so. "You're my son. I love you, no matter the crime. God help me. God bless your your soul, Giovanni. This is my fault. I should have fought harder to keep you from this… from him. I'm weak. I failed you."

"*Madre*, no, no. It's my fault. Don't cry."

Eve nodded but the tears continued to fall. "Please, Gio. Do as I say. Do you understand me? Stay away from your father until his temper cools."

Giovanni nodded and blinked away his tears. "Armando Mancini deserved it. He deserved it, Ma-Ma!"

"The reason doesn't matter now, Gio. What you did will put your father at war with the Mancinis. Rocco is on his way. Stay out of your father's sight. Do you understand me? Say you understand! Say it!"

"*Sí, sí, Madre,* I understand." He nodded.

"And I will pray for us all," she said.

Four Days later –

Giovanni wiped the damp rag down his face. The swelling to his left eye had ripened to the point of shutting. But he could see out of both. His nose was broken. The *dottore* had insisted he wear a splint to keep it from misshaping horribly. It was the bruise to his stomach and back from *Patri's* kicks that made his aunts weep whenever they caught sight of him without his shirt. Still each day the physical pain hurt less and less.

"Gio!"

"Avanti," Giovanni answered.

He walked out of the small bathroom into his room. Lorenzo and Santo entered. Carlo and Nico were noticeably absent. Though he was still angry at his friends, it was Lorenzo's betrayal that hurt him the most. However, he'd rather have them visit than continue to suffer under forced exile alone.

Santo closed the door.

"Is he dead?" Giovanni asked.

"Who? Armando? No. But the pig squeals."

Giovanni's gaze slowly lifted. Lorenzo looked to Santo and then back to him. "Alejandro is dead. They bury him tomorrow. It wasn't your fault, Gio. He got in the way of your strike. I told *Patri* this. The fight with Armando got out of hand."

The news of Alejandro's death did not catch him by surprise. He heard his aunt's whisper about it days ago. Giovanni went to his bed and sat. He had never imagined he'd be responsible for taking someone's life. He'd seen it from his father's and uncles' hands, but never his own. He closed his eyes and accepted the grim responsibility. It was Lorenzo who approached him. It was Lorenzo who betrayed him.

"You made me do this," Giovanni said to his cousin. "I think it was you that set me up, to see her that way. Wasn't it?"

"It was him, Gio," Santo confirmed. But Santo couldn't look him in the eye. He didn't trust the opinion of anyone who could not look him in the eye.

"Shut the fuck up!" Lorenzo hissed. Lorenzo stared down at Giovanni but offered no explanation. He knew they treaded carefully around him. None of them had killed a person before. Giovanni had unintentionally garnered respect among his friends and cousin that would shadow him for the rest of his life. His cousin spoke in a low contrite voice. "We can't visit long. Vito isn't here but he will return. He's out with *Patri* now. They meet with the Mancinis."

Giovanni nodded. He again looked at his hands and remembered the knife and blood.

"Gio, I am sorry. What we did. What I did. I shouldn't have. We were in trouble because of your obsession with that *puttana*. It made you look weak! I only did this to make us strong. I make you strong, Gio," Lorenzo said.

"It is time for you to shut your fucking mouth!" Giovanni slowly stood. "Santo's right. You betrayed me. You have blood on your hands too!"

"She's a whore! I didn't force her! You saw her, Gio. Did it look like I forced her?" he shouted. "What is my crime? I'm your brother! Your blood brother! You had us fighting with Mancini in the streets for her. They laughed at you. They don't laugh anymore do they?" Lorenzo smiled.

Giovanni cast his gaze away. Lorenzo put his hand on his shoulder. "Yes, I was wrong. But so were you, Gio, about her and everything. You see that now. Eh? With me at your side I will always make sure you do the right thing, because I love you, brother. I will protect you."

The words failed Giovanni. He could barely process any of it now. Walking in on his girlfriend sucking the dick of his greatest nemesis, while his cousin and friends laughed, broke something in him. It wasn't just her betrayal, but his inability to not see it in her. It made him weak and Lorenzo was right to wake him up.

"Where is Carlo? Nico?" Giovanni asked. "Why aren't they here?"

Lorenzo looked back at Santo, who again kept his eyes trained to the floor. And then Lorenzo's gaze swung back to Giovanni. "It's Carlo. He's in trouble."

Giovanni frowned. "What kind of trouble?" he asked.

"Gabriella now accuses him of rape. First she's fucking him behind every tree they can find, and now she says she was raped. They came for him. Dragged him from his bed in the middle of the night. His sister said they are going to send him away for the crime. I tried to talk to *Patri* but he won't listen. Gabriella is a Mancini. And with what you did to Armando… Alejandro… Gio, Carlo will not come out of this without your help."

"My help? My help!" he knocked Lorenzo's hand away. "How am I to help, cousin? *Patri* has banished me here. My mother has taken to bed sick with worry. They fear she could lose the baby. I haven't spoken to anyone outside of here in days. And I still don't know my punishment. This isn't on me alone! You do as you please and then circle back for solutions. I have none!"

"This is Carlo!" Lorenzo shouted. "We must all help him!"

Giovanni shrugged. His father had taught him something four days ago. He would not shed a tear for a woman or friend again. He cut his gaze to Santo. He looked back to his cousin. "I can't do shit for Carlo now."

Santo cleared his throat and spoke up. "Armando is being released from the hospital today. He has a broken collarbone and several cracked ribs. The blade you used on him didn't go deep. It wasn't the worst of his injuries. He can't stand. I hear he is wheeled around in a chair and pisses in a bag." Santo chuckled. "You're right, Gio. We are all to blame. But Carlo is our brother, our friend. And he has no father to speak for him."

Lorenzo nodded in agreement. "Help us, Gio. Help him."

"*Va bene*," Giovanni said. "I make no promises."

Two Weeks Later –

"*Avanti!*" his father said.

After visiting with his mother he was summoned. Giovanni's legs felt like jelly, but he stepped inside. He kept swallowing saliva and nerves. For the first time in weeks his father looked him in the eye.

"Close the door," Don Tomosino ordered.

He did as he was told. *Zio* Vito was with him. His uncle chose to take a seat on the sofa next to Flavio. Giovanni had to approach Tomosino alone. He glanced over to see that Dominic sat on the floor near his father's desk playing with his toy soldiers. He looked up at Giovanni and smiled. The fear in his heart lessened. Most days his father kept Dominic close to him when he was in his office working. A privilege Giovanni only experienced when he too was Dominic's age.

"Come closer," his father said.

Giovanni walked in and stopped before his desk. His father didn't speak. Giovanni lowered his gaze and found his voice. "I want to apologize, for my behavior, for everything. I regret my actions."

"I hear this was all for a girl who hurt your feelings?" Don Tomosino asked.

"Pussy," Rocco chuckled.

He lifted his head and looked at his father and then his uncles. "No, sir. It was a matter of respect. Armando Mancini and my friends disrespected me. I handled the insult poorly."

Tomosino cut his eyes over to Flavio who stared directly at Giovanni. He knew what the men thought of his father's weakness for his mother. Whatever Giovanni did, he was always an extension of his father. It was a lesson he'd never forget. He had hoped his response gave them some explanation.

"You will pay Armando a visit today and apologize to him and his mother." Flavio informed Giovanni.

The news was an unexpected blow to his gut. He glanced to his father to see if they were his wishes. His father stared back at him expressionless. He turned his gaze to Rocco who smoked a cigar and winked at him. *Zio* Vito was the only one who couldn't look Giovanni in the eye. He stared at the floor with his hat in his hands.

"*Patri*? I am the one that is wronged." Giovanni tried to reason. "Armando Mancini is no victim."

"You are the one to react with emotion and without thought. Wronged or not, you are to never let our enemies see you humbled. So I intend to humble you before them. Give you a taste of the humiliation. In the future, no matter what is at stake, you remember the bitter taste of such defeat. And you will make the better choice." His father leaned forward. "You are my flesh. My progeny. I am you and you are me. But if you ever strike another without my consent, I will not hesitate to strike back. Do you understand, Gio?"

"*Sí, Patri*," Giovanni nodded.

"Take Dominic and go!" The Don commanded. Dominic rose with only one toy soldier in his hand. He came over to Giovanni and he took his hand.

"*Patri*, my friend Carlo is in trouble. He needs your help. He has been falsely accused of rape."

"I don't give a shit," Don Tomosino said. "Leave!"

Giovanni did as asked. He walked out of his father's office and closed the door.

"Gio? What is the matter?" Dominic asked.

"Nothing. Nothing is the matter," he said and led him away.

"But what of Carlo?" Dominic asked.

"There is nothing I can do for him now. Someday when I do have control I will not be like *Patri*. We will be different, Domi."

"*Sí*, Gio. You already are," Dominic smiled.

CHAPTER ONE

May 1994 – Sorrento Italy, La Famiglia—

THE AFTERNOON WAS NEARLY DONE. The heat from the day had caused the staff to open every window in Melanzana. Life in Sorrento was as pleasant as the tropics of Sicilia. Alone, on the second level of the 18,000 sq. ft. estate, Giovanni Battaglia sat behind his desk. A cool breeze blew in through the open shutter doors, and ruffled the papers he reviewed. He closed the ledger and reclined in his leather wingback chair. Outside of his veranda his children's laughter beckoned. Since his return home he hadn't seen his wife or *bambini*. He felt sour over the separation.

Giovanni stood. He walked around his desk. From the open doors of his office the sky was streaked in colors of red, orange, and purple. There were only two possible hours left to daylight.

Three weeks away from home exhausted him. The later part of the day he preferred his office in Melanzana than the one in Villa Rosso to make his calls. He missed breakfast. He had two glasses of wine for lunch. Dinner might be the same. And all that he craved for sustenance was a peek at his children, and a sweet kiss from his wife. Giovanni stopped to the end of balcony to lean against the iron banister. From his top-level view he could see his family.

"I can do it, Mommy!" Eve said. She pinched her nose and puffed her cheeks.

"Okay, sweetie. On the count of three."

Mirabella, and their four year-old daughter Eve, were poised to jump from the edge of the pool into deeper waters. Marietta was with them. She too cheered the children from the sidelines. Giovanni frowned. Over the past two years he'd had to watch the sisters bond. He pretended at wanting this union, but deep down inside he resented it. Marietta had a connection with his Bella that rivaled his own. And he'd never be okay with having his wife's loyalties split.

Marietta began counting: "One…two…."

Eve dove into the water first. Bella squealed and dove in after her. The two submerged in the crystal blue waves, then both began to swim to the surface, to the other end of the pool. Giovanni chuckled. He nearly clapped. His little girl was a champion. She kicked her feet and swiped her arms across the water with grace. Often he was excluded from playtime. He wished he could enjoy an evening poolside with his girls.

Mirabella emerged and stood in the shallow end. Eve pedaled in the water with floaters on each arm to the finish line. Mirabella clapped, as did everyone over Eve's accomplishment. The twins were both at the edge of the pool with Cecilia. One splashed in the water while perched on the middle pool step. The other twin was in his caregiver's arms.

"I won, Mommy! Did you see? Did you see me?"

"Yes, baby, you won. *Brava!* Cecilia, give me Gino," Mirabella reached for her son. There once was a time when his sweet wife feared open bodies of water. She fought him at every turn when he offered to teach her to swim. After her near death experience while delivering his children, she began to appreciate the role of wife and mother. And also the responsibility. It was their job to protect their children—equally. Now she taught his *bambini* how to swim. The Donna was stronger.

"Gio?"

"Out here," he answered.

Mirabella lifted Gino up above her head. He grinned down at his mama. She then started to climb the stone steps out of the water with him on her hip. In her white bikini she redefined beauty. Her brown skin was slick and bronzed thanks to the hours spent in the sun. All of which reminded him of the melting softness between her thighs. Mirabella had a body made of curves. She was a walking fucking fantasy for any man. He loved everything from her round ass, heart shaped hips, shapely thighs, slender legs and firm high-perched breasts. And that included the little imperfections of belly fat left from birthing three *bambini*. She carried Gino in her arms. Her hair was slicked to her scalp in deep waves that lay against the sides of her face, and reached just past her shoulders. She kissed his son's face and walked around the pool.

"Ah, here you are," Lorenzo said. His cousin stepped to his side. "I thought we were going to meet in Villa Rosso? Dominic has returned with Carlo. They are ready to see you."

"I was headed in that direction," Giovanni replied.

Lorenzo's gaze narrowed on the girls. Marietta, his wife, lounged in a chair under a large floppy yellow hat and oval shaped sunglasses. She wore a yellow bikini that was a bit more string than bikini. Giovanni glanced up at his cousin. Lorenzo looked upon his wife with the same adoration Giovanni expressed for his Bella. At first he doubted the two of them as a couple. And if one were to consider how they came about, the doubt would be deemed justified. However, Giovanni had seen a different side of Lorenzo as a married man. His cousin even boasted at fidelity to him and the other men. Possibly the saints' prayers for them both had shown the Battaglia men favor with the Mancini sisters.

"How did your meeting go?" Giovanni asked.

Lorenzo shrugged his broad shoulders beneath his tailored blazer. "Armando is a bitch. How do you think it went?"

"You still play this game with him?" Giovanni shook his head and half-smiled.

"Whether he likes it or not. We play this game." Lorenzo chuckled.

"Come, let's get it over with. I don't want to be late for dinner." Giovanni stepped away.

"We really are blessed," Lorenzo said. He hadn't moved. He continued to stare out toward the pool. Giovanni glanced back. Mirabella sat in the chair next to Marietta. The women side by side did resemble each other remarkably.

"I want a son," Lorenzo announced. "Like you, I want to be a father."

Curious, Giovanni eased his hands in his pockets and stared at his cousin. "Then make one."

Lorenzo leaned over the balcony when he spoke. "She and I try, but she isn't pregnant. What if my mother's curse is true? What if I can never be a father?"

Giovanni returned to his cousin's side. The differences between them had passed. Lorenzo was his trusted council, his left hand. He deferred to him often on matters of business, or the family.

"See a doctor. It may be something simple, something correctible," Giovanni advised.

Lorenzo scratched his chin. "I'm a man, Gio. You think I want a fucking doctor to tell me I can't use my cock?"

"Maybe it's her," Gio said.

"It isn't her!" Lorenzo said his voice was low with malice. He glared at Giovanni with the temper of a cobra. "Don't dismiss her like that."

"I wasn't trying to dismiss her…"

"She's perfect. Just like Mirabella. They're fucking twins!" Lorenzo shouted.

Giovanni shrugged. The subject was far tenderer with his cousin than he first considered. If Mirabella were sterile at the beginning of their marriage it would have broken his heart. And even now it makes him uneasy with the doctor's prognosis about the scarring of her uterus, and the slim chance she could conceive again. He loved his wife being pregnant, being his. He loved seeing her swollen with life that they made. He understood Lorenzo's pain. "You need to get to the bottom of it, Lo. See a doctor. Get answers."

Lorenzo looked back out to his wife. He let his temper cool before he spoke again. "You're right. I will talk to Marie," he said under his breath.

"Come, we have work to do." Giovanni patted his shoulder.

Lorenzo followed him out.

—*B*—

"So I have a request," Marietta removed her large floppy sun hat. She gestured for Eve to come over so she could fix her swimsuit bottoms sucked in to her tiny butt. All the while Mirabella struggled with calming her rebellious son Gino. He was now banned from the water.

It was hard to understand her little boy's daredevil acts. Gianni was far more docile and accepting of the rules. Gianni was the stronger of the two when born, Gino fought for his life. And since then it has been Gino who defied her, challenged her. Her baby boy refused to be mommy's little panda anymore. Now he wanted to be daddy's tiger.

A nice afternoon swim turned disastrous when her son ran from Cecilia and dove off the poolside to the deep end of the water. He did so without his floaters. Gino sank like a stone. Mirabella had to go in after him and it scared the shit out of her.

"Hush now, Gino. Mama is very upset with you," Mirabella said in her sternest voice. Gino fought against her holding him like a baby. Despite the fight she managed to keep him on her lap.

Marietta kissed Eve and then popped her on the butt. "*Va bene!* Show auntie what you can do!"

"*Grazie, Te-Te!*" Eve said. She hurried over to the side of the pool where Cecilia played with Gianni. She eased in the water and splashed around trying to swim on her back. "See? I can do it! Just like Daddy!" Eve laughed.

"*Brava!*" Marietta clapped. Mirabella smiled with pride. Gino's face rested against his mother's breast. He held back his tears and let his mother calm him.

"What is it you have to ask?" Mirabella asked her sister.

"Huh?" Marietta answered. She never took her eyes off Eve as she began to doggy paddle around in the water. Marietta got to her feet and began to remind Eve of the rules to stay closer to Cecilia. Often Marietta stepped in as a surrogate mother with the kids. She and Eve had the most special of bonds.

"You said you had something we needed to talk about?" Mirabella reminded her when Marietta sat back down.

"Oh, yeah. The party. We're turning thirty. That's huge."

"I suppose. Some days I feel more like I'm forty," Mirabella smiled.

"What? Please! Honey, I feel twenty-two."

"You look it! Lorenzo comes home and sees you in that bikini around his men he's going to go for his gun." Mirabella teased.

"What? This innocent little thing? You think this would get his attention?" she posed. Mirabella laughed. Marietta loved pushing her husband's buttons. Mirabella not so much. She learned early on that pissing Giovanni off was never fun for either of them.

"How has it been for you? I mean with them gone? I'm about to climb the walls," Marietta shivered.

"Me too. Sometimes I have to call him to... you know, talk me to sleep," Mirabella winked.

"Oh yeah? The Don talks dirty to his wife?" Marietta laughed.

"You have no idea, the man... never mind. I'm just glad he's coming home. I'm about crazy."

"Me too." Marietta agreed.

"Go on with your request," Mirabella said.

"What request?" Marietta stretched out in the sun.

"You said you had a request?"

"Oh! Shit! Ooops, sorry, Gino," she chuckled. "I forgot. It's our first big party together. We are going to burn Italy to the ground with everything I've got planned." Marietta rubbed her palms together.

Mirabella shook her head. "I don't know about that. Nothing too flashy. Gio is grumbling about having it in Bellagio. I agree with you it's the best location since we have my show in Milano. The man trusts nothing unless he's the organizer."

"Which is exactly why I planned it." Marietta grinned. She turned on her chair and faced Mirabella. "Catalina and I will handle everything. It's going to be huge. Everyone's coming."

"I don't like the sound of this," Mirabella chuckled. "We said a private intimate affair. Close friends and special guests."

"Girl? What the hell are you complaining about? We've closed the New York offices. We've just launched our Parisian line. And you, Ms. Sassy, are officially hot shit again. The world gets to see you in Milan in two days. After what? Four years? Seriously! This is big!"

Mirabella chewed over the news. She glanced to the upper level of their home. She wondered if Giovanni was back from his business. His final stop was in Naples so he was close. He had been short with her on their call last night when she mentioned her desire to do a few interviews with the press. She had to temper her excitement around him. And then came the guilt. Yes, they agreed the kids were older, but her babies had her at every turn, and so did her husband. How could she manage to juggle them and work full time?

"Hello!" Marietta snapped her fingers in front of her face. Mirabella smiled. Marietta continued. "Thing is, I ah, I've invited someone," Marietta said. She squinted out of one eye as if expecting her sister to disapprove.

"Who?" Mirabella frowned.

"A girl from back home. Her name is Shae. Shae Dennis. She's been my friend since I was sixteen. When I first ran away she took me in. We were the same age but she always had this hustle about her. Shae was in her own apartment and running her own business by then."

"What kind of business?" Mirabella frowned.

"The kind a sixteen year old stripper could run," Marietta said.

Mirabella nodded that she understood.

"She's flying in tomorrow. I want her to stay here and go with us to Milano."

"Oh? Okay, well that's fine. It's your house too." Mirabella smiled.

"Please. This kingdom belongs to the high and mighty, and I know how your husband can be toward strangers. Either they're an irritant or a threat, but never welcomed."

Mirabella laughed.

"I'm serious. Clear it with King B please. Make sure it's okay. She's a little on the wild side. You know what I'm saying?"

"I'll make sure Giovanni is aware of the house guest. Now can you please tell me what you and Catalina are concocting for the fashion show? I'm being kept out of the details. Even Kyra is quiet."

"Don't worry. It'll be tasteful and up to your standards. We have it under control. I have something else to tell you." Marietta whispered. This time Marietta looked away. Mirabella wondered if her sister was finally pregnant. She knew Lorenzo wanted a child. He mentioned it often. But something about Marietta's silence and reluctance to speak on the subject troubled her. Her sister was very strong willed and secretive, even now.

"I invited Armando to the party," Marietta confessed.

"You did what?" Mirabella gasped.

"Wait for the explanation before you flip out!" She threw up her hands in defense.

"No! Absolutely not. Un-invite him. Now! Before my husband and yours find out," Mirabella warned.

"Why? Lorenzo works with him."

"Against him—" Mirabella insisted.

"With him, Mirabella! He's trying to secure our future. We are Mancinis."

"Are you out of your freakin mind?" Mirabella demanded. She covered Gino's ears when she almost cursed. He bucked on her lap not liking the hold she had on his head. "We are not Mancinis, and don't you ever say we are aloud again!"

"But?"

"No buts damn it! I don't want my husband upset about something that doesn't matter to me. And shouldn't matter to you. Un-invite him!" Mirabella stood and put Gino on her hip. "I mean it. Call him and tell him to stay away."

"Hold up! You always do this." Marietta blocked her in. Mirabella heaved Gino up on her hip and faced off with her sister. "You always put Giovanni before you."

"Are you crazy?"

"No! This is not about our husbands. It's about us. We have a connection

15

that we can't just ignore!"

"Watch me," Mirabella said.

"It's been two years since our father died. Two years since we found each other. Enough time has passed for us to move on. To heal! Armando has no one. He—"

"Can not be trusted. The only reason he talks to you is to find a way to divide you and Lorenzo. He doesn't want to be our big brother, Marietta. He wants his company back. The man tried to poison me."

"That's not true. He said Carmella did that without his knowledge."

"You heard her on the phone with him!" Mirabella shouted. Gino gripped tighter to his mother in fear.

"I heard her talking to someone. I don't remember who."

"Lies! You knew. What is wrong with you?"

Marietta's eyes began to tear. "I'm sorry. Maybe he is lying. But I think he's doing it because he's trying to start over. I make mistakes, I've made mistakes!"

"Not the same thing!" Mirabella insisted.

"I'm so frustrated with this! If we could all just sit down and start over we can be a family."

Mirabella grabbed her arm. "You have a family. Hear me? Me and your husband. Gio, Catalina, Zia and Rocco, we're your family. You can start a new family by giving your husband the child you know he wants. Stop reaching back in the past before it destroys all of our futures. We know these men, I know my husband. You keep this up and it will end badly. Not for them, but for Armando. Do you get it now?"

"Did you ever ask Gio why he hates him so much?" Marietta asked.

"Because he tried to kill me." Mirabella answered.

"No. Before he even met you he hated Armando. And do you know why? Because when he was fifteen he caught Carmella, his girlfriend, sucking Armando's dick. And then he picked up a knife and stabbed Armando and his friend. He killed the friend."

"Where did you hear this crap?" Mirabella demanded.

"Pillow talk. My point is, the two of them have been lashing out at each other since they were kids, and using the women they cared about to do it."

"It's a lie. Armando is twisting things." Mirabella waved off the comment. She rocked Gino on her hip. She shook her head with disbelief.

"Is he a liar? Or does your husband have ulterior motives? Could Gio be holding an ancient grudge over losing a woman who tried to kill you?" Marietta marched off. Mirabella watched her go. She shook her head. She loved her sister but even now she didn't understand what motivated her. Marietta lived as if each day wasn't promised to her. That was fine considering her history, but dangerous considering their future. Something had to change. Marietta had to change.

—ℬ—

Carlo paced.

Dominic glanced up at him and then shook his head. The constant pacing began to wear on his patience. "Stop with the worrying. It's a good proposal for Gio. He'll accept it."

"It's the first time I've come to the boss with my own… idea. Lorenzo shot it down," Carlo said.

"And I say it's a good idea," Dominic insisted. "Lorenzo doesn't run this family. Gio does."

"You sure about that?" Carlo chuckled. "Gio listens to him more and more. And less to you!"

The truth hurt. Dominic was allowed to pursue legitimate business for the family. But they were knee deep in the illegal affairs once again. With Lorenzo at Giovanni's side he'd acquired the extortion businesses Mottola left behind, and some of their old territories as well. That included the gambling houses. The only rule that was severely enforced was the one of no trafficking of women and prostitution. Giovanni would never disrespect his mother, his wife, and his daughter by ever picking up that business again. Still the Battaglia men weren't altar boys. Dominic had to turn his head to Lorenzo's dabbles in the drug trade through the *Campania*. Giovanni accepted Lorenzo's methods and reasons, but Dominic secretly despised them. They were once so close to atonement. Instead, Giovanni's thirst for respect, and Lorenzo's thirst for power, was now a deadly and greedy mix. Carlo's idea was a good one. And if Giovanni signed off on it Dominic hoped it would be the first step to influence his brothers in the right direction.

The door opened.

Carlo froze. Giovanni glanced to him and Dominic. Dominic stood as Carlo greeted Giovanni with respect. He walked over and kissed Giovanni on both cheeks.

"We've been waiting, Gio," Dominic said.

Lorenzo was the last to enter. He closed the door behind him.

"What is this that you two insist we discuss today?" Giovanni asked. He went to his bar and poured another drink. He'd promised his wife that he'd not do so much drinking casually. But he was a man of habits. And this habit kept him calm and rational, contrary to her belief.

"A proposal, Gio," Carlo spoke up.

When Giovanni turned he could not miss the glare Lorenzo leveled on Carlo. An exchange between the men that revealed more than he was sure either intended. Carlo was speaking out of turn. And it wasn't like Carlo to do so. Giovanni glanced to Dominic and recognized the encouragement lied there. He wished Lorenzo and Dominic would come to terms on business matters. It would alleviate a lot of his stress.

"I take it both Domi and Lo have heard your proposal?"

Carlo nodded.

"It's not the time for this discussion," Lorenzo said. "We have enough to contend with in the *Campania*."

"Let him be heard," Dominic said.

"He has been heard by me!" Lorenzo shot back.

"And since when is your decision law? Last I checked Gio ran this family." Dominic said.

"Enough of this bullshit," Giovanni said. He nodded to Carlo. "I'm listening."

"I have a brother," Carlo began. Giovanni's brows lifted. He'd learned that Carmine was Carlo's brother after the kid was dead. He knew that Carlo's family was split, with his father having fucked half of Sicilia, and populating the island. Carlo continued. "His name is Ciro. And he's a fighter."

"Fighter?" Giovanni frowned.

"Boxer," Dominic clarified.

"Sí," Carlo said. "He's been trained. He's really good. He wants to join the *Federazione Puglisitica Italiana*, maybe even fight in America. He has the skill. I'm talking the grace of Angelo Palma, and the finesse of Arturo Gatti all rolled up in a one-two punch. Pow!" Carlo threw a few shadow punches to demonstrate. "He's my blood. He's tough like my Pa and me. He has it."

"Then why see me about him? If he's this good?" Giovanni asked.

"It takes a lot to get him to the EUBC."

"You mean money. It takes money!" Lorenzo scoffed.

Carlo flinched after the bite of sarcasm. "Lo is right. To make him a contender he needs sponsorship. His first manager wasted his talent. But I've found him now. I can manage him, Gio. I need… the family behind me. If you see him fight you'd understand."

Dominic cleared his throat.

"Something to add, Domi?" Giovanni asked.

"I've seen him. He had a match a week ago in Rome. He's good. Consider this, Gio. Boxing is very hot right now in Rome. The Russians dominate the AIBA now. When was the last time a Sicilian made the rankings?"

Giovanni took a sip of his drink. He loved boxing. He even sparred with a few of his men to keep himself strong. It was an idea that stroked an itch in him he's had for some time. "Go on," Giovanni said.

Dominic stood. "I've been looking for new business. Legitimate ones." Dominic glanced to Lorenzo who continued to glare at Carlo. "If we back him and hire the proper trainers, we could have him ready in weeks. We'll put him on the circuit and walk through doors closed to us now."

"It exposes us, Gio." Lorenzo spoke up. "What if the kid is good like Carlo says? What then? The Battaglia name would be in the press all over. Strangers will stick their noses into our fucking business. The world once again pays attention to the *Camorra*. That's the plan?"

"Lorenzo misses the point. We are exposed, Gio. You have Mirabella about to re-enter the fashion business. The press is already running features on her, and you. I field calls daily wanting to know how Giovanni Battaglia makes his fortune. And the shit Rocco puts out from that vineyard doesn't cover it. The real estate deals haven't baked long enough. We need more legitimate investments to wash the blood clean from our name. This will distract the media."

"Bullshit!" Lorenzo laughed. "This will put us in jeopardy."

"No! You put us in jeopardy with your extortion rackets, drug trafficking, and gambling!" Dominic pointed an accusatory finger at Lorenzo. "It sullies the family!"

"Chiudi il culo!" Giovanni sighed. "Shut the fuck up. The both of you!"

The men fell silent.

"I tire of the constant bitching like women. Enough. Neither of you can decide on anything without this competition bullshit." Giovanni drank his glass dry and slammed it down on the desk. "Legitimizing the family is the future. I have not forgotten that, Domi. Lorenzo!" His cousin's gaze flickered up to Giovanni. "Find a way to contribute to Domi's plans." Giovanni turned his gaze to Dominic. "And you. The blood we've spilled will never be washed from the Battaglia name. I don't fucking want it to be. So find a way to live with it, Domi!"

Giovanni returned to the chair behind his desk. He sat. "This fucking fashion business," he threw his hand up in disgust. "She wants it. And I have struggled with being the generous husband. I know the exposure her business costs us all." He lifted his gaze to his men, all of them like brothers to him. They guarded the family secret. He shared it with every man working for him. And in two years no one had uttered it aloud to strangers. Mirabella Battaglia was the bastard daughter of Marsuvio Mancini. The more his beautiful wife danced near the flames of celebrity, the harder it became to keep her true identity contained to their world.

Taking a deep breath he exhaled his frustration. "The bottom line is, a happy Bella gives me peace. And I need it. We all need it. So if I must be in the media as her husband, then I do agree something new and distracting should shield me. A boxer might be the right choice. When is his next fight?"

"Tuesday, in Bergamo. It's perfect," Carlo said.

"I will be willing to see this fighter," Giovanni said.

"Gio," Carlo said. "I wish to manage his career. He's young. I ask that if any deal is to be made I am his manager. Only me."

"He's your blood." Giovanni reclined in his chair. "I would never stand in between you and *famiglia*. But understand your loyalties are always to me first, Carlo. As far as my compensation, we'll save that discussion for another day."

Carlo nodded. He clapped his hands together in celebration and then rubbed them together. *"Grazie,* Gio!"

"Are we done?" Giovanni asked.

"Can I have a word with you? Alone?" Dominic asked.

Giovanni shook his head. "No. Lorenzo stays."

Lorenzo unbuttoned his suit jacket and walked over to a chair and sat in it. He smiled up at Dominic. Carlo left and closed the door behind him. Giovanni felt the tension of a headache forming. He'd definitely have to eat dinner or he'd be on his ass for the rest of the night. And after three weeks away from his bed and his wife he had no intention of returning to her weak.

"It's Mancini," Dominic said.

"What about him?" Lorenzo answered.

"I need to know what your plans are, Gio," Dominic asked. "We are talking about an eighty million dollar fortune. For the past two years we've not finalized things with the women's inheritance. If we sell their shares back to Armando we will get half of eighty million dollars."

"Fuck half. We should take it all," Lorenzo said.

Dominic continued to address Giovanni. "On your terms, Giovanni, we can maintain the truce. The press does not know the women are Mancinis. We've kept this quiet. The clans have not been told. The Sicilians have not been told. Armando doesn't want the exposure."

"But they suspect, Gio!" Lorenzo cut in. "No one would dare say it aloud because they fear us. As they should." He boasted.

"We should sever ties, Gio. Armando is willing to negotiate, hell he's begging for a sit-down with you," Dominic said. "You have him on his knees."

"Armando is a fucking weasel! A cock sucker." Lorenzo hissed. "Have you forgotten what he did to Carlo? How he has taunted and mocked Gio for years. That he put a hit out on Mirabella? Have you forgotten his sins?"

Dominic sighed. "That is childhood bullshit! And the hit was called off. He never acted on the threat again. We are men now. This is business!"

"And Giovanni is the *capo di tutti capi*. He takes it all. Always," Lorenzo pounded his fist into his hand.

"You take it all. Last I heard you were running the deals with Mancini." Dominic replied. "What are they exporting into Napoli?"

Giovanni put up his hand. Both of them fell silent. "Lorenzo, I need a plan from you."

"Plan? I've given you one." Lorenzo frowned.

Giovanni leaned forward. "For two years you've been playing this game with Mancini. The money coming in from the Mancini business deals aren't enough for the aggravation. And I hear your wife has been in communication with the bastard."

Lorenzo paled. "I've told her to not reach out to him again."

"And she disobeys you. Get your fucking wife in order and either sever my ties with the Mancinis, or find a way to crush him. I don't want him near my Bella."

"Gio? I am close to gaining more leverage. We have him up against the wall. If we only—"

"Bring it to an end!" Giovanni said.

Lorenzo nodded.

"Good. Now can the day be over?" Giovanni reclined in his chair. The men exchanged looks. Lorenzo was the first to leave. Dominic hovered.

"What is it, Domi?" Giovanni asked.

"Do you trust me?"

"With my life," Giovanni replied.

"Then listen to me. Lorenzo is good for many things, but not business matters. Give me the control to deal with Armando Mancini and I will spare you the aggravation."

"Lorenzo keeps Armando in line. Selfish or not, he has Armando by the balls," Giovanni said. "And let's not forget, Lorenzo has succeeded in dealing with the clans, where you and Santo failed. He's been loyal to this family and me. We are good together."

"But for how long, Gio? There is risk here. For over fifty years the *Camorra* and the *Mafiosi* have kept this truce. Do you not see the risk?"

"I see it. We agree. The truce is best. I have no desire to put this family or my men through another war, especially with the Sicilians. But I will not let the Mancinis off easy."

"Drugs. *Patri* never, ever, agreed to drugs. Neither have you. But in the past two years with Lorenzo as your left hand, you have changed, Gio."

"Have I? Or has the world? Drugs are here, Domi. There is no golden rule or moral high road to who we are. All I've done is agreed to allow the clans to do what they would try to do behind my back. Mottola gained power because of my refusal to accept the truth. The clans are prosperous now. The clan bosses are content."

"Not true, Gio. You are strong because you hold to beliefs higher than our fathers. The drugs poison our people, and could eventually destroy our men. "

"We don't sell drugs!" Gio shouted.

"But we allow the trafficking through our ports, we make the money off of every ship that docks."

"And we will continue to. Lorenzo is right on this. Patri was wrong. I was wrong. You are wrong. That is the end of it. I trust Lorenzo and you need to learn to."

Dominic nodded. "Of course, Gio."

Giovanni smiled. "Where's my sister? Will she be here for dinner?"

Dominic wiped his hand down his face. In that moment he could see how stress and tension had aged his brother. Giovanni felt a pang of regret for being so tough on him. "She's in Milan," Dominic said. "I'm leaving to join her first thing in the morning."

"Oh. She spends a lot of time there," Giovanni said, unable to hide his disappointment.

"It's this designer business. If Mirabella can't be there then Catalina must."

"And that is okay with you?" Giovanni pressed. Dominic didn't answer. He started for the door. "What about the wedding?" Giovanni called out. "I've given my blessing. What is the date? I want to… you two should be married."

Dominic stood at the door for a moment. His back was to Giovanni. "When I know the date I will tell you," he said and walked out. Giovanni nearly called out to him. When Dominic was just a boy he was his only protector, mentor, confidant. He missed being that council for his young brother. Giovanni drummed his fingers on the surface of his desk. After a contemplative moment he picked up the phone. After a few rings Mirabella answered. "I'm home," he said.

"I know. Let me guess. My husband, the one I've been missing so much, is now locked behind a closed door," she said.

"You were told?" he asked.

"I was told," she replied. Underneath her sweet pleasant voice he heard a tinge of disappointment. He could have returned home sooner. But he needed the time away to focus on his affairs. He'd been to Europe and back, and not seen her. But he spoke to her every night. Did that not count for anything?

"I need you. Just you," he said.

"I have a big dinner planned, Gio."

"Just you," he said.

"Giovanni? The kids missed you. Sweetheart, for heaven's sake it's been three weeks. Have dinner with them and then we—"

"Bella."

"Okay. Okay, I understand. I'll be waiting for you."

He hung up. Giovanni rubbed the tension in his brow. He exhaled deeply and pushed up from his chair. He walked around the desk to the coffee table. On top he saw his gift for her. He slid his hands in his pockets and stared at the bouquet. It felt good to be home.

—B—

"Is this a bad time?" Marietta asked.

"Never for you. I'm surprised you called. Didn't you say your husband would be returning today?"

"Yes, he's around here somewhere," Marietta smiled.

"How are you?"

"I'm okay. I wanted to call you to tell you I spoke to Mirabella. She's not really open to the idea of meeting with you," Marietta said.

"I understand."

"You do?"

"Of course," he chuckled. "Tell her to know me is to love me."

"You're a real funny guy," Marietta chuckled. "It'll take time. My sister is very loyal to her husband and the family. She thinks you want to hurt us."

"And you aren't loyal?" Armando asked.

"Oh trust me, I'm one hundred percent loyal to Lorenzo. He just doesn't try to control me. I can do and think what I want."

"Interesting." Armand said.

"Besides, I think you deserve a second chance."

"It's possible I don't," he told her.

"True. Anything is possible I suppose. Why say that to me?" she frowned.

"I'm not perfect, Marietta. None of us are. I just want a chance to know my sisters. A lot has changed in the past two years." Armando said.

"It has. I won't be able to meet with you for dinner like we discussed. Like I told you, Lorenzo is back. I need to tell him that we've gotten closer," Marietta sighed.

"Are you sure that's wise? He hates me more than Gio," Armando chuckled.

"It's not funny. I'm sick of the fighting." Marietta said. "Well all need to get past it."

"Forgive me. Lorenzo and I meet frequently. I think he and I will come to terms soon," Armando said.

"I have to go. I'll call you when I can," Marietta said.

"I look forward to it. *Ciao, bella*," Armando said and ended the call. Marietta dropped the phone on the receiver. She inhaled deeply and exhaled slow. She couldn't believe how nervous and excited she was to see Lorenzo. When Leo told her the men were back she hurried and changed. Three long weeks with her beloved absent had left her bored out of her mind. She hated the separation between them because of their competing schedules. Three damn weeks was the final straw.

"Non me ne frega un cazzo!" Lorenzo bellowed and received a roar of laughter as applause. Marietta peeked out at the gathering. Lorenzo sat at the table with an empty plate. The others fed and stuffed their mouths as they listened to Lorenzo and Carlo bicker over who the best player in some sport was. It was Carlo who saw her first. Their eyes met, and once again she felt that flutter she hated. It stirred at the pit of her stomach and spread like a wildfire through her gut. She stepped from her hiding place and his gaze lingered on her face. There were several questions in his eyes. *How was she? Did she think of him when he was away? Did she ever think of him at all?* Marietta broke her gaze away from him when his piercing gaze slowly descended down the curves of her sunshine yellow summer dress.

Lorenzo looked behind him and saw her. His warm smile pushed all thoughts of Carlo aside. He was home! She gave him one in return.

"Cara mia!" he extended his hand.

She walked over to her husband and leaned to kiss him on the cheek, but he turned up his chin and offered his mouth. His tongue flicked up and beckoned hers in. The kiss became inappropriate, and the smell of him left her rubbing her thighs together discreetly to calm the heat spreading up into her pussy. How many times had she sniffed his bottle of aftershave at night because she missed him so much?

He hooked his arm around her waist and brought her in close to him. Immediately he buried his face between her breasts and shook his head. She loved it! Tickled, she hugged his head and laughed, as several of his men looked away out of respect. Carlo did not. His gaze was unwavering and Marietta felt it strongly. She pushed Lorenzo's face up and cupped it in her hands. Her man was home. It was time to celebrate.

"I'm so glad my bad boy is home. I've missed you, sweet baby," she kissed him again but drew back before he turned the kiss into something obscene.

He squeezed her ass and bit down on his bottom lip. "Mmph! I have missed you, *bambina*!" He stared at her breasts with such hunger and lust she felt her nipples peak.

"Behave," she brought his face up once more. "Are you hungry?" she asked him.

Lorenzo nodded. She peeled his hands off her ass and picked up his plate. Lorenzo drank from his beer and watched her. No matter how long they were married he always looked at her as if she was the last woman on earth. And it made her heart beat faster. Marietta went to the buffet Mirabella and Ana had arranged for the men. Everyone was present. The kids were being served and fed by Zia and Cecilia. Even Dominic was at the table eating. The only person missing was Catalina, her sister, and King B. She found the Don and Donna's absence odd. Typically they were at the head of the table.

Marietta returned the plate of Lorenzo's favorites and put it before him. Carlo looked up again and she gave him a friendly smile. He smiled in return. They were respectful of each other now. The kiss shared between them happened two years ago, and never happened again. Carlo was however very much present in her life, and his constant stares or passing whispers did trouble her at times. But more and more they made attempts to keep their distance. And after years of drinking, laughing, and being a family with Carlo, her feelings for him were strengthened. The truth was she'd always care more than a woman in her position should.

After she fixed her plate she sat next to him. Lorenzo had large hands, she felt dwarfed by them when they reached for her, and protected by them when he touched her. His right hand eased between her thighs. She parted them and scooted forward on her chair so no one seated across from them would notice. He ate as if his actions were normal. And for them it was. She tried to eat with him stroking her pussy using his two middle fingers, but she could barely swallow. She glanced up. Carlo's sly smile revealed that he knew the game they played. She looked away and closed her thighs on Lorenzo's hand to stop him. But he persisted. She sipped her wine and tried to ignore the passion from her husband, and the intense stares from his best friend. Inside she knew she failed miserably.

—*B*—

"*LE PIACE, DONNA?*"

"Yes. Well done. This is perfect. I'm sure he hasn't eaten, and you've brought everything he loves. *Grazie* Ana," Mirabella said.

"Prego," the cook replied with a curt nod. Ana Marcello was a short stout woman with chubby arms and legs. She'd served the Battaglias for over thirty years under two mistresses, Eve and Catalina. Now she took orders from Mirabella only. Once dismissed, Ana snapped her fingers and her two helpers left with her. Mirabella saw them to the door. Alone, her attention returned to the dinner setting. She inspected the meal. Giovanni preferred that Mirabella prepare his supper with only Ana's help to serve the rest of the family. Zia spent countless hours teaching Mirabella how to cook traditional dishes. And when Marietta joined the family she too took on the lessons from Zia's apron, and flourished under the attention. Her sister loved to cook. Mirabella only enjoyed the way it made her children and husband happy.

Tonight, however, Mirabella had Ana do all the cooking. She anticipated a house full of men and couldn't manage the deed and the children. As usual she tasted his food and found everything to his liking. Though it was customary to have a glass of his favorite Merlot ready with dinner, she'd chosen water for him. She was sure he'd already swallowed his belly full of the grape while away.

Now came the waiting game. Mirabella paced. She stopped when she spotted his guitar. She smiled. When was the last time he serenaded her? She exhaled. She craved the sweet love moments in their marriage. Lately it felt like neither of them made enough time to enjoy it. Mirabella put a hand to her heart and looked away, but her gaze fell upon the bed. The last time they made love she woke up to her wrists being bound with her red silk scarf and tied to the headboard. That was some night.

What time was it? He'd called her over a half hour ago. He should arrive any minute. Mirabella went to the mirror and checked her appearance once more. Her hair was damp from the swim. She decided to let it air dry into its natural curl pattern. It drew up to her neck thick and curly. She wore a long pearl-white satin robe and nothing underneath. She loosened the front of the sash to reveal more of her breasts. Then she thought it was a bit of overkill and tightened it again. She repeated this action twice before finally deciding that less was more for her husband. If her breasts or thighs were revealed to him when they ate together it would only excite him too soon. But at the right time, an excited Don would bring on the sweetest pleasures. Tonight she would not leave him or see their children until sunrise, unless summoned because of an emergency.

Tonight was theirs.

Mirabella fluffed her hair. She puckered her lips and turned sideways to look at her body. She'd gotten plenty of sun lately. Her skin was a richer, deeper, shade of brown. She moved the robe aside a bit to reveal how nicely toned her legs were. The jogging with Marietta had tightened and firmed her ass too. After giving birth to three children, her hips spread a bit but Giovanni loved the curves. Often she woke to find him on top of her entering her from behind because he couldn't get enough of making love to her with the cushion of her ass between them.

She smiled.

Dinner, the seduction, all of it wasn't necessary. If she dropped her robe and lay in bed he'd walk into the room and not hesitate to join her. Mirabella looked to the bed once more and considered doing just that. She chuckled and pushed her naughty thoughts aside. He'd been gone from home and not been fed properly. Probably survived on cigars and alcohol. Her lust could wait. At least that's what she told herself.

The evolution to become the wife to a man as powerful and cunning as Giovanni Battaglia had not been an easy transition. She couldn't recall when she passed the test and became Donna Battaglia. It happened some time after their scare with the birth of the twins, and the discovery of her being half Sicilian. She and Giovanni decided on the needs in their marriage—hers and his—mostly hers because his were very explicitly understood.

The door opened. Her husband entered with his arm behind his back. He looked like a boss in a black tailored suit with matching shirt and tie. His gaze volleyed between the private dinner arrangement, and then to her evening attire. She found approval in his smile. She started towards him and paused. He revealed a vibrant, fresh, long stemmed bouquet of blue-bloomed roses wrapped by a blue silk ribbon. Her heart stopped at their beauty. Even more remarkable was that the color of the roses matched the color of his eyes.

"Oh my gosh," she covered her mouth.

"I've missed you, Bella," he said and closed the door behind him. She went to him immediately. He welcomed her into his arms.

"Bentornato a casa, tesoro." She welcomed him home. She kissed his chin and then brushed her lips across his. Her arms circled his neck and her robe parted all the way up to her waist. She didn't hesitate to rub her exposed sex against his thigh by bending her left knee and moving against him. He didn't let her go. She had to pull her lips from his by dropping her head back. She held to his shoulders and looked up into eyes. "Long day at the office, sweetie?"

Giovanni cupped her ass with both hands and squeezed. He seized her lips once more. His tongue swept in and flicked at the roof of her mouth. The smoky liquored taste of his breath, and his strong aftershave weakened her. She didn't dare break away until he released her.

"*Santo cielo!* Somebody is happy to be home," Mirabella chuckled.

"I've missed you, Bella," he replied in a deep whisper that curled around her heart and squeezed.

"Have you eaten?" she stroked his jaw. She looked into his eyes for the truth about his diet during his absence. The glazed weariness and smell of wine on his breath clued her into what had been served for his breakfast and lunch.

"You haven't eaten, sweetheart. Have you?" she asked with mounting concern.

"I intend to." He looked down at her cleavage that was heaved up from the front of her robe and crushed against his chest.

Mirabella peeled his hands off her ass before he made good on his promise. She was right to not take him to bed immediately. Her husband needed to be fed. She took him by the wrist. "Come on. Eat first. Food. Please."

There was a slight pull of resistance from him but she forced the issue. She took the roses from his free hand and brought him to the table. He sat. Mirabella went for the vase on the bookshelf in their room. She brought it to the table and put the roses inside. "They are so beautiful. They remind me of the ones in your mother's gardens at Villa Mare Blu."

"I know you like them, so I had them brought in," he said.

"From Sicily?" she gasped in surprise. That was so sweet and considerate of him. She went over to stand behind him. She uncovered his meal. This one had all his favorites.

"Mmm, looks good, Bella. *Grazie*," he said.

She kissed the top of his head. She put her hands to his shoulders, and began to squeeze and massage the hard muscle until they became manageable under her fingers. He devoured his favorites. He glanced from the water she filled in his glass goblet, to the corked bottle of wine on the table. After a pause he picked up the glass of water and drank. The drinking troubled her the most. He'd lessened his intake, but still it was part of him. A scary part of him.

"I saw you at the pool today," he said after he swallowed.

Mirabella smoothed his hair down and massaged his scalp like she did her curly haired sons. "Why didn't you send for me sooner? The babies would have loved to see you, Papa."

"I miss them," he admitted.

Mirabella smiled. The day before he left for his trip he showered with both of his sons. It was a sight to see. Gianni was in his arms. The toddler used his tiny hands to wash and lather up suds in his thick curly hair as Papa instructed. And then Gianni laughed and bucked with enthusiasm when Giovanni held him under the water to rinse. Gino at Giovanni's feet, was covered in suds. He jumped, stomped, and splashed in the puddles disappearing down the drain. She could hear Giovanni's laughter in the room before she discovered them.

"You'll see them tomorrow," she reassured him. He glanced up and grinned at her between chews and swallows. He shoveled food in his mouth bite after bite. She had to wonder if he truly digested the mouthfuls he wolfed down.

"I'm glad you're home. You need to spend a little more time with them, Gio. Especially Gino."

"Why? Something wrong with my boys?" he asked.

"Gino is a baby but—"

Giovanni glanced back. "What's wrong with my Gino?" he asked with a mouthful.

She nearly laughed at the comical way his face twisted. "Sweetheart, you aren't listening. He needs Papa! He's growing, testing boundaries. No. He's very disobedient when you aren't here."

Giovanni turned and continued to eat. Mirabella could see in his eyes he was amused not concerned. She shook her head and tried to explain. "He climbs furniture and jumps off. He climbs the stairs and jumps from them. He even jumped into the pool today. And Zia and I have tried everything outside of a spanking to discipline him." She kissed his cheek. "Gianni listens to Mama, all I have to do is call his name. Gino runs the other way. He only lets me hold him when I give him food or drink. He wants to run everywhere and not walk. He's a little rough with the way he plays with Gianni too."

"You spoil Gianni. Stop coddling them so much. Gino is a boy. Let him be one. They can't grow into men if you smother them," Giovanni said.

Mirabella rolled her eyes. "They just stopped breastfeeding two months ago. And it's my job to coddle and smother. It's your job to discipline." She walked around the table to take a seat. "I want your approval to send Eve to school."

"She's four!" Giovanni nearly choked. "Why so soon?"

"They have a primary program at the church. It's a really good pre-starter program that will accept her at four. I've met with sister Aggie and Father Álvaro after mass on Sunday. The church agrees it would be good for Eve."

Giovanni shrugged and mumbled something under his breath.

"A yes would be nice?" Mirabella desired explicit consent. After all she was sending her baby girl outside of the compound walls. If there were any danger, a hint of it, he'd object without question.

"Whatever you say," he waved off the discussion. Mirabella watched him finish off his meal. He ate too fast and drank the water pitcher clean.

"Did you eat at all while you were gone?"

"Never this good," he grunted.

Mirabella chuckled. She poured herself a glass of wine, sipped and watched her husband.

Giovanni glanced up from his plate. "Tell me what you've been up to since I've been gone."

"As if your spies don't report back my every move," she half-joked.

"Tell me," he winked. She nodded and began to share. All of her news centered around the company he couldn't give a shit about. He got rid of the woman Carole Montague for her, but it was a big mistake. Once the office in New York was closed, and his wife and her sister rebuilt her team, the company became her joy. He understood her passion and hid his secret jealousy. He guessed that's what a good husband would do. And after his scare of almost losing her during childbirth, he swore to be better, a more attentive husband. His method was to ask what would his father do, and then reverse that decision. It worked well for him so far. After all she was a good wife.

"Kyra is coming to Milano. I've decided to incorporate my shoe line in the show." Mirabella prattled on. "She's trained in Paris and taken some lesson from expert shoemakers out of Florence. I've signed the papers. Dominic said I own the warehouse space next to Fabiana's."

"We own it," he corrected between swallows.

"Yes, sweetheart. We do. Did he tell you? Kyra and Jamie can make their shoes there," she asked.

"Who the fuck is Kyra?" Giovanni asked. She sliced bread and poured some olive oil with cracked peppercorn in a dish for him. He plucked a thick slice and dipped it in his sauce.

"Renaldo's fiancée. You remember her, from America."

Giovanni shrugged. *What the fuck did he care?* Renaldo had disappointed him. But he was done with the entire matter. Mirabella had convinced him to leave the lovebirds alone.

"The event is going to be so nice, Giovanni. You will be so proud of me," she giggled.

"I already am," he said. "You are the best in your business. The very best."

She nodded in agreement. "Every media outlet has requested an interview with me."

"No interviews," he stated.

"Okay," she said. He heard the disappointment in her voice and looked up. She poked out her lip for him in a playful pout. Giovanni considered the request. Mirabella stared him back in the eye, her gaze never wavering. He sighed. "One interview. You choose. Only one. Please, Bella, I don't need the headache."

"Thank you, baby," she blew him a kiss.

He chuckled and rolled his pasta up on his fork. His gaze however lingered on the separation of her robe while he did so. He ate, chewed, and stared at her breasts. Each time she breathed in they threatened to fall out of their flimsy confinement. After the birth of the twins his wife's body changed. Her breasts were fuller and her hips a little wider. She had a nice round ass he touched and fucked every chance he got. No matter how many runs she did with her sister, there was a little fat to her lower belly that he found soft and sexy when he was on top of her, inside of her. It's the mark of her being a mother and beautiful as fuck to him. Giovanni continued to chew remembering the last time they fucked. Of course he couldn't tell her this. She was so sensitive about her weight and how she looked in her clothes. Especially now that *Donna Mirabella Battaglia* was to replace *Mirabella Ellison* for the fashion industry.

"And she arrives tomorrow."

He blinked out of his thoughts of sex and dominance. Were they talking of this Kyra person again? "Who arrives, when?" he asked.

"Have you been listening to me, *mio caro*?" she chuckled. She set the wine glass down and leaned forward. Her robe opened further and her breasts breeched. His brows shot up and he smiled.

"I said Marietta has a friend coming to visit us, from America. She will be staying with us and traveling to Milano. She will attend the party in Bellagio. I okayed all of it."

"Did you?" he asked with an arched brow.

"Yes! As the Donna it's my decision," she said.

"Damn right!" he said with a smile. She beamed with beauty when he encouraged her. He made a mental note to remember to encourage her more. Giovanni reached for the napkin and wiped his mouth. He didn't give a shit about the houseguest lists, or all the festivities for the next week. In fact he was ready for his wife to be silent and serve dessert—her.

Mirabella blew him another kiss from across the table and then wagged her finger at him. "I know what you're thinking," she teased.

"If you did you'd take off that robe," he said.

"Oh yeah?" she sipped her wine and held his gaze. When he didn't blink she traced her hand down her throat. Her hand went lower and lower. She slipped it inside the front of her robe and squeezed her breast. She massaged it, tweaked her nipple, he saw her fingers moving underneath the silk fabric. Giovanni's dick went stiff. Mirabella set the glass down. She kept her eyes trained on him as she used the other hand to slip between her thighs, which he sensed she parted. And then she began. She masturbated and massaged her breasts in front of him. Her long dark lashes fluttered. She began to move her shoulders, her hips to her own rhythm. In his mind's eye he could see her hand beneath the table, between her thighs, titillating her clitoris as her fingers slipped inside her pussy, doing his job. Mirabella's head dropped back, her luscious lips parted in a silent cry. She rolled the tip of her tongue over the top of her lip and climaxed for him.

"Shit," Giovanni breathed.

"Mmm, baby," she moaned and slowly came down from her climatic high. When she was spent she shook her head as if woken from a dream. She looked at him under her veil of long lashes and a tease of a smile curled the corner of her mouth.

"Bella? You do that often when I'm gone?" he asked.

"Yes. When you call to tell me goodnight I'm touching myself, in that bed over there. Alone," she smiled.

Giovanni wiped his hand down his face. "I need to be home more often," he said more to himself than to her.

"*Va bene,*" she said. "That's enough talk, sweetheart. I want my Don."

Mirabella pushed back her seat and stood. She leaned in to smell the roses that he brought her. Her breasts swayed out of her robe. The sash to her robe slipped further to her hips and the front parted to her navel. Why even bother to tie the robe together? She should have greeted him at the door in nothing. She walked over to him. She smelled like a rose. He knew her body was covered in perfumed lotions and oils. Mirabella extended her hand to him and he took it in his. He turned her palm over. He pressed a kiss to the center.

"You smell so nice, Bella, come closer," he said. He scooted his chair back and turned it so she could stand between his parted legs. He untied the front of her robe. His nose brushed the transparent trimmed fuzz just above the lips of her vagina. He kissed her there. She had the prettiest pussy, and he'd seen plenty of pussy as a man. In fact he was a man who appreciated the unique physical qualities of his woman. He'd wage war and cut throats over this woman, and he had.

Giovanni stood. His wife was forced to step back so he could. She went for his tie first. He stared down at her hands as she ran the silk tie through the knot and pulled it free of his neck. She tossed it aside. She smoothed her hands over his chest to help him shrug off his blazer. And when it dropped she unbuttoned his shirt. He didn't bother to stop or offer assistance. While she worked on his belt and lowered his zipper, he touched her damp, crinkly hair. It took the longest time for moisture to leave her hair once wet. But he liked it best this way, the curls were tight and spiral looking. The texture was different than his own. Eve had fine silky curls. Bella's hair thickened, puffed, frizzed from the root to the ends like his sons'. He let his fingers sink into her tresses, and her head went back. Her lovely golden brown irises, under thick lashes, snared his heart. She eased her hand in the front of his pants and touched his dick.

"For me?" she asked as she gave it a tug.

"Mmm," he moaned, unable to respond.

"You shouldn't stay away so long, Giovanni. It's not healthy for either of us," she said.

Her husband smiled.

His gaze bore into her, glittering with triumph.

"I'll make it a habit not to," he replied.

The robe came off her shoulders. His trousers dropped to his ankles. She went to her knees and pulled down on his boxers. Mirabella literally let go a deep exhale of appreciation when his erection sprang free. She ran her hands up both sides of his muscular, hairy, thighs.

"Come ti va?" she asked him what he was in the mood for. She hoped he'd prefer she take him down her throat. She loved his cock. The smell of it, the texture of its veined rigid skin over her tongue excited her. Her mouth went dry and her gaze slowly climbed up his length to look into his face. He looked down at her and his violet blue eyes sparkled like the rare gems they were. Mirabella didn't need permission. He belonged to her—cock and all. She flicked her tongue at the dimpled head of his dick and it tasted salty. She swallowed the head of his dick and then more. He gripped her hair and pushed and pulled as his dick glided over her tongue and reached into her throat.

"Leccalo! Succhiami!" He demanded she suck him faster. Mirabella complied. Her lids fluttered and her jaws caved with tension from suctioning and then swallowing. He pulled her hair, not hard, only to instruct the rhythm of a good cock suck. And then she sensed his breakdown and released him from her mouth. Slowly she stood. As soon as he could reach her, he drew her up into his arms for a kiss.

The woman could still make him crazy. Though the bed was only a step away from them he lifted her in his arms. Bella laughed lightly when he tossed her playfully on top.

"I'm going to make you pay for that!" she teased and shook her finger at him. He toed out of his shoes and stepped out of his pants and underwear trapped at his feet. She scooted back to the pillows. She parted her knees. Bella used her pointer finger with a beckoning gesture. He greeted her between her thighs first. His tongue gently plied apart the lips of her sex, and his fingers spread the top folds wider to reveal her clit. Giovanni inhaled her feminine fragrance. He lifted his gaze to see her slowly sinking into the pillow, and the dark berry tips of her breasts undulate upward with a deep intake of breath. He licked his two fingers and inserted them in her pussy. Bella was tight for him. He groaned with lust. And then he teased her clitoris into his mouth for sucking. The harder he sucked and finger fucked her, the more he enjoyed her reaction. Her ass began to move in circular motions up off the bed sheet. He could tease and please her this way all evening. But his cock's aches became unbearable.

He eased up her, running his tongue over her pussy to her navel. All the while he kept the rhythm of his fingers delving in and out of her channel.

"Giovanni... *dammelo... dammelo...*" she pleaded.

He loved it when she begged to be fucked. He lost his concentration when her plump nipples brushed his chest. Drawn to the breasts he loved to suck, he lightly bit her nipple with his teeth and she hissed. He kissed away the sting and sucked the morsel into his mouth. His two fingers tunneled further into her tightness. Three babies later, the snug fit of their union went unchanged. He withdrew his fingers. She opened her eyes and looked at him, still moving and pumping her pussy up against his groin under the pangs of ecstasy shocking her channel. He hovered with his hands pressed to the headboard unable to resist the challenge gleaming in her eyes.

His cock surged against her opening, and his shaft plunged deep. His pelvis pressed against hers. She would have spread those warm thighs of hers and welcomed him in if his knees hadn't settled on either side of them and kept them closed. She ran her hands up and down the sides of his chest and lifted her head to flick her tongue at his nipple as he gave her another thrust and sank deep.

"Yes, mmm, yes," she groaned.

Giovanni clenched his ass and pumped his pelvis to give and receive the ultimate pleasure of loving his woman. Breathing between them broke apart like sobs, as he fucked her harder and harder. Pleasure burst from her in a startled cry, and he dropped on her to take over. However, all her warmth and softness weakened him. She seized the moment. They rolled on the bed. She straddled him. Giovanni closed his eyes, rocked by the wicked swirls of her hips.

"Talk to me, baby... please," she begged as she arched her back and gripped his knees. She rose and fell on his cock with mounting speed.

"I love the way your pussy smells, then you move it, like this," he groaned.

"Mmm..." she said. "Yes, say more," She dropped forward and began her rhythmic rise and fall.

"This is how a real woman fucks her man," he said. "Fuck! Fuck!" he panted. He gripped her hips to keep from releasing. She groaned and kept putting her little maneuvers on him. He pressed his palm to her pelvis and the other just above the curve of her ass. With this control he stilled her and was able to thrust into her with hard bangs. It made her crazy with excitement. Giovanni smiled as she clawed at his chest and cried out for mercy.

"Oh, oh, it feels so good, oh..." she panted.

He bit down on his tongue and kept with his counter maneuvers, putting her pussy in distress. But he was no man of steel. He could only endure so much, and soon his hold slipped and his own passion consumed him.

"Mannaggia!" he breathed and flipped his wife. She gasped at the roughness. He was too far-gone to care. He pinned her leg over his shoulder and fucked her until his entire body seized and every drop of his seed was spent. Exhausted he dropped his face in the crook of her neck and shoulder. He lowered her leg and lay there for several moments, struggling to capture a breath.

She whispered she loved him and was glad he was home. He drifted on the whispers with his cock still in her.

—*B*—

"HELLOOOOOOOO? Has anyone seen my husband?" Marietta knocked. She peeked inside the room. Lorenzo looked up from his ledger. He'd forgotten the time. He'd only intended to visit his office for a few minutes and then join his wife in the shower.

"Forgive me, Marie. I got distracted."

She came inside and closed the door. "Aww, honey! Are you seriously working? Tonight? I've missed you. You've been gone for three weeks. What the hell could be more important than me?"

"Nothing," he smiled. "It's just Dominic is trying to make Giovanni question me again, and if I don't come up with a plan to shut him the fuck up I'll—" The words lodged in his throat when his eyes drank in her sex appeal. Marietta wore a peach satin robe that tied around her curves nicely. She had scooped her wild locks up into a messy ponytail to the back of her head. Her face was free of makeup, it made her look younger. How many nights when he was away did he pull and tug on his dick until it was raw because he missed her so much? He had been neglectful. It wasn't his fault entirely. Giovanni trusted him now. And he wanted to prove to his cousin that he was more than a fist. He had brains too. He was just as loyal as Dominic. Hell if he could find a legitimate business win for the family it would give him all the respect he needed. He could be the one to help Giovanni take the family into the future. First he had to set a trap to gain control over Mancini's business. And he was close. Maybe his wife could get him closer.

"I want you to come with me now!" she pleaded.

"I need to talk to you first," he extended his hand.

She came over and sat on the edge of the desk. She lifted her foot and put it on his lap so that her robe opened and he saw between her inner thighs.

"Damn *bambina*!" Lorenzo chuckled.

"See something you like?" she asked. She leaned back on her hands. Lorenzo smiled. But she would not distract him.

"Have you been in contact with Armando Mancini behind my back again?" Lorenzo asked. He ran his hand over her foot and caressed her ankle.

Her naughty smile dimmed. "Honey, I only—"

"Don't lie to me, woman," he said in a low serious voice. "You know I know the answer before you speak," he warned.

"He's my brother. A few conversations over the phone is all. We're trying to fix things between us."

"Fix things?" Lorenzo picked up her foot and began to massage it. "What kind of conversations are these?" he asked.

"Nothing personal or about your business. I swear. Just stuff about Mirabella and me. He tells me stories about… my father. I should have listened to Mirabella when she begged me to talk to Marsuvio before he died. I regret it now, Lo. No matter how evil he was, he created me out of love."

"Or rape," Lorenzo said.

"What did you say?"

"I'm sorry, Marie. My mouth gets ahead of my brain," he replied.

"You're an asshole." She tried to pull her foot away but he gripped her ankle tighter to keep her still.

Lorenzo tugged on her foot. "Go on. Tell me what's wrong. I'm listening."

"I need… sometimes I need to understand why the things I've been through happened to me. Don't you?"

"You said I was all you needed," Lorenzo reminded her. "On our first anniversary what did I give to you?"

She pressed her lips together. Her large eyes watered with the brink of tears. She didn't answer.

"What did I give to you, Marie?" he demanded.

"You killed that bastard Octavio Leone for me. My adoptive father. You gave me my revenge," she said and a few of her tears spilled. Not in sadness or grief. They spilled because she felt joy over such a heartfelt gesture. He sent Renaldo to America to do the deed. And one call home confirmed it. Octavio was executed coming out of a local neighborhood bar. Lorenzo made sure

Renaldo told him why before the bullet split his skull. "It was the sweetest gift I've ever received. I... I'm grateful."

Lorenzo smiled. "So why look elsewhere, for happiness when I'm your husband? Your protector."

Marietta nodded her head in agreement.

"I want an answer, Marie," Lorenzo demanded.

She sighed. "All I need is you, Lorenzo. That doesn't change the fact that I want to know who I am. I have family. A history. Hell I'm part Sicilian. That's something I never knew. Armando and I talk about a family, a very powerful family I was born from. That's all. If you want me to stop I will."

"You're lying to me. You think I can't tell?" his gaze sharpened. Marietta couldn't counter. No one knew her rebellious nature better than him. He could raise hell and put his fist through every wall in Melanzana, and the damn woman would do whatever settled in that thick skull of hers. Not many men in his world would put up with a wife that tested him as much as his *cara*. He wasn't like most men. And when it came to women, only one that equaled him in strength and stubbornness could own his heart.

Marietta owned him.

"Let's not fight, sweetheart. I'm sick of talking about Armando. Fuck me, baby." She scooted over. She removed her foot from his hand and placed each foot on either side of his chair. Her knees parted and the treasure before him made his loins tight with lust. Marietta untied her robe. Damn woman left the room with nothing underneath. He shook his head in admiration. "Didn't you miss me, Lo? Haven't you missed me, baby?" she said. She moved from the desk to straddle him in the chair. The heat of her pussy pressed down on his bulge.

"Mmm, you did miss me," she whispered in his ear. Her tongue dipped inside and did a lovely swirl. Lorenzo exhaled through his nose. "You leave all of this home waiting for you, and the first thing you do is work in your office? Naughty husband," she shook her head with disappointment. She began to unfasten his belt with her knees awkwardly pushed through the opening on either side of the chair.

He grabbed her by the chin and forced her to look into his eyes. But her fingers worked fast to down his zipper and pull out this cock. "I won't forbid you from talking to him. Or even seeing him, which I know you already have."

"You mean it?" she paused. Her hand froze on his dick and her touch alone made his breathing shorten and quicken. He again refocused his mind.

"I need you to pay attention to Armando's questions about *la famiglia* business. And deliver a little information for me, when the time is right. Especially if he ever does or says anything that means he is trying to get closer to Gio."

"But we don't talk about you and the Battaglias. I don't like the sound of this. You want me to spy for you?" she removed her hand.

"*Cara*, he isn't talking to you to be your long lost big brother. He's prepping you, making you his ally."

"I would never betray our family or you, Lo," she said. "You do believe me?"

He chuckled.

"You do believe me?"

"Yes. Still there will come a day when he asks something of you. It will be something small, insignificant. Your first reaction will be to answer or give it. Has he already?"

She bit down on her bottom lip and lowered her gaze.

"What did he ask for?"

"A picture. A picture of Mirabella and me. He wanted to have one, something of us. So I tricked Mirabella into posing for one with me. I got the film developed and gave it to him. And he gave me pictures of my father."

"And you did this without discussing it with me?" he asked. Marietta opened her mouth to explain but he cut her off. "I've taught you better than being so impulsive. Haven't I?"

"Yes."

"Damn it, *bambina*!" Lorenzo slapped his forehead with his hand. "Maybe I've been too liberal. Gio doesn't have these issues because he and Mirabella have boundaries. Where are our boundaries, Marie?"

"We have them, Lo. It's just that you can't control me like he does her. I won't put up with it."

"You think I can't control you? You think I don't how?" he asked and the darkness in him surfaced in his eyes.

She lowered her gaze. Lorenzo's ruthless reputation had been mentioned to her over the years. She heard the stories. But he never showed any of his rage to her. Not since their fated meeting when he discovered the cassette player in her purse.

"I'm sorry. I should have told you." She wrapped her arm around his neck. "It won't happen again." She kissed his lips. "I promise."

He pinched her on the ass and she squirmed a bit for him. "I will decide how to deal with Armando Mancini. If a brother is what you want to play with, Marie, I will bend him for you. After I break his knees and dust his empire."

The threat tickled Marietta, she giggled. She didn't care if Lorenzo wanted the Mancini empire. She learned early in her marriage that her husband's ambitions would lead him toward some goal such as this. What thrilled her was his willingness to do anything to make her happy. Never in her life had she had that kind of unconditional love.

She kissed his brow. "You're so bad, Lo! I love it! And for the record there is no man, no one, who will ever make me forget the lessons you've taught me. I will do whatever you want me to do. I swear it." She bounced on his lap with excitement.

Lorenzo laughed. He shook his head smiling. Marietta climbed off him. She stood between him and his desk. Her lips were more persuasive than her words. If she kissed him again he'd do whatever she asked. But she didn't. Instead she slowly untied the sash to her robe and let the delicate fabric drift down her arms. Again he drank in her beauty. Her body was flawless. The diamond piercing in her bellybutton sparkled. Marie fluffed out her hair and turned to give him full view of her ample butt cheeks. She leaned on his desk. She cast him a look over her shoulder that challenged the beast in him. Then she spread her feet and dipped her spine to give her ass life.

"I've missed you so bad, Lo. Fuck me. Now," she pleaded. Lorenzo scooted his chair closer. Her pussy was now level with his mouth. He closed his eyes and inhaled her rich scent.

"Kiss me, Lo," she said and reached between her parted thighs to ply her pussy lips apart. He kissed his wife appropriately. His tongue swept and licked from her clit to her forbidden zone. She cried out the way she often did when he fucked her with his tongue. He heard several items push off his desk and crash to the floor. Lorenzo put an iron grip on her thighs and she lifted on her toes. His lids fluttered shut as her cries for mercy only made him want to feast and feast.

Lorenzo couldn't believe how lucky he was to have her. He wanted it all with her—his very own legacy. A dynasty to leave to his sons. Men like him didn't live until old age. Lorenzo had no intention of dying, but even he and his brothers knew the reaper would come for them, like it had for their fathers before them. That's why having sons was important.

"Don't stop! Don't!" she shouted.

Lorenzo stood. She turned her gaze back over her shoulder to watch as he freed his cock. He lifted her by the hips for the strike. Her knees buckled but she stayed in position for him. That tight pussy of hers squeezed the head of his dick after the first plunge. The breech was glorious. He exhaled hard. Three weeks and he hadn't touched his wife. What the fuck was he thinking? He gave her another shallow thrust and Marietta's forehead dropped on the desk. He pushed down on the center of her back to keep her cherry ass nice and high for his invading cock. His mouth formed the perfect shaped O. And his head dropped back. The spasms of her pussy were intensely tight as she worked her ass for him. He learned early on that his woman savored this part. Fuck! It was his favorite part too. He loved to fuck her from behind. He didn't want to explode. He was so close. Slow and easy he fed her pussy more of him, and then withdrew. He closed his eyes and willed his dick to not rush to the finish line. But the pain for release hammered his pelvis and sent cramps through his groin.

"Fuck! Fuck!" he shouted, and started thrusting in her harder once more. "Fuck! Damn it!" he wheezed as he felt his control slip.

"More, baby, give me more," she whimpered. Lorenzo bit hard on his bottom lip, nearly drawing blood. Marietta danced and moved like no other woman he'd ever known. Even now with him bending over his desk she made her ass cheeks bounce and clap with the working of her feet, she forced him to thrust his hips with such frenzy he was struggling to keep control.

"No! No damn it!" he grunted. His control slipped. It was too much too fast! He exploded in her sweet pussy with a cry of defeat.

Marietta stopped moving and frowned. "You're done? Already?"

"Marie, *bambina*, I just got home. I haven't had you in a week. Give me a minute to catch my breath," he chuckled. He pulled back. She turned and slapped him. It was a love tap, and usually happened if she was frustrated. He grabbed her hand and kissed it. "Let me shower. I'll take care of you tonight. Don't I always?"

"You better," she pouted.

Lorenzo shook his head and smiled. "I love you, woman."

She sat on the desk and stared at him. "I love you too."

Before she entered his world he had resigned himself to being second in life. He knew now that his dreams were achievable. Why would the saints give him the daughter of one of the most powerful Dons in Sicily as a bride if it weren't his destiny? It was because he had a higher purpose. Marietta would give him his destiny.

"What is it, baby?" She looked down at his erection. Did the woman always have his dick on her mind? She reached for it. He knocked her hand away.

"Let me suck it, Lo, I'll get it back up for us," she came off the desk for him. He grabbed her hand. "What's wrong? Why are you staring at me like that?" she asked.

"A son. I want a baby, Marie. It's what you want too? Isn't it?" he squeezed her chin tightly.

She hesitated, and then her resistance softened. "Some day. Yes."

"No. I want a baby now. Today. Let's see a doctor. Have a test done to see what the problem is—"

"Lo, stop." She grabbed his hand that held her face. "We don't need a doctor, sweetheart. We need each other. You are constantly out there trying to prove yourself to Giovanni. You're barely in my bed anymore. You want a baby, then eat a little pussy and fuck your wife."

A gust of laughter exploded from him. He hugged her to him unable to stop. When he caught his breath he confessed. *"La fregna che te ceca!"* It was a phrase said in central Italy where he met her. He said it often since the day she fought him in her hotel suite and then fucked him like a goddess. It meant: *pussy could blind a man.* And it was ever so true about his naughty wife. A dark part of him whispered that she deceived him about wanting to give him sons, but his heart would never let him believe it.

CHAPTER TWO

The Guest

"Buon giorno! Buon giorno papà!
Buon giorno! Buon giorno… buon giorno papà!
Batta le manine! Batta le manine!
Buon giorno papà!
Ora viene papà! Ora viene papà!
Buon giorno… buon giorno papà!"

The children sang. Eve led the chorus holding the hands of her brothers on either side of her. The twins mocked their sister. They swayed side to side. Giovanni groaned. He put the pillow over his head. The singing got louder. He turned over. He peeked out of one eye at his grinning *bambini*. They were only a few feet from the bed, and their voices raised louder than that of a bullhorn. He had his wife to thank for the sweet harmony. It was a song she taught them, and they sang it often when he returned from a trip.

Unable to deny them their welcome, he woke and lifted his head. All three cheered with delight and rushed the bed. Eve climbed on first as the bigger of the siblings. Gino was able to keep up. Gianni, however, fell behind and immediately screamed with an explosion of frustrated tears. Giovanni reached for him and brought him on the bed while taking tackles from his other son and daughter.

"Not so rough!" Mirabella said. "Gio, be careful, he's too close to the edge of the bed. Eve, sit down before you knock Gino off, sweetheart!"

Giovanni threw Gianni and he bounced on the bed nearly rolling to the edge. He giggled, got to his feet, and charged at his father again. Giovanni flipped Eve. He tickled her while Gino climbed on his head. Mirabella threw up her hands in defeat. She joined them on the king size bed.

"*Grazie* for the wake up call, Bella," Giovanni chuckled.

"*Prego,* sweetheart. Your children wanted to wake you," she said as she tried to stop Gino from jumping on top of the mattress. He then dove at his father landing on his lap. Giovanni would take hold of his feet and flip him again. "Stop playing so rough. Gino, you could fall off the bed and hit your head."

Giovanni heard her plea and gave in. He let the kids fight over him. He dropped back on his pillows and drew them all into his embrace. He had long enough arms to hold them. *"Come sta, bambini? Eh?"*

The children spoke at once. He couldn't hear one over the other. He laughed and pretended at understanding Gino. This was his boy. He could see it in his son even now. Of course he loved all his children, but Gino was special. He pulled him in for a bite on his cheek.

"Papa! Listen to me!" Eve whined, trying to push Gino away. "I was talking to you!"

"I'm listening, Lucciola. I always listen, *mia cara.*" He kissed her next.

"Give me my baby." Mirabella reached for the whining Gianni. He passed his son over to his mother. The boy silenced the minute Mirabella cradled him in her arms and put him to her breast. Giovanni took hold of Gino and Eve. Both kids sat on his lap but the two shoved at each other for dominance.

"Okay, that's enough. Be still." He scolded them. He was a sucker for their pouting. So he tried to make them smile again. "Have you been good?"

"Yes," they sang and glared at each other.

He looked over to his wife. "Has Ma-Ma been good?"

"Nooooo!" they sang.

He laughed.

"Mama was on the phone, Daddy, all day!" Eve tattled. He glanced to his wife and she looked at her daughter surprised by the accusation. Eve nodded that the story was true. Giovanni felt a pang of guilt. There was a fight once in front of the kids when she spent an entire day on the phone with business calls, and dinner was left to Ana and Zia. He knew the kids heard them arguing but he dismissed it as a forgotten event. Eve was very observant. He wouldn't allow her to disrespect her mother.

"Mama was on the phone with me, Lucciola," he smiled.

"Oh?" Eve frowned. He shot Mirabella a wink and she cut her eyes at him unimpressed.

"I brought your coffee," she told him in a dry tone. Now she was pissed. He glanced over to see the mug on the nightstand. Steam swirled up and the aroma made his mouth water.

"Thank you, my beautiful wife," he said.

The compliment softened her frown. Mirabella leaned in closer. She kissed his shoulder. "Spend a little time with them this morning okay? I need a break," she sighed. She put Gianni on the bed. He settled on the pillow without complaint. "I'm going to go shower," she waved him off and went into the bathroom. Giovanni had to give credit to his wife. She made sure he found time for all that was important. Gino eased out of his arms and started to jump on the bed. Gianni stood and began to jump with him.

"Gino needs a spanking, Papa. Mama told him no jumping!" Eve huffed. "Look at him. He's a bad boy." Eve stuck her tongue out at her brother. The boys plopped down laughing, and stood and began to jump again. Giovanni kissed his daughter and hugged her. She began to tell him about her swim adventure. Resigned to the morning of father duties he listened. After a check of his watch he knew the time would cost him. Santo returned today.

He needed to be ready to receive him.

"*SVEGLIA!*" LORENZO SMACKED MARIETTA ON THE ASS. The pain jolted her awake. Her head lifted from the pillow. She tried to swing at him but he was off the bed and out of her reach. "What time does your friend arrive today, *cara*?" he grinned.

"That hurt!" she said. She rubbed the sting out of her warmed left buttock. Lorenzo moistened his lips with eyes glued to her ass. He buttoned his shirt. His gaze lingered on the lower half of her body as if trying to decide on temptation.

"We made a baby last night. I feel it!" he grabbed his dick and tugged it at her. God her body hurt. He wasn't great in the beginning, but after he showered and joined her in bed, her tiger had returned. Her pussy hurt so bad she found it hard to close her legs. Marietta rolled over laughing. She stretched her arms above her head so her breasts lifted, nipples peaked, and her belly flattened. She parted her thighs in a suggestive manner. She didn't mind a little discomfort with her morning loving, just as long as she had more of him.

"Do you want to try again to be sure?" she teased.

The offer put a sly smile to his mouth. She knew he was tempted. He paused and then blinked out of his lust. "Later. Definitely later," he said and walked way from the bed.

Marietta rose on her elbows. "What time is it? Come back to bed now. I'm serious. I'm sick of this, Lo. You owe me more time."

"Can't. I want to meet with Carlo first thing. Need to straighten something out with him. And plus I have a few calls to make before Dominic wakes and is riding my ass."

Marietta turned over and pulled the sheet to cover her nudity. "I thought you would take me to the airport to pick up Shae?"

"Send a car for her." Lorenzo replied.

"She's flying into Napoli!" Marietta shouted. "The girl has never been out of the States. I need to meet her there."

"Don't bust my balls!" He threw up his hand and walked away. Marietta watched him march around the room in search of something. He was dressed except for his shoes. He turned and went to the dresser drawer.

"Wait!" she yelped. He ignored her. He found a pair of socks in the bottom drawer instead of opening the top one. Her heart started beating again. She watched him put on his socks and shoes and tried to mask her discomfort. How could she have been so careless as to leave her pills in the top drawer?

"I'll tell Renaldo to take you to Napoli. Gio and I have business to tend to here. Santo arrives today. It's a very important day. Gio needs me."

"Oh? Santo's out of prison?" she asked.

"Been out for a week. The motherfucker has disrespected Gio by not coming sooner," Lorenzo grumbled.

"You know we leave for Milano this evening. Will I see you before?" she asked.

"Ring Villa Rosso when you return from picking up your friend. I'll meet her and you can give me my afternoon snack," he winked.

Marietta threw her pillow at him. He stood, grabbed his watch from the dresser and walked out. As soon as the door closed she bolted from the bed, rushing to the dresser. With him gone the past few weeks she'd been careless. She pulled open the top drawer and there on top of her undergarments was her pack of birth control pills. She quickly took one and swallowed the pill dry. Marietta closed her eyes and exhaled. She tried on numerous times to muster the courage to explain to Lorenzo the reasons why she wouldn't be a good mother. But he'd never listen. It was easier to pretend for now.

She looked down at the pills and felt the stab of regret. How could she deny her sweetheart the only thing he'd ever asked of her? Lorenzo was her world. There had to be a compromise. But what? She prayed with everything in her she'd find the strength to make him understand.

Fabiana's, Milano – Italy—

"Ciao a tutti!" Catalina greeted her staff. She passed her coat off to Mateo. He kissed her on both cheeks and fell in step at her side. Though the hour was very early her staff was up and bustling. Mirabella would arrive that evening, and possibly stop by before the office closed. Though if Giovanni was with her, Catalina doubted it. Everything had to be perfect just in case. "Sorry I'm late. There was traffic. Have Kyra and Jamie arrived yet?"

"Um, no. But, Catalina, I must tell you—"

"When they arrive I want them both brought to me immediately. Renaldo has rented a place for Kyra here. With the success of her shoe line the Donna wants her working between Milano and Sorrento for the rest of the year. Send flowers as a house present. No! No! Send flowers and a nice bottle of champagne. Oh! I think Jamie is staying at the *Pierre Milano*. Make sure he, um, she has a bottle of champagne too."

"*Signora* Catalina, *per favore…* I must tell you—"

Two men with racks of clothes came down the hall at full speed. Catalina sidestepped a near collision. *"Minchia!"* **Catalina shook her fist at the man to her left. "Watch where the fuck you are going! What is the damn hurry?"**

"Scusi signora, Catalina. Scusi!" **The man stammered**. Catalina marched off with the toss of her hair. She headed for Mirabella's office. "I'm still not sure if the Donna wants to feature the new red bottoms Kyra designed in the show, or the platforms that Jamie recommends. We must decide that soon. I need the girls' shoe sizes to make sure they are fitted and rehearsed. *Mio Dio!* Let's not have Zenobia trip over herself in the finale! I could see it

now. Marietta would blame me for it."

"Signora!" Mateo grabbed her arm to stop her.

Catalina paused and looked at the men when they crashed the dress rack into a few mannequins. She groaned in her throat. "Is this place the zoo? Get it under damn control, Mateo! Or fire them! He nearly ran me over."

"Sí, Signora, but—"

"Now that I've had time to think about it, all of this may be too much overkill." She gestured to the decorative red scarves and extra lighting on the floor. "We don't want to look gaudy for Mirabella."

"Sí!" Mateo replied.

"I shouldn't have listened to Marietta. We have Fabiana's and Mirabella's lines on the same runway. What should distinguish the two? And the platform shoes are too flashy. It'll take away from the clothes... too much! I think I made a mistake."

"Signora!"

"Yes, Mateo, I'm right here! What is it?" Catalina asked. Mateo pointed. She and her men glanced to the glass doors of Mirabella's office. A man paced. His hands in his trouser pockets and his head bowed she didn't recognize him immediately. He was taller than Dominic and dressed in a tailored dark suit.

"It's what I wanted to say to you. *Signor* Armando Mancini is here," Mateo began. "He arrived just a few minutes ago. I didn't know where to take him, so I brought him to the Donna's office."

Catalina glanced back to the hired men that followed her everywhere. Both tensed at the sight of Mancini. She found it even more peculiar that Armando would show up without his entourage. Men like him and her brother had to be shadowed by guns constantly. It was a matter of safety. Armando had arrived alone.

"It's fine, everyone. I'll deal with him," said Catalina.

The men disobeyed her and marched straight into the office. Catalina hurried after them. The last thing she needed was her brother's men making a scene and embarrassing her in front of Armando Mancini, or worse her staff. The people working for her were out of America and France. Many only half-believed in the Mafia. All of them were tense with anticipation over who and what the Battaglias were.

"Wait! Wait!" she said through clenched teeth. She was too late. When her brother's men stormed inside the office, Catalina barely arrived behind them. Armando looked up with not a hint of fear in his eyes.

One of the men demanded his reason for the visit. The other circled Armando and stopped directly behind him. It was Umberto, an enforcer with the temper of Carlo and the cunning of Dominic. Umberto parted his blazer to reveal his gun in his pants. Catalina saw the anger and heard the threat in their tones.

"He's here to see me!" she announced. "Enough of this. Get out. To the door. Now! It's a private family matter. I requested the meeting with Don Mancini."

The men exchanged looks. Catalina shoved Umberto in the chest—the taller of the two. "Go! Go now! Just to the door. It won't be a long meeting. Go!"

They heard her wishes and obeyed. Not before they both gave Armando a warning glare. Catalina shook her head. She waited until the door closed to turn and look upon her visitor. "Are you insane? Coming here uninvited?"

"Aren't I family?"

"No," Catalina frowned. Armando's gaze pierced her. He had very compelling brown eyes ringed with dark lashes. Dominic had those bedroom eyes. It was the first time she saw that in common with both of the men. She had to look away from his piercing stare. Men like Armando could see through a woman's curiosity to her hidden interests. Of course she had none. It just felt weird.

She went to the desk and pretended to straighten some things there. "I will tell Marietta that you came by and have her call you."

"Catalina? I am here to see you," he said.

"You what?" she glanced back at him with surprise. Again she was taken with his physical appearance. His hair was combed back from his face, tucked behind his ears. Silky and black it dusted his shoulder. She didn't know much about him. As a little girl she had little access to him, and as a woman even less. However, she'd have to be blind not to be affected by his fearlessness. Deep down Catalina always craved men of power. It was why she constantly tried to encourage Dominic to achieve higher ranking with her brother. And a *consigliere* was as high and respected as they come. But a *consigliere* was no Don.

As he flipped back his jacket to slip his hand in his pocket, he raised the line of his trouser leg to draw her gaze to his feet. Jamie once told her that she could tell a lot about a man by his shoe size. Armando Mancini had an impressive shoe size. He stepped toward her. His aftershave greeted her and drew her eyes back to his. Secretly she inhaled the spice and tried to name the scent. His gaze swept her and the perusal felt intimate. Nervous, because of the attention, Catalina glanced back to the glass doors to see if the men noticed.

Today and every day she worked at Fabiana's, she wore red. That's what House of Fabiana's was about, the color scarlet. And the dress flattered her curves. She knew this. She'd chosen the garment for Dominic, but Armando smiled as if she dressed that morning for him.

"*La piccoletta.* My how you've grown," Armando said. "*Bellisima!* You are one beautiful woman.*"

"Why do you want to see me?" she asked again. The man made her pressure rise by the minute. She was actually beginning to sweat.

"I'm here about my sisters. They have a birthday coming soon. No? It's just a few days from now." Armando walked around Catalina toward the desk in the room. Behind it was a wall portrait. It was a very striking image of Mirabella and Fabiana posed back to back. He stared up at the portrait for a moment. "Interesting painting. Never had the pleasure of meeting the other woman, her partner. What was her name?"

"Fabiana. They were the dynamic duo. Gio had this painted for Mirabella over two years ago when he opened her boutique in Milano."

"She is beautiful, as is Mirabella," Armando said.

"You aren't invited," Catalina informed him. "To the party. You aren't invited."

"Oh but I am," he corrected her and cast his gaze her way. "Marietta extended the invitation."

"She did? No she didn't!" Catalina said. "Gio would never allow it."

Armando stepped again into her space. Catalina refused to show fear, but there was weakness. Whenever he stared at her too long she found herself smiling. That was definitely disrespectful to Dominic. So Catalina took a step back and cast her gaze to the portrait and not him.

"We've kept our little family ties private. But make no mistake. There are rumors, whispers, and it chips away at Giovanni's credibility, and mine," he said softly. His voice was too deep for whispers, but when he lowered it, the soft approach came across more sensual than she was sure he intended. She looked up into his eyes and realized her mistake. His attentions were far from innocent.

"Why do you care?" she asked and crossed her arms over her chest.

He faced her. "Because soon the truth will come out. It always does.

Everyone will know your brother married the bastard daughter of one of the five Dons."

"I'll ask you one last time before I have you escorted out. Why did you come to see me?"

Armando tried to mask his amusement, desire, and appreciation for her beauty, but the question nearly demolished his smirk. Should he be honest? Should he share that the other day between meetings he caught a glimpse of a television in his office. On the screen was Catalina being interviewed about the fashion house Fabiana's in Milano. She wore an all white dress with a heart shaped bodice that revealed a tasteful hint of her breasts. He had heard from his men that the young sister of Giovanni was beautiful. She often visited her family in Sicily. But he had no interest in a child. The woman on the television screen was far from it. He'd spent many sleepless nights thinking about her.

Her dark raven locks flowed like silk to her shoulders. The side part she wore caused some hair to drift over and cover her left eye. She had curves that were graceful, but voluptuous in the hips, breasts, ass, and thighs. The hot red dress was like a siren announcing her femininity with every step she took. And lastly it was her eyes. Sultry with innocence and warmth, under long dark lashes, he couldn't stop staring into them.

When he arrived he told her they were family. It was not Mirabella and Marietta he spoke of. It was another half-truth. Armando's mother lost her own *madre* when she was just a babe. Her father had to take a new wife to raise the infant. That woman that Armando's grandfather married was a Baldamenti. A blood relative to Tomosino Battaglia. Though Catalina and he had familiar *famiglia* ties, they were not blood related. Just as she wasn't blood bound to Dominic. He smirked at the irony when he considered his plans for her. What if Catalina was the one to tame him? Stranger things had happened between their families.

Catalina tossed her dark bangs from her eyes and glanced once more to the men outside. The Battaglia bodyguards itched to make this a more dramatic event. However, even in Milano, Armando had no fear that anyone would.

"I want to get to know Mirabella," he said. "I want you to convince her to let me come to her birthday celebration. To mend the bad blood between myself and Giovanni. It's time for us to move past the mistakes of our fathers. No?"

"I can't do that. Besides I won't. I know Gio hates you and has good reason to. That's where it stands," Catalina said.

"You have a lot of influence in this family now, Catalina. Look at you. Running a fashion business. I'm impressed, *piccoletta*."

"Grazie," she smiled. "I have grown up. Nice of you to have noticed."

"Oh, I've noticed." Armando chuckled. Flattery seemed to be the key with her. She blushed for him when complimented. Her olive skin flushed with a deeper rose tint that was lovely. What did Dominic know of unlocking the passions of a woman like her? Armando had to resist saying more. She wasn't ready. If she kept smiling and looking into his eyes, he had secret hopes that some day soon she could be ready. He took a careful step toward her. He sensed that the men were already back inside the door without looking up to confirm.

"Can I be honest with you, *cara*?" he asked in a voice so low and insistent only she could hear. She blinked those round eyes of hers at him and nodded. "I'm struggling to make sense of my life now. I lost my father. It's wounded me deeply. You know how that feels. No? It leaves you empty inside." He touched his chest.

She nodded. "Yes, I do. When Papa died I couldn't get out of bed for weeks. I could barely attend his funeral. I miss him still."

"Sí, now I have sisters I never knew. The bad blood between your brother and me goes back to our primary years. It's *non importa*. I want peace not war." He took another step closer and she didn't back away or turn her gaze. "I need an ally, a friend. You are allowed to make your own friends? Aren't you?"

Catalina chuckled. "I don't want to make friends with a Mancini… ah, I mean with you."

"Famiglia, bella. Remember it's all for family. Mirabella has my blood in her veins. She belongs to me too. The both of them do. The party would be a good step in the right direction." He winked. He gave a curt nod and started for the door.

"I'll talk to Mirabella," she said after him. Armando paused. He turned his gaze back over his shoulder. Catalina blushed for him again. *Damn.* It was hard not to touch her. "I can talk to her. It's all I can promise you."

"It's all I can ask," he smiled.

—*B*—

"You wanted to see me?" Carlo asked.

"Close the fucking door!" Lorenzo said.

Carlo did as he asked. Lorenzo reclined in Giovanni's chair. They were in Villa Rosso awaiting Giovanni's arrival. It surprised Lorenzo when he woke to discover Dominic had already left for Milano. Typically Dominic would stay for such an important meeting, nipping at his ankles, making Giovanni question Lorenzo's every move. He was happy he was gone. Still it didn't settle his anger over Carlo's betrayal.

"I told you we would hold off on the fighter. Not tell Gio until I decided if the business was needed."

Carlo wiped his hand down his face. He sucked in a deep breath before he spoke. "I brought the idea to Dominic. I've done that before. He's *consigliere*. He said it was a good investment and Gio should hear it."

Lorenzo slammed his fist down on the desk. "I had already given you an order!"

"No disrespect, Lo, but you aren't the only man in this family to give me orders. Dominic is my boss too."

"Don't bullshit me! It is disrespect. Every time you find a stray brother you drag them into this family as if we're a fucking orphanage! Did you not learn anything from Carmine! Do you want his blood on your hands too?"

"*Vai a farti fottere!* Don't ever throw Carmine in my face! Ever!" Carlo slammed his fist into his hand. Lorenzo held his glare with equal malice. Carlo paced away. He threw his hands up in the air and cursed under his breath. Once calm he turned and addressed Lorenzo again. "I am not going to make the mistake of bringing a brother of mine into this family again. Ciro is a good kid. A fighter. What I propose is a legitimate business. And last I checked, the Battaglias wanted to legitimize their affairs!"

Lorenzo stood. He leaned in on the desk with his fists. "You don't know shit about what the Battaglia business is built on. You don't know shit about anything other than the orders given to you! Fuck this nonsense about legitimizing my family. There is honor in who we are. Who Gio is now thanks to me! You step back, Carlo. Stay behind me. And don't you ever get in front of me again! *Capisci?*"

The stare off between them lasted longer than Lorenzo could tolerate before Carlo nodded his head.

"Get the fuck out of my sight," Lorenzo told him.

Carlo turned and walked out. Lorenzo dropped back in Giovanni's chair.

At some point he would have to make Giovanni understand that no one, not even Dominic needed to be his advisor. They are best and stronger with him as the trusted council.

—*B*—

"Morning!" Mirabella said.

Marietta looked up from her plate. She smiled as her sister walked in and joined her. They gathered in a smaller kitchen. It had a four-chair breakfast table, a brick oven that was older than them both, pots and pans hanging over the gas stove, sink, and a kitchen island. Typically the women retreated here, the bigger kitchen was left to Ana and her team.

"What time does your friend arrive?" Mirabella asked.

"I'm leaving to go get her in an hour," Marietta swallowed.

Her sister poured herself a cup of coffee. She pulled out a chair and sat at the table. Marietta loved how beautiful and vibrant Mirabella looked in the morning with no makeup. Each morning they met in the kitchen to share a cup of coffee and discuss any and everything. Mirabella mostly confided her feelings and frustrations. Marietta mostly listened. Even now she found it hard to really open up and tell her sister her deepest secrets, such as, her wish to never have children. And she could never tell her that Lorenzo was inadvertently responsible for the death of Giovanni's father. Some things were better left unsaid.

After seeing pictures of their mother, and learning more about the family she never knew in Virginia, she felt on most days that Mirabella looked like their mother. It was ironic that she had found her mother and sister all rolled up into one.

"So did it work? Your plans to seduce Gio?" Marietta asked.

Mirabella laughed. "Of course it worked. He was mine all night."

Marietta chuckled. "I decided to do the same when Lorenzo called himself working last night."

"Working?"

"Yes," Marietta cut her eyes. "I found him in his office. It didn't take long to convince him to come to bed."

"I bet," Mirabella smiled.

"Where's King B and those little blue-eyed devils of his?" Marietta asked.

Mirabella chuckled. "He's taking a break to spend some needed daddy time with his *bambini*. I hope."

"You hope? What's that comment about?" Marietta asked.

Mirabella shrugged. She stared down at her coffee, silent. Marietta reached over and touched her arm. "Hey? What is it?"

After a brief pause Mirabella looked over with tears in her eyes. "I'm a little scared."

"Scared? Of who?"

"Not who. What. I don't know if I can do it," she confessed. "I'm about to launch two different fashion houses, and step up as the head designer for both? Even Gio doesn't know the level of work ahead of me. And then there's my return back to that world. All of it. You know everyone is going to be waiting to see me, I… It's going to be hard to walk back into a life I left behind four years ago without… Fabiana, Teddy." Her voice trailed off. Mirabella glanced back at her sister. "I wish you would have known her."

"I don't!" Marietta said. She was sick to death of the ghost of Fabiana. And she was jealous of her sister's inability to let Fabiana's memory go. She hated that fucking portrait in Mirabella's office. It should be her and Mirabella standing back to back, not that red haired bitch. When she saw the hurt in Mirabella's eyes she decided to fix her tone. "What I mean to say is, I am glad it's us, doing it together. I want to be with you, at your side."

"What if I'm not that good? I've changed."

"Bullshit. You haven't changed that much. You don't lose your talent or forget it. You've evolved. Mirabella, you've been designing in Sorrento, and running the business in Paris and Milano through me and Catalina for over a year. We may be the face of the company, but you have always been the heart."

Mirabella nodded. She blinked away her tears. "My husband has needs, expectations. I know you don't believe this, but I love being his wife. Taking care of him and my babies. I like that they need me. I don't want to have servants and Zia step in and care for them while I'm split down the middle with the company."

"This doesn't sound like you? Is Giovanni trying to get in your head?"

"No. He's a sweetheart about it all."

"Yeah right!" Marietta said. The man barely smiles, always barks when he talks, and scares the shit out of most of the people that work for him."

Mirabella laughed. "You really see him that way?"

"Girl, I can never get the two of you. He's so stiff." Marietta shivered.

"He's complicated. Trust me, he's everything I ever wanted in a husband. Treats me better than any man ever has in my life, other than my grandfather. I won't make the mistakes I've made in the past."

"Mistakes? Stop it! This isn't a mistake. This is your dream. Giovanni needs to be supportive," Marietta said.

"He is," Mirabella quickly replied. "I keep telling you that!"

"You were fine until he came home. You were excited. Now listen to you."

"It's not him. I missed him when he was gone. Last night I had him all to myself and it felt good. I love that feeling. I can't explain it."

Marietta arched a brow as if she didn't believe her. Mirabella only smiled. She sipped her coffee before she spoke again. She tried to explain herself a different way. "I have three small children. We are moving fast. If I fail I won't get another shot at this. I know it. And what scares me is that I won't even try again. I'm different now. My priorities are different. Lord listen to me. I think I'd rather be a housewife than a fashion designer. When did that happen? "

"You won't fail! You can be both, though I can't imagine why you would want to wipe butts and fix dinner for your grumpy husband rather than be in the spotlight again!" Marietta moved her chair closer to Mirabella so she could reach her. She took her hand in hers. "I'm the last one to give you advice on how to handle your man. Listen to me. I've spent two years with you, learning from you. I see you with him and the kids, and I know you love them deeply. But I see you when you create something all your own, and know you are destined for greatness. Don't doubt yourself now, sis. You can have both worlds. You're strong enough. I'll help you. Catalina will help you. Kyra and Jamie will help. You've got one helluva team. Believe in us."

"I do."

"Then separate them, work and family, separate them."

"I don't understand. Separate how?" Mirabella asked.

"Leave Giovanni out of it. The party we have tonight to celebrate. Let's keep the men out of it. Let's get you to focus on just the fashion show and your company. Really give it a shot. You said he isn't pressuring you. And if I know them, then I know that they can give a shit about how we make dresses and shoes. So let's keep it separate, and that way you can keep focused on your goals without mixing them up."

Mirabella smiled. She hugged Marietta tightly. "I love you so much," she said.

"I love you too," Marietta said. She let her go. "Are you hungry? I can cook you one of my famous omelets before Zia comes down and chases us out of here to make one of her pies."

Mirabella laughed because she knew it was true. "Sure. I'm hungry."

—*B*—

"PAPA?" EVE SAID.

Giovanni tossed his underwear on top of the bed. Cecilia had come for the twins to dress them and take them downstairs for breakfast. Only Eve remained at his side.

"Yes, Lucciola?"

"Can I go with you today?" Eve asked. "To Villa Rosso?"

"No. Stay close to your mother."

"But, Papa, I don't see you anymore. Can I be with you today?"

"You will go with Mama to Milano. We discussed it," he said. He went to the closet to find the suit. Then he paused to see it hanging on the inside of the door for him. He should have known that Mirabella had done this for him. When he was home his clothes were pressed and arranged for him. She never forgot his needs.

"It's boring in Milano. I get stuck with the twins and Mama is always too busy for me. I want to be with you."

Giovanni cast his gaze down to his daughter. Eve wore a light green leotard, matching tights, and a green tutu. Her hair was smoothed up into a ball on the top of her head. She looked every bit of his ballerina. He wondered if her mother had dressed her for some lessons he didn't know about? She looked up at him with those expectant blue eyes and determined will. He had to admit their time-shared was now split with her brothers. When Eve first came into his life she was with him as much as possible. That had changed. His heart suffered a blow of sadness. "I will be coming to Milan with you. So we can be bored together."

"Really? Yay!" she cheered. She walked over to him and he picked her up. She'd grown so much and far too fast. He missed the little one with the cherry red pacifier. He kissed her cheek and inhaled her baby scent.

"What is this you're wearing?" he asked.

"Mama made it for me. I'm tinkle bell. I have wings too. She said I can wear them after when we have lunch."

"Who is this tinkle bell?" he asked.

"Peter Pan, silly. She's a fairy and does magic!" Eve grinned.

Giovanni chuckled. *"Vabene piccoletta."* He kissed her brow, her nose, and her tiny rosy mouth. "Go find Mama and have her give you breakfast. I need to shower."

"You're Peter Pan. Okay," she hugged his neck. "Papa, I love you. Forever."

"I love you too, Lucciola. Forever." He set her down and she ran from the room in her stocking feet with her tutu bouncing around her hips. He couldn't stop smiling. The phone rang. He marched over and picked it up.

"Pronto?" he answered.

"Gio, it's me, Santo."

Giovanni sat on the edge of the bed. "I have been looking to hear from you. It's been a week."

"Perdonami. I had to see to my family. My brother has been ill and it was important."

"But we are your family. Are we not?" Giovanni asked.

"Sí, you are. And I am grateful. But I must ask that I have another few days. There are personal matters that I need to attend to in Napoli."

Giovanni frowned. Santo was never expected to be jailed for so long. Unfortunately the press got hold of the crimes committed by Mottola, and Giovanni had to step aside to let the *Polizi di Stato* posture for the media. In doing so Santo had no cover from the *Camorra and* the tribunal proceeded. The judgment wasn't as severe as the attorneys advised it could be. Still the sentence was received bitterly by Santo. It never set well with Giovanni that Santo was condemned with so little proof of treachery. Especially after knowing how loyal his friend had been over the years.

"You will be here today, to see me. No more excuses," Giovanni said.

"I understand, Gio. I will see you soon."

"Santo, I've known you since we were kids. I love you like a brother. I'm pleased the nightmare is over for you, and I intend to make sure you receive the rewards you deserve for your sacrifice."

"Grazie, Gio. Tante grazie," Santo said. *"Ciao."*

"Ciao." Giovanni set the phone down. He stared at it for a moment. Santo

would fall in line. He had little doubt of his men.

Aeroporto Internaizonale di Napoli, Napoli, Italia—

"What time is it?" Marietta asked.

She checked her watch once more. The plane should have landed thirty minutes ago. She glanced over to Renaldo. He stood at her side, tall, silent, and watchful. His gaze remained shielded behind the dark lenses of his sunglasses. His hands clasped together in black leather gloves. When she spoke to him he looked right through her.

Marietta cut her eyes. It was always the same with Renaldo. She had no idea how he could ever have such a torrid love affair with the young beautiful shoemaker they brought back from America. The girl was feisty, and Renaldo was cold and brooding. Marietta smiled to herself. Those two did make some pair. Too bad it cost him his position as top enforcer to the Don. He no longer shadowed Giovanni and Lorenzo on important affairs. Nico was now the man who assumed the responsibility. Renaldo was more like a personal errand boy to the women, and a baby watcher for the kids.

She felt sorry for him, but safe whenever he was around. She could never tell if the demotion mattered. Kyra confided in her that it did. That Renaldo worked constantly to regain Giovanni's favor. But he was either ignored or dismissed for the effort. Even still, when it came to his responsibilities, he took every assignment given to him with the utmost seriousness. At that moment Renaldo could give a shit about her friend's arrival. He watched Marietta like a hawk. No danger present or unseen would come near.

"Marietta!" A voice shouted from above.

Shae rode down the escalator with a wide grin. She waved hard with her free hand. On her other arm was her large designer carry-on bag. Of course her friend stood out. She bounced in high heels. She wore flashy large gold earrings and bracelets, with the tightest fitted jeans a girl with her curves could squeeze into. Underneath her blazer Shae wore a white cut-off shirt that said 'Rock Steady' and revealed her navel piercing. A few men riding in front of her turned their heads and stared with appreciation. Shae was fierce. Her hair was cut in an asymmetrical bob with a long swoop of pink streaked across the left bang that hung to her nose concealing the side of her face.

It would be so much fun having her in Italy. Marietta glanced to Renaldo who was staring at Shae as well. Her girl had an immediate effect on men. Of course with Renaldo she couldn't tell if he'd noticed her flare, or just wanted to put her in his sights for protection. And though Marietta appreciated Shae's style, she'd have to ask her tone it down with the Battaglias. Shae may be a gem, but she was by no means the caliber of class Marietta had adapted as Lorenzo's wife and Mirabella's sister.

"That's her," Marietta grinned. She started off toward her.

"Oh my God! Look at you! Damn girl!" Shae rushed her from the final step. She bumped a woman and her child to do so. She dropped her carry-on bag and grabbed Marietta. They hugged, screaming and laughing.

"I have missed you, bitch!" Shae shouted to the entire airport.

Marietta hugged her back. "Girl! You have no idea how much I have missed you."

"Come on let's get your luggage," Marietta said. Renaldo reached down and picked up Shae's dropped bag. It was then her friend noticed him.

"Hold up. Who is he?" Shae asked.

"Huh? Oh! That's Renaldo. He works for my husband," Marietta told her.

"Mmmm…hi there, baby!" Shae grinned up at him.

Renaldo stared at her. Marietta shook her head. "Don't go there. In fact we need to talk." She hooked her arm in Shae's and forced her to turn and walk toward the luggage depot. Her friend smelled like berry scented lotion and expensive perfume. "I told you who I married. How things are here in Italy."

"Yeah, yeah, I know how those Italians in the 'Chi' roll." Shae grinned. "But girl they don't come like that. Most of them Italians are short with big bellies and receding hairlines." She smacked her gum, and shot Renaldo a sexy wink from her over shoulder.

"These men aren't like the Italians at home. They're Sicilian, and even the short ones are different than the men from home. My husband… well he's different. Shae, you have to respect them. Don't come out of the mouth all crazy. Okay? You said you could do this."

"Alright!" Shae shrugged her off. "What's with the attitude? You think I can't hang with your fancy life? Girl, please. I was the one that taught you how to tone it down with your crazy ass." Shae then took a long sideways look at Marietta. The white linen sundress that tied around the neck and flared at the hips was a Mirabella original, and her strappy sandals were from Gucci. She didn't have time to do anything with her hair so she let it air dry with big loose curls after the shower. Still her attire was understated, classy, and

Marietta knew it.

"Well I guess you have changed, Ms. Priss. You look… all prim and proper," Shae said with the wrinkle of her nose.

Marietta swallowed her smile. "Liar. Bitch, I look sexy, pampered, rich."

Shae rolled her eyes and giggled. "That's my Mae! I knew you were in there behind that fake smile."

"Oh cut the bullshit and point out the luggage!" Marietta laughed. Shae did. Renaldo was able to handle all the bags, and Shae travelled with three. One empty suitcase for all the shopping she intended to do in Italy. Shae was what Marietta would call hood-rich. She worked the clubs and did private parties in her early twenties. When business got really good she started her own escort company. She had girls who did bachelor parties and special events for sports stars and rappers. Shae said music videos were where the money and future clients were. Those video shoots sent her all over the world. Marietta was once one of those girls for hire. They were the same age, but Shae always had more confidence and business savvy. She gave Marietta her first loan to open her furniture business, and helped her when her adoptive parents turned her away.

Once in the car and on the road Marietta relaxed. Shae had a client, or boyfriend, that was some big time general. The man flew to Chicago regularly to see her.

"So how's Joe?" Marietta asked.

"Dead," Shae answered softly.

"Wait what? Dead?" Marietta asked.

Shae glanced over at her with tears in her eyes. "He had a heart attack. I wasn't with him. His son called and told me. I couldn't come to the funeral. His wife would take one look at me and have her own heart attack on the spot." Shae chuckled, but it was a sad empty chuckle. "I'm done, girl. I'm done being the side chick. I think you had the right idea. I need a change."

"I can understand change," Marietta smiled. "Lord knows I made a big one when I married Lo."

"So tell me all about him. This Sicilian you married?" Shae asked.

"He's my man. All mine. I can't describe him. You have to meet him. Trust me, when you meet him it will make sense."

"I'm confused. You were all worked up to find your mother and father in Italy. Then bam!" Shae snapped her fingers. "You call me and say you got married?"

"Yeah, it happened fast. He knocked me off my feet. Literally." Marietta laughed.

"What's funny?" Shae asked.

"Nothing. Private joke. I love him, girl. I've never loved a man so much. He's like part of me in a weird way. We both fuck up, but we get each other. I love him with all my heart."

Shae cast her a funny look. Marietta shrugged. It was the truth. She didn't care about the tough girl act she had with Shae. What she had with Lorenzo was one hundred percent real, and she'd kill any bitch who tried to come between them.

"And your sister? That's the real mind-fuck. Shit, people at home I told didn't believe it until we saw you on the news. Girl! I would have met you in New York when you came. I turn on the TV and see you walking out the Waldorf in a mink coat. Bitch! I almost fell over. What is she like? Mirabella? That bitch is the baddest in—"

"Shae, drop the 'B' word. Okay?" Marietta sighed.

"What? Bitch? It's a term of endearment, you know that!" Shae laughed. What she said was half-true. She and the girls used the word 'bitch' as a compliment of the fiercest, or as a deepest insult for treachery. It depended on how you phrased it in a sentence.

"Here they call my sister 'Donna'. And everyone gives her respect."

"Why is that her middle name or something?" Shae frowned.

Marietta laughed. "No. It means lady in Italian. For the family, she's the head next to her husband. He's the Don and she's the Donna. Get it?"

"Oooooh, okay. I get it." Shae nodded.

"Good, because you will call her that too. She's really sweet, Shae, not stuck up at all, but… well the people you meet treat her special. She gets respect from everyone. At all times. I told you about this… it's different with the Battaglias."

Shae nodded. "Calm down. I'm not an idiot. I won't go to anyone's house as a guest and act up." Shae chuckled. "I got your back. I always have. You need to relax. Remember my people skills." She popped her gum with the toss of her pink bang from her eye and grinned.

The tension eased out of Marietta. She missed her friend. It was hard being one hundred percent herself with Mirabella. With her sister she just wanted to please her and be accepted. Deep down she feared losing the connection that they just discovered. With Shae she was her old self again.

"Are you excited? This is your big event too, the fashion show. You helped coordinate it right?" Shae asked.

Marietta nodded. "I did. It's going to blow your mind. My sister has given me part of the company too. It's our thing. I told you she is really sweet."

"Yeah, yeah, but what about you, Mae? What is it you do?" Shae asked.

"You know I love to decorate and stuff. The set designs and the choreography for the runway show is all me. The music and entertainment. Girl I have celebrities calling me to get an invite. You are going to be blown away by the guest list for our party."

"Wow! Check you out!" Shae elbowed her. "Bitch… ah, sorry, I mean, girl, you are doing your thang!"

"Wait until you see Bellagio. It's so beautiful. The house there is mine. Lorenzo gave it to me for a wedding gift," Marietta grinned.

"I went to the book store," Shae said. She reached down in her bag and started to pull out books and maps. "This here is my translation book." She passed it to Marietta. "So I can communicate with the cuties. I learned the curse words, and some of the naughty ones too. I just love Italian!" Shae looked up at Renaldo who kept driving.

Marietta laughed. "They're Sicilian, Shae."

"Same thing! And oh! This! Here is my map of the places we're going. I got one for Sorrento, Milano, Bellagio, and I want to go to Venice. Please! Please take me!" Shae pleaded. "I want to ride in a gondola with Renaldo! You interested, baby?"

He glanced up and looked at her in the rearview mirror over the top of his sunglasses. Shae winked at him. Marietta shook her head amused. "Okay, I'll talk to Lorenzo and see if he can take us. If not there's the train. We can take it and the ferry into Venice. No problemo."

"Goodie!" Shae clapped causing her bracelets to jingle. "Wait, Mae, I'm sorry. Shit. Here I am going on and on about partying and I didn't ask you how you're holding up. The death of that bastard father of yours."

"Octavio Leone was never my father," Marietta said dryly.

"He was shot in the back of the head leaving Smithy's bar, and his body dumped behind it. You know it. The old dive off Crescent street."

"Yeah I know it," Marietta mumbled.

"The police still can't figure out who was responsible. I checked. Your mom, ah, your adoptive mother has moved to New York with her sister. It's all so fucked up. Random."

"I don't care about either one of them. Dead or alive." Marietta said.

"Sorry for bringing it up, girl."

"You will have a great time. Italy and the *Campania* is the most romantic place in the world." Marietta smiled.

"Romance huh? Well I can believe that, if all of the men look like Mr. Sexy up there. Does he speak English? Pass me my translation book!"

Marietta laughed. "You so damn crazy! I'm going to love having you here!"

—*B*—

THERE WERE TIMES WHEN Catalina found it hard to recall all of Mirabella's wishes from notes and previous phone conversations. On the eve of Mirabella's return, the biggest test of Catalina's career was at hand. Self-doubt and fear crept in. She had difficulties now making the simplest decisions. She had to get it together.

"Yes, Catalina. We can definitely do this for you. I'll see to it personally. But may I suggest we go with the pre-season selections you and Marietta chose for the opening? It was something Mirabella mentioned on her phone call. I think it may be an expectation."

"Mmm, I'm not sure," Catalina's gaze lifted from the sketches before her in time to see Dominic and his men arriving. She stood upright and straightened her skirt. "Clara and Mateo, I need a moment please."

"Sì, signora," her assistants nodded and gathered the plans they brought in for her review. Dominic held the door for them to pass through. He had to know of Armando's visit. Would he be angry? Would he be disappointed in her? Either way she was nervous and a little afraid. The ruling emotion was guilt. And even now she couldn't quite determine what she was guilty of.

"Ciao, my love," Catalina said. "I am so happy you're finally here!"

"Why was Armando Mancini here?" he asked.

The question stopped her approach. Catalina glanced to the men who were behind him. They glared at her. The damn bastards couldn't wait to give her up. "You just got here and that's the first thing you have to say to me?" she asked. She walked over and put her arms around his neck. *"Ciao, mio amore...* let's greet properly."

The last of her words were smothered under the press of his lips. She glanced over his shoulder at his men and they turned and walked out. She rose on her toes to welcome him with her tongue. His breath was warm against her mouth. And the feel of his body pressed against hers was what she craved. His kiss felt tender, forgiving. It delivered the sweet remembrance of the promises they made to one another. No girl on the planet deserved to be as lucky. When their lips parted he cradled her face in his hands and looked at her with so much love she blushed. "How's my girl?" he asked her.

"*Bennisimo*. I'm so glad you're back."

"I was only gone a few days," he chuckled.

"So you didn't miss me?" she asked.

"Of course I did," he kissed her once more. He released her face to wrap her up in his arms. He kissed the top of her head and squeezed her ass.

Catalina shivered. She was so horny she had a mind to take him to the bathroom and reunite properly. "I know, but still, I need you." It was the truth. She took good care of Dominic Battaglia, her future husband. Whenever he could plant himself in Milano between business trips, she made sure to be the dutiful fiancée. And the pressure eased on her for a wedding date. However, Catalina was far from naïve. She knew after two years of delaying the inevitable she couldn't hold his desire to wed off much longer.

"Now. I want an explanation. You requested a meeting with Armando Mancini. Why?" he asked.

Catalina let go of him. She looked up into his eyes. "I didn't."

"What do you mean you didn't? You told the men you invited him here," Dominic said.

She stepped back. "I didn't, Domi. He just showed up."

"*Mannaggia!*" Dominic paced away.

"It really wasn't bad, Domi. He wanted to ask that I speak with Mirabella. He asked for a favor."

"Who is he to ask a favor of you?"

"He told me that Marietta invited him to the party in Bellagio," she said. Dominic stared at her. She continued. "He wanted me to speak to Mirabella to see if it was okay with her. He didn't want to come and make it a problem with the family. Especially on their birthday."

"If this is truly what he wanted then he should speak to Gio about the impropriety. He knows this. He's fucking with me by coming here to see you."

"You? It had nothing to do with you?"

"Really?" Dominic lowered his brows. "Are you telling me it had everything to do with his wanting to see you?" Her sweet lover tensed. Dominic didn't rise to anger quickly. But she'd learned with Franco that if a man got in between them and hurt her in any way he wouldn't hesitate. Armando Mancini was a Don. He shouldn't be challenged over some petty jealousy.

"No. No of course not. Oh Domi, stop. It wasn't that sinister. He's trying to find a way to make this work with our families. He hasn't gone public about the twins. He keeps the family secret. Giovanni may have told the men in the family, but the press and the world still don't know that Mirabella is a Mancini. Isn't it wise for us to come together and manage the risk of how the truth comes to light? Armando coming to the party is a good start."

Dominic waved off her logic. "Fuck him. *Che palle!*"

Catalina waited. She watched Dominic pace in front of her. There was no need to try to reason with him when he was like this. She let him decide on what to do next. He stopped pacing and looked over at her. "How much longer here? I want to take you to lunch. I want to spend some time with you."

Catalina nodded in agreement. "I'll go with you now. No problem. Wait!"

"What is it now?" he asked.

"What time does everyone arrive? I need to make sure everything is ready for them."

"They won't be here until late in the afternoon. You're mine now," he smiled.

"Andiamo!" She kissed him. "Then let's skip lunch. Take me home so I can welcome you properly." She squeezed his groin. He chuckled and nodded in agreement.

A HAND PRESSED AGAINST HER LOWER BACK. Mirabella wiped the sweat from her brow with the back of her hand and continued to slice through the tenderloin. She'd warm and sauté the meat, then make fresh panini's for lunch.

"What is it, sweetie?" she asked.

The touch was that of a man's. No man in or out of this family ever touched her but Giovanni. When he didn't answer she glanced back. He stared into her eyes. She put down the butcher knife and turned to face him. He took her by the hand. Without a word he walked her away from her tasks. Zia glanced up.

She was cutting fruit for the salad and chatting with Ana the cook who sat at the table rolling pasta with her hands. They both ignored the Don's mission to steal away his wife. He walked her into the hall and to the first room they came to that offered privacy. It was a guest room on the lower level. The moment she entered she was pushed up against the door and it closed.

"I have meetings today," he said with a soft groan of regret. He brushed his lips over hers. He kissed her cheek. Mirabella held to his side.

"I know. I was working on lunch. I'll send some sandwiches for you and the men." She touched the side of his face. "Make sure you eat. Please. We've got a busy day with our traveling out to Milano."

"About last night?" he said. "I haven't been able to stop thinking of you, Bella," he shared with her. His hand rubbed up her thigh. She wore blue leggings and a long, loose-fitted, white button down shirt. He started to push loose each of the buttons.

"Gio, I can't, not right now. We both have so much to do before we leave," she reasoned. When his lips brushed her neck she fell silent. He lifted her by the hips. She wrapped her legs around his waist as he turned and carried her to the bed.

"I'll be quick, Bella. Just a taste and I'll let you go." He and she went down on the bed together.

She grabbed his face. "We should have taken a shower together. That would have worked. I'll have to shower all over again."

"Shhhh…" He kissed away her protests. "I want to fuck you right here, right now, say yes."

"Yes," she breathed.

He pulled down her leggings until they were snatched from her ankles. She helped by rolling her panties off her hips and down her legs, kicking them off her feet. He drew his shirt over his head and tossed it aside. He undid his trousers and let them drop. His erection had nearly punched through the front of his boxers. Mirabella tingled with excitement.

Giovanni dropped on her before she could remove her shirt. It didn't matter. All she craved in the moment was him. It was always like this between them after they'd been separated. Marietta and Catalina didn't believe her when she said she made love to her husband every night. No exceptions.

There was no woman on the planet that excited him like his wife. Each time he fucked her it felt as sweet as the first. He thrust into her. Mirabella gave a thin soft moan. She gripped his arms to steady herself as she simultaneously pushed her pelvis down on his thrust so she could take him in deeper. They were on the edge of the bed. He eased up on her and brought her left leg up and over to press it down on her right. She gripped the sheets as he thrust into her again. And even though she was pinned into position she was ready. He rocked his cock into her and her tight little cunt lips tugged and clenched to draw him even further.

"Yes!" she cried out in joy. It was easy to turn her over so that she was on her stomach as he slipped out of her. She crawled on the bed on all floors. He staggered, a bit dazed by the pleasure. But he came behind his wife, gripped her by both hips, and plunged into her again. He gave her sharp thrusts that churned within her silky walls. Giovanni's balls tightened. He gritted his teeth. Every sensation felt amazing. And the sounds they made when fucking fanned the flame of his wild obsession to posses her. Wet slaps sounded at his belly and thighs as he slammed into her pussy over and over. He started to tease and play with her clitoris while fucking her with targeted strikes. Mirabella's entire body shivered and short breath pleas for mercy filled the room.

Her back dipped.

Her pussy convulsed around his dick, squeezing him with strong rhythmic pulses that made a chump out of him. He broke. "Shit!" he cried out and dropped on her. His weight drove them flat to the bed. He kept rising and falling in and out of her pussy until every ounce of his seed was spent.

"Bella, Bella, Bella," is all he kept repeating.

He lifted off her for fear of causing her discomfort. She rolled to her side and held herself. He spooned with her and held her to him. They both lay on their side, trying to capture their breaths.

"Gio, you'll be late for your meeting," came her soft, sweet, caring voice.

He closed his eyes and smiled. "Fuck the meeting. Run away with me. I'll get the jet and we can be in France tonight. Just me and you. Somewhere alone, forever," he breathed.

She laughed. "And our children?"

"Oh? Yeah, bring them too," he panted.

She turned over and hugged him. He held her close to his heart. "Sounds like you are in love with your wife," she said.

"I am. I love you, Bella. *Ti amo*," he kissed her brow.

"Clean up and go to your meeting. I need to finish lunch."

"Wait! Let Zia do it," he tried to pin her down. She eased from under him. She smiled and he groaned over the loss of her. He watched as she put on her lace panties. He thought to ask to keep them, but it might distract him if he sat in his meeting sniffing them all evening.

She pulled up her leggings. She blew him a kiss and was gone. Giovanni touched his deflated dick. He lifted his head to look at it. If he could get it to rise again he'd kidnap her to another room and do it all over again. Nothing happened. He slapped it and it fell limply over to his thigh. "Fuck!" he groaned.

—*B*—

"Is HE HERE?" Giovanni asked. He rolled his cigar between his thumb and pointer finger. The ash lengthened but didn't flake away. His mind once again conjured images of his wife masturbating for him. He smiled.

"He just arrived. Carlo and Nico will bring him in." Lorenzo frowned. "What's so funny?"

"Funny?" Giovanni asked.

"You're smiling," Lorenzo said.

"Nothing. Nothing," he took a drag from his cigar.

Lorenzo took a seat across from Giovanni in the other chair. The sitting room in Villa Rosso was Bella's idea. She did a little decorating and remodeling. Despite his initial protests, he liked the improvements over the musty office where he usually conducted his business affairs. Here in this extension to his villa, were large leather sofa chairs and an air filtering system for his cigars. The tall windows on either side let natural light in and gave him an obstructed view of Melanzana where his wife and *bambini* slept. If he stood and went to the other side of the room he could see the land and horses he kept. It soothed him and put his visitors at ease.

"Gio? About this fighter in Bergamo."

"I want to see him. It might be a good investment, Lorenzo." He looked up and he could read his cousin's disapproval. Giovanni sighed. "What is your objection?"

"I think you and I agree that we need legitimate affairs, it's wise that we don't let our attentions divide too quickly. Too much exposure may not be wise now. We already have the press at our door."

Giovanni chuckled and exhaled tobacco smoke. "I have no intention of forgetting what we have planned for the triangle. Boxer or no boxer, I won't be divided on the direction of this family again. I have you to thank for that."

Lorenzo smiled. "We make a good team, don't we?"

"We always have. The bullshit is behind us. I lost my way. Forgot what was important. You kept me from losing the *Camorra* and the respect my father found here in the *Campania*."

"I'm your brother."

"No," Giovanni shook his head. "You're more than a brother. You're my best friend. I punished you for your rebellion in the past. But I see now I was to blame for some of it. You deserve respect."

Lorenzo smiled broadly. Giovanni shook his head and took another long drag from his cigar. He spoke through his exhale.

"You will be heard, on everything. I trust you enough, Lo, to give you back your voice."

"Grazie," Lorenzo replied.

"As for Mancini."

"I'm working on it, Gio. I think there is more to consider than just a truce. Think of it. The women are blood to Mancini. If you were to take him down, after all these years, it would be within your right."

Giovanni sighed. "I don't trust him. But the war between us as kids is over. I'm not interested in moving in on the Sicilians."

"Aren't you?" Lorenzo pressed. "Have you not been trying to prove yourself to the Sicilians since you were a kid? It's me you're talking to, Gio. Mirabella is Don Mancini's daughter. She and Marietta are the key—"

"That's enough!" Giovanni said. "My wife is no key to your fucking ambition. Watch your fucking mouth!"

"I didn't mean it that way."

Giovanni leveled a warning finger on him. "I'll give you some rope on this, Lo, but bring it to an end. Bring me something other than this bullshit talk of taking down the *Mafiosi*. Do it soon or I'll end it for us both."

"I can handle it," Lorenzo said.

Giovanni ran his hand over his face and let go of his anger. He had no time to be riled over this. He needed a clear head to deal with Santo and his business matters.

"How is Mirabella? Is she excited over the fashion show? Marietta can't stop talking about it." Lorenzo asked.

"I suppose. It will happen. Enough said." He flicked his ash into the crystal ashtray. "I will say she was happy to see me when I came home," he boasted. Another surge of love shuddered through his heart. Lorenzo chuckled in agreement. Apparently he had his own homecoming. There was a knock at the door. Lorenzo got up and walked over to open it. In walked Carlo and behind him Santo, Nico entered last and covered the door. Giovanni set his cigar in the ashtray and stood.

Santo had changed. He'd gotten thin. He had dark circles under his eyes and pasty skin from a poor diet. He looked older than them all. The Neapolitan prisons were hard on a man. And Santo had now served two terms in the name of the Battaglia family. Giovanni hadn't seen him in over two years. It wasn't wise for a man of Giovanni's reputation to visit the prisons for a man who the authorities believed betrayed the *Camorra*.

"*Ciao amico mio, bentornato!*" Giovanni said. Santo walked over and the two embraced and exchanged cheek kisses. He grabbed Santo by the face. "Let me get a good look at you. Ah? You see this?" he asked the room. "This is the look of a survivor." Giovanni kissed Santo on the left and then the right cheek ceremoniously once more. "Come, and sit!"

"*Grazie, Gio*. I apologize I didn't return sooner. As I said my brother is ill."

Giovanni put up his hand to dismiss the insult. "You've been gone for two years. I understand your family matters needed to be attended to."

The two sat down. The only other person to sit across from them in a chair was Lorenzo. Carlo and Nico stepped back but kept an eye on Santo. Until Giovanni cleared Santo, his absence made him a threat. He'd have to prove to Giovanni that his return came with the loyalty he professed before he left.

"*Sì*, I was supposed to be inside for two weeks, but two weeks became two years." Santo's gaze slipped over to Lorenzo when he spoke. Giovanni picked up his cigar and reclined in his chair. He would make no apologies for the past. It was done.

"My life is ruined," Santo continued. "I've lost my clan. My family is in shambles. My sons don't respect me. I have the money you set aside for me… but…"

"Go on," Giovanni said.

"I've lost so much for the Battaglias. For you. I did so in respect of *omertá*. The vows we took as men. But who am I now, Gio? I don't think there is a man in this room that has made the sacrifices I have for the brotherhood!" Santo made a point to look at all the men gathered. He settled back in his chair and addressed Giovanni. "I need more than my life back. I want my honor. Only you can give it to me."

Giovanni cast his gaze to Lorenzo. His cousin cleared his throat and Santo stiffened. Lorenzo spoke with a smile. "We understand honor. Don't we boys? Santo is our hero. Bravo!" Lorenzo gave a slow clap. "Unfortunately, brother, to the other clan bosses you are a fucking *pentito*. *Mascalzone!* You testified against Mottola's men."

"I did, because Giovanni wished it! And Mottola the true *pentito* had killed himself in his jail cell. I had to testify. I had no fucking choice." Santo shouted. "And don't call me a betrayer. Remember I know you too, brother. You are as loyal as the leash Gio keeps on your neck!"

"There you go insulting me," Lorenzo chuckled. "It makes my dick hard to hear you beg."

Santo shot to his feet. Nico and Carlo stepped forward. Giovanni smoked his cigar and observed. The taunts weren't what interested Giovanni. It was Santo's refusal to look him in the eye for longer than ten seconds. He didn't like it. Lorenzo continued. He was unfazed by Santo's anger. "Own your misery. You testified. Giovanni can't change that. You know how this works."

"I have paid in blood!" Santo slammed his fist in his hand. "I have never failed this family. Never! I've proven myself." He glanced to Giovanni. He then looked back to Nico and Carlo. "Where is Domi? I want Domi here."

Lorenzo laughed. "I'm to Giovanni's left. You address me!"

Santo put his hands in his hair. He pulled it at the root. Giovanni understood the struggle. Santo had the discipline from living in a cage for years to know restraint. Everyone paused to see what Santo's next move would be. Giovanni secretly hoped he passed the test. "*Non ne posso più!* Gio, I can lower myself no more. I need *famiglia*. I need my soul back! If begging is what I have to do—"

"I've heard enough," Giovanni said. Santo looked up at him and this time he managed to hold his gaze. "Lorenzo is right. You testified. I can't change the fact. The clan bosses need to approve your return to the *Camorra*."

"But you are the *capo di tutti capi*. You can decide this, Gio," Santo said. "No disrespect, but don't bullshit me! It's your blessing they need to hear. None of them would dare challenge it."

"I say you've done enough, Gio," Lorenzo answered. "Mottola came to rise under Santo's watch. You spared Santo's life. You took care of his family while he was in prison. We owe him nothing."

"You fucking bastard!" Santo seethed. "Since we were kids you played this game. Constantly whispering in Giovanni's ear against all of us!" Santo looked back to Nico and Carlo. No one gave him the agreement he sought. He turned his attention back to Giovanni. "I'll ask it again, Gio. Who in this room has laid his life and soul out for you and you father other than me? Who has rotted in a cell for years and kept the secrets of this family? Who has been tried, convicted, tested other than me?"

Giovanni sat forward. "I believe you are the brother I've known since we were kids in Sicilia. And I believe you deserve a chance to reclaim what is lost to you. But just as you were loyal to me, you failed me. And that failure came at a price. You get no fucking mercy from me. You owed me those two years, just as Mottola owed me his life and the life of his sons." Giovanni stared into Santo's eyes to make sure every word he spoke was heard. Santo's gaze wavered and lowered. "Look at me when I'm speaking to you!"

His gaze lifted.

"I will meet with the clan bosses and tell them of my wish to pardon your sins. Mottola was the rat, *la pentito*. Mottola is dead. I still have use for you, Santo."

"Gio?" Lorenzo started to object. Giovanni leveled his gaze on his cousin and Lorenzo immediately fell silent.

"Where are you staying?" Giovanni asked Santo.

"My brother is in Firenze now, at a medical center barely hanging on to life."

"What ails him?" Giovanni asked.

Santo's gaze lifted. "He's eaten up with cancer. I've been with him and then tried to visit my kids in Roma. Their mother refuses to let me see them. I have no place in Sorrento."

"Make sure Santo has a villa and a car in Napoli," Giovanni told Lorenzo. He kept his gaze trained on Santo. "I'm on my way to Milano. See me at the end of the week. I'll be in Bellagio for Mirabella's birthday party. The clan bosses have all been invited. You can be heard then."

"Grazie, Gio! Grazie!" Santo righted the chair he kicked over. Giovanni stood and approached. Santo kissed his ring. He embraced Giovanni once more. Before leaving he cast Lorenzo a look of contempt. As soon as the door closed Giovanni's anger surfaced.

"Don't ever question me in front of these men!" Giovanni warned. "I gave you a voice but learn when to hold your fucking tongue!"

"Perdonami, Gio. It wasn't my intent. Why do you keep bringing Santo in? He isn't trustworthy." Lorenzo said.

"He's blood. He's been blood since we were thirteen. And he's gone to prison twice for me. Have you?" Giovanni asked.

Lorenzo stared on. "I've been in jail plenty of times for this family, Gio. I'd go again willingly. We had a gun to Santo's head before he agreed to the same sacrifice. Do you not remember?"

"My point, Lo, is he made the sacrifice to me. That is a step toward redemption. What would any of these men think if I just cast him aside after all he's done for us?" Giovanni leaned forward and held his cousin's stare. "Do you not understand the tenants of loyalty? Forgiveness? Unless it only serves you?"

"You're right, Gio. I give up," Lorenzo sighed.

Giovanni shook his head. "Slow down, cousin. Learn from our mistakes. Even if we can't trust every man under the gun, we must make him think we do."

Lorenzo nodded.

—*B*—

"Good Lord!" Shae pressed her hand to her heart. It beat so fast with excitement she swallowed her gum. Never in her life had she seen a place so beautiful. It was like a page out of a storybook. First they travelled along the Amalfi, which was a narrow road that threaded along high cliffs, and dropped down to quaint little villas and the sea.

The coast had a colorful splash of flowers blooming everywhere. She took out her camera and snapped a few shots. Mostly she looked on with her mouth gaping. The drive changed from scenic, to an isolated hillside. The car drove up a single lane road between trees with umbrella shaped branches heavy with palm leaves. And then came the unveiling. Out of the clearing Melanzana sat perched upon the highest part of the land, and it was at least three stories tall. It nearly blocked the afternoon sun. Shae leaned forward to look out of the front driver's window.

The vehicle slowed to a crawl and stopped before large gates with a family crest at its center. She glanced to Marietta. "You have got to be kidding me? This place is gorgeous!"

Marietta laughed. Shae grinned as well. Her feisty best friend Marietta

Leone, who carried fake designer bags, and bought that favorite Shalimar perfume of hers bootleg, had really come up. At the gates the men opened them for Renaldo to continue through. Shae saw the guns on both men. They wore them in the open.

"Ah? What's up with that? Guns?"

"I told you. The Battaglias are very private. And different," Marietta replied.

"No shit. I can't believe this is where you live?" Shae chuckled.

"One of the places I live in. Yes." Marietta corrected her.

"One? How many do you have?"

"We have a place in Milano and Bellagio. My husband has real estate in Napoli and Sicilia. Melanzana is where the Don and Donna nest. Not many people are invited to stay, especially women."

Shae sat back in her seat. "Why not women?"

Marietta shrugged. "It's just one of the house rules. Only family come through these gates. And in this family it's mostly men. I think my sister was the first woman to live here who wasn't family, and wasn't married to the man she was sleeping with. And then came me. So it's a honor that you have an invite."

"How big is Melanzana? How many rooms?" Shae asked.

"I don't know how big it is. I haven't been in all of the rooms. But it's big. And there is land to the back, two pools, stables with horses, and a guesthouse. All of it belongs to the family. You travel far enough west on the land and you reach the end. The cliff drops off to a deep valley that leads out to the sea. You travel East and you reach our neighbors but that's after crossing three hundred acres."

The car circled a marble fountain of what looked like the goddess Aphrodite pouring water out of a pitcher. Renaldo parked. Shae couldn't wait. She threw open her door immediately. Before she got out a hand reached in to help her. The young man was just a few inches taller than her. He was cute except for the scar to the side of his face. He said something in Italian and Shae pretended to understand with a polite smile. She glanced back to see Marietta being helped out of the car.

"This way!" Marietta called to her.

Shae winked at the man and sashayed around the car. Her heels kept sinking into the dirt-paved drive but she straightened her spine and tried to keep from stumbling. "I have to take plenty of pictures. No one is going to believe me, Mae, when I get back home. Damn!" Shae giggled.

Marietta grabbed her arm. "Wait." She stopped her on the step. There were at least eight of them to climb before they reached the doors. "Remember what I said. Represent, respect, Shae. Don't act all loud and bossy. Okay?"

"I said I understood. Calm down. I'm not some ghetto queen. If you remember I was the one who taught you how to 'represent'," she said with air quotes on the last word. The door opened, and Shae froze. A black woman stepped out. She wore dark slacks and an emerald green satin shirt. Her hair was in a blown straight style with a center part. She had Marietta's eyes and smile. She also had a trim figure that made her clothes look classy. It was the fashionista she'd seen in magazines, Mirabella Ellison Battaglia. Next to her was a short older woman in a shawl. The old lady had a nest of gray hair pinned to the back of her head, and very dark piercing eyes. She stared directly at Shae and there was nothing welcoming in her smile.

"They told me you were here. *Benvenuto in Sorrento!* It means welcome to Sorrento. I'm Mirabella, Marietta's sister."

Shae glanced to Marietta. Her friend let go of her arm. She smiled and nodded for Shae to continue on up the stairs. She did so, but this time she could feel the thaw of nervousness overcome her excitement. It dawned on her what her friend worried over. Not Shae being uncouth and embarrassing her. Marietta wanted Shae to charm her sister, the Empress.

Mirabella stepped forward and kissed Shae on the left and then the right cheek. She then glanced behind her with a broad smile for the old woman. "Oh, forgive my manners. Please meet our Zia. She's like a mother to me and Marietta."

The old lady nodded at her but didn't speak. Shae nodded in return.

"We are so happy to have you come all this way to visit with us. Please! Come inside," said Mirabella.

The Donna took Shae by the hand and pulled her inside. Shae blinked at the grandeur but tried to mask her excitement. Suddenly she didn't feel as giddy with happiness. In fact she felt a bit overwhelmed. Several men were inside. They passed and nodded at the designer with respect. Mirabella kept walking with her arm hooked on Shae's. She spoke to her about the few visits she had made to Chicago.

"How long will you be staying?" Mirabella asked.

"Uh, two weeks. If that's okay? Maybe longer," Shae answered.

"Of course it's okay. Trust me, most people that visit *la Campania* have a hard time leaving. We'll make sure you see all of Italia and have a wonderful visit," Mirabella said.

Shae's gaze swept left and right in appreciation of the polished villa. What caught her eye for a stretch was a portrait that hung between the front and back of Melanzana on a hall wall. On one side was the family crest that had a cursive letter B in gold carved through it. And the other was a portrait of the Battaglia family. From the Donna sitting with a baby boy on her lap and little girl to her right, to the Don behind her with an identical baby boy in his arms. To his left was Marietta, and Shae guessed the man standing behind her to be her husband. To their right was another striking woman and a young man. Also both the old woman and an older man were in the portrait. Shae wanted to see more of the family but she was marched through the hall and could barely keep up.

The journey ended out on an open terrace. There was a long table made of wood with enough chairs for a family of thirty to sit down to dinner. There was food, wine, bread, and lots of different cheeses. Shae's stomach clenched and her mouth watered. The food on the plane was bland. She hadn't eaten in over ten hours.

"Zia and I prepared this for you. I know you've been travelling and would like to freshen up. But first would you like to join us for lunch?" Mirabella asked.

"Sure. I'd love to. Thank you," Shae smiled.

"Let's eat!" Marietta clapped her hands together. She pulled out the chair in front of her and sat at the table. They all chose chairs to the center of the table. Zia did not join them. At some point the old woman left their company. Marietta sat next to Shae and Mirabella walked off to bring plates to the table.

"The food smells so good. Do you always dine outside like this?" Shae whispered.

"Most days. Unfortunately we won't be here long. We all leave for Milano in a few hours. So I suggest you eat up," Marietta said.

Shae glanced up at Mirabella who put a plate in front of her. "I've been a fan of your clothes, I mean I've loved your work for years."

"Oh, that's sweet. Thank you for taking care of my sister all these years. She told me how much you helped her." Mirabella used mitts to bring over one potted dish and then another tray with flat meat sandwiches oozing cheese.

The compliment lifted Shae's confidence. She looked over to Marietta who winked and reached for the decanter of wine. She poured her glass and then Shae's, just as three men climbed the steps to the side of the terrace. Shae had found Renaldo the driver handsome, mysterious. Nothing she'd seen so far prepared her for the troop of men approaching them.

"Who do we have here?" A tall handsome man with a deep tan asked. His accent was thick. He looked tough. His muscles rippled but did not strain the silk threads of his tailored suit. The very way he stared at her made her want to explain herself. She'd met men like him before. The kind you couldn't bring home to meet your girlfriends, but you'd welcome to your bed to pin you up against the headboard. He had dark curly hair that tapered low to his long sideburns. His eyes were the darkest shade of blue, almost black. Marietta scooted her chair back and stood.

"Come here, baby, and meet my friend," Marietta said.

This was her husband? Shae remembered the glimpse she got of him from the family portrait. Seeing him in the flesh was a totally different experience. She pushed back her chair and stood. Two other men accompanied him. The one to the right was big. He had height, a wide chest, muscle in his arms and legs, even his neck bulged with muscles. She imagined his dick would be too. He stared at her but didn't speak. Shae's eyes reverted to the other man. This one made her blink. He was tall like Marietta's husband, and athletic enough to keep up with the other man, but it was the way he stared back that felt sexy. He had the eyes of a predator; a sexiness about him she couldn't resist. He leaned against the column on the terrace and let his gaze do a slow walk up her body.

"*Ciao, bella,*" Lorenzo said and kissed her on the left and then right cheek. Shae had to snap out of her trance to accept the greeting. She swallowed and found her voice.

"Hi. Nice to meet you, Lorenzo. Mae... ah, Marietta has told me so much about you. Congrats on getting my girl down the aisle."

"Down the aisle? *Che cosa?*" he looked at his wife.

"She means congratulations on convincing me to agree to marry you!" Marietta smiled.

"Ahh!" Lorenzo laughed. "Yes! Marie is my greatest accomplishment." He pulled Marietta in close and bit her on the neck. The bite looked yummy. And she could see how it tickled Marietta. Her girl really had scored. Shae cut her eyes over to the other man. He stared back. The challenge lay bare in his eyes. He wanted to be introduced.

Lorenzo whispered something to his wife and Marietta giggled. He kissed her again and then walked off. The other two men weren't introduced. They both followed him out. Shae grabbed Marietta by the arm. "Who were they...

the other two?"

"Huh?" Marietta blinked out of what trance kissing her husband had put her in.

"That was Carlo and Nico. They both work for my husband. I heard Santo was here earlier," Mirabella answered for her sister.

"In the house? Why don't you tell Giovanni that you don't like the man?" Marietta returned to her seat. Shae strained to see the men leaving. Carlo never glanced back, and that was disappointing.

"Sit down!" Marietta laughed.

"Oh? Okay," Shae tried to mask her flushed state. She sat back at the table.

"If I told my husband of every man who works with him that made me nervous he'd never let anyone through the door," Mirabella chuckled. "Besides it's been two years since Santo has come here, I'm over it."

Shae didn't get the joke but Marietta did. She laughed and chimed in. Shae pretended at listening as she ate her lunch. His name was Carlo or was it Nico? Either way she was determined to find out.

CHAPTER THREE

The Dragon

Macau – Asia—

Isabella Mancini had ventured into dangerous territory. The stench strangled the last of the breathable air. She lifted the red silk scarf around her neck and pressed it over her mouth and nose. Her eyes watered. Nausea clenched her stomach and dried her throat. Darkness beckoned inside and she found it hard to take the next step. Since the ferry brought her from Hong Kong across the Pearl River Delta, nothing but misery and poverty greeted her. However, in the deepest recesses of hell came something else—the sounds of laughter and celebrating. She had to go inside. The problem persisted. Her legs wouldn't move.

"Gǎnkuài! Gǎnkuài!" An Asian man, barely five-foot tall with dark scraggly hair and hard eyes, shouted at her. He wore a stained shirt and cut-off shorts. He smelled as bad as the building he held the door to. Isabella was a risk taker. Her father, Flavio, had taught her that no reward came without a price. But even she knew traveling this far without her men to protect her, and uninvited, could prove to be a fatal mistake.

"Come! Now!" he shouted at her.

She nodded and continued on. The only discernable scent she could put to name varied between that of animal's blood, rotten meat, and excrement. Isabella stepped over stains in the floorboards and garbage in designer heels. She clutched her Chanel bag to her chest.

The front of the warehouse looked to be some kind of open market that had closed for business. Tarps covered several vendor booths. The few that were left bare had traces of rotting food with large black flies swarming. She swiped a few flies away from her face as they buzzed around her head, attracted to her perfume. She followed her guide through the open space to a musty hall. On the way she had to be cautious of her steps in the dark. She sidestepped buckets positioned to catch the water as it dripped through the cracks of the tin ceiling above. Once they descended a few steps to another passageway she began to understand the destination. Since making an alliance with Kei Hyogo, she'd visited several opium dens in mainland China which were owned by the Triad. This must be one of some other purpose.

The laughter and raised voices in a foreign tongue grew louder.

"You. Wait. Here." The Asian man pointed at her and then the floor. Isabella nodded that she understood. He pushed open a tall aluminum door bringing forth the musty heat and liquored rank of the celebration beyond. She could only glimpse the men inside. The door closed.

Isabella checked her watch. Two years ago Kei Hyogo saved her life. A bomb planted by her adoptive father's men nearly claimed it. Before then she had no faith in the Triad bringing Kei to power. His extradition had landed him in one of the most brutal prison camps in China. And for several months he was beaten, starved and tortured. Before all hope was lost he was freed. In just two short years the Wall Street business tycoon had turned into the head of the Dragon. Kei was now the leader of one of the most ruthless and successfully cunning Tongs, a secret Chinese society, on this side of the world. Access to him wasn't as liberal as she hoped. After the bombing she had to go through his vanguard, what most considered an assistant or counselor, for all communication. And the message was always the same. "In time, in due time."

Well the time was now. She'd waited long enough.

The door opened. Gone was her scraggly runt of a guide. Before her was a tall Chinese man with a shaven head. He wore a dark business suit and a welcoming smile, the first she'd seen since she left Hong Kong.

"Isabella Mancini?" he asked.

"Yes."

"I'm Bao Zei." Isabella recognized the name. They spoke over the phone two months ago. "Kei has been told you are here. Come with me." The man said in polished Italian. His ease with her native language made her tense. She knew predators, and it was always the polite, cultured ones that proved most deadly. She stepped forward with her head high. Inside gathered a large crowd of men on bench seats, and some standing. At the center were kick boxers fighting each other. Blood and sweat flew from their mingled bodies as they kicked, punched, and tackled one another.

"This way," the man whispered in her ear.

She turned and followed. Every spectator she passed stopped to stare at her. Most with looks of disapproval. This was a man's game. There wasn't a woman anywhere in the arena. That was until she was brought around to a private booth. Three beautiful Asian women scantily dressed in low cut blouses, and very short mini-skirts, sat around one man. Kei Hyogo leaned back on the bench seating that was clear of anyone that wasn't part of his harem. He wore a long black silk shirt that was unbuttoned to reveal what she thought was a serpent on his chest. But the closer she drew she knew it was something far more sinister. A multi-leg dragon snaked its way up his torso. A dark eye patch covered his left eye, and his hair was longer and tucked behind his ears.

He smiled. He sat forward and watched Isabella approach. The women sitting around him all stood at once and began to walk down the bench steps and away without being told to do so. Soon she stood before Kei with his vanguard to her back.

"I didn't send for you," Kei said.

"I know. I apologize if this is inappropriate, but you haven't returned my calls in months. I've written, I've called."

Kei moistened his lips and held her stare. He then looked away from her. She turned her head to see a man pounding his fist into another man's face until blood squirted from his nose, ears, and mouth. It was gruesome. "Can we please go somewhere private and talk?" she yelled over the jeering.

He said something in Mandarin to the man who stood behind her. Bao Zei offered her his hand. Isabella accepted it and was aided as she stepped up the bench seats to take her place next to Kei. She supposed this was as private as it could get. Now she was forced to look upon the barbaric fight scene with him.

"Santo will be released soon."

"He has been released," Kei informed her.

Isabella glanced over at him. She knew it was coming soon but she had no idea of the date. It took her close to three weeks of negotiating and traveling through China to bribe her way into locating Kei Hyogo. She had hoped she would return home before Santo left prison to greet him.

"You should have been there. Instead you come here to see me." Kei sat forward. He leaned in on his knee, riveted by the kill scene.

Isabella forced an obedient smile. Obedience was never a good trait of hers. "It's been close to two years. I've given you everything on the Battaglias. Years of research, planning, information no one has, I handed it all over to you on a silver platter. I've visited the prisons and buttered Santo up for you. Still Giovanni and his…" Isabella bit her tongue. Strange enough Kei was a very dangerous enemy to the Battaglias, but Isabella had once made the mistake of speaking ill against that black bastard whore Mirabella. The man put a knife to her throat. "Ah… his wife and he are living life as if they have no care in the world."

"Mirabella likes her men broken," Kei said.

Isabella frowned. "Broken? I don't get your meaning?"

"Do you know why I left China fifteen years ago?" Kei asked. It was the first time he spoke to her directly without his riddled questions and answers. She was rendered speechless. He glanced over to her and had to turn his head to see her fully with his good eye. "Do you?"

"No," she answered. "Of course not."

"But you're the woman to do all of the research, planning." He cast his good eye to her. "Are you to tell me that the day you visited me in the American prison you had no idea of who I once was, and would become if I returned to China?"

"I only know a little of your history, Kei. I knew more about Mirabella's betrayal than… this," she turned her gaze to the fight arena.

"My uncle Dao raised me after my mother's throat was slit by his brother, my father. He was what these men out there would call the Mountain Master, dedicated to the purpose of serving Guan Yu. More powerful than the Yacazza, or the *Mafiosi*. A very disciplined and righteous leader."

Isabella didn't understand where the conversation was going. The death cry of the poor man in the center of the ring before his neck was broken, shattered her nerves. She fidgeted in her seat. Kei stared at her with a sly smile. "Uncle Dao made sure I was educated. He spared no expense on my education in Europe and then America. All for a single purpose." Kei glanced back to the ring. The man at the center faced Kei and bowed. He too was badly beaten and bloodied. The room fell silent as all others looked to her and Kei in expectation. After a brief pause Kei nodded his head and the men cheered. The man was declared the winner.

"I was to never return here, to become Dao. When I did my uncle was very disappointed." Kei removed his hand from the side of him and held it out. Isabella had always seen it in a glove. It was now harnessed in a steel glove-like contraption that gave him very sharp, pointed steel nails. He worked it with mechanical ease. "I say Mirabella likes her men broken because Giovanni and I have a lot more in common than either of us knew. Our only blind spot is our love for her. And your quest for revenge," he glanced to her. "You knew this when you visited my uncle and told him of my crimes in America. When you handed me back over to the Triad."

"I—"

"Shut your fucking mouth." Kei seethed. "I'm not someone to toy with. Giovanni is weak, so you play shadow games with him. You cause little fires for him to put out. Games!" he shouted at her. "When I strike it will be a decisive blow, and I will have my woman and child returned to me after I snap the necks of his sons." He grabbed her chin with his iron hand. The sharpened nails cut into her cheek and she feared he'd broken skin. She double blinked away tears of pain. "Go home. Fuck the Sicilian Santo, and get him ready for me. I will be coming to Italy in my time," he said.

"I thought you should know that Mirabella is having her fashion event in a few days, and a private birthday party in Bellagio. She's finally leaving that compound. She'll be more accessible now."

Kei let go of her face and Isabella recoiled from his touch. He pressed his lips together as if hesitant at first to speak. Then he spoke with a graveled voice and he did so in Mandarin. Whatever he said sounded like a threat. Bao Zei nodded to him understanding his order. Kei stood and shouted something to the men gathered in their language. They all cheered. A pair of men raced out to pick up the dead, or near dead fighter, left broken on the dirt floor. As they carried him off, other men dragged in three others who were weeping visibly and bound at the wrist.

Kei looked down at her with his good eye. His dark hair fell over the side of his face. "I know everything about Mirabella and Little Rabbit that I need to know. Go home, Isabella, and never come here looking for me again."

Three men dressed in long sleeved black jumpers with red sashes and their faces covered except for their eyes, carried sharp swords with them into the ring. They greeted the weeping prisoners with a bow akin to a Japanese Ninja instead of a Chinese assassin. Isabella's stomach clenched. Before she could say more Kei walked down the steps of the bench and was immediately flanked by six men who trailed him as he left. She sighed. The slaughter was hard to watch, but all she could do was wait for an escort out. If Kei Hyogo didn't deliver on his promise to help her exact revenge she'd find another way to get it. She was done with the waiting game.

Milan, Italy –

"Who was it?" Catalina asked. She turned over under the sheets and ran her hand across his chest. Dominic hung up the phone and dropped back on the pillows.

"The family will be landing soon."

"Oh?" Catalina kissed his chest. Something weighed heavy on Dominic's heart. She could tell. He was still semi erect. He didn't release when they made love earlier. And that was never like him.

"The place is ready for them. I made sure of it."

Dominic sat up and threw back the sheet. Concerned, Catalina lifted on her elbow. He sat on the edge of the bed with his face in his hands. She waited a minute and then spoke softly to him. "Talk to me, Domi. What's wrong now?"

"Nothing. Everything!" he threw his hands up in the air. "Giovanni! He… he listens to Lorenzo now."

Sitting up she put her back to the headboard. She waited for Dominic to share more. But he didn't. He stood and stretched and then walked off to the bathroom. The phone rang. With a curious frown she reached for it and answered. *"Pronto?"*

"Catalina?" a deep voice asked.

"Yes? Who is this?" she answered.

"Armando."

"What?" she gasped. "Why are you calling here?"

"I wanted to thank you for—"

Catalina slammed the phone down. She exhaled deeply and watched the phone as if it were to jump and tell Dominic who the caller was. Her heart raced so fast she nearly thought it would stop. The phone didn't ring again. Catalina bit on her nail, concerned. She'd tell Marietta and Mirabella about their brother's strangeness and let them deal with it. She didn't need anything to upset Dominic further.

When Catalina heard the shower come on she eased out of bed. They were in the new villa Giovanni bought for Mirabella. The odd thing was, in the past two years Mirabella had only visited it once. Catalina had to take pictures of every room for her to decorate. The place had eight bedrooms and three large entertainment rooms. It was perfect for the kids because she made sure one of the rooms was equipped with everything they'd like to play with. There was little she could do to help Dominic but offer him support. Whatever divided the men now would pass. It always did. Dominic was smart. He'd find a way.

Catalina opened the door and peeked inside. The steam billowed up out of the top of the shower and clouded the atmosphere in the bathroom. "We will have a great homecoming dinner when they arrive, all of the family will be gathered again. And we're the hosts," she said.

Dominic didn't answer. She went over to the shower and eased open the glass door. He reached for her the moment she stepped inside. He took her into his arms and just held her. He then kissed her cheek tenderly. Catalina smiled. She touched the sides of his face and kissed him back. She drew his face up and looked into his eyes. "Do you know what the real problem is, Domi?"

He stared into her eyes and let her speak.

"You're so loyal. That's what makes you different from Lorenzo. And Giovanni knows this. It boils down to jealousy, Domi. You can never see yourself the way we do. I don't care if Lorenzo is older, or Giovanni tougher, you're the wise one Domi. You keep us all going. You're the one with the real power and heart."

"It's more to it than jealousy. Lorenzo is my brother and a good man. He's loyal to Gio, to the family. He just doesn't respect me because I haven't earned it. Every man in the clan has shed blood, been to jail, even Gio. Not me. I'm the baby brother they all protect."

"Domi, let Lo play big man now. You are the heart of this family. Without you neither Gio nor Lo can survive. Neither can I."

First came the kiss of agreement. He cupped her ass with both hands. The tip of his tongue licked at the crease of her lips and drew her mouth to his. She curled her tongue around his and deepened the kiss. Dominic squeezed her ass like a vice. She felt the bottoms of her feet rise as she was forced to her toes. Crushed up against him, she kissed him deeply. The warm spray of the shower, and her rising temperature, flattened her hair to her skull and dampened her body with moisture all over.

"I don't care if I'm never Gio or Lorenzo. All I ever wanted was you," Dominic said. Catalina's eyes teared over his devotion. He pinned her to the shower. Up against the tiled wall, with her legs wrapped around his waist, she held to his face and kissed him. She drove her tongue deeper as he screwed up into her with repeated hard strikes. Catalina's pussy expanded and contracted. She felt him reach her pelvic bone. Dominic held her up by the back of her thighs and she bounced under his instruction. The friction scraped her back up and down the wall. Her pussy accepted and released the tension. It was glorious and far too much. There was tenderness in his kiss and voice, but he was all masculine strength in the ways he drilled her pussy. She whimpered. He kept fucking her and she was barely able to breathe. Dominic broke the kiss to love on her breasts. He could suck her nipples for an eternity, or until they were tender and bruised. She didn't mind. She closed her eyes and let him have her.

"Yes! Yes, Domi!" she panted.

He dropped his head on her shoulder and squeezed the cheeks of her ass. He slammed up into her repeatedly until she felt the aftershocks in her pelvis. And then he released. She kissed the side of his face, and held him as he shuddered through an orgasm he denied himself all evening. She didn't mind that she didn't have one. All she truly wanted was for Dominic to be confident and strong when he met with Giovanni and Lorenzo. Maybe there was something she could do to help.

"Domi?"

"Mmmm," he groaned, unwilling to release her.

"I'm ready," she whispered in his ear.

His head lifted and he looked into her eyes. Those dreamy long lashed eyes of Dominic's were the color of cola. She melted the moment she saw her reflection in them when she was a young girl. They still held power over her. "I'm ready to get married. Let's do it this summer. Okay?"

"This summer? You sure?"

"Yes!" she screamed.

Dominic let go a deep laugh. He kissed her brow, nose, and then lips. "*Ti amo, Catalina*. With all my heart."

"I'm going to make so many babies with you, Domi. The sooner the better. We can have it all. Right, Domi?"

He kissed her again and she giggled. His cock was so flaccid it slipped out of her and she was lowered to her feet. Still his mouth remained glued to hers. She could feel his strength return in that kiss.

—𝓑—

THE CHAUFFEURED CAR DROVE OUT of the airport. Her husband rode in the front seat next to the driver. Mirabella sat with Gianni in one car seat, and Gino in the other. Gianni was the only baby she had left who sucked a pacifier and clung to his mama. Gino never accepted the habit, and Eve gave it up once she found her independence, after her brothers were born. Gianni blinked his round blue eyes up at his mother and sucked. She smiled down at him. She let him hold her hand. Her only wish was that Eve could ride with them. Her daughter had protested when they left the plane, and she was relegated to the car with Marietta and her American friend. Next time she'd remind her husband to have passenger vans for the family, not these cars.

Giovanni laughed and joked with Nico. Her husband was in a good mood. It would make him more accepting of her first request. Marietta may be right. Tonight she should step out on her own. Really go for it. She needed to practice what she preached to Giovanni during their long discussions about her company and independence. Instead of dinner together tonight, she wanted to visit her office at Fabiana's, meet with the girls, and have a celebratory dinner with them. Mirabella drifted on all the things she would have to prepare for. The closer they drew to leaving and returning to Milano, the more nervous she felt.

"Bella? I spoke to Dominic. He said he needs you to meet with the attorneys first thing in the morning. And he wants to know about the interview we agreed to."

"Will you join me? In the interview?" Mirabella asked.

Silence greeted her. Giovanni had only committed to one interview with the press, but still he was unwilling to get in front of the cameras.

"I think it should be you and your sister," he eventually answered. "Don't you? You two are both the face of the company now."

"Yeah, I guess," she said trying to mask her disappointment. "Sweetheart, you have to pose for my press pictures. I want you at my side. I want the world to know I'm your wife. Please consider it."

"I will," he mumbled.

Gino hit at her. He leaned forward in his seat and blinked those doll baby eyes up at her. He said something in his baby voice. She picked up the toy truck he'd tossed to her lap and gave it to him. He settled back down. Gianni's lids were lowered. Even in his sleep he held tight to her finger.

"The new woman, did she arrive okay?" Giovanni asked.

"Yes, honey. She was on the plane with you. I introduced you. Remember?" Mirabella said.

He didn't answer. Mirabella rolled her eyes. Their new home was a bit more snug for their large family and entourage. But the home Lorenzo had in Bellagio was far grander. She imagined her husband would grow restless in Milano, and try to convince them to stay there instead. It would hamper her efforts to work fulltime. With Giovanni she had to be one step ahead of him on these matters. It was sometimes mentally exhausting. They drove up a hill to the gate of their new home.

"Mama! Mia camera! Mia camera!" Gino exclaimed.

Mirabella chuckled. "Yes baby, that's your house and inside is your bedroom." Her son nodded in agreement like a big boy. She had told all the children they were going on an adventure, and would have a new bedroom to sleep in. She'd probably split her time between sleeping with her babies and her own bed. The layout of the villa meant their bedroom was further up the hall.

The car stopped and the men got out. Mirabella helped unfasten Gino first and he was nearly climbing out of his car seat as soon as the belt was removed. When she turned to help Gianni she saw Nico had already opened the car door and was removing her sleeping boy. Nico may be her husband's shadow, but often their family giant found time to sneak away and play with the boys. Eve clung to him like he was a big teddy bear. She smiled her thanks and exited the car last. Mirabella glanced up to the villa. It was quite charming. A neat two-story, square shaped villa with yellow wildflowers banked around the edges.

"Everything okay, Bella?" Giovanni stepped behind her. Gino pulled her hair.

"Ah, yes," she said and winced. She untangled her locks from her son's hands. Giovanni heaved him up above his head proudly. She smiled at her boys and then followed her husband from around the car. Marietta and the rest of the family followed. The men began to unload the luggage.

"You're here!" Catalina screamed. She ran from the front door. Mirabella was the first person she hugged. But Eve was now at her mother's side and Catalina lifted her up into her arms and showered her face with kisses. "I have missed you all so much! Hi, my Evie! Nippy has missed you! Come inside!"

Mirabella took Gino from Giovanni and followed her sister in-law. The villa was much cooler than the muggy afternoon temperature steaming up outside.

"I want to show you the room I did for the kids first," Catalina told her. "It's right down here. These little ones we must make happy. Right, Eve?"

"Yes, Nippy!" Eve laughed.

Catalina put her down and took her hand. "And oh! Wait! I have a surprise too." She continued. Gino began to twist in Mirabella's arms so she set him down as well. The toddler turned and ran in the direction of his father. Mirabella accepted a sleeping Gianni from Nico instead of chasing after her son.

"I will see to him, Donna," Nico said.

"Thank you. If Giovanni starts smoking those cigars can you please bring him back to me?"

"*Sì,* Donna," Nico said and walked off.

"Slow down, Catalina, I need to introduce you." Mirabella called after her. She did so in time for Shae and Marietta to catch up with them.

"Introduce?" Catalina paused in the hall. She looked directly at their houseguest with surprise. In her haste to greet everyone Mirabella was sure Catalina missed her.

"This is Shae Dennis from Chicago, America. She's Marietta's friend. She has come to visit."

"Oh? *Perdonami! Ciao, sono Catalina.*" She extended her hand. Shae shook it and smiled. "I love your pink hair!" Catalina grinned.

Shae touched the streak of pink to the front of her hair and smiled. "Thank you, I mean *gracias,*" Shae said.

Catalina looked to Mirabella who hid her smile. Confusing Spanish with Italian was cute. But they didn't want to make Shae uncomfortable so neither of them corrected her.

"Now everyone come with me. It's just right here." Catalina pointed to a room door at the far end of the hall. When they passed through it Mirabella was reminded of the screened in terrace at Villa Mare Blu. But never in all her efforts to spoil her children had she seen anything remotely like this. Toys and treasures for the kids were everywhere.

"Mommy! Look!" Eve gasped and ran through the room. Mirabella put Gianni, who was now awake, down, and he joined his sister's enthusiasm. It looked like a screened in terrace. Catalina had a six-foot tall, two story princess castle erected in the corner of the room for Eve to crawl inside and play with. It was equipped with life sized prince and princess dolls seated at a table and chairs.

"This is too much," Mirabella frowned.

"Are you kidding? It's a fucking kid's paradise," Marietta laughed.

Catalina grinned with her hands over her mouth. She looked giddy with excitement. "We have so much work to do, and I know you are on thin ice with my stubborn brother. We need to keep the *bambini* happy and entertained, and you less stressed. No? This is perfect."

"They'll be bored with it in a week," Marietta joked. "Nice try though."

On the floor was a train track and large locomotive engine that two little boys could ride around the room. Cecilia picked up Gianni and sat him on it so he could ride. There were two activity tables and painting easels for all the kids. A television was mounted from the ceiling with a VCR attached. Mirabella saw blocks of all sizes, floor puzzles, dolls, and a baby doll crib. There was so much for her children Mirabella did feel at ease. She walked over to Catalina and kissed her.

"*Grazie.* You did well. This is perfect," she said.

"Wait a damn minute. Where did Shae go?" Marietta glanced back to the door. Zia stepped inside. She paused and then smiled at the room. "Did you see Shae, Zia?"

"She asked to use the toilet," Zia dismissed the concern.

"Everybody, it's time for Mirabella to open her presents!" Catalina exclaimed. The announcement took Mirabella by surprise. She looked over to the table Catalina pointed out. There were several wrapped packages. She initially thought they were for the kids.

"Who sent me gifts?" she asked.

"Are you kidding? Everybody! The entire fashion world is on the brink of hysteria because my sister has returned." Marietta joked. Catalina pointed to a large bright red leather chair for Mirabella to sit in. She had no choice but to comply.

"Let's see. We got Chanel, Lagerfeld, Versace, Gucci, House of Fendi... and wait, who is this from?" Marietta held up a beautifully wrapped red silk box. "There's no card here."

Catalina walked over and inspected the package. "Hmm... I had Mateo bring the gifts over. The card must have fallen off."

"Hand it here. Let me open it," Mirabella said.

Marietta brought the package over and Mirabella inspected the rectangular gift box. The wrapping was extremely elegant. "Well they got the color right. Everything we do at Fabiana's is scarlet red," Mirabella chuckled.

She carefully lifted the seams and peeled the paper away. The box was red beneath. She lifted the top of the box. Inside was black tissue paper. She parted it and found a card against silk. She handed the black card over to Marietta and carefully lifted the garment.

"It says: Congratulations, I have missed you," Marietta said.

"Who from?" Catalina asked.

"No name, just this symbol of a dragon." Marietta frowned.

"Let me see that," Catalina took the card from her.

Mirabella shook out the long black kimono. Hand stitched on the back was a beautiful Chinese dragon with many legs like that of a centipede, and interwoven with red and gold stitching, there were colorful beads woven throughout. "It's adorable," Mirabella grinned.

"Who the hell is the Dragon? A new designer?" Marietta asked.

"It doesn't sound familiar," Catalina said.

Mirabella stood and held out the kimono. She eased it on. She loved beautiful garments, but it was rare that she received one that captivated her like this. "I haven't worn pretty kimonos since Kei—" she paused. She glanced up to see if anyone heard her say his name. Marietta and Catalina seemed fixated on the card. And Cecilia and Zia were with the children. Mirabella shrugged off the robe and held it out in front of her once more. She knew Kei was sent to prison in China, but that was all she knew. A robe like this reminded her of the intimate gifts she would receive from him before every big event in her life. It was too damn similar. He even insisted that she wore them with nothing underneath so he could make love to her in it.

The black tide of dread she used to carry when she thought the mafia was hunting her surfaced. She folded the garment and tucked it back in the box. She suppressed the urge to throw it in the trash.

"We'll find out who the sender is, trust me," Marietta said.

"Yeah, let's forget it. Trust me we will get plenty of gifts from up and coming talent looking to impress us," Mirabella forced a grin. "What other goodies do we have? Help me open them," Mirabella said. The girls were eager to assist. She glanced once more to the kimono and frowned. She'd have to show it to Giovanni. Was she overreacting?

—*B*—

SHAE WASHED HER HANDS. She found a towel and dried them. The Battaglias were interesting. Marietta was much more grounded with them. Shae used to get a kick out of her black girlfriend who could speak Italian fluently. Now she wished she had learned from Marietta when she tried to teach her. It would have given her a bit of independence on this visit.

And then there were the kids. She and Marietta hated the little ankle biters. Shae was shocked at how patient and nurturing Marietta seemed with Eve when they got saddled with the kid. Marietta was totally taken with her. She sang along with her in the car, and played hand games with her. The wild parties and hook ups she had heard so much about in Italy weren't going to happen if they spent too much time babysitting.

She walked out of the bathroom and headed back out into the hall with her purse on her shoulder. She had a client who said he would be in Lake Como during the time of her visit. She intended to find a phone and call him. Then she heard the voices of two men approaching. Curious, Shae followed their voices and saw the men just as they went through the door to the outside.

The one named Renaldo was speaking with another. The man's head turned and she could see his profile clearly. She found out his name, it was Carlo.

Earlier –

"Where are we going?" Shae asked.

"To the villa," Marietta answered. "I told you. We are staying in Milano and then Bellagio." She continued to point to a letter on a page and the little blue eyed, brown girl with a head full of curls pronounced it perfectly. Shae cut her gaze up to the driver. Marietta's husband Lorenzo rode in the passenger side, and another man drove. But it wasn't the man she'd seen earlier. This man wasn't as handsome as the others.

Shae leaned over to whisper so the men up front who talked and ignored them would not hear her. "Hey?"

Marietta glanced up.

"What's with that guy?" Shae asked.

"What guy? Renaldo?" Marietta frowned.

"Shhh!" Shae said.

Marietta frowned. "I told you he has a girlfriend. You'll meet her soon."

"No, the other guy. His name is Nico, or Carlo."

Marietta doubled blinked as if surprised. "What are you talking about?"

"Damn it, Mae. The tall guy, not the big muscular one. What was his name?" Shae asked.

"Carlo."

"Yes. Carlo. Is he married?"

"Did he say something to you?" Marietta asked.

"Huh? No. When could he? I've been with you. I was just curious. I didn't see him on the plane."

"He was there. Ignore him. He's trouble." Marietta turned the page for Eve and started asking her to say her colors.

"Shit who isn't? I'm trouble," Shae chuckled.

"I'm serious, Shae. I told you not to flirt with these men. I'll take you out, I promise, as soon as we help my sister get everything off the ground with her fashion event. There will be so many celebrities and cuties coming at you, you won't be able to keep up. Trust me."

"Okay, I can't wait. Girl, you know I'm restless. So far I'm bored to death." Shae pouted.

Shae stepped out further to be sure the man speaking was the man she thought he was. The men started to walk off toward the grass. "Shit!" she mumbled.

"Hey?" Shae whirled around. Marietta stood there smiling. "What are you doing peeping around corners?"

"Oh, I was just seeing if, ah, I was lost."

"Girl, come on. I'll show you to your room. I think later we'll go in to Milan for dinner. We have a meeting with Mirabella and her team. Go over the plans for the meetings we got scheduled tomorrow."

"Oh, okay. Yeah, let's do it," Shae said. Her opportunity was missed. But she was almost certain it was Carlo she saw. If it was she'd make sure she got another chance at him.

— 𝓑 —

GIOVANNI LIFTED GINO TO HIS KNEE. His son turned and scooted up his chest so he could stand on his lap and face the men. Even now Gino surprised him. He had to chuckle. Lorenzo dropped his mud caked boot on the coffee table. A clunk of dirt broke off.

"Where the hell is Domi?" Lorenzo grunted. He checked his watch for the third time.

"I'm here," Dominic replied. He walked in with both hands shoved down into the pockets of his slacks. "How did the meeting with Santo go?"

"Let's keep an eye on him for now. I'll meet with the other clan bosses and see what is left to be divided. I'm feeling generous."

Dominic nodded. He looked from Lorenzo to Giovanni, then back to Lorenzo again. "I've arranged for you to see Carlo's brother train tonight, in Bergamo. The fight is in two days."

"What time? Bella has her show in two days," Giovanni said.

"It's in the evening. You could slip away and see the match, or wait until next month and see him fight in Roma. Up to you."

Giovanni lifted Gino and held him up above his head. His son grinned and kicked his feet. Each day his boys looked more and more like their mother. But Giovanni felt that way about all of his children. They were his Bella, through and through. "I'll go tonight." Gio said. "I won't see the fight. I can't miss Bella's big day. Any of it."

Lorenzo didn't speak. He stared straight ahead as if Dominic wasn't in the room. Dominic stepped in closer.

"I have an announcement. Something I want to clear with you both before we share it with the family," Dominic began. Giovanni set Gino down and the toddler walked over to a chair next to his father and tried to climb it.

The door opened and everyone paused. Rocco entered. Giovanni hadn't thought to see the old man so soon, but he knew he would be traveling to join the family.

"Welcome, old man!" Giovanni said. Rocco gave Dominic a hug and then walked over to give one to Giovanni.

"I just arrived. Have I interrupted?" Rocco asked.

Lorenzo didn't stand to greet his uncle. He just nodded a hello from his chair.

"No, Zio. You are right on time. Sit. I have an announcement and I want you to hear it from me." Dominic continued. "You all know I've asked Catalina to marry me, and Gio has given our wedding his blessing."

This time Lorenzo's gaze did switch from the window watching to Dominic. And little Gino was on the chair jumping up and down. The toddler got down from the chair and pushed it over to the desk that was at least four feet tall. Giovanni observed his son climb the chair and then scale up to the top of his desk. He smiled at his son's ingenuity. Little Gino grinned and stomped his feet in triumph. He clapped his hands while rocking his little hips side to side.

"Ah yes, the wedding missing a real wedding date," Lorenzo chuckled.

Giovanni nodded for Dominic to continue. Dominic found his breath and did so. "We have set a date. It will be July 1st. We're going to do it."

"Are you sure? Seems like you two have had a hard time agreeing on the event?" Lorenzo asked.

Dominic nodded. "We're sure."

"Congratulations, Dominic. I think it's about time you and our sister settled down." Dominic didn't react to the comparison. After all these years Giovanni still couldn't help but see them as brother and sister. Although he'd given up on trying to break them apart. Marriage was a hard journey. Maybe this would be the final test to put some hair on Dominic's balls. He also liked the idea of Catalina being a wife, instead of the jetsetter she was becoming working in Bella's company.

Before Rocco could offer his congratulations Gino jumped from the desk with his arms stretched out as if he expected to fly. The men were all too startled to act. The baby landed on his side with his arm pinned behind his back. Gino immediately howled through his tears of pain.

"*Basta!*" Giovanni shouted. He stood to go for his son but at some point Nico had joined them, he wasn't sure when. Nico reached Gino first.

"Is he hurt?" Dominic asked.

"I don't know," Nico said.

Giovanni took the weeping boy into his arms. Gino stopped crying as soon as he held him. But when he touched his little wrist Gino screamed. "Call the doctor. Have him come."

Dominic went to the phone and called a physician that they used in Milano. They were never keen on hospital visits unless absolutely necessary. Giovanni checked Gino's hands and knees. There was no visible scar. Still the fall wasn't something he could easily dismiss. Giovanni kissed Gino's face and tried to rock him as he had seen his wife and zias do to comfort babies.

"Where's his mother?" Giovanni said.

"I came to see to him. I'll take him to her and tell her the doctor has been called." Nico reached for Gino but lowered his hands when Giovanni glared at him. He looked Gino over once more. The boy's face was wet with tears but he stopped crying. The panic tightening Giovanni's lungs loosened. "Are you okay *piccoletto*?" he asked.

Gino blinked at him and then dropped his head on his shoulder. When Gino was a little baby he was small. It took more time for him to put on weight. He never cried like Gianni. Never seemed to fuss when he needed a bottle or changing. Bella and he took Gino back to the doctor to see if something was wrong with him. The doctor assured him Gino was fine. There was something inherently strong about his son. He rubbed his back and soothed him.

He glanced to Nico who stood there waiting. Reluctant at first but not wanting to come off too panicky in front of his men, he passed Gino over to Nico. "Take him straight to Bella. Call me when the doctor arrives."

Nico took Gino from his father and the toddler immediately began to cry. His screams were piercing, and Giovanni felt his own eyes mist over with tears. He made a step to take his son when Lorenzo stepped to his side and squeezed his left shoulder.

"Let the women see to him, Gio. He'll be fine."

Giovanni nodded. Appearances, no matter how small, always had to be maintained with his men and family. He watched Nico leave.

"The boy thinks he's a frog. Did you see that jump?" Lorenzo chuckled.

Rocco chuckled. "Yes, Zia often complains about his jumping."

"I should watch him more closely." Giovanni shrugged. "But boys jump. It's what they do."

"Lorenzo's right, Gio. The boy is fine. Don't stress it," Rocco said.

Dominic hung up the phone. "Doctor Vanzetti will be here within the hour." Lorenzo started for the door.

"Where are you going?" Giovanni asked.

"If we're to go to see this orphan in a boxing ring I need to tell my wife I'll be missing dinner." Lorenzo stopped in front of Dominic. He smiled. "Congratulations, brother. I'm happy for you."

Dominic nodded, and Lorenzo left. Giovanni looked to Rocco who observed the men but didn't say anything.

"Where do you want to get married? Here or Sicily?" Giovanni asked.

"Melanzana. We want to do it in Sorrento, if that's okay with you?" Dominic asked.

"I'll call the cardinal," Rocco offered.

"Are you okay with it? Truly?" Dominic pressed Giovanni.

"Do you want my truth or that of your godfather?" Giovanni replied.

For a moment Dominic hesitated. Giovanni waited for his answer.

Dominic's gaze returned to him. He nodded his head slowly. "I want the truth of my brother," he answered.

"Catalina's my heart. No woman other than my wife has that position. I thought protecting her was to marry her off to Franco. And look where that led us. Do I want my sister and brother to wed? No. I can never want such a thing. I would have liked for you to find a woman outside of this family, Dominic. Start a family on your own terms. It doesn't mean I don't see how much you love her, and I know no one will protect my *piccoletta* better than you."

"*Grazie,* Gio. I've given her time. I've let her be her own person. I love her. I always have. I will never let you or her down. I swear it," Dominic said.

Giovanni arched a brow. "Hmmm... this means I get to plan your bachelor party."

Dominic smiled. "You didn't have one."

Giovanni reclined "That doesn't mean I don't know how to throw one."

Dominic grinned. "I will see you later, bye Rocco. I need to meet with the men before we leave for the gym."

"Gym? What gym?" Rocco asked.

"Ciro, Carlo's brother. Giovanni has agreed to be his promoter." Dominic walked out.

"Is that true, Gio? You are now a boxing promoter?" Rocco asked.

They were now alone. Giovanni had an urge to rise and see about his son. He resisted. "I've agreed."

"And Carlo has another brother?" Rocco asked.

"Carlo finds a brother at every corner," Giovanni chuckled.

Rocco did not take to the humor. "Whose idea was it to enter boxing? To own a fighter."

"It was mine!" Giovanni snapped.

"I understand that, Gio. What I mean is who brought the business to us? Carlo?"

"Yes. And Dominic."

"So Lorenzo doesn't agree?" Rocco asked.

"Is there a point to this interrogation old man?"

"I've stayed out of the family affairs for the past few months. I think it would make my brother happy to see you with Lorenzo at your side running the family." Rocco said.

"You think?" Giovanni said.

"Dominic is a better counsel. With him you are… you make very solid decisions."

"You talk as if I'm a fucking puppet with no mind of my own!" Giovanni said.

"No. You are the *capo di tutti capi*. You own the lives, and control the minds of many. Every decision you make, every day, decides the fate of so many. That is why it is good to have a *consigliere*, a left and a right hand. To balance scales."

"So?"

Rocco sighed. "There is balance there for you, Gio. But you sway more toward Lorenzo. I know of the drugs. Gio? Drugs?"

"I'm not selling them."

"No. You've become a traffic cop," Rocco said.

"And if I am? Mottola was able to divide the clans and nearly destroy this family. The drugs are here. They come from every port. My fucking *Campania*! I can not close my eyes to it."

"Your father—"

"Was a smuggler. How many wars have we armed? How many weapons from the Irish have we pushed out through those to Turkey? Lorenzo is right. You cannot be half in. My father was never what I am today, because he didn't understand that fact. I own the *Campania*. And now I own the drugs."

Rocco sighed. "And with ownership comes a price for us all, Gio. A price we as men will all have to pay. Think about it when you kiss your sons good night tonight."

—*B*—

"COME HERE." Lorenzo swept in and scooped his wife up with his arms fastened around her waist. Marietta squealed in shock. Everyone looked up in the family room. Marietta saw her friend's curious frown before she was carried from the room.

"Put me down!" she yelled. He did. She whirled on him and started backing away. He winked and she turned and ran. Lorenzo was taller, stronger, but she was fast even in her heels. She nearly made it out the back door before he caught her again in the kitchen. She laughed and kicked her legs. He carried her into the food closet and closed the door.

She had to catch her breath. She stood on her toes and kissed him. "If you wanted to talk all you had to do was ask," she grinned.

"Where has my wife been? I've been looking to talk to her all day," he said.

"Right behind you, baby. You're too busy building our empire to notice."

Lorenzo lifted her chin with his finger. "Don't even think about it," she said.

"What am I thinking?" he asked as he traced his index finger from her chin, down her throat to the dimple separation of her breasts.

"It's the pantry, Lo. Our room is just down the hall," she said. "I know you, Lo. The dirty and nastier the better."

"Nothing dirty or nasty about fucking my wife," he said and squeezed her breasts.

"You know what I mean! This is where the food is kept. It's obscene."

He chuckled. She watched as he reached down in his pocket. "I have something for you, my good luck present before your big day."

"What is it?" she asked.

He removed a twenty-two inch diamond strand tennis necklace. Her breath caught at the sight of it. Even in the dark the baubles sparkled like priceless gems. "It's beautiful."

"Turn around," he said.

She turned and put her hands against the closed door. Lorenzo brought the necklace around her neck and fastened it. She touched the diamonds. "I love it. So sweet, thank you, baby."

His hands went to her hips. She barely noticed when they caressed around to the curve of her ass. He pulled up her dress and she glanced back at him from over her shoulder.

He kissed her and cupped her pussy. Marietta swallowed his tongue. She reached behind her to stroke his face. And his fingers felt delicious as they fondled and molested her pussy. "So proud of you, Marie. You're going to show them all. Wear it for me on the big day."

Lorenzo pressed her up against the wood surface of the door as he ran both hands to the front of her thighs. He rubbed and spread her thighs. His erection was pressed between the cheeks of her ass. She closed her eyes as her body responded to his touches and caresses. The panties she wore were forced off her hips and further down until they were trapped at her ankles. She was hot. Not just with sexual anticipation. She was hot thanks to the cramped quarters, and the excitement melting the walls of her pussy. The silk dress she wore was sticking to her skin. He freed himself. He released his cock so swiftly and thrust inside of her, Marietta's nails nearly broke as they scratched down the line of the wood. He thrust into her again and her mouth gaped in pleasure. Faster and faster his thrusts went. His hard length stretched her walls to the maximum. She was dry for the invasion, but the friction stirred heat and pre-climax wetness that eased his glide.

"Ah yes!" she laughed when he lifted her out of her shoes. Her panties dropped off her ankles. And she hooked her feet behind the back of his calves. She was as open as she could get for him. She beat her hand against the door in celebration. It was so good to her. "Do me, baby," she wheezed.

Her husband was tall. Taking every inch of him this way was only bearable if she was elevated. Hip and pelvic thrusts drove him deeper and deeper. His hands were now to the front of her thighs, keeping them parted while his index fingers played with her clitoris. Before long the hurried thrusts of his thickness slowed to a teasing rhythm, delivering enough pleasure to overcome her discomfort. And with his large frame pressed into her, she barely captured enough air in her lungs to keep breathing. Lorenzo grunted against her ear one last time before he exploded inside of her.

Together they melted down the wall. He went to his knees and she joined him. Dazed they sat with their backs to the door. She looked down at her necklace and smiled. "I love it, Lo," she said. "Why not give it to me last night?"

"I forgot," he wheezed. "I was going to surprise you in bed after I finished work, but you surprised me in the office. It slipped my mind. And then today—"

"We both were going a mile a minute in opposite directions." She finished for him.

He took her hand and kissed it. "I want us to take a trip soon, *cara*. Just you and me."

"I'd like that," she said. She reached over and grabbed a roll of paper towels. She ripped the plastic off it and pealed off several pieces to clean her self. It was useless. The dress was stained and ruined. His seed ran in a steady stream down her thigh.

He worked up his zipper. "I have to go with Gio and Dominic to a private meeting this afternoon. I'll probably miss dinner," he said.

"Oh, okay," she said.

He flashed her a lopsided grin. He squeezed his dick.

"I have plans too," she said as she pulled up her underwear.

"What plans?" he asked.

"Dinner," she said.

"With who?" Lorenzo asked.

"Catalina and Mirabella. We're having dinner with our team at Fabiana's," she said.

"Is Mirabella going?" Lorenzo asked with a serious frown.

"Of course she's going, it's her team."

"Gio won't be happy. The boy, Gino was hurt today," Lorenzo told her.

"How?"

"He jumped from a desk," Lorenzo said.

"Is he okay?" Marietta stood and smoothed out her wrinkled dress.

"He's fine, Marie. But I saw the concern in Gio's eyes. He will want Mirabella here with the kids."

Marietta rolled her eyes. "If he's fine then there is no reason for her not to go. Besides we've been planning this for weeks. It's what Mirabella wants."

"I'll make sure Renaldo is there for you both. He'll take some men. I'm sure Gio is fine with it."

"Thank you, baby." Marietta took a step toward him when he stood. "I love my necklace."

He lifted her chin. "I'll pick you up from Fabiana's."

She smiled and hugged him. Lorenzo squeezed her ass. Sex in the closet was the most romantic thing he'd done since he returned.

— ℬ —

MIRABELLA SENT THE KIDS OFF with Cecilia and Zia. She kept Gino. Nico arrived with her weeping son, and explained he'd jumped from a desk earlier. To her surprise a doctor was called but her husband didn't appear to offer any explanation. Nico was left to explain how the hell Gino managed to get on top of a desk to jump. The doctor said that Gino's wrist didn't appear broken, and wrapped it to give the toddler some comfort after a quick exam. She was advised to call him if she saw any swelling. Still she worried about how weepy he was. Mirabella broke her rule and fixed him a bottle. Her heart finally calmed down when the toddler fell asleep in her arms. She paced in their room with him in his arms.

The door opened and she glanced back. Giovanni stepped inside.

"Is he okay?" he asked.

"You tell me. He was with you," she whispered.

"Yes. He was playing. He fell. It was an accident," Giovanni said.

"That is not what happened. He jumped." She turned and faced him. "I've told you that you have to watch him, discipline him about the jumping. You encourage it. You think his rebellion is funny. He's a baby. He doesn't know any better unless you teach him better."

"Bella…"

"I don't think you should have the boys with you at Villa Rosso, or while you are working."

"Isn't that extreme? The boys are fine with me."

"Not anymore," she informed him. "You're there working, distracted, meeting with people like Santo!"

"Wait, what does Santo have to do with this? He wasn't even there today," Giovanni said.

"That's not the point. When you are working it's not a place for kids. I've decided. They will not be with you when you are working!"

"You decided?" Giovanni asked.

"If you can't be bothered to keep your eyes on your son, then you can't be bothered period! Besides you don't always take your boys. You take Gino. Do you know Eve comes to me crying when you close the door and keep her out?"

Giovanni narrowed his eyes on her. "Don't scold me."

"When it comes to my children I will have this discussion," she said. Gino lifted his head from her shoulder and began to whine. She rubbed his back. "You send Nico in to tell me our child was hurt. Call a doctor, and then show up an hour and a half later to ask if he's okay. It's ridiculous to think I wouldn't be upset. I'm sick of this, Giovanni."

"Sick of what? Me being the man who has to juggle time with my business and my kids, because their mother is too damn consumed with playing with fabric to be of any use!" he shouted.

The accusation fileted her. Not only was it not fair, nor true, but she had spent the entire day beating herself up over not inviting him to her staff party. Marietta was right. She should be able to enjoy her independence without guilt. It was evident her husband didn't burden himself with the emotion. She rolled her eyes and continued to pace.

"Nothing to say?" he challenged her. Now he was ready for the argument. When he first arrived she could tell he struggled with an explanation. If she took the bait he'd turn it into some stupid argument about her working. Those days were over. They agreed the company was part of their lives and she'd return to it.

"It's not going to work. You are not going to turn this around on me. You were distracted, and my baby was hurt."

"Our baby. Our son," he addressed her without raising his voice.

"You know what I mean," she shook her head. "Gio, please. You have to be the same for all of them. They love you equally."

"Wait a minute. Are you accusing me of loving one child more than another? First I'm a bad father because I don't discipline Gino, now I only favor Gino? Any other failures at fatherhood I show know about?"

"No! I only meant—"

"I made a mistake. I turned my head for a moment and he was hurt. How could you think I'd want that to happen?" he asked. "I love all my children equally. But like any parent I see the potential and strengths in them. Maybe I could handle Gino differently, but this is new to me, Bella. I'm more of a father to them all than mine ever was to me!"

"I know, sweetheart. I didn't mean to hurt your feelings."

"It's not about my fucking feelings! It's about you thinking I'm capable of not caring that my son was hurt!"

"Why are you shouting at me?" she asked.

"Because you're pissing me off! This was an accident. I apologized."

"No you did not!"

"I did," he said. He then thought on it. He wiped his hand down his face and groaned deep in his throat. Then leveled his gaze on her. "I'm sorry he was hurt and I didn't come sooner, Bella. Now don't you think I'm owed an apology?" he teased her with a smile. It wasn't going to work. He was not going to charm his way out of this.

Mirabella shook her head in refusal.

Giovanni threw his hands up in defeat. Her heart softened. He was right. To accuse him of being a bad father was extreme. He was far from it. Only she knew of the nights he would leave their bed to go and check on their little boys. And how worried he was when Gino developed a little slower than Gianni the first months of his life. Gino almost died. Giovanni was always sensitive to that fact.

She walked over to the bed and put her son down in the center. She positioned the pillows so that he wouldn't roll off. When she stood upright Giovanni was right behind her. He folded his arms around her.

"Bella, don't be angry with me. You know I hate disappointing you." She tried to shrug him off but he was too insistent. He put his chin on her shoulder. He stared down at their sleeping son.

"I love my *bambini* the same," he repeated. "Gino is the most adventurous of them. He loves life. I think it's because he struggled to be born. I see it in him and I want to encourage it. My father never did with me. Do you understand?"

She turned around and looked in his eyes. She wasn't blinded any more. She knew her husband's strengths and his weaknesses. "If he was hurt would you want me to send one of your men down the hall to tell you?"

"Never."

"Okay. I'm sorry for my accusations. I get so scared when it comes to the kids. They're the best of us, Gio, but the most vulnerable. I panicked when he came to me holding his wrist. And when you didn't come I—" her voice choked with emotion.

He kissed her softly. She blinked away fresh tears and hugged his neck. She felt sane again. He kissed the side of her face. He kissed her neck. He caressed her back.

"Woman, you sound like my mother not my wife," he chuckled. "Give your man a break once and a while, and not assume the worst in him."

"I love you." She pressed her face to his chest. The truth was she hated arguing with him, even when he was wrong. And in the end, every fight was a lesson for them both. He ran his hand down her back. She pushed out of his arms and moved around him before he got more amorous. She needed to dress and tell him about her dinner plans. Before she could speak he did.

"I came upstairs to tell you that I have business to tend to. I won't be here for dinner," he said.

"Oh? Okay. You sure?" she asked.

"I'll try not to be out late," he smiled.

"Uhm, well I have an idea. I think maybe I should have dinner with my staff tonight. At Fabiana's."

Giovanni frowned. "Why there?"

"I haven't been 'there'," she said with air quotes, "in months. They want to celebrate with me. And since you won't be here for dinner I can meet with them and be home before you miss me."

Giovanni dropped his hands in his pockets. "You had this planned didn't you?"

She chuckled. "Confession time. I planned it with the girls. Yes."

"Am I invited?" he asked.

"Why would you ask that?"

"Because it's the first I'm hearing of it. If I were invited you would have told me sooner," he said.

"You don't want to come—"

"I do," he insisted. "I could have changed my plans. Be there for you."

"Giovanni?" she gave a nervous chuckle and walked away. "It's just us talking about dresses and shoes. Stuff you hate. You don't want to come, trust me."

"I can come afterwards, if you want," he smiled.

"No," she said.

"No?"

"I think I just want to meet with them. Don't be upset. Why don't you come tomorrow and do the photo shoot and interviews with me? That would make me happy."

She avoided his eyes. She knew he stared at her while she unpacked their things.

"Okay," she heard him say. She glanced back up at him. He smiled at her. Mirabella grew increasingly concerned. Nothing was ever that easy with her husband.

"Just okay?" she asked.

"We're in Milano for you, Bella. This is your business. If you want to have a dinner with your team I understand. I accept it."

"You continue to amaze me, Gio," she said. She looked into his eyes trying to gauge his sincerity.

"What's all this?" he asked about the boxes and packages all over the floor.

"Gifts from other designers. They sent them to wish me luck on my big day," she said.

Giovanni knelt and picked up the satin Kimono. He shook it out and studied it. He turned it around and looked at the dragon. Mirabella chewed on her bottom lip. It was silly to think that Kei, after all this time, would have something to do with the gift. The man was in prison.

"I like this," Giovanni said. "Wear it for me tonight?"

Mirabella's smile changed. "I have something special to wear for you tonight. We won't need that."

"I like this," he insisted.

"Better than me naked?" she teased.

He looked at the robe and then to her. He tossed it aside. "I'll let you decide on what's best."

"Good boy," she winked. He left. When the door closed Mirabella glanced to the kimono.

"It's nothing," she said to herself. She picked it up, put it in the trash, and then dusted her hands. She looked over to Gino, who was now sleeping on his back. She smiled. A family trip with just them, and not his entourage, is just what they both needed.

CHAPTER FOUR

Bella Mafia

APPLAUSE GREETED HER. Mirabella wore a long flowing black dress. It wrapped around her curves and parted to the front with a seductive split. The plunging neckline revealed the contour of her breasts. The only accessory on her neck was a two-carat diamond solitaire that matched the studs in her ears. The moment she stepped through the doors of House of Fabiana's the staff exploded with excitement.

Humbled she put both hands to her mouth. A sheen of tears blurred her vision. In Milano she employed a team of two hundred, and in Paris she had twice that number of people working for her. So many smiling faces from both operations welcomed her, she couldn't possibly count them all.

"Is everyone here?" she asked in disbelief.

"Almost everyone," Catalina replied.

"Go on, sis, don't be shy," Marietta pinched her on the side. Mirabella was giddy with excitement. The fashion house was decorated beautifully. Red balloons, red and gold silk streamers, and hundreds of red roses in crystal vases were posted on several pedestals. Large and tall red candles provided the lighting to the front of Fabiana's. They collectively illuminated the stairs that circled and went up to the top floors. Every woman on her staff wore a red dress, and every man a red tie.

"Congratulations!" Shouted the crowd.

Marietta kissed her cheek. "Take a bow! This is all for you."

The celebration left her speechless. She had prepared for crises, and last minute changes that any designer faced before the biggest day of their career.

After all, most of the garments were cut in her design room at Melanzana, and hand stitched with specific instructions to her seamstresses. She hadn't had time to touch and review each one. The Milano Fashion Gala would be the first time in her career that she'd introduce a new line and Fabiana wasn't there to encourage and manage things. Even Teddy's absence had filled her with doubt.

"Thank you, everyone! *Grazie, grazie!*" She stepped into the crowd and stopped to kiss many cheeks.

"Donna Mirabella, ben tornata!" exclaimed one person.

"Congratulazioni, Mirabella!" cheered another person.

"Complimenti, Donna Battaglia!"

She hugged the necks of several. The crowd circling her became so overwhelmingly tight that Catalina and Marietta had to tell several people to step aside. Mirabella made a point to greet every single person who came before her. In the past two years she'd only met with a handful of her employees. The cheek kisses and hand squeezing was put to an end. Catalina pulled her through the praise by the elbow. Again Mirabella was struck by how elegant everything was. Music serenaded the guests from a violinist and a cello player. The back room was cleared out for tables with black cloths and red china.

"Upstairs, go, we'll have our meeting first before we join the staff and eat," Catalina whispered. Mirabella had to hold the sides of her dress to keep from stepping on the long hem as they climbed the stairs.

"You okay?" Marietta asked Shae. Together they climbed the stairs side by side. She'd given Shae one of the designer originals from her closet for the evening. Her best friend glammed the dress up with her trademark style. She'd put loose curls in her pink streaked hair, then styled the asymmetrical bob-cut with puffy thickness and bounce. Shae turned the heads of gay and straight men with her voluptuous hourglass figure in a t-shirt and jeans. But the dress she wore flattered her figure even more so, fitting snug around the hips and ass. Marietta dropped her tomboy jeans and big sweatshirts the moment she and Shae became friends. She learned from Shae how to love her body and take care of it. It was a lesson that influenced her choices in diet and exercise to that very day.

Shae smiled. "Why are you so nervous around your people, Mae? They like me."

"Yeah, they do. But my sister doesn't know everything about me, and my past. Not like you do, Shae. I just want, never mind. Forget it."

"Mae? I'm your girl. You think I want to fuck this up for you? That fancy sister of yours is no saint. Trust me. I know women, she has her own freaky secrets."

"Shut up!" Marietta hissed.

Shae chuckled. "I'm joking."

Marietta glanced up to Mirabella ahead of them walking off the final stair. Once Mirabella confided in Marietta that she had an abusive boyfriend when she was a teenager. It was something Marietta shelved to the back of her mind. But she always wondered why her sister up and left Virginia, and rushed to her dreams in New York. The death of their grandfather only partly explained it. There could be more to the story.

"This place is the bomb. I'm loving it." Shae glanced back at the others on the lower floor when they reached the top. "Is this all you, Mae? The decorating I mean?"

"Yeah, it's me. But I do other things. Catalina and I are pretty much the eyes, ears, and voice for my sister."

"No shit? You got your head on straight. Can handle business now?"

Marietta cut her eyes. She couldn't balance a checkbook if she tried. Lorenzo threw money at her. And when she moved to Sorrento, everything in southern Italy was given to her. She'd walk into a store and they'd recognize her as a Battaglia and never question payments. One time when drinking with Lorenzo and Carlo she heard them talk about the money they used to collect when they weren't high ranking officers for Giovanni. Extortion was big with the *Camorra*, among other things.

Shae looked at her with a frown, and then glanced to Mirabella who was continuing toward the conference room. "Why did she give you so much control?" Shae whispered. "I get the feeling it's the first time she's stepped in the building of her own company. It's weird."

"Long story. Trust me, nothing goes down here without her approval. But yeah, she can't really be here physically like Catalina and me, or in Paris. It's complicated."

"It's her husband," Shae replied.

"Yeah. It's him. Don't the decor remind you of the parties we used to throw, huh?" Marietta asked, effectively changing the subject. Shae grinned and nodded. Together they entered the conference room. Catalina talked so fast Marietta was sure Mirabella missed most of what she said. She didn't jockey for Mirabella's ear. She had it on most days at Melanzana. Also the first rule enforced by her sister was there was to be no competition between Marietta and Catalina. So they worked together fine. It was Fabiana that Marietta secretly loathed. And the damn building stunk of her. On every wall hung portraits of Fabiana from her life as a fashion manager. And the larger than life portrait in Mirabella's office of her and Fabiana back to back irked her the most.

"Kyra! Jamie! You've arrived!" Mirabella laughed. The welcome brought Marietta out of her thoughts.

"*Ciao, Donna Mirabella,*" Kyra said in her soft sweet voice. Marietta noticed how beautiful Kyra looked. She had cut down her thick curly fro lower to her head. It was tapered so neatly, and framed her face so nicely, she rivaled the models who walked the runway. Kyra was in her early twenties. She wore long fashionable golden earrings, and a red mini dress that revealed her dark brown legs, and outlined her petite figure. The young girl walked over and hugged her mentor. Kyra was a rare gem. The talent she and Jamie brought to their business often surprised Marietta. Especially since she was so vocal of not bringing them on from America.

"How are you?" Mirabella asked her. "The wedding? How's the planning going?"

"Getting settled here in Milan. Since we are buying a place here I have Luca with me now. Renaldo's mother and my mother are planning the wedding. We've decided on two ceremonies."

"What? Two?" Catalina frowned.

If a black woman could blush Kyra would have. "It's best this way. Renaldo is Catholic and we must be married here. And of course my family we… have our own traditions. We will be going to Nigeria to be wed there afterwards. It makes everyone happy."

"Is she serious? That's Renaldo's woman?" Shae whispered.

"Yes. I guess this is her way of making everyone happy." Marietta chuckled and shook her head. Kyra was pretty young to be stepping into the role of stepmother so soon. Luca was Renaldo's son, and though Kyra and Renaldo were engaged, she didn't expect her to take on his motherless kid. Lorenzo had told her that Renaldo was orphaned and considered his dead wife's mother his mother. The arrangement had to be an appeasement for everyone.

"*Benissima!*" Mirabella grinned. "I love Nigeria. I will talk to Giovanni to see if we can attend."

Inside the conference room they found seven other people from Mirabella's design team waiting. Jamie of course was the one with presence. She wore red glitter, platform boots that reached to her thighs, and were so tall they could have been stilts, a leather red mini-skirt, and a fitted red corset with the same stones as on her boots. *Did she have her boobs done again?* In the corset they looked huge. Jamie's hair and makeup were flawless as always. In the fashion industry there were both male and female gay, bi-sexual people. They held jobs in makeup, event planning, and were even more notable as fashion designers. However, no matter how much the world was changing, many people, including the men she and her sister were married to, had a hard time accepting this aspect of the business.

Jamie was a woman now. She had the surgery in Switzerland soon after moving from the States. Mirabella took care of all the expenses, and Marietta knew for a fact she did so without telling Giovanni. After Jamie's transformation, Marietta and the rest of the girls never addressed her as anything else.

"Ciao a tutti!" Mirabella said. She kissed and hugged Jamie. "Please have a seat, everyone."

Shae, who seemed extremely impressed, asked Marietta, "So this is the team? The people who make the magic happen?" She held a glass of champagne in her hand. She must have scooped it when they came inside. The one weakness her friend had was alcohol. In fact she could become a raging, cursing bitch if she drank too much of it.

"This is it. Watch and learn," Marietta instructed. "You are about to see Bella Mafia at her finest."

Mirabella lowered to the seat at the head of the table and gazed upon her team. It had been a hard fought journey to bring them to this point. She ran her hands over the smooth tabletop, and glanced around at the office where many meetings had occurred without her. She took a deep breath before she spoke.

"Catalina, you first." Mirabella said.

Her sister in-law flashed a look of surprise to be singled out. Mirabella had learned yesterday that Catalina was talking of making some last minute changes. It troubled her that Catalina didn't tell her and she had to hear this third hand. Everyone around the conference table stared at Catalina and waited.

"I… ah… my issue is too much, too soon. It's your first… event. I don't know if everyone can handle two fashion houses, and the shoe line all in one show. Maybe we focus on Mirabella's, with a preshow to feature a few pieces from Fabiana's and the red bottom shoe line."

"What? Are you fucking kidding? We are one day from the show. The itinerary and schedule have been sent out. The models are here. We have…"

"Marietta, let her finish," Mirabella said.

"Maybe we should discuss this privately." Catalina mumbled.

"I understand. I had many of the same reservations, at first." Mirabella smiled. "Don't think of this as just a Mirabella event, or just a Fabiana's event. Think of this as a Battaglia event." Everyone stared at her waiting for her meaning. "Whenever any of you address the press you say Battaglia first. Are we clear?"

Everyone nodded his or her head in agreement.

"Good. Our work is a reflection of my family. Every garment, every shoe, every model that wears them strengthens the Battaglia family. Including you. We step out in front of the world and show them *la famiglia*. And it's as colorful, vibrant, and layered with beauty as a peacock." The others laughed and looked around the room at each other. Fabiana and Mirabella had made sure to celebrate diversity. She hired talent, and what came through the door off the streets of New York was a variety of colors. They were yellow, brown, pink people. None of it mattered. It felt good creating with people from all walks of life.

Mirabella continued. "We don't follow the guidelines of the industry. We make them. That's the difference between them and us. Of course the show is big, overwhelming, and a risk. What in life worth having isn't?"

After nearly five years of loving a man unwilling to compromise, Mirabella had finally understood the way to achieve happiness and success in her life and marriage. On the eve of her biggest day, it was time to teach them all the same. Nothing is unachievable as long as they acted as a family.

"Kyra, are you ready?" Mirabella asked.

"Yes, Donna. Jamie and I have rehearsals and fittings tomorrow. We're ready. Right, Jamie?"

"Honey cakes, I was born ready, the shoes are the candy. Kyra and I have brought the sweetness." Jamie winked.

Mirabella and the girls laughed. "I agree," she said. "This is huge. Everyone in Paris is coming."

"The features they are running on you are almost daily in the States," chimed in Kyra.

"It's why we start red hot! Flash and sparkle! That's Fabiana's." Mirabella said. "We end with class and sophistication. That's Mirabella's. It's the fashion that they want to see. It's what we work for."

"Thank you, for your updates, Kyra and Jamie." Mirabella smiled. "Marietta, what about you? Any concerns?"

"I agreed with Catalina in the beginning. But I thought we all accepted the bigger picture. I'm just ready for this to happen. For you to be out there again, sis."

Mirabella went down the table and continued to hear of last minute changes, and preparations that needed to be made. Catalina forced a smile, but Mirabella could sense her concerns persisted. She was a worrier, like Fabiana. It's why Mirabella was convinced that the show would be a success. Catalina and Marietta balanced the scales for her.

"I'm ready. Let's see what we have." Mirabella clapped her hands together.

Mateo picked up the remote and turned on the projector that dropped from the ceiling. Mirabella smiled as the video production team gave her a preview of her dream. It was happening. Fabiana would be so proud of her.

Nicosia Boxing Gym, Milano Italy –

The gym was in the heart of Bergamo. Buildings were huddled together along a cramped one-way cobblestone street. Storeowners leaned against their shop doors, and patrons dined at small tables on the sidewalk. The only discernable distinction for the gym sandwiched between a tailor and bakery, was the creaking signboard posted several feet above the door, flapping in the wind. Dominic and Lorenzo entered first, with Rocco and then Giovanni following. Three of his best men took up the rear. One remained outside.

This was no ordinary gym. Nicosia was the training ground for the toughest and meanest men in the Italian and Sicilian fighting circuit. It was owned and financed by Father Nicosia, an excommunicated Sicilian Catholic priest. Father Nicosia was the only man who Giovanni knew held the respect of the *Camorra*, *Ndrangheta,* and the *Mafiosi*. His gym was neutral territory in the heart of the triangle.

As for Nicosia's sins against God, there were many that led to his excommunication. His final offense should have landed him in jail. The Papacy spared him that disgrace. Giovanni was told the Pope himself made the call. To be excommunicated meant Father Nicosia was officially excluded from participation in the sacraments, and performing the services of the Catholic Church. In other words, Father Nicosia's soul was now more damned than any of the ruthless crime bosses he offered blessings to. The priest continued to wear his collar and practice his beliefs behind the church's back.

When the Battaglia men entered the gym Giovanni didn't see the fallen priest. Two men danced around the ring with boxer helmets on their heads, and bright red boxing gloves covering their fists.

"Is that him?" Giovanni asked as he stood observing between Dominic and Rocco.

"No. He's over there, Gio." Dominic replied.

He looked to his left and saw Carlo. He was with a younger man, lacing his glove. The boy was shorter than Carlo. He couldn't be more than nineteen or twenty.

"Look at that runt. Probably has no hair on his balls," Lorenzo chuckled.

"Name is Ciro. Remember?" Dominic interjected.

Giovanni nodded. One look at the kid and he wasn't really sure he'd be a contender for this match or any other. Why the fuck did Carlo think so?

"Buona sera, Don Giovanni!" Father Nicosia appeared from the right in a dark suit, priest collar, and pectoral cross. He wasn't tall like Giovanni and his men. He put his hands together and bowed his head a bit at Giovanni, and then clasped them behind his back. *"Come sta?"*

"Molto bene. E lei?" Giovanni asked.

"I'm well," the priest who was the same age as Giovanni answered. He had long, dark curly hair that reached just beyond his nape. He tucked it behind his ears. Skin darker than most Sicilians, the priest had very piercing hazel-brown eyes, and a very athletic build like the men who trained in his gym. "I was told of this visit. You come to the triangle often but I rarely hear from you. Why is that, Gio?"

The priest was aligned to no one. Either you were in Giovanni's world or you weren't. And if you weren't, Giovanni had no use for you. Also the Calderone war years ago made Giovanni an enemy of many people in this region of Italy. They may fear him and the *Camorra,* but they didn't all respect him. The priest gave him a friendly pat to his arm. "It's fine. You're here now. Please, we have prepared for your visit. Maybe you and I can meet before you leave. I know of some opportunities in Genoa you might want to hear about."

After a handshake Giovanni and the others were led around the ring to open bench seating that gave an elevated view to the boxing ring. Giovanni unbuttoned his blazer and settled down to the middle seat, with Dominic on one side and Lorenzo on the other. Rocco sat on the row beneath them. The priest nodded his head in respect and stalked off. Giovanni and his men tracked the priest with their eyes until he was gone.

"I hear he is now counsel for the Bonaduces," Lorenzo whispered. "Don't let him suck your dick, Gio. He can give a shit about the Battaglias."

Giovanni accepted the information.

"Ciro has fought sixteen matches so far," Dominic said. Giovanni's gaze swung back to the young fighter.

"Sixteen?"

"*Sí*, He won two of them with knock outs, and only one was a draw. No losses, Gio," Dominic said.

"Who were the challengers?" Lorenzo chuckled. "Preschoolers?"

Dominic leaned forward with his elbow to his knee to look around Giovanni and address Lorenzo. "Locals mostly. But since Carlo took him on he has had a few challengers out of Roma. No one noteworthy."

"Figures!" Lorenzo gave a snort of disapproval.

"I've done some research, Gio," Dominic began. "There's a boxer in London who is undefeated in the IBF. He's in Ciro's weight class."

"Russian?" Giovanni asked.

"Asian," Dominic replied. "Santo happened to mention wanting to see him fight the other day."

The trainer blew his whistle. Ciro climbed into the ring. The sparring partner given to him threw shadow punches in the air while bouncing on one foot and then the other. The men met at the center of the ring. They bumped gloves and stepped back. Carlo was on the outside holding on to the ropes. He shouted instructions to his brother. Giovanni observed Carlo's concentration more than his tutees finesse. Carlo behaved as if the boy was a son.

"How long has Carlo been keeping up with this one?" Giovanni asked Lorenzo.

"Not sure. It's like he lives a double life. Always searching for the lost boys that belonged to his father. He only recently told me about this one," Lorenzo answered.

"I don't think the kid is his brother," Dominic said. "Made a call. The mother was a whore and says she doesn't remember who the father is. Carlo scared the *puttana*. When he was done with her she swore up and down the kid belonged to Carlo's father. He's been this way since he lost Carmine."

Giovanni nodded that he understood. They were all kids in their hearts. Lost boys searching for an identity in their fathers' shadows. Giovanni didn't know a man who stood beside him or behind him that didn't have a broken story to tell. It may explain why they were so willing to accept the darkness of their business. Carlo was one of the more ruthless men under his employ. There wasn't a job he'd turn down. It was now, when Giovanni watched Carlo coach his bastard brother, that he saw some of the spirit he'd lost when he was sent away at fifteen.

"I've made my decision," Giovanni announced.

"You have?" Lorenzo sat forward.

"How?" Dominic asked. "They've just started and we haven't seen him with—"

"Sponsor the kid. Get him the best trainer. Make sure his papers are in order so he can compete outside of Italia. And keep that fucking priest away from the deal."

Giovanni looked down at Rocco. Though his uncle didn't turn to comment, he knew he heard him. Rocco's words and warnings regarding his dirty business deals plagued him.

"Gio? Look at the kid. He's scrawny, weak. My wife can throw a better punch!" Lorenzo wrinkled his nose.

"Look at Carlo," Giovanni replied. The men all looked back at Carlo who had now gotten in the ring against the trainer's orders. He stopped the boxing and was speaking sternly to his brother. He made the boy put up his gloves and showed him how to stretch out his swing. "In all the years we've known him, what has he been passionate about?" Giovanni asked.

"Killing, whores, drinking, and gambling," Dominic chuckled. "In that order."

"Now we see this. Carlo's a good soldier, and he lost a brother because of the family," Giovanni cut his gaze over to Lorenzo. "Do you not think this is something we should give him?"

Lorenzo's face flushed. He rubbed his jaw. "Fuck it. The kid can be trained. I guess. I don't give a fuck about this boxing shit. We have more important business."

Giovanni looked over to Dominic. His young *consigliere* smiled with what looked like pride. "You're a good man, Gio. I'll make sure this investment pays out."

"*Basta.* Now take me to my wife's party. I want to see it." Giovanni stood.

"I thought it was some women's party and we weren't invited?" Lorenzo frowned.

"I don't give a shit. I want to see it," Giovanni said and walked down the bench seats.

Lorenzo grabbed Dominic's sleeve and stopped him from leaving. Giovanni and Rocco continued to the door. "I want to meet with you. Private. To go over some of my ideas for Mancini. *Presto?*"

"*Sí, domani,*" Dominic said and followed Giovanni out. Lorenzo hung back. He'd watch the sparring match and deliver the news to his best friend. After several minutes he smiled. Giovanni just bought Carlo a brother to play with. It wasn't a business investment. It was bullshit.

— *B* —

"*ATTENZIONE! ATTENZIONE!* Everyone, please! Can I have your attention?" Marietta said. She tapped her spoon against the glass to quiet the staff. Mirabella glanced up at her sister. They'd laughed, eaten, and drank bottles of Merlot for close to two hours. She spent most of the night wiping tears of joy from her eyes.

"To my beloved sister. For four years the world has speculated, gossiped, and lied about who you are, and on your talent. They credited Carole Montague for your success. *Diavolo!*" Marietta made a gesture of false spitting to the left as her husband did often when pissed. Mirabella and the others roared with laughter. "She was never you! Together we will show the world who you really are: *Donna Mirabella Ellison Battaglia.* My sister, my mentor, my best friend, and the best damn fashion designer in the world! *T'amerò per tutta l'eternità.*"

"*Cin! Cin!*" Catalina raised her glass in tribute. Everyone raised their glasses and yelled. "*Cin cin!*"

"Speech! Speech! Speech!" Jamie beat her hands on the table. Several others started to beat their hands on the table and chant the words as well.

Mirabella stood with applause.

"*Grazie!* Thank you all." The staff quieted. "We have one day before we reveal to the world our talent. I say *our* talent because it's you, all of you that made this event possible. *Mia famiglia!*" She paused and allowed the applause to settle down. "I want to give a special thank you to my sisters Marietta and Catalina. For two years you have worked tirelessly to bring my vision to life. I am nothing without you. I love you, I thank you!" she raised her glass. Everyone raised his or her glass in return. "*Viva la Battaglia! Salute!*" She drank her glass of wine down and giggled uncontrollably once done. Clearly she was intoxicated. Marietta poured her more wine.

"No, I've had enough," Mirabella gasped between giggles.

"Girl, please. Let's get fucked up! It's our party! Drink!" Marietta chuckled.

Mirabella nodded and picked up the glass to take another sip. And then her vision focused and she noticed three men watching from the side door.

"Is that Giovanni?" Catalina asked.

Mirabella lowered her glass to the table.

"Oh shit," Marietta said.

Several heads turned. Soon every eye in the room looked to her husband. She wanted to invite him to the celebration but decided against it. This was her night, and she kind of liked the idea of keeping him separate. Her heart couldn't beat faster to have him appear from out of thin air. He strolled in with Dominic and Rocco trailing him with his cane. His focus was singular. It was aimed at her. Mirabella walked around the table to greet her husband properly. Lucky for her she managed her steps in her heels with grace. It was an accomplishment. She'd drunk so much wine she could have easily stumbled. Once within reach of him she threw her arms around his neck and pressed up against his chest. She loved the smell and feel of him, and loved it even more when she'd been drinking.

"*Ciao, bambino,*" she whispered. She kissed him so hard he went stiff as if to reject her enthusiasm. "*Baciami,*" she said and felt him soften under her persistence. Giovanni wasn't prone to such acts of affection in front of strangers. Well to hell with appearances. She wanted to kiss her man. She was happy.

"That's enough, Bella," he said and brought her arms down from around his neck. She reluctantly let him go. She stared up into his blue eyes. Was he angry? He sure as hell didn't look happy. "Remember where you are."

She nodded and stepped back. "Thank you for coming, sweetheart," she said in a deeply formal voice and then giggled. He didn't crack a smile. "I thought you had a meeting?" she asked to mask her hurt feelings. Maybe the wine made her feel his scorn too deeply.

"The meeting's over," he replied. "I came to collect you."

"Collect me? Did you?" she crossed her arms. She had half a mind to remind him that he wasn't invited. But his unwavering stare broke down her courage.

Mirabella tossed her hair. "Do you see? Do you see what we've done?" She gestured around. Giovanni glanced to the others. She put her arm around his waist. He eased his arm around hers. "What do you think?" she asked. Her head cleared a bit and she was steady on her feet.

"I'm very proud of you," he whispered in her ear. "Have you been drinking in front of your staff?"

She blushed. His deep authoritative voice, mixed with the wine, diluted her commonsense. The words translated like that of a sexual proposal instead of chastisement because it started with a compliment. Mirabella walked with him back to their table. "Everyone, many of you have met him, and some of you haven't. I want to introduce my husband, the love of my life, Don Giovanni Battaglia."

A few people exchanged glances and Mirabella knew it was the title she used. To hell with propriety he was her Don, and theirs too if they continued to work for Mirabella's. Of course many applauded, and soon everyone gathered did so as well.

"It's time for you to come home with me," he said softly in her ear. "You've had too much to drink. Let me take care of you."

"Not yet, sweetie. Come. Sit, and let me get you something to eat," she said. She double blinked to clear her head. He checked his watch, and then looked at her guests. Reluctant but supportive, he agreed. He, Rocco, and Dominic all joined them. Marietta gave up her seat so Giovanni could sit next to Mirabella.

"You must be very proud of your wife, *Signore* Battaglia," Francesca her marketing manager said. "She's brilliant. We have been starved for her talent and guidance."

Giovanni stared at the woman expressionless. Marietta chuckled over the awkward silence. Mirabella cleared her throat. "Sweetheart, let me introduce you." She went down the line. She introduced everyone outside of the family, including a few people Giovanni did know. He nodded and dropped his arm over her chair and rubbed her shoulder. People continued to eat and chat up each other over the tasks and responsibilities planned for the big day. A few celebrity names were tossed into the conversation. The entire affair went on with her husband gently caressing her shoulder. He only smiled when she glanced at him. And that wasn't often. But he was there, at her side, and it meant the world to her.

"We have an early morning. I think we should start at six? What do you think, Mirabella?" Catalina asked. "Is six okay with you?"

"Six sounds fine. What time will the lawyers want to meet with me, Dominic?" Mirabella asked.

"*Non c'é una problema.* I can have them here in the morning," Dominic said. "Don't worry."

Mirabella glanced to her husband. He hadn't touched the plate put in front of him by the server. Instead he stared directly at Jamie who sat at another table across from them. Jamie was hard to miss. She too had too much to drink and laughed loudly. She yelled across the table at Kyra a few times. Giovanni's brows lowered and his violet-blue gaze narrowed on the transgender shoemaker. Mirabella placed her hand on his thigh. His gaze slipped over to her. "Can you come here tomorrow, around two?"

"Why?" Giovanni asked.

"We have a reporter coming. I was thinking we could do the interview together and let them take some pictures of the children. It's what the P.R. team suggests. And since Thursday promises to be crazy it's best to do it before then."

Giovanni winked. She exhaled a sigh of relief. Why she was so tense about his approval, when he'd done nothing so far but offer it, was beyond her. She leaned in to kiss his cheek. He liked the attention. She could tell. Marriage changed her and him. They both found it hard to compromise. No matter what his words of encouragement were, she knew his true feelings. It was like a sixth sense of hers.

"All right, I think I'm done. Since we have an early start in the morning we should probably leave." Before she could say more Giovanni scooted his chair back and stood. He stepped behind her and pulled out her chair. "Good night," Mirabella said. "See you in the morning." She left the party with her hand in his. Mirabella didn't bother to look back.

"What just happened?" Shae asked.

Marietta downed the last of her champagne. "Party over. The King has come for the Queen."

"He's pretty intense. Barely spoke to anyone. Is he mad at her?" Shae asked.

Marietta laughed. "No. I think that was him being supportive."

"Hey, are you two going to leave? Now?" Catalina asked.

"Looks like the party is over." Marietta said with a pout. "I was just getting Mirabella to loosen up, and he had to come in and spoil the fun."

"Oh leave Gio alone. He was being supportive. It was cute," Catalina said.

"Whatever." Marietta shrugged.

"Dominic is going to stay and wait for us, Marietta. Let's go up to Mirabella's office. I haven't seen you in weeks. We have the party in Bellagio to discuss. I need your permission, and signatures."

"Excuse me, ladies," Shae spoke up. "Is it okay if I head back with the Don and his wife? I'm worn out."

"Oh shit. Yes, girl, I'm sorry. You've been on a plane twice today and the time change and all. Go on. Get some rest."

"Thanks!" Shae got her purse and hurried after Mirabella and Giovanni.

Catalina elbowed Marietta. "I like her. She seems like fun," she said.

"She is. She'll be the life of the party. Trust me." Marietta yawned. She glanced over to Dominic. "Where is my bad boy husband, Domi? He said he would come and pick me up."

Dominic continued to eat. He didn't even look up. Marietta cut her gaze away. She'd be lucky if she was awake when Lorenzo came home. "Yeah, let's go upstairs and finish things. We have so much left to do we should get it over with as soon as we can."

They said their goodbyes to a few and walked off together.

MIRABELLA GLANCED OVER TO HER HUSBAND. He hadn't spoken. Leo drove. Shae rode in the passenger seat, silent as well. Rocco travelled in the car behind them with their men. The silence felt like an order from her husband as opposed to a natural settlement within the group. Giovanni stared out of the window for most of the drive home. Typically that meant he was deep in thought. She reached over and took his hand. He squeezed hers but didn't look her way. That confirmed it. He wasn't happy, and that made her sad.

"Everything was so beautiful tonight," Shae said.

"*Grazie.* I can't wait for tomorrow. So much to do," Mirabella replied.

The car drove up the hill and through the gates. Giovanni's hand left hers as soon as the car stopped. Mirabella sobered. She was helped from the car and met her husband at the steps. She glanced back once to Shae and winked. "See you in the morning."

Shae nodded. She watched the Don take his wife inside without a backward glance. As she started toward the steps she caught the shadow of movement to her left from her peripheral vision. Three men emerged. The one who glanced up in her direction was the one she'd noticed before. Their eyes met. Carlo's brow arched at her refusal to lower her gaze.

Was he going to walk right up to her? *God she hoped so.* Shae sucked in her diaphragm and let him get a good look at her. She knew under the moonlight, the red satin material of her dress looked like liquid draped over her curves. To her disappointment Carlo and his men walked over to a car. He got behind the wheel. He glanced up at her again from the inside. He said something to the men in the car and they all looked to her. Carlo shook his head, and the men laughed. He started the car and drove out of the drive.

Was that a dismissal? Shae stood there stunned. Not many men, black, white, or purple turned away when she looked them in the eye. She crossed her arms in disappointment. Another man approached her and asked her something in Italian. Shae cut her eyes and stormed up the steps. This was far from over.

— *B* —

"ARE YOU GOING TO GIVE ME the silent treatment the rest of the night?" Mirabella asked. She glanced up to the reflection of Giovanni's piercing blue stare in the mirror before her. It never wavered.

"Did you check on Gino?" he asked.

"You know I did. Maybe you should go in and say goodnight." Mirabella removed one diamond earring, and then the other. Giovanni turned and walked back into their bedroom. With a burdened sigh she decided in that moment to deal with her husband's sulking. She would not let his mood ruin the great days she had ahead of her. And she was horny. Wine always made her horny. He always made her horny. Mirabella followed him back into the bedroom. He paced before the bed. Sex was the last thing on his mind. She waited until he worked through whatever he had to say. He stopped and looked at her.

"Say it? What have I done now?" Mirabella threw her hands up.

He sat on the bed. He wiped his hand down his face and exhaled a deep breath. "You looked beautiful tonight."

"You're angry because I look beautiful?" she asked.

"You looked like my wife. Beautiful," he clarified.

Mirabella paused. She waited for more. He didn't speak. "Thank yo—"

"Why were you drinking?" he asked. "In public."

Mirabella laughed.

He did not.

"I had a glass of wine," she answered.

"You're drunk now," he accused.

"I am hardly drunk. I was celebrating. I had a few glasses of wine—"

"More than a few," Giovanni narrowed his cold hard gaze on her.

"I have more than a few here with you. And you never complain. Besides you of all people need not lecture anyone on drinking."

"My drinking and yours is not the same," he said.

"Oh Giovanni, let it go. I'm not in the mood to fight."

"The people work for you, Bella. You must always behave like my Donna and theirs in public. Always. Who do you think feeds the tabloids stories about your life?"

"My staff does not—"

"You barely know half of them," he reminded her.

"And why is that? Huh? Why is it I can never meet with them? I can never travel to see them?"

"Because you are a mother. A wife! Bella, you know the rules!" Giovanni reasoned.

"Rules! Rules! Rules! Oh my God. Would you stop with these damn rules?"

"I knew it. I knew this company would be a problem. This is a bad idea.

You aren't ready for this," he said.

"There it is!" She pointed at him. "Right there. You said it. You want to stop my show. You're the one that's not ready!"

"I didn't say that." Giovanni's brows shot up in surprise.

"No." Mirabella shook her head in refusal. "I'm not going to take the bait. You want to fight, and all I want to do is rejoice. Oh tonight was so much fun. I had a great time! A fabulous time! Tonight has been one of the best nights of my life," she smiled though the action hurt to do so. She neared the verge of tears. If she cried, if she gave in to her emotions and let him box her in, she'd lose. And it was always a damned battle.

"I thought our wedding night was the best night of your life," he said.

She ignored him and continued. "All day I've been so nervous. So worried about how things would be. I had second thoughts, Giovanni. I love my life as it is. I was thinking that maybe you are right and I don't need to be a designer again. Believe me, I'm happy being your wife, a mother. I take pride in it."

He smiled. She wasn't finish. "Then I get there and it was all about me. My passions. It was like I finally saw what Fabiana and Teddy used to tell me. The company isn't dollars and cents. It's my heart. See? See?" she held her hands out. "My hands are shaking I'm so excited thinking about it."

"And you didn't want to include me?" he asked.

Mirabella blinked in shock. It dawned on her the reason for his attitude. Why he kept pushing for the argument. Not her drinking, not even her having a party. He was jealous because she purposefully excluded him. And she did. A measure of her anger softened. It was a big night and she could have invited him. Part of her did want to. She struggled with finding the words to explain her conflict. She decided honesty would be the best approach.

"To be honest, sweetheart, you're a big distraction."

"Why? Why can't I be part of this and not a distraction?" he frowned.

"Because you take up so much of my heart, Gio. It's hard to explain. I look at you and I see love. I look into your eyes and I see our family. I see myself the way you see me. You never see me as Mirabella Ellison." She let her words sink in. When he was unable to look her in the eye she knew he agreed with her. "The night was not about you. The truth is, Gio, tonight I didn't put you first for the first time in two years, and it felt good."

"Is it possible I could love my husband and my company differently? Is it possible you could love your business and me differently?" she asked.

"You're twisting my love for you to say it's exclusive, my way only," he said. "I love you, Bella. All of you. I never knew you didn't understand why I prefer the woman standing before me. The woman who returned to me after I thought she was dead, with a daughter, and gave me sons, my own family. She's special to me. I live for that woman."

"And you're twisting my actions tonight. It's what we do when we talk around our issues instead of hearing each other. It's the same sad cycle. It's exhausting."

He nodded. "Yes. It is exhausting."

He ran his hand back over his head and cursed under his breath. He refused to let go of his hurt. She wanted to apologize for hurting his feelings. She was on the verge of doing so but held back. She believed the truth was important to say. No matter how hurtful. It kept them honest. It kept them focused. That's what she told herself. "I may have drunk a little more than I intended. Some of the things I'm saying may be coming out wrong, Gio. I don't want to hurt your feelings, sweetheart. You're right. I'm wrong. Let's forget about it."

"I heard you," he said.

"Good. Finally! It's over," she sighed.

"Not my meaning, Bella. I heard you. Tonight," he said.

"I don't understand?" she frowned.

"I heard Marietta's toast. I saw you with those people. I saw you give your speech. The way you… spoke, it… it reminded me of us. Before."

"Before what?" she asked.

He sat down. She decided to join him by sitting at his side on the bed. "With all that we've been through I don't understand why seeing me give a speech to my employees would bother you so much."

"It's not the words you used. It's the way you looked. The way you sounded. It reminded me of who you were." He scratched his brow. "I wasn't prepared to see you as her again. With those people," he said.

Mirabella shook her head at his logic. She wanted to smack him. He was acting like a toddler. *Why couldn't he just be heroic, or accepting of change? Why must he always be this man who hid his insecurities from everyone else, but punished her with them privately? Why was he so damn insistent that anything that divided her heart was a threat to be eliminated?* Every man she ever loved had been this way. It was her mother's curse.

"Bella?" he said.

"You saw the woman you fell in love with and that upset you? You saw people that I respect and love celebrating my accomplishments, and that pissed you off? What am I supposed to say to that, Gio?"

"It's my issue. It's a feeling that I have in my gut. I can't explain it. The faster we move toward this thing, the more my gut tells me we should slow down."

"It's our issue. How could my happiness ever make you uncomfortable? It hurts my feelings."

"Cara," he said softly. "I don't mean it that way. I don't want to hurt your feelings."

"I know you don't mean to, but it hurts. I thought you loved the woman that I was?"

"Love her?" Giovanni smiled. "Love isn't a big enough word to explain how I feel for her. For you. Of course I love her. I worship her."

"Yeah right," she turned to stand. He stopped her.

"Look at me," he said.

She looked into his eyes. "I chose her. I fell in love with her. I'll burn my life to the ground before I ever let her go."

"But I've changed. Right? You prefer the new and improved me. Right? That's what you said."

"It's not a fair question," he said.

"It's an honest one. A simple one. You do see us differently. That woman you saw laughing and drinking was the one you met in Napoli, and then again in Milano, Bellagio. The one you convinced to come to Sorrento. She was not the one you found in Switzerland. The mother of a toddler who had witnessed the death of her best friend. The woman you found and brought back was different, afraid, guilt ridden, she wasn't half as confident as I am now. I feared her return too, Giovanni. Doubted I could be her again. And then tonight I finally understood, I am her."

"I'd kill for either of them. That's my point," she said. "I understand, Bella. I do. You are stronger, but you aren't that different. The world is different. I can't protect you from everything I fear. When you slip away from me, we are vulnerable. That's my biggest worry," he said.

She leaned in and kissed his lips. She wiped her lipstick from his lips and chuckled. "Remember how it felt the first time we kissed, made love?" she asked.

A sly smile lifted the right corner of his mouth. "I remember how soft I thought you were."

"Soft?" she laughed.

"Your skin. Soft."

"Ah, I remember. In your room, when you went up under my dress. You were very naughty to molest me, and we'd just met."

"Mmm, yes," he groaned deep in his throat. "The first time my hand went up under your dress and I felt your thighs." He ran his hand along her thigh, and the split to her dress parted. The fabric concealing her thigh dropped off to reveal and expose her leg all the way to the hip. He nuzzled her breasts. He rubbed and caressed her thigh, first the curve of it, and then he brought it over to ease between. They parted when he caressed his hand an inch closer to her sex. "Yes, soft. And your pussy, all I could think of was how soft you would feel if I were inside of you," he kissed her neck.

Mirabella shivered and swallowed her smile. Desire tickled her intimately. She closed her eyes and tried not be distracted by the feel of his lips, the caress of his hand.

"I've never been attracted to a man who didn't know how to pursue what he wanted. But you, Gio? You always take it to another level," Mirabella admitted. "When your hand went under my skirt I couldn't believe you knew I'd like it."

"Ah! Shy, yes that's what you pretended to be," he kissed the side of her mouth.

"I was not pretending!" she protested.

He looked at her. She cut her gaze over to him. "Well maybe a little bit."

He chuckled. "I'm glad. I wanted the chase. I like arguing," he nipped her earlobe.

"You do?" she asked.

"I like it when I get my way. I always get my way, Bella." He now had her thighs parted enough for him to rub three fingers over her sex. She sighed again. It came out as a soft moan. She put her hand between her thighs and covered his. Her fingers stroked his knuckles. His fingers parted the thin fabric of her thong. He eased two fingers into her and she gasped.

"I just want you to be proud of me, baby," she said moving against his hand.

"I am, always, Bella. Very proud," he said watching her intensely. She rode his hand. She pumped her hips and worked her pelvis. It wasn't his cock, but it felt delicious. Mirabella bit down on her bottom lip as her back bowed and her breasts heaved.

"You like that?" he asked.

"Yeah, oh yeah," she said.

"Tell me, Bella, what did you like about me? The money?"

"No!" she gasped and dropped her head back. He kept fucking her with his two fingers.

"The power?" he asked.

"NO!" she cried out now squirming and rubbing her pussy up on his hand as he slipped knuckle deep.

"My temper?" he asked.

"A little," she chuckled.

"What was it, Bella?"

"Oh, ooooh," she breathed when his thumb began to circle her clit as he fucked her with his hand. "Yes, Gio. Like that."

"Tell me what it was you liked about me? In the beginning?"

She glanced over at him. Confused he would make her use her brain when her pussy was singing for him thanks to his hand. "Your... your... eyes. I love your eyes. It's why my babies have your eyes. Beautiful... love...it's your eyes," she gasped and shuddered. She slammed her knees shut and climaxed for him.

"I remember everything." He licked her nipple through her dress as she melted into bliss. "When Nico brought you to me in Lorenzo's club, and you rejected me. I loved it. I wanted that woman."

"You did?" she panted.

"Yes. I wanted to fuck her, make her shut up, be mine."

Mirabella laughed out loud and hit him playfully. He bit her cheek softly.

"What else?" she asked.

He pulled his fingers out of her and she groaned.

"And then I just wanted her to love me." He paused. She looked again into his gemstone eyes. "I wanted to be loved by her."

"Why?" she asked.

"I didn't know why then. I think I finally understood when I learned about your father and mother. When I discovered what my father did to keep them apart."

"What did you discover?" she asked. Loving to hear him talk like this to her.

"Destino," he kissed her cheek. *"Il mio destino."*

"We are destiny, to have found each other across an ocean of lies and deception. That is fate, sweetheart, and true love," she smiled.

"Do you?" he asked.

"Do I what?" she asked.

"Do you still love me, after everything I've done? Knowing everything I am capable of doing?"

"More and more each day." She took his face in her hands and brought it down to kiss his brow. "So much it scares me. You worry about me, Gio, what about my worries? Some nights when you're off working and gone from me, I can't sleep from worrying. Sometimes our life can be quite scary. Every day I pray for your soul, mine, our family, our future. If I ever lost you it would kill me."

He pulled her dress down her shoulder and her breasts were uncovered. This was not easily done because she had taped her breasts to the fabric to keep them from spilling out of the dress.

Mirabella stopped him as he tried to remove her pasties. "You trust me right? You know, I can live in two worlds without becoming some uptight bitch who will plot to steal your children."

He laughed. "Yes, Bella, I know this. I am..." He said. "It threw me tonight. You drinking, celebrating without me."

"You were jealous—"

"Mannagia! I am not jealous!" he protested. He dropped back on the bed in defeat. *"Ammazza!"*

"I'm killing you?" she chuckled. "Is that what you said? How?"

"I'm ready to make up," he sighed. "Enough with the talking."

"You said you liked it when we talked."

"Yes. But aren't we finish?" he asked.

"Not until we agree," she said.

He ignored her. His arm was thrown over his eyes. Mirabella refused to give up. She turned and straddled his waist. He lay still on his back. She put her hands flat to his chest and she could feel how fast his heart beat. "Donna Mirabella Battaglia, they know who I am, Gio. They respect who I am."

"And who are you now?" he asked. He removed his arm from his eyes.

"A wife, a mother, a sister, a fashion designer. A woman who isn't afraid of life, even though she knows it can get scary. She welcomes the future, her future, inside or outside of this family. I'm not my mother. And you aren't Tomosino. We are Mirabella and Gio."

He smiled. "You're right. I don't want to be a bastard. It's never you, Bella. It's me. I hold on too tight. I get… confused."

"Jealous," she corrected him.

"Confused!" he insisted. She smiled and nodded that they could substitute the word. "*Perdonami.*"

Long ago she used to tell Fabiana that the reason her red-haired friend failed so miserably in love was because she liked her men broken. Love shouldn't be hard or complicated. Love should be the easiest, most fulfilling experience in life. Was it Fabiana she was speaking about or herself? Every man she'd ever loved has been complicated and stubborn. Yes it was hard, but moments like the one they shared now when he lowered all defenses and gave himself to her, were the most fulfilling. Nobody saw her Giovanni the way she did. She feared for his life, for him period. The only power she had was her love for him.

"*Ti perdono.*" She lowered the back zipper to her dress and pulled down the sleeves the rest of the way. She peeled off the pasties stuck on her nipples. The dress was left gathered at her waist. She leaned in until her nipples brushed over the silk threads of his shirt, and smoothed her hands down to his sides. A deep moan slipped up from his throat. She felt his erection beneath her, and that too excited her. She kissed his chin and then his neck as she started to undo the buttons to his shirt. "You like that, sweetheart? Can you now please fuck your donna?" she whispered.

"*Sì,*" he answered. And made to rise to undress.

"No," she said and pushed him down. "Is this the suit I tailored for you?"

"One of them, yes," he smiled. "You set it out for me to wear, remember."

"Yes. It's one of my favorites. Keep it on." He arched a brow to her request. She ran her hand over the fine threads. "You look like my Don in this suit. I want to fuck the Don," she teased. Their lips met. His tongue slipped inside. Within his kiss she tasted his strength, his weakness, and his apology. It tasted like sincerity and acceptance. Sweet.

Giovanni loosened the tie to the side of the evening gown she'd worn. She wore these dresses for him. Each came from an exclusive collection of formal evening and casual wear that allowed a woman to wrap her curves by day, to be unwrapped by her lover at night. She called the line of dresses *Bella Donna*, inspired by her husband. The dress was cast away and she was exposed in nothing but her black lace garter belt, stockings and designer heels.

"I love my wife." His large hand gripped her hip and flipped her beneath him. "You pray, Bella?"

"Often," she said.

"Pray that I can control myself," his gaze lifted to latch to hers.

"I don't need to. You never have to control yourself with me," she teased.

Giovanni eased her nipple in between his lips, and the suction of his mouth sent another spasm of heat through his groin, making his dick bulk behind his zipper. He released her from the kiss and went down between her parted legs. When her inner thighs pressed against both sides of his face he remembered again how soft she felt. He kissed her there too. Not a lot of tongue, only his lips. A sweet soft kiss to her core. The first of many apologies he intended to make to her tonight.

She bit her bottom lip against the moan trapped in her throat. *Oh merciful God,* her heart cried out.

"Don't tease me if you have no plans to please me," she giggled. The wine continued to fuel her desire and her anger. Or was it now just pure happiness diluting the blood in her veins? She laughed and arched her back. She gave him a show with her raised arms above her head, and the sultry roll of her hips. Giovanni released himself from the confinement of his zipper. He remained fully clothed, his shirt only loosened by a few top buttons. She however was stripped down to her garter belt and stockings. After a single thrust his dick breeched tight heat, and she could feel her passion curl and tighten like an iron vice around her pelvis. His thick cock spread her channel. He thrust into her with measured force until his reach was balls deep. It was too much and not enough at the same time. Mirabella crossed her legs and locked her ankles to trap him between, willing to endure.

"Mmmm, Gio. Yes!"

Distressed she clung to him, wanting him to fuck her harder and faster. Without realizing it, she was shouting out her desire between thrusts. The wine made her forgetful. The walls were thin in their temporary residence, and her children were not far away.

She tried to quiet herself and could not. A thick thumb pressed against her other hole. Mirabella's breath seized when it pushed down inside of her.

His thumb pumped in and out of her forbidden zone in time with his thrusting dick. He kept her pinned beneath him, driving them both to climax. Giovanni kissed her face, rubbed his jaw against her soft face, and fucked her slow and then harder and faster. His body went rigid and stiff, but his dick kept tunneling. Mirabella wept from the relief as they both collapsed under the weight of a renewed climax.

"Yes, baby! Yes!" she cried out.

The heat their bodies generated made his shirt wet with their shared sweat. She blinked away the tears of comfort and bliss while she clung to him. There was nothing left of her but submission. He lifted his head after a few minutes and stared down into her eyes. "I am proud of you, Bella."

"I know. I know, sweetheart." She smiled up at him. He dropped his head on her chest and pulled his flaccid cock out of her so he could rest against her breast. She stroked his head and relaxed. Mirabella decided to give him an hour tops and then he'd have to rise to the occasion again. The wine and trip down memory lane had her body purring for a repeat performance.

—*B*—

"OKAY, CATALINA, I THINK I'M DONE!" Marietta closed the folder. She'd signed every invoice and contract. The party in Bellagio would be the biggest event she'd ever thrown in her life for her birthday. And to think all of it would occur in her house. When Giovanni gave Bellagio back to Lorenzo, her husband put her name on the deed. She couldn't believe she owned the palace by the lake. She absolutely loved that place.

Catalina had left to go downstairs and tell Dominic they were ready to leave. She also wanted to say goodbye to the rest of the staff. When she heard the door open, Marietta assumed it was Catalina. She glanced back. Lorenzo stood there observing her.

"What are you doing here?" she asked with a smile.

"Are you done?"

"I am now." She turned and leaned against the desk. "I wish you would have come with Gio. Joined us for dinner. I want to show off my man to all the girls."

Lorenzo gave her a sly smile in return.

"Miss me today?" Marietta teased.

"Don't I always? I was hoping I could take you home and you'd cook for us." Lorenzo stepped toward her.

"Us? I already ate."

He crossed the distance separating them. He pressed his hand to her lower belly and looked into her eyes. "My son needs to eat too. How do you feel?" he asked.

She found it incredulous that the man would think she would be pregnant because he said so. He was so cute though. "I don't know if I'm pregnant yet. It might take some time."

"I made you a doctor's appointment, Marie."

"I told you, Lo, I don't need a doctor. I just need you." She tried to get around him but he grabbed her by the arms and stilled her.

"Wait," he said. "Calm down, Marie. I'm not trying to piss you off. This is important to me, to us. Okay? We need to see a professional. Gio thinks it's a good idea."

"What if we take a break?" she asked.

"Che cosa?" he replied. "Break from what?"

"Let's stop trying so hard. What if maybe in two or three years we try for a baby then?"

"What the hell are you saying?" Lorenzo let her arms go. "Two or three years? It's been two years! We have been trying."

"I'm saying that I have a lot going on, and so do you. A baby, Lo? You are barely here anymore. I don't want to be my sister. Stuck between her mean husband and some bratty kids."

Lorenzo's eyes narrowed on her. His nostrils flared. "What are you keeping from me?" he asked through clenched teeth.

"Huh?"

"Are you trying not to get pregnant?" Lorenzo asked.

"No! How? Have I ever done anything? Stop grabbing on me! I'm just trying to talk to you." She stepped closer to the door. Her heart beat so fast it staggered her breathing. She put her hand to her head and tried to calm herself. Her husband tracked her with his eyes. His face was flushed with anger. He didn't believe her. *Oh God, what if he found out?* She was so stupid to run off at the mouth. The man was Catholic, Sicilian; if he discovered she was on birth control pills her marriage would be over.

"I confess," she said. "I admit that I haven't been praying for a kid. And maybe my attitude is why we don't have one. Okay? I'm sorry for being a bitch about it. You put so much pressure on me. And Zia is constantly asking me if I am pregnant. Do you ever stop to think of how it makes me feel?"

Lorenzo stared at her. Marietta held his stare. She held her breath. She waited for what felt like an eternity for him to react. His scowl softened. He managed a weak smile.

"It's my fault too, Marie. I know you, *cara*. You can't be forced or bullied into anything. I should listen more. Come here."

Relieved, she went to him. He brought his arm around her shoulders and held her to his chest. He kissed the top of her head. "Do you know what having a little Marie would do for me? How sane it would make us both?"

"You're the crazy one not me!"

He smacked her ass. *"Dio mio!"*

She kissed his chest. She wrapped her arms around his waist. "I'm enough for you, Lo. I can love you. Protect you. I don't want to share you with a kid."

Lorenzo chuckled. "Marie? Woman, the things that come out of your mouth! Of course you want my child. What woman doesn't want to be a mother?"

Marietta rolled her eyes. She held tighter to him.

"Give me a baby. It's what I need," Lorenzo insisted. He loosened his hold on her and lifted her chin. "Stop wishing against what will naturally occur between us. We will have children. As my wife you will give me sons. Three. Do you understand?"

"Yes," she said bitterly.

He kissed her and she loved the kiss. Having a child was inevitable. No matter what, she'd not be able to put it off much longer. Maybe this summer she'd stop taking the pill. Maybe then she'd be willing to stomach the idea. For now, she'd take care of him and make him happy. Her way.

"Let's go."

"I need to get my purse. I left it in Mirabella's office," she said.

He nodded and she walked him out of her office. Lorenzo had never visited Fabiana's. Even when they visited Milano over the years and she had business to conduct, he took no interest. She led him to Mirabella's office and then walked over to her sister's desk to get her purse out of the bottom drawer.

"I'm ready," she said checking in her purse for her things. When he didn't answer her she looked up. He was frozen. Curious Marietta's head turned to see what he stared at. It was the larger than life portrait of Fabiana and

Mirabella.

"That's her? The one who died," Marietta said. She studied her husband's reaction. It was as if the woman had risen from the dead. He looked away and ran his hand down his face.

"What? Seeing her upsets you?" she asked. Her voice was tight with jealousy.

"I didn't expect to see that." He said. He put his hands to his waist and turned away. Marietta couldn't believe how affected he was. She glared back at the portrait.

"She wasn't a fucking saint, Lorenzo. I wish you all would stop acting like she was!" Marietta said.

He cast a look at her from over his shoulder. "No, Marie. She wasn't a saint. But I did love her. And she died because of me."

"So! People die because of you all the time!" Marietta said.

Lorenzo's eyes stretched. He looked physically wounded. She didn't mean to be so heartless, but she hated Fabiana. She hated her, and now she knew why. Before she came Fabiana was the center of Mirabella and Lorenzo's life. She felt second best next to her memory.

"She wasn't perfect, Marie. But she did want a life with me. You two are nothing alike. She couldn't wait to give me children," he said and walked out.

Marietta's mouth fell open. If he had struck her it would hurt less. She turned her angry gaze back to the portrait. She was grateful she didn't have a knife in her hand to shred it. Wiping at her tears of frustration she went after her husband.

KYRA WISHED JAMIE WOULDN'T DRINK. Especially around their co-workers and the Donna. It was embarrassing. She had to ask Etienne to see Jamie back to her hotel. There were last minute changes to be made before the Donna visited their workspace tomorrow. The work would now be left to her.

The steel tip shoe sewing machine-gunned. It's piercing needle stitched along the seam of the shoe, perfectly binding the sole. She wore a mouth mask to keep from inhaling the fumes she used to polish and soften the leather. Each pair of shoes was hand made by her, Jamie, or one of the ten people trained under them. Kyra picked up the sponge and wiped down the sole to soften the leather and the seams. She'd work on the heel of the shoe next. But first her work needed to dry.

The door opened and closed behind her. Its hinges were rusted so it did so nosily.

"I only need another hour!" she said to her chaperones. It's what she called the men that Renaldo kept hovering around her. The man never exhibited any sign of jealousy, but he found a way to keep an eye on her in Paris, and in Italy. Her sisters thought it weird. Her father thought it dangerous. Kyra didn't. She tingled with excitement when the men showed respect to her fiancé. What girl wouldn't love the protective side of her hero? And no matter how many years passed, she never forgot the night Renaldo's protective nature saved her life. She loved him.

The Red Bottom shoe factory, under the House of Mirabella's, was adjacent to Fabiana's. The front section was boarded up and under renovation. It was going to be a fabulous showroom and boutique. Better than the one they opened in Paris.

The door opened and shut again.

Kyra paused. She removed her goggles and looked back. The lamplight brightened her workstation, but did very little for the rest of the open space. It was darkest near the door.

"Hello?" she cried out.

No one answered. Kyra pulled down her mouth mask. "*Ciao?* Anybody there?" she asked.

The door opened and slammed shut. Kyra jumped. Nothing but silence greeted her. She was certain the door opened and closed twice before. Someone had returned. Kyra stood. She looked around for a weapon, anything. It was instinctual. The dark. The isolation. Her mind replayed trauma from years ago. She should run. She'd be damned if she did so without a weapon. The tips of her fingers connected with something. A very sharp blade lay flat across a cutting board. It was to be inserted into a machine that sliced through leather like butter. It reminded her of a machete.

"Eduardo? Gustavo? Are you here?" she asked. She picked up a towel and wrapped it around the end of the blade. She managed to hold it firm in both her hands.

"Eduardo? Gustavo? Dove sei?"

Silence greeted her. It was possible that her reaction was because of Italy. Kyra and Renaldo talked on many long nights about her move from France. She knew whatever danger he perceived in their lives was greater the closer they were to the man he served, Giovanni Battaglia.

For bravery she sucked down a deep breath and exhaled. Slow and cautious, she stepped around the benches with shoehorns and leather slates piled upon them. There was a noise. It was very faint but she heard it. It came from her left. She swung in that direction. The blade cut swiftly through open air. She found herself alone.

"Shit! Shit! Kyra, calm down. You're scaring yourself." She panted. She squinted in the dark. "Who's here? I know someone is here. Show yourself. Now!"

There was a corner she turned, it led to a door that connected to Fabiana's fashion house. Maybe it was the door the person had entered. Kyra's hands were shaking. Her arms ached from their frozen position.

"Gustavo? Eduardo?" she called their names again. *"Dove sei?"*

A cool hand touched her back. Kyra screamed. She swung the blade and the person ducked. The sharp edge hit the wall and was embedded into the paint and plaster.

"Renaldo?" she gasped.

He stood upright and chuckled.

"I could have killed you!" she shouted at him. It was a dirty joke to play on her. However, it turned out to be the best moment of her day. She flung herself at him. She kissed the side of his face and neck. "You scared me so bad."

"*Sono perdonta.* I was closing the place so we could leave. I came in and you were working. I went upstairs to make sure we were alone. When I came back I see my little warrior with her blade, and I have to have her." He squeezed her ass and groaned in his throat. She felt the massive might of his erection rising between them.

"Oh," she panted. "I could have hurt you though!"

He took her face in his hands and smiled. "*Ciao, bella.*"

"I've missed you so much!" She touched his erection and squeezed it.

He kissed her brow, and his lips soon found her mouth. It became a slow mint flavored kiss that made her heart sparkle. The man's breath always smelled divine. She always prided herself on being a very well groomed person, but Renaldo took good hygiene to another level.

"Are you done?" he said when their lips drew apart. "Can I take you home?"

"Home? It's finally happening. Italy is my home."

"I've waited too long not to have you with me," Renaldo said.

"Me too. Luca is waiting for us. Your mother called me and said they arrived safely. They are staying with her sister. We can go by there and see him tonight."

"I know," he said before he kissed her again.

"I have so much to tell you. So much!" she said between kisses and turned her face away. He was growing more amorous and it excited her. "Let me go," she pushed free. When she tried to step around him to locate her purse he revealed he had it in his hand. She laughed. He eased his arm around her waist. Together they went for the door.

Later –

Shae couldn't sleep. Never in her life had she felt more exhausted. The plane ride was long, but the day with the Battaglias went on forever. She closed her eyes and tried to settle her restlessness. Nothing, worked.

"Damn it!" she pounded her fist on the mattress.

Sounds of laughter answered through the window in her room. Shae sat up and listened intently. It came again. Laughter. Men laughing. Muffled whispers. Unlike Melanzana, the villa they stayed in was much smaller and intimate. The rooms weren't that far apart. In fact Marietta's room was so close she heard her when she came home with her husband. They laughed and stomped all the way into the room before things got more amorous.

Was that them she heard now?

Shae pushed the sheet aside and got up from bed. She walked over to the window covered by drapes. When she parted them she nearly jumped back in surprise. The men stood so close she could be seen. To be discreet she peeked out from the left side of the window as opposed to looking through the center part in the drapes. And there he was. He smoked something. He laughed with another man. One spoke in a low Italian voice until the others began to laugh. Carlo turned from friendly to angry. He shoved the man and cursed him. Or at least that's what it looked like to Shae. *Why were they roaming about outside at three in the morning?*

Carlo and his companion started to walk off toward the shadows.

"Shit! Shit!" she hurried over to her suitcase. All she could find was a pair of jeans and a thin t-shirt. Shae hopped around pulling on her jeans and shirt, forgetting the bra. She slipped her feet into thong sandals and snatched off her headscarf. She tried to comb out her limp curls that lay listless and flat on her head. She gave up. Maybe she should heed Marietta's warning and not seduce one of these men. She toiled over it for a moment, and then she remembered how Carlo rejected her earlier.

"I'll just introduce myself. No harm done." She went to her purse and found her translation book. Good enough. She crept from her room. The halls were empty. Somewhere upstairs a baby cried. Nothing else stirred. Shae went to the back door, deciding it was best to start there since her window faced the back of the villa. Once outside she regretted the thin shirt sans jacket. It was far chillier than she believed. Her nipples peaked and her arms were covered with goose bumps.

With only the moon and stars to light the way, Shae ventured out across the damp grass. She wasn't three feet away from the door before a man walked up to her with a gun in his hand. Startled she froze.

"C'é un problema?" he asked. His gaze lowered to her nipples and then lifted to her face. *"Che cosa!"*

"Ah, wait a second," Shae fumbled through the translation book to passages she marked. She found it. *"Dove si trova…?"*

"Chi é?" A voice spoke from the darkness. Shae looked up. Carlo approached with the man she saw him laughing with. He stopped when he saw her. He frowned and walked toward her. Shae lost all train of thought when he drew closer. Damn it, she tried to find the page to talk to him but couldn't in time.

Carlo questioned the man who found her. He spoke to him and then looked to her. Both of them stared at her. Shae decided to start with something simple.

"Mi chiamo Shae from America,*"* she smiled.

Carlo's eyes narrowed on her. She tried again.

"Lei mi piace," she said. Carlo chuckled. She thought she told him that she liked him but she couldn't be sure. The other men were snickering too.

"Parla inglese?" she tried again. Carlo said something to the men. Without another word spoken both men turned and walked away. Shae smiled. He understood her. Carlo's gaze swung back to her. He snatched the book from her hand.

"Hey? That's mine!" she said. He turned the book up toward the moon and read the passages she had highlighted. He looked down at her.

"I can't talk to you if you don't give it back. I don't speak Italian," Shae said.

He handed the book back to her. Shae nodded her thanks and thumbed through the pages. She had wanted to ask him if he wanted to make a friend. She highlighted the damn line in the book somewhere.

"Why are you out here?" he asked.

Floored, she glanced up. He spoke English, and perfectly. "This is a surprise. I thought you didn't know English?"

"Why are you out here?" he asked again.

"I came to see you. Make a new friend."

Carlo's brows lowered. He glanced to the door behind her. Shae's head turned. She half expected to see someone watching them. No one was there.

"I'm Shae, Marietta's friend. From America."

"I know who you are," Carlo said.

"Good. I know who you are. Marietta has told me all about you."

His brows drew together. He didn't seem angry. But the question in his eyes demanded an explanation. "Good things! Marietta said good things," Shae chuckled.

"Go to bed." He turned away and she grabbed his arm. He looked down at her touch and then back at her. *What the hell was his problem? Was he gay?*

"Don't walk away from me. I saw the way you stared when I arrived. I'm just trying to be friendly. You don't have to be rude."

To this Carlo looked at her again with renewed interest. "You want to be my friend?"

"Is that a problem? You married? Engaged? Gay? What?"

He again looked to the door as if he expected someone to discover them. Maybe that was the issue. He didn't want to get caught by that mean Don. Marietta said the men aren't supposed to flirt with the women.

"I'm new in town. I don't know anyone but Marietta. I don't speak Italian. And I'm locked up here with strange men carrying guns." She nodded to the one to the front of his pants. "I'm bored. Conversation? Anything? Okay?"

"Come for a walk with me. We can have conversation," Carlo said to her breasts. Shae hesitated. Exactly where did he expect her to walk to? And what was with the way he smiled at her tits. Did she expect them to rise up out of her shirt and greet him? It was kind of off-putting. He arched a brow and waited for her to decline. She stuck the small translation book in her back pocket. Carlo shrugged off his blazer and handed it to her. She eased it on. His dark eyes gleamed in the moonlight. Maybe walking off to the woods with him wasn't a good idea. But Shae never backed down from a man who gave her a look like that. She liked this one.

Zia lifted Gianni on her hip. She had his bottle for him when she glanced to the window in the kitchen. In the moonlight she could see Carlo standing and talking to a woman. She leaned on the sink to be sure she saw the woman. The pink hair to the front of the woman's face revealed her identity. Zia frowned.

"Is that Gianni?" Mirabella asked, from behind her. "Oh Zia, don't give him a bottle. Gino has stopped taking one and we talked about this with Gianni."

Zia kissed Gianni's cheek and he dropped his head on her shoulder. Mirabella entered the kitchen. "Of course it's my Gianni. You need Mommy? Come here, baby," she said. Zia handed Gianni over to Mirabella. The toddler sucked his bottle and looked at her with those round beautiful eyes like his father's.

"I'll take him upstairs. You go back to sleep," Mirabella said.

"Wait!" Zia grabbed her arm. "That woman doesn't belong here."

"What woman?" Mirabella asked with concern. Zia glanced to the window. She was sure the woman was in the woods now with Carlo. Doing whatever harlots do.

"The woman Marietta brought here. I saw her. She is out there, with Carlo. Now!"

Mirabella glanced to the window with concern. She walked over to the window and looked out. As Zia suspected, they were gone.

"She and Carlo went to the woods. Gio should be told, immediately. Carlo knows better. *Che schifo!*"

"No. Do not tell Gio," Mirabella said. "*Figurati.* I'll take care of it, Zia."

"She's trouble! I see it when she come here. She has pink hair!"

Mirabella smiled. She kissed Zia on the cheek. "Go back to bed. Gino is in the bed now alone? Right? Go on. I'll talk to her."

Zia nodded and shuffled out.

Mirabella looked out the window again. She didn't see them but she had no doubt that what Zia told her was true. If Giovanni got wind of it he'd pop a blood vessel. Gianni eased his hand in Mirabella's robe and reached for her breast.

"No you don't, sweetie. You can have the bottle, but Mommy's breast is off limits." She removed his hand. It had been weeks since she unlatched him from her breast. Gianni often tried. He dropped his head on her shoulder and sucked his bottle. She'd have to accept the compromise Zia offered, at least for now.

She decided it best to deal with their houseguest's wanderlust in the morning. She returned upstairs to bed. The moment she put Gianni between them and pulled up the covers her husband woke. He rubbed his eyes. He glanced down and saw Gianni next to him.

"Put on your pajama bottoms, sweetie," she whispered.

Giovanni grunted. He sat up and reached for them. She watched as he slipped them on before he lay down again. "I was hoping to have you to myself tonight," he mumbled before he turned over on his side. He rubbed his hand over Gianni's curly head.

"Eventually you'll need to cut their hair," she said.

"No. I like it like this," Giovanni said.

"It'll grow. Their hair is lot like mine."

He glanced up not understanding her meaning at first. And then he smiled. He nodded and agreed. His sons' hair would be as thick as their mother's soon if she didn't trim it down. Eve's hair was always combed down into two braids because it was so long and crinkly.

"I have something I want to ask of you," she said softly.

"Okay?" he replied.

"It's my brother."

Giovanni's gaze flashed up to her face. The alarm in his eyes was quick and precise. He stared at her. "Brother?"

"Armando Mancini. My father's son," she smiled. "I spoke to Catalina and Marietta. We agree, he should be welcome to come to my birthday party."

"Are you out of your mind?" he asked.

"Hear me out, Giovanni."

"Nothing to hear. The answer is no," he said. Gianni's head lifted. Mirabella stroked her son's back. Giovanni dropped over to his back. He threw his arm over his eyes. She knew the conversation would start this way. It was best to push forward.

"I know you don't trust him. And I have not forgotten what he's done. I haven't forgotten any of it. I asked you to get rid of him and sell him back my inheritance. Instead you gave it to Lorenzo to manage. He's in our lives and that's your choice."

Giovanni lowered his arm and looked at his wife. Mirabella sat up. "Sweetheart, I am in a very delicate situation right now. The world is looking at our family closely. They're watching us. What you do is invisible to them. I'm not questioning that. However, I do have a secret. Who my father is, and how my mother died is something I want to keep buried. For two years you and Armando have done this. Inviting him under your watchful eye keeps it under control. Right? Right?"

"You think I haven't thought of this?" he asked.

"No. That's not what I'm saying. I know you have. But I also know you don't like him around me, or our family. And that might cloud your judgment. However you decide to handle it is fine. I just wanted to tell you that he was extended an invitation. You should let him come."

"Is that right? It's up to me now?"

"Isn't it always?" she smiled. She eased down under the covers and kissed Gianni. She reached over and put her hand on her husband's chest. He picked up her hand and kissed it. He then pressed it to his heart. He kept it there until he fell asleep.

"So do you sleep?" Shae asked.

They walked around the back of the property and stopped between two trees. Carlo glanced down at her. He removed what looked like a cigarette and lit it. As soon as he puffed out the smoke she inhaled a whiff. It wasn't an ordinary cigarette. He took a long drag and then handed it to her.

"Why yes, I'll have some." Shae took a toke of the joint. "Hmm...good."

Carlo dropped on the tree. "Why do you have pink hair?" he asked.

"It's not pink. It's strawberry. And strawberry is my natural color," she passed him the joint.

He flicked the ash and took another drag from it. "Strawberry is not a natural color for a black woman," he said as he held the smoke in and exhaled slow.

"Sure it is. And it used to be my name… stage name… a long time ago."

"Stage? You a singer?" he asked.

"Dancer."

Carlo stared at her. He smoked the weed down without sharing. He kept staring. Shae wasn't sure if it was desire in his eyes or something else. Suddenly she didn't feel that adventurous. In fact he was acting a little creepy with the way he kept lowering his gaze to her crotch.

"Were you a dancer like her, like Marietta?" Carlo asked.

The question threw Shae. "You know about Mae dancing in Chicago?"

"Mae? You call her Mae?" he smiled.

"Yes. We all call her that back home."

Carlo extended the weed again as if it were a peace offering. She accepted it. Shae continued, "She worked for me. I taught her everything she knows." Shae smoked and exhaled. "I'm surprised she would tell any of you about her dancing. Mae… well she wasn't into it like the rest of my girls."

"Why? Why wasn't she like the other girls? What made her different?" Carlo asked.

"What do you care?" Shae asked.

"I'm curious," he shrugged.

"Nope. Wrong answer, playboy," Shae said. "You're more than curious. In my business I deal with all kinds of men. So don't hustle me. You want some dirt on Mae. Why?" He didn't answer. Shae shook her head. "This is bullshit. Thanks for the smoke." She flicked the smoked out joint at him and it tumbled to his feet. At least she thought it did. She didn't wait to see. She started back down the path he walked her through. In minutes she felt his hand tighten on her arm. She turned, ready to reject his offer, when he gripped her chin. The way he held her face still silenced her.

"Tell me your name again?" Carlo asked.

"Shannon Dennis, but my friends call me Shae."

He let her arm go and then her chin. "*Sono Carlo.* Maybe I can teach you Italian or Sicilian. Whichever you prefer."

"Really?" She took a step toward him. "Tonight?"

"*No, cara.* Not tonight. You go back to bed before you're missed. My boss wouldn't like you out here, alone, with me."

"Oh yeah? Why is that?" Shae asked. "Something wrong with me?"

"I thought you said Marietta told you about me?" Carlo asked.

"She told me to stay away from you. What's so dangerous about us being friends?"

He leaned in and looked her in the eye. "I'll show you. Soon."

Shae smiled.

"It's that way." He glanced behind her.

"What's that way?" She said and stepped closer. If he kissed her she wouldn't mind. He had sensual lips. The kind of lips a girl loved for a man to brush over her body.

"The way back," he answered.

"You're going to let me walk to the villa alone?" she asked.

"You're safe. My men are around." He glanced to the woods.

Shae began to get the meaning. They had an audience. This is why he was turning her away. After all, what did she expect for him to do? Fuck her up against a tree? The rejection still burned at her pride. She didn't want the night to end.

"Why did you ask me those questions about Mae? I am her friend you know. I don't want to cause her any trouble."

He wiped his hand down the side of his face. "No worry. I have... I won't cause her any trouble. Forget I asked."

"Are you staying here? Inside?" she asked.

"No," he smiled.

"So you walk around the house all night? Playing in the dark. Why?"

"It's my turn," he replied. "To play in the dark."

"When do you sleep?" she teased.

"At sunrise," he answered.

"Will I see you again tomorrow?"

"If you answer a question for me," he teased.

"Ask it."

"Strawberry? The color in your hair. Is it everywhere?" he asked. His gaze lowered to the delta between her thighs. Shae laughed. She was right about him. She knew it. Beneath the pretense of politeness lurked a beast.

"You'll have to earn the privilege to see." She put a hand to his chest. "Teach me how to answer you in Italian when the time is right, and I will show you."

He chuckled. Shae smiled. She shrugged off his blazer and passed it to him. Carlo accepted it with a gentlemen's bow. *Sexy!* Shae turned and hurried off down the path and back to the villa. It was much closer than she thought. He hadn't taken her too far into the forest. And as he said, she saw three men before reaching the door. Each one stopped to stare at her. Inside she closed the door and crept back to her bed. Her panties were soaked. She had to go to bed without any on. Thank God she packed her vibrator. Italy had so much promise. She couldn't wait for what tomorrow brought.

Marietta heard the door next to hers close. Shae must have gotten up and went to the bathroom or for a drink of water. She was already up watching her man sleep. What he said at Fabiana's, and the way he reacted to seeing his old love cut her so deep, all her insecurities surfaced at once. Before they drove off she apologized. Kissed him. Made up with him. Lorenzo slept with his arm thrown over her waist. She turned to her side and propped her face in her hand with her elbow pressed down in her pillow.

A swath of wavy hair was damp against his forehead. Like most of the Battaglia men, Lorenzo had dark curly hair tapered short around the temples and nape. She loved the texture most of all. The locks felt as soft as feathers. She rubbed the hairs between her finger and thumb, and two years of memories surfaced. Oh how they fought and loved one another. He wanted a child, progeny. Each time he demanded a son he made it sound like a trophy instead of a human being. That is how arrogant Octavio Leone used to be with her adoptive mother when he was drunk. He'd rage about how much better life would be if he had a son, not some bastard half-black daughter.

Marietta felt a pang of guilt. Her troubled husband was nothing like Octavio. She hated herself for even making the comparison. She had to wonder what kind of father Lorenzo would be? She was not as selfless as her sister. The competition was constant between Lorenzo and Dominic to be Giovanni's favorite. What about the motherly instinct? The thought of a baby sucking her nipple freaked her out. She could barely change the diapers on either of the twins without gagging. And then came her deepest fears. What if Lorenzo's secret was revealed? What then? What if some assassin in their very own family was ordered to put a bullet in her husband's skull? *It was possible.* Or worse, there was an even more important question to consider. What if she just plain sucked at being a mother, and fucked up a kid as badly as her adoptive mother fucked her up?

She played the questions over and over in her head. There were no guarantees in life. No matter how many excuses she came up with, or justifications, it was hard to live with her decision to not try to become pregnant. He was her world. And if he wanted her to create a family for them both, she damn well had to try.

Marietta blinked away her tears. She leaned in and kissed Lorenzo on the brow. *"Ti amo da morire,"* she whispered she'd give her life for their love.

He snored.

She kissed his brow again and again. She loved him with all her heart. Turning over she eased from under his arm. She left the bed. When she reached her dresser she glanced back at him. He didn't stir. With quiet care she went to her purse and dug out her secret. She found her birth control pillbox. She crept into the bathroom and closed the door. Marietta stood at the toilet. She had never missed a day of taking the pill in close to ten years. Would that cause her problems with conceiving? She hadn't considered the risk to her reproductive health before. What if all this time she didn't want to get pregnant, only to now discover she couldn't? Her mind struggled with that irony. Could Lorenzo love a wife who was barren?

She pushed out the first pill from the foil, and then the next. Each one dropped in the toilet. In a few minutes she had emptied them all.

Marietta flushed. She watched the pills circle the drain. "Okay, Lorenzo, you win. I'm all in. We gonna do this. We're going to have a baby." Before she left the bathroom she caught a glimpse of herself in the large mirror. Her belly piercing gleamed in the darkness. Her stomach was flat. It would grow and stretch like Mirabella's. She already knew what she had to look forward to. Marietta smiled and tried to poke out her belly. Mirabella said she was super horny when pregnant. Marietta had no doubt she would be too.

Before she left she tossed the pill compact into the trash. And then she considered her error. She fished it out. She didn't need him finding it. And if the trash was emptied and the staff found it they would certainly tell her husband. These damn men had eyes and ears everywhere. Marietta went under the sink where she put his toiletry bag and hers. She put the pill compact inside her bag and vowed to dump it when she got a chance.

She walked out of the bathroom and paused. Lorenzo was on his back. His hands were behind his head. He grinned at her. "You woke me up," he smiled.

"Go back to sleep. I have an early morning."

He drew down the sheet and his erection bounced up. "Sit on it," he said.

"Lo? Seriously, let's play tomorrow. It's been a long night."

"Sit on it, Marie!" Lorenzo held his cock by the root and shook the stalk at her. Marietta chuckled. She crawled over the bed and stopped to run her tongue over the head of his dick. He drew in a breath deeply when her mouth sank and she swallowed several inches. Lorenzo's dick was so hard she didn't need to hold it. Instead she gripped his thighs and dug in her nails for balance. Her jaws caved and she dragged her mouth up, making sure to lay her tongue flat for the glide. She loved it. There was nothing like a little dick sucking to get her man ready for some real fun.

"Mannaggia! Non fermati! Dammelo!" he wheezed deeply and demanded she not stop. Lorenzo snatched the scarf off her head and gripped her by the hair. The tug to her hair stung her scalp, and his frantic pushing down and pulling up to instruct her head bob almost made her gag on his girth. She dug her sharp nails deeper into his thighs to punish him, and he behaved. He groaned, arched his back twice, and she knew his strength weakened.

Marietta released him with a final lick. She eased up on her knees and he positioned the head of his dick at her opening. As usual her body was getting way ahead of her discipline. She wanted to ride him wild and free. But her man needed the slow tease, and she wanted to be sure to satisfy all of his needs. On the drive home he finger fucked her while he steered the car along dark roads at a dangerous speed. Marietta could still remember bracing one stiletto heel against the car dash and dropping her seat back for the pleasure. How he played with her pussy and drove two fingers into her until she was climaxing all over her designer original was beyond delicious.

Oh yes she'd give him a ride to knock his head back and put his mean ass to sleep. And hopefully she could squeeze another hour or two of rest in before it was time for her to rise.

With her hands flat to his abdomen she made her descent. Lorenzo's hands were hard, unyielding vices on her hips. He guided her progress as she repeatedly glided up and down, until the swollen hurt in her pussy from when he fucked her earlier while having her pinned to the headboard eased. There was nothing left to feel other than his body heat and strength.

Lorenzo's head lifted and he stared down the line of his body to where her pussy greeted his cock. He watched. He liked to watch. He loved a midnight ride on his dick. The in and out action turned them both on. She made sure to lift on her knees to rise high enough to give him a show.

"Ti sei eccitato? You like that huh, baby?" she teased him. She bounced harder and faster with increased frenzy to take him to the vanishing point.

"Sì, bambina, sì!" Her husband dropped his head back into the pillows and his Adam's apple bobbed in his throat. He grunted loudly.

"Yea, you're mine, all mine," Marietta said. And for the first time she actually believed they could possibly have created a life. She fell over on him and kissed his sweaty chest and neck. His body spasmed through his release and she held on to his face, sweeping his tongue up into a kiss and dragging the last of his breath from his lungs. She let him go when he went still, breathless.

"You okay, baby?" she asked stroking his jaw.

"Fuck, Marie. You trying to kill me?" he chuckled. "My dick is broke."

She laughed. He hugged her to him and laughed with her.

"Let's go to the doctor, Lo, get me checked out. It's time I make sure we start our family."

Lorenzo grabbed her face and lifted it in his hands. He stared at her with the biggest grin on his face. She didn't need to reaffirm her words. Instead she kissed him. A renewed promise for the man she'd give her world to.

CHAPTER FIVE

Pre-Show

"CAN I TALK TO YOU?" Mirabella said to her sister.

Marietta glanced up from her work and looked around her team. She had everyone gathered in her office going over last minute changes made by the engineer in charge of the lighting for the event. They'd just finished the music selections. Mirabella had observed it all from the door before stepping in to summon her.

"Continue working, everyone. I'll be right back." Marietta said. Mirabella glanced to the friend Marietta brought into the family from Chicago. Shae seemed to be taken with Jamie. They were on the sofa eating candied almonds from a crystal dish, and flipping through one of Jamie's portfolio books. Kyra was probably in the shoe warehouse obsessing over her designs.

"Something wrong?" Marietta asked.

Mirabella nodded to the open huddle room, a smaller office fit for a more intimate conversation. She closed the door behind Marietta. Her sister sat down with a look of concern. "What is it? What?"

"We've been so busy since this morning, I haven't had a chance to talk to you," Mirabella smiled. "You're doing a great job. You and Catalina are made for this business."

"Oh?" Marietta put her hand to her chest. "Girl, I thought something had happened."

"Relax. I, ah, just wanted to talk." Mirabella glanced to the window. Every office was made of clear glass walls. One could look from their meeting room into the next. She saw Shae up on her feet. She danced and pranced around in some platforms Jamie must have located for her.

"Okay, what is it? You're acting funny," Marietta said.

"Your friend," Mirabella began.

"Shae?"

"Yes. I like her. I really do," Mirabella said.

"But?" Marietta narrowed her eyes.

"You need to talk to her," Mirabella said.

"About what?" Marietta asked.

"Last night, she was outside with Carlo. Zia saw her. It might be totally innocent. But you know my husband and his rules. Look at poor Renaldo and what became of him because of his affair with Kyra. I promised Gio that there would be no more trouble with his men and the women who work for me."

"Carlo? You sure?" Marietta asked.

"It's what Zia saw. I can't be sure. Talk to her, okay? Remind her of the only house rule."

"Right. No fucking the help. I got it," Marietta said.

Mirabella smiled. "I'm nervous." She checked her watch. "Gio and the kids should be here in a hour. Margot Duval is doing the interview from Vogue. She wants it recorded for their cable television show."

"Don't be nervous. We went over all the acceptable questions. You'll do fine."

Mirabella scratched her brow. She expected a few pictures taken of her family and a print article. She had not prepared Giovanni for a film crew.

"Is everything okay with you and King B? He isn't fighting you on this?"

"Huh?" Mirabella came out of her thoughts.

"Are you and Giovanni okay?" Marietta asked.

"Yes. He was so cute this morning. Asking me all kinds of questions about the show. He was just tired last night," Mirabella smiled. "A little grumpy. He's fine."

"Yeah right, grumpy." Marietta laughed.

Mirabella stood and started to pace. She practiced her breathing. Fabiana would always make her breathe in deep from her nose, and exhale slowly out of her mouth. There was plenty to do. She needed to get back in the design room and continue with the models' fittings. The interview would be fine. She could handle it.

—*B*—

Giovanni stepped over toy trucks. Gianni held to his pants leg and matched his steps while sucking his pacifier. He wanted to prove to his Bella that he'd be supportive of her day. Spending time with the kids was a good start. He glanced over to Gino who sat with Eve playing with some toy. Neither child looked up. He reached down and picked up Gianni, went to the door and opened it. Leo nodded at him and he turned and went back inside. In less than an hour he would have to take the children to their mother. There was no reason why the meeting should extend past that.

Nico escorted his visitor in. Giovanni sat on the sofa and put Gianni on his lap. The children stopped playing to stare curiously at their uncle. Armando Mancini stepped inside with one of his men.

"Gio, ciao."

"Join me," Giovanni said. Typically he'd have Lorenzo and Dominic with him for this type of meeting. Lorenzo was dealing with the *Ndrangheta,* and Dominic had Bella and her attorneys to tend to. Rocco had gone to the gym with Carlo and the other men to watch their new boxer train. Before walking over to take a seat in the chair across from Giovanni, Armando paused to look upon the children. He smiled at Eve and she smiled up at him.

"My time is short," Giovanni said.

"Of course. She's grown, they all have," Armando said. He occupied the seat. Nico escorted Armando's shadow out of the room.

"I think a conversation between us is long overdue," Giovanni began.

"Lorenzo acts as your proxy. I've offered a seat at my table to discuss family matters, but you have declined," Armando said.

"We aren't family," Giovanni reminded him. Gianni scooted off his lap to go over and play with his brother and sister. Gino walked over and reached for Giovanni to pick him up. He did and sat his boy over to his right side.

"If we aren't family, then let's sever ties. On more than one occasion I've wanted to discuss the compensation to my… sisters. I believe my father's guilt made him impulsive. If you are willing to put a figure to the inheritance, I'm open to hearing it."

"I've left it to Lorenzo. He's working on a proposal for you. I believe you two will come to terms soon."

"How soon?" Armando snapped.

"Soon," Giovanni replied with a smile. "Until then, I've received your payments. I've had the accountants review the financials. Everything appears to be in order."

"Let me be clear, Giovanni. I will only tolerate you in my family affairs for so long. Two years is more than any man in my position would be willing to accept. It is to both of our benefit that we conclude our business, and continue the truce between our families."

"Is that why you continue to reach out to Marietta? Why you paid my sister a visit at Fabiana's? And now you have my wife asking for you to attend her birthday party. This brotherly love act of yours is just you seeking to keep a truce?"

"Partly. Another part of it…" Armando paused as he looked to Gino who stared directly back at him. Giovanni looked down at his son. Gino was oddly silent and observant, adapting the disposition of his father. It wouldn't seem strange if Gino wasn't so young. Most toddlers couldn't sit still for more than two minutes. Giovanni had to smile and worry about Gino.

Armando chuckled. "He is truly your boy, Gio."

"He makes his papa proud," Giovanni agreed.

"Mirabella is my sister. She has my blood. Your children have more Sicilian blood in them than you. I think I see my father in *il piccoletto*."

The insult burned as if a hot coal was thrown in his lap. And if it weren't for his children being present he might have reacted. Instead he let his temper chill over the truth. In this game Giovanni held the cards, not Armando. A far different balance than the war games they played when they were kids.

"Of course, there's a blood tie. I've accepted it. And my men are aware. Are yours?"

Armando didn't answer. Giovanni cocked his head to the left and studied Armando. The motherfucker was obedient because he was a coward. "How will *la cosa nostra* feel about your connection to me? The bastard Don of the *Camorra* owns two-thirds of your legitimate companies. The same bastard Don who has now put the *Ndrangheta* on their knees? Who wiped out the Calderones, Mottolas, and still evokes fear in the Bonaduces."

"Don't stroke your dick in front of me," Armando seethed.

"You're right. I prefer you do it." Giovanni smiled.

The silence lengthened. Giovanni was the first to speak. "Stop with the bullshit of them being your sisters. Admit your cowardice. Ask me again nicely and I'll put a price on your release."

"This war between us is a waste of time and energy. We aren't kids anymore, Gio. We belong to different worlds and it should remain that way. But if that has changed and you want to make an enemy out of me…"

"I agree we need to reach a compromise," Giovanni cut in.

Armando looked unconvinced. Giovanni continued. "Presently the press is at my fucking door. My actions, finances, everything accessible to those bloodsuckers is being picked apart. Do you understand?"

"You're being investigated?" Armando clarified.

"Aren't we always? It's why I asked you here. There is a need for discretion with the severing of our ties. A necessary delay." Giovanni reached over and put Gino on his lap. "Come, bring your men and join us in Bellagio for my Bella's birthday. We'll show the world we're friendly. Consider it an act of good faith."

Armando swiped his hand back through his hair. For the first time since he arrived he saw the torment and conflict in his nemesis. He also understood why Lorenzo wasn't so willing to let this fish off the hook. At first all Giovanni could think about was keeping Mancini from his wife. Now he had a taste of something he's wanted since he was fifteen. Revenge.

"I will see you at the party." Armando stood.

To Giovanni's surprise Eve walked over to him. *"Ciao!"* she said.

Armando looked down at her. *"Ciao, bella."*

"Sono Evie," she grinned.

"Mi chiamo, Zio Armando," he replied.

"Zio?" Eve wrinkled her nose. She looked to her father for an explanation.

"We're done," Giovanni said. His daughter immediately came over to her father and climbed on the sofa. She found a place on his lap next to Gino. Armando looked to her once more and then winked. He nodded at Giovanni before he left.

"Who is he, Papa?"

"A ghost. You won't see him again."

—ℬ—

"Thank you very much, Mirabella, for inviting us here today with you. I know you must be under such pressure with the show less than a day away."

Mirabella walked Margot Duval through her show room. The Vogue fashion reporter and critic had a new television show in the States that was even broadcast in the U.K. Not only did Mirabella invite her for an exclusive, but she refused any payment for the interview. She wanted a genuine honest critique of her work. She needed it.

"Larry, get that shot," Margot said. She pointed to Zenobia, Mirabella's model, being fitted for one of her dress slips. Mirabella waited for the cameraman to get the footage Margot requested, and then they moved on.

"I'm excited to sit down and have this conversation. It's long overdue."

"Yes! The last time I saw you was six years ago in Paris. Remember Fabiana had the party at Chateau Vicci?" Margot said.

Mirabella smiled fondly at the memory. "That was some night."

"One of the most memorable," Margot agreed.

"This way." Mirabella led the reporter to the private room she had polished for the interview and photos. Fabiana taught her many things about the press. Today she hoped to make her mentor proud. They passed through the door where Giovanni and the kids waited. Gino and Gianni wore matching blue knickers with tweed vests and bowties. They chased after each other, playing merrily. Eve wore a blue and white tea dress with blue ribbons on the ends of her two long French braids. She sat next to her father reading a book to him. Giovanni glanced up. Of course he was as handsome as ever. And with the studio lights burning bright in the white on white room, his violet blue eyes sparkled like gems. Mirabella smiled with pride. "Meet *mia famiglia*," she said.

"Oh my! They are adorable. May we?" she signaled for the cameraman to film the boys wrestling over a toy. Giovanni's gaze narrowed on the man but he didn't object.

"Only for a few minutes," Mirabella said.

"Of course. Hello, sweetheart, what is your name?" Margot asked Gino.

He glanced to his mother and then to the reporter. She knelt in front of him with the microphone. He grabbed it with his hand and turned the bulb. The reporter laughed.

"This is Gino, and he's Gianni."

"They're identical. Blue eyes? My, their eyes are striking," the reporter said with a confused frown. She glanced to Mirabella and she understood the surprise. Brown, blue-eyed children were not common.

"And my oldest daughter Eve," Mirabella said. She picked up Gino, and took Gianni by the hand. The reporter turned her attention to Giovanni and Eve.

"All of your children have blue eyes? That is very rare for black… ah children of mixed race."

"They all look like their father," Mirabella corrected her.

"Tell her that's enough, Bella," Giovanni said in Italian. She knew the American reporter didn't understand his statement. So she gave a pleasant smile. "Okay, babies, let's go. Come on, Eve," Mirabella said.

She walked over to the door, and her assistant who followed them in opened it. Cecilia waited outside. Mirabella passed Gino to her, and handed over Gianni and Eve. The first part of her mission completed. The interview would be her greatest challenge.

"Is that the reporter?" Marietta asked.

Catalina stood at the top floor balcony and peered down. "Yes. Giovanni is in there." She pointed to the private show room. "He's with the kids. Mirabella wanted to bring the reporter in. Look at her. She looks beautiful."

Together they watched Mirabella. She wore a knee length black pencil skirt that had a high waist, with a crisp white blouse tucked in. Marietta had put curls in her hair and the make up team had done their magic. She was flawless. The scarlet red shoes and matching lipstick were the right amount of flare needed.

"He's going to do this? He's really going to do it," Marietta said in disbelief.

"My brother loves her. Of course he'll do it. Did you see the twins? Oh my goodness they are so cute," Catalina said.

"Yeah, those devils will be heart breakers," Marietta chuckled.

"I'm proud of Gio," Catalina said with the upward toss of her chin.

"Don't give him too much credit yet," Marietta chuckled.

"What the hell does that mean? Too much credit?" Catalina frowned.

"Nothing. I have to admit I didn't think she'd convince him to sit down for the interview. And with the kids too? The man barely lets them see daylight. Now he has cameras in their faces. It's a big compromise."

"Oh stop. You always have to say something negative," Catalina turned to walk off. Marietta caught her by the arm and stopped her.

"I'm not trying to be negative. I'm saying you and I should make sure nothing goes wrong. Give him a way out of the interview after about ten or fifteen minutes. And then sit at her side and take over the rest."

"I don't think that's what Mirabella wants."

"What she wants is to be her self again. And this industry is cutthroat. There are so many people wanting her to fail. Read the fucking papers. They aren't all predicting a success."

Catalina nodded. She glanced to the reporter who walked into the private room. Marietta continued. "Your brother is only tolerant of her fashion business because he loves her, and it benefits him. Right? Right?"

Catalina nodded again.

"How long do you think he will sit through an interrogation by an American reporter? Trust me that bitch is all smiles now, but she will try to provoke him."

"Why isn't Domi in there with them?" Catalina frowned.

"Because this has to be done by Mirabella and Gio. Let's give them fifteen minutes and pull him out of there." Marietta raised her hand and Catalina gave her a high five like she taught her. They nodded. It was done.

— *B* —

"*SIGNOR* BATTAGLIA, my viewers are dying to hear about the love story. I've read a little about you." Margot smiled.

"Don't believe everything you read," Giovanni joked. Margot gave a genuine laugh. Mirabella smiled at her husband's relaxed demeanor.

"Before Mirabella you were one of the top ten most eligible bachelors in Italia, hell in the UK. Can you share with us how you two met?" the reporter began.

Mirabella's hand was in Giovanni's. He stared at the reporter. For a moment she didn't think he'd answer. And the next moment she was afraid of his reply. To her he spoke like a poet about their love. She'd never once heard him speak of his devotion to her to strangers. Not intimately, not from the heart.

"I first met Mirabella in Napoli, at a restaurant my *cougino* owned. The most beautiful woman in all of Italy walked in through the doors and I couldn't turn my eyes away. Do you remember, Bella? We talked about this the other night." He kissed her hand. She glanced over to him. His eyes sparkled with mischief. She remembered his hands between her thighs as he told her about how it felt to fall in love with her. She felt flushed and was rendered speechless as the memory overcame her. More to the question she recalled him in the hall chasing away that rude man who wanted to pursue her. She remembered that same look in his eyes when she thanked him.

"I didn't know who she was," he continued. "I soon learned. She was American, successful, a talented woman who was invited to my country to share her creativity. I had to see her again. Here in Milano I made that happen."

"Do you often pursue beautiful strangers like Mirabella?" Margot asked.

"No. They often pursue me," he corrected. It was Margot who blushed as she stared into Giovanni's eyes. Mirabella saw it all over the woman's face. That heated look of desire he evoked from women. She didn't like it. "Mirabella was different. Rare. I touched her hand and it was soft." He brought her hand to his lips and kissed it. "She smelled beautiful, the dress she wore," he stared into Mirabella's eyes and her throat went dry. A sly smile tilted the corner of Giovanni's mouth. "*Benissima*. I attended her fashion show. I watched as she walked the runway in another beautiful dress. Her long legs, and sway of her hips, she was again the most captivating woman I'd ever seen. At the end of the runway she looked me in the eye. She owned me. It was *amore*," he confessed.

"So you met here in Milano?"

"No, in Naples, and then again here," Mirabella smiled. She drew Margot's gaze back to her. The woman was now flushed and kept looking over to Giovanni, finding it hard not to stare into his eyes. "He's quite charming."

"Yes, he is," Margot tossed her hair and crossed her legs for Giovanni. Mirabella narrowed her eyes on her. Was the woman flirting in front of her? Giovanni held Margot's gaze every time it slipped his way. The bitter bite of jealousy clenched Mirabella's gut. She tried to not let it show. She continued.

"My husband's a little intimidating too. I'd never met a man like him before."

"How nice. And that was when your business partner Fabiana was alive, correct?"

"Yes," Mirabella answered.

"And you've named your new fashion house after Fabiana. She was quite a force in your company. I know the loss of her must be hard on a day like today."

"She is missed. Deeply. Fabiana's my inspiration. Red was her favorite color. I feel like each garment I make for House of Fabiana's is a tribute to her style, passion, love for life."

"Can we talk about her death?" Margot sat back and crossed her legs. "The world was shocked by it… and your supposed death. I attended your fake funeral. The first lady attended your fake funeral."

Mirabella squeezed Giovanni's hand. She knew this part of the interview would come. She had hoped it wouldn't happen so soon. "It was awful. What do you want me to say? My best friend died in a terrible accident. And the man I trusted, Kei Hyogo, he made me believe that disappearing from my life was the only way to cope with my trauma. The press has lied and exaggerated my story to sell magazines and papers. The truth is I fell in love with this man, and made a life for myself. A life I wouldn't trade for anyone or anything in the world."

"Yes, you were pregnant when you went into hiding. You kept the pregnancy from this man you *say* you loved. Surely there's a reason why."

"She's answered your question. Move on," Giovanni said.

The reporter frowned. "*Signor* Battaglia, there has been much speculation on who you really are. Interpol has you listed as one of the clan bosses of the *Camorra*, a crime organization that has terrorized southern Naples for close to a century. Do you want to respond to any of these allegations?"

"I'm a husband, a father, and a business man, in that order," he replied. "Americans romanticize the mafia. Interpol has a file? So what? I have nothing to hide."

"Giovanni's family has been in the export wine business out of Chianti for many decades. Trust me you'd be bored to death if you get him talking about it," Mirabella chuckled. Giovanni didn't. She cleared her throat and continued. "As for, ah, uhm, Fabiana died in an accident. I lied to my fans, colleagues, and friends by faking my death. I accept that. I can't change it. Kei and I both have paid a heavy price for the deception. He manipulated me. I trusted him when I shouldn't have. But today isn't about the past. It's about the present. You want drama? Wait until you see my show," Mirabella smiled.

"I can't wait… but I have one more question before we move on. *Signor* Battaglia, only recently have you and your wife been seen in public together. Even your wedding excluded the press. If there is nothing nefarious about your lifestyle, can you or Mirabella explain the secrecy around your lives? I'm told it's because of you. If you are a simple business man, then why all of the security?"

The door opened. Mirabella looked up to see her sister and Catalina appear. The reporter looked a bit startled by the intrusion as well.

"Oh, I'm so sorry. I hate to interrupt, Mirabella. Giovanni you have a very important phone call. You have to take it," Catalina informed them.

"But, we've just started," Margot protested.

"And you will continue," Marietta replied. "With an exclusive. Me and my sister."

"Oh yes? You are Marietta Battaglia. I've wanted to meet you," Margo stood. She extended her hand. "I'd love to interview you."

Mirabella leaned over and kissed Giovanni on the cheek. "Thank you, sweetheart."

"I will say goodbye to the kids before I leave," he said. "It was nice meeting you, *Signora* Duval," he said.

"*Signor Battaglia, grazie.* You're quite a man," Margot batted her long lashes at him and held his hand a little longer than Mirabella liked. Giovanni smiled at the woman. *He never smiles!* Mirabella's brows lowered and gathered together. Now she was certain the heifer was flirting with her husband. It happened so naturally between them she had to wonder how many women he came across when he was away on his trips did the same thing. She hated it.

Marietta occupied the seat Giovanni vacated and tossed her curls from her shoulder. She crossed her legs and smiled. "Mirabella? What's wrong?"

"She better sit her ass down and get out of his face," Mirabella said. Marietta gaze swung to Margot. The reporter said something else to Giovanni and he nodded before he cast his gaze over to Mirabella once more. He gave Mirabella a wink and left.

"I'm here now. Let's handle the bitch," Marietta said through clenched teeth.

Mirabella nodded.

Margot took her seat once more.

"Now. Where do we start?" Marietta asked. "Ask me anything you want."

—*B*—

"WHERE'S THIS CALL?" Giovanni asked.

"No call. It was time to put an end to that little circus, don't you think?" she asked.

"You did this?" he smiled.

"It was Marietta's idea. The interview should be about Mirabella. Not you." Catalina hugged him and kissed his cheek. "Don't worry about her, Gio. We have her. She'll be fine."

He kissed her brow. "I'll see you at dinner." She nodded and let him go. Giovanni headed for the door. He remembered the kids and glanced up to the stairs. He made sure to go and pay them a visit first. He had no idea how long the day would be.

Later –

"Do they mind if I smoke?" Shae asked. She lit her cigarette without waiting for a reply. Marietta sat next to her in a wicker chair on the terrace. They both looked out to the sun hovering just above the mountains.

"Today was fantastic!" Shae exhaled. "Oh my God! I had so much fun. And Jamie? She's so damn cute. She's going to make me some shoes. Girl, I loved it. I had a chance to see their shoe factory. Have you ever seen how shoes are made? Quality leather shoes?" Shae prattled on. "I watched Kyra cut and die the leather. She sculpted each shoe by hand."

"What happened last night?" Marietta asked.

Shae put her cigarette out on the side of the wicker chair. She exhaled through her nose and frowned. "What do you mean?"

"Last night, you and Carlo. What happened?" Marietta asked.

"Oh? How do you know about that?" Shae asked.

Marietta's gaze slipped over to her friend. The last thing she wanted was to get into an argument with Shae, or ruin their visit. But she would not have her disrespecting her. "I told you one rule. Only one. Don't approach these men. Did you meet with Carlo last night?"

A nervous chuckle escaped her friend. Shae averted her gaze. "I saw him outside and he was…smoking. I could tell it wasn't a cigarette." Shae cleared her throat. "I stepped to him to ask for a hit. We went for a walk and smoked out. That's it."

"Got damn it. Who saw you 'smoke out' with him?"

"No one."

"Stay away from him!" Marietta insisted.

"Him? Or the men?" Shae asked.

"Both!" Marietta said through her clenched teeth.

Shae chuckled.

"I say something funny?" Marietta asked.

"He only wanted to talk about you," Shae teased with a smile.

"What?" Marietta frowned.

"You heard me. He kept asking me if I was a dancer like you, how I knew you, stuff like that. Seemed quite interested in where you came from," Shae said. "You and Carlo close?"

Marietta glanced to the left when she heard voices. Two of her husband's men walked past them. Neither looked up. She knew Shae. Even a direct answer would lead to more probing questions, and ultimately Marietta would say more than she intended.

"Stay away from them, Shae. Cut the bullshit. I won't say it again."

"Sorry. I'll keep my distance." Shae reached over and touched her hand. She squeezed it. "What's going on with you, Mae?"

"I'm trying to get pregnant," Marietta confessed. Relieved to change the subject.

"No shit? You and a kid? What's our number one rule, Mae? No fucking brats to get in our way. Remember? I can't believe you turned on me," Shae teased. The truth was Shae had a very bad ectopic pregnancy when they were teens. Doctors removed her fallopian tubes. She was barren. Though Shae made it seem like she hated kids, Marietta knew differently. Her friend was always dismissive of her pain.

"Trust me I fought it, girl. I've been sneaking birth control behind Lo's back for two years. I decided last night to stop taking them."

"Sneaking? Why are you sneaking the pill?" Shae asked.

"Lorenzo, all of these men here, they're real funny about birth control. Catholic and all. And I wasn't sure I wanted a kid."

"But you do now?" Shae asked.

"I want to make my man happy. This will make him happy. I'll do anything for him, Shae."

"Oh honey. That sounds pathetic," Shae sighed.

"You've never loved anybody but yourself so how would you know?" Marietta snapped.

"Ouch," Shae said.

"Sorry. Lorenzo is my heart. Don't talk smack about him."

"Okay. Make your man happy. But be careful, Mae. Honey, we from the

Chi. We both know the truth. The fastest way to get rid of a man is to give him a kid. He'll lock you up in some golden tower and creep out the back door at night."

"I wasn't married, in love, and living in paradise back in the Chi. My life is different here. And my man… he's different. You've seen them. That's why you all hot in the panties for Carlo."

Shae chuckled but didn't deny it.

"Motherhood is in the marriage contract. Took a minute for me to accept it, but I have. I can do this. I can be a good mother," Marietta said.

She looked over. Shae reclined in her chair. She closed her eyes as if relaxing. And then Shae spoke. "Carlo is interesting."

"Stay away from him. Agreed?"

"Yes. I got it. I'll stay away."

"Good. And no smoking. Not because it's not allowed, it's just not… a good habit. Take care of you, Shae. You're the only friend from home I got."

Shae smiled. She reached over and extended her hand. Marietta took it in hers and they held hands watching the sunset.

— ℬ —

"SWEETHEART? YOU DOWN HERE?" Mirabella asked. She put her hand to the wall and braced her hand there as she stepped carefully down the stairs. She heard the moving of crates. Leo told her he went to the wine cellar.

"Giovanni?"

"Over here, Bella," he said.

"Turn on the light. It's dark down here." She reached and flipped the switch. More light flooded the dank musty wine cellar. There were rows and rows of shelves. Possibly stocked by the previous owner. Giovanni was at a crate opening it.

"What are you doing?" she asked.

"Looking for something to celebrate." He glanced up at her. "How did everything go?"

"It went good. Very well. The interview was a success. Dominic will see the footage with the lawyers, as agreed, before anything airs."

"Ah! Here it is." Giovanni pulled out the vintage label he was searching for. He charged Mirabella and scooped her up against his chest with one arm.

He spun her around and she laughed. She hugged his neck afraid he'd drop her or the bottle of Merlot.

"I'm so fucking proud of you!" he lowered her to her feet.

"You are?" she laughed.

He smiled down at her. "I had a short tour on my way out. You've done it grand, Bella. I had no idea."

"I thought… I thought you might have been upset about the interview."

He laughed. He kissed her brow. "Fuck the reporter. She did what reporters do. Tougher interrogators than her have questioned me. And tonight we celebrate!"

"You seemed to like her though," Mirabella said.

"Like her?" Giovanni frowned.

"She flirted with you. And you encouraged it." Mirabella said.

Giovanni let go a roar of laughter. Mirabella frowned and then smiled not sure what was funny. He kissed her and spun her around again. "I have never seen it! Never!"

"Seen what? Stop before you drop me!" She forced him to put her down.

"I've never seen my wife jealous." Giovanni grinned.

"I am not!" She pushed back from him.

"Yes you are!" He nodded.

She laughed. She was aggravated the rest of the day. Especially when Margot asked if she could get another exclusive with Giovanni. She politely put the bitch in her place. "Okay, maybe a little."

"Come here, woman," he pulled her close. "I was being nice. Charming. I wanted your fans to like me. To give their approval of my love for you."

"You don't care what people think." she frowned.

"No. I don't. But you do, Bella. And all I care about is making sure you have everything you want. Especially if it is within my power to give."

Mirabella grabbed him by the face. She kissed him. "I love you, Giovanni. With all my heart!"

"I love you too, my sweet sweet Bella." He swept her up with his tongue this time and the bottle nearly slipped from his hands. She couldn't believe how beautiful he had made their life.

—*B*—

CATALINA LOOKED AWAY from her computer screen when the phone rang. She was left to tend to all of the last minute details. Mirabella and Marietta had left over an hour ago. Dominic was just down the hall dealing with legal matters. If he didn't love working for her brother, she swore his job should have been as a lawyer. They made a hell of a team. She glanced over her computer monitor past her office walls to the conference room where he sat with three other men. He looked up and their eyes met. She winked at him. He winked at her. Though she told him she was ready to marry, she hadn't shared the news with Mirabella or Marietta. Between the fashion show and the birthday party there was too much to do.

The phone rang.

"Pronto," Catalina said. She tucked the phone between her face and shoulder. She kept typing. Silence greeted her. "Hello?" she said.

"Catalina?" a man's voice answered.

"Who is this?"

"Armando."

Catalina stopped typing. "Why are you calling?"

"To thank you," he replied.

"Me? Why?"

"I met with Giovanni today. He gave his consent. I am sure I have you to thank," he said.

"Oh? Okay. Well I'm glad for you. Do you have the details? The date and everything?" she asked. She glanced to Dominic who was standing and shaking hands with the men.

"I do. I have one more request," he said.

"Look, I have to go."

"It's the gift. A special gift I am having made for them. Something my sisters won't expect."

"What do you need from me?" she asked.

"I want to show it to you. To be sure that it's appropriate before I bring it to Bellagio."

"No. I can't," she said. Dominic was walking straight toward her office. "Thank you for calling. See you at the party."

She hung up the phone. Dominic smiled as he came through the door. "Are you ready, beautiful?"

"I sure am. Let me get my purse."

She couldn't stop her heart from racing. She'd be lying if she didn't admit Armando Mancini had crossed her mind a few times since he came to visit her. The strange attraction she felt was unlike her. She made a mental note to put an end to his niceties. If he ever called her again she would tell Dominic. That would stop it for sure.

—*B*—

MARIETTA THREW HER DRESS ON THE BED. She decided to change for her husband. The dinner planned for the evening was going to be a celebration. All of it was Mirabella's idea. She wanted the Battaglias gathered for the fashion show. A real event.

The phone rang.

Marietta walked over and picked it up off the base. *"Pronto?"*

"Marietta, it's me, Armando," the voice answered.

"Oh, hi. I was going to call you." She sat on the edge of the bed.

"We must think alike. I needed to call and thank you," he said.

"For what?" Marietta smiled.

"For convincing Mirabella to allow me to come to your party."

"So Giovanni agreed? You're coming?" she asked.

"I am."

Marietta breathed out a sigh of relief. Lorenzo didn't think Armando could be trusted. And she agreed on some levels. To be honest none of them could truly be trusted. Everyone had agendas.

"So will you make sure to save me a birthday dance?" he asked.

Marietta chuckled. "Ah, no. My husband would not like that."

It was Armando's turn to release a soft laugh. "Then maybe when everything is over we can meet. For lunch."

"You're in Italy?" she asked.

"I have some business here in Milano. I'm staying for a while." Armando informed her.

"Oh, wow. You must come to the fashion show. Please say you will come."

"I'll be there."

"Great! See you tomorrow," she said.

"Ciao."

The phone line disconnected. Marietta set the phone back on the base and stared at it for a moment. Things were changing. She could feel it. Change would be good for all of them.

There was a knock on her door. She walked away from her nightstand and opened it. Carlo leaned in the frame. The moment she looked into his eyes her heartbeat slowed. She felt calm. Relaxed. "You told Umberto you wanted to see me?"

"Yes. I want to talk to you," she said.

"Really? Can I come inside?" he teased her with a smile.

She glanced back into her bedroom. Then she looked up into his eyes. She stepped out of the room and closed the door. He didn't move much. He was closer than appropriate. "There's a study down the hall. Let's go in there."

"After you," he said.

Marietta had no choice but to lead the way. Carlo walked behind her. She wore a long maxi dress that draped around her hips and ass. When she looked back at him she noticed where he was staring. She shook her head. She opened the door to the study and held it for him. He walked inside. Marietta decided to keep the door open. Though Lorenzo wouldn't find anything wrong with her speaking to him, she would never disrespect her husband by having a closed-door conversation with another man, friend or foe.

"You look beautiful, Mae," Carlo said. He moved the toothpick around in his mouth and lowered his gaze to her hips. She crossed her arms in defense.

"Don't call me Mae."

"Why not? It's what they call you back home. Friends. We're friends right?" he asked.

"So you've been speaking with Shae?"

"Strawberry," Carlo smiled. "I've always had a fondness for strawberries."

"Not funny. You know the rules. Gio is very clear on his men not flirting with women in this family." Marietta reminded him.

"She's not in the family. She's a stranger." Carlo said.

"She's a guest. And I consider her family. It's wrong and I want you to be respectful. My friend is off limits," she said. "Please."

"She reminds me of you," Carlo said. "I find her interesting. Maybe I should travel to the 'Chi' and meet my own woman?"

"Carlo, stop it okay. Seriously this isn't cute. You're Lorenzo's best friend. The comments. The winks. The looks at my ass. I want you to stop. It stresses me out. I feel bad that I encouraged it that one time. But I've done nothing to make you think that this is okay."

Carlo sighed. "I'll stop. I don't want to upset you."

Marietta sighed. She ran her hands back over her head and through her curls. "Can you answer a question for me? A very personal one about Lorenzo?" she asked.

"Depends," he said.

She looked into Carlo's eyes. It was something she tried to avoid doing but could no longer. She stepped toward him. "Fabiana. When they were together. He was in love with her. Right?"

Carlo nodded.

"Do you think he would have married her?" she asked.

Carlo shrugged. "Lorenzo does what he feels. I didn't think he'd marry you and he did."

"Why? Why didn't you think he'd marry me?" Marietta asked.

Carlo didn't answer.

"Because he knew me for a short time like Fabiana? But he wasn't as in love with me as he was with her. Right?"

"No. You and Fabiana are nothing alike. Don't make the comparison."

"Right. Because she was sweet, and beautiful, white."

Carlo's brows lifted. "White?"

"Oh please! I know what most of you think of the color of my skin. We may be family now, but I don't see you befriending Africans, people of color." She said.

"Wait. What are you talking about? You think your husband is prejudice?" Carlo chuckled. His toothpick moved around to the other side of his mouth and his eyes sparkled. She had to smile when he did.

"No. I'm saying she fit into his world easier than I did. She was Italian. I'm saying if he had married her he'd have kids now. Right?"

Carlo's smile faded.

"Having a son is important to him. Fabiana would have understood that. She would have given him babies without a second thought. But I..."

"Lorenzo loves you, Marietta," Carlo said. She looked over to him. He nodded at her to believe him. "I've seen him with all kinds of women. You are the only one I've heard him speak of loving. No question."

"Then why does he still feel so guilty about Fabiana's death?" she asked.

"Because he's human. If he felt nothing, then you should worry," Carlo said.

Marietta wiped at her loose tears. She smiled. "Thank you."

She walked over to Carlo and hugged him. He stiffened at first, and then hugged her in return. "Thank you for being a friend to me."

He lifted her chin. He kissed her brow. "I promise to hold back my desires to be more."

She let go of him and stepped back. "I need to get back to the family. Thanks again."

"Any time," he smiled. She walked out and didn't look back though it took more effort than it should have.

LAUGHTER EXPLODED FROM those gathered at the outside table. Dinner was over. The wine flowed, and more desserts than the heart could yearn for, were shared amongst the family. It was a night for celebrating. With warmth and love in her heart her gaze shifted over to her husband. He was up from his seat throwing Gianni in the air. The boy squealed with delight, and grinned so wide Mirabella couldn't help but smile too. Eve was seated in Catalina's lap whispering in her ear. Nico wrestled with Gino. The toddler would go down and then get back up with Nico's help, only to charge Nico with his full force again. He seemed fine and full of energy after his fall.

"Bella, dance with me," Giovanni said. At some point he'd let Gianni go into the waiting arms of Zia. His hand was extended to her. The setting sun was to his back giving him a halo of sorts. She could not deny him or the smile he favored her. There was always music playing around Melanzana, and it seemed the tradition would continue in Milano. This time however it was a few of his men on their guitars harmonizing with Rocco who played a harmonica. Mirabella pushed back her chair and stood. She accepted her husband's hand and let him pull her in close with his other arm around her waist. She swayed with him and felt as carefree as she ever had. Mirabella dropped her face against his chest. Her hand slipped from his. Her arms circled his waist and she let the warmth and love consume her.

"It will be your birthday soon," he said softly.

"I can't wait," she replied.

"What do you wish for?" he asked.

"More days like this. Look at our family, Gio," she said. As they danced together they looked around at the happiness. "I think Cecilia is in love," she said.

Giovanni glanced to Nico who was now laughing with Gino in his arms and talking to Cecilia. "Yes. They started their romance when she left us."

"I hope they get married. Nico deserves someone to look after him," Mirabella said. "You see how he is with the kids? He'd be a wonderful father."

"True. Your sister is trying for a baby. Did you know?" Giovanni asked.

"No. She didn't say she was ready." Mirabella frowned.

"Lorenzo says she is," Giovanni kissed Mirabella's cheek. "Maybe they can all have what I have with you, Bella. Every man should be as blessed."

"Grazie, mio marito," she kissed his lips. *"Ti amo."*

CHAPTER SIX

Carlo & Shae

THE AFTERNOON FELL. For a girl brought up on the tough concrete streets of Chicago, spring in Italy was wonderful to behold. The sun bled all over the sky in warm colors of red, purple, and pink. Every branch, on every tree, held bright and colorful blooms. Shae typically loved the urban landscape of neon signs, skyscrapers, and streets congested with traffic. However, Italy's rich history, food, and music had begun to induce a peaceful contentment inside of her she could grow accustomed to.

That evening the Battaglias celebrated the Donna's achievement with a lavish dinner on the outside terrace of their Milan home. Shae had eaten her belly full. She'd consumed a few too many glasses of wine as well. If she didn't lie down soon it would be impossible for her to make a gracious exit later. Shae scooted her chair back from the table. Marietta was the first to notice. Her friend sat upright between her husband's legs and looked at Shae with a questioning frown. Shae winked to signal she was fine. Marietta reclined back against Lorenzo, as he continued to talk to her about something that made her friend smile.

The night was over. Every woman was either paired with her significant other, or tending to the needs of one of the Battaglia children. For a restless girl like herself, all she saw was temptation. Handsome men came and went. Some ate and drank wine with the Battaglias. A few serenaded the Don and Donna with their guitars as the couple danced and laughed in each other's arms. And other men, the ones who didn't speak or smile, patrolled the perimeters of the property watching Shae with dark piercing stares if she dared to step out into the gardens or in their way. To make matters worse, she couldn't speak or engage any of them because of the house rules and the language barrier. It was ridiculous.

Shae's attention kept returning to the Don and his Donna. They were in a world all their own. She saw them whispering to each other and smiling. The man never smiled. Tonight however, he laughed and even blushed with his wife in his arms. She wondered what they truly had in common. Mirabella seemed much more cultured than her brooding husband. And he didn't seem to relax around anyone but his wife and children.

In her experience, men with his temperament rarely could maintain lasting love affairs. And usually kept mistresses on the side if they did to act out their aggression. Did the Don have a whore stashed somewhere? Shae wouldn't be surprised if he did.

The evening became a bit boring. The disappointment for Shae was she hadn't seen Carlo. After making her promise to Marietta she figured that it was for the best. Forbidden fruit had always been her biggest weakness.

"You okay?" Catalina asked.

Shae smiled. "Yeah, excited about tomorrow. I think I'll go to my room and lay down."

"Really? It's early. After the kids go to bed it really turns into a party." Catalina winked. Shae liked Catalina. She hadn't had a chance to truly get to know her. But she'd seen how she interacted with the staff and everyone.

"I'm not going to bed. Papa says I can stay up late," Eve said to Shae.

Catalina chuckled. "We will see, Evie."

Shae almost felt compelled to stay. Eye candy kept arriving through the doors. Carlo could show. She had so much fun with her vibrator after going to bed with him on her mind last night.

"I might come back. See if the party's still going. Good night, Eve."

"Buona notte!" Eve smiled.

Shae dragged in a deep breath of resignation. She sidestepped a few to leave the terrace and walked back inside the villa. And there were even more men to avoid inside.

"Excuse me, pardon me, excuse me," she said a few times and caught a few appreciative stares. She thought someone had touched her hand. When she glanced back every man stared so she couldn't be sure. And when she dared to hold the gaze of a man, it never lingered for long. Eventually she found her way to her room through the kitchen. Once she entered her hall she froze. Shae's heart pulsed hard. Hooded brown eyes stared at her out of a tanned face. He pushed out of his lean against her door. He had a hard-edged masculine beauty. He'd been there all along waiting on her, for her.

"*Ciao, bella,*" he said.

"Hi, ah, *ciao*," she replied, annoyed by the quake in her voice. "Waiting for me?"

His gaze swept over her with appreciation, and she held her breath for his response. He spoke the words so low she had to read his lips to understand him.

"How is learning Italian coming?" he asked.

"I don't have a proper tutor. So it's a struggle," she smiled.

"We need to begin lessons," Carlo said.

"Okay," she said. "How do you say let's get out of here in Italian?" she asked.

"*Andiamo,*" he replied.

"*Andiamo,*" she repeated.

"Can you leave?" he answered.

"Leave? Right now?"

"Yes. Leave. Come with me. Away from here? That's what *andiamo* means," he said. "How else am I to give you your next lesson?"

"Hmm? Should I leave with you, Carlo? Is it safe?" she asked. She stood only a centimeter apart from him. His gaze narrowed on her as if he were insulted by the question. His reaction had to be an act. They were after all his boss's rules not hers. Closer to him with the light of the hall to illuminate his features, she could not mistake the handsome hard angles of his face and body. He had chiseled cheeks and dark hair that curled around his temples. His eyes were the color of brandy. The hairs to his mustache over his lip and under his chin were jet black and wavy.

She took a step closer. Her nipples brushed his chest.

"Marietta asked me to stay away from you," she said as her mouth moved in close.

"Did she say why?" he asked.

"House rule? You live by a code, don't you, Carlo? The big bad Battaglia men are off limits. Isn't that the code guests are supposed to honor?"

"Ah yes," he smiled. He glanced behind her. She turned her head, half expecting to see someone else in the hall. There was no one. But Carlo seemed conflicted on his offer to teach her Italian, his way.

"Let me know if you decide to break any rules like we almost did last night," he said and started to walk off.

She stepped in front of him. "And if I do… say… want to go with you. How exactly do we get away?"

"We walk out of the front door," he answered.

"That easy?" she chuckled.

"I said it is," he answered.

"I got a better idea," she whispered up to him.

"I'd like to hear it," he said, as he moved her hair from her eye with a finger.

"What if I requested an escort? I've noticed one thing. The women here don't go anywhere without an escort. Right? What if tonight I need someone tall, handsome, and strong to guard my body?" She ran her hand down his chest. "To take me into Milan to meet a friend?"

"A lie?" he frowned.

"An untruth," she corrected him.

"Why not tell the truth?" he asked.

Okay, now he is fucking with me. She tingled over the tease in his smile and knew his game. "Do you really want to take me away from here or are you playing games?"

"You're an interesting woman. A little rule breaker. It's sexy. Show me how brave you are. I'll wait for you outside." He walked off. Shae went to her door. She glanced back and Carlo cast a second look from over his shoulder as he left the hall and turned the corner. She hurried into her room to change. She took a quick shower and rubbed some oils and lotion over her skin to make sure she was supple and soft. She chose a dark purple summer dress that was strapless, with a shifting skirt that belled out from her hips and barely reached her knees. She thought of the thong she wore underneath and smiled. Shae reached up the skirt and pulled it down. She stepped out of the thin gossamer and tossed it back to her open suitcase. After a touch up of her makeup she felt complete.

There was a knock at the door.

"Come in," Shae answered.

"Shae? What's up? You headed out?" Marietta asked.

"Yes. I was on my way to come and find you. Do you remember my friend Harry?"

"Guilleti?" Marietta asked.

"That's him. Guess who's in Milan?" Shae turned and smiled. "Finally, girl. I can get out and have a little fun. See the city and mix it up. You know how I like to do!"

"You still date Harry? The man is in his seventies." Marietta laughed.

"Don't laugh. He has strong will power. And trust me it does get better with age." Shae teased.

"Old men have worms, Shae. I've told you that."

"Bullshit." Shae giggled. She dabbed her lips with one more touch of gloss. Then pressed them together to smooth the gloss over.

"Well you can't drive into Milano alone. I'll tell Lorenzo to get you a driver. He'll have to stay with you for the evening." Marietta turned for the door.

"Already have one. Asked a man out front, don't remember his name, one of them cuties. He's cool with it."

"Oh? Okay," Marietta walked over and smiled at her friend. "You gonna stay out all night? We have an early morning remember."

"Not sure. Trust me, I'll be back in plenty of time for your big day," Shae said.

"Have fun. *Ciao*." Marietta kissed her right and then left cheek. Shae nodded to her and watched her leave. She waited for the sound of Marietta's door closing next to her room before she grabbed her purse and shawl and hurried out.

—*B*—

THE WOMEN IN THE FAMILY were off limits. It was a commandment that every man who worked for or served under Giovanni respected and obeyed. This oath, along with his vow of friendship to Lorenzo, has kept him from acting on his desires for his best friend's wife. Though Marietta rarely glanced his way, there were times when he caught her staring and saw temptation in her eyes. At least that's what he told himself.

Carlo reasoned that the American woman was different. She was an outsider. And he'd seen her watching him. He tried to ignore her beauty, her sexy body, and that teasingly sweet voice of hers. However, last night, in the woods, she reminded him of the sweetest temptation life had to offer. There was no better pussy than new pussy.

He waited outside of his car. A two-seater, canary yellow Ferrari he'd taken off the hands of a businessman in Napoli who couldn't pay his debts after he broke his jaw. He opened his father's pocket watch and checked the time. The watch was sterling silver and the only token of affection he ever received from the old man. He was considering giving it to Ciro. He just might before the kid's next fight. The watch could boost his kid brother's confidence.

"Leaving, boss?" Eli asked. He walked up and flicked his cigarette to the grass before crushing it under his boot heel. Carlo didn't bother to answer. Eli got the message. He moved on. When was the last time Carlo had gone through the actual effort to plan a date? He was out of practice. He'd take her for a drive and a drink, maybe some dancing. He'd be a fucking gentleman if she wanted him to be. He had hopes she didn't. Contrary to what his friends believed, he could be as charming as Gio if need be. Yes. He'd be a gentleman and maybe learn what it is that made these American women so fucking special.

Earlier —

"Carlo, aspettare. Un momento!" Lorenzo jogged toward him. "What's your hurry? The ladies have a big dinner prepared. Family will celebrate tonight."

"Beh! Need to leave and check on Ciro," Carlo said. The conversation with Marietta rattled him. When she was upset he wanted to comfort her. When she was happy he wanted to be near her and share in her excitement. The only remedy for his conflicting emotions was to keep distance between them.

"Why?"

"Why what?" Carlo asked.

"Why run out to check on the kid constantly?"

"He has another fight in Bergamo, and if he wins it we will be accepting a match in Napoli." Carlo answered. He continued on toward the door.

Lorenzo caught him by the arm. "Christo! Would you slow down a minute? I need to know. Did you make sure Marie's birthday gift is ready for her?" he asked.

Carlo glanced up at him. "I have. The staff in Bellagio will make sure it's as you wanted."

"Grazie!" Lorenzo grinned. "She's going to love it. I hurt her the other day. I made a comment about Fabiana. Never mind. I want to show her I support her."

He was in no mood to listen to Lorenzo brag on his wife. He tried to step around him but Lo effectively blocked his pass and pushed him further from the door. "What is it between you and me? Are you still pissed over the boxing thing?" Lorenzo frowned.

"Ciro will be a boxer. Why would I be pissed? Giovanni believes in me. It's my turn to prove myself. I can do it." Carlo glared at him.

"Sure you can," Lorenzo taunted him with a sly smirk. "And for the record, you asshole, I convinced Giovanni to approve it."

"Bullshit!" Carlo scoffed. "I know it was Domi. You bust my balls for going behind your back."

"Dominic has no influence. I do! I bust your balls for stepping out of line." He poked Carlo in the chest. "It's a good business plan and I always agreed on its investment. Giovanni wanted my opinion and I okayed it. You can do this. I support you. Make the kid into a champion. I'll help slap him around and toughen him up if you need me to."

Carlo looked down to Lorenzo's hand of friendship extended to him. He set aside his aggravation and shook it. Lorenzo pulled him into a brotherly hug. His best friend kissed his jaw. "I am glad it is settled between us."

Free from Lorenzo's hold, Carlo nodded and started to walk off again when they heard the laughter of the women. Carlo glanced back and saw Marietta and Shae giggling as they walked down the hall toward the back of the villa where everyone dined.

"I hear you've made a friend?" Lorenzo asked.

"I did nothing wrong. The woman comes to me. Flirts with me," Carlo said. "I never crossed the line."

Lorenzo chuckled. "You curious?"

"Not my thing. You and Gio like American women like them." Carlo shrugged it off. "I prefer my own kind of woman."

"Bullshit. I see the way you look at Marie!" Lorenzo laughed.

Carlo frowned. Lorenzo shrugged off the awkwardness. "I trust you, brother. My wife is beautiful. I know men see it." Lorenzo stared Carlo in the eye. "So you're curious about the pink hair lady? At least admit it."

"I don't have time for this shit," Carlo grumbled.

"Why don't you take her out to the city? Take her to Corso Venezia, spend some money on her, maybe the Diana afterwards, and have some pink pussy for dessert?"

"Gio would be pissed if I—"

"I've okayed it with Gio. There won't be any trouble from the boss." Lorenzo patted his arm and started to walk off. Lorenzo stopped. *"Be a gentleman, Carlo! I trust you with my wife's friend. Treat her with respect. I don't want no shit from Marie."*

Carlo stood there for a moment conflicted. He should go see Ciro and train with him tonight. Keep his mind focused. He was however the man to do exactly the opposite of what he was supposed to do.

—ℬ—

AFTER AN HOUR-LONG WAIT Carlo had begun to consider that Shae might have changed her mind. He checked his watch again. It was early. He had time to catch his brother in the practice ring. When he lifted from his lean on the car, the door to the villa opened. A vision of beauty walked out.

"Hola!" she said, greeting him in Spanish.

A jolt of lust hit him hard. Shae smiled for him and started down the steps. She wore a dress that presented her larger than average bosom to the front, and fit snug on her hips, before fanning out around her thighs. The fabric had to be light because the night wind caused it to lift and ripple, revealing a hint more of her shapely legs.

"All ready," she said. Her voice had a smoky seductive pull to it that made his loins stiffen. Or was his dick hard for another reason? Carlo opened the door to the passenger side of the car. He glanced over and saw two of his men. Both stared at him.

"Gracias," she said as he helped her get in the car. He was forced to swallow his smile. *Gracias* was Spanish for thank you. This beauty still failed at his language, but he appreciated her effort to try. He closed the door and hurried around the Ferrari. Once behind the wheel he lowered the top. He glanced over to her crossed thighs and smiled.

Men didn't make Shae nervous. They never did. But this one gave her the jitters like a virgin on her wedding night. Although she had many male suitors, she didn't sleep with every man with a big wallet. The men she took to her bed, married or not, were always those she'd seen and dated for months. Those lucky blokes worked tirelessly to earn the pleasure.

Carlo hopped in the car and they were off. Shae rolled her passenger window up. It helped to block the wind from tangling her hair. The car was made for speed. It didn't take long for them to arrive on the busy city streets of Milan. The Italian city was far different than the subdued beauty of the Amalfi. The buildings were tall, box shaped, with medieval architecture. Train cars carried people through the heart of traffic. Several cars they passed had left the passengers gawking at them. She felt like royalty in his golden yellow chariot. This was the life! He glanced over at her and then to the road. She caught a couple of his sideways stares. She didn't acknowledge any until his quiet nature got to her.

"How did you learn English?" she asked.

"My brother taught me," Carlo said. He shifted the car into a reduced speed and slowed to a crawl behind the others congesting the two lanes.

"Really? Your brother is American?"

"He was Sicilian. He left for America as a baby and returned later to find me," Carlo told her.

"Oh? That's cool. Wait? You said was?"

"He's dead, *cara*. Died two years ago," Carlo replied.

"Sorry to hear that," said Shae. "What was his name?"

"Carmine," Carlo told her.

"Have you been to America?" she asked.

"No. You inviting me?" he answered.

"Sure, you would love Chicago," she smiled. "It's like Milan, busy, lots of buildings and people."

"Do you have sisters, brothers?" he asked.

"No. Well yes, but I don't know them. My mom was my father's sixth wife. He had other families and kids before me, but the kids were never around. I grew up as an only child." Shae turned her gaze away. Her parents were still married and estranged from her. That's what she and Marietta had in common. They both despised the people who raised them. Shae's parents were never open or trusting of her free spirit. And when they discovered her profession in adult entertainment, they actually called the police on her twice to have her shut down. She cut all ties. She hadn't seen either of them in years.

The sad memory evaporated when she looked up at two twin buildings lit by green spotlights. The monuments had columns enclosed within its walls. Carved along every angle were three-dimensional images like the raised stamps of dead presidents on American coins. The closer they came she saw more of the details. The classical architecture told a story of ancient times in the way Egyptians recorded their history.

"What is this? Where are we?" she asked. Her head went back to look up at the gargoyle statues peering down at her from the tops of the buildings as they drove through.

"*Corso Venezia* is the avenue we traveled, and there, those twin buildings are called the gates of *Porta Venezia*," he told her.

"Gates?"

"*Sì*, twin buildings hundreds of years old. I think it used to be part of the gates to keep invaders out of the *rione*."

After turning off the main road they travelled down a few narrow streets before he parked the car. Shae pondered her predicament. A night walk along these side streets in her heels would wreck her feet. She should have thought better of her shoe choice.

The top lowered and snapped shut on the Ferrari. Carlo turned in his seat. "Do you drink?" he asked.

"I do."

"And you are a dancer?" he asked looking again to her breasts as if they would speak back. She lifted his chin to draw his gaze back up to hers.

"I used to be. I'm a business woman now."

"What is your business?" Carlo asked.

"Pleasure. What's yours?" she countered.

"Pain," he winked. He threw open the door and Shae waited for him to open hers. She was helped out of the car and brought to her feet only a few inches apart from him. Carlo took her hand in his and began to walk her past some of the closed stores to the street. They broke left. There were plenty of people out. Some of them dressed impressively, while others appeared to be the dregs of society. Carlo marched down the center of the sidewalk. His tall brooding stature knocked several people out of his way. Shae found herself giving apologetic smiles because of his rude behavior.

The restaurant served its patrons under the stars. It was overrun with customers. The waiters bumped into each other delivering trays of food and carafes of wine. She had thought to tell him she wasn't hungry, but soon learned the Italian eatery wasn't their final destination. Along the side of the establishment was a narrow stairwell that descended down. Carlo glanced back at her and she nodded she would stay close. She did. She gripped the cool metal rail. She measured each step. Slender cinderblocks smoothed over from age and weather felt slippery under her feet. There was no way she could drink and climb her way back up. He'd have to be her hero. Shae smiled at the thought of him carrying her like some gladiator into his arena.

"Where are we going?" she shouted to his back.

He didn't respond. Music blared and possibly drowned out her words. His tall frame blocked her view. Carlo stepped down and reached to make sure she did so with grace.

"Thank you, sweetheart," she said to him.

"Prego, bella," he replied.

Several tall and very dark skinned men were outside the doors of the dance club. One of them appeared to be the bouncer. He looked directly into Shae's eyes when he spoke to Carlo in Italian. A few words were exchanged and the door was opened. Outwardly she ignored the stares of these men. Inside she was turning to jelly with nervous energy. Carlo's long arm dropped over her shoulder and she was pulled in closer to him. Initially darkness was all she could see. But the smoky atmosphere opened up the scene under the flashing glare of strobe lights. The place was hot with excitement. There was something fast, rhythmic, and thrilling about the DJ's choice in music. Vibrant drumbeats mixed in with acoustic instrumentals, gave the song a reggae dance hall semblance. And the partygoers were mostly black. Confused, Shae's gaze swept beautiful dark skinned men and women gyrating, dancing at the bar, or on the dance floors. At home she might have mistaken the music for something Caribbean, but the language and harmony was clearly African.

"Keep close, *cara*," Carlo whispered against her ear. "You're mine tonight."

He removed his arm from around her neck and took her hand. Due to the overcrowding, he took the lead and parted the way as he pulled her behind him. They walked to the back of the club toward black doors guarded by two giant African men in dark suits. Both looked at her and then each other before seeking an explanation from Carlo. She noticed Carlo was one of three men in the entire place she'd seen so far that wasn't black.

Again he replied in Italian. The doors opened for him. Inside was a very posh and more exclusive arrangement. The walls must have been sound proofed. She could no longer hear the African music out front. The musician was a solo saxophonist serenading the crowd with a small band behind him, and a woman in beautiful African green and gold regalia, including head wrap, harmonizing on a microphone. Again they were all black.

A hostess greeted Carlo. A short woman with a shaved head and very curvy figure led them to an elevated booth. There were only four of them posted in different corners of the club. To the left Shae noticed a group of men with hardened glares that rivaled the men out front. They watched Carlo. Gangsters? They had to be by their silent intimidating behavior. Carlo didn't blink in their direction. Why had he chosen this place? The other three booths were all occupied. The one they approached was being cleared for them. The men and women were forced to give up their seats, and did so with grumbled complaints. Carlo waited a beat for drinks and plates to be removed before helping her to step up into the reserved seat.

Shae couldn't hold back her curiosity any further. "I'm confused. Why did you bring me here?"

Carlo scooted in next to her. "Do you not like it?"

"I'm expecting to experience Italy. This looks more like home."

Carlo laughed. "The *rione* has a long history with immigration in Italia. Milan's casbah is a mix of Africans, Asians, and South Americans. They eat, party, shop for whores, fashion, and drugs here. You wanted to know where the fun and good times are in Milan, and I bring you to it."

"Oh gee thanks?" Shae replied. "Here it is I thought you brought me to this place because I was black."

He stroked his chin. "That too."

It was her turn to laugh. Shae wasn't easily insulted, but she did expect the finer things in life. Romeo would have to step up his game if he thought she'd be his. She picked up the menu and it was all in Italian. She put it down.

"I'll order for you," he said.

"I've already eaten," she replied.

"You'll like this. It'll go good with the drinks," he replied. He scanned the menu. "Have some chicken suya, and fried yams." Carlo told the waitress. He gave the rest of his request for them in Italian.

"So you've been here before?" Shae couldn't help but glance across the club to the men who watched them.

"No," he answered. Shae noticed he spoke with his hand on her knee. She didn't object to his forward touch. And typically she would so early into the night.

"Why are those men staring at you like that?" she asked.

Carlo glanced in the direction she referenced. It was as if he saw them for the first time. He smiled. "They don't like me very much."

"Am I safe here?"

His gaze shifted to her. "You are always safe with me."

"I hope you don't have to prove it tonight," she half-joked.

The saxophonist ended his solo and the songbird took over. Again, she appreciated the lovely harmony. It felt oddly comfortable for her. Since she landed she couldn't keep up with everyone speaking a different language, and all the excitement focused on the fashion event. She appreciated Carlo trying to make her feel at ease. And though she vowed to make him chase, she did want a little taste. Shae parted her knee an inch and his hand slipped a little further in between. She pretended to not notice and sip her water. But he stared directly at her, so she was forced to look over into his eyes.

"Why do you keep teasing me?" he smiled.

"Me? You're the one with your hand on my thigh," she chuckled.

His caress went further. He brought his mouth closer to her ear. "I like this dress."

"Do you?"

"Yes. It looks nice on you. I like your ass in it. You're pretty," he said.

"Say it in Italian," she replied. "Maybe I'll believe you."

"Ti sta bennisima. Bel culetto! Sei bellissima," he said between soft kisses to her cheek and neck. Shae's lids fluttered. He stroked her kitty now and she was slipping fast.

"Carlo?" a man spoke.

Shae's eyes flashed open. Her knee bumped the underside of the table nearly toppling over their drinks. A man stood before them watching. He was tall, imposing, and not very attractive. She could see his eyes clearly. Carlo eventually pulled away from touching her to address their guest.

"What the fuck do you want?" Carlo demanded.

The stranger smiled. "A word."

Shae glanced between the men. Were they friends? Enemies? She couldn't tell. The silent stare-off made her cautious. There was an unseen tension between them.

"Ciao, bella. Mi chiamo Santo," he said. The man extended his hand to her in greeting. Unsure how to respond, Shae decided it best to be polite.

"Hi," she replied.

When she reached for his hand he leaned in and brought hers up to his chapped lips for a kiss. She forced the smile on her face to remain. Carlo stared at Santo.

"May I?" he asked Carlo.

He joined them in the booth seat. Shae was now forced to sit between the men as they faced off. And the rest of the conversation continued in Italian. All she could do was sip the wine the waitress brought to the table and wait for the exchange to end.

"You like living dangerously? The Nigerians aren't happy Battaglias are in their house," Santo lit a cigarette. He exhaled and locked eyes with Carlo. And this time his gaze shifted over to Shae as if she were the reason for Carlo's choice.

"You following me?" Carlo asked.

"Needed to speak with you. So yes. I followed you here," Santo confessed. "How long have we been friends, Carlo? Since we were what? Seven or eight?" Santo asked.

"What the fuck does it matter? We aren't friends now," Carlo said.

Santo exhaled another long stream of smoke. "We're brothers in blood."

"You're a rat."

"And you're a fist turned boxing promoter." Santo smiled. He gave him a nod. "Congratulations."

"My business is not yours," Carlo seethed. "Who the fuck told you that I was managing Ciro?"

Santo drummed his fingers on the surface of the table. He dropped the cigarillo into the ashtray. "Nicosia the priest told me. I saw your boy in the ring. He's got talent. And after my time away I'd know."

"And?" Carlo asked.

"I've made a few connections that could help put him in the ring with a real bad ass contender."

Carlo laughed. "Fuck off."

Santo leaned in. His voice dropped to a threatening low tone. "Boxing is hot right now. It's a good direction for the family. And the word is the boss is now backing Ciro. Everybody will want a shot at him. You have to be careful to choose a worthy opponent. I know Gio. If this doesn't bear fruit he will not give you this liberty again. Right?"

"I got it under control."

"And as I said, I've learned a lot in prison. Made a few contacts. This Asian fighter out of London wants to come to Rome. He's winning matches. Almost undefeated. Ciro needs ranking. He needs the IBF. A fight with this guy will guarantee it."

"Name?" Carlo asked.

"Chao Lee," Santo replied. "Take the meeting. See him for yourself. If a deal is to be made I'd ask for ten percent."

"Three," Carlo replied.

Santo's brows shot up. "For putting the meeting together I deserve fifteen. It'll take a year for Ciro to make the ranks in the IBF."

"Three percent if what you say is true." Carlo countered. "And of course it will have to be approved by Gio."

"Of course. Three percent." Santo said with reluctant acceptance. Carlo noticed how Santo kept looking to his companion. He waited for him to say something in regards to her but Santo didn't. He gave a respectful nod, eased out of the booth and left.

"That seemed intense," Shae said.

"Are you done? We should leave," Carlo mumbled.

"The food?"

"Fuck the food!" he said.

Santo was once a close friend. But when they were kids and a young girl accused Carlo of rape, Santo could have easily stood up for him. The night in question he was at Santo's house sleeping on the floor. But Carlo was to be sacrificed by the Mancinis for Giovanni's tantrum and assault on Armando. Everyone kept their mouth closed and turned on him. Everyone but Lorenzo, his true friend.

"Carlo?" Shae touched the side of his face. He opened his eyes to realize how easily he slipped into his darkness. She stroked his jaw and her touch felt good. Her large round brown eyes looked into his with a question he couldn't answer. And to his relief she didn't ask.

"Let's not spoil the night. Okay?" she smiled.

"*Mi perdo nei tuoi occhi,*" he replied.

"Mmm," she kissed his lips softly. "When you speak Italian to me it sounds yummy."

"I say to you, I get lost in your eyes," he answered. He captured her silky lips with a kiss and she tasted nice. Her tongue darted into his mouth, at first shyly. But he devoured her in a kiss. And she responded to his aggression with enough of her own. He should turn over the table and fuck her on the spot. He moved his mouth from hers after devouring its softness, and returned his lips to the hollow pulse of her throat. Before he knew it he had his hand under her skirt and was trying to push her down in the booth.

"Whoa! Wait, playboy!" Shae laughed. He pinched her clit. Her pussy was wet and sticky from her arousal. She liked it. If he couldn't fuck her he'd at least feel her pussy.

"Carlo! I'm serious. Slow down."

With a deep throaty groan he withdrew. She smiled and pushed him all the way back.

"I love this song. She's singing Mariah Carey. Do you know her?"

Carlo glanced to the singer and frowned. He didn't care much for American music. He had recently started to listen to the rap music that spoke of pussy and killing police thanks to Marietta and the tapes she made for him. It was the only kind of American music he could tolerate.

"No," he replied. He picked up his wine and drank his glass clean. Santo's visit still burned his gut. Not even the idea of fucking his pink lady could calm him. Several things troubled him. First was the location. This was *Ndrangheta* territory, and not many spots were open to the Battaglias. Especially since the Calderone war and the Nigerian massacre. That meant Santo had to be his shadow for quite some time to follow him here. Which led him to the other troubling thought. How did Santo, who has been out of the loop of things with the family, know that Giovanni approved him to manage Ciro? Not even Nicosia was aware that Giovanni had given his final blessing. Had Gio taken Santo in confidence so soon? That would be a mistake.

"Carlo? Dance? Don't make a girl beg," Shae brushed her lips over his jaw. When he turned his head to tell her no, she flicked her tongue at his lips. And then she moved in on him. Holding his face, she would have been on his lap if it weren't for the table. Her lips were so soft and her tongue so sweet, it knocked his head back and cleared his thoughts. She dragged her mouth to his ear and breathed a kiss there.

"Dance with me, please," she said. She then caressed his jaw with her lips. His mouth, nose, jaw, brow, all were touched by her petal soft lips. "I'm not ready for the night to end."

Shae pulled away. A look into her beautiful, long lashed eyes sent the pit of his stomach into wild swirls. Most of his women pleased him with physical aggression to match his own insatiable appetite. She felt soft, lovely, and seductive against his chest.

"*Mannaggia!* Let's dance." He scooted out of the booth. He reached back and pulled her out. She wrapped her arm around his waist and went with him to the dance floor. He could tell that she'd had a couple of glasses of wine too many with her light stumbles. But with his assistance she found her balance. He drew her back into his arms. Shae intertwined her fingers behind his neck.

He was tall, handsome, and dominant. What else could a girl want on a night like tonight? The hot and solid length of him made her heart pulse. She shouldn't have had those three glasses of wine. The conversation between him and the other man felt intense. She kept drinking to keep from asking for the man Santo to leave. Hell the stranger was killing her fantasy. Now Carlo was hers.

To her surprise Carlo could dance. Most men let their ego get in the way and stood stiff while a girl grooved all over them. Carlo held her up against him with a firm grip to her hips. And his movements were hip and pelvic thrusts that kept in time with the music. The man had a natural rhythm that made her eyes flutter with wonder. *I wonder if he's this good in bed? I wonder if I should break my rule and give him a taste without the chase. I wonder, wonder, wonder...*

Shae melted against his hard frame. When his large palm squeezed her ass, she parted her legs and rubbed her sex up and down his muscle packed thigh. She began to roll her ass and grind down the heat and passion burning her core against the top of his thigh. The side of her face was pressed to his chest. Her eyes were closed. And he smelled good; that raw spice and tobacco smell that was all male.

"Stay with me," he said, and his voice was deep and commanding enough to be heard over the music.

"Hmm?" she smiled and held on to him.

"Stay with me. Tonight." He proposed.

Shae's eyes opened. She lifted her head from his chest and stopped trying to fuck the man on the dance floor. He looked down at her with expectation.

"Where?" she asked. "Stay where, Carlo?"

Carlo smiled. He let her go to walk her out of the club. They didn't bother to pay the bill and no one stopped him to question why. They made it back to the car without incident. The bustling street was teeming with nightlife. And the muggy evening weather cleared her head. In the car with Carlo speeding and swerving around traffic, Shae braced for the final destination.

On the avenue she was again taken by all of the fancy stores and fashion boutiques. The buildings' architecture was richly designed. Carlo drove up to a corner hotel that looked like a museum. The valet opened her car door and helped her out.

"Thank you," Shae said. She glanced up to the flags flapping in the wind. "Where are we?" she asked.

Carlo hooked his arm around her waist. "Hotel Diana Majestic. It's one of the oldest and most famous hotels in Milan. The Milanese host their private fancy affairs here. It's where the Donna will have her fashion event tomorrow."

He walked her inside. She absorbed the posh décor.

"You stay here?" she asked.

"Me and the men are here. Yes. We will make sure nothing goes wrong tomorrow," he said. "Let me take you through the gardens. You have to see it at night."

"Okay."

Shae had been disappointed over the little nightspot he chose for them. She had hoped his taste improved. It was as if she'd entered a roman palace from ancient times. They walked through the lobby across black and white marble floors to the side doors, which were all made of glass. Carlo's pace was casual. Shae absorbed every detail of the palace. It was a good choice for Mirabella's fashion debut.

Together they passed through two inside doors to reach the outside veranda. She could see the gardens and the lanterns giving the blooming flowers a majestic beauty. Maybe that's where the hotel got its name from?

"It's really pretty out here," she said.

"The hotel is close to two hundred years old," Carlo said. He walked ahead of her and then jogged down the steps to the lawn. She followed but at a much slower pace. Shae looked up to the stars in the sky. The lanterns around the outside gardens dimmed the beauty of the night above her but still she could see the moon clearly. It was a crescent moon that softened and bathed the landscape in shimmery silver. For a brief moment the moon hypnotized Shae. She'd never appreciated it before.

When she looked back toward Carlo he was gone. Shae paused. She knew he hadn't gone around her.

"Carlo?" she called out.

Shae heard a couple laughing as they strolled up the path. They nodded politely to her when they passed. She wrapped the shawl around her arms tightly and hurried her steps. Of course her only choice was to take the path that led into the gardens. Confused she kept glancing back wondering if he had indeed gone around her and back inside. Maybe she should go back the way they came. Shae rounded the next corner of rose bushes, now alarmed. "Carlo? Carlo, where are—"

"Rah!"

"Aaargh!" Shae screamed. She was swept from her feet and spun around. Her purse was thrown from her hand. And her body slung over some man's shoulder. Shae choked on her screams and then they were off and running. Actually Carlo was running while carrying her through the garden. Of course it only took her a moment to realize who had assaulted her. And it felt like an attack. She hit her chin on his back and nearly bit through her tongue from the jostling and bouncing. Hanging upside down she blinked out of shock and fury, and tried to summon her voice to demand her release. Not only had he scared the shit out of her, but he was running with her. Faster and faster he ran around one corner of bushes and then another. What if he fell? What if he dropped her?

Shae screamed and kicked "Carlo, please! Please stop! Please put me down! Stop! We'll fall. Stop!" He bit the side of her ass and pain shot through her thigh. Shae froze. The bite hurt but the shock of his attack scared her. Her head bounced up and down and banged against his rock hard back. She had to use her hands to brace herself. He ran for what felt like forever. The blood rushing to her brain left her dizzy and weak. She feared if he didn't stop running she'd pass out or throw up.

And then he stopped.

Shae dragged in a deep startled breath. He brought her down on legs of jelly. As soon as she was on her feet she slapped him. He grabbed her wrist painfully tight and yanked her toward him. She crashed into him and his lips crushed hers. She tried to break away but he held on to her wrist and twisted her arm. *Was he crazy? Yes! He's crazy!* The fight was on. She fought with everything in her. Carlo let go of her wrist but grabbed her by the neck to maintain the kiss. The strangle hold made her gasp and wheeze. She bit his bottom lip but he didn't stop. Lord help her but he was too strong. When his tongue slipped into her mouth she bit it hard.

Carlo laughed. She pushed at his chest, but her right hand cramped from the pain in her wrist. And he held her by the throat and forced her to walk backward. Soon she was pinned to a column. She could tell by the cool smooth curved surface.

"Carlo! I can't breathe!" she wheezed between kissing him back. She knew a woman's defense when a man became uncontrollable was to lessen the resistance and ramp up her strategy for escape. There was no fun in his overpowering her. And his demands were too aggressive. He was scaring her. She kissed him and tasted his blood on his tongue from her bite. He reached up under her skirt.

Shae squeezed her eyes shut and winced when he scratched her thigh as he tried to force them apart. It was then she seized the moment. She drove her knee up so hard and swift she was certain she'd forced his gonads up into his throat. Carlo buckled. He stumbled back and Shae hit him. Punched him in the face hard. He stumbled back another step holding to his dick. There was madness in his eyes. He glared at her with the look of a predator. Shae had been in some tough spots before, but this one was quite different. Here she was in another country, with a foreigner, hell she had dropped her purse when he grabbed her. She was cornered.

Carlo glared at her under the moon. He didn't speak. He licked the blood from his lip. And rubbed the soreness from his dick. The hatred she saw in his eyes hurt her feelings. Who was this madman? She really did like the jackass, and he turned barbarian on her for no discernable reason.

"What the fuck is wrong with you? Why did you attack me?"

He looked away. He stepped back and away from her. Shae felt a greater sense of relief for the distance. But the fear was still there. Should she run? *Yes!* She should run and the get the hell away from him. Pray he didn't catch her and finish whatever the hell he was trying to do. The man was bat-shit crazy, a killer, and possibly a rapist. What the hell was she thinking? Marietta had warned her. She fucked up. Carlo ran his hand back through his hair. He said something in Italian or Sicilian, she didn't know. He began to pace as if panicked. He knew he hurt her. She could tell by the way he looked at her. And she licked the sting of her lip to taste her own blood.

"Why?" she asked.

"I didn't mean to," he said.

"Bullshit! What was that? Were you going to rape me?" she shouted at him.

He shook his head. "I was playing… ah, I didn't mean for it to happen."

"Bullshit!" she shouted at him again. "You hurt me! On purpose!"

"I apologize, *bella*. I will take you home. I will make it right," he said. "Don't tell. Don't worry. I'll make it right."

Shae wiped her tears. "What are you schizophrenic?"

"Che cosa?" he asked.

"What the hell is wrong with you?" she pronounced every word clearly.

"It got out of hand. I wanted to play with you." He reasoned.

"Play with me? I'm a grown woman. Play with me? Are you fucking kidding me?" she asked. He made no sense. How could he be so awkward and lack control? It wasn't sexy. It was pathetic.

He turned and started away.

She walked toward him. "Wait a minute. It was the alcohol. We both had a lot to drink. I'm fine," she tried to reason the attack away. The problem was her throat hurt something awful. She feared it would be bruised in the morning.

He stared at her in disbelief.

"Carlo? It's okay," she tried to swallow the tremor in her voice. She blinked away her tears. "I'm fine," she smiled. "See?"

She turned for him. She looked back at him from over her shoulder.

He shook his head and stepped back with his hands forced down into his pockets. He said something in Italian again. His face was flushed red.

"I don't understand. Speak English."

"I will take you back now. I'll confess to my actions. It's time to end the night."

She almost agreed with him. Hell she should get the hell back to the Battaglias, pack her shit, and just leave Italy. The entire family and these men were too intense, even for her. But Shae had seen the Don and his cold ice blue stare. She had heard the underlying warning in Marietta's voice about what would happen if these men were to break their boss's rules. Carlo was fucked up in the head. Immature. Dangerous. Possibly a psychopath. But she broke the rules too. And she wouldn't let him be hurt because of her impulsive choices.

Carlo could not hide his shame. He wanted to hurt her. Choke her. Strangle something. And the urge persisted. When he was angry, frustrated, and horny, the urge to crush something soft often overcame him. Never a good mix if he added alcohol. This is why he could never have a woman, any woman's heart. Who would want such damaged goods? It was why he fixated on Marietta, and her wild intolerance. Seeing her as the woman who tamed his friend, secretly wishing for someone with her strength to do the same for him.

He should take Shae back to the Battaglias and go see Elsa. At least with her his aggression would be accepted, even welcomed. In the morning he'd face Gio and confess. He'd take his licks. He just hoped his brother Ciro didn't pay the price. Shae stepped toward him. He could sense her fear by the way she clenched her hands into fists, and see courage in her fearless smile.

"Is that a pool?" she asked.

The question confounded him. Pool? He glanced back over his shoulder. The biggest draw for the Milanese who frequented the Diana Majestic was the pool. They called it the Diana bath. It was a hundred meters long and twenty-five wide. Access to it was often restricted. This area was under some reconstruction. But from their position in the garden they could see down the hill to the clear blue waters sparkling under the moonlight.

Before he could answer Shae started to remove her shoes. She ran down the hill. Carlo watched her, curious. And then it dawned on him what she was going to do. If she breeched the pool area and went in she could be arrested. It would definitely cause a scene. From every angle of the hotel guests had aerial views of the pool.

"No! No, *cara*, wait!" he warned and went after her. But he was too late. Shae went around the blockade and dove in the water from the edge of the pool. Carlo froze. She submerged and began to swim like a mermaid in her purple silk strapless dress. She came to the surface at the center of the pool. Her hair was slick to her face with the pink strands in her eyes. She floated there smiling at him.

"Get out. The hotel will call the *polizia*. It's forbidden."

"Take me upstairs, to your room. I can't very well go back to the Battaglias like this. Can I?"

The request was foolish, and reckless of her to ask. Carlo walked to the edge of the pool. Could it be possible that he met someone as crazy as him? Or was this a trap? He'd take her upstairs and she'd scream for the authorities. Get her revenge for what he put her through. He glanced around and saw no one. His hands slipped into his pockets. He stared down at her. She was very beautiful this way. He was fucked no matter the choice he made. And it dawned on him. Did Lorenzo set him up? When had he ever been given the green light to date a woman associated with the family? Did Lorenzo know he'd fuck this up, and he'd be brought to Gio on his knees? Stripped of his honor. Had he ruined Ciro's chances to be a boxer?

"Maledizione!" Carlo hissed. *He was so fucking stupid.* Shae waved her arms over the surface of the water and kicked her legs slowly to stay afloat. The way the water glistened like iridescent pearls over her brown skin made his heart race.

"This is no game, sweetheart," he said. "The night is over. You and I both know it."

"Why did you try to scare me? Back there?"

"Get out of the fucking pool! Now!" he extended his hand.

Shae shook her head left to right slowly.

"Answer my question first. Why did you try to scare me?"

"Did I succeed?" he asked her.

She nodded. "Yes. You are scary. But I think you want women to fear you. Keeps them from getting close to you."

Carlo smiled despite his anger. *"Per favore, cara,* enough of this. I can't have my boss called because of this bullshit. He'll have my balls."

"Sounds like you're damned either way. Right?"

"Please…" he extended his hand. "Come out of the pool."

She looked at him for a minute. He thought she'd swim to him. Instead she submerged.

"Signor! Signor! Che cosa è questo? Cosa fai? She can't swim in there! She must get out now! *Signor!"* One of the hotel managers and two of his staff raced toward him. Carlo looked up to see a small crowd had gathered to watch. Shae began to back stroke in the water. Her dress was dangerously high on her thighs and Carlo remembered she wore no underwear.

"Signor! Per favore!" the manager said.

"Perdonami. She's American, a guest of mine. She doesn't know better. I will have her out immediately.

"Now! She must get out now!"

"I said I'd fucking do it didn't I!" he shoved the short chubby man. "I work for Giovanni Battaglia. She's a friend of his."

The man glanced to Shae who waved at him. He looked back to Carlo and nodded his head repeatedly in respect. "Of course. *Sí, signor.* Of course."

The manager snapped his fingers and marched his employees away. The staff began to herd the guests and other spectators away from the area. Carlo knelt by the pool.

"Wow! So you drop your boss's name and get all the respect, huh?" Shae grinned.

"That's going to cost me, sweetheart," he said with a smile.

She swam over to him. She rested her folded arms on the edge of the pool and dropped her chin on top "You're weird, Carlo."

"So I've been told," he replied.

"Do you want the night to end?" she asked.

"I think it should," he said. "Don't you?"

"But do you want it to end?" she asked again.

"Stop fucking with me, *bella*. Get your sweet ass out of the pool so I can take you back to the Battaglias."

"Wrong answer!" she pushed off the edge of the pool and started to do the backstroke in the water.

"Shit!" Carlo hissed. "Okay! I don't want the night to end!"

"Good!" she laughed. She swam to him once more. "You don't have to rush to the finish line with me. I'd rather we get there together." She extended her hand up to him.

He took her hand and kissed it. Then pulled her up out of the water. Her purple dress clung to her curves, and Shae had the body of a goddess. He especially liked her wide hips and round ass.

"I dropped my purse somewhere along the way," she said. "We need to find it, caveman."

He tore his eyes away from her pointed nipples straining against the front of the dress and nodded. "This way, *bambina*."

Shae followed Carlo back up the grass. She put her wet feet in her shoes and he walked her back the way they came. Soon they found her purse and an earring that had fell. He dusted the purse off and gave it to her with care. Her shawl was lost in the dark. He was quite charming when subdued. She wasn't sure which version of the man she preferred yet. But she knew she'd soon discover the answer.

Arriving through the hotel lobby was an interesting experience. She caught the stares of men and women. Carlo draped his blazer over her shoulders. At the very least her breasts were covered. Jumping in the pool was a reflex reaction. That water was cold. She was frozen all the way to the bone. Things got intense too quick between them. She had to take measures to turn it around. Still, Shae worried if her reckless nature would only cause her more harm than pleasure. Any other woman would have run for her life. Shae was not like other women.

His hand slipped over and covered hers. She squeezed his hand and walked off the elevator with him. "So this is your hiding place?"

"One of them. Yes."

"Oh, it's not just for the visit?" she asked.

He opened the door and held it for her to enter. Shae walked inside. The room temperature was frigid with cold and she shivered. Carlo must have understood her discomfort because the very first thing he did was raise the temperature. "Like I said we have business here this week. But when I visit, I often stay here. I keep a room."

Shae inspected the suite. There was clutter everywhere. It was like the man walked inside and opened his suitcase to toss his things all around. And whatever he ate or drank from was left behind. Empty cartons and bottles covered the coffee table, desk, and tops of the dresser. She stepped over the mess.

"They do have maid service?" she asked.

"I don't like people touching my things," he said and tossed his keys to the sofa.

"Are you kidding me?" she laughed. "Who doesn't want maid service when living out of a hotel?"

Carlo went over to a cabinet and grabbed a trash bag. Apparently he kept them on supply. He started picking up everything and shoving it into the bag. In a few minutes there was enough cleaned up space to make the place worthy of her.

Shae helped. They worked together in silence. One thing was certain. This man didn't have a woman to care for him. He was a lone wolf like her. When she was done she went into the bedroom. The bed was made. She began to undress in front of it. The wet dress clung to her skin and made her feel itchy all over.

"Need some help?" he asked from behind her. She let the soggy garment drop to her feet. Carlo stared at her in the dark. His face registered no emotion.

But his eyes possessed that dangerous glint she'd seen from him before. Shae stepped out of her shoes. Her feet still had the grit from the grassy hill she climbed to get her shoes.

"You like what you see, Carlo?" she asked.

"Tu sei la donna più bella che io abba mai visto," he said.

"What does that mean?"

"You are the most beautiful woman I've ever seen," he smiled.

"There he is. My Romeo," Shae laughed. "I'm sure you've seen a lot of beautiful women before." She walked over to him and put her hands on his belt. She loosened it and unzipped his pants. "But after being such a bad boy, I sure would like to hear sweet words from you."

"I tuoi occhi sono come diamanti," he leaned in and whispered into her ear.

"What does it mean?" she smiled.

"Your eyes are like diamonds," he pressed a kiss to her cheek.

"Go on," she exhaled. Her hand slipped into his boxers and she touched the snake between his legs. "My, my, you are a man."

"Hai le labbra squisite," he said and brushed his lips over hers. "I say you have thick sexy lips."

"And you have a thick, yummy dick," she replied kissing him under his neck. She stroked his penis in his pants.

Carlo groaned deep in his throat. He gripped her by both cheeks of her ass and nearly lifted her off her feet. *"Mi dai la pelle d'oca quando mi tocchi cosi,"* he said when he heaved her higher. She didn't bother to ask for a translation. Shae wrapped her legs around his waist and his pants dropped to his knees. His cock was freed from his boxers. Carlo slammed her down on it. She dragged in a deep yet stunted breath and clung to his massive shoulders. While standing, Carlo held her hips and pumped his cock up into her hard and strong. She nearly bit down on the inside of her jaw over the force.

Her pussy convulsed. Spasms of pain stretched and ripped through her tender walls. "Carlo! Mercy!" she pleaded.

He pulled her off his dick and carried her to the bed. He laid her on it and then dragged her to the edge. She sat up. He went to his knees. She closed her eyes to the softness his lips brought to her ravaged cunt. Her bottom lip still stung from earlier, but she drew it in to suck on instead of crying out her pleasure.

Carlo teased her by tracing her slick entrance with the tip of his tongue before plunging it into her tight channel. When he walked in the room and found her undressing nothing prepared him for the vision. He saw her pussy and nearly went to his knees to beg for it. The woman had shaved a lightening bolt above the pretty dark lips of her sex and dyed it pink. He'd never met anyone like her.

And damn if her pussy didn't smell and taste like strawberries. Her inner muscles contracted around his tongue when it dove in deep. Oh, how he liked that. The juices from her arousal dripped from her sex to his chin. And he feasted. She gyrated against his mouth, smashing her sex into his face. And then she chanted his name.

"Carlo! Carlo! Carlo!" her voice pitched to a soprano as she climaxed.

He wanted to be gentle, fuck her slow and easy. Worship her body. Bury his cock in and let her ride it, take him there. But he had to have her. He could put his fist through the wall the need was that fiery hot. He got to his feet and stepped out of his pants. Shae curled up into a ball and shivered.

Maybe he'd give her one last kiss below to ensure she was ready. He turned her over and laid her out, feet flat to the headboard. Carlo put a pillow under her abdomen. Shae parted her legs on instinct and lifted her ass for him with the bend of her knees.

How much more could she stand? Carlo licked and kissed her pussy. Every second of his tongue's plunder sent spirals of pleasure through her pelvis. She slammed her thighs shut and he forced them up and apart. He was now a gentle tiger. Pleasure came in pulsating waves. He kept her pinned down to explore. Before long Shae's body was racked with tremors and she was hollering her pleasure. This time he dragged his tongue down from her pussy to her forbidden zone. Shae pulled another pillow on the bed to her and bit into the soft cushion. She squeezed her eyes tightly shut. Her feet lifted and pointed north.

She collapsed during her next release and let herself go. Shae hugged her pillow and smiled with pleasure. She didn't hear or see him. She didn't care. She had that warm tingling feeling sending ribbons of contentment around her pelvis. Her legs were useless. Her body was limp.

After several seconds with not a single touch from Carlo she opened her eyes. Her head lifted. She glanced to the left and the right in the darkness. When she looked back he was sitting back against the headboard stroking his dick. Watching her.

Shae rolled over to her back and parted her thighs. She was stunned by how wet her pussy was. She plied open the lips of her sex for him. She fondled herself and smiled. Carlo stopped stroking his cock. At last he decided, and Shae still remained clueless as to what that decision was. Instead she drove herself to another pleasure point. He got to his knees and hovered above her with his angry cock pointed directly at her. His body was magnificent. She paid little attention to the scars and tattoos, and more attention to the physical build of the man. Every angle of his chest was sculpted muscle.

Shae sat up and faced him. The man was hairy. A black wave of silky hairs lay flat to his lower abdomen and arrowed down his pelvis. His dick was thick. It was average length but really thick.

"More than a mouthful," she said with a tease. He smiled down at her.

"Put it in your mouth, *cara*, and I promise not to choke you," he replied.

With her eyes fluttering shut she flicked her tongue at the dimpled center and tasted him. Her mouth formed a perfect shaped O, and her cheeks caved inward as she swallowed the first inch. Carlo's scent unfurled in her nostrils, spice and musk, everything male. She loved the smell of a man.

There was a technique to fellatio. A skill Shae had learned early in her business, and schooled her girls on soon after. It wasn't about sucking. Not totally. The glide over the tongue and the moist heat of the mouth is what really melted the cock. Carlo responded, as she expected. With his hands behind his head, fingers intertwined, his breathing went from shallow to deep. His chest bulked with deep inhales, and deflated after exhales. After sensing his weakening she sucked him to the back of her throat and squeezed his balls. Carlo groaned. Shae dragged her tongue over every veined inch of him until she sensed his collapse.

Shae released his cock but kept stroking the stalk. "You're ready now, baby," she teased.

Carlo pulled her hand off his dick and Shae turned around. He pushed on her spine until her face was flat on the mattress.

He thrust into her hard. She grunted. At first the invasion was smooth and thick. But the fucking consumed them both. He circled his hips and screwed her deeply. She could tell his fucking her was more about his pleasure than hers, and that was disappointing. Carlo covered her with his massive body.

His powerful thrusts, accompanied by his weight pressing down on her. were too much. She collapsed. And he kept punishing her. Shae vowed to endure, but there was much pain with her pleasure. He was too thick to be so rough. Had he not taken the time to learn how to make love to a woman without torturing her?

Damn him!

Shae whimpered and gripped the sheets to keep from crying out for him to stop. Deep down she wanted more. But at what price? He was so deep when he plunged. She squeezed her eyes so tight she wept. And he grunted at her in his native language, curses of his own torment. His powerful plunging hips shredded her pride. She began to whimper for mercy. Then she began to shout for it. He didn't stop. Refused to stop. Up and down he went, each thrust more forceful than the other. And Shae held on until her body collapsed and his did too.

—*B*—

SHAE WOKE IN CARLO'S ARMS. She looked directly into his eyes.

"Ciao, bella," he said with a boyish smile.

"Hi. What time is it?" she asked.

"Late," he answered.

"Did you sleep?" she asked.

"I could not."

"Why?" she asked.

"I don't know," he answered.

She stared into his eyes not sure of his truth.

"Are you okay, *cara*?" he asked.

"Am I okay? Yes, Carlo. I'm fine," she touched the stubble on his jaw "What kind of question is that?"

"Was it, nice? Good for you?" he asked. "Things may have gone further than I intended."

"I know," she kissed his lips. "I enjoyed it."

"You're lying," he said.

"I'm not. I enjoyed you, Carlo," she kissed his chin. "It was… rough, but pleasurable."

"And yet you're still here?" he asked.

"I am," she said and blinked at him.

"Why?" he asked.

She caressed his jaw. "Because I like it. Because I want to be here, with you," she continued to caress his jaw.

He turned his face to kiss the inside palm of her hand. *"Mi dai la pelle d'oca quando mi tocchi cosi,"* he whispered.

"It's the second time you've said that to me. What does it mean?"

"You give me goose bumps when you touch me like that," he smiled. "Time for me to take you back to the Battaglias."

"What if I don't want to go?" she hugged him to keep him from turning away and leaving the bed.

"You must," he replied.

"What is it? Why can't you smile, relax, go with it?" she asked.

"I am relaxed," he replied.

"Carlo?" she lifted on her elbow. "You're a passionate man. I can tell."

"Che palle," he snorted.

"Let me finish. When I say passionate I mean you feel deeply. Even in sex I can tell you struggle with feeling and uh, releasing. Thing is… you need to learn how to let go of your anger enough to enjoy the nectar."

"That's bullshit. Are you saying I don't know how to fuck?" Carlo scowled.

"I'm trying to explain to you what I felt. What I think the problem is."

"Problem!" he said in a raised voice. "I don't have a fucking problem!"

"I think you're wound too tight, Carlo," she said. "You're tight as a spring. The simplest gesture of kindness from a woman and you go off!"

"You don't know me," he said.

"So what? Who better to see through you than a stranger?" She turned his chin and looked into his eyes. There was an unnamed pain reflected in his eyes. Every muscle in her heart tightened. Shae brushed her lips over his and his arm eased around her waist. She parted her thighs and lifted her leg over his. His cock nudged at her pussy. "Gentle, I've let you fuck me how you wanted. Now I want you to make love to my body," she ran her hand down his chest to grip his erection. "I'll teach you how. No one has to know about our lessons. It's just me and you."

She guided his breech and received him inch by inch nice and slow. Carlo's face was hard. His eyes glittered with deep shadows beneath his thick and severely creased brows.

"Mmm, yes, slow, baby, easy, easy, like that," she said. Her labia swelled and constricted around her opening so each measured thrust he gave her was felt deeply. Her forehead rested against his, her hand to his face. She closed her eyes as he worked his way deeper and deeper. "Wait, wait," she said and stopped him. She moved and he slipped out of her. Shae turned over on her side to back up against him. Carlo eased his arm around her waist and pulled her closer. He pushed her top thigh up and parted the lips of her sex.

"Touch me right there," she said to his fingers grazing her clitoris. "Aaah, yes. Soft, like when you use your tongue," Shae moaned. His calloused fingertips were soft and pleasing as they teased her clit.

"Now. I want you inside of me," she breathed. She reached behind her and held to his neck. She turned her face and kissed him as he slipped into her again. The measure of his thrusts matched her breathing and his. He stopped tickling her clit and squeezed her breast. He twisted her nipple gently, ran his hand down her flat tummy to the mowed hairs over her mound. He pulled the short pink hairs and her pussy tingled warmly.

"Yes, like that. Mmm," she moaned. He returned his hand between her thighs. He rubbed her clit while working his pelvis against her backside. "Yes, Carlo. Oh yes. I like it."

She reached behind her and grabbed his ass. She dug her nails into his buttocks. He pumped a little harder, a little faster. "Move, I'm ready, go faster. Deeper, deeper."

"Like this," he whispered into her ear. "You like it like this?"

"Yes! Oh yes!" She gritted her teeth when the friction increased. Sharp, targeted friction ignited heat in her channel. He curled his body up against hers to deliver powerful plunging thrusts until the pain of their first tryst dissolved into her bliss. It felt so good. She savored each stroke and braced for the next.

"Like this," he breathed and pumped a little faster. His finger worked up the rubbing of her clit until she neared a cataclysmic explosion.

"Yeeeeessssss," she cried out.

"Or like this," he rolled his pelvis a bit which almost made his dick turn in her before he kept thrusting.

"Yes! Yes! Yes!" she chanted.

"Move your pussy. *Uau sei bagnata!* Talk to me, Shae. Tell me again how to make love to you."

"I… I…" she couldn't find the words. Her mind had blinked off. All she felt now was pleasure. He withdrew and eased on top of her. His hands went under her ass and cupped each butt cheek before slipping back inside of her.

"Yes!"

Carlo dropped his face to the side of hers. She could see his ass rise and fall underneath the cover of the sheet. She locked her legs around his waist. He pinned her arms above her head and kissed her as he drove them both to the climactic edge. Scalding spurts of his seed erupted and filled her. He went faster and faster until his hips lost rhythm and he cried out her name before his collapse.

— *B* —

THEY SAT IN THE CAR STARING AT THE VILLA. Neither of them spoke. The sun was fast approaching, and Shae knew she had to leave him. For some odd reason she couldn't make herself go.

"It was a strange, and wonderful night, Carlo. Thank you."

His gaze turned to her. He smiled. "Can I tell you a story?"

"A story?" she said. "Now?"

"I think I owe you an explanation, for my actions. My temper," he confessed.

"Okay?"

"When I was fifteen I was sent to prison." Carlo said.

"Prison?" she asked. "You mean a juvenile center?"

"No. I mean prison," he said.

"Why?"

"For rape," he glanced over to her.

"Did you do it?" she asked after a long pause.

"I was innocent. The girl was my friend, girlfriend. She was forced to accuse me. At least that's what I first believed." Carlo tapped his thumb on the steering wheel but his grip locked tight. He stared straight ahead. "Later I found out she was never my friend, girlfriend. She lied to set me up, to get revenge. She used me."

"How long were you locked away?"

"Until I was twenty. When I came home my father was gone and my mother was very sick. My sister was the only family I had left. Her and the Battaglias."

"Oh. I'm sorry for that." Shae reached over and touched his hand. She squeezed it.

"I don't have anyone… ah, anyone special. Most women run after ten minutes alone with me."

Shae chuckled. "I find that hard to believe."

"It's true. I do it mostly on purpose. I love women. I'm not gay or anything. But when I was sent away I was tortured for being naïve. I think… I know I have some issues with what happened to me."

"I am sorry it happened to you. We all have a past, Carlo. We just can't let it rule our future."

"*Grazie* to you, *bella*." He kissed her hand. He leaned over and kissed her lips. He didn't seem to care if any of the men lurking outside the doors of the villa saw him. And Shae didn't mind. "Tonight after the event there will be a big party in the Diana. Come to my room, *cara*. I need more lessons," he said.

"My pleasure, *signor*. Bye, Carlo."

"*Ciao,*" he said.

Shae left the car and hurried up the steps. She had to wear his blazer to cover the front of her purple dress and it swallowed her. A man opened the door for her. She turned her head and waved at him and then went inside.

CHAPTER SEVEN

Little Rabbit

"SLOW DOWN! SLOW DOWN!" Marietta said. She couldn't keep up. Her sister ran through the changing room to the next. She stopped to yell at one person and then the other. Staff looked up and nodded with respect, but Marietta knew they didn't hear or understand her erratic orders. There were no last minute changes. There was no crisis. One wouldn't know it by Mirabella's demands and shouting. Marietta had never in the past two years she'd spent with Mirabella seen her behave this way.

"Where is Catalina?" Mirabella asked. "I need Catalina. Find her! Now damn it! No. No. Bring Kyra and Jamie to me. I want to see the shoe choices again. I can't remember what we decided on for Zenobia."

Marietta shook her head no to Clara. "I have it. Go see if Jamie needs anything."

"Did you not hear me?" Mirabella whirled on Marietta with her hands on her hips. "I said I want to see them. Where the hell is Catalina?"

"She's outside. The doors open to allow everyone to the gardens soon. We have less than an hour to get you ready."

"Okay. Okay. Then we're set." Mirabella put her hand to her forehead. "I think we're ready."

"Girl! Would you calm down please? Damn, I can't keep up," Marietta put a hand to her heart.

Mirabella started to pace "I'm so nervous. God help me. I'm so nervous."

"Hey? Look at me. You're going to be fine. Everything is planned down to the simplest detail." Marietta took her sister by the hands. "Can you please get dressed now?"

Mirabella glanced down to her jeans and white t-shirt. "I forgot my dress."

Marietta hugged her. "No you didn't. We brought it over for you. It's fine. It's your nerves. We can do this. Together."

"Okay. Together. Is Giovanni here yet? I need to see him."

"Probably not. Lorenzo said they had a meeting and then they'd be here." Marietta hooked her arm through her sister's and started to walk her to the room she reserved for her. She needed to get her beautiful before her debut.

"My babies. I need to see them before we start. Can you have Cecilia bring them down to me?"

"Mirabella! If those boys see you they will only be upset by you sending them away. They're with Cecilia. Later Zia will come with Rocco and collect them. Like we planned."

"Yes, I know but I need to check on them. They haven't seen me all day." Mirabella fretted. "Just ten minutes."

"You don't have ten minutes. And that's your fault for running around here like a mad woman. Go in, now. I can't risk the press taking a picture of you looking like this. And I need to do your hair."

Mirabella chewed on her bottom lip for a second as if she were set to say no. Marietta dropped her hand to her hips. Mirabella sighed. She nodded and went into the dressing room.

—*B*—

"DO YOU KNOW WHO I AM?" Giovanni asked. He sat in the chair closest to the window. Young Ciro sat next to his brother on the sofa facing Giovanni. He looked over to Carlo and then to Lorenzo. He finally returned his gaze back to Giovanni.

"Sí, Signor Giovanni, Don Giovanni," Ciro answered.

"That's who I am to them." Giovanni answered. "Who am I to you?"

Ciro looked to Carlo for help. He cleared his throat and spoke. "You are my benefactor, my boss."

"He understands what's expected, Giovanni. I've explained it all to him," Carlo spoke up. Giovanni's gaze volleyed between the brothers. Everyone in the room waited in silence for Giovanni to decide.

"Hand them over," Giovanni said.

Dominic passed his boss the contracts. Giovanni leaned forward. He put them on the coffee table. He licked the tip of the pen and scrawled his signature across several pages. He eased the contracts across the coffee table and Ciro was given a pen by Dominic. The young man signed without reading a single page. He looked to Carlo twice who nodded his encouragement. Once done, Ciro passed the pen to Carlo. He sat while his brother signed the documents. It took all of ten minutes to finalize their business.

"Grazie, Don Giovanni. Tante grazie!" Ciro smiled.

Giovanni nodded and Carlo patted his brother on the back. "Let's go. Need to get you back in the gym," Carlo said. The young man picked up his ball cap and went to the door. Giovanni checked his watch. He had less than an hour to be there for his wife. He couldn't be late.

"Carlo," Giovanni said as he headed out behind his brother. "A word."

"I'll drop these off at the lawyer's and meet you at the Diana," Dominic said. He walked Ciro out. Lorenzo was seated in a chair to the left side of the parlor, his leg thrown over the side. He toyed with a sterling silver lighter. He flipped the cap and released the flame, then closed the cap and extinguished the flame repeatedly.

"Yes, boss?" Carlo asked.

"I hear you had an eventful night," Giovanni said. He leaned forward with his gaze leveled on Carlo. "With our house guest?"

Carlo glanced to Lorenzo for a reply, but Lorenzo kept playing with the lighter. His gaze swung back to Giovanni. "I ah… we went… I took her into Milan."

"You know the rules. Why the fuck would you break them?" Giovanni asked.

"I cleared it with Lorenzo," he said. "Tell him, Lo. You asked me to take her out."

"You knew about this?" Giovanni asked.

"Tell him!" Carlo demanded. "You said Giovanni was okay with it."

"I said no such thing," Lorenzo smiled. "I said I would handle it with Gio."

Carlo paced away and cursed under his breath.

"She's Marie friend, Gio. I thought it would be okay for him to take her out if he could manage being a gentleman. From what I hear about her being thrown in the pool at the Diana, he failed," Lorenzo said.

"I fucking did not! She jumped in the pool. She—"

"I don't want anything to upset Bella. And you're the last motherfucker here to know how to show a lady a respectable time." Giovanni pointed a finger accusingly at Carlo.

"No harm came to her. It was a stupid prank," Carlo tried to explain.

"I don't give a fuck why she did it! Men that work for me are to stay away from the women in this family. What do you think the boys think when they see you behave this way? First Renaldo, now you! I don't need this shit!" Giovanni shouted.

"Gio, it's harmless." Lorenzo reasoned. "She's a stranger. She'll be gone in a few days."

"I didn't hurt her. She fell in the pool at the Diana. It was an accident. I apologized to the manager."

"Apologize to me." Giovanni seethed.

Carlo sighed. "*Perdonami, Gio. Mi scuso.* I swear to you no harm came to her. We had dinner and dancing."

"And?" Lorenzo teased.

"And I brought her back here afterwards. Nothing happened that she didn't want to happen."

"This is on you!" Giovanni pointed at Lorenzo. "You and these fucking games you play. Anything goes wrong it's on you."

Lorenzo put up his hands as if in surrender. "It's fine, Gio, on my honor. I'll keep Carlo in line. He had his fun. It's over now. He'll stay away from her."

Giovanni was done with the subject. He smoothed his hands back over his hair. He hadn't seen his wife this nervous and excited in years. He was really proud of all she accomplished. Returning here, for this kind of event, brought back a flood of memories. The woman he fell in love with was back. He needed to be at her side.

"Is everything ready for Bella?" Giovanni asked as he put his gun in the back of his pants.

Lorenzo stood and nodded. Carlo stood silent.

"Who's in charge?" Gio asked.

"Nico and Renaldo are running point on security."

Giovanni arched a brow to the appointment of Renaldo.

"He can handle it. His fiancée Kyra is not an issue. Trust me nothing will get past them both."

"I've asked Santo to work with them," Giovanni said.

"What? Why?" Lorenzo said.

"He's here. We need to start bringing him in with the men." Giovanni headed out. "Let's go. Bella's waiting."

Lorenzo started for the door. Carlo seized the moment and stepped in front of him. His best friend looked up at Carlo with a sly smile. He knew in that moment that what he suspected of Lorenzo was true. Lorenzo set him up. He wanted to make him look like a fool in front of Giovanni. The betrayal hurt.

"Don't be pissed. It was a joke. Gio isn't mad—" Lorenzo began.

Carlo's punch connected with the side of Lorenzo's face and knocked him off his feet. Lorenzo landed on his side. Carlo stood over him glaring, fist clenched. "You're a brother to me. But if you do anything to derail my position with Gio I'll treat you like a fucking enemy! You and your fucking jealousy!"

Lorenzo wiped the blood from his busted lip and smirked. He didn't understand Lorenzo's jealousy. He was at Giovanni's side. The boss looked to him on everything. Even Dominic was seen less and less in front of the men. Still it wasn't enough. Lorenzo was jealous of any attention given to any other man in the family. And though he didn't think it possible, he knew his friend had now become jealous of him and his business deals with Gio. *Why?*

Carlo extended his hand in friendship to Lorenzo. He regretted striking him. In fact the action could put a bullet in his skull if Lorenzo took it as an insult.

Lorenzo stared at his hand for a moment. Carlo waited. Lorenzo accepted it and was brought to his feet.

"How was she?" Lorenzo asked.

"She's a lady. I treated her like one," Carlo said.

"Bullshit! You wouldn't know what to do with a lady if she sat her prissy pussy on your face," Lorenzo chuckled "My guess is you fucked her until she bled and she wants nothing more to do with your ass," he said and walked out.

The remark stung. Carlo thought of Shae and the night they shared. He wiped his hand down his face. They were wrong about him. Shae proved it. He was going to be a better man. He could do it.

—*B*—

"Are you ready?" Marietta knocked on the door.

Mirabella had gone in to dress. She'd wear white. The dress was made especially for the event and no one, not even Marietta had seen it on her.

"Ready!" Mirabella said.

Marietta stepped back and waited. The door opened. Her sister emerged with a smile. Marietta put her hands to her mouth. Mirabella's dress was a long garment with a low V neckline. A golden clasp to her right hip made the fit snug around the lower waist and ass. The front split that parted to reveal her legs only did so when she walked.

"Holy shit!" Marietta clapped. "Girl, you can go from cold to hot in zero to one hundred."

"Let me explain," Mirabella said as she hurried over to the floor length mirror. "Every show I preferred to wear a business suit, and most times I was able to. Fabiana would be pissed. We fought about it constantly. This," Mirabella ran her hands down her hips. "This is what she would want me to wear."

"Fuck Fabiana!" Marietta said.

Mirabella looked up at her surprised. "What did you say?"

"I said fuck her! I'm sick of her ghost haunting this day, haunting us! Mirabella this is you and me, the new beginning. Must everything be a tribute to your dead ex-business partner?" Marietta regretted her words as soon as they escaped her mouth. "Mirabella, I'm sorry. I shouldn't have said that."

Mirabella smiled. There was sadness in her voice when she spoke. "You're right."

"I am?"

"Yes." She walked over to Marietta and cupped her face in her hands. "I'm about to face the world again. The new and improved me. And I got the biggest gift of all, you, the other half of me. When I think of how much time we spent separated it tears at my heart. And I wish our mother could see us now."

Marietta's eyes began to tear. She hugged her sister. They hugged each other tightly. Marietta was the first to let go. "You look so damn hot. King B is going to bust a vein when he sees you in this dress."

"Lord I hope not." Mirabella laughed. "I finally got the man to relax and enjoy this."

"Don't you worry, sis, we all love you. It's show time!"

—*B*—

EVE SET HER BOOK DOWN. She yawned and stretched her arms over her head. Gianni was seated on Cecilia's lap sucking on a bottle. Mama had said no more bottles but everyone gave Gianni one to calm him down, even Mama. He was a big crybaby. Gino was in the corner stacking pillows and then throwing his body on top of them. She shook her head. He'd hurt himself and Mama would be upset.

"Chi Chi, Gino is jumping again," Eve said. "He'll hurt himself."

Cecilia looked up. "It's okay, Evie. Why don't you read a book to him?"

"I finished my book."

"What about that one over there?"

Eve smiled. She rose and went to the books they brought from home. She loved to read. Her favorite book was Peter Pan.

Cecilia couldn't believe how much Eve had grown. The little girl had a photographic memory. If a stranger were to observe Eve they would think the four-year old tot could read. But every book she had in Italian or English she had put to memory. Cecilia told this to the Donna who laughed. She told the Don and he smiled. No one thought it odd that little Evie was so smart and attentive to detail. Even Zia just babied and kissed on the little girl ignoring her achievements. It was Cecilia who sat with the Donna and told her Eve should go to school. And she was happy that soon she would be.

Eve walked over and grabbed her brother Gino by the hand and pulled him to the sofa in the suite. She had her book Peter Pan in her other hand. Cecilia read to Eve from that book every night. The pictures inside were bright and colorful. Gino climbed on top of the sofa like a good boy and put his hands in his lap, while Eve got on the sofa with her book and opened it to read to him.

"Everything okay in here?" Nico asked.

Cecilia looked up and her heart skipped a beat. Nico smiled at her. She hadn't seen him in two days. He was so busy with making sure the Donna's event was a success. She missed his company. "Yes. We're fine. Is it time?"

"They'll be starting soon. I'm leaving Leo here. The entire floor of the hotel is for the Battaglias. If you need me have me paged. I'll come."

"We're fine, Nico," Cecilia chuckled.

"Nico! I love you!" Eve said. "You're mine!"

"I love you too, Evie," he winked at her. Cecilia had to laugh. Eve made a point to get his attention whenever she found Nico with Cecilia. As if there was a competition. Cecilia knew there wasn't. Nico loved Eve with all his heart.

"Go!" she said. "Make sure the Donna has a good event."

Nico hesitated. Their love wasn't forbidden. She started dating him after she left the Battaglias for some time. And even now she felt her heart race whenever he looked at her as he did now. "Shoo! We're fine."

He winked and left. Cecilia looked down at Gianni. He was asleep in her arms. The twins were the cutest little boys she'd ever seen. They had darker skin than Eve's, and bright blue eyes. Gianni was the Donna's baby, though Cecilia doubted she would admit to any favoritism. Cecilia could tell. His father and all the men favored Gino. Countless times Cecilia found him with one of the men playing roughly or riding on their shoulders. And Eve was the light of both parents' eyes. Though lately Eve had been sensitive to the Don's attention to Gino. She constantly asked Cecilia if she believed her to be her Papa's favorite *lucciola*. The Donna had her concerns on this as well, and they both made sure that Eve got equal time with Giovanni.

Cecilia felt grateful for her job and the Battaglias. She was able to take care of her family on her salary. And soon she hoped Nico would propose to her. One day she'd have babies and a home of her own. She lived for that day. Her life was a blessing because of these kids. She'd give her life willingly for them all.

—*B*—

SANTO WALKED INTO THE HALL. Leaning against the wall was Leo. He looked up with surprise. Renaldo and Nico had secured the hotel. No one but top ranking officers with the Battaglias could gain access to this floor. Santo smiled.

"Why don't you take a break?" Santo said to Leo.

"I can't. Nico said I'm not to leave the kids."

"I'll stay. Gio wants me to make sure the kids are safe. This fashion thing has taken over the hotel. You won't get this chance for a smoke again."

"Grazie, Santo," Leo said with a nod and walked off toward the elevators. Santo watched him go. He opened the door to the suite and peeked inside. The young girl Cecilia wasn't there. However the Battaglia brats, Eve and one of the twin boys, were on the sofa. Eve looked up from her book and then continued to read to her brother.

He entered and closed the door.

"Nico?" he heard Cecilia call from the bedroom. Santo waited for the young woman. She walked out with a bottle in her hand. "Oh? *Ciao,* Santo. Did you need anything?"

"You alone?" Santo asked.

"Leo's outside," Cecilia smiled.

"The fashion show is starting. I came to make sure you were okay," Santo said.

"I just put Gianni down for his nap. We're fine." Cecilia smiled. "You can leave."

Santo looked her over. She was quite pretty. Her hair was cut in a short style and she wore very little makeup. She had that natural tan, deep olive skin like his ex-wife. And though her dress was modest he could not miss the curves that lay hidden beneath. How long had it been since he enjoyed a young fresh woman like her?

"Ah, is there something else?" she asked. This time her smile was a bit dimmer and she looked at him with concern.

Santo stepped toward her.

Cecilia stepped back.

"Lunch?" he smiled.

"What?" she frowned.

"Lunch. You need to get lunch for the kids. Giovanni doesn't want any strangers near them. I can't allow the staff to come up."

"But there's a servant's entrance to this room. Nico said lunch would be brought up."

"No. You should take the elevator down to the lobby and meet with the receptionist. She has the menu selections from the Donna. She said you were aware. I came up to stay with the kids. They're safe with me."

"Oh?" she sighed. "Oh, okay. Eve?"

"Sì, Chi Chi?*"* Eve answered.

"Zio Santo is going to stay here with you and the boys. I won't be long," she said.

"Okay, Chi Chi," Eve said. "I'll watch Gino."

"Good girl." Cecilia looked to Santo and nodded, then she walked out. Santo glanced around the room. He checked his watch. He locked the door Cecilia left through. Eve looked up at him curiously. Her brother turned the page on the book. Eve began to read to him again. Santo wouldn't have much time. He walked over to the back of the suite. The reason Nico chose this room was the very secure access. Even the wait staff had different access to the room. Of course Cecilia didn't know Santo's intentions. Santo found the service door and unlocked it.

"You have ten minutes." Santo said.

Kei stepped into the suite. He passed Santo. When he first saw Eve, the heart he thought was dead in his chest began to beat again. She had grown so much. There was little access to pictures of her. Mirabella never let 'little rabbit' out of her sight. Gone were her chubby cheeks and red pacifier. Too much time had passed. Eve had blondish brown curls in two ponytails separated by a center part. She wore a yellow dress and white sweater. She kicked her little feet as she read to a boy next to her in Italian. Kei observed her. It was the boy who looked up at him first. The child met his stare. It was Giovanni's spawn.

"Get rid of the toddler," Kei said.

Santo approached the children. The boy, who could be no more than two, flipped over and scooted down from the sofa. He ran for the door.

"Gino! Come back!" Eve yelled in confused surprise. Santo nearly crossed his legs and tripped over his own feet trying to catch the kid who hollered and ran from him.

"Gino! Gino!" Eve said alarmed. Eve got down from the sofa. She ran for her brother but Kei intervened. He held her hand to keep her close. "Gino! What's the matter?" Eve said trying to pull away from Kei's touch.

Santo grabbed the boy by one arm and lifted him from the ground. The toddler swung his other arm and kicked his little legs. The kid was wailing so loud he was certain to be a problem.

"Put him down, Zio Santo! Put Gino down now!" Eve shouted, with tears brimming her eyes.

Santo carried the kid roughly into the other room and slammed the door shut.

"Let me go! Let me go!" Eve struggled in Kei's hands.

"Little Rabbit, it's okay." Kei said to her calmly. "Shhh... it's okay, darling." She didn't hear him or didn't care to listen. She struggled. "It's me Poppy. Don't you remember me?" Kei asked.

Eve looked into his eyes. She looked so much like Mirabella in that moment it burned his chest. Kei's heart melted. He loved her so deeply. He took her little hand in his iron glove and kissed it. Eve pulled her hand from his immediately. She blinked at him confused. "I want my Papa," she said and her bottom lip trembled.

"I won't hurt you. I came a long way to see you," he said softly.

She touched his eye patch. She then touched his face.

"That's right, Little Rabbit. It's me Poppy. Do you remember?"

"Poppy?" she said and shook her head with confusion. "I don't know you."

"It's okay. I know you. I've known you since you were this little," he pinched his fingers together.

Kei remembered it all. The day she was born. The many nights he picked her up from her bassinet and put her to Mirabella's breast to nurse. He remembered the long days by the fire with Mirabella talking about her future. So much time had passed between then and now. But those memories never faded.

"What happened to your hand?" Eve asked.

Kei looked down at the iron sleeve covering his fingers and palm. After a brutal beating by his uncle's men in prison, his hand was crushed, every bone broken. To make it halfway useful he wore the glove and relied on the mechanisms to bend and stretch his fingers.

"It's my special hand," he told her.

"And your eye?" Eve touched his eye patch.

Kei smiled. "My magic eye."

"Like Captain Hook from Peter Pan. Mama reads the book to me. It's my favorite," Eve smiled.

"Yes. Exactly. And do you know what would make Captain Hook happy?"

he asked.

Eve blinked at him again. "No?"

"A hug. Can I have a hug, Eve?"

"Yes!" She threw her arms around his neck and hugged him. He pulled her close to his heart and kissed her cheek. "How is Mommy, Little Rabbit?"

"She's pretty." Eve grinned.

"Yes she is. I miss her. I miss you. Would you like for us to go somewhere? Some place far away."

"To Neverland? Where Peter Pan lives?" Eve asked, her eyes stretched with wonder.

Kei nodded slowly. "To Neverland. Me, you, and Mommy on a special trip."

"Yes!" Eve grinned. "I want to go!"

"Times up," Santo came out of the room carrying two boys in his arms. Isabella had shared the news that Mirabella carried twins and nearly died during their birth. He looked upon Giovanni's sons and seethed with rage. How sweet would justice be if he snapped their necks now? Kei resisted the urge. He had far greater plans of pain and torment for Giovanni.

"Are you leaving?" Eve asked.

"I'll come back for you. Neverland, remember. I promise."

Kei let Eve go. Santo set the boys down. Both of the toddlers went to their sister giving him a wary look. Kei clenched his fist and narrowed his eyes on the boys.

"Poppy loves you," Kei said.

"Bye, Captain!" Eve said in return.

Kei reluctantly turned and left out the way he came. He stopped at the door. "Name the price to put a bullet in the boys."

"I told you, I will not kill children." Santo said. He glared at Kei. "No harm will come to them."

"I should take Eve with me now." Kei said.

"And if you do, even if you manage to get out of Milan with her, you'll never get next to her mother. We stick to the plan. She's yours, the both of them. Soon."

Kei nodded. He glanced back at Eve who smiled at him. Though it killed him he had to turn away.

CECILIA POUNDED ON THE DOOR A THIRD TIME. Santo opened it. "Is everything okay?" she stormed inside. "Why was the door locked?"

Santo held the door open for the server to wheel in the lunch cart. "I was taking a piss. Didn't want the kids to get away from my sight."

"Oh. Leo is back. We are fine now. Please leave." Cecilia requested.

Santo nodded his head and walked out. Cecilia felt much better once he was gone. The server left the tray. She thanked him and saw him to the door. She could barely turn around before Gino was clinging to her knees and crying. Gino never cried. She knelt down and touched his little face. Gianni stood next to Eve holding her hand.

"What is it?" she asked. "He's trembling. Why is he so upset?"

"Captain Hook scared him," Eve said.

"Who?" Cecilia asked.

"Captain Hook. He came here, and he scared Gino. Santo took Gino to the room and closed the door so me and Captain Hook could play. Gino got upset." Eve walked over to her books. She picked up the one she read to Gino. Cecilia lifted Gino in her arms. Eve handed her the book. It was the children's fable of Peter Pan.

"He told me he was my Poppy and I was his little rabbit," Eve smiled.

"Wow. That's amazing. Well it's time for lunch. How about we eat? Huh, Gino? You want to eat, *bambino*?" The little boy rested his head on her shoulder and tears continued down his cheeks. "Oh sweetheart, it's okay. I promise. Zia and Zio will be here soon for us. And we will go have fun, after lunch."

"Yay!" Eve said and Gianni grinned up at her. Cecilia laughed. She looked at the book once more. Little Evie had a very vivid imagination.

ZENOBIA STRUTTED DOWN THE CATWALK with a long leg stride and swaying arms. The couture gown she wore shimmered like a polished pearl. An off-white ensemble of webbed fabric, that Giovanni assumed was some kind of futuristic wedding gown. The crowd celebrated. A standing ovation was given for the final Mirabella original to come down the runway. Zenobia struck a pose at the end of the catwalk. She slung her neck with a dramatic turn, and headed back to the other end. Giovanni stood. He applauded.

And then the models returned. First came Fabiana's fashions in shades of red and pink, and then Mirabella's originals, which were a mix of dark greys, blues, and black.

Each turned at the end of the catwalk and then kept going.

"The women did good," Dominic said. "Mirabella is very talented."

"Yes, she is," Giovanni agreed.

He held his breath and waited. Soon Mirabella walked down the runway. She waved at those applauding, and held hands with Zenobia. His wife was a vision in white. Being married to a fashion designer he'd become aware of the fit and compliment of clothes on his woman. In this dress she had fine hips and shapely thighs. The golden clasp to the right of the dress made the fabric tight to define her small waist. Her throat and breasts looked like warm brown satin thanks to the low cut bodice. He preferred modesty when she was on the world stage. When she reached the end of the runway their eyes met. She blew a kiss to him. He winked at her. Bella bowed for her admirers and turned and walked her models back up the catwalk.

"Andiamo," he told Dominic and Lorenzo. The crowd consumed them. Two of Giovanni's men fought back reporters who shoved a microphone at him for a comment on his wife's big moment. They left as the excitement and applause reached a deafening pitch. The back stage production was as rowdy and chaotic as the crowd to the front. Several champagne bottles popped and a fountain of bubbly poured out of the tops.

He glanced over and saw Kyra leap into Renaldo's arms, and him swing her around with delight. It was rare to see Renaldo show any emotion. Giovanni shouldered his way through the celebration in search of his wife. He saw and met with his sister first.

"Gio! Did you see? Did you?" Catalina exclaimed. She rushed to him and hugged him. "Did you see? It was fantastic! They love her again!"

"I saw. Where is she?"

Catalina ignored the question and rushed to Dominic's arms next. Giovanni cast his gaze over to Lorenzo. His cousin nodded in the direction of the right side of the room. Mirabella and Marietta were side by side grinning and speaking with a reporter. He told her one interview and he sat for it. But there she was in front of reporters. He started toward them. When his wife finally recognized his approach she ended the interview and walked over to him. He swept her up in his arms and spun her in a half-circle. Mirabella hugged his neck tight. She put her face to his cheek, and he buried his in her neck. She smelled as beautiful as she looked.

It was hard to put her down or let her go. He just wanted to hold her. "What did you think?" she asked with tears glistening in her eyes. "Did you like it?"

"I loved it. I love you. *Ti amo, Bella!*"

Lorenzo now celebrated with Marietta. He held her up in the air above him and she kicked her legs with laughter. They made such a scene that the reporters ran over and started snapping pictures. Marietta squealed with delight. She grabbed her husband's face and leaned in to kiss him with the passion of a porn star, while he held her up with his arms locked around her thighs. The sisters were a team now.

"Let's go see the kids," he told Mirabella.

"But… Gio I have to give a few more interviews."

"I told you no interviews, Bella. We granted one. And now you've given them plenty."

"But these are different. I have to make a statement," she smiled. She kissed his jaw. "A few more. Just a few and I'll be yours. I promise. Go see the kids and wait for me."

His face went slack. He opened his mouth to object but she breezed away. Marietta was lowered to her feet. She hugged her husband once more before being pulled away by her sister. Giovanni stroked his jaw. What was he to do? He couldn't drag her out in front of the media. He felt awkward and dismissed around nothing but strangers.

"It's her moment, Gio, let her have it," Lorenzo said.

"What have I done? I didn't say she couldn't have it!" he snapped.

"No? You look like you will draw Danny-boy and empty the room." Lorenzo teased.

Giovanni scratched his brow. He tried to mask his irritation but he could never hide much of his emotions from his cousin. "I'll go see the kids."

"They're gone. Remember? Zia and Rocco came for them."

"Oh?" he said. "Yes, I remember." Giovanni felt further agitated. His family was scattered. In Sorrento he kept Bella and the kids safe in Melanzana. Here in Milano they were in enemy territory. Though no one would dare make a move on him, he couldn't shake his agitation. Too many strangers. Too much noise. Flash bulbs kept exploding in his face. It was chaos.

"I'll check on things. Nico and Renaldo have been running tight security.

Santo too, I'm told. We're still doing the party afterwards. In the gardens?" Lorenzo asked.

Giovanni groaned. He'd forgotten that there was a party after the show. The Prime Minster and his wife were going to attend. If he had it his way he'd take his family and head to Bellagio. "Yes. We'll do the party."

Lorenzo patted him on the shoulder and walked off. Giovanni stood there with his hands in his pockets. He felt awkward in the mix of these strangers. Too many faces he didn't know. He decided to focus his attention on his wife. She laughed with Marietta for a reporter, and then turned sideways and around so they could get the full view of her dress.

"She's beautiful," a voice spoke behind him.

He cast his gaze left and Armando stepped to his side. His nemesis dropped his hands into his pockets and parted his blazer. "She looks a lot like her mother. More so than Marietta."

"How would you know?" Giovanni asked.

"I found a few pictures in Papa's things. I should give them to the twins," Armando replied.

"What are you doing here?" Giovanni asked.

"Catalina gave me a pass. She said it would be okay if I came and wished my sisters well after the big event."

Giovanni shook his head and smiled. "Your sisters? You continue with this bullshit."

"We continue, Gio. Remember? Neither you nor I can change the blood in their veins. They are Mancinis. Sicilian. My father's baby girls."

Giovanni looked up into Santo's eyes. He approached them then paused at the sight of Armando. "Don Mancini," Santo said with a nod of respect. The men had known each other since primary school, but Santo addressed Armando formally.

"Santo, I heard you were out of prison. *Come va?*" Armando asked.

"I'm well."

Armando nodded and glanced to Giovanni. "We'll speak again soon."

Giovanni watched him walk away.

"*Problemo?*" Santo asked.

"Unfinished business," Giovanni said. Santo was the only man in his camp who didn't know the truth about Bella and the Mancinis. When he told his men Santo was in prison. Giovanni considered sharing the truth but held back. Santo was still proving himself to him.

"The children and their caregiver left two hours ago with Rocco. Leo accompanied them. I thought you should know."

"You've been working with Nico and Renaldo?" Giovanni asked. "Has it been difficult? There are so many damn people here."

Santo shrugged. "The crowds are manageable. To be truthful it's the men I'm concerned about."

"What about them?" Giovanni asked.

"They are still a bit hesitant around me. I guess it's to be expected. I'm anxious to meet with the clan bosses and be heard, to have my own clan again. Under you of course."

"You will get your chance," he reassured him. "One chance, don't fuck it up."

"I don't intend to," Santo smiled.

—*B*—

"THAT'S ENOUGH," Mirabella whispered to Marietta when the reporter spoke to her cameraman who had equipment failure. She could see Giovanni across the room staring at her. Even when she didn't look into his eyes she felt his impatience. And she had disregarded his wish to limit the interviews. It was time for it to come to an end.

"Okay, you go, I'll finish with them." Marietta kissed her cheek.

Mirabella smiled. She cheek kissed the reporter and thanked her for coming. She stopped twice to hug and speak with her staff. When she returned to her husband's side he took her hand and walked her away. Mirabella glanced back to see Santo smiling at her. It felt like a sneer.

"Why is Santo here? I thought you didn't trust him?" Mirabella asked.

"He's family, Bella. He's earned my trust," Giovanni answered.

"He's been in prison," Mirabella said.

"Who told you that?" Giovanni glanced back at her.

"I'm not stupid, Gio. I know where he's been." Mirabella said. "It was on the news when he was arrested."

"Don't worry about it. He's family." Giovanni pushed the button to the elevator and it opened upon request. Inside he pulled her to him. He squeezed her ass. Mirabella lifted her arms to his neck. She gave her husband a slow teasing kiss with her tongue, and their tongues dueled for control with unrelenting passion. He turned her to the back of the elevator and pushed her against it. She giggled. She stepped out of one shoe and hooked her leg around his. When his face went to her neck she caught her reflection in the glass doors of the elevator. His kisses smeared her lipstick over her mouth and chin. Mirabella's eyes fluttered when he sucked her pulse and eased his hand between her thighs.

"The elevator, it's stopped!" she whispered. The door opened. Giovanni forced a finger up into her pussy and she gripped the sleeve of his suit jacket. "Gio, stop. We need to get off," she pleaded. She pushed at him but the door closed again and they started to descend. "Gio! Stop."

He groaned and let her go. They returned to the bottom level. Mirabella fixed the front of her dress when the doors parted. A few of her staff members saw her. She blushed. Giovanni pushed the button to the upper floor again. The doors closed.

"I have a surprise for you," he said.

"I love your surprises," she laughed.

"How long do we have before the party?"

Mirabella felt so happy she was light headed "It's starting now. People are already headed to the gardens. I need to be there, you too."

"Two hours, Bella," He touched her chin. Lifted it with one finger. "We will return to the party and I'll be by your side for the rest of the night. I promise."

Mirabella pulled his black silk tie that was tucked neatly inside his suit jacket. The elevator door opened. "Well come on, sweetheart, and show me what you got," she said pulling him by the tie.

SHAE FOUND MARIETTA. She laughed and sipped a glass of champagne in the garden. Marietta was now a socialite, and very well liked. It amazed her how much her bitter, introverted friend had changed. Shae began to walk toward Marietta. Her mind and back was blown from the night with Carlo, and then the day with so many of her favorite celebrities.

"Shae! There you are! Come here, girl!" Marietta waved her over.

Shae greeted Marietta with the customary cheek kisses she'd been giving and receiving since arriving in Italy.

"Pierre, this is my best friend from home, Shae." Marietta made the introduction.

The man wore a black velvet suit, with a long sleeved, wide collar pirate's blouse beneath. He had a curled mustache and very thick dark brows.

"Enchantée de faire votre connaissance." He bowed his head and kissed her hand.

"He said he's delighted to meet you. He's from our Paris office." Marietta grinned.

"Nice to meet you too," Shae smiled. Pierre whispered something to Marietta in French. Since when did her friend speak French? She knew Marietta spoke Italian but not any other language.

"Pierre says he loves your hair. He wants to know if pink is your favorite color." Marietta winked.

"Tell him it's strawberry, and yes," Shae smiled.

Apparently he knew the word 'strawberry' because he laughed. Shae's gaze slipped away when Pierre and Marietta chatted her up. Like a magnet she was again drawn to Carlo. Several of the Battaglia men stood around the perimeters of the gardens. Carlo was one of them. He apparently had been staring at her. The moment their eyes met he winked, and she felt her cheeks warm from the flattery.

Marietta waited for Shae to answer. When she didn't respond to Pierre's question she glanced back to see what had Shae's attention. Carlo was staring directly at Shae. He wore a sly smile to his face. Marietta looked to Shae and recognized the same gleam of interest in her eye.

"Ah, Pierre, *excusez-moi, s'il vous plait,*" she said. They gave each other cheek kisses and Marietta took Shae by the hand to pull her away. Shae nearly spilled her champagne by Marietta's abrupt pull of her.

"What's wrong?" Shae asked. She forced Marietta to stop.

"What's that about?" Marietta asked.

"What?" Shae asked.

"You flirting with Carlo? I told you not to," Marietta said.

"Relax. I just smiled at the man," Shae chuckled.

Marietta stepped into Shae's face. She was forced to look her friend in the eye. "I told you to stay away from him."

The tone of Marietta's voice gave Shae pause. In the past Shae and the girls at the club they worked for gave Marietta the nickname firecracker. Everyone joked and feared Marietta's explosive temper.

"Why is he off limits, Mae?"

"I told—"

"No. In fact you never did. You said it was some kind of house rule. But that's not true. Is it? Why can't I smile at Carlo? Why does that piss you off?" Shae asked.

Marietta could think of no quick reply. No quick denial. But she was not going to be disrespected. She told Shae to back off. Had she defied her? She glanced to Carlo who was now staring directly at her instead of Shae. His dark penetrating stare asked the question. *Why are you upset?* Marietta rolled her eyes.

"Stay the hell away from him, or your visit will come to an end," Marietta said.

Her friend double blinked. Marietta turned and walked away. She needed air, space, and a fucking drink.

"Slow down," Lorenzo grabbed her hand.

She glanced up and her husband's smile greeted her. Marietta's anger softened. "Hi, baby."

He pulled her in to him. He kissed her cheek. "*Bravissima, amore mio. Sei bella,*" he said. He made her step back and looked down at her attire. She wore a white leather pencil skirt that fit like a glove over her heart shaped hips, ass, and thighs. Her white silk shirt was tucked in and was so thin it was nearly see through. Of course she too had on scarlet red shoes from Kyra's designs. She, Mirabella, and Catalina all wore white. Lorenzo appreciated her look. Marietta's hair was so thick and wild with curls they nearly covered her brow and fell into her eyes.

"You like?" she teased.

His lids were heavy with desire. It was the only answer she needed.

"You saw the show, the production? All of it?" she asked him.

"I saw all of it. You and your sister work well together." He kissed her other cheek.

"Better than what she and Fabiana used to do?" Marietta asked.

Lorenzo's brows arched. "*Che cosa?* Why ask me that?"

"Am I better than Fabiana? Everyone is making the comparison. Even my sister. What about you, Lo? How do I compare?" she asked. Her heart raced. From the beginning she competed with Fabiana's ghost. And today she fielded questions from the press who constantly mentioned the red haired *puttana*! It hurt.

Lorenzo lifted her chin and leaned in so his words were felt and heard. "There is no comparison, Marie. You are the original. And what you did today is far better than anything I've ever seen in Milano."

"I love you, Lo," she hugged him.

He chuckled and held her. "What am I going to do with you, Marie?" he asked. She closed her eyes and exhaled. Lorenzo kissed the top of her head. "Let's go and celebrate, privately," he said.

"We can't. I can't. Mirabella hasn't come back down yet. We have the Prime Minister coming and so much—"

"Gio has his wife now. Do you think he'll let her go?" Lorenzo asked.

Marietta smiled. "You have a point. Maybe an hour? Then I have to be here. You understand?"

Lorenzo squeezed her ass and she plied his hand off. "The press!"

"Beh!"

She touched his chin. "I have a room upstairs. You have one hour. We can keep working on making that baby you want."

Lorenzo groaned. She pulled him by the hand leading the way.

—*B*—

CATALINA SMILED HER THANKS to the reporter for the compliment. Dominic's arms slipped around her waist. She'd know his touch anywhere. The reporter looked to Dominic and pointed her microphone in his face.

He ignored her and kissed Catalina on the neck instead.

"*Signor*? And who are you? Do you have any comment on the event this evening?"

"This is my fiancé, Dominic Battaglia," Catalina made the introduction.

"Aah, yes I've heard of your engagement. Have you love birds set a date?" the reporter asked.

Catalina opened her mouth to respond. At that moment her eyes connected with Armando. He stood several feet away staring at her. She found it hard to look away from his stare when she spoke. "This summer. It will be the biggest event in the *Campania*!" she declared. She turned and kissed Dominic in front of the reporter. Several photographers snapped the picture. She didn't care. She wanted the world to know her love for her man.

"Staring at that one could be bad for your health," Santo chuckled.

Armando cast his gaze over to Santo. Prison must have been hard on him. Santo had changed physically. He didn't have that tall domineering physique like the men who worked for Giovanni. He was thin, with a gaunt, haunted look to his features. He dragged his leg a bit when he walked. Armando was well aware of what they did to '*pentito*' in prison. *Pentito* was the name given to those who once arrested decided to cooperate with the authorities. Armando knew that Santo's loose tongue had to be under Giovanni's order. If not Santo would have had it cut out of his mouth before he ever showed his face again. However, there was one solid truth from the order: once a *pentito* always a *pentito*. The title could not be lifted.

"Welcome back," Armando said.

The glare Santo cast toward him was void of humor.

"I'm surprised you're here," Santo replied.

"Surprised? And why is that?" Armando asked.

"The Battaglias and Mancinis aren't known to mix socially." Santo said. "Are you into women's clothing?"

Armando watched Catalina flash her ring to the reporter. She was beautiful. She wore a white mini dress that showed her creamy legs and thighs. And the bright red shoes on her feet could not be missed. She grinned and giggled when Dominic lifted her in his arms and hugged her. It was official; *la piccoletta* has decided to marry her brother. He couldn't look away from her when he spoke.

"You know why I'm here," Armando answered.

Santo's brows lowered. "I've been in prison for two years. I'm afraid no one has filled me in. Are you and Gio considering the benefits of an alliance?"

Instead of answering, Armando walked off. He approached the happy couple who had ended their interview. Dominic noticed him first. Catalina's gaze met with his and she smiled for him.

"*Complimenti*. You and my sisters have put on quite an affair."

"*Grazie,*" Catalina said. "I know it meant a lot to Marietta and Mirabella that you came today."

Armando extended his hand to Dominic. He was not surprised when Dominic looked at him with distrust.

"Domi! Don't be rude," Catalina said.

Dominic accepted the handshake.

"Will you please give my congratulations to my sisters? Tell them I will see them in Bellagio," he said to Catalina.

She nodded.

"Dominic," Armando nodded. He turned and left.

"That was rude, Domi. You should have said something to him," Catalina said.

Dominic turned her to face him. "I am so proud of you, Catalina. So is Giovanni. You made this event a success for Mirabella."

"We all worked so hard. I can't believe this is my life now. Can you?"

Dominic's gaze swept the crowd of strangers laughing and mingling. He shook his head no in agreement. "A lot has changed for our family."

"We are at peace now, Domi. No threat. Just love and happiness. Isn't it time we celebrate and heal?"

"Heal?" Dominic laughed. "You aren't talking about accepting Mancini into the family?"

"Mirabella and Marietta are part Mancini. We can't pretend it's not the truth."

"Slow down, Catalina. Focus on today, on the family. Let me and Gio worry about Armando Mancini." He touched her face. "I have news."

"You do?" she asked curiously.

"I've bought a place for us in Sorrento. No more traveling to Naples. We'll be near the family. But we will have our own."

"When did you do this?" she frowned. "I thought we'd look for a home together?"

"It's a surprise. We're going to be married soon. We need to look to start our own family."

She forced a smile. "Okay. Yes. Whatever you think is best, Domi."

He kissed her cheek. "Introduce me to your guests. I want to know all about how you made today a success."

Catalina grinned. She eased her arm around his waist and his went around hers. She walked him toward Jean Carlo and several other designers. She couldn't believe how sweet life was for them all now. She loved her family.

MIRABELLA LOOKED OUT OF THE WINDOW. There was so much traffic congestion that the narrowed street that cornered the Diana was frozen with cars, vans and people on Vespas. From her view she saw the arrival of men and women dressed beautifully. Cameramen were all a buzz fighting to get a celebrity picture. Giovanni stepped behind her. He brought her a crystal flute of sparkling champagne.

"Grazie," she said. She turned. He looked devilishly handsome in the suit she made for him. The bowtie was a nice touch. Not since their wedding had he worn a bowtie for her. She loved being the tailor for men of his stature. She brushed off invisible lint from his shoulder. Her man looked good!

"I want to toast my wife," he raised his champagne glass.

Mirabella raised hers.

"To the woman who brings love into everything she touches and does. The woman who knows the true meaning of beauty and shares it with the world. To my Bella. *Congratulazioni! Sono veramente entusiasta del riconoscimento che ha ricevuto il tuo lavoro!"*

She took a sip from her champagne, then a deeper swallow. She drank the glass clean. He took the glass from her hand. He set them both down on the desk in the suite. He captured her lips in a sweet kiss. She loved the taste of him. He looked into her eyes when their lips parted. "I am so very proud of you, Bella," he said.

"That means so much to me, Gio, so much!" she hugged his neck. He let her go and she touched his face. "Do you see? Everyone is here!"

She turned again to look out at the city again. Giovanni stepped behind her. He eased his arm around her waist and held her to his heart. "Look at them, Gio. They all came. Fabiana is in heaven right now smiling down on us. I have my sister, my children, you, my life is so sweet now. I'm so happy, Gio."

His lips brushed the column of her neck. She reached back and let her fingers graze his scalp, and grip his silky hair. One of his hands traveled south down her tummy to the split at the front of her dress and then between her thighs. The other squeezed her breast and then eased inside to massage and caress it.

"I want you, Bella,"

"Okay," she sighed. The party would have to wait. Her body was aflame with desire for her man. She turned and reached to undo his bowtie. He ran the zipper down the back of her dress and rubbed his hand over spine. She removed his blazer and then unbuttoned his shirt. They walked back from the window. Not before Giovanni grabbed the rope tie to the curtain and released it. The drape fell across the window and the room was shrouded in shadows.

She lifted her gaze up into his. "You look so sexy, baby," she told him.

"I do?" he chuckled and blushed.

"Yes. Like a boss," she said and took his hand. She walked him over to the bed. He was very good at making love to her. But she didn't need his worship of her body. She was too excited about worshipping his. She knocked his hands away and he raised them as if he were her prisoner. She took her time undressing him. When she released his trousers she could barely contain her excitement.

"Sit down," she told him. He did as she asked. She removed his shoe. First his left leather loafer and then his right. "I'm thinking the next thing I want do is a men's line. Inspired by my husband."

"I like that," he said as she removed his socks.

"I'll call it: He's the Boss," she said.

Giovanni chuckled. She stood before him and he rubbed his hands up her thighs to her hips. He pressed his face against her pelvis and kissed her pussy. She pushed his shoulders for him to go back. He tried to bring her down with him but she resisted. Mirabella scooted back. She shed her clothes quickly. Giovanni scooted back on the bed. The phone to their private room rang. He glanced toward it, and then looked to her.

"Let it ring. It's just you and me."

When it didn't stop ringing she walked over and picked it up and then hung it up. She then took the receiver off the base. "Now. No interruptions."

She crawled over the bed to him. She stopped to run her tongue up the length of his shaft before swallowing him. He filled her mouth after only a few inches. She grabbed the root of his dick and suctioned her jaws to drag her tongue up and over to the head. He let go a soft moan and she loved it.

Her head lifted. His eyes opened. "Get me ready for you, baby," she said.

He extended his hand. Mirabella accepted it and he pulled her closer as he slid down a bit from the headboard. Giovanni gripped her ass and lifted her. She fell forward. Her hands fell flat to the headboard. He lowered her pussy on to his mouth. Mirabella's lips parted as air rushed out of her lungs. His tongue pushed between her folds and slid into her entrance. She felt him down in her soul. His tongue withdrew and then feathered upward. It toyed with her hard little knob before swirling over it wetly. Her hips gyrated forward and back, and then circled his mouth. The pleasure curled and spread throughout, as light and gentle as smoke. It didn't take long before she came apart. Her head dropped to the headboard. Her ass bounced on his face as his tongue licked in and out of her pussy and she creamed.

Mirabella was ready. She slid down her husband and kissed him. Instantly their kiss went from loving to carnal. Their tongues dueled for supremacy. Her man was a master at kissing. His tongue slicked over the edges of her teeth and stroked up to the roof of her mouth.

She pulled her mouth away and sat up. He had that glazed over, lust drunk look to his violet-blue eyes. "Hold on for me, baby," she said and kissed his sweat-slicked chest. She reached between her legs and grabbed his cock. She held it steady for her descent and made sure she clenched her pussy walls, and ass cheeks as she did. His back bowed from the bed. He let out a gust of breath, and she knew it pleased him.

Once she was seated and full of him she began to move her hips back and forth. It was a slow ride. She put one hand to his lower abdomen and the other rested behind her on his thigh. She went up and down rocked her hips. He began to thrust up into her when she descended, and the rhythm rocked them both. This time instead of crying out with joy, the air hissed out between her teeth. They found a rhythm that was all their own. She fell forward with her hands braced to his shoulders. She bounced on his dick with rapid hard strikes, crying out. Sweat covered them as the smell of sex wafted through the air. He put his hands under her thighs and gripped them to instruct her up and down strokes. He flipped her. It was so sudden she cried out in surprise. He put her legs on his shoulders and fucked her into oblivion. They crashed hard, with her legs pinned to her shoulders, and his dick tunneling deep. Mirabella's eyes rolled in her head.

It was damn good.

Giovanni withdrew. He did so with a deep groan of regret. She was in his arms again and held to him. "Oh, Bella," is all he could say.

She kissed his sweaty chest and smiled.

CHAPTER EIGHT

The Dinner

"SHAE! WOULD YOU LIKE TO come open the wine? Keep me company?" Kyra asked from the kitchen. Shae's gaze lifted from Carlo's hand of cards. Through the cloud of smoke hanging over the poker table she saw Kyra's smile. Carlo's free hand continued to rub between her thighs. He had effectively pushed her skirt all the way back to her panty line. To be honest she preferred where she sat rather than standing over a stove. Refusal, however, would be impolite.

"Sure," Shae said. Kyra turned and went back into the kitchen. Jamie shuffled the deck of cards. Jamie had her hair wrapped in a colorful turban like some kind of African queen, and her face was clear of makeup. Still she was undeniably beautiful and all woman. Jamie had flawless pecan brown skin and severely arched brows. Everything about Jamie exuded femininity. From her nails to her floral perfume, her confidence and presence drew envy instead of contempt from the women that crossed her path. That was until one was to notice the cigar hanging out the side of her mouth ready to be lit. Or hear her spew her truck driver language to a group of mobsters.

Earlier that day Jamie told her about the poker game she wanted to have at Kyra's. It was something she suggested when Shae fretted over how she couldn't get an evening of fun and relaxation with Carlo. Poker was something she had taught to Carlo and Renaldo when she first arrived in Italy. Jamie did it to break the ice with the men who would glare at her when she entered a room. Once they started gambling and drinking, the bonding set in. Tonight Carlo, Jamie, Renaldo and Carlo's little brother Ciro were all dealt in. Shae knew how to play but settled on being an observer.

"Alright boys, grab your dicks because your wallets are mine!" Jamie said as she began to toss out the cards.

Ciro laughed. Renaldo and Carlo only smirked. Jamie had already won one out of the first three hands. And now it was her turn to deal. Shae pushed back to stand. Carlo reached up and grabbed her arm to stall her escape.

"My good luck kiss, brown sexy?" he said. The nickname wasn't all that hot but when he said it with that wicked smile of his, it always made her tingle. She leaned in to kiss his cheek. He turned his face and gave her a much more provocative tongue lashing before he let her go.

"Good luck, baby. Win some money for me," she whispered in his ear and ran her hand down his chest. He chuckled. Shae joined Kyra in the kitchen. "Hi, miss lady, how can I help?" Shae asked with concern. The kitchen was a disaster. Kyra had pots boiling over, dirty dishes piled everywhere, and the fridge, freezer, and oven doors were all open. The destruction was an affront to the immaculate order of the small villa.

"Open the wine. It's over there."

"Where?" Shae asked. She scanned the counters and saw bottles of everything but wine.

"Over there, silly," Kyra pointed at the bottle.

"Maybe I should clean up a bit for you? While you finish dinner."

"Don't bother!" Kyra laughed. "Renaldo will take care of it."

"Are you serious?" Shae had to stop herself from laughing. Renaldo had smiled and spoken a little of his broken English since she arrived, but he seemed as intense as the other men. He definitely didn't strike Shae as a guy into domestics. Kyra turned from the cutting board. She wiped her hands on the apron.

"I'm his little *uragano,*" Kyra said.

"What does that mean?" Shae asked.

"It means hurricane in Italian. That's what he calls me," Kyra smiled. "No matter if I tried to clean this up I'd never get it to his liking. He'll handle it. He likes my chaos."

Shae had to admit their home was spotless. Nothing was out of place. Even the shoes at the door were aligned in perfect symmetry. What she didn't understand was why Kyra had to take everything out of the fridge and cabinets to cook a simple meal.

"He's a neat freak. I'm a messy freak. Together we make perfect harmony," Kyra said as if hearing Shae's inner thoughts.

"Hey, I get it, sweetheart. Opposites attract," Shae said. She closed the fridge and freezer door. "How old are you?"

"I don't like saying my age," Kyra said.

"Why?" Shae asked.

"I work with a lot of ambitious people. Jamie protects me some, but mostly I have to work a bit harder for respect. And mostly I'm always the youngest in the showroom other than the models. I think my age distracts people."

"I understand," Shae said with a newfound respect for Kyra. The girl at first seemed flighty to her. But to be best friends with a six-foot tall transgendered woman, and be engaged to a Mafia enforcer, Kyra had to have some toughness about her.

"I wanted to thank you, Kyra, for having me over. Jamie invited us, but I know you had to approve. Marietta is really busy with her sister after the big fashion show," Shae said. She went over to the wine and located the bottle opener.

"Yeah, the show was awesome yesterday! Wasn't it?"

"The party was hot too! I've never seen so many celebrities in my life," Shae grinned.

After twisting the screw down into the bottle, Shae gave it a hard pull up. The cork popped out.

"Voila!" Shae said.

Kyra smiled. "I have a question for you."

"Sure," Shae said. "Ask."

"Do the Battaglias know you're dating Carlo?" Kyra asked. She turned back to the cutting board and continued cutting the bell pepper.

"Ah, dating?" Shae gave her a nervous laugh.

"I heard you. When you told Marietta that you were hanging out with Jamie and me tonight. You conveniently left out that you were coming with Carlo."

"Did I?" Shae shrugged.

Kyra stared directly at her. "Yes, you did."

"We're just friends. Marietta is weird about it. I hope you don't mind, and keep our visit discreet."

Kyra didn't answer. She scooped up the veggies and dropped them into a pot. She picked up a spoon and began to stir them as they sizzled in olive oil.

Shae felt a little uneasy by her silence. Carlo told her that Renaldo and Kyra would be cool with them hanging out. What if he was wrong?

"Is it a problem, Kyra?" Shae asked.

"Don't worry. I won't say anything. But it can turn into a serious problem for Carlo if Giovanni doesn't approve," she warned.

"I don't understand that? Why would Giovanni care?"

"Why?" Kyra laughed. "I don't know much about what the Battaglias do. But they aren't trusting of strangers. They live by very strict rules. Renaldo broke this rule once, and it cost him his position with the family—almost his life. If you care about Carlo be careful. Harmless fun can… well it can get you into a lot of trouble."

"How did you and Renaldo meet?" Shae asked. She poured herself a taste of wine in a Merlot glass.

"America," Kyra smiled. "He visited, and it was love at first sight. He saw me and just had to have me. That's they way he tells it. I like to think of it that way too."

"Sweet," Shae smiled.

Kyra giggled. "I love him to death. When we first met he was intense, really serious about his job. But I got him to loosen up. Now he's my teddy bear." She showed Shae the bedrock of a diamond perched on her finger.

"Teddy bear?" Shae chuckled. "He's a damn grizzly bear to afford this ring, honey!"

Kyra laughed aloud. "Mmhmm, and his son, Luca. Oh he's so cute. He's teaching me Italian. Soon he and Renaldo and I will be one family. We're building a house in Sorrento. We already have one here in Milan."

"What about Paris? The shoes, all of it?" Shae asked.

Kyra didn't answer. Instead she put the meat in the oven. "Look at me. I could cook before. Growing up I had no choice but to learn how. But I never liked it this much. Now I can't wait to make his favorites. His mother and mine are constantly giving me recipes."

"Mother? I thought he was an orphan?" Shae frowned.

"His wife, she died young. Her mother is his mother. She keeps Luca and treats him like a son. When we get married she will move in, help us. They are with family tonight."

"Strange arrangement." Shae scoffed. She has never understood the tenets of family. Especially since hers was so rigid and unyielding in their strict beliefs.

"Family. Love. I've always wanted these things. I just wanted to be a shoemaker too. Now I can have all three. In my culture we take care of our parents. Same for the Italians. American blacks… well… you don't value these things."

The comment hit Shae hard. She narrowed her eyes on the girl. "American blacks take pride in family and culture! I'm so sick of everyone stereotyping 'American blacks' but reaping the benefits of our hard fought battle for rights in America."

"I didn't mean to offend—"

Shae ignored her failed apology. "American blacks believe women have just as many rights as men do. And we don't try to suppress or silence them to make men feel superior."

Kyra smiled. "I said it wrong. I apologize."

"Oh, you said what you meant!" Shae snapped.

"I really didn't mean to offend you. Trust me. I am all for women's rights. The fight to be here, right now and marry Renaldo has been a hard one for me. I love America, and everything about it. I miss it terribly. I love working for Mirabella. Having my creations walk the runway of one of the best designers in the world. I only meant to say that I've been raised to believe that this…" she gestured around the messy kitchen. "Is love too. Do you agree?"

"Not quite," Shae gave her a half smile. "But I get your point."

"You and Carlo make a cute couple too. He's a bit… different, huh?" Kyra asked.

"What ever do you mean?" Shae chuckled.

"Renaldo doesn't have many rules. But the ones he gives me I obey without question. He saved my life once. Long story. Let's just say I trust him completely."

"Okay? Now you have me really curious," Shae said.

Kyra walked over to the door to the kitchen that was open. She peeked out at the men playing cards. Shae waited as Kyra drew the door shut. It was one of those that swung inward or outward with no doorknob.

"The rule is I am to never be alone with Carlo. Ever. And if he does come here without Renaldo, or any of the men that work with Renaldo that I've been introduced to, I am not to let him in."

"Are you fucking kidding me?" Shae asked.

Kyra shook her head slowly to answer.

"That's bullshit. Why?"

"It's not just me, it's the women in the family. He's never allowed around any of us alone. He… I think he hurt someone or something. I think he's a rapist."

"He is not!" Shae said.

"I don't want to speculate. I'm just telling you what they say about him."

"It's bullshit. Calling a man a rapist is serious. He's not a danger to you."

Kyra arched a brow. "Are you sure?"

"I'm dating the man. Of course I'm sure," Shae said.

"A minute ago, you said you were just friends."

"And you know what the fuck I meant by that!" Shae hissed.

"Look, I like him. He's really funny. And he's very loyal to who they are. But he's mean at times when he's drunk, and a bit scary."

"He's a fucking man, like all the rest of them. Trust me not even yours is destined for sainthood."

Kyra laughed. "That's true. As Jamie would say, if you like it I love it, honey!"

Shae drank a bit more wine. "Well I like it!"

"Duly noted," Kyra nodded.

Shae considered Kyra's comments in silence. Carlo was different, complicated, but he wasn't a rapist. She really felt sorry for him. Who did he have in his corner?

—*B*—

"FUCK THIS!" Carlo threw in his hand. Jamie squealed and dragged the money over to her end of the table. "You wear a dress, but play cards like a man!"

"And you carry a gun, but lose at cards like a *puttana!*" Jamie teased.

Ciro and Renaldo roared with laughter. Carlo didn't enjoy the humor. Jamie winked at him. Carlo couldn't help but shrug the insult off. Not long after meeting Jamie he began to respect the fearlessness in her. She didn't lower her gaze when stared at. She didn't walk out of a room when ignored. She took a seat at any table with an open chair. That took guts considering the world she was now thrust into.

Of course she soon came under the boss's radar. Carlo was present when Renaldo was called in to tell them who Jamie was. He explained to Giovanni that the Donna had gone behind his back and funded a sex change operation for a man. Carlo believed the doctors cut Jamie's dick off and did away with his balls too. The mere idea of it went against their faith. Giovanni didn't challenge this news, though everyone knew it enraged him. The men were given orders to be watchful of her. After a few drinks, and cards played between them, Carlo had grown to accept Jamie for who she was. It was clear that Jamie was part of Renaldo's family, and a very good person. Who was he to tell her she needed a dick to be respected?

"Vieni con me," Renaldo patted Carlo on his back. "Let's talk."

Ciro nodded that he was okay to be left behind. Carlo pushed up from the chair and took his beer with him. They walked to the front of the villa and out the door. To have any conversation they couldn't do it in front of others. They both took a seat on the front step.

The moon had risen. Yet traces of the sun hadn't completely faded away, which made the evening cool and pleasing.

"Grazie for having us over," Carlo said.

"Va bene," Renaldo said.

Carlo glanced over to him. "If any questions come I'll take the heat."

"Yes, you will, because I've already told Dominic."

"Perchè?" Carlo asked.

"Dominic asked. I don't lie," Renaldo said simply.

Carlo nodded. Renaldo was one of the most loyal, by the gun and by his word, men he worked with. He did nothing without orders and approval from the bosses. His first act of rebellion cost him dearly. Which was total bullshit when one was to consider how many times Lorenzo broke the rules and got a slap on the hand. Not once since Renaldo's return from America had he seen Renaldo complain or gripe. He took the demotion and cut in pay in stride. And he worked harder at the menial tasks given to him. Carlo would consider him weak or a chump if Renaldo wasn't equally crafty and deadly when provoked.

"You of all people should understand forbidden fruit," Carlo said.

Renaldo hung his head. He shook it slowly. "What are you doing with this one? The truth, Carlo?"

"What kind of question is that to ask? What does a man do with a woman?"

"It's a direct question. Why are you with her?" Renaldo pressed. "And in secret? You bring her to my home after you know how it will be perceived."

"I meant no disrespect. The women came up with the dinner plan. I should have confirmed it with you."

Renaldo didn't accept the explanation. He continued to stare straight ahead and sip his beer.

"Why are you with Kyra? Why is Lorenzo with Marietta? We all know why Giovanni chose Mirabella. But why did you make the choice?"

"It was made for me, by my heart," Renaldo said.

"And how am I different?"

Renaldo's gaze was slow to turn to Carlo.

"A man can't live on whores alone," Carlo said.

"You are no average man. Are you?" Renaldo asked.

"I've done things. I've been paid to do things. I don't go around the country terrorizing women." Carlo stood on the step. He was growing agitated. He expected others to doubt his intentions. But why did his brothers constantly have so little faith in him?

"She's American. A stranger to our ways," Renaldo said.

"So is Kyra!" Carlo said.

"But Kyra is to be my wife. Are you ready to marry? Take a permanent woman?" Renaldo asked.

Carlo turned up his beer and swallowed the last of it.

"She's a friend. I can be friends with a woman and it not lead to trouble or marriage." Carlo answered while keeping his voice dead even. Anger tightened like an iron knot in his gut.

"You have a lot to lose now. The boss has invested in your brother. Ciro becomes a real boxer in the IBF, it's going to be good for you."

"I'm not trying to make big moves, just my own," Carlo said.

Renaldo nodded that he understood. "We can't all be boss. We do what we do for respect, independence, money."

"The brotherhood," Carlo said.

"And the brotherhood. Fatherless sons always gravitate to brotherhood," Renaldo said. "Things can be different for you now, Carlo. You are about to achieve it all from outside of the family. Be legitimate."

Carlo cast his gaze to Renaldo. None of them had hopes of legitimacy. Especially once they turned their lives over to the *Camorra*. To be his own man was a rare opportunity for a thug with blood on his soul.

"Don't screw it away playing games with that woman you barely know."

"I can handle her," Carlo assured him. "She's far safer than the other option."

"And what is the other option?" Renaldo asked.

"Me being alone," Carlo said. "You remember that feeling don't you? After your wife died? Before you met her?" he tossed his chin to the door. "Do you remember the man you were before? The man you are now, Renaldo, is he different?"

Renaldo didn't answer. He sipped his beer.

"I thought so," Carlo said.

—*B*—

CARLO REMAINED OUTSIDE WITH RENALDO. Jamie and Kyra were in the dining room setting the table for dinner. Shae chose to sit next to Ciro on the sofa. "Are you excited?"

He looked to her. She had never spoken to him before. The only time she heard him speak was when he did so in Italian. She forgot to ask if he knew English.

"*Sì, signora*, I am excited," he said.

She sighed, relieved. Finally she could have a conversation with one of them. "Carlo has a lot of faith in you."

Ciro nodded. "My brother," he said with pride.

Shae found it cute. Carlo rarely smiled unless she made him do so. But when he and Ciro were training, he laughed and joked with the young man as if he were his son instead of a brother.

"How long have you two known about each other?" she asked.

He frowned as if to say he didn't understand. Shae reformulated her question. "Carlo and you…brothers?"

Ciro nodded again. "Same father. Found each other."

Shae smiled. "I'm happy for you both."

"Carlo likes you," Ciro said.

Shae's brow arched. "Really?"

"*Sì*. A lot. *Amore*," Ciro winked.

Shae nearly coughed up her wine. Ciro patted her back. She shook her head smiling. "I know what *amore* means, Ciro. We aren't in love."

"Soon," Ciro assured her. In his way he was giving her his endorsement. The door opened and the men returned. Carlo looked at her and winked. Shae smiled. She may not be in love with him, but she sure did like him a lot.

Later –

"Dinner was nice," said Shae.

She watched Carlo pull his shirt over his head and toss it. He wore a black t-shirt underneath. It fit snug against his muscular diaphragm. Carlo's muscles flexed in his arms and chest, and she found it hard to look away. Shae fantasized about him often. During the day, and the evenings, when she couldn't see him. She was glad to see the night end.

They were back at his hotel room. After dropping his brother off, they returned. She had initially thought they'd stay longer at Kyra's, but all through dinner Carlo was sullen and quiet. He barely touched or acknowledged her. The shift in his attitude soured her mood as well. She was ready to go, and was relieved when he ended the evening.

"Carlo?"

"Take off your clothes," he said and started off to the bathroom. He slammed the door. Shae stood there dumbfounded. Prince Charming was gone. She had no desire to spend the night with who was left. She opened her purse and checked to see how much cash she had on her. A cab ride back to the villa shouldn't cost too much. Shae started for the door.

"Where are you going?" he asked.

"I'm leaving," she told him.

"Why?" he asked.

"Because you're in a mood. It's late. I'm tired. Hell, pick a reason. The night is over." She opened the door.

"Stay."

Shae walked out. In the hall she turned left for the elevator, when the door opened again. She glanced back at him.

"Stay," he said again.

"It might be best that I leave."

"Stay," he insisted. It sounded more like a plea from him than a demand.

He opened the door wider. She walked back inside. Once in he locked the door. She tossed her purse to the chair.

"What happened? Before dinner you were fine. And then bam." She snapped her fingers. "You changed."

"I didn't change. This is who I am." he rubbed his brow. "I'm not angry. I'm…"

"What?" She waited for an answer. He didn't respond. She stepped closer. "What? Are you disappointed? Aggravated? What?"

He smiled.

"So now it's funny?" she asked.

"Will you stay the night?" he asked.

"Of course," she smiled in return. "I'll stay. Marietta thinks I'm spending the night with Jamie."

He took her hand in his and kissed it. Carlo walked over to the bed. He sat on it and she joined him. For a moment they didn't speak. And then it struck her. The room was clean.

"You cleaned up?" she asked.

"I knew you were coming," he said.

She put her hand over his and covered it.

"I may come to America some day soon," he said.

"Really?" she asked.

"Ciro will be a boxer, a good one. He'll have fights all over the world. I will travel with him. Manage him."

"You're a good brother to him," she said.

"He's a good brother to me. He makes me… less angry," Carlo said. He then glanced to her. "So what do you think? About me coming to America?"

"I'd love to show you Vegas," she said.

He turned her chin. "I prefer you look at me when you speak. What's in Vegas?" he asked.

"Don't you know?" she teased.

"I want you to tell me." He said, keeping his tone even.

"Vegas is huge for boxing."

"Is it?" he said with his eyes focused on her lips. She licked the plump pair, and it made him lick his in return.

"I know you've heard of it. The city has the coolest party scene, with lots of gambling," she said as she began to scoot back on the mattress. He pursued her and kissed her tummy, breasts, and then her cheek.

"Big shows, and celebrities too," she sighed. "It's like Milan at night, but with many more lights. So many blinking and flashing lights they blind you. Shae reclined at the center of the bed and kicked off her heels. He took hold of her wrists and brought them both over her head. The kissing stopped. She looked up into his eyes. Her legs parted and he fit between her thighs nicely. Her dress was up to her waist. He moved his hips in a slow circular motion that pressed his erection to her exposed sex. She chose to go without panties for the evening. She tried to maintain his stare. It was hard.

"How long do you plan to stay in Italy?" he asked.

"For as long as it takes," she answered.

"Takes? To do what?" Carlo asked.

"Tame my lion," she smiled.

He laughed. It was the first laugh she heard from him since the dinner. He dropped his mouth on hers and his tongue swept in. She wanted to touch him but couldn't be freed. She met his kiss with equal vigor until he released her lips, and left her panting for more. "I won't be tamed."

"You sure about that?" she asked. "Seems like your behavior is improving each time we're alone."

His brows drew together. "Why would you say that?"

"Say what?" she asked.

"What you said. That my behavior is improving," he said.

"It's nothing."

"It is something. What have you heard about me, Shae?"

Shae sighed. She bit down on her bottom lip. Carlo stared at her. "I've heard that not many trust you with their wives, daughters, girlfriends." Shae answered.

"I've never—"

"Shhhhhh." She put a finger to his lips. "Don't explain, Carlo. Not if you don't need to," she said. He dropped over to his back. They lay side by side staring up at the ceiling.

"And I don't need to explain with you?" he asked.

"You've told me enough. I'm here because I like lions," she smiled.

"I like lionesses," he turned and made her face him by rolling her to her side, gripping her hip. He kissed her brow, her cheek, and her lips. "I wish you to stay longer, with me. I will tell Gio."

"Whoa... slow down..."

"Stay, and let me know you. Have you with me."

"I can stay an extra week. Maybe. But not longer," she said.

"You'll stay longer," he answered with a sheepish smile.

She chuckled. And then he buried his face in her neck. The kisses and sucks to her throat were so nice with him squeezing her ass.

"Leave bruises this time," she whispered in his ear.

It was Carlo's turn to chuckle. He ran down the side zipper to her dress. They were nose to nose. Carlo's brown eyes were dark, very dark. She was mesmerized looking into them. Tonight she wanted to play. He sat up and she did too. The dress was brought over her head and cast away. She wore a half bra, but nothing else. Shae unhooked it as Carlo unfastened his belt. His eyes never left hers.

Shae set her hands to his shoulders and smoothed up to his thick neck. She drew his face down to hers and gave him another soft kiss. This kiss meant acceptance. It was the greatest gift she could give him next to her heart. Slowly she turned on her hands and knees to put her back to him. Shae brought her hands behind her back and waited.

Carlo wrapped the belt strap around her wrists and fastened it.

"Tighter," she said. "I can still move my hands."

"Is it too tight?" he asked after tugging on it.

"No," she said. She glanced back over her shoulder. "Feels good."

He looked into her eyes. He yanked the strap and her arms were forced straight behind her back. Shae had learned a few things about Carlo's desires in the stolen moments they shared. She always felt his restraint after the first night. She wanted to feel his release tonight.

Carlo pushed up from the bed and began to remove his clothes. Shae tried to look back but couldn't.

"Lay down," he ordered her.

Shae walked on her knees further up the bed and then managed to drop flat on her stomach with her wrists bound behind her back. A quiver worked its way down her spine.

"I've changed my mind," he said.

"Have you?"

"I want you on your knees. I want you face down. I want to look at you.

Open your thighs for me."

She jerked up and got to her knees with her bottom lifting up to him in offering. Without the use of her hands she had to put her face in her pillow. Carlo reached across the bed to touch her ass. Just the fingers brushed her left cheek at first. He liked how soft her skin felt she supposed, because he knelt on the bed behind her. He used both hands to rub and squeeze, parting the globes with pleasing massages.

"I like giving it to you in the ass," Carlo said through a deep breath. He pinched her clit, and she squeezed her eyes shut to the warm tingle it sent through her core.

"I know. I like it too. When you behave, Carlo," she tossed him a challenging look. There was a girl in every woman who craved to be pushed beyond endurance. The problem was finding a man who understood that darkness and nurtured it, not turned her inside out because of it.

"I'll behave," he promised. His palm cupped her sex. Shae's eyes closed. His fingers strummed the lips of her sex. She began to shake her ass slowly in response. A low, sexy chuckle escaped Carlo. Before she had a chance to respond he bent and licked her from behind. It was glorious. The stroke of his tongue moved over her clit as it eased in to slide up to the tender region between the folds of her pussy.

"Ah, yes," she sighed.

The tip of his tongue trailed to her forbidden zone. Shae nearly lifted, but her bound arms and position kept her from doing so. He swatted her vagina after the kiss. Repeated strikes were delivered until his hand was wet with her juices. Heat arched through her, and then his hand landed on her backside. The spanking was brief, only meant to tease. And only given because the last time they were together she asked for it. Carlo's aggression would come after. She braced for the adventure.

The bed pressed down behind her when he joined. She remained in a kneeling position except her knees were parted, and her ass was turned up. "Your only job, *bella,* is to enjoy me and—" he kissed her shoulder. He kissed the back of her neck. "And let me know if anything I do becomes uncomfortable for you."

The low, resonant sound of his voice against her ear melted her insides. Her hands cinched together with her fingers entwined.

"Ah yes, *cara mia,* so nice your body is. I love it," he said. He kissed down her spine to the separation between her buttocks. The feel of his breath and tongue, mixed with his words, was such a sweet turn on. And his mouth on her clit was just the beginning. He sucked and toggled the tender flesh before holding it hostage between his pressed together lips. The slick wet sounds he made were sloppy but sweet. So few men knew the path to a woman's g-spot. They treated it like a target to hit at the end of a woman's cervix. She considered Carlo at first one of those men. But even Shae would freely admit that despite his brutish manner, he could lick and finger fuck a girl to heaven. In his excitement he nudged her sex with his face and she nearly went flat again to her stomach. She held on. The muscles in her vagina contracted and his tongue began to do the swirl licks up and between her folds before returning to task.

And then she exploded.

Wave after wave of blazing pleasure shocked her womb. He teased her further. He traced the tip of his tongue at her entrance before plunging it into her tight channel. When his tongue repeatedly thrust into her, it was only a tease of what his hard cock would bring. She gyrated against his mouth. Emotion clogged her throat and prevented her from celebrating by calling out his name. In doing so, her pussy smashed against his mouth and lips. It felt even better. It felt glorious.

His name became a chant that pushed higher and higher up her throat. And he feasted on her pussy until she neared madness.

Carlo loved the way she tasted. Her pussy was so wet and tight, he found it hard to not force himself on her on the spot. Shae's essence smeared over his lips and chin. *Mannaggia!* He wanted her to come but not so soon.

"Relax, goddess, we haven't begun yet," he said in a voice tight with frustration. He lifted his head and sat back on his haunches. He'd brought the bottle of lubricant jelly to the bed. Her cherry was on full display for him still. Carlo smiled. He never understood why women liked spanking before sex. He preferred to give licks during.

Not wasting any time, he returned to his position behind her. Without warning he gave her the dick. He pushed hard and fast into her, and as a reward he sank deep. The walls of her sweet nectar quivered around him. There was a fever inside of her. Hot melting heat that paved the way to pleasure so intense it nearly shriveled his spine. Carlo pulled out and thrust forward, rocking her back and forth with his motion. And soon they found a rhythm all their own.

It took insurmountable strength to keep from climaxing. He smacked her ass in timing with his thrusts. He hit her harder and harder. She whimpered but didn't object. Searing waves of arousal struck him until every nerve in his dick was seized with need.

The vibrations of her ass jiggling when he swat it while pumping into her pussy, made it harder to hang on. He gripped both of her hips to steady her and himself, and fucked her harder. "Hang on, goddess, just a little longer!" he grunted.

"I'm trying," she wheezed.

Carlo felt her body cinch tighter around his cock. Pleasure spiked through him with unrelenting intensity. Her bottom slammed her pussy against his groin. And all he could think of was the need to go deeper, fill her to completion, never let their passion end. The tension in his groin built steady and steady, until he rocketed into an orgasm that brought her flat down on the mattress.

"Carlo," she said weakly. "Get. Up!"

"We've just started." He wheezed. "I'm not done."

—*B*—

KYRA ROLLED TO HER SIDE ON THE BED. She wrapped her arms around her breasts and pressed her thighs together to stop the tremors between them. Renaldo had dropped over to his side of the bed. His body was slick with sweat. Hers too. He looked over at her and smiled. Without him requesting for her to do so, she turned over and stretched her naked sexed-out body across his. He rubbed her ass and then smacked it. She groaned in frustration and eased off him. Kyra watched as he went to the bathroom and rinsed his dick in the sink, then gargled with mouthwash. He returned with a rag. She giggled as he cleaned her sex-beaten pussy.

"No! We aren't changing the sheets. We'll just mess them up again anyway," she teased. She knew he wanted to, but he relented. He returned the washcloth to the bathroom and then joined her.

"Do you have to work tomorrow?" she asked. She snuggled in close.

"Yes."

"Renaldo, your mother arrives tomorrow. She's bringing Luca. They were only to stay a few nights with her sister. I want you here."

"I have to go with the Battaglias to Bellagio," he said.

"Did you ask for the day off?" she asked him. When he didn't answer she lifted her head from his chest. He looked down the tip of his nose at her.

"Well did you?" she asked. He only shrugged. She gave up and dropped her head on his chest. "You promised that when we get married you'll be here more. Luca needs you."

"And what about you? Do you need me?"

"I need you," she smiled and hugged him. "I do."

"I will be here. Trust me. I've spoken to Gio. The Donna will be working out of Milan and so will her sister. I'll be at the factory every day. We'll have lunch. Take walks together."

He smacked her ass. Kyra chuckled. She lay there listening to his heartbeat for a moment before she lifted her head once more. "What do you think of Shae and Carlo?"

"Trouble," he said and closed his eyes.

"Carlo or Shae?" she asked.

"The both of them."

"I think they are seeing each other behind the Battaglias back."

"Possibly," he yawned.

"It's a free country. They should be allowed to date if they want to. Just like us?"

He rolled her to her back. And pinned her down. Kyra parted her thighs and welcomed him.

"They are nothing like us. No woman is like you," Renaldo smiled.

"Will you love me when I'm fat and swollen with a baby?" she asked.

"With all my heart," he said.

"And our little brown babies? Will you love them?"

"With all my heart," he teased her with a kiss to her nose.

"We're going to be so happy together, Renaldo. A family."

"We already are," he said.

She kissed him and he settled in her arms. She held him close to her heart until they both drifted to sleep.

—*B*—

SHAE RUBBED THE SORENESS from her wrists. The bruised skin had left reddish welts rising. And she knew there were bruises to her buttocks and the backs of her thighs. The kind that faded quick, but left aches for days. She could barely lie on them. Carlo returned to the room. He paused. He flashed his boyish smile at her and flopped on the bed.

"You okay?" he asked.

She smiled and extended her hand to him. Carlo eased back in under the covers and joined her. She scooted into the snug fit of his embrace and closed her eyes.

"How much longer do we have?" she asked.

"Two hours," he yawned.

"I'm going to tell Mae. I have to," Shae said.

"*Sí.* I was thinking the same thing. Dominic knows. There is no need to keep it a secret any longer."

"It?" she asked.

"What?" he frowned.

She lifted her head. "You said 'it'."

"I meant… us… this… it."

"Ah, and what is this?" Shae teased.

"Friends, no?" Carlo asked.

"Friends with benefits," Shae smiled.

"Benefits? What are the benefits?" Carlo pinched her butt and she smacked him. It really hurt. Shae lifted her wrist and showed him the red raw skin. He laughed, and nodded that he understood. She lay back and he turned on his side to stare at her. "Tell me, why aren't you married?"

"Because I don't want to be," she said. "I've had proposals. Plenty."

"I know you have, my strawberry lady. You have many men who want you."

She rolled her eyes at the lame nicknames he gave her.

"I can't have kids," she shared.

Carlo's brows shot up. He blinked at her as if in disbelief. "Are you sure?"

"I'm sure. I can't have them. My lady organs to make babies are gone. Bad pregnancy when I was a teen." Shae looked at her nails. She picked at her cuticle while she spoke to keep from looking into his eyes. "Never wanted any brats. Not really."

"I'm sorry, beautiful," Carlo said.

"Don't be sorry. Some women can and some can't. I can't. End of story."

Carlo turned her chin and she looked into his eyes. "I'm sorry."

The sincerity in his voice, and her weariness from the night overcame her. She blinked away her hurt and tears. He drew her to his arms and held her. Shae held on to him. She wasn't domestic. She had a very successful, thriving business at home. She had money. She had lovers. And nothing she had made her feel as safe and comforted as the way she felt with him.

"Carlo?"

"Yes?" he answered.

"I can stay the night. The Battaglias think I'm with Jamie. I want to stay all night."

"Good. I wasn't ready to let you go."

CHAPTER NINE

Happy Birthday Bella

"BELLA? BELLA. WAKE UP?" Giovanni said.

Mirabella opened her eyes. The car had stopped. She blinked over at her husband and smiled. The past two days had been a whirlwind of activity. There was so much to do after the fashion show she barely saw her husband and kids. But now they were in Bellagio. She looked down to Gianni sleeping in her arms. Gino and Eve were with Zia and Rocco. Gianni, however, refused to let anyone touch him but Mirabella. Her poor baby.

The door opened. Mirabella was exhausted. The sun had yet to rise, and in less than ten hours the party would begin. She desperately needed sleep.

Nico accepted Gianni from her and she eased out of the car.

"I'll bring him inside, Donna," Nico said.

Mirabella yawned. She nodded. Giovanni wasn't in sight. She didn't bother to wait for him. She followed Nico and heard the others behind her. Mainly her sister, who was shouting orders to the men, and letting everyone in earshot know they were at her villa now. Mirabella smiled and shook her head. She climbed the stairs.

"Gio?" Dominic said.

Giovanni looked back and recognized Dominic. He was surprised. He hadn't spoken to him in two days, not since the big celebration at the Diana. The next morning he and Lorenzo flew back to Naples to deal with the

Racchini clan and some unfinished business. Dominic was with Bella and the ladies.

"I need to meet with you and Lorenzo now," Dominic said.

Giovanni glanced up. Mirabella and the family disappeared inside. Their reunion had been brief. She was asleep as soon as she joined him in the car. He had hoped to spend a little time with her before the sun rose and the children needed her.

"Can't it wait?"

"I'm afraid not. It may be nothing, but I need to speak with you both. Now." Dominic said.

Giovanni nodded. They walked inside and Lorenzo fell instep. Apparently Dominic had already summoned him to this meeting as well. Lorenzo kept a private wing in his villa by the lake. It had a pool table, and a large television with sofa chairs for sports watching. He had two full stocked bars, and a dartboard. Dominic drew both the doors closed when they entered. He then looked to Giovanni with concern.

"What is it?" Giovanni asked.

"Kei Hyogo," Dominic said.

"What?" Lorenzo asked.

"I was at Nicosia's with Carlo. The IBF has agreed to let him fight in Rome. It's in a week."

"What the fuck does that have to do with Kei Hyogo?" Giovanni asked. He sat in the chair behind him to keep his calm. Standing only fueled his anger and clouded his judgment.

"The challenger, he's out of London. Asian. Chinese is what he is."

"So?" Lorenzo asked.

"The money trail leads to the Triad. At first I thought it was a coincidence, Gio. Carlo knows nothing about this. The boxer is legit in the IBF. He's a real opponent. But I can't accept the coincidence. So I made some calls. I can't confirm it, but I don't think Kei is in prison."

"You can't confirm it? Where the fuck is he?" Giovanni asked.

"I don't know. We don't have the contacts that can tell us. He's not dead. But where he went, what he does? There's no way to really know. He could be back in the Triad."

"Gio, we knew this could happen when you let the worm live," Lorenzo said.

"He was beyond my reach." Giovanni said. His gaze volleyed between Lorenzo and Dominic. He rubbed his brow. "I don't like this."

"We should have killed that bastard years ago. Domi, you were supposed to keep an eye on him," said Lorenzo.

"He's a fucking hedge fund or stockbroker sentenced to a prison camp in China. What the fuck else could I do?" Dominic asked.

"He's connected to the Triad. We don't know who he really is. He sent an assassin here for me." Giovanni stood. He pushed his hands in his pockets. "Reach out to the Armenians. See if they have some inside track with the Triad. Or friends we can get information out of. I don't care the cost. I need to know where Kei Hyogo is."

"I'll make sure we tighten security, Gio. Until we know we'll pull the women out of Milano," Lorenzo advised.

Giovanni nodded in agreement. It could be a coincidence. But he didn't believe in such things. Something was missing. He didn't trust the unknown. It would be a costly mistake.

— *B* —

"MIRABELLA?" ZIA SAID.

Mirabella had just laid Gianni down. She was about to curl up with him in her arms when Zia appeared. She glanced back. "Are the kids settled?"

"Yes, they are both still sleeping. I made sure of it," Zia said.

"*Grazie,* Zia. I'm so grateful to you. For the past few days I've been so busy. I feel really guilty about leaving you with the kids."

"No! No worries. I love my babies. They are fine. It's Eve I'm worried about," Zia said.

"Why? What's wrong?"

"She keeps telling these fables. Lies," Zia shook her head. "She says a man named Captain Hook is coming to take you and her to Neverland. She goes on and on about it. I think she is behaving this way because she misses you and Gio. Today before the party will you spend some special time with her? Talk to her?"

"Yes. I should have known. I'm sorry." She glanced to Gianni who screamed and cried the moment she saw him today. He clung to her trembling. As soon as the sun rose she'd make it up to her babies. "I need to lay down, just for a minute. In the morning, tell Marietta the kids and I will eat up here in the room with Gio. Just family time."

"Bene!" Zia smiled.

Mirabella kissed her left then her right cheek. *"Grazie mille, Zia. Ti amo,"* she said.

"I will help. I love to help." Zia kissed her and left. Mirabella sighed. She kicked off her shoes and climbed in bed. She pulled Gianni over to her and put his small face against her breast. Stroking his curly head she drifted to sleep.

Giovanni returned. They had less than three hours before sunrise. He wasn't sleepy. He was anxious. The news of Kei Hyogo kept him unsettled.

"Bella?" he whispered.

She slept in the middle of the bed. Gianni was in her arms as she lay on her side. He unbuttoned his shirt and stared at her. The Americans loved his wife again. He saw it on the tele. Every news station buzzed with excitement over the reclusive black fashion designer who had returned. He worried that it would be costly to put her out in the front of the limelight. Not only to his family and their personal time. The greatest threat remained their enemies who would once again be focused on her.

"Bella?" he said when he slipped in behind her. He spooned her, drawing her backside up against him. He kissed her shoulder. "Bella, wake up *per favore?*"

"Giovanni, no. Please stop. I need a little more sleep," she groaned.

He turned her chin and her eyes fluttered awake. He kissed her. She returned his passion and he ran his hand down her side. "Let me take Gianni to Zia. So you and I can be alone," he said between kisses as his hand cupped her sex.

"No," she turned her face away. "Go to sleep. We'll make love in the morning."

"It is morning now, Bella. *Mi manchi!*"

"Gio—" He turned her away from the baby so she could come into his arms. She kissed him. But he could see her exhaustion in her bloodshot eyes. She rested her face against his chest. He sighed in defeat. Giovanni held her and stared into the darkness of the room. He didn't see any point to delving into paranoia. He'd find out where the bastard had crawled off to and make sure someone put a bullet in his skull.

—*B*—

IN LESS THAN A WEEK Shae had fallen hard for her new lover. Nothing prepared her for how good and protected Carlo made her feel. After the fight with Marietta and her sworn promise to stay away, she and Carlo were careful. Shae found the perfect excuse to sneak away with him. Marietta was so busy with the business and planning for her big in party in Bellagio, that Shae spent her days with Jamie, and her nights with Carlo. Two days ago she and Carlo dined with Kyra and Renaldo.

Unfortunately the romantic interludes could only continue if she were to come clean with Marietta. Shae didn't look forward to it. Marietta could be unpredictable when challenged. They arrived in Bellagio. The trip out of Milan to Bellagio was done under the cover of night. She could see little of the mountainous landscape so she slept in the car. She couldn't shake her restlessness now. As soon as the sun rose she thought of exploring. Marietta said Lorenzo had a boat she could take out on the lake. She looked forward to it.

There was a knock at the door.

"Who is it?" she asked in a hushed voice.

No one responded. Shae planted her feet on the floor. It was quite late. Maybe Marietta decided to check on her? They weren't on the same floor. She stood and felt the tension in her lower spine tighten. Shae should have considered a cool bath to soak in when she arrived. She went to the door and opened it. Her breath caught at the sight of Carlo. He leaned in and kissed her cheek. "Can I come in?"

"Get in here before someone sees you!" she held the door open.

He walked inside and looked around her room.

"How did you know which room was mine—" Shae was pulled up into his arms. He kissed her. She lifted her arms around his neck and kissed him back. "What are you doing here? You said you wouldn't arrive until tomorrow night? How's Ciro?"

"He's a pain in my ass. He wants pussy. I told him he can't have any while he trains. I've brought him with me to keep an eye on him."

"And the trainer? Can he have some?" Shae smiled.

"Only if the lady agrees," Carlo spun her. Shae had to swallow her cry of excitement. She hugged his neck tighter.

"So? Did he win?" Shae asked.

Carlo nodded. "And we have the fight in Napoli. It is going to happen."

"IBF?" she grinned.

"IBF!" his smile broadened.

"You did it! You fucking did it!" Shae laughed. She wanted to go to the fight, but Jamie and Kyra had to return to work. She had no cover. Carlo put her down on her feet and held her face with his large hands. This time his kiss crashed on her lips and robbed her of breath. "Wait. Wait, Carlo. We can't." She tried to push him off.

He brought her down on the bed.

"We could get caught. I haven't told Marietta about us," she warned.

"She knows. Dominic knows, so I'm sure they all have been told." Carlo grinned.

Shae put up her hand to stop his approach. "No. She doesn't."

He reached behind him and pulled his shirt over his head. "My room isn't far from here. No one gives a shit. Everyone is in bed." Carlo reasoned. He then pulled down her pajama bottoms. She scooted back and kicked them off her feet.

"Can you be quiet for me?" he asked.

"Can you be gentle for me?" she teased him with a sexy smile.

He shook his head slowly no, as he lowered his zipper. Shae bit down on her bottom lip and waited for the unveiling of the cock she loved to suck. Her gaze flickered up to his eyes once more. "I'll try for the both of us," she said.

"Good girl."

MARIETTA POURED HER HUSBAND a glass of their family wine. Lorenzo kicked off his shoes and reclined in the chair in his entertainment room.

"Everything okay?" she asked. She walked over and gave him the glass.

"Not sure. Got some troubling news from Dominic," he said before he sipped.

"Should I be concerned?" Marietta asked.

"For now Giovanni wants you and the women to stay close. After the party we're taking you back to Sorrento. Until things cool down."

"But I was thinking of going to Paris. Jamie leaves in a few days. I got maybe two weeks of work ahead of me in Milan. Mirabella and I were going to stay with the kids. That was the plan. Fuck, Lo, don't change it now!"

"Not my call. You will return to Sorrento," he said.

Marietta sighed. Lorenzo lived a life that required obedience. If he felt there was danger then there probably was. She rubbed her hands together. She looked around the room and smiled. They were home. She'd missed this place. She hadn't been there in months. Her staff greeted her and everything was polished, dusted, and the decorators had already erected the tents for the evening party by the lake.

"Vieni qui," he said and set his wine glass down on the table next to him. "How do you feel?"

Marietta eased on his lap and turned sideways so her legs dropped off the arm of the recliner. She rested on his broad chest and relaxed. "Excited."

"Happy birthday, *cara*," he lifted her chin with his finger. She looked into his beautiful eyes. "I'm proud of you."

She brushed her lips over his. Her tongue eased into his mouth and she teased him with a slow kiss. Lorenzo's eyes closed and she stroked his jaw. Her lips trailed from his lips to his chin, and then his neck. He dropped the recliner back even lower. She unbuttoned his shirt and eased her hand inside. She loved his chest. She could rub his chest all evening.

"Scusi, Signora Battaglia," a soft voice spoke.

Marietta lifted her gaze from her husband's face. Talia gave a respectful nod. The housekeeper and her family had tended Lorenzo's palace by the lake long before he married Marietta. And they showed her respect and humility soon after. She liked Talia. She trusted her.

"Yes?"

"Your guests are settled in for the evening. I was told that you wanted to prepare breakfast for them?" Talia asked.

Though breakfast wasn't customary in Italy, at least not how Marietta prepared it, the family was quite used to Marietta's culinary skills. "That's correct. I'll begin at seven."

"Sì, signora. I will make sure Marcie and Emilia are available to assist. *Buona note, signora* and *signor."*

"Buona note, Talia," Marietta smiled.

She glanced down at Lorenzo. His eyes were closed but there was a content smile on his lips. "Aww, sweetie, you're tired. Let me put you to bed."

"I'm okay," he sighed.

She kissed his brow and brushed the back of her hand over his jaw. She loved it when he was like this. The most passionate times in her marriage were shared between them here in Bellagio. Her very own castle by a lake, with servants, and a prince who made love to her every night, and woke to bake hand made pizzas for her in the morning.

"Lorenzo?" she whispered.

After a few deep breaths he opened his eyes. His lids barely parted, his pupils were dilated. Fatigue had a strong hold over him, but still he managed to give a sly smile. "Time for your birthday present, Marie," he groaned.

"Now?" she asked.

He patted her thigh. "Today is your birthday, no?"

"Where is it?" she glanced around. She saw nothing. Then she looked back into his eyes. She put her hand over his erection. She grinned. "Ah, here it is."

"No, *cara,* that would be my reward," he said.

She squeezed his dick and he groaned. He sat the chair upright from the reclined position. Marietta stood. She pulled him by the hands and brought him to his feet. Lorenzo dropped his long arm around her shoulder and pulled her closer as they left the room. She wouldn't be disappointed if he led her directly to their bedroom. Most often Lorenzo's gifts were jewelry or a fancy Chinchilla coat. However, just before they reached their bedroom door he stopped her.

"Not that room," he said.

Marietta glanced to the door to their left. He winked at her as if to encourage her to go in. "What have you done?" she laughed when she went to the door and he pinched her bottom. The room next to theirs was cleared out months ago. It was Lorenzo's orders. She hoped he'd turned it into an office. That way when his working extended into the late hours during one of their visits, she could easily entice him to bed. Marietta opened the room door and was greeted by darkness. She reached inside and flipped up the wall switch.

"Sweet Jesus." she gasped.

The walls were painted a light shade of powder blue with a navy blue, white, and yellow trim. There was a decorative wall painting of sailboats, balls, and teddy bears above the crib. A train set traveled the entire room by rails tacked on a very high shelf. She stepped inside the room. She glanced to the left to the rocking horse, playpen, and changing table. The crib near the window was antique and reminded her of the crib the twins once shared. It was dark wood. The mobile was blue and white. He walked over and turned the tiny crank. It spun slowly playing Twinkle Twinkle Little Star.

"Lorenzo?" She turned around looking at it all with disbelief.

She was immobile with shock. He hugged her from behind. He squeezed her tight. *"Buon compleannu."* He wished her happy birthday in Sicilian.

"This? This is my birthday present?" she put her hand to her forehead. "I'm not even pregnant."

"How do you know? We haven't seen the doctors. I made an appointment."

"Lorenz…"

"Carlo brought the crib up here for me last week. It's mine, from when I was a *bambino*. I brought it out of the old house. I keep promising to take you to Chianti to see the house I grew up in with Mama. We'll go some day."

"Lorenzo—"

"I asked Zia how I should paint for a boy. What a baby boy would like." He stepped back and admired the room. He pointed out things he wouldn't commonly know. For instance, the need for a changing table, and a rocking chair for her to breastfeed, was explained to him by Zia. Marietta felt sick.

"Marie? Are you crying?" he asked with concern.

She was. She didn't know when she started but she was. She put her hand to her face. "I'm trying, Lo, but you promised no pressure. Why did you do this?"

"This is not about pressure."

"It is dammit. It is. A baby room and I'm not pregnant is pressure! Doctor appointments made without my permission is pressure!"

"I don't need fucking permission to take you to the doctor!" he yelled. *"Santo Maria!* Why must everything be so difficult with you, woman?"

"Stop it!" she over shouted him.

He seized her by the arms. He shook her. Not hard but firm. "From my heart, Marie! This is from my heart. You stop crying. Look at me. Look at me!" he demanded. She looked up at him.

"Sei l'amore della mia vita." He told her she was the love of his life. "How much jewelry can I buy you? Eh? How many cars, how many villas? How much can I give you before it means nothing to either of us?" He kissed her brow as she tried to shove him away. He kissed her tears from her cheeks and grabbed her face to keep her still. "This isn't about you giving me the baby. My present is my giving you me."

"That makes no sense!" Marietta sniffed.

He lifted her chin. "Me. When you are pregnant we will come here, just you and me. I've already told Gio. I'll take whatever time off I need to. I found a doctor here in Bellagio for you. I will put you first. Our *bambini* will always come first. Trust me, *cara*."

She smiled. "Why would you promise that?"

"Because I know you, *cara*. Giving me my son scares you for some reason. It'll be a sacrifice that we make together. I am selfish in everything in my life. I know that. But not when it comes to you, Marie. My love for you is the only thing that makes me a better man. *Voglio stare con te per sempre*. I want little Maries and little Lorenzos."

Love filled her to the brim as Marietta hugged her husband's neck. She looked into his clear eyes. "You always know what I need. I will give you so many sons!" she laughed through her tears. "I love you so much!"

She rubbed her nose with his and kissed him. "I love you so much!" she laughed louder. "This is the best birthday gift you could give me!" she squealed and leapt on him.

"That's my girl," Lorenzo chuckled.

Morning –

"Eve?" Mirabella said. She found Eve alone in the room. The boys were downstairs having breakfast.

"Ciao, Mommy!" Eve said. Mirabella walked into the room and observed her daughter. She was completely captivated with combing through her doll's hair.

"Why aren't you downstairs, sweetheart? Eating?" Mirabella asked. She sat on the bed and stroked her daughter's curly hair.

"Not hungry," Eve shrugged.

"Everything okay?" Mirabella asked.

Eve ignored her. She ran the comb through her doll's hair and then set it down and started to braid it. She mimicked Mirabella in the way she sectioned the hair and combed through it.

"Zia told me that you've been telling her stories?" Mirabella asked.

"About Poppy?" Eve asked.

Mirabella's heart dropped. "What did you say, baby?"

"Poppy. He's coming to take us to Neverland. Isn't that right, little rabbit?" she asked the doll. She looked up at Mirabella and smiled. "He's a pirate, Mommy!"

"Sweetie. Do you remember who called you 'little rabbit'?" Mirabella asked.

"Um hmm," Eve nodded.

"And who was it?" Mirabella asked.

"Poppy. I told you." Eve set the doll aside and scooted off the bed. She went over to her bag of toys and pulled out the book. She brought it back to Mirabella. She put it on her lap. She opened it and flipped the pages to the one of Captain Hook. "Here he is, Mama. See?"

Mirabella stared at the image of the pirate with his hook for a hand. What was her daughter telling her? Were memories of Kei surfacing for Eve? If they were, then why now? Mirabella always assumed her daughter was far too young to remember the role he played in her life. And though she never admitted it to her husband, Kei was the person who nurtured Eve when she was born. Post-partum had settled in and robbed her of that joy.

"I saw him, Mama," Eve told her "I tellin' the truth! He come in the room and tell me that he taking me and you to Neverland. No one believe me. He scare Gino. Make him cry. No one believe me."

"What room?" Mirabella asked.

"The room," Eve shrugged and her eyes brimmed with tears.

"Sweetheart," Mirabella set the book aside. "Look at Mama." She took her hands and kissed them. "I believe you, baby. Okay?"

"You do?" Eve's eyes stretched.

"Yes," she smiled. "You're a special girl, and it's okay to have special friends. Even ones we don't see."

"He coming again. He is. You'll see him. I promise." Eve grinned. She was such a remarkable child. So beautiful and sweet, she could have possibly been made here in Bellagio.

"I promise, tomorrow we will have our own party. Go on the lake in the boat. Just you and me?"

"I want to be with Papa. He always takes Gino with him, never me anymore. He says he doesn't do it, but he does. He likes Gino more."

"He loves you, Eve," Mirabella said.

"No. He loves Gino. And you love Gianni. No one loves me. Poppy does. He said so." Eve's bottom lip quivered and fat tears rolled down her cheeks.

Mirabella took her daughter into her arms. "I'm sorry, baby, so sorry."

Zia had a good reason to be concerned. She hugged Eve to her heart. "Mama has been really busy. So has Papa. That's going to change, I promise."

Eve pushed out of Mirabella's arms and looked up at her mother. "Don't cry, my Mommy. I don't want you to cry," Eve wiped her mother's tears. "I'll let you play with me today. Okay? You'll feel better."

"Yes, baby. Mama's fine. You are my beautiful special girl. Our only baby girl. Papa and I love you to the moon and back!"

"To Neverland and the stars?" Eve grinned.

"Absolutely. Do you want to go downstairs and eat breakfast with Mama? I'd like it if you did. Marietta has made your favorite!"

"Pannie-cakes?" Eve's mouth opened with wonder.

"Yes! With strawberry syrup!"

"Yay!" she stomped her feet.

"Yay!" Mirabella cheered. She stood and took Eve by the hand and walked her out of the room leaving the fable of Captain Hook behind.

—*B*—

GIOVANNI WOKE ALONE. He tossed the covers away and picked up his watch from the night table. The time was a little after eleven. He hadn't intended to sleep in so late. With the big party happening that evening, he'd hoped to have Bella in his arms.

"Cazzo!" he said.

Barefoot he went into the bathroom and pulled out his dick. He pissed. He shed his clothes and turned on the shower. His room was one of two with the larger shower and closets. Giovanni was able to step in and let the cool jets massage away his weariness.

When Mirabella entered the room she noticed the empty bed first, and then heard the shower. Her prince was supposed to be asleep. The original plan was for them to all have breakfast upstairs together. After seeing how exhausted he was, she changed gears, and time got away from her. She knew his schedule. He never slept in this late. Mirabella opened the door to the bathroom and barely saw through the cloud of steam. She turned to leave and reconsidered. She remembered his touch in the middle of the night. How tired she was. How frustrated she left him. She went to her suitcase and found her cosmetic bag. She found his treat tucked inside. Slipping it into the palm of her hand she returned to the bathroom. She disrobed.

"I was waiting for you," he said.

"Were you?" she answered. "Lucky I came up here when I did or else you would have shriveled up into a prune."

She opened the glass door and stepped inside. She kept the gift in her hand concealed behind her. Giovanni stepped back to let the water rinse the suds from his hair and face. His dark hair was slick and flat to his head. The water left his skin in a fine spray, polishing it with moisture. She went to him. She couldn't help herself. Mirabella ran her hand over his broad chest to his muscular arms. As he turned her so her back was against the shower wall, he rested one hand against the tile above her head. He had the body, and long reach of muscle packed arms like that of a prizefighter. The steam of the shower covered his skin with moisture that glistened under the shower lights. Giovanni leaned forward. He looked at her with unrequited desire. He was so close she could see the crinkles in the corners of his violet blue eyes.

As time went on in their marriage, he never questioned her about birth control. They never once discussed future children. And she didn't bother to take any contraceptives. She didn't need to. The doctor told her there was a very slim chance she would ever carry a baby to term again if she were lucky enough to conceive. It was all due to the extensive scarring along her uterus. After two years of caring for her husband it seemed the doctors were right.

She was barren.

"Are you finally mine now, Bella?" he asked. The question came through a deep sigh. She loved it when he spoke to her with such restraint in his voice.

His head cocked over to the side and his gaze swept down to her breasts before landing on her lips again. "Say yes."

Mirabella rose on her toes.

"Yes," she said.

Their lips met. His mouth was hot on hers. Like a wildfire it sparked searing passion in its wake from one kiss. The heat wave flashed up between her thighs. She stretched against him, brushing her nipples over the wall of his chest. Then his questing fingers found the lips of her sex as he stroked her clitoris nice and slow. One touch from her man and she was ready. Her body shuddered with the sweet familiar tingle of pleasure. Her lips parted as she breathed in the steam, soap, and heady scent of anticipation. And his tongue swept into her mouth to delve deeper. It swept the roof of her mouth and tangled with hers. She nearly dropped what she clutched in her hand behind her. Instead she bent her left knee and rested her foot to the tile. Giovanni had the freedom to continue to love her with his hand.

"*Bon compleannu, Bella*," he said through their kiss before their lips parted. His breath feathered her cheek, ear, and then his mouth was on her neck.

"Don't bite me, Gio," she pleaded. The dress she wore tonight would reveal everything. She stroked his cock. She gave it a long and steady touch that lengthened and strengthened his desire for her with each tug and pull.

"Can I have my birthday wish now? Right now?" she tugged a bit harder.

"What's your wish?" he said through clenched teeth.

"You, me, and the kids. Our day. Before the party starts," she whispered. "All day, you're ours. Promise me. Nothing takes you from us."

He stopped the nibbles to her neck and lifted his face to lean and kiss her. She turned her mouth away. Giovanni grabbed her chin and enforced his will. And it was then she revealed the gift she kept in her hand behind her back. He let go of her chin. His gaze bore into her when he accepted the tube of lubricant from her hand. He set it in the soap dish before bringing her up into his arms and kissing her once more. Mirabella wanted to feel him deep inside of her. She hooked her right leg high and across his hip. She was pushed up the shower wall when he thrust into her and she felt the full power of his love. His lower body moved, and the thick length of his dick needed no guidance to enter, and reenter her again. Mirabella rode his dick. Giovanni sucked and laved her nipple. Up and down she went until her spine melted and she clung to him for existence. Giovanni's face buried between her breasts, and his breathing was reduced to shallow gasps. Every sensation she could name, and a few she had never known, pulsed through her vagina. She whimpered with pleasure.

Giovanni stopped working his hips and fucking her. Mirabella immediately sobered. Panting she looked down at him with disappointment. He eased out of her and she landed on her shaky legs. She turned toward the wall, and placed her hands flat there. Her head dropped between her outstretched arms.

Each and every time he was gentle, attentive. He parted her buttocks. Two fingers stroked up from her sex to her anus. He squeezed a dollop of lubricant into the crease of her ass. Mirabella tried to relax. The anticipation often made her clench her buttocks and thighs with trepidation. Giovanni nestled his hips up against her ass and slowly fed his cock into her. She bit down on her lip as her sphincter muscles stretched beyond belief, before surrendering to his thick invasion.

Mirabella squeezed her eyes tightly shut. Hands glided over her back, and then down the sides of her butt cheeks. Her husband had taught her the art of wicked pleasure. He massaged her ass with one hand and plunged in between the parted globes. He pinched her clit with the other. He pumped his hips with a slow motion and went deeper, ever so deep.

"Mmm. Oh Gio… oh my God," she panted.

Slowly she found the ability to gather strength in her trembling thighs to brace for when he thrust harder. And it happened. His hips thrust faster and faster in opposition to the tender massages of her clit by his thumb.

"So good, Bella, you feel so good," he wheezed.

"Gio, I can't hold on much longer!" she warned. His deep humorless chuckle vibrated through her. Her nails scratched and clawed at the tiles as his thrusts became sharper, more insistent. He slid a hand under her and pressed it against her diaphragm as the other gripped her hip and held her still. It seemed there was no end to his fucking. She now had her forehead pressed against the wall and was trembling hard. She reached between her parted thighs and grabbed his groin. She squeezed hard. He howled through his release.

Mirabella drew in a long breath and joined him.

Before The Party –

"Donna Battaglia, you have a visitor," said Talia.

Mirabella glanced up. She wore sunglasses over her eyes. In less than three hours they would have to dress for the party. However, the morning and afternoon was spent with the kids. Giovanni was in the pool with Eve helping her swim. Family was scattered. This was the only stolen moment Mirabella had to herself.

"I do? Who is it?" she asked the housekeeper who only smiled in return. Mirabella squinted, even though the dark lenses of the sunglasses blocked the sun from her eyes. She hadn't seen Marietta in over an hour. Her sister and her friend were very busy with getting everything ready for the party.

"Give him to me. I'll watch him." Catalina reached for Gino. Her sister in-law wore a sheer red cover-up over her white bikini. Mirabella looked to her son who was now sucking his two middle fingers with tears in his eyes. She held him on her lap as punishment for his behavior earlier. Giovanni was able to witness his son defiantly jump from the edge of the pool into the water. He had to go in after him and bring him out. He spent time chastising Gino, who only grinned at his father.

"Keep him from the water," Mirabella said. She handed her son over. Gino bucked and fought over the exchange, and then settled down into his aunt's loving arms.

"Ah, Gino, stop your fussing. Is it okay if I get in the pool with him, Mirabella? He's truly sorry. Aren't you, *piccoletto*?" She kissed his face and he fought her.

Mirabella eased on her sheer white cover-up. She glanced to the pool. Eve was in her father's arms as he circled the water. Her daughter floated above the waves. She kicked her feet and splashed, laughing. Giovanni's attention was solely on her. That might explain the agitation Gino felt. Mirabella smiled at her son.

"Yes. Take him in, but keep your eye on him. And, Catalina, can you make sure Giovanni focuses on Eve. She needs her father today."

"Don't you worry!" Catalina grinned. "Auntie and Gino will have their own fun! Eh?"

Gino flashed a smile for them both.

"I knew you were faking," Mirabella wagged her finger at her son. Mirabella walked off. Zia was upstairs with Gianni who had a slight fever. They agreed he'd stay out of the water. Her son was the only one out of her children who suffered from ear infections. She might need to take him to the doctor again.

"This way, *signora*," Talia said.

Mirabella followed the servant back inside and though the craziness of people scrambling and yelling orders to each other as they marched to Marietta's drumbeat. She knew her sister relished having the event in her home. Here she was the Donna.

"She waits for you in the lake room, Donna," said Talia who then took her leave. The lake room was what they called the room made of total windows. It gave a spectacular view of the blue lakes of Como with white sailboats coasting.

When Mirabella entered she didn't see her visitor at first. And then she caught sight of her from the corner of her eyes.

"Sophia?" she asked.

"Donna Mirabella," Sophia smiled. "*Grazie* for seeing me!"

"Oh my! Sophia!" Mirabella went to her and gave her a hug. It had been over two years since they last saw each other. "I had no idea you were coming."

"I'm sorry, Donna. I saw in the paper that you were to be in Milano. I speak to Zia and she tell me you come here for party. I have to speak with you, *per favore*. I've travelled so far." The old woman's voice broke with emotion. "I beg you!" she wept.

"Of course, come here, sit down." Mirabella helped the old woman sit.

"Prego," said Mirabella. She sat next to her on the sofa. Sophia dropped her head and wept. Mirabella stroked the woman's back. She waited patiently for her to share her troubles.

SHAE HURRIED. Marietta needed her to check on the liquor shipment and make sure everything ordered was taken to the rooms that were designated for entertaining. It was a simple task she thought at first. Then she discovered otherwise. How the hell was she to do anything when she could barely speak a word of Italian? No one bothered to translate. She felt like a fool. And even more frustrating, she couldn't find a fucking solitary moment to pull her friend aside to tell her about her feelings for Carlo.

When she entered the hall she heard a woman crying. Confused she stopped. Curious she continued, but was very careful not to be seen. She peeked inside. She saw an old woman weeping and Mirabella next to her, comforting her. Mirabella spoke in Italian to the woman. There was no way to understand them. Before she turned away the woman spoke in English.

"I would not have come. I'm desperate. I need your help," Sophia said.

"Tell me. What is it?" Mirabella asked.

"It's Carmella, my girl. She's dead," Sophia said.

"Dead? When? How?" Mirabella found a box of tissues and gave it over to Sophia.

"You know how, Donna. She was taken after you delivered your sons."

Mirabella drew back in surprise. She hadn't been back to Mondello since the boys were born. And she didn't inquire about Carmella. Why would she?

"Taken where?"

Sophia glanced around. "I mean no disrespect to you or the Don. I know Carlo was sent for her. The day she went missing from Marsuvio Mancini's funeral I hear he was at her car waiting for her. I know the Don... ordered it." Sophia's voice broke again around her sobs. Mirabella comforted her the best she could. "I have no defense for what my daughter has done. Carmella has always been troubled, and in love with Giovanni. I never thought she would try to hurt you or the kids."

"Sophia, I can assure you, Giovanni did not hurt her. I wish you had come to me sooner."

"*Donna, per favore*. I am not questioning you or Giovanni. What Carmella did... I had nothing to do with. I am her mother. I wanted to protect her from herself. I failed. I can't fail my Anthony. *Per favore, Donna*. I beg. I beg." Sophia got down on her knees. She kissed Mirabella's hands and wept. "I beg for you to help my son. He is just a boy. Only seventeen. They have him."

"Who has him?" Mirabella asked. Her heart raced so fast and so strong she felt it would seizure. "Who has him, Sophia?"

"He is with the Mancinis now. He works for them. Soon he will belong to them. Donna, I know your secret. I know that you are Marsuvio's daughter. *Per favore*. I've kept many Battaglia secrets. I do so for decades. I've given you my life in service. I closed my eyes to my daughter's murder. I never asked for anything. I am begging you, Donna, spare my boy. Give him a chance to be something more than his father. Help me. He is all I have left in the world."

Sophia buried her face in Mirabella's knees. Unable to summon the words of comfort, Mirabella stroked her head instead. A mother's love for her children, when tested, was unwavering. Mirabella couldn't imagine having to beg for the life of any of her kids. And no argument she could raise to excuse her husband and brother's actions seemed justified. What could she do?

"What the hell are you doing?" Marietta snatched Shae by the arm. Startled Shae couldn't speak. Marietta looked into the room and saw her sister comforting a weeping Sophia. She glared at Shae. "Answer me!"

"I-I-I-got lost," Shae stammered.

Marietta dragged Shae to the nearest room and forced her inside. Shae stumbled back rubbing her arm as if it were wounded. "Were you eavesdropping?"

"Calm down," Shae answered.

"Were you?" Marietta shouted.

"I was only doing what you asked. I can't understand them. I don't speak Italian. You know that!"

Marietta paced. "I warned you, Shae. This is the second fucking time I've caught you peeping around corners."

"Mae?"

"I told you not to meddle. What if my husband found you? Huh? What if one of his men saw you? Damn it!"

"Okay! You and these fucking rules! I can't talk to the men. I can't speak unless spoken to. Fuck this! I should have never come here!" Shae shouted.

Marietta put her hand to her head. She looked to her friend and calmed herself. She was on edge. Everything was on her for this event, and the stress was mounting. She shouldn't have yelled at Shae. "I'm sorry. I didn't mean to flip out, girl. But you get it. Don't you? My family. We live by rules to keep our husbands out of jail, and our children safe. So please, pretty please. Stop the bullshit. Okay?"

Shae smiled. "I got your back. Like always. There's something I need to tell you."

Marietta rolled her eyes. "What now?"

"Oh, ah, forget it. It can wait."

"Good, come on. Let's check on the liquor."

MIRABELLA HAD A HEADACHE. She found a pill bottle and dumped two Tylenol into her hand. She took them without water. She closed her eyes and swallowed.

"Mirabella? You should be getting dressed," Catalina said. She walked into the kitchen in her robe. "I came to your room to borrow your earrings. What's wrong?"

Mirabella turned from the kitchen sink. She smiled. "Have the kids left?" she asked.

"No. Dominic said they have to stay. Zia and Cecilia will keep them upstairs."

"Why? We agreed that they'd go into Bellagio and visit with Zia's friends for the evening. It was all arranged."

"Gio's orders. We are to go back to Sorrento right after the party, first thing tomorrow. I had to cancel our follow-up meetings with Kyra and Jamie. I'm on a travel ban too. I thought you knew?"

"My husband and his orders. I can't keep up." She pulled out a chair from the table and sat down.

"What's wrong?" Catalina asked.

Mirabella couldn't say. She stroked her brow. Her sister in-law put her hand over hers for comfort. It helped. "Is Armando coming to the party?" Mirabella asked.

"He said he would," Catalina said. "Wasn't easy getting the men to agree."

"Nothing is ever easy in this family. Is it?" Mirabella asked.

"No. I suppose not."

"Catalina, I have a question for you. It's… it's about Carmella."

"Puttana!" Catalina spat the word.

"Have you seen her?" Mirabella asked.

"No. I haven't been back to Sicilia in over a year."

"Have you spoken to her since… well after the twins were born?"

Catalina pushed back her chair and stood. She went to the sink and picked up a glass to run tap water into. "There was a lot of drama going on when you were in the hospital. A lot of chaos."

"You didn't answer my question." Mirabella said.

"Why ask it now? It's been over two years. Who cares what's going on with Carmella?"

"Is she dead?" Mirabella asked.

"What?"

"Dead. Is she dead?" Mirabella asked.

Catalina walked back over to the kitchen table. She pulled out a chair and sat down. "Yes, she's dead," she said.

"Jesus Christ," Mirabella sighed. "Do you understand how insane that is?"

"No one told me she's dead. No one had to, Mirabella. She tried to kill you." Catalina looked Mirabella in the eye. "Anyone ever tries to harm us, Gio won't forgive. He won't forget. He never does and never has. It's not your fault or your concern. She's gone."

"Sophia came to see me. She knows that I'm Marsuvio's daughter."

"How?" Catalina asked.

"These people who fix our meals and change our linen. They have eyes and ears, Catalina. She knows. And she came to me begging for me to save her only child's life."

"Anthony?" Catalina asked.

"He's working for the Mancinis. The kid's about to disappear into their world. Our world."

"There's nothing you can do about that. It's Mafioso business. Best to stay out of it." Catalina waved the matter off.

"I won't have any more blood on my hands. If I can help her—"

"You can't," Catalina said. "Giovanni wouldn't bother with it no matter what you say to him, and… wait? Are you going to ask Armando to intercede? Giovanni would be livid. Never ask a favor from his enemy. The debt becomes Gio's."

"Enemy or my brother? I was born into this life, just like you. Too late to stay out of it now," Mirabella said.

"Not exactly. Being a Mancini has no meaning to you. You married into this life, Mirabella. You're a Battaglia. Period."

Mirabella sighed. She cut her eyes and walked away.

"Mirabella? Mirabella!"

She left the kitchen and headed for her room. Suddenly her headache was gone.

The Party –

"How many people did you invite?" Mirabella whispered through a frozen smile. Marietta gave a single hand wave as if she were on a parade float alone. Mirabella scanned the faces of those applauding. Only a third of these people she recognized. Bulbs flashed in rapid succession blinding her. She squinted twice.

Marietta took the first step and Mirabella followed. Together they descended the stairs of the outside veranda to the lawns, where lanterns swayed in the breeze, and lights were strung up around white and blue tents. Mirabella had to pause over the exquisite draping of wild flowers in bloom under the moon and stars.

For the evening Mirabella had designed golden toga dresses that draped over one shoulder, had two front slits that reached up the thigh, and were long enough to cover their feet. The dresses tied snug around the waist with a golden rope sash. With their hair both styled in loose but long spiral curls, wildly picked out and pinned on the left side, they looked identical down to their lipstick choice. If it weren't for the different skin tones between them she knew many would struggle to tell them apart.

"Bella," Giovanni greeted Mirabella first. He took her hand and kissed her cheek. She blushed. Not from the attention, but from the adoration banked in his violet blue eyes. She smiled and hugged him, pressing her cheek to his.

"Attenzione!" Lorenzo shouted down the applause.

The grand entrance was orchestrated by Marietta. But Lorenzo made sure to pull his wife close and address the crowd of partiers as the lord of the manor.

"I, and my beautiful wife, want to welcome you to our home. We celebrate! Together!" he said to another burst of applause. "Marietta and Mirabella are together. It is a miracle, a Battaglia miracle, that they have found each other. This is their celebration and announcement to the world. With family we are stronger! Always!"

"Cin-cin!" Giovanni raised his glass. The crowd followed with their salute and toasted them. After the toast, they were rushed by well-wishers. Mirabella took her position at her husband's side. Marietta and Lorenzo stood to the left of them. They received each guest and envelope of money with a smile and humility. So many had come to celebrate.

"Ciao, piccola." Carlo pressed in behind Shae. The moment she felt his erection against her backside, the muscles along her inner thighs tensed. He kissed her bare shoulder. Her hair was short enough, and here sleeveless dress granted him the privilege. She pretended not to like how gentle and pleasing his lips brushing against her skin felt. The kiss was a very brazen act. Shae sipped her champagne and observed the twins, hoping no one would notice.

"Come with me," Carlo whispered with his lips only a centimeter away from her ear. "I want to give you something hard and stiff." His hand slid across her midriff and she was drawn back into his chest.

"I can't. Stop," she chuckled.

"Sei una ragazza aqua e sapone," Carlo whispered in her ear. "I say you are a natural girl. You don't need this dress, makeup. You smell so good. Let me take this off you."

"Carlo, you're so bad."

"Andiamo," He took her hand and pulled her away. She was forced to go with him. It was then she glanced back, and to her dismay Marietta was now looking directly at them.

Through the sea of people Marietta saw them. Carlo leaned in and kissed her friend's shoulder, then pulled her away. The intimacy between them didn't appear new or awkward. In fact, in all the time she'd known Carlo, she'd never seen him whisper to another woman or touch her the way he did Shae. And when Shae glanced up and looked into Marietta's eyes she knew.

"Marie, meet Frenchie. My old friend from Genoa," Lorenzo swept Marietta closer.

Forced into a greeting she gave her pleasantries in Italian and listened to Lorenzo brag about his bachelor days with Frenchie, whose real name was Arlo Capriani. A man who loved French women so much he'd married French three times. Marietta tried once more to locate Shae and Carlo in the crowd, but they were gone. She fumed.

—*B*—

"Buon compleannu, Donna Mirabella," Armando said. Her brother had always appeared handsome, but in a tuxedo he was dashing. She was rendered speechless at the sight of him. Was he the image of their father? It was no wonder Lisa's choices and life ended so terribly.

Armando leaned in and gave her a cheek kiss. He nodded to Giovanni out of respect, and then extended his hand. Mirabella observed her husband's tolerant handshake. It was progress. Or at least she hoped it was.

"I'd like to give the sisters their birthday gift, in private. Before family only of course." Armando said. "Dominic approved. Your men had it brought in to a private room for showing." He pointed back to the villa. "Shall we?"

The others had moved on and were socializing. It appeared that Armando waited to be the very last one to extend his birthday wishes.

Mirabella was the first to speak. "I'd love to."

She glanced to her sister and gestured for her to come closer. "I'll get the family and we'll all meet in the conservatory," Mirabella said. "Gio, show him the way."

Armando and the men watched her walk away.

"What is this about?" Giovanni asked.

"A gift. I couldn't travel all the way to Bellagio without one," Armando said.

"If you do anything to disrespect my wife or the family I won't be restrained." Giovanni warned.

Armando patted his arm. "I come in peace, Gio. Don't you trust me?"

"Let's go, honey!" Mirabella called out. She waved to him. She'd gotten nearly all of the family to return inside. Giovanni's jaw twitched. He hated having to coexist with the Mancinis this way.

"After you," Giovanni said to Armando.

He nodded and followed the others. Dominic appeared at Giovanni's side. He hadn't seen him walk up. He was too consumed by his own thoughts.

"I'm not sure of this gift," Dominic said.

"Did you not see it?" Giovanni asked.

"Yes. Well I saw it. Looks like it might be a portrait of some kind. It's large."

"And you okayed this?" Giovanni stopped.

"You okayed his attendance. I assumed he, like everyone else, would bring a gift," Dominic said.

"Assume nothing when it comes to a Mancini. Have I not taught you that?" Giovanni glanced to the others. "If he embarrasses me or..."

"I'll handle it, Gio. Right now it's good form to be gracious. No?"

"Gracious?" Giovanni scoffed. "*Che cazzo!*"

Mirabella waited for the last of the family to arrive. Marietta had set up a room for the family to leave their gifts separate from the guests. So many had come in from Sicilia. The tables were lined with presents.

"Mirabella, Marietta," Armando spoke and the room silenced. Giovanni observed by the door. Mirabella wished he'd come over to her side.

"I want to thank you for inviting me. I'm honored," Armando said. He pressed his hands together flat, with fingers to fingers. He gave them a very charming smile. "I know that you are all aware of who Mirabella and Marietta are to me, to my father. In honor of that bond I would like to gift my sisters something special from the Mancinis."

"Do you know what this is about?" Mirabella asked under her breath.

"Just play along," Marietta said with a tight smile.

Armando signaled to one of his men who brought over a large flat gift covered in brown paper. It stood taller than Armando. One of Vito's sons walked over to help hold up the other side. Mirabella didn't like surprises in their family. None of them ever ended well.

"For you both!" Armando proclaimed.

He reached up and tore off the paper until the portrait was revealed. There was an audible gasp. Mirabella realized that it came from Marietta. Hell she was too stunned to dare blink. The portrait was spectacular. The likeness was uncanny. It was as if they had actually posed for it. And that would have been a pleasant enough gift. Instead he went a bit further. Seated in a chair between them was the late Marsuvio Mancini. She and Marietta stood on either side of him. He stared out of the portrait as if he were alive and strong enough to stand, step back into life.

"My father's dying wish was to know you. On his deathbed he asked for this gift. It is like the one he and I had done several years ago. Two years have passed. We are all wiser. Please accept this from the Mancini *famiglia* to you."

"Grazie!" Marietta applauded. She did so alone. She walked over to Armando and hugged him. She kissed both his cheeks and hugged him again. Mirabella could see Lorenzo standing off to the side, chuckling and shaking his head. She wished her husband had the same sense of humor. Giovanni stared at the portrait and nothing else.

"Isn't it wonderful?" Marietta asked Mirabella. "Well? Isn't it?"

"It's very… nice," she said. *"Grazie, caro fratello."*

Lorenzo clapped. Every head turned to look at him, and then slowly the rest of the family applauded. Catalina walked over to Mirabella and hugged her.

"I had no idea," she whispered in Mirabella's ear. "I told him to come, but not to bring this."

"Va bene," Mirabella smiled.

Catalina let her go and addressed the family. *"Prego!* Let's open presents! Mirabella, Marietta, have a seat. It's time." She glanced to Dominic who nodded to the family members to take the portrait out discreetly so non-family members could not see it.

Armando stepped in front of Mirabella before she could join her sister. "I hope I didn't offend you, Donna."

"No. It's a lovely gesture. I ah, I do have a request." Mirabella glanced toward her husband. He was watching them both. She wouldn't get a chance to speak to Armando again. And with the family laughing and chatting each other up this proved to be the perfect cover.

"Ask anything of me," Armando replied. "It's your birthday. As your brother I'm bound to grant any wish you have today."

"Anthony. You know him. He's Carmella's little brother."

Armando's brows lowered. His handsome features grew serious. She didn't dare lower her gaze. After all it was he and Carmella who plotted to kill her.

"Yes, I know little Anthony. I call him Biscuit. He's always at my home bringing the boys his mother's biscuits. Nice kid."

"Innocent kid," she corrected him.

"Children aren't always so innocent," Armando said. "When Giovanni and I were fifteen, his age, we were far from it."

Mirabella chose to ignore the sly humor in his comment. "His mother is concerned. He's being brought into your family. I went—" She glanced to Giovanni who continued to observe them from across the room. "I'm asking that you let him go. Send him to school. Give him a future, just one different than that of our father."

"Or your husband?" Armando asked.

"Or you," she clarified.

"Why would you ask this of me?" Armando asked.

"Because you owe both me and Sophia peace after what you and Carmella tried to do. Because you keep telling my sister that you want to get to know us. I need proof. Help him and I'll consider it a gesture of goodwill between us."

"Is that so?" Armando asked. He leaned in and Mirabella stiffened. He whispered in her ear. "Consider it done, sweet sister."

And then he walked away.

Mirabella looked for her husband. She found him once more. He met her stare. She gave him a small smile and decided it was time to join him.

—*B*—

"WHY DON'T YOU COME AWAY WITH ME?" Carlo asked. His hand inched further up her thigh. He had Shae pressed into the wall. There was no desire in her to escape. He'd already kissed her lips clean of lipstick. And she was so hot for him that thoughts of propriety were dismissed. She got such a rush from sneaking around with him and their sex games.

"I can't leave," she said. She kissed his neck. His face buried into her shoulder and her legs wrapped around his waist.

"Not now, after. I know a place for us. We can be alone." They heard laughter it followed the cheering of the family.

"I need to come clean with Marietta. I'm tired of lying to her," she said.

"Let's play once more before the big confession, eh?"

She chuckled. "What's the name of this game?"

"Find the snake," he smiled.

Shae laughed. She laughed until tears brimmed in her eyes. "I think I'm good at this game!"

—*B*—

"WHERE'S GIO?" Benicia, the boss of the northeastern Neapolitan clan in the *Camorra* demanded. He had great influence amongst the municipalities of Saviano and Nola. He was of medium height. He had a large frame and belly that hung over his belt. "We've been kept waiting for close to an hour. *Che cavolo!*"

"Be silent, Benicia! It's his wife's birthday, we agreed to this meeting," said Mario Racchini whose clan operated in the neighborhoods of Secondigliano, Scampi, and Miano in Naples. He was known for his love of guns. Out of the other clan bosses, Racchini had extreme loyalty for the Battaglias, who had kept his position elevated over the years.

"It has been some time. It's disrespectful to keep us waiting," said Luigi Tacchi. His clan operated in the remote areas of Naples. He and several other lower end clan bosses were in attendance. Each of them felt envious of

Giovanni's claim of being the boss of all bosses.

"Signori, grazie per la sua pazienza," Dominic Battaglia said as he entered the room. Benicia stopped pacing. The other men stood.

"Where is he? *Che palle!* We've been pulled away from the party to wait?"

"You are free to leave. We can discuss business in your absence." Dominic replied.

Benicia pulled up his belt over his gut. He fell silent. Dominic cleared his throat and addressed the other men. "You know the purpose of the meeting."

"Santo the rat!" said Tacchi. "He's out of prison and back in your family."

"He is. But he is kept on a short leash I assure you."

"Still, there is one vow that should be never broken," Tacchi said. "He pissed all over it."

"And I will say that Santo kept his vow. Did he not? His complicity helped us squeeze the true traitor, Mottola, and send the *polizia* on a different chase. Too bad the punk hung himself in jail. We should have tied the noose."

"We are not convinced that he hasn't been corrupted. What if the *Polizia di Stato* got to him? What if he now plots with them? To bring your boss down?" Benicia asked with an accusatory finger pointed at Dominic.

"What does Lorenzo think of Santo joining the clans? Having rank?" Racchini asked. "As I recall he wanted a bullet in his skull."

Dominic masked his annoyance with a coy smile. "Lorenzo and I defer to Giovanni on this decision. You will hear from Giovanni soon." Dominic stepped closer. "I will ask you to consider the other side of the coin. If we do not bring Santo back into the family, what do you propose a man who has lost his life and identity is left with? I can assure it isn't loyalty."

"How would loyalty be a problem if we traded in his Battaglia leash for a *Camorra* noose?" asked Racchini.

Tacchi removed his cigar to light it. "We vote against this boys, and the noose is already around our own necks, and Giovanni holds the rope."

—*B*—

"At last. We're alone," Mirabella smiled.

"Bella…"

"I had no idea he would bring that portrait here." She walked away.

"Thank God he gave it to me in front of the family and not all of them. What was I to do or say? No thank you? We are Mancinis. Maybe it's time we let the rest of the world know? Stop with this war between you both. Peace? Right? Let's have peace."

"Are you done?" Giovanni asked.

She rubbed the nervous sweat from her hands down her sides. "I suppose. Yes. I'm done. What do you have to say?"

He waved off the concern. "I don't care to discuss Armando or his gift. It's time for me to give you mine."

"Really? Where is it?" she asked. He'd given her so much over the years, and still he managed to surprise her. She couldn't wait to see what he had for her now. Giovanni reached inside his suit jacket and removed a black letter envelope.

"Here," he handed it over.

"Oh, whatever could this be?" she chuckled. She fanned herself with the envelope. "Should I open it now? Huh?" She began to run her finger under the seal. Inside she found a commercial airline packet.

"Giovanni? What have you done?"

"This summer, after Dominic and Catalina wed, you, me, the kids, Lorenzo and your sister are going to America," he smiled.

"Are you serious?" she gasped.

"To Virginia. Your home," he clarified. "I want to see where you grew up. I want to meet the people who knew you."

"But I thought—"

"Dominic has been working on it. The Americans approved my Visa. I can enter the country. Lorenzo and I both can." He took her hand and kissed it. "You wanted the family to spend time together, wanted my focus on the kids. Well I think our children should know where Mama is from. We go for two weeks."

"I can't believe this!" she laughed. "Oh my God!" She leapt on him and he spun her around in his arms. He let go a deep chuckle. She kicked her feet excitedly.

"Thank you! Thank you! It's the best gift. Gio, it's the best gift ever!"

"Even better than a portrait of your lousy father?" he teased.

She laughed and bit his cheek. He squeezed her tight to his heart.

"Yes. Nothing can compare!"

—*B*—

"In a hurry?"

Carlo wiped the lipstick from his mouth with the back of his hand before he glanced back down the hall. Marietta marched toward him. She was angry. She was beautiful. And the combination made her tempting. He turned to continue on and avoid confrontation.

"Wait! Stop right there!" She demanded. "You missed the gift exchange for me and Mirabella. That was rude!"

"I'm not family," he reminded her. She was fucking gorgeous. The dress fit her curves perfectly. Her hair bounced long curls on her shoulders, and several fell over into her face. It was wild and curly like Lorenzo preferred it. Like he preferred it. The way her hips swayed, and her legs emerged from the front slit to her dress when she walked, made it impossible to not feel enticed. He chose to avert his gaze. The better idea was to keep walking.

"Oh, you're family and you know it. You used to be a man that respected the rules of *our* family. I guess that has changed too. Huh?"

"*Bon compleannu, Marietta,*" he said.

"Don't walk away from me damn it!" she hissed.

Shae fixed her dress and hurried. Carlo was addictive. Like the dance a moth did to an open flame she kept dancing around him hoping to not get burned. She needed to tighten up, and not attach so much emotion to a man as emotionally wounded as him. IF this were home she would have already put him on a rotation, and moved on to another conquest. It was Italy. The beauty from city to city, the wealth and prominence of the Battaglias, the danger and sexual adventures with Carlo, were all as addictive as any drug.

The only thing left to do was come clean. She needed to tell Marietta. She had no choice. Carlo wanted her to abandon the visit with her friend and spend time with him in Rome. Ciro would be training there for his next big fight.

When Shae opened the door she heard them. Carlo's voice forced her to stop and listen. Shae stepped back inside but kept the door open.

"You're doing this to piss me off! Going after my best friend! That's really scummy, even for you," Marietta said. "Even for a low-life like you."

"Not everything is about you, sweetheart." He gave a weary sigh.

"Since when?" Marietta challenged.

"Since you told me that you loved your husband and didn't want to have anything else to do with me. Remember?" he asked.

"Right. Because you care about what I want? Well here is what I want now. I want you to end it with Shae!" Marietta crossed her arms.

"Or what?" Carlo asked. He stepped in close. "What will you do?"

"I'll tell her the truth. You're using her to get to me. And she'll hate you for it." Marietta smirked.

"I give up! I'm done with this bullshit, Marietta," Carlo shouted.

She sidestepped him. She kept him from escaping and stepped so close he was forced to step back. "It's what you do. Right? Use and abuse women? That's who you are. Deny it! Go ahead! Deny it!"

"Deny what? That I'm in love with my best friend's wife? That if he ever found out he'd kill me, and then kill you for these fucking games we play? Do you want me to deny that? How about the fact I spend every day thinking about you?" he touched her face. She turned it away. "I'll admit it. For two years I've hurt anyone who has tried to get close to me, to keep from hurting you. Doesn't mean I'm not tired of being the big bad monster in your eyes." He lifted her chin and she couldn't resist looking up into his eyes. "Your turn. Admit the real reason you don't want me getting close to your friend? Can't, can you?"

He kissed the side of her mouth and then brushed his lips over hers. Her eyes fluttered shut as his tongue pushed inside. And then she shoved him off. He grabbed her hands and yanked her closer. This time he owned her and the kiss. And she didn't know how to stop it.

"No. I don't want to, Carlo. Stop it."

He grabbed her up into his arms and deep tongued her.

"I said stop it, damn it!" she broke off and slapped him. "Don't do that! Ever!"

"Then stay the fuck out of my life!" he shouted in her face. "Let's be honest, Marietta. You don't want to be in it. Shae is who I want, not you. Get over it. I have!" He shoved her out of his way and walked off.

Marietta put both her hands to her face and held back her tears.

"Shit! Shit! Shit!"

—*B*—

"SANTO?" GIOVANNI WALKED up to his old friend. Santo paced by the door and he looked desperate.

"They're in there, boss. I just arrived. Didn't want to walk in unless you, well unless invited. Should I go in there with you?"

Giovanni looked him over. "No."

"Boss? You said I could be heard. They don't trust me. Maybe if I can explain to them that I'm loyal it'll make them see me again. As a brother."

"I'll speak for you," Giovanni said.

Santo was a man that feared little. As were all the men in his inner circle. The thing with men, especially ones lethal enough to be high ranking in the Battaglia clan, was that none of them feared looking into the eyes of their Don. Because every man that served under him was loyal. Giovanni stared at Santo, and for the first time in countless years Santo could not meet his stare. This gave him pause.

"Is there something you need to say that I haven't heard?" Giovanni asked.

"No. I'm just anxious. I want to clear up any misunderstandings. Today decides my future."

"Time to get this over with!" Lorenzo announced. He approached them both. Santo glanced to Lorenzo. His gaze never returned to Gio. "What are you doing here? He can't be in there, Gio," said Lorenzo.

"I want a fair hearing."

"You get what you deserve, *pentito*!" Lorenzo said.

Santo took a step as if he'd swing at Lorenzo for being labeled a rat. Lorenzo arched a brow "Something you want to say, *pentito*?"

"Basta!" Giovanni said. "Lorenzo is right, you aren't needed here."

"Grazie, Gio," Santo took a step back. "I'll wait at the party. For whatever you decide," Santo said. He bowed his head and walked off. Lorenzo stepped to Giovanni's side and they watched Santo disappear out of the hall.

"Having doubts, cousin?" Lorenzo asked.

"I'm not sure," Giovanni replied. He went to the door and opened it. The Dons of the *Camorra* were gathered. All thirteen were present. But of course only the men who held the most wealth and influence were seated. The others stood in silence.

Giovanni addressed the three. "Benicia, Racchini, Tacchi."

The men nodded their hello.

"Thank you all for coming. I regret keeping you waiting," Giovanni said.

"Everyone is clear on why you wished to have this meeting," Dominic began.

"Some of us think it's premature, Gio. Santo hasn't proven himself." Benicia was the first to speak.

"The man has lost his family and clan," Racchini responded.

"Doesn't make him loyal," said Tacchi. "In fact it makes him weak. Have we not forgotten why Santo put us at risk? We've all been in meetings with him and Mottola. Where was his loyalty to Gio then?"

"No one has forgotten," Lorenzo replied. "Including us. Gio has reason to believe that Santo has paid his debts to the *Camorra*. That we should reward his dedication."

"I will speak on my beliefs," said Giovanni. Lorenzo nodded. Giovanni walked over to the window. He gazed out at the party. He could see his wife amongst her admirers. He again was reminded of how fragile their happiness remained.

"Santo isn't trustworthy," Giovanni said. The men exchanged baffled looks.

"Gio? We discussed this. Santo's punishment and rewards guarantee loyalty, not only from him, but from all our men. The clan bosses have to show compassion. What are the men to believe if they make a sacrifice? That there is no justice?"

"Benicia is right. Nothing is certain with Santo. I propose we give him the legs to walk on, for now. But each family, each clan, keeps a close watch on him. Including my own."

Giovanni ignored the shocked and confused look on Dominic's face. They knew better than to question him further on the subject in this forum. The men nodded in agreement. And after a brief discussion of other business affairs they left and returned to the party. Soon he was left with his brothers.

Lorenzo closed the door. "Gio, you surprise me."

"What is this, Gio? Why have you changed your opinion on Santo? We agreed he has paid enough for his mistakes. We agreed."

"Am I not allowed to change my fucking mind?" Giovanni asked.

"I meant no disrespect," Dominic began.

"Then shut the fuck up." Giovanni went to the bar and poured himself a drink. The gnawing feeling in his gut persisted. He turned with his whiskey glass in hand. "Something is off. I felt it earlier with Santo. He's desperate."

"Can you blame him?" Dominic grumbled.

"Desperate makes a man weak. And a weak man can be bought," Lorenzo agreed.

"But who made him weak? That's the fucking question!" Dominic said. "How many years of loyalty and sacrifice until he's broken?"

"I've decided. We keep a close eye on him. He rides with you, Lorenzo. Give him some false hope that it's to bring him back into position. But keep the family business closed to him, for now. It could be nothing."

"Or it could be everything, Gio," Lorenzo said. "It's what I've been saying all along. Santo is a snake. He is not to be trusted. Don't worry. I will appease him or put a bullet in his skull."

Lorenzo winked at Dominic and then left. Giovanni sat and stared into his drink. He loved all his brothers. It didn't feel right to question the motives of any of them. But Santo had a price.

"Carlo didn't lie." Giovanni said.

"About what?"

"Santo," Giovanni took a sip.

Dominic looked confused. Giovanni continued. "You were too young to remember when they took Carlo away. I went to Patri and asked him to help Carlo."

"And Patri said no," Dominic said. "I do remember."

"Yes. He did. But Lorenzo wouldn't let up. He loved Carlo. He knew it was a setup. We later found out that Santo could help him," Giovanni said.

"Are you saying that Lorenzo and Carlo's hatred of Santo is because Carlo went to jail for raping that girl?"

Giovanni nodded. "He didn't rape the girl. He was at Santo's house that night. His father had beat him up. He needed a place to hide from him. Mancini paid Santo's father, and Santo was forced to go to the prosecutors and lie. Or so he says. What choice did Santo have really?"

"He had a choice. We always have choices, Gio," Dominic said.

"True. It's why Lorenzo never trusts Santo not to be bought off."

"If you forgave him then, why convict him now?"

"The only time Santo was unable to look me in the eye in all the years

I've known him was when he was guilty in his heart." Giovanni finished his drink and looked up at Dominic. "I trust you the most, Domi. I love Lorenzo, but he is what he is. You're my conscience. My heart. Prove me wrong and I'll reward Santo. But I will not risk any of my men and family again if my gut tells me not to."

"Of course, Gio. You're right," Dominic said.

"Check into his story about the sick brother. Put a man on him and see where he goes, where he sleeps, eats, fucks, everything. You know what must be done."

Dominic nodded and left.

CHAPTER TEN

Who Can You Trust?

LORENZO HAD MANAGED TO REMAIN STANDING. All night he drank, smoke, laughed and argued with his friends, cousins, and uncles. The last of their guests left just before dawn. When he staggered into his room the shadows hadn't departed. He flipped up the light switch. The lamps on either side of the bed vanquished the dark. Marietta wasn't there.

"Damn it!" he grunted. He glanced to the bathroom and found she wasn't there as well. "Where the hell is my wife?"

—*B*—

"YOU STILL UP?" MARIETTA ASKED.

"I wanted to help. Is everyone gone?" Catalina yawned. She plopped down and kicked off her shoes. "What time is it?"

"Five or four, not sure," Marietta sat. She needed to find Lorenzo and have his men carry him to their bed. But she was in no mood to deal with his drunkenness. Carlo's words to her burned through the chambers of her heart all evening.

"Something wrong?" Catalina asked.

"I hear you and Domi have set a date?" Marietta asked.

"*Sí,* we have. It was time," she replied.

"I thought you wanted to wait another year, stay in Milano with Kyra and Jamie. Build up our offices in Paris—"

"It's time." Catalina cut her off. "No need to discuss it further."

"Then let's change the subject," Marietta said. She put her face in her hands. "I'm worried, Catalina."

"About what?"

"It's hard to explain." Marietta lifted her face from her hands. "I'm just concerned. When things are at their very best for me, somehow I manage to screw it up. I've already started to screw it up." She wished she could say more to clarify but the words were lodged in her throat. Catalina sat forward. She stared at Marietta with concern.

"I know it's hard to trust the good when you have had so much bad. I know it's easy to be tempted to test everything for proof of love. Trust me. Sometimes love is just enough. There is no dark cloud looming. This is our family being happy now. Enjoy it," Catalina said.

"I know. I know. You're right. Lorenzo and I are trying for a baby," Marietta smiled.

"I can't wait to see you as a mother," Catalina chuckled.

Marietta had to laugh at the thought. "You sure about marrying Domi? Now?"

"Am I sure?" Catalina tilted her head so her dark locks cascaded past her shoulder. She was so young and beautiful. Sometimes Marietta saw that beauty and was taken aback by it. Catalina let go a girlish giggle and closed her eyes as if she were wrapped up in Dominic's arms. "Of course I am. I have wanted to marry him since I was eleven years old." She opened her eyes and looked at Marietta. "It's time. I just wished my mother were alive to be part of my wedding. My real wedding. The one that lasts forever."

"Do you think your mother would approve?" Marietta asked.

"I don't know. I miss her. I miss her everyday." Catalina sat upright. Her eyes were bright with excitement. "I know she would approve of you! And she would love Mirabella for Gio. My mother had no prejudices. Not like the rest of us. She suffered so much scorn in her younger days, she could never be mean to anyone. And she always loved the good in people."

"She sounds like a sweetheart." Marietta smiled.

"Your turn. Do you think your mother would approve of Lorenzo?" Catalina asked.

"All I know about my mother is her pain and her murder. I would like to think that she's happy for me. I don't know what it would even be like to understand her."

Catalina stood. She stretched. "I'm going to bed. You coming?"

"In a minute." Marietta smiled. "Go on. I have a big brunch planned for us before we head home. Sleep in."

"I intend to," Catalina winked. She started to walk off and stopped. Marietta could sense her staring at her. When she looked over she saw concern on her face. "Did you know that Armando was going to gift you and Mirabella that portrait? Is that why you're worried?"

Before Marietta could answer Catalina continued. "Don't be. I was thinking about it tonight. Maybe I was wrong and you were right. Armando is your family too. Gio and Lo will have to accept it. Mirabella will have to accept it. Maybe together we help to make sure they do." Catalina looked at the covered portrait. "I think the gift was sweet. A nice gesture."

"Sweet?" Marietta frowned. "It's creepy how he did this. The damn thing looks like we actually posed for the portrait."

"But you said you loved it," she said.

"I only said that to avoid the awkwardness. To be a gracious hostess. The more I look at it I have to ask myself if Armando truly did this from his heart or for some other reason."

"Coming from a man like Armando Mancini, trust me, he doesn't have a gentler side," Catalina turned and left the room. Marietta hadn't thought of the gift. She had been too busy seething with jealousy over Shae and Carlo to be bothered. She stood and went to the corner of the private room. She removed the draped cover from the image.

Marsuvio Mancini stared into her eyes. Marietta stepped back and stared at the portrait. Her father had a cruel unwavering look. Armando had found a way of softening him. Marietta knew who she was because she was depicted as the fairer skinned of the two. She stood to the right of her father on the portrait, with her hand on his shoulder. Mirabella was to the left. She didn't touch Marsuvio in the portrait but she did smile in that gentle manner that her sister often did.

"Why are you in here?" Lorenzo asked from behind her.

She glanced back. He staggered into the room. He closed the door too abruptly and straightened his back. When Lorenzo did he stood taller than most men. But his bloodshot eyes, and that sly smile tilting the edges of his mouth, revealed plenty. He was drunk.

"What do you think of this?" Marietta asked. She turned her gaze back to the portrait

"I think we should throw it in the trash," Lorenzo said. "Let's go to bed. I want to fuck."

"I'm serious, Lorenzo. I really think it has meaning. How did he get our likeness so well done? It looks like we posed for it. Is this how you remember Mancini? He was a powerful man, larger than life. Wasn't he?"

"He was an asshole." Lorenzo said as he stepped behind her. "I believe he's part Spanish."

Marietta ignored the comment. Lorenzo was the only one who constantly mocked or commented on who was a legitimate Sicilian. But he never cared to explain to her how he too had blue eyes like his bastard cousin.

"We're all mixed with something. The point is, he's my father. And Armando was very generous to give us this. Look! It has the Mancini crest."

Lorenzo pushed the portrait and it fell over to the side. Then it dropped flat on the ground. Shocked, Marietta whirled on him to shove him in retaliation. But he caught her by the wrist. "I told you, Marie, you can't trust the fucking Mancinis. Especially Armando. He's a *figlio di puttana*!"

"You're jealous, and an ass," she shouted.

He grabbed her by the hair and pulled so hard her chin was forced up. Marietta grimaced. She closed her eyes when the tip of his tongue traced her neck to the diamond stud in her earlobe.

"You're drunk!" she said and fought harder. This time she got him off her. He stumbled back. She slapped him. His inebriation reduced his balance and he fell to his hands and knees. "You're such an asshole!"

Lorenzo laughed. He looked up and grinned at her. Marietta rolled her eyes and started to smile. He managed to stand. He wiped his hand down his face. He put up both his hands in surrender as if she were going to strike him again, and then laughed harder. He went to the portrait that was lying facedown. He stood it upright and placed it back against the wall. And then he dusted it with his hands.

"Welcome to the family, you fucking cocksucker," he said to Mancini and gave him a salute.

"Let's go to bed." She turned for the door but he caught her by the arm and pulled her up against his chest. "You smell so good, *bambina,* and your hair. Yes. Your hair smells good too."

"Lorenzo, stop pulling on my hair!" she pushed at him again. She tried to turn in his arms to lead him away, but his grip was too strong. She struggled with him as they both went down to their knees. "Jesus! Why must you be such a jackass?"

"Happy birthday, Marie," he kissed her face and neck as he pinned her beneath him.

"Lorenzo, stop!" She kicked her legs and tried to buck underneath him. She broke free and grabbed his face. "Stop," she said. "It's a turn off."

He grabbed her wrists and pinned them above her head. His focus became the rise and fall of her breasts beneath him. "They're so pretty. Your tits, Marie, I fucking love them. Will they get bigger when you become pregnant?"

"Shut up!" she said.

"I love them. I love your pussy, sweet, sweet, pussy!"

"Lorenzo, you're heavy!"

"Your skin, and your thighs. I love your fat ass. I love to fuck you in your ass."

"Stop it!"

"I've fucked a lot of women, Marie."

She stopped struggling. She lifted her gaze back up to him.

"I haven't fucked anyone else since I met you. No woman has had everything I wanted. Not even Fabiana. No woman." He kissed her face. "There is no woman like you, Marie. My dick gets hard when I'm sleep just because you're next to me. Gio said Mirabella was different when she was pregnant."

She laughed. Lorenzo laughed. He dropped his head and laughed. "He said her body felt different. He said he loved her more. It'll be like that won't it? And your breasts. I'll suck on them every night." He dropped his face between her breasts and started to bite and nibble on them.

"Damn it that hurts, Lo!" she started to fight him off her again. He lifted his head to her screaming.

"Do you love me?" he asked.

"Don't be stupid." She shoved at his immovable shoulders. Her heart beat hard, and then harder in her chest. Even though she doubted her ability to protect her love for him, she could never deny it. She kept her expression carefully neutral when she answered.

"Yes, Lo, I love you. With all my heart," she said.

He looked up at the portrait. His gaze hardened as he stared at the man who was her father. "You cannot trust Armando. I'm the only man you need, Marie. The only man you trust."

"Only you. Now stop," she said. "You're drunk. You stink with liquor breath. Let me take you to bed."

Lorenzo grinned. He dropped his face to the side of her neck as he clawed at her designer original. He forced himself between her thighs. He was in her. Swift and hard he thrust into her. Marietta held to his sides to try to slow down the invasion. She turned her face away to avoid his sloppy kisses. She locked eyes with her father. He stared at her from the portrait. Was it her imagination or did he smirk?

—*B*—

"CIAO?" SHE WHISPERED.

"Ciao," he answered.

"What are you doing in here?" Mirabella asked. "I thought you had a meeting?"

"I missed them," Giovanni carried Eve to the bed. He put her on top of the mattress gently. Mirabella adjusted the covers over the kids. The bed was large enough for both her and Giovanni to join them.

"I had a talk with her while I waited for you," Giovanni said.

"Good," she eased her arm around his waist.

"Eve loves Captain Hook, but not as much as she loves Papa," Giovanni smiled.

"Maybe we should stay a few more days. Go out on the lake. You and I both have been distracted," Mirabella said.

"True," he kissed her brow. "Unfortunately we need to return home."

"Why?" she asked. "Why so soon?"

For close to two years the tension in the family had eased. If it returned it only meant one inevitable truth, there was more conflict and danger in his world. "Should I be worried, Giovanni?"

"Never, Bella. Cautious. Always. But as long as I'm alive and by your side, you should never be worried," he replied.

She lowered her arm from around his waist. She took his hand and squeezed it. "They are so beautiful," she said.

"Like their mother." He turned her and she came into his arms. His hand held hers and the other was snug around her waist. They danced to their own music. And she smiled with happiness.

"We're going to America!" she silently cheered.

"You will show me where you grew up," he kissed her brow.

"And where my grandfather preached. I'm so excited. I wanted to tell Marietta, but I'll wait. I plan to call home. There's an aunt and cousins that I haven't spoken to in many… many years. They probably have questions since we've gone public."

"I find that curious, Bella," Giovanni said.

"Why?" she asked.

"You never speak of your family there. Why haven't you called them to introduce your sister?" he asked. "Do you keep in contact with any of them at all?"

"We're not that close. Don't worry, I'll introduce everyone soon enough. Look at me I'm rambling."

He kissed her cheek. She squeezed him and felt so much love swell in her heart it made her light on her feet. He spun her in a half circle and they continued to dance.

"I love my life," she told him. She danced in his arms with her face pressed to his chest.

The Next Day –

"Are you avoiding me?" Carlo asked.

Shae kept walking. She managed to dodge both him and Marietta by returning to her room well before the party ended last night. Brunch was at noon, and so many Battaglias remained, she blended and disappeared in the chaos. Where Marietta had gotten off to she didn't know. She didn't care. She hitched her purse higher up her arm and started toward the cars. The Battaglias were on the move. All of them now headed back to Sorrento.

"Shae?" Carlo touched her hand. "Can you look at me?"

The first reaction she had was to turn and shove her fist into his face. Anger hit her like an electric surge. How she managed to resist was a mystery.

Instead she glared at him. He looked stricken by the anger he saw on her face. The damn hypocrite. Here she was foolish enough to think he was more than the murdering thug they whispered he was behind his back. He'd made a fool of her.

"Stay the hell away from me," she said.

Carlo stepped back. When she glanced up before getting inside the car she saw Marietta behind Carlo. The two of them watched her. She cut her gaze away and eased inside.

"What's wrong with the wild one?" Renaldo asked.

"*Vaffanculo!* Fuck off," Carlo grunted. He had no time for the bullshit. Ciro was his focus. They were meeting today to talk to the commissioner of the IBF. The fight would be in Naples. Giovanni wanted the match closer to home. Thanks to Father Nicosia it was a strong possibility. That was something Carlo hadn't shared with Gio. He understood why his boss didn't trust the priest, but he had to make moves, and he needed to make them quickly.

"Wait," Renaldo matched his stride. "I need to know about the venue. Where in Napoli will it be?"

"Why?" Carlo frowned.

"The boss. He's giving me my position back. He likes the way I handled the fashion show. I'm in charge of security for him."

"Bully for you," Carlo snickered.

"Not really. My woman wants me in Milano. I'll have to convince her to move into the small villa I'm building near the Amalfi. We'll be staying close to the coast now."

Carlo still didn't care.

"The China man is out there," Renaldo said as they got in the car.

"Oh, I get it. The challenger is Chinese so now Gio thinks it's some kind of link to that Kyoko piece of shit."

"His name is Kei Hyogo and he is out of prison." Renaldo turned over the engine and steered the car in line with the rest.

"*Che minchia!* It's bullshit! The fight was arranged by me. I've done all the necessary checks. The challenger has been out there for nearly four years. Longer than Ciro. He's had over a hundred and fifty matches."

"He's connected to the Triad," Renaldo said.

"Chao Lee? He's in the Triad? *Porca puttana!* So the fuck what? I did the necessary checks! Father Nicosia doesn't fuck with the Triad. He's been working with me," Carlo shouted.

"Gio doesn't want the priest involved," Renaldo said.

"Gio has left it to me. The priest's payment comes out of my salary. It's my deal."

Renaldo nodded. Carlo hated Renaldo's cool manner. He sulked in his seat trying to solve the mystery as to why Shae would be angry with him. And there was only one reason. Marietta. *Did Marietta threaten her?* He chewed on his bottom lip. He'd have to speak with her and clear it up.

"I need the information for the venue," Renaldo repeated.

"I already said it once, I'll say it again. Fuck you," Carlo flipped him off.

Renaldo chuckled.

"SOMETHING WRONG?" Mirabella asked her sister.

Gianni was in the car seat between them. Her other babies were riding with Rocco and Zia behind them. Gianni cried until she relented and kept him with her. Lorenzo was behind the wheel and Giovanni was in the front passenger seat. Both of them laughed and joked like brothers. They completely ignored the battle to calm Gianni in the back seat. It was finally won when Mirabella found her son's pacifier.

"Hey?" Mirabella snapped her fingers in front of Marietta's face.

"I'm sending Shae home," Marietta said.

"Oh? I thought she had another week with us?" Mirabella asked.

"I think she's over-stayed her welcome. She can't be trusted," Marietta said.

"Wait? I'm confused. What did you say?" Mirabella asked.

"I said she can't be trusted."

"What has she done?" Mirabella asked.

"For starters I caught her listening in on conversations she shouldn't have been twice," said Marietta.

Mirabella chuckled.

"What's so funny?"

"You. Here, sweetie," Mirabella gave Gianni his toy truck to play with. He again threw it on the floor. He clapped his hands and grinned with his pacifier tucked in the side of his mouth. He thought it was a game.

"Me? Why am I funny?" Marietta asked.

"Everyone eavesdrops, Marietta. Even you when you came to stay with us. Hell, how do you think I knew you liked to dance around naked like some stripper for your husband?"

"Hmph! You weren't complaining when I was teaching you lessons," Marietta reminded her.

"And I still need practice," Mirabella said.

They both laughed. Giovanni looked back at them and they reduced their laughs to giggles. Mirabella shook her head smiling. "All I'm saying is, the temptation is great in that big ol mausoleum we call home. Especially for strangers."

"She's fucking Carlo," Marietta said through clenched teeth.

"I beg your pardon?" Mirabella asked.

Marietta cut her eyes at her. "You heard me."

"Let's talk about it later," Mirabella whispered.

"No need to discuss it. When we get to Melanzana I'm booking her a flight and sending her ass home."

"She's your friend. You barely got a chance to spend time with her. I can deal with Giovanni," Mirabella said. "It's not like I haven't had practice."

"This isn't the same as Renaldo and Kyra," Marietta said.

"Why isn't it? It's a dumb rule anyway. Cecilia and Nico are dating and—"

"It's not that. I think the two of them already know." She tossed her chin up at Giovanni and Lorenzo. "I told Lo this morning and he just gave that stupid grin of his. They know," Marietta whispered. "Like you said I haven't spent much time with her. I'm sure she has things to do. It'll be fine."

"You still haven't told me why you want her gone. Did you two fight about Carlo?"

"What? No! No! I don't care about Carlo!" she said too loud. Marietta noticed Lorenzo's eyes flipped up to the rearview mirror and he looked at them.

"Okay. Sorry," Mirabella said.

"I've been feeling a little tired. I guess we've been going so fast lately, I need to slow down." Marietta sighed. She dropped her head back and closed her eyes. "Lorenzo wants this baby. I need to focus on getting pregnant."

"Okay, sweetie," Mirabella agreed.

Gianni passed his bottle to Marietta. He said something neither of them could understand. Marietta smiled. She leaned over and kissed his lips. She then kissed his forehead. "Did you hear? No travel."

"Yes. Giovanni said it should be fine in a couple of weeks. We'll go back to Milano before summer comes."

Marietta nodded. The car steered up the sloped hilltop road, and she knew they neared the airport. She tried to change her attitude. She didn't want to have one when she confronted Shae.

Melanzana –

Catalina loved home. She had missed everything, from Ana's cooking, to lounging by the pool with Mirabella and the kids. She even missed the horses. Too much time was spent in Milan, and not enough in Sorrento. She tossed her purse to her bed and the men dragged in her luggage.

"Grazie," she said to the men and they left.

She heaved an affronted sigh. The thought of unpacking bored her. Catalina sat on the edge of the bed. She kicked off her shoes and scooted back into her stack of pillows. It felt nice and comfortable. Her schedule had been non-stop for weeks. Some time under the covers with a good book would be a lovely change.

The phone rang before her eyes closed. She glanced over in search of it. Her private line was on the dial list of everyone on their staff. For a brief minute she considered ignoring it. But she reached for it despite her weariness.

"Pronto?" she answered.

"Catalina. *Ciao, bella.* It's Armando," said the person.

"Why are you calling? How did you know we were home?" she asked.

"Marietta phoned me to say thank you for the birthday gift. She told me you returned to Sorrento."

Catalina turned over on her side. She closed her eyes and exhaustion weighed the lids to her eyes. Armando had the kind of soothing voice that was very easy on a girl's ears.

"What do you want?" she yawned.

"When a beautiful woman asks a man what he wants he better have an answer."

"I'm hanging up."

"Wait. Catalina, don't hang up," he said.

"Don't flirt with me."

"Understood. I called to thank you again. Because of you my sisters are now open to new relationships with me. I'm grateful."

"You've thanked me twice already, Armando. No need."

"When do you return to Milano? I've extended my stay. Maybe you will allow me to take you to dinner?"

"That's a flirt!" she said.

"No. That's an offer to take you to dinner."

"Listen to me, Armando. I do want Marietta and Mirabella to learn to accept you. I think you and Giovanni need to both work at a new relationship. But please leave me out of it. Don't call me again. Don't stop by my office. Don't try to be overly gracious. I'm not Marietta or Mirabella. I know who you are. I know what friendship between you and I would mean."

"If you know who I am then you know I won't easily give up on something I want."

"Keep calling and I'll tell Domi."

"My question to you, beautiful, is why haven't you told him already?"

She hung up the phone. "*Che stronzo!*" she cursed. She threw the phone back on the night table and turned over to let sleep claim her.

—*B*—

"WE NEED TO TALK." Marietta walked into Shae's room without knocking. She found her friend seated in a chair by the window. Shae stared out of it. Her luggage was unpacked.

Good, thought Marietta. She'd already confirmed that an evening flight was available for Shae to leave for America.

"Yah. I guess we do," Shae said. She stood and faced Marietta. Gone was the friendly smile or sassy charm that she loved about Shae. She looked at Marietta with equal distrust. She put her hands to her hips. "I was waiting on you," she said.

Marietta tensed. It was a natural response to Shae's defensive stance. She knew Shae like she knew herself. Whenever her best friend faced off with an enemy she had her hands to her hips.

"You lied to me," Marietta began.

"Looks like we lied to each other," Shae said.

"To each other? What the hell does that mean? I asked you to respect my family, my home, by not seducing these men. And all the while you've been sneaking around behind my back!"

"Same ole Mae," Shae smiled. "It's everybody but her." She looked Marietta over like she used to whenever Marietta tried to elevate her status from a stripper. "You know you almost had me fooled. All that talk about being changed, and happily married. It was kind of funny watching you run around that fancy house of yours and imitate your sister. But I know how Mae pretends. I shouldn't have forgotten!"

"I am happily married. I don't need to imitate my sister because she's part of me. This is my world. Do you remember yours? Managing whores for modeling gigs that pay you how much I spend on a pair of shoes."

Shae laughed. "Chump change was your game, Mae. Not mine. I'm not a whore. I'm a businesswoman. And you're a fraud."

"I don't give a shit what you think about me. This isn't about me." Marietta clarified. "This is about you and Carlo."

"Me? He doesn't give a fuck about me! Your American friend who's a whore! You and Carlo started your affair long before I came!" Shae shouted.

"A-a-a what? Affair? What the hell has he been telling you?"

She shook her head. "I remember when you first showed up at the club. You were green, awkward, and homely. A fucking joke. I taught you how to survive, and now you look down on me? Bitch please! Let's get it straight, Mae. We aren't that fucking different. When the rubber hits the road we are still the best whores in the business. Only thing is, I do it with generous boyfriends, and you do it with your husband's best friend!"

"Watch your fucking mouth!" Marietta shoved her.

Shae's eyes glistened with tears. "Why, Mae? I've always been the one to give it to you straight. Why do I have to watch my mouth now? Afraid someone will tell that big bad husband of yours your fucking his boy?"

"I never got as low as you. I didn't sleep with anyone for money, now or then. And I have never cheated on my husband. NEVER!"

"You took their money and sold your body every night, but the first thing that comes out of your mouth is to call me a whore! There is no difference!" Shae shouted.

"There's a big difference! I did what I had to do for survival. You did it because you got off on being some Queen Bitch." Marietta took another threatening step. "Some mother bee teaching us how to use our bodies and hide our pain."

Shae wiped tears. Marietta could see her words cut deep. But her heart was pumping adrenaline through her veins. Shae had accused her of something and she wanted to get to the bottom of it. "I have never had an affair with Carlo!"

"That's right. Because that's not your style! *Mae the tease*. That's your style!" Shae shouted. "You just string him along. Toy with his feelings. Keep him confused and on his knees begging for a chance. Huh, Mae? Like you did Earl, Ray, Eric, Chip!"

"Shut up, Shae," Marietta clenched her fist.

"No! You don't even know how fucked up in the head Carlo really is. Every one of you whisper and snicker about him being some kind of animal behind his back. Then throw him a stick for him to fetch and bring back."

"Shut up!"

"You sure as hell got him convinced he's a monster. In your little game of tease and catch me, did you ever notice how he is the one left with nothing? And we both know how it feels to have no one. The man can barely touch a woman without being aggressive. Sound familiar?"

"I don't care! It's none of my business! And it's none of yours!"

Shae smirked. "Is that why I saw you in the hall kissing him?"

The invisible band of restraint holding Marietta back snapped. She charged Shae. Neither woman was ready for the sudden eruption of violence. It sent them both crashing into the tallboy dresser. It nearly came down on them both. On the ground they kicked and clawed at each other. Marietta kept trying to gain leverage, to keep her hands on her throat.

Women screamed. Catalina shot up in bed. At first she thought the screams were in her head. She was off the bed and running. Every time she's ever heard screams in her home disaster followed. From Fabiana's death, to Mirabella's collapse in Sicily, the worst always came after a scream. In the hall it only took her seconds to find the door the screaming came from. She threw it open and paused. Shae and Marietta were fighting. All she could see was arms thrashing, legs kicking, hair pulling.

"*Mama mia!* Stop!" Catalina ran inside. She grabbed at Marietta first. Shae was underneath, fighting to get Marietta off her. Catalina tried to pull them apart but it was crazy how wild and strong they both were. "Stop it! Stop!"

Two of the men ran inside. One grabbed Catalina and threw her to the side, and then they both went for the fighting women. They literally had to drag them apart.

"You fucking hypocrite!" Shae shouted at her. "Calling me the whore when you're the one sneaking around this damn place to fuck Carlo!"

Catalina's heart seized. She looked to Marietta in shock for a response.

"I'll kill you, bitch! I'll kill you!" Marietta battled hard to get to her. Ringo had to tighten his hold on her. But Marietta's kick landed its mark. Shae was hit in the stomach and gagged with agony. Shae coughed and started shouting in retaliation.

"Tell your family how long you and Carlo have been sneaking around. How you take birth control to keep from getting pregnant. Fool your husband so you can fuck his best friend! Tell them!"

"You fucking liar! I'll kill you! I'll kill you!" Marietta screamed.

Panic set in and Marietta couldn't think through what to do next. All she knew was she had to get her to shut up. The men heard Shae. Soon everyone would be in this room. Some things can't be said or unsaid.

"Shut up! The both of you!" Catalina warned. "Stop it! Let her go!" Catalina said to Eduardo who held Shae by the arms. He did as he was asked. Shae backed up, but she had a wild look in her eyes. One of her earrings was gone. Her face had scratches on the cheeks. Catalina stepped in front of her. "Go in the bathroom. Fix your face." Catalina said. "Please! You're bleeding."

Shae backed away touching her cheek, and then checked her fingers for evidence of blood. She turned and went into the bathroom.

"Go get the Donna. Tell her it's an emergency. Do not say anything to my brother, Eduardo. This is for the Donna! Do you understand me?"

He nodded and left.

"Let me the fuck go!" Marietta yelled. She bit Ringo on the arm and he howled in pain. He was forced to release her. "I want that bitch out of here now!" Marietta charged for the bathroom door. Catalina stepped in front of her.

"Stop it!" Catalina said. "Calm down."

"I never slept with Carlo!"

"*Che cazzo dici!* Shut up. Don't say another word." Catalina warned. "I'm serious. Stay silent."

Marietta pulled at her own hair with both hands as she paced away. It looked as if she did so to calm herself, but it was having no effect. She breathed hard and was flushed with anger. Catalina noticed Ringo held his arm. Marietta had bit him hard enough to draw blood.

"*Merda!*" Catalina said. "Ringo, go find Zia. Tell her... tell her... tell her I sent you. Tell her she needs to take care of your arm. And listen to me, Ringo. Until the Donna has a chance to deal with this, keep your fucking mouth closed. Domi, none of them need to know about the fight. It's ... it's women's business. Okay?"

Ringo was very close to Carlo. He worshipped him. The men knew what an accusation like the one Shae leveled would mean for Carlo. He looked to be relieved to have the orders to not say anything.

"Go!" Catalina pushed him. Ringo walked out holding his bloody arm.

"I didn't do anything," Marietta began to cry. "She's fucking lying."

"Don't say anything else. Just wait until Mirabella gets here. *Cavoli!* I need to think."

"What the hell is going on in here?" Mirabella walked in. Marietta and Catalina both whirled around. The destruction in the room only then became clear to Catalina. She was still reeling from what she overheard. Everything had either been broken on the floor or smashed. A chair was turned over. The sheets were dragged off the mattress. Mirabella closed the door.

"Marietta? Explain this." Mirabella demanded.

"Stay there. No more fighting!" Catalina warned Marietta. Mirabella walked over to her sister. She took her in her arms and forced a hug on her. Catalina went to the bathroom door and opened it. Shae was at the sink tending to the long scratch under her eye.

"Come out please," Catalina said.

Shae glanced up at Catalina in the mirror.

"Nothing will happen to you. I swear it. Just come out," Catalina said. "Mirabella wants to talk to you."

Shae did as she was asked.

"I want her gone!" Marietta shouted. "Out of this house! Now!"

"Not until someone tells me what happened," Mirabella demanded. She let go of Marietta and smoothed back her hair. Her sister refused to look at her. "Talk to me?"

"I don't know," Catalina began. "I was taking a nap when I heard screaming. I came in here and they were fighting. It was crazy. Eduardo and Ringo were the first to arrive. They pulled them apart. And then—"

"She's a liar!" Marietta shouted.

"I don't lie! Why the fuck would I need to?" Shae shouted. "It is not a lie! I saw you both kissing! You told me about the birth control pills!"

"Fucking bitch!" Marietta charged at Shae, but Catalina tackled her and brought her down on the bed.

"Stop it!" Mirabella shouted. Catalina and Marietta stopped wrestling with each other. "I mean it. Stop it now, Marietta, or I'll go get Giovanni and Lorenzo and have them sort it out!"

Marietta's eyes stretched with fear. She pushed Catalina off her and scooted off the bed. "She's lying on me."

"I am not!" Shae insisted.

Mirabella turned on Shae. "You are a guest in my home, and my sister's home. You will either shut the hell up, or I'll have someone make you be quiet. Do you understand what that means?"

Shae narrowed her eyes. "Are you threatening me?"

"I don't make threats. I don't need to," Mirabella said.

Shae glanced from Mirabella to Catalina, who stood glaring at her. She threw up her hands. "You're all fucking crazy. All of you."

Mirabella arched a brow. Shae became silent. Catalina was grateful because she truly didn't know what else to do.

Mirabella turned to Marietta. "What happened? Talk fast before one of our husbands show up!"

Marietta began to cry and shook her head. Mirabella turned to Shae. "What did you accuse her of?"

"Oh now you want me to speak?" Shae replied.

"Answer me!" Mirabella demanded. "What did you accuse her of?"

"I saw them," Shae said.

"Saw who?" Mirabella asked.

"Her and Carlo kissing in the hall. They're having an affair. And she's been taking birth control pills so she wouldn't get caught with a baby with two daddies!" Shae spat.

"That's not true!" Marietta leapt to her feet.

The accusation knocked the breath out of Mirabella. She turned and looked at her sister with disgust, shock, and outrage. If it was true then Marietta would have put Carlo's life in danger, and her own.

"I swear it's not true!" Marietta wept. "Please don't tell Lorenzo that lie. It'll cost me my marriage. I swear I didn't do anything. I swear it."

"Who heard her, Catalina?" Mirabella asked.

"Eduardo and Ringo. Remember, I told you. Marietta bit Ringo. His arm was bleeding. I sent him to Zia."

"Shit. Oh shit," Mirabella said. She put her hands to her head. She felt dizzy. "Oh shit."

"It's not true!" Marietta swore to them both.

"It doesn't fucking matter if it's true!" Catalina shouted. "She said it in front of the men. The accusation alone will get Carlo killed."

"Killed?" Shae said. "I didn't mean to—"

"*Sei stupida!* You didn't mean what?" Catalina whirled on her. "To get him killed? Too late, bitch!"

"Fuck you!" Shae shouted through her tears. "This isn't my fault. Marietta attacked me. Came in here and confronted me for dating the man. She was the one! Not me!"

Marietta tried to swing at Shae again. This time it was Mirabella who blocked her. She shoved her sister so hard Marietta hit the window with a loud smack.

"Are you insane? Are you?" Mirabella asked through her tears.

"I didn't do it," Marietta wept. "I... Carlo and I... we kissed. Once. And not in the hall!" she said the latter to Shae. "I was telling him to not sneak around here with Shae, and he kissed my cheek. Not my mouth. Before then... I was drunk and—"

"And what?" Mirabella yelled.

"And nothing, Mirabella! You were in the hospital. I thought you were dead. He found me and I was drunk. We kissed. That was it. And for two years nothing has happened between us. He and I are friends. That's all."

"And the birth control?" Catalina asked.

Marietta sniffed. "I told Shae because I thought she was my friend. I didn't want to have a baby. But I do now. I stopped taking them. I told her that too!"

Mirabella looked over at Shae. She looked back at Marietta. She didn't know what to believe. "Catalina, take Shae to your room. And… uh…"

"I'm leaving. I'm going home," Shae said. "I don't want to be here."

"Oh, I agree. You are leaving. But first we need to clear this up. Make sure that no one breathes a word of it to my husband, and yours!" Mirabella pointed at her sister. "Take her to your room, and then find Ringo and Eduardo and have them come to the room."

"What are you going to do?" Marietta asked.

Mirabella approached her sister. Marietta could barely look her in the eye. She hugged her and whispered in her ear. "I will always protect you. But I swear to God if you're lying to me I won't be able to."

"I never slept with Carlo. I swear it," Marietta said.

No matter if it was true or not, Mirabella loved her sister. She wouldn't let her world be destroyed. "Go to your room and clean yourself up. Then meet us in Catalina's room."

She lifted Marietta's face and held it with both hands. "No more fighting and running your mouth. Don't say anything. Do you understand?" Marietta looked back at the other two women. "Does everyone understand?"

"Yes," Catalina said.

"Yes," Shae said.

"Then go!" she said.

Shae took her suitcases with her. She would change her clothes and fix herself in Catalina's room. When they were gone Mirabella let Marietta go.

"It's just me. You have to be honest with me. Did you sleep with Carlo?"

"I swear on our mother I never did," Marietta repeated.

"Did you want to?" Mirabella asked.

"What kind of question is that?"

"Answer me. Did you want to?"

The look of shock in Marietta's eyes was all the answer Mirabella needed. "If you ever cross that line it will destroy our family. I can't control Giovanni, and you can't control Lorenzo. Not on this. If you care about Carlo, in any way, stop this. Don't flirt with him. Don't encourage him. If he's coming down the hall you go the other way. Do you understand me?"

"I understand. I never will. Never again. I told Carlo I love my Lorenzo. I do love him. I just mess things up sometimes."

"It's okay. Lorenzo likes your crazy, remember?" Mirabella smiled. Marietta managed to smile and nod for her. "Don't cry, sweetie. We'll fix it. Together. I got an idea. You pray it works."

Marietta nodded in agreement.

"Go change."

Marietta left.

Mirabella exhaled. She looked around the room in disbelief. One lie always led to another. What could she really do but be the keeper of this lie?

—$\mathscr{B}$—

RINGO WAS THE LAST TO ARRIVE. And Mirabella breathed a sigh of relief that Zia didn't accompany him. She looked to the women. They were all given instructions on what to do. The only person Mirabella couldn't trust fully was Shae, and her role was the most important.

"Come in, Ringo," Mirabella said.

He walked in and saw Eduardo waiting. Mirabella nodded for him to take a seat. He did so. There was a last minute change of plans. They had to reconvene in Catalina's room to keep the situation contained. The kids were in Mirabella's room sleeping. Catalina sat on the bed next to Shae. Marietta stood at the window looking out. Mirabella cleared her throat.

"You both were our heroes today, dealing with this nonsense." Mirabella laughed. The men exchanged a look with each other and then glanced to the Donna with a slow nod.

"Marietta?" Mirabella said.

Here sister glanced from the window to Ringo and then Eduardo. She sighed. "I'm sorry, Ringo, for biting your arm."

"No problema, signora." Ringo nodded to Marietta.

"Things got out of hand. A misunderstanding between me and my... my friend. I behaved badly. I apologize to you both."

The men nodded.

"You know the rules." Mirabella addressed the men. "None of you are to date or mess around with the women in this family. Right?"

The men nodded.

"Shae and Carlo have been dating. And it happened against the wishes of Giovanni and this house. Marietta found out about it. They argued." Mirabella glanced to Shae. "Can you please explain to them the things you said earlier?"

"I was angry. Marietta was throwing me out of the house. I wanted to upset her. To hurt her. So I said things that weren't true. She never had an affair with Carlo. I thought she was jealous of my friendship with Carlo and accused her. It wasn't true. I apologized to the Battaglias for the insult."

Earlier Mirabella explained the hard truths to Shae. She either cooperated or the man she claimed to care about would be destroyed. It was pretty clear to them all that Shae had to recant everything she said.

"So you can see why I've decided this matter is settled," Mirabella said. "There is no need to upset your bosses about this. It was a petty fight amongst the women. And it's over. *Capice?*"

"*Sí,* Donna. We understand," they both said.

The men started to the door. Eduardo hesitated. He glanced to Marietta. Mirabella noticed the conflict in his eyes.

"Something wrong, Eduardo?" Mirabella asked

He shook his head no and left. Catalina stood as soon as the door closed.

"Do you think they believe it? That they won't say anything?" Shae asked.

"They won't say anything," Catalina said. "They better not.

—*B*—

RINGO AND EDUARDO STARTED FOR THE STAIRS. Eduardo grabbed Ringo's arm and stopped him. "Do you believe the Donna?"

"About Carlo and Marietta?" Ringo answered. "Yes. Carlo would never betray Lorenzo. Never. And I've seen him with the woman Shae. It was a stupid fight. Forget about it."

"But the birth control," Eduardo said. "The Donna didn't mention it. None of them did. She isn't pregnant. It's been over two years," he said.

Ringo nodded. "I don't trust her. She's not like the Donna. Some of us think she's not really her sister."

Eduardo nodded. "The Donna did not forbid us from mentioning the birth control."

Ringo grabbed Eduardo by the collar. "Don't mention any of it. It could backfire on you, and then on me. Just forget it happened. Do you understand?"

Eduardo shoved him off. He threw up his hand in an obscene gesture and walked away. Ringo looked back down the hall. Whether the birth control was a lie or not, it wasn't their business.

—𝓑—

"*ANDIAMO,* CATALINA. Let's leave them to talk." Mirabella said.

"Are you crazy? They'll kill each other!" Catalina objected.

"It's okay. We need to finish this," Marietta said. "We've had worse fights. Trust me."

Shae nodded in agreement. "We'll be fine."

Mirabella took Catalina by the hand and walked her out.

"I'm sorry," Shae said. "I heard you two in the hall and I thought the worst."

"No, you saw me kiss him. That was me at my worst." Marietta sighed. "What you said about Carlo was true. About me. I've always teased and pushed men away. I even do with him. I don't know why. But I do."

"My psychiatrist said it's the 'daddy syndrome'," Shae smiled. "We both have it. Remember?"

Marietta gave a hollow laugh. "Yea, I got daddy issues alright." She looked up into Shae's eyes. "I never cheated on Lorenzo. The kiss was wrong. I regret it. But I never slept with Carlo. I love my husband with everything in me, Shae."

"Then why even risk anything with Carlo?" Shae asked.

"I don't know. I've been selfish, controlling, meddlesome, jealous. I can't explain it."

Shae shook her head. "Carlo's a good guy, Mae. You're right, I do sneak around here and listen in on your family. The things they say about him. You wonder why he feels like an outsider? Everyone, even his friends, treat him like he's a madman. And he is. Do you know why? This place? What they do. It could drive any of them mad. Lorenzo and Giovanni are lucky to have you and your sister. Carlo has no one."

"You care about him?" Marietta asked. "How much time did you two spend together?"

"Every chance we got. Jamie and Kyra were my cover," Shae confessed.

Marietta rolled her eyes.

"I could easily fall in love with him," Shae said.

"You? Love?" Marietta scoffed. "Not likely."

"*Amore!*" Shae grinned and threw her hands up as if giving praise. "I learned the word. If I can learn Italian I can learn how to be in love and not fuck it up."

"Then date him. You don't have to be here to see him," Marietta said.

"I can't," Shae said.

"Why? I said I don't care."

"I think he's in love with you," Shae said.

Marietta smoothed her hair from her face. "He's not."

"You're sending him mixed signals. He's sending you only one. He's in love with you."

"Even if he is, nothing will ever happen between us."

"It'll get him killed, Mae. He's knows that. Still he kissed you in a hall where anyone could see. I know what I saw with my own eyes. No man as dangerous as him takes those kind of risks if he can control himself. He's in love with you," Shae said. "I don't play second to anyone. Especially not my best friend."

"Nothing is ever going to happen between us," Marietta said.

"Then stop making him think it might." Shae stood. She crossed her arms. "Can I tell you something?"

Marietta looked up at her.

"I was so jealous of you back in Chicago. So fucking jealous. Mae, you'd get up on that stage and dance, and clear more money than I made hustling in a week. Men would pay to just talk to you. Have you on their arm. It made us all feel cheap. I raised my game because of you."

Marietta gave her a weak smile. "I didn't think I was better than any of you. I just didn't think I mattered."

"But you do. And your life matters more now than it ever did. Forget what the Leones did to you, look around you at the family you found. You did it, Mae. You got another chance at happiness."

Marietta smiled. Shae smiled. "That sister of yours is fierce. She loves you, Mae. You don't need me anymore. She has your back. Trust her."

"And you? What about you?" Marietta asked.

"It's funny. I don't want to be a domesticated wife with a mafia husband." Shae laughed. "But if Carlo was really an option, I sure as hell would give him a second and third try."

"I shouldn't have hit you. I'm sorry."

Shae walked over and hugged her. "Remember the time we fought at the club because I thought you took my Gucci watch?"

Marietta smiled though her heart hurt. "I remember."

"I found it two days later in my purse. It took me a month to apologize to you." Shae let her go and looked into her eyes. "I was a selfish bitch back then. You brought me into your new family and I lied to you. I'm the guilty one. I'm sorry, Mae. I never meant any disrespect. Just a creature of habit."

"Me too." Marietta smiled. "I'll go with you to the airport."

"No. Let one of those non-English speaking men take me. That way I can stick to it and not try to see Carlo before I leave."

CARLO NEEDED A PHONE. The pager on his hip buzzed non-stop. He glanced up to the ring. Ciro was throwing and landing punches on time. The trainer, a cousin of Carlo's, was ducking and weaving but taking the blows.

"Be back!" he yelled at the men. It could be Renaldo paging him. They were supposed to meet up to make rounds and collect some debt. He went to the back hall and found a payphone. Carlo dug deep in his pocket for change. He dialed the number.

"Carlo?" came the hurried answer.

"Who is this? Ringo?"

"It's me. Are you at the gym with Ciro?" Ringo asked.

"Why? What's wrong?"

"The women. They were fighting." Ringo said.

"Who was fighting?" Carlo asked.

"The American woman. Shae and Marietta. They fought. The Donna separated them. They were pretty angry."

"Does Giovanni know?"

"It's not why I'm calling. The one, the one from America with pink hair, she's leaving. The Donna is sending her away. They are driving her to Napoli."

Carlo checked his watch. His heart beat so fast he nearly dropped the phone. "When did she leave?"

"Thirty minutes ago. Renaldo was called to take her."

"What was the fight about, Ringo?" Carlo asked.

"I... ah, I'm not sure. I just thought you'd want to know," Ringo said.

"*Grazie.*" Carlo hung up the phone. Ciro walked down the hall. He was dabbing at his face with a towel.

"Carlo? I want to spar with you," Ciro said.

"Enough training. I need to get to the airport." Carlo started for the door. "Shae's leaving!"

"I'm coming with you!"

— *B* —

SHAE SMILED AT THE LADY standing behind the counter. She was glad the woman spoke English. She accepted her ticket and hitched her strap up her arm.

"*Grazie,*" she said to the woman. It was funny but after all this time she finally figured out how to say 'thank you' correctly in Italian.

"Travel safe," Renaldo said.

"Tell Kyra I want an invite to the wedding." Shae smiled.

Renaldo turned and walked away without a second glance. Shae stood there with her plane ticket in her hand and watched him go. She was pretty sure this would be the last time she'd visit Italy. She could never return and not think of Carlo, and how wild and crazy he made her feel.

"Are you done, lady?" A man with a strong British accent barked at her.

"Oh, sorry. Yes." Shae picked up her carryon bag and started toward the customs line.

Carlo drove his car up to the curb and threw the gearshift into park. "Circle the airport. I'll get her and bring her out," he said.

Ciro nodded that he'd obey. He'd already expressed to his brother his plans to invite Shae to stay with them for a few days. He knew she was moody, but the news of her leaving shocked him. He hit the sidewalk fast and eventually started running. He didn't know what airline, or her flight number. He was going in blind. Carlo rushed through the automatic doors. He looked left and right. People were everywhere.

"Shit!" He ran his hand back over his head. "Shit!"

"Carlo?"

His head turned. Renaldo was looking at him curiously. "Where is she?"

"What are you doing here?" Renaldo asked.

"Where?" he shouted.

"Gone. She's probably through customs. I left her at the counter ten minutes ago. The line for the toilet is around the—"

"Fuck the toilet! Which airline? Which one?"

"American." Renaldo pointed. "Let her go, Carlo. The Donna sent her away."

"*Vaffanculo!*" Carlo said. He ran toward customs. He immediately caught the stares from the *Carabinieri*. Carlo stopped running and tried to walk fast. And then he saw her. The customs line was apparently as slow moving as the line to the toilet. She was closer to the front.

"Shae? Shae!" he shouted.

An officer put his hand to his arm. Carlo shrugged off his touch. "She forgot her passport," he said. Shae had heard him. She refused to look back at him again. He could tell by her stance she was purposefully ignoring him. He grabbed her arm and made her look at him.

"I need to talk to you."

"I can't. I'll miss my flight," Shae said.

"Fuck the flight. Don't go. Talk to me!" he demanded and grabbed her arm.

She looked up at him and tears were in her eyes. "Go away, Carlo. We had our fun. It's over. Okay? It's over!"

Carlo let her arm go. "I can fix it if you tell me what the fuck I did!"

"No. You can't. There's nothing to fix."

"So your plans to stay with me, and see Ciro's match were all bullshit? You changed your mind."

"You changed my mind." She looked away.

"What the fuck does that mean? What is my sin now, Shae? Nothing happened between us that you didn't want to happen."

"I'm going home. It was all a game remember? A stupid game. And now it's over." She walked up to the window and gave the customs agent her passport. He stamped it.

Carlo grabbed her by the arm once more. "It was never a game to me."

She snatched free of him and this time he saw the tears had spilled on to her cheeks. She gave him a faint smile before she walked away. Carlo made a step to follow. He could grab her and drag her out the airport. Force her to tell him how the fuck she could go from being his sweet strawberry, to a cold bitch in just under a day. She was gone. Nothing worthwhile was meant to last.

CHAPTER ELEVEN

Before the Storm

"WHY ARE YOU SITTING IN THE DARK?" Lorenzo asked. He turned on the light. The brightness hurt her eyes. She squinted through the glare. Marietta sipped her tea. Zia made her a special cup that drained the stress from her headache.

"I was waiting for you to come home," Marietta said.

Lorenzo walked into the kitchen. All evening Marietta thought of this conversation. Mirabella and Catalina had coached her on what to say. However, this was her marriage. And she knew her man better than any of them. She'd need to tell him something that protected them both from her mistakes if they ever surfaced to destroy her life.

"I sent Shae home," she began.

"I heard. Why did you do that?" he asked.

"You heard? From who?" Marietta asked.

"Renaldo told me when I arrived. He said he took her to the airport."

"These men tell everything we do! Jesus!" Marietta sighed.

"*Che cosa*?" Lorenzo asked.

"We had a fight. It got out of hand," Marietta said. "We said some ugly things. Our friendship is over." A hand covered hers. Marietta looked up into Lorenzo's eyes. "I messed up. I love you, Lo. You know that. But I did something terrible."

"You didn't. You fought with your friend. Fuck her," he smiled. "Come on smile for me."

"Lo, you aren't listening," Marietta said. He kissed her. She kissed him back, afraid of the truth she wanted to share.

"Let me run you a bath." Lorenzo pulled her up and then his arm went over her shoulders. He didn't ask her for any further explanation and she was grateful. She just wanted the entire day to be washed away.

—*B*—

"WHAT HAPPENED HERE? TODAY?" Dominic removed his tie. Catalina looked up from her vanity mirror. She watched him undress.

"Catalina?" he asked.

"What are you asking?" she answered.

"Today. The women. I hear from the boys that there was some kind of fight. The American was sent home."

"Who told you that?" Catalina turned around on her stool.

"Should I be concerned?" he asked.

If Eduardo or Ringo had told what they heard and saw, they wouldn't be having this conversation. She smiled at Dominic. "Marietta and her friend had an argument. The Donna thought it was best that she leave."

"That woman is a hot-head just like her husband," Dominic said. He kicked off his shoes.

"Marietta's sensitive, Domi. That's all. The Donna handled her," Catalina said.

Dominic stared at her for a moment. He shook his head smiling. "You know Patri had an old saying. It goes: a man should believe half of what he sees, and none of what he hears from a woman."

"That's a stupid thing to say. What does it mean?" Catalina frowned.

"It means there is more to this story than you are telling me. But, it's women's business so why bother?"

Catalina threw her brush at him and he ducked. He grinned. She smiled. "You're so romantic, Domi," she blew him a kiss.

He smiled. "I'm staying here tonight."

"In my room? I thought Gio forbid it?" Catalina rose. She walked over to Dominic and stood before him. He sat on the edge of her bed. His hands stroked up her thighs and she ran her fingers through the crown of curls at the top of his head.

"Gio complained the entire time you were in Milano. He's happy we've set a wedding date and you're home. I know we have his blessing. You're mine tonight."

"I was always yours," she hugged his face to her stomach. He rubbed her ass and it felt nice. "I can't wait to get married."

"Me either." She lifted his chin. "How about we practice for the honeymoon." She pushed him back down on the bed and straddled him. She planned to spend the rest of the night in his arms.

—*B*—

"IT'S GOOD TO BE HOME," Mirabella said. She found Giovanni in bed with his reading glasses on. He was staring at his paperwork. She cut off the light in the bathroom and walked over to her dresser. She picked up her hand lotion and began to rub it into her hands and elbows.

"Giovanni?" He glanced up. "I decided to send Shae home."

"Who is Shae?" he asked.

Mirabella sighed. "Marietta's friend. My God the woman has been with us for over a week."

"I forget her name." he continued to read his documents.

"She and Marietta had a fight… an argument," Mirabella said.

He glanced up over the top of his glasses. She smiled. "It's nothing to worry about, really petty stuff. I didn't want it to get out of hand. So I had Renaldo take her to the airport."

"Well it's handled then. And from now on keep them out of our home. These friends you and Marietta have. A hostel would be nice. I own a few in Sorrento."

"How generous of you," Mirabella chuckled. She eased into bed. "What are you reading?"

"Boring stuff." He tossed the papers to the side.

"Is it true? What the men say?" she scooted over and rested on his chest. He removed his glasses and put them on the night table. He turned off the lamp.

"What do they say?"

"You have a boxer. Carlo's brother?" she asked.

"Yes. It's true. He has a fight in a few days in Napoli." Giovanni kissed her forehead.

"I love boxing, Gio. Love it!"

"You do?" he asked.

"Yeah. I never told you? I used to… ah… I had a friend back at home, he was a boxer," Mirabella said.

"No. You never told me."

"It was a long time ago. Oh! I have an idea!" She sat up in bed. She must have startled him because she could see how bright his eyes flashed.

"Date night," she said.

"Date what?"

"When was the last time we went out? Me and you. I want to go to the fight."

"No, Bella."

"Please, Gio! I would love it. A date. What do you think?" she grinned.

He chuckled. "Let me think about it."

She ran her hand over his groin and he grunted. She gave him a kiss.

"Maybe I can convince you," she said and eased him out of his pajama pants. Before he spoke she eased down the bed and guided him into her mouth. Giovanni rubbed the top of her head and she swallowed him down her throat, stroking his stalk. She worked her jaws until her man had the ultimate release.

The Next Day –

"Gio?" Rocco said.

Giovanni's head turned and Rocco entered the room. He gestured for his uncle to join him. He was in need of the old man's wisdom. Rocco closed the door behind him. His uncle could visit Villa Rosso whenever he chose. He couldn't, however, enter a closed-door room without invitation.

"I spoke to my contacts in Firenze. They tell me the same as Domi. There is no Kei Hyogo running the Triad. The name has no meaning to their contacts."

"And you believe them?" Giovanni asked. He glanced over to Santo who was invited to the conversation. Santo remained silent.

"What do you think, old man? Am I paranoid?" Giovanni asked.

"About the Triad?" Rocco asked.

"The China man. The one who stole my Bella away. He's out of prison. No one can tell me where he went."

"If he's out of prison it would take him years to get the kind of muscle to return here after you, Gio," Rocco said.

"Thank you!" Lorenzo said. "It's what I've been saying. Gio, fuck the China man. He's not a threat. If he is out there plotting, let him. He'll play right into our hands. Then bap!" Lorenzo made the gesture of a gun firing. "I'll do him myself."

Rocco chuckled and nodded with glee.

Giovanni remained unimpressed. His gaze swiveled to Santo. "What do you think?"

Santo cleared his throat. "I think being cautious is wise, Gio. At least until we can pin down where he is. My cousins tried to put him down in New York." Santo's gaze switched between the men. "The closest they could get to him was one hit when we carved out his eye. He's connected. He's protected. He's a threat, Gio. I just don't think he's an immediate one."

"Keep looking," Giovanni told Lorenzo. His cousin threw up his hands in defeat. Santo sat forward.

"Gio, I didn't get a chance to thank you."

Giovanni nodded.

"I'll be starting out with the sanitation boys. I have a few Lorenzo put under me."

"Yes, Gio. Santo is our new garbage collector," Lorenzo winked.

Santo held back from reacting.

"Let me know how it goes," Giovanni said. Santo heaved a deep sigh and gave a nod to them all as he headed to the door.

"I'll check in tomorrow," Santo said and then left.

Rocco sighed.

"Something to drink, old man?" Giovanni asked. He stood and started toward his bar.

"You know Zia forbids it," Rocco said with a sly smile. Giovanni took that as a yes and poured them both a glass.

"So, Santo is back in the family?" Rocco asked.

Giovanni handed Rocco his whiskey glass. "He's being watched."

"I saw the gift from Mancini." Rocco switched gears on him. Giovanni took a swallow from his glass. "You allow a man to come into your home and disrespect you, Gio?"

"It was my Bella's birthday. She wanted him there. Besides it was Lorenzo's home, not mine."

"It was disrespectful. What if the other clan bosses saw the portrait?"

"They didn't." Giovanni assured him in a flat tone.

"He's mocking you. He's trying to get next to your wife, trying to bring your business down."

Giovanni looked at the empty glass. He turned it in his hand so that small traces of amber liquor swirled. "Have I been too tolerant, uncle?"

"In my day lines were never crossed. If they were there was a cost or consequence," Rocco said. "Either you crush him and take what is yours, or you cut and sever all ties. There is no room for *la cosa nostra* in *la Camorra* or your *famiglia*."

Giovanni nodded. "Agreed."

That Evening –

Lorenzo laughed. He slammed the cards down on the table and picked up his cigar with a big boastful grin. The door opened and Carlo entered. Of course the boxer wannabe kid brother tagged along. The two greeted several of the men. Lorenzo hadn't spoken to Carlo in several days.

"Deal me out, boys," he said. He left the money on the table with no concern over its return to him. The men never disrespected him. When he stood, another man eagerly took his seat. Carlo walked through the gambling house headed for the back where others from different clans drank and gathered.

Lorenzo followed.

His best friend only saw him when someone in the room called out Lorenzo's name in excitement. Carlo glanced back with that wounded lion look in his eyes. Lorenzo cocked his head left gesturing they leave the crowd and find a corner to chat. Carlo dug out a lager of his choice in a cool bottle with ice crystals covering the glass. He nodded and followed Lorenzo to the crates near a closed door.

"Where have you been?" Lorenzo asked.

Carlo glanced to his brother. The kid was laughing and demonstrating his technique with a few shadow punches for the younger men.

"Is he ready?" Lorenzo asked.

"I'll stake my life on it," Carlo said. "He's ready."

"It seems like we don't talk much anymore. I rarely see you. I don't hear from you." Lorenzo said.

"Are you my wife?" Carlo asked.

Lorenzo chuckled. He stared at the men with Carlo in silence. "I need my friend. Things are getting complicated."

"What things?" Carlo mumbled.

"For starters you missed the meeting with Santo. Giovanni has given the sanitation routes in the Arenaccia district to Santo."

"Renaldo told me that Santo wasn't promoted," Carlo said in a dry tone.

"He wasn't. He'll watch the men pick up shit and trash. It's an appeasement while Giovanni and the other bosses keep an eye on him."

"And this pisses you off?" Carlo asked.

"He's a *pentito*. A rat," Lorenzo said. "And not just for Mottola. Have you not forgotten how he turned on you? How he let you go to jail and did nothing to help?"

"Don't do that," Carlo said.

"Do what?" Lorenzo said.

"Don't use that bullshit to gain my alliance in whatever plan you're hatching. Santo paid his price. I don't like the fucker, but he is a brother. If Giovanni wants to forgive, then you'll forgive."

Lorenzo fumed. He didn't trust Santo. He didn't have the time to dig up more dirt on the *pentito bastardo*. "Keep an eye on him. It's all I ask," Lorenzo said.

Carlo didn't respond. Lorenzo glanced over to him. "What happened with you and the American woman? Marietta tells some story of an argument and sending her away."

Carlo didn't answer.

Lorenzo thought to press for an answer and decided against it. Instead he approached another subject. "I've been meeting with Tacchi."

"Why?"

"He has his concerns. He thinks Gio is trying to squeeze the lower clans out," Lorenzo said. He reclined back against the wall. "He's hungry."

"Who gives a fuck? He's not of any importance."

"He understands the trafficking that comes through the bay. He understands the future. *La Cosa Nostra* is already bringing in heroine through Turkey. Tacchi has contacts. He tells me—"

"I get it," Carlo said with an exasperated sigh.

"You get what?"

"You don't give a shit about Tacchi's contacts. You're going after Mancini's drug business. You want to hand that over to Gio," Carlo said.

"Bravo," Lorenzo chuckled.

"It's a dangerous plan, Lo. We keep the *Polizi di Stato* and the *Carabinieri* in their place because we don't cross borders. Even if you take down Mancini from the inside, he has two hundred years worth of loyalty and history on that island. The *Mafiosi* will never bow to you."

Lorenzo smiled. "It's possible. Can you imagine it? Gio runs the *Camorra* and I run the *Mafiosi*. Think of the power we'd both have. And we would be equals. We'll rule the world."

"It's a death wish. You'll weaken us if you divide the men that way," Carlo said.

"I have a plan. I just want to know when the rubber meets the road, which way you will roll?"

Carlo sighed. When he held back on giving an answer Lorenzo looked over. Carlo continued to stare at his brother.

"Well?" Lorenzo asked.

"I have my own plans. Ciro is my plan. All the way to America."

"America? Bullshit!" Lorenzo laughed. "With your record they will never let you in the fucking country!"

Carlo sat upright. "It's not bullshit!" he said through clenched teeth. "We could eventually move to America. I can find Shae and who knows. I can be my own man."

"You don't have the fucking balls to be anything other than who you are. You swore your life to *la Camorra*!"

"Yes! But I didn't swear a life to being your bitch!" Carlo threw the glass bottle at the wall and it shattered. It nearly hit a man who jumped out of the way. Lorenzo chuckled after Carlo's flash of rage. "I have my own life! Go play in your drugs. That shit is poison. It'll destroy you and Gio."

Carlo stood and walked away. Lorenzo cursed under his breath.

"I'm going to go talk to him," Eduardo said.

"Don't!" Ringo grabbed his arm. They glanced over in time to see Carlo throw a bottle at the wall and then storm away. Lorenzo didn't look pleased.

"He's in a mood," Ringo warned. "Bad timing."

"He's always in a mood," Eduardo reasoned. "Now is the time."

"It won't work!" Ringo warned.

"It will. Look at Renaldo. He tells the Don everything on those women. No matter the news. They respect him for it. I hear he's back in his old role again, guarding the Don. Lorenzo needs to know."

"We swore to the Donna that we would not mention any of it. Ever," Ringo said.

"Not the birth control. We did not make that promise. The Donna didn't even ask for us to make that promise because she too knows it's blasphemous. If I tell Lorenzo that his wife is tricking him he will be grateful. He will reward me and you. I can get out of this errand boy bullshit. Be an enforcer. Maybe even get promoted to work with Renaldo and Nico."

The plan sounded solid. But when Ringo glanced over to Lorenzo he recalled the time before when he delivered him news he didn't want. Lorenzo came to a party and shoved a gun in his mouth. It was just a package, and Lorenzo was willing to kill him. What would happen to his friend?

"Don't do it!" Ringo tried to grab Eduardo by the arm but Eduardo snatched away. He almost called after him when he saw Carlo from his peripheral vision watching him. Ringo nodded at Carlo and turned and went in the other direction. He didn't want anything to do with it.

Lorenzo stood. He would go home to Marietta and let her calm him. Without Carlo at his side he felt open and vulnerable. Tomorrow he'd apologize and gain his friend's trust. He'd just have to find a way to wake him up. The boxing dreams he had were nothing more than bullshit, not a reality. His idea was best for the brothers, and the brotherhood.

"Boss, can I speak to you?" asked Eduardo.

"Get the fuck out of my way," Lorenzo started for the door.

"It's about *signora* Marietta."

Lorenzo paused. He glanced back at Eduardo. He barely knew the kid. More and more Nico hired the youth to do the errands, and some were elevated enough to be given more important jobs. This one hadn't taken a vow to be anything other than a foot soldier, relegated to patrolling Melanzana and keeping an eye on the women.

"I ah, I wanted to say—" Eduardo stammered.

Lorenzo looked the boy over. What was he twenty, twenty-one? He was scrawny with mousey brown hair and a sleepy eye. The kid shoved his hands down into the front pockets of his jeans and continued to mumble through his words.

"Spit it out!" Lorenzo said.

"I was there, the day the women fought. I was there first to break them apart." The boy lowered his gaze. "They argued. And… boss, see, I ah, I thought you should know why."

Lorenzo took a step toward him. "What the fuck do you have to say about my wife?"

"She lies to you. She takes the pill so she won't become pregnant." Eduardo said.

"Che cazzo dici! Say it again!" Lorenzo drew down on the boy with his gun.

Carlo heard Lorenzo's voice pitch high over the laughter and the music. He looked up and saw Eduardo now staring directly into the barrel of Lorenzo's gun. Several men began to back away.

"Shit!" he got up quick to get to the scene but he was too late. Lorenzo fired and blew the kid's head clear off his shoulders. After the cannon blast, silence echoed through the room, except for the ringing in everyone's ears because of the discharge.

Lorenzo stepped forward and stood over Eduardo. He unloaded his gun into the body until the poor sap was shredded to a bloody pulp. The blasts were deafening. No one moved. Carlo was the only one brave enough to approach his friend.

"Lo, check yourself," Carlo warned. Lorenzo's position was one of strength. He could not show weakness in front of these men. Lorenzo didn't move. He stared down at the boy as if in shock. No matter how dirty the deed, Carlo had never seen Lorenzo shocked by his actions. Something was wrong. What could Eduardo have said to unleash such fury?

"Tutto va bene. Leave." Carlo said. "Leave."

Lorenzo blinked. He looked to Carlo as if only then could he hear, think, and breathe. He turned and walked out. Carlo ran his hand over his head. "Arturo, Elian, Umberto, get garbage bags and a mop." He glanced around at the other men staring. Most of them lowered their eyes. Those that loved murder and mayhem met his stare with an amused smile. A few laughed. Among the faces he didn't see Ringo. His protégé was Eduardo's shadow. The kid would know the reason for the hit. He stormed out of the villa and into the night.

SANTO CHOSE TO ENTER THROUGH the back doors no matter the establishment he visited. His routine had to be natural and repetitive. He had men who he used to call brothers watching and tracking his every move.

The manager glanced up from his magazine. It was late. The lobby was dark except for the small portable television with the bent antenna in the corner. Santo nodded at the man and headed up the steps. The lift hadn't worked in years. He kept glancing back over his shoulder to see if he was being followed. At first he thought it was his paranoia. He however picked up his tail at a restaurant in Pompeii. It took him two hours to lose the fuckers.

He arrived at the door and knocked only once.

After a second it opened. Isabella smiled at him. She wore a black satin robe parted enough to reveal her voluptuous breasts. She stepped aside for him to come in. The strong patchouli smell of incense burning greeted him. Isabella was a beautiful woman. After one night between her creamy thighs he considered himself an addict. Often they fucked first and reserved the talk of business for after. To be as refined and elegant as she appeared in her expensive shoes, she let him fuck her any way he chose.

"You're late," she said. She closed the door.

He reached for her. A thin sash tied around her waist closed the robe she wore. He yanked it off to reveal her nudity. She had flawless buttery tanned skin. Her large breasts were tipped with even larger rose-colored nipples. She didn't shave her pussy. He was grateful. The downy nest of curls over the delta of her sex was where he loved to bury his nose while he licked and fucked her with his tongue.

The excitement of her being so close overcame him. His head bent to capture her mouth, but she grabbed his face and stopped what should have occurred naturally.

"He'll call in a hour. Do you have something for him?" she asked.

Santo smiled. "Gio's agitated. Like you said he would be, he now sees Kei's shadow everywhere. We have to make our move now. Let's discuss what kind of move that is later."

He shoved her to the bed. Isabella grinned. Santo began to undress.

"I need more that that, Santo. Where is he vulnerable? When is she out of his sight," Isabella asked.

"The Donna is taking the little one Eve to the church for school. I know who will be driving and which men will be following. You can have your boys pick them off easily."

"Mmm, sounds yummy," she started to rub her breasts for him. "I'm so ready."

"Me too."

—*B*—

MARIETTA TURNED OVER. She expected to find Lorenzo in bed with her. When her hand smoothed over the cool sheet she sobered from sleep. He arrived. She was certain she heard him return to the room in the middle of the night. Marietta sat up. She reached for the lamp switch next to her bed and flipped it on. Lorenzo was across the room seated in his favorite chair. Though the corner of the room where he sat had the deepest shadows, she could see his penetrating stare. He was awake.

"Sweetheart? What time is it?"

He didn't answer. If he had been drinking he'd already be in bed wrestling with her.

"Come to bed." She turned off the lamp. Marietta slipped back under the covers. When he didn't move or respond she opened her eyes again. Marietta sighed. Whatever was bothering him would keep him sulking all night. She tossed the covers aside. She sat up. She wore a black silk negligee that barely covered her thighs. The front triangular cups revealed her breasts as well. It was one of his favorites. If he had come home early like he promised she would have given him his treat.

"Lo? What's the matter?"

"Are you pregnant?" he asked.

"Huh?"

"Pregnant," he repeated. "Are you?"

"No. I dunno, maybe," she said.

"Because you're trying to get pregnant?" Lorenzo asked. "We fuck all the time now, Marie. And you're trying, right?"

"What the hell is the matter with you? It's an act of nature. I can't predict when it's going to work, Lo."

"Why? Why can't you predict it, Marie? Don't you know your own body?" he stood and kicked the chair back. Marietta took a step back. "I thought all women knew when they could become pregnant? Do you keep track. Mark it on a calendar, Marie?"

"Stop being an asshole! Get the hell out of here and sleep in another room if you're going to be like this!" Marietta said. Her vision clouded with fresh tears. Lorenzo seemed unmoved. This was different. He wasn't drunk. He was angry.

"Why are you mad?" she asked. Had the men told him about the argument? They couldn't have. Did they?

"I'm going to ask you only once, Marie. I want the truth. Do you take birth control behind my back?"

Inside of her head she screamed and screamed the answer. Marietta let go a nervous chuckle. It was her only defense. Lorenzo arched a single brow to her humor. This was not a question to laugh at. What other reaction could she have? Tears wouldn't work. Honesty wouldn't work. She smiled. She stepped closer. "Lo? Why would you even ask that?"

Mirabella and Catalina had warned her of this moment. The back-up plan was simple. The three of them would ban together against any accusation of her fucking Carlo or taking contraceptives. She made a mistake. She would make it up to him. He didn't need to know the truth. Especially since the majority of what Shae said were lies. He didn't deserve that level of betrayal.

"That's not an answer, Marie," Lorenzo said.

"No," she said. "I would never do that to you, us." She touched his face. "You trust me right? With your life, Lo." She ran her hand slowly down his neck and then over his chest. "It's me, baby. *Cara.* Look at me. Have you ever seen me take anything? I wouldn't do it."

He closed his eyes. Relief washed over her. Marietta hugged him. She put her face into his chest and silently prayed once his arms folded around her and he completed their embrace. In an instant she was swept up in his arms and carried to bed. He lay her down gently. He kissed her belly first. He ran his hand softly over the flat surface. Marietta lay still. She closed her eyes and squeezed them tightly shut. He had to believe the lie. Just this one little lie, and she would not tell any other.

Lorenzo didn't ravage her body as he often would after one of their more explosive fights. Instead he rested his head on her belly and snuggled with her. Fully clothed he laid this way on top of the covers. She stroked the top of his curly head. She was only able to restart her heart when she heard his light snoring and knew he was asleep.

Marietta smiled.

—*B*—

"VIENI QUI!" CARLO SAID.

Ringo didn't move. Arturo shoved him and forced him to walk. Soon after the shooting, Ringo fled. Carlo sent the boys after him. They brought him to the beach near the bay. When Ringo didn't walk fast enough, Carlo marched over and grabbed the boy by the neck. Ringo gasped.

The tractor rumbled. It's cranky engine drowned out Carlo's voice. This part of the land was near a few ruined buildings, and perfect for a burial since the construction would cover the area with concrete soon. The sea wasn't too far ahead. The long arm of the machine reached and dropped its claw in to the earth and dug up large clumps. They would bury Eduardo here. They would leave no traces of him.

"I want answers!" Carlo shouted over the noise.

"I had nothing to do with it, boss," Ringo wheezed. Carlo let go of his throat and Ringo took several steps back. He bowed his head in shame. Running was an act of cowardice. It was also an act of the guilty.

Carlo looked to the men. "Make sure no cars are on the road until this is done."

The men nodded and walked off. Carlo shoved Ringo and forced him to walk. Soon they were on the beach, headed toward the sea. Though the night was darkest near the water, the moon glowed like the sun in the sky. There was plenty of moonlight cast over the bay. Carlo kept his gaze trained on Ringo. The kid was shaking with fear.

"Start talking. Why did Lorenzo kill Eduardo?" Carlo asked.

"He… we…" Ringo's voice faltered.

"What happened?" Carlo demanded.

Ringo shook his head no. Carlo understood his fear. Many feared Lorenzo. And he outranked them all.

"Dica!" He grabbed Ringo by the collar and delivered slaps to both sides of his face. *"Dica!"*

"The women. The Donna asked it of us!" he shouted. "To lie. To be silent. I told Eduardo to keep his mouth shut. He thought if he told Lorenzo the truth he'd get respect."

"Explain!" Carlo shoved him. Ringo fell to his butt. He looked up at Carlo in fear. He spoke fast.

"They fought. The women fought. The American one with the pink hair and *signora* Marietta were trying to kill each other. Eduardo and I were in the house. We heard the screams upstairs. We ran in and found them fighting. Catalina was trying to pull them apart."

Shae left him without even a fair goodbye. He knew something happened. He figured Marietta had told her his sins and she finally realized he was not her wounded bird, but a monster. So he accepted her truth for now. He had already thought of how he'd visit America and find Shae again.

"Go on. Finish the fucking story."

"The pink hair lady, she said she heard you. She saw you in the hall kissing Marietta. She said Marietta and you were having an affair. She said… Marietta was on birth control because she didn't want to get pregnant and caught with a baby she didn't know who it belonged to."

"This is bullshit! Are you sure Shae said these things?" Carlo asked.

Ringo nodded his head yes.

"What did Eduardo tell Lorenzo?"

"The Donna met with us. She told us to never speak of the incident. The pink hair lady said she lied. She was upset and it was words of anger. But Eduardo thought the birth control part of the tale was true. He said it explained why *signora* Marietta wasn't pregnant. He thought if he exposed her to Lorenzo he would be rewarded. I told him not to. I remember when I got a package for Lorenzo and gave it to him, how he put a gun in my mouth and threatened me. No disrespect but he's a psycho. I told him not to. I called you to tell you about the pink lady leaving. I didn't want anything else to do with it."

Carlo remembered the time when Ringo and Carmine were at his place, and Lorenzo walked in with a gun and beat Ringo. He never really understood why.

"Eduardo didn't listen. He said he would not say anything against you, but he would tell Lorenzo this thing of birth control. I think it's why Lorenzo killed him."

"Get up!"

Ringo refused.

"Up!" Carlo extended his hand. He helped Ringo stand. "It was a lie. A stupid fight. I have never betrayed my brother. Never slept with his wife. And she is not on birth control. You forget everything about this. If Gio asks, Domi, anyone, you play dumb. You know nothing. Do you hear me, Ringo?"

"I do. I understand. I have already forgotten," Ringo said.

"Go back to Sicilia for a few days. I'll tell you when it's safe to return." Carlo reached in his back pocket. He pulled out all the money he had on him. He handed it over to Ringo, who took it and nodded. "Wipe your fucking tears before anyone sees them. Be a man. Go stay with Ciro until I'm ready to leave."

"Grazie."

Ringo ran as if the devil was after him. Carlo looked to the sea. Shae saw through him. She was right to leave him behind. He turned and started back toward the rumbling engine of the tractor. In the dark of night they would bury Eduardo and the secret of the kiss. Tonight he vowed never to cross that line again.

—*B*—

THE PHONE RANG. Isabella's head lifted off his chest. "That's him."

Santo sat up and so did Isabella, she covered them both with a sheet. He reached over after the third ring and picked up.

"News?" asked Kei.

"Giovanni is suspicious. He knows you are out of prison, and he's tried to confirm your whereabouts."

"What else?" Kei asked.

"I say it's time you take her. He's got the men heavily guarding the women. However the Donna and little Eve will be visiting Our Lady of Lordes church about her attending school. It's the perfect time to grab them both."

"I want the boys dead," Kei said.

"I'm not a baby killer. I told you—"

"Kill the boys and deliver Mirabella and Eve. And then our business is done. Non-negotiable."

The line clicked off.

"Well? What did he say?" Isabella grinned.

"I'm not a fucking baby killer!" Santo threw the phone across the room. "I'll get my revenge on the Battaglias, but I'm not killing Giovanni's sons."

"Slow down. Why be upset? You are a man who will do anything to have what he wants. Kei Hyogo still doesn't know that he is half-blind because of your order to have his eye carved out of his head." She laughed.

"How do you know that?" Santo frowned.

"Oh, *caro*, I know many things about you," she smiled. The agitation he felt pitched. "Kei believes he's in control but is he really? We are loyal to our cause. Not his. Correct?"

"Cause or no cause, I won't kill children for him or you."

"Wait!" Isabella put a hand to his chest to keep him from rising. "Don't lose focus. If you can't kill the boys bring them to me. I'll see that it's done."

"Get off of me!" Santo left the bed and paced the floor. "What is wrong with you? Killing *bambini*? What kind of woman are you?"

Isabella smiled like a hungry serpent. "What kind of man are you? In your feelings about two half-breed brats? The bigger picture, Santo. Stay focused on the bigger picture. We aren't doing this for Kei. You break Giovanni and the clans will feed on themselves. The plan has always been to give you control. I have the money, the influence, and the men to make you king. You tried with Mottola and you failed. Giovanni is a weak man, and yet your *Camorra* calls him *capo di tutti capi*. You must hit him hard. The best strike is to take his sons. You cut out their little hearts out, you break his. After Mirabella and his daughter are gone, he will be on his knees. He will give it all over to you. We stick to the plan."

He grabbed his pants and pulled them on. Isabella laughed at how hurriedly he dressed. She sounded wicked. And when he dared to look at her again her beauty had faded. She was pure evil. "I'll deliver Mirabella and that daughter the psycho is crazy about. I'm not killing his sons. You want those kids dead, you find a way to do it."

"Whatever you say." She shrugged. "I have plans for them all."

He walked out with his heart lodged in his throat. Giovanni was like a brother to him. He'd been stripped of everything. Reduced to a trash collector in the *Camorra*. The boss of all bosses deserved this misery. But there were lines to never cross. Killing children was where he drew his line. No matter what the sacrifice he wouldn't make that one.

Morning –

Lorenzo opened his eyes. He had a cramp in his neck that reached down to his spine. Marietta was wrapped up in his arms. Her naked body pressed against his. At some time in the night he removed her negligee and made love to her. He now lay with her with no pants or underwear on, just his button down shirt and blazer.

He moved. She curled up tighter on him. Lorenzo didn't want to let her go. Last night was a blur. The motherfucker Eduardo had the nerve to speak against his wife. Make him question her. The hell he spiraled down into at the thought of Marie betraying him was the darkest place he's visited in his soul. He loved her. It wasn't the average kind of sweet kisses and sweet promises love. It was much deeper. His love for Marietta consumed him. It kept him balanced. And though he fucked up regularly in presenting that love to her, it was the purest love he's had in his life. Each day he obsessed over their future, their life, and the perfect family dynasty he wanted them to have. God gave him a second chance after he sinned against Patri Tomosino. He gave him a third chance when Marietta agreed to be his wife. And then God visited and gave him another. Mancini's legacy could be his for the taking if he played everything right. He was close to having it all.

Lorenzo felt no guilt. He knew he was right to put a bullet in the *leccaculo*. After he showered he'd explain himself to Giovanni before the other men spread the news. He reached over and grabbed the blankets. He dragged them up and covered her. Marietta smiled but didn't fully wake. She was most beautiful when she slept. He kissed her brow and eased off the bed to not disturb her further. Later he'd have one of the men go get her another diamond bracelet from their private jeweler. It would make up for his falsely accusing her last night.

The temperature in the room felt cooler. He shrugged off his blazer and unbuttoned his shirt. As he walked into the bathroom he scratched his jaw. It itched. Unlike Gio he could never stand facial hair. He shaved regularly, and if he forgot his skin became irritated with bumps. Lorenzo removed his shirt. He stood naked before the mirror and sink. He picked up his razor. The shaving cream can was empty. Lorenzo knelt and opened the cabinet. He reached inside and pulled out his bag. Marietta's makeup bag fell over. Lorenzo tossed his to the sink. He righted her bag and then paused. Countless times he caught her in the bathroom fiddling with her cosmetic bag.

"Why are you constantly with that damn bag?" Lorenzo asked. He reached around her to pluck the bar of soap from its dish, and then turned to go to the shower.

"This is my magic bag, baby. It's where I keep all my secrets. How else do you think I stay so beautiful for you?"

He glanced over at her and she removed her lipsticks and then blew him a kiss. He shook his head smiling.

"Bag of secrets? Che palle," he chuckled. "That's where you keep them women things."

"What women things?"

"For your period. Those things."

"I swear, Lorenzo, you act like a cave man sometimes," she laughed.

"Bag of secrets," he said. Lorenzo stood. He unzipped the top. Inside were tubes of crèmes and lipsticks. He turned the bag over and dumped its contents in the sink. A circular plastic disc was one of the last items to drop out. He studied it. *What the fuck did he know about birth control pills and how they were packaged?* The thing looked odd enough to be something. Was it contraception? He flipped it over. The foil was a circular wheel of broken capsule slots. Lorenzo flipped the compact open. It was a prescription in his wife's name. The date was just under a month.

"Lo? What are you doing?" Marietta entered through the bathroom door as she tied the front of her robe. She looked to the sink first and then to his hand.

"What is this thing?" he asked.

She turned and walked out of the bathroom. Lorenzo blinked. He was surprised by her immediate retreat. He went after her. She was by the bed twisting her wedding ring over and over.

"Marie?"

"I can explain. I swear!" she yelled at him.

"Why are you yelling?" he asked her.

Her bottom lip began to quiver and her eyes pooled with tears. She stood there twisting her ring over and over on her finger.

"Explain it. Start talking!" he said.

"I-I-I-took those pills before. Not after," she answered. "And, I tried to tell you before. But you wouldn't listen. Then we talked about it and I changed my mind. So I didn't need them anymore. So I didn't take them."

"You took them before what? You don't need what?" he asked. He threw the packet at the wall. "Tell me what they are."

Marietta put her hands in her hair. She pulled her hair at the root. "I made a mistake."

"Did you lie to me? DID YOU LIE TO ME?" he shouted loud enough to raise his mother from the dead. Her silence fileted him. It was like she'd taken a blade and carved out his heart. "Did you? DID YOU LIE TO ME?"

"Yes! I lied."

The confession was not what he wanted. It was not something he was prepared to hear. She could have lied to him again, and he would have convinced himself that it was the truth. He could forgive so many things, but not her betrayal. Not this betrayal. She made a fool of him.

"You did this. You did this," he said in disbelief. He took a threatening step toward her. He could see his hands wrapped around her throat. He could actually feel her gasping and begging for life as he squeezed the lie out of her mouth once more. But her weeping turned his rage inward. Just like his mother, when the hurt became insufferable, she wept and made him feel guilty about his own pain.

Just like his mother.

Of course she tricked him. Of course it was a lie. No one could love him completely. Her tears were further sullied by her pathetic apologies and garbled excuses. He could hear none of it. Marie yelled and screamed at him while crying. He went deaf. He heard nothing. She didn't want his child. She never did. And she'd do anything to keep from having it.

"Lorenzo, please forgive me!" Marietta wept. She reached for him but her touch had the adverse affect. It unleashed the fury he kept caged. He grabbed her by both arms and threw her to the bed. And then he turned and destroyed everything in the room he could lift, throw, and rip from the walls. The chair to her vanity went crashing through their window outside. It landed on a car that sounded a car alarm.

"No! No! Stop it!" Marietta screamed. She ran to him to grab him and he threw her off him. She hit the dresser. Her head landed with a loud smack. She nearly lost consciousness. He either didn't notice or didn't care. She crawled away. Lorenzo smashed his fist into the wood dresser drawer, and nearly put it through it. He shoved the heavy tallboy and it too went crashing to the floor, barely missing her. Marietta screamed. She kept screaming because her heart hurt too bad to fight back.

Lamps, clocks, even the television was hurled at the wall.

"How could you fucking do this to me? How could you fucking do this?" he shouted.

Marietta put her hands to her ears and closed her eyes, begging for him to listen, to forgive. Praying that she could find a way out, but realizing she was trapped.

—*B*—

"WHAT WAS THAT?" Mirabella turned from the mirror and stopped braiding her hair. The car alarm blared. Giovanni sat up in bed. They listened for the noise again. A woman's screams could clearly be heard. Next came pounding on their bedroom door.

Mirabella fled to the kids' room connected to theirs. Giovanni was up and putting on his robe. He was half dressed when he opened the door with his gun in his hand.

"What is it?" Giovanni asked.

"Boss, it's Lorenzo and Marietta. They're fighting. We can't get into the room."

"Fighting?" Giovanni asked in confusion. He stepped out into the hall where the screams and shouting could be clearly heard. "It sounds like they're going to war."

Mirabella heard Leo. The twins were still sleep in their bed, but Eve was sitting up now looking around. She locked eyes with her mother and pulled back her covers. She was going to get out of bed and come to her. "Stay there, baby. Mommy will be right back." Mirabella raced from the room. In the hall she could hear Lorenzo's shouting clearly, and they were on the hall beneath them.

"What is it? What's going on?" Zia asked her.

"Watch the kids," Mirabella said. She went after Giovanni and hoped to reach her sister's room in time.

—*B*—

"*SMETTILA DI MENTIRE E INIZIA A RACCONTARMI LA VERITÀ!* Stop telling me you're sorry. You're a fucking liar!" he shouted.

"I didn't do it to hurt you. I stopped taking the pills over a week ago. I just threw them away. I tried to explain it to you."

There was nothing left in the room to hit or kick. Lorenzo started to get dressed. He put on his underwear and pants. The men were demanding the door be opened. He ignored them. Marietta found the strength to stand.

"Please don't leave me," she said softly. "We have to... talk... work it out. Right, baby? We can figure it out"

"*Vaffanculo!*" he said.

"Lorenzo, please!" she pulled at his arm.

"Get the fuck off of me!" he yanked away.

"No!" She panicked. She jumped on his back. Marietta wrapped her arms around his neck as tight as she could to choke him. To make him come down to his knees, or at the very least stop him. He was too tall and too strong. She didn't know what else to do. He struggled to get her off him. He swung left and right. He finally got a hold of her when the door crashed open.

Marietta shrieked and screamed to the top of her lungs.

"What the hell is going on in here?" Giovanni demanded. The men took the question as an order and charged in to break up the fight. Lorenzo must have resisted throwing her off him to keep from hurting her. But Giovanni couldn't tell if his theory was correct by the look of the destroyed room. The way Marietta screamed and hit at her husband, he again was curious over who was attacking who. Everything but the bed was either shattered or broken.

"No! No! Noooooo!" Marietta screamed like a mad woman. The woman wouldn't stop screaming. Mirabella pushed past him. He didn't even know she entered the room. She grabbed her crying sister, who was being restrained. Marietta clung to her when released.

"Take her out of here, Bella. Now!" Giovanni ordered.

Mirabella nodded. She had to help Marietta walk. The woman wailed so loudly that they all believed her pain to be physical. And that further outraged Giovanni. He grabbed Lorenzo and punched him in the face. He slammed his fist into his face twice more before driving him to his knees. He pulled him by the hair. "Did you fucking hit your wife? Did you?"

Lorenzo shook his head no. Giovanni let him go. His cousin fell forward on his hands and spat blood. "Out! Everyone, get the fuck out!" Giovanni shouted.

The men left and closed the door behind them. He immediately turned on Lorenzo. "Convince me that you aren't insane enough to beat your fucking wife in my home!" Giovanni shouted.

"I didn't hit her!" Lorenzo said. "I was trying to get the fuck away from her!"

"That's not what I saw when I walked in. Look at this fucking place?" Giovanni kicked the splintered wood.

"It's personal, Gio. Stay out of it." Lorenzo staggered to his feet.

"I will not! I will not have you fucking hitting your wife!"

"I didn't!" Lorenzo shouted him down.

"Then tell me what I walked in on."

"It's private!" Lorenzo sat on the bed. "It's my private hell," he said. "None of your fucking business!"

Giovanni wiped his hand down his face. He stepped over what looked like a dresser drawer. He sat on the bed. "Tell me or leave my house. Push me and I'll make the boys get it out of you. Do you want to confess your private hell to them?"

"She's not pregnant." Lorenzo said. "And don't worry, I was leaving your fucking house." He got up and went to the closet and brought out his suitcase.

"You went crazy because she can't make babies?" Giovanni asked.

"Not can't. She won't," Lorenzo said.

"I don't understand?" Giovanni said.

"She's not pregnant because she doesn't want to have my child. She's been taking birth control pills behind my back," Lorenzo said.

"You sure about this?" Giovanni asked.

"I caught her lying. I… last night… fuck," he said shaking his head. "Everything I am, I touch, it all turns to shit."

"Get it together. She's your damn wife. Figure it out."

"Fuck figuring it out! I'm done!" Lorenzo dropped several suits in the suitcase and zipped it. "I can't look at her. I need to be away from her, from all of you," he said.

Giovanni had to agree. What else was there to say? If his Bella had done this thing behind his back he wouldn't know what to do with the betrayal. And then it dawned on him how he recovered from sin in his marriage. "Do you remember what you told me when I found out that Mirabella had run away with another man and kept little Evie from me?" Giovanni asked.

"No."

"You told me to not let my anger cost me the woman I love."

"That was Domi, not me." Lorenzo said.

Giovanni frowned. "I don't remember if it was you or Domi, but the advice was solid." He pointed a finger at Lorenzo. "I didn't believe that you two belonged together. I thought you married her to piss me off, or to manipulate me, or maybe because you finally wised up and found someone to love."

"I have loved her! What did it get me?" Lorenzo said.

"Maybe. Maybe not. She lied, she betrayed you, but she is your wife. And that bond you only make once. Forever. Be careful where anger takes you. Never close doors in your marriage that you want to return through."

"I'm leaving," Lorenzo said.

"Go. Get over it. Then bring your ass back to deal with it. She's your wife. I don't care if you married her under a full moon, on the back of a donkey, you married her. That's not going to change! We clear?"

Lorenzo looked him in the eye. He shook his head and finished packing. Giovanni walked out.

—*B*—

"I HAVE TO GO TO HIM. I have to talk to him." Marietta paced the floor. She twisted and turned her wedding ring.

"What exactly does he know?" Catalina asked. "Does he know about what Shae said about the birth control? About Carlo?"

"Yes!" Marietta shouted. "Oh God. I don't think so. He came home last night and asked me if I was lying to him about taking birth control. So they told him. My marriage is over because of lies!"

"He doesn't know," Mirabella said. "You talked to him last night and he was fine. You said he found your birth control pills this morning. If he knew, trust me they would have come for Giovanni last night," Mirabella said. "Giovanni is with him. He'll calm him."

"No! He won't. He'll side with Lorenzo. You know how they are. He'll tell him to leave me. I'll kill myself!" Marietta began to hyperventilate. Mirabella rubbed her back and encouraged her to breathe through her anxiety. She looked up at Catalina who shook her head in disbelief.

"Stop with the crazy talk!" Catalina stood. "You will not kill yourself, and Lorenzo will not leave you. Not if Gio has anything to say about it. And he does. He'll get Lorenzo to calm down, and then you'll talk to him and make it right between you two."

"She's right," Mirabella said. "He just needs to clear his head."

"Why would you keep the birth control pills?" Catalina asked. "Why keep them if you didn't plan to take them?"

"I forgot to throw the empty package away. I couldn't just toss them in the trash. We've been crazy the past week. Here and there, and back again. I didn't remember… damn it! I'm human!"

"It's fine. We're just trying to understand," Mirabella said.

"It's not fine. You didn't hear him. You didn't see how he looked at me. He's going to leave me. He's going to punish me."

"I'll call Domi and tell him to come home. See what he thinks," Catalina said.

Mirabella agreed. She pulled Marietta down to the sofa and sat with her. Marietta laid her head in Mirabella's lap, and lifted her feet to stretch out on her side on the sofa. Mirabella stroked her hair. "I promise you when he's not so angry he'll listen. Let him cool off."

"Okay," Marietta said weakly.

Mirabella began to hum as her grandmother did when she was a child and confused or hurting. She stroked Marietta's hair until he sister stopped trembling. Giovanni peeked in at them. Their eyes met. He then disappeared. Mirabella continued to comfort her sister.

—*B*—

DOMINIC FOUND GIOVANNI in his smoking room. The door was open. Gio saw him and gestured for him to come in closer. He was on the phone.

"Yes. I'm not sure where, just handle it," Giovanni said.

He ended the call.

"What's happened?" Dominic asked.

"Lorenzo. He and Marietta had a fight. He's packed and left."

"A fight? Do you know what about?" Dominic asked.

"He didn't give me the truth. Not all of it. I just got off the phone. Apparently last night Lorenzo killed Eduardo."

"He killed him?" Dominic said.

"Carlo says the boy told him that Marietta and the women were fighting because she was sneaking birth control behind Lorenzo's back. Lorenzo shot the kid when he told him the truth, came home and lost his fucking mind." Giovanni picked up his cigar and cutter. He snapped off the end. He flashed his lighter and took a toke from it. "I told Carlo to find Lorenzo, get him off the streets. I don't need him out there in this state."

"Where will he put him?" Dominic asked.

Giovanni glanced up and Dominic knew. There was no reason to name the place.

"Birth control? I can't say I'm surprised with those two," Dominic said.

"He's been thinking she's infertile."

"Ah… what a mess," Dominic said. "Anything you want me to do?"

"Domi! Gio!" Catalina charged into the room. "Where's Lo? Is he ready to talk to Marietta now?"

"He's gone, Catalina. He'll be back after he cools off," Giovanni said and dropped his cigar in the ashtray.

"Gone? No. He has to talk to her. Make him, Gio. She's really upset." Catalina pleaded.

"She made her bed. Betrayed her husband. Everyone stay out of it," Giovanni said.

"I can't believe you would say that. We all make mistakes. Look at what I did with Franco. Look at what Mirabella did with Kei Hyogo. She made a mistake and she deserves forgiveness."

"Mistakes do not come and go without consequences. We all pay them." Giovanni said. "They are married. It's a personal lesson between them. Let them figure it out. I'm going to shower."

Catalina turned to Dominic. He had to admit that he agreed with Giovanni. He smiled at Catalina and she spurned his touch.

"You know Lorenzo. He'll do something stupid. He's not Gio. He's not you. When he's hurt he hurts himself. He self destructs," Catalina said.

"He's like any man, Catalina. He'll remember what's important when it matters. Trust me."

She shook her head in defeat. "I hope so."

CHAPTER TWELVE

The Storm

One Week Later—

"YOU ASSHOLE! I want my FUCKING husband!" she screamed. "DO YOU HEAR ME? *STO CERCANDO LORENZO!* DO YOU HEAR MEEEEEE?"

"That's enough!" Mirabella grabbed Marietta by her arms to keep her from advancing on Giovanni.

"Let me go, Mirabella! He knows where he is! It's been a week. You said he would help! He's done nothing!" Marietta wept. Mirabella glanced back to her husband. He sat behind his desk glaring at them both. She pleaded with him with her eyes. The stress was killing all of them. He had to do something.

"I will talk to him," she said to Marietta. "Go back to the villa. Wait for me."

"No! No more talking! You keep saying that. They know where he is. They won't tell me. Nobody will. If I don't find him I'll go crazy," Marietta said through her sobs. And her sister looked a sight. She hadn't bathed or eaten anything in a week. Her hair was tangled, uncombed. Her eyes were swollen with puffy dark circles underneath. Nothing they did or said calmed her. She was making herself ill.

"I promise you I'll talk to Giovanni. He'll bring him back." She cupped Marietta's face. "You trust me right? Right?"

"No," Marietta said softly.

"Yes you do," Mirabella smiled. "I'm your sister. I love you. Go back inside. I'll be there with you in a minute." Mirabella gave her a gentle shove to the door. She watched and waited until Marietta left with the men who would escort her back to her prison. She looked to Giovanni.

"Why won't you put an end to this?" she pleaded.

Giovanni didn't answer.

"It's killing her. She made a mistake! A horrible one. I agree. Hasn't she suffered enough?"

He slammed his hand down on the top of the desk. "She did not make a mistake!" he shouted. "It was intentional. It was deliberate. It was a lot of things, but not a mistake!" Giovanni said.

Mirabella sighed. She put her hands in her hair. This was making her just as crazy. She needed peace in her family. The constant hysterics from Marietta were putting an unfair strain on her marriage now. She sucked down a deep breath and exhaled slowly.

"Have Lorenzo come back and talk to her. Or take her to him. Whichever you think is best."

"If she comes down here again I'll have the men lock her in her room. Do you understand?" Giovanni replied.

"She's upset. I would be too if I were her."

"But you aren't her. And this is not your battle," Giovanni reminded her.

"She's my sister. My twin sister!" Mirabella said. Giovanni didn't blink. She walked over to the desk. "Where is he? Do you even know? Do you?"

Giovanni scratched his brow. Something he did when she knew he struggled with telling her the truth. "Lorenzo is dealing with this his way. He'll return when he's ready. You have my word, Bella."

"Can't you see we're beyond that now? It's not good enough, Gio. You can put an end to this. One phone call and he walks through that door. Do it! Now!"

"Basta!" Giovanni said. "You don't give me orders. This is her fault! She betrayed him. He has been a loyal husband to her, and she betrayed him. If she suffers she deserves it."

"She was right. You can be a real asshole at times!" Mirabella said before she too stormed out. The door closed and she dropped against it. She closed her eyes and tried to catch her breath. She should go back inside. She knew how to convince him to act against his strong beliefs. One thing was clear, Giovanni and his men believed in the most traditional rules of marriage. No birth control, ever. Only Mirabella could help him be reasonable. She'd done it before. This approach wouldn't work. *It has never worked!* She put a hand to her head to keep away the lightheaded feeling stress brought on. Marietta had her on edge and she was now taking it out on Giovanni.

Tears pooled under her tightly shut lids, "Damn it!" she said. She had to be stronger than this. She'd never seen her sister so manic, crazed. It terrified her.

Three nights ago Mirabella brought food to Marietta's room. The bed was empty. She found her sister in the bathtub. She wore the same floor-length white gown she had on for days, while sitting in lukewarm water that reached the brim of the claw foot tub. It was the strangest sight. And then Mirabella's heart stopped. A pack of unopened razor blades floated on the surface of the water. Marietta stared at the package. It was her only focus. When Mirabella tried to coax Marietta out of the tub she didn't blink. When she took the razors from the water and put them in the trash her sister didn't blink. It was when she touched her that she went crazy. She screamed and fought her, splashing water until it covered the floor. Mirabella had to run from the room and bring back Catalina to help drag her sister from the tub.

Something was wrong with her sister. It wasn't Lorenzo leaving. Though she imagined Marietta was scared for her marriage. There existed a much more troubling reason for her erratic behavior. She'd seen her sister throw tantrums, and show rage, but nothing like this. It was as if a switch was flipped and all her demons surfaced at once.

It dawned on Mirabella who Marietta reminded her of in that moment. Her grandmother's twin sister. A feisty grand-aunt they all referred to as Sweetie. She was a fun loving, gun-toting woman who was never diagnosed for her manic bouts of depression. Sweetie had made several attempts to take her own life through the years, and Mirabella was too young to understand why. It was only after her grandmother died, and Sweetie drank herself into a hospital bed, that a cousin told her what the doctors called it. She was bipolar. Sweetie's erratic behavior and drinking habit drove even her children away. Only Mirabella's grandmother could keep her calm. And when she died Sweetie's demons eventually caught up to her.

Marietta may not be bipolar. But there was something broken in her that pushed her dangerously close to Sweetie's edge.

Mirabella had done the only thing she knew to do. She channeled her grandmother's patience and took care of her sister. She'd been so worried about Marietta's depression she took to sleeping in her room with her. That infuriated Giovanni. He didn't say so. He didn't have to. She knew it. If she had to leave Marietta to see about the kids she'd check on him to either see his pacing shadow behind a closed door, or to be told he was downstairs in the cellar hitting his punching bag to work off stress.

They always slept together, whether angry or not. No exceptions, until she introduced this one. If she had just lain in his arms and talked it out with him, she might have convinced him sooner to bring Lorenzo back. This had to end. Add to it that she hadn't been physical with her man since the drama started, and she was unraveling a well. Her body craved Giovanni like an addict. Her heart craved him too. She fought down all of her own turmoil to do what she could to heal her sister. But could she?

"Are you okay?" Dominic asked her.

Mirabella looked up and saw his familiar smile. She glanced around at the other men waiting to go in. She was keeping them from their meeting.

She wiped her tears. "Yeah, sorry. I'm fine. Ah, I…" she looked back at Giovanni's door. "Tell Giovanni when he's done to come see me. I want to fix dinner for us, or something. Tell him I wan to talk. Excuse me," she said. She hurried for the door and didn't look back.

It made him sick with frustration. All he did was argue with his wife. Night after night they fought over Marietta and Lorenzo. He had enough of it.

Dominic, Renaldo, and Nico came in. They had been in a meeting when Marietta charged inside screaming for them to tell her where her husband was. He had no idea how she got around the men outside. Marietta should be thankful Mirabella showed up before he had her dragged out.

"How the fuck did she get in here?" Giovanni asked.

She attacked Umberto. Hit him in the head with a stick from behind. The men were caught off guard.

"What bullshit story is that? A stick?" Giovanni shook his head. "He carries a fucking gun and she beats him up with a stick?"

"He couldn't shoot her, Gio," Dominic chuckled.

Giovanni waved the comment off. "My wife hasn't been in my bed in close to a week. She sleeps with her now. Where the fuck is Lorenzo?"

"I spoke to Carlo. He says he's at Maria's," Renaldo said.

Dominic put his face in his hand. Maria's wasn't a woman. It was a place. A whorehouse that Giovanni's father owned, and Lorenzo inherited. Giovanni did away with the business of prostitution. Maria's was now managed and owned by the Tacchi clan. The place was full of a bunch of gypsy whores who robbed and hustled men who came through the door. It was not the agreed upon place they went to escape.

"Do you want me to bring him out of there?" Nico asked.

Giovanni tapped his finger on the surface of the desk. He thought it over. "Pay him a visit. Tell him to clean up. I expect him to return to his wife no later than tomorrow morning. He needs to walk through that door and not be dragged in. The man has his fucking pride." Giovanni shook his head in disgust.

"Pride? Gio, he's at Maria's. The women find this out and he can't walk through that door." Dominic said.

"Not our concern. If he's stupid enough to take a whore into his marriage, there is nothing we can do to prevent it," Giovanni said.

"The Donna asked that I tell you to come see her when you are done. She says she wants to talk," Dominic said.

"I'm done talking about this bullshit." Giovanni grumbled.

Santo appeared at the door and knocked. Giovanni granted entrance with a glance. Nico left.

"Ciro?" Giovanni asked Dominic.

"He's ready. I just left the gym. This fight will make him a star, Gio. All the clan bosses will be attending. Everyone in the *Campania* is going to show support." Santo boasted.

"Carlo's been working hard with him," Dominic agreed.

"I want to take Bella to the fight tonight," Giovanni announced.

Santo sat up. Since the Lorenzo and Marietta drama, his wife hadn't answered a phone call from her business, or handled any other matters. In fact his little one was supposed to start school, and Mirabella had called it off. The women were standing together in their support of Marietta.

"She likes boxing," he explained though he didn't have to. "She needs to get out and have some fun. With me." Giovanni smiled. He was ready to make up. Boxing could be the key. "Marietta's draining the life out of my wife," Giovanni said. "It's time I put an end to it."

"It's a good idea, Gio," Santo spoke up. "I think the family should be there. The press will be. It's a good way to give your endorsement of Ciro." Santo stood.

"Where are you going?" Dominic frowned.

"I, uh, excuse me, Gio. I need to make a few calls," said Santo.

"I agree with him," Dominic said and watched Santo curiously as he walked out. "I'll bring Catalina."

Giovanni shook his head no. "I don't want Catalina to come. I want it to be my night with Bella. Catalina comes and it'll just distract her, or the women will worry about Marietta. Her attention should be on having fun with me."

Dominic smiled. "You making other plans for the evening?"

The thought of an evening of just the two of them did lessen his anxiety. "Yes. We'll stay the night in Napoli."

"I'll make sure it's all arranged." Dominic smiled. Giovanni again gave his nod of approval. He wanted his wife back. He knew exactly how to make that happen.

"WHERE IS SHE?" Mirabella asked Catalina.

"In her room," Catalina said. "In the bed."

Mirabella turned and headed down the other direction of the hall. Catalina was on her heels. "We have to do something. She won't eat. Zia has been making her soup and she won't eat it. I made her bathe today. She was beginning to smell."

"I know. I know," Mirabella said.

"Will Gio help? Did you talk to him?"

"Damn it, Catalina, I have! What more can I do?" Mirabella snapped.

Catalina nodded. "I'm sorry. I hate seeing her like this. Even Zia is treating her coldly. They all blame her. But I understand why she did it."

Mirabella glanced over. "Don't ever do anything like that with Domi. If you don't want kids tell him. Don't do anything sneaky behind his back. It's hard to come back from lies and deception in a marriage."

"I won't. I wouldn't. That's not what I mean. It's just that it's hard to tell these men anything. They're so stupid sometimes," Catalina said. "Marietta loves Lorenzo. Anybody can see it. But she's different, Mirabella. Something is wrong with her."

"She's fine," Mirabella said.

"No she isn't. We both know it," Catalina said.

"She's fine! She's just stressed out. We'll get Lorenzo back here and they'll talk it out. She'll be back to her normal self in no time."

"Okay. Yes, you're right. I feel bad for her. She tries so hard but she always does things the tough way. Lorenzo should understand her more, not try to crush her spirit. It's cruel. If I were a man I'd kick his ass!" Catalina said.

Mirabella nodded that she agreed. She wished Marietta confided in her fear of having kids with her and not Shae. Why hadn't she confided in her? She pushed open the door. Marietta lay on her side. She didn't look up when they entered.

"Nico is leaving. Is he going to bring Lorenzo back?" Marietta asked.

"No, sweetie. I don't know. Giovanni said he'll take care of it, so yes, that might be the reason Nico left," Mirabella lied.

Marietta put her hand to her face. "I don't feel good."

"You need to eat. What if they are going to find Lorenzo and he comes home and sees you like this?" Catalina walked over and sat on the edge of the bed. "Get dressed, and come downstairs and eat with us. Okay?"

"No. I need to stay by the phone. I paged him again. He might call back." Marietta pushed Catalina's hand away. Catalina looked to Mirabella for a suggestion. She only nodded for Catalina to give her space.

She walked over to her sister. "She's right you know. He could walk through that door any minute. Look at you. You need to eat and comb your hair. Be pretty and confident when he comes back. Let him see he didn't break you. No one can set Lorenzo straight like you."

For the first time in an exhaustive week Marietta didn't respond with tears. "You think I'm crazy?"

"No." Mirabella sat on the bed. "Well maybe a little."

Marietta let go a burst of laughter. Her smile broadened. Mirabella and Catalina both exhaled in relief.

"Zia is angry with me. She's not talking to me." Marietta said. She sat upright.

"Zia will get over it. Lorenzo will get over it. That's what's special about our family. We learn to love, forgive, and get over it." Mirabella put her hand on top of her sister's.

"Mirabella's right. You know the story of me and Franco." Catalina sat at the foot of the bed. "The entire family was mad at me. I thought it would never end. Now we're planning a wedding. They get over it," Catalina said.

"Okay! Fuck this!" Marietta stood and heaved several deep breaths. "He better not be with another woman. That's all I got to say. I swear to God I'll cut off his dick and feed it to him in a bowl of Zia's ziti."

They watched her go to the bathroom. The door closed.

"Do you know where he is?" Mirabella whispered to Catalina.

"I got an idea. I'm praying I'm wrong. But it's Lorenzo we're talking about." Catalina said.

Mirabella nodded. "I know."

— *B* —

"I CAN'T SPEAK LONG," Santo said.

He peeked out the door of the study and then closed it. "Tonight. We do it tonight."

"What. Why now? You've been putting it off for a week. Suddenly you're ready to make a move?"

"There's been trouble here. Lorenzo is missing and his wife is distraught. Mirabella and the kids haven't left."

"And what's different about tonight?"

"You asked if I could get her to the arena for the boxing fight. I thought I couldn't. Today I found out Giovanni is bringing her. If I can separate them it might work to your favor."

"Might? I want guarantees."

Santo grimaced. "This is the fucking best I could do. I am putting my life on the line by even trying it."

"I want Eve," he said.

"Not possible. I'll deal with the children after. Do we do this or not?"

The silence on the phone was like the cold steel sharpened edge of a knife being slowly dragged across his throat. Santo kept glancing over his shoulder. He was inside Melanzana. One of the men could walk up on him at any moment. He waited.

"I'm impressed. I think it's a perfect plan. Yes. Do it. Tonight."

The line went dead. Santo hung up the phone and considered what he'd have to pull off. It wouldn't be easy.

—*B*—

"BELLA?" GIOVANNI SAID.

"Give me a second," Mirabella said. She picked up the stack of folded clothes and went to the dresser drawer. He couldn't tell if she was angry or not. All he knew was he missed his wife and the tension was draining them both.

"I told Nico to find Lorenzo and tell him to come home," Giovanni said.

She paused at the dresser. "You did?"

He approached her. She turned and stared into his eyes. He could see the fatigue and stress on her face. She looked exhausted. "Are you well, Bella?" he asked and touched her hair.

"I'm scared for Marietta. I think we might need to get her some help, Gio." She went into his arms and burst into tears. She wept so hard it shook him. He stroked her back and held her until her sobs lessened. "Something is wrong with her."

"She's upset about her marriage. Marriage is private, Bella. We can agree on that much?"

"Yes. We can agree on that." She lowered her arms and looked up at him. "I just didn't know what to do. She's my sister. I don't know what to do when she acts this way. It's extreme, and scary. You didn't see her this week. Do you understand why I've been concerned?"

He cupped her face. "I do now, Bella. I only ask that you don't punish me when we don't agree. Don't push me away. Come to me if you're scared," he told her.

"I tried."

"Bella? You've tried harder for that business than you did with Marietta. You shut me out. That's not like you. What is it that makes you so terrified of your sister's pain?" he asked.

Mirabella lowered her gaze. "I—my family. I think, I think there's depression in my family."

"I don't understand." Giovanni said.

"Nothing. Forget it. It's probably nothing. Marietta was upset and she reminded me of someone. But it's nothing. You're right, sweetheart." He held her face and kissed her lips twice before kissing the tears from her cheeks.

"I've been so lonely for you," she said softly. Her hands slipped around his waist. "Have you missed me, baby?" she rubbed his back. Giovanni chuckled. His wife was really good at evading. He could press the issue and uncover what scared her about Marietta's depression. But to be honest he had to be selfish on this. He missed her smile.

"Let me cook us a special dinner. You and me. And then we can make up." She rubbed her jaw across his. "Any way we please."

"Let's go out," he said.

She looked into his eyes. "Out? Where?"

"A surprise."

"I don't know if I should leave her tonight. When Lorenzo comes home we both need to be here. Don't you think?" she asked.

"He's coming in the morning, and I'll have you back before then."

Mirabella chewed on her bottom lip. He saw how torn his wife was. He loved her loyalty, but on this one he needed to insist. He needed to make her feel good again. Feel safe and protected. It was the best way he knew how to love and nurture her. She may have pushed him away, but he did little to comfort her. He watched her run between the children and her sister for a solid week. He could have easily put an end to it by bringing Lorenzo back home. Part of him wanted Marietta to suffer. It was blasphemous of her to pull such treachery in her marriage. But these women were American, foreign to their customs and ways. Maybe he was too quick to judge. When she didn't agree he finally relented.

"Okay. I'll tell you the surprise," he said.

She lifted her gaze. He smiled down at her. "Ciro fights in Naples tonight. We got ringside seats."

"Really?" she smiled. His heart expanded with relief.

"Sounds like fun doesn't it?"

"It sounds like so much fun!" she said barely able to contain her excitement.

"*Dà retta.* I love you. I'm sorry we argued. This isn't something either of us can fix. My *cougine* is as stubborn as I am. I do know he loves her. He will come home and make things right with his wife. Believe me."

She hugged him. Mirabella was her sweetest to him when she offered him forgiveness. The week had been hard on the family. Marietta's wails, ranting, cursing, tantrums, were an all day and all night event. He'd spent a couple nights at Villa Rosso to escape his loneliness for his wife.

"I'd love to go on a date with you. I need to be with you away from here," Mirabella said.

"We need each other. Away from here," he agreed.

Later –

Marietta saw Nico arrive from the downstairs window. She had changed into a red summer dress that tied around her neck and draped her hips. The hem was mid-thigh. Lorenzo loved her in this dress. She spent hours fixing her dry tangled hair. She even managed to cover up the dark circles of fatigue under her eyes with makeup. She dabbed Shalimar at all her sensitive spots to carry the fragrance with her wherever she went. She was ready for him.

She stepped closer to the window. Her breathing fogged the glass. Nico exited the car alone. Lorenzo was not with him. She glanced up to the gates, and to her disappointment she saw no car follow. Her heart sank.

She turned and hurried out of her room. *Where was he? Why hadn't he come?* If Giovanni gave him an order, would Lorenzo disobey? Her mind said he had no choice. Her heart knew the man best, and it told her he'd not come to her on anybody's demand, unless it was what he wanted. When she reached the end of the hall she saw Cecilia with one of the twins on her hip. She greeted Nico. They kissed. Together they walked off toward the front parlor. Marietta went in pursuit.

"Did you find Lorenzo?" Cecilia asked.

"Don't worry," Nico told her.

"*Signora Marietta* is not well. Did you tell him, Nico?" she asked.

Nico sighed. He took Gianni from her arms and raised him above his head. He grinned up at the baby. "Lorenzo is drunk, too wasted to return home."

"Where is he?" Cecilia asked. "I swear I won't tell a soul."

"He's at Maria's." Nico said sadly. "Surrounded by gypsy whores. He's been there for the week."

"Oh? How awful for Marietta. She can't know that. It'll break her heart," Cecilia said.

"I told Elsa to call me when he wakes. I'll go back and make sure he knows to come home. I couldn't bring him out of there in that condition. He's my boss."

"I understand. But you have to tell the Don. He and the Donna are going to the boxing match in Naples. He needs to know."

"I will." Nico threw Gianni up above his head. The toddler squealed with delight. He caught him and kissed his face then threw him up in the air again.

Marietta clenched her fist so tight her knuckles went white. Here she was torn up with guilt, and that rat bastard of a husband had gone to a whorehouse. She'd kill him. She'd kill him nice and slow. And she'd do it after she murdered those sluts.

—*B*—

"YOU LOOK PRETTY, MOMMY!" Eve clapped from Catalina's lap.

Mirabella checked herself in the mirror. The black dress she chose flattered her slender waist, and curvy hips. And though her breasts were sculpted elegantly to the front, they were not revealed. However, when she turned, the backless cut was so low she couldn't wear underwear.

"You should wear your hair down," Catalina said.

"In this dress I think I should wear it up," Mirabella lifted it from her neck.

"Gio likes it down," Catalina said. "This is to make up with him so he can bring Lorenzo home. Right?"

"Yes! Papa wants it down. He told me." Eve nodded.

Mirabella laughed. "Yes, I intend to make up with him. Papa is more willing to be reasonable when he isn't agitated." She turned from the mirror when her sister walked in. Marietta surprised them all. She looked beautiful. Her smile had the familiar radiance they all loved about her.

"Auntie!" Eve said and scooted off Catalina's lap. She ran over to Marietta who picked her up. Eve kissed her cheek and hugged her neck. "Do you feel better?"

"I sure do, little diva." She set Eve down.

Catalina stood. "Come on, Eve. Let's see if Zia and Ana need help in the kitchen. I know they're baking today," Catalina stopped by the door to kiss Marietta on the cheek. They gave each other warm smiles, and then she walked Eve out.

"You feeling better?" Mirabella asked.

"Yes. Where are you headed?" Marietta asked. She came over to fix the back of her sister's dress.

"To dinner and a boxing match in Napoli. It's a date night with Giovanni. We've been... arguing. He's trying to make up."

"I'm sorry," Marietta said softly. "That's my fault. I've been a terror these past few days."

"Hey? It's okay. You and Lo need to work it out. Is he here?"

"Not yet," Marietta beamed with a smile. "But I'll see him tonight."

Her sister walked into the bathroom. Marietta's gaze swept her surroundings. This room was the grandest in all of Melanzana. Fit for a king and queen. Next door was the adjoining room for the kids.

"Where do you keep your gun?" Marietta mumbled under her breath. She heard Mirabella with her combs and brushes.

"I think I am going to wear my hair pinned up. What do you think?" Mirabella asked.

Marietta went to the cabinet and then checked the top drawers. "Good idea, with that dress it's perfect," she answered. She remembered that Mirabella always kept the weapon close.

"I have a surprise for you. I was going to wait to tell you, but I think I should tell you now," Mirabella said.

"Oh yeah? What is it?" Marietta asked. She ran over to the closet next to the bathroom and began her search there.

"America!"

"What about America?" Marietta asked.

"Giovanni and I are planning a trip. I want to take you to Virginia, to see where I grew up. To Mama's grave."

Marietta walked out of the closet and Mirabella had a curious frown on her face. "Oh, I was looking for your red bottoms to wear with that dress. The ones Jamie made for you with the steel pointed tips."

"Good idea. They're on the top shelf." Mirabella winked. "So what do you think?"

"About?" Marietta asked as she returned to the closet. She found the shoes on the shelf with over two hundred others. She brought the pair out.

"About America? Going to Virginia? Me and you. I can introduce you to our family. Cousins, aunts, and take you to Granddad's farm. We still own it. What do you think?"

Marietta handed the shoes over to Mirabella. "We have cousins and aunts? You never mentioned them before."

"They… well we aren't that close anymore. Long story. Still you need to meet our family. And they need to meet you. I know by now with all the press coverage and our interviews they are curious about us both."

"I'd love it. I think Lorenzo will too. I'll tell him about it when I see him tonight," Marietta smiled.

"You sure you're okay?" Mirabella touched her face.

"Yep. I'm fine. I feel better."

"Okay." Mirabella sat on the bed and put on her shoes.

"Hey? You gonna take your gun with you tonight?" Marietta asked casually.

"No. Why would I?" Mirabella frowned.

"You know why. Giovanni made you keep it on you when we were in Milano. Even Lo doesn't make me carry one," Marietta smiled. "I guess he doesn't trust me not to shoot him."

"That's not funny," Mirabella frowned.

Marietta shrugged. She refused to take it back. Especially since she had plans to do just that tonight.

"I hate the thing. Besides my husband has plenty of guns around us tonight. I don't need mine," Mirabella chuckled.

"Where do you keep it?" Marietta asked.

"Over there, to the back of the bottom drawer in the gun case. It's under the sweaters. The bullets are in there too. It's not loaded. Gianni loves to open drawers and pull clothes out. I know I should move it."

"Oh? Okay." Marietta sighed. "Want me to help you finish your makeup?"

"Nope! I have it. I'll see you in the morning. Good luck tonight," Mirabella said.

"Thanks, sis," Marietta kissed her cheek. She started for the door. Mirabella had already returned to the bathroom when she reached it. Marietta was quick to double back. She went to the dresser and quietly opened the bottom drawer. She found the gun, and bullets. She never took to the weapons her husband carried. Worse than her sister, she was a terrible shot. All she needed to do was point and aim. How hard could that be? She closed the door and crept from the room.

—*B*—

GIOVANNI CAST HIS GAZE over to his wife. She was at his side with her hand in his. He checked his watch. The fight started in less than an hour. Mirabella stared out at the city lights. Perched at the top of the Vomero Hill, it was the city's grandest landmark, *Castel Sant'Elmo*. A medieval fortress that overlooked the gulf of Napoli, was host to everything from sessions of Congress, to music festivals. And in the bottom chambers was an auditorium that could house close to a thousand spectators. The huge event would draw thousands, but not everyone would gain access.

His wife crossed her legs. He let her hand go to rest it upon her thigh. It dawned on him how little they ventured out and enjoyed the city as man and wife. The fashion show and party in Bellagio had been big events for them both. He intended to enjoy their life, and give her the liberty to be more than just a wife. He had warmed to the idea of being the husband of a highly acclaimed fashion designer.

Giovanni squeezed her thigh. He wanted to touch and feel more of her. His dick was killing him. But they were running late.

"What time does it start?" she asked.

"We're almost there."

"Yes, but what time does it start?" she asked.

"In about half an hour. We're close."

"It's like a castle," she said and leaned forward. At night the city lit up *Castel Sant'Elmo,* which stood next to *Certosa di San Martino,* a former monastery turned museum.

"It's beautiful," Mirabella said. "I saw it when Fabiana and I were shopping nearby."

"You'll love it. Everyone is coming out for the big event."

Mirabella glanced back at the glare of headlights trailing them. "Looks like it. Did we leave anyone back home to guard our castle?" she joked.

"The men are as excited as you. Many are coming to support Ciro and Carlo." Giovanni reclined his head on the seat and continued to caress her thigh. The further his hand moved up the more he wondered of the choice she made for the evening. With the body of a goddess, the dress made his men lower their eyes out of respect when she walked past them. The dress teased and flattered her curves. Was she wearing underwear? Typically when she wore a dress that was backless she wasn't. He glanced down and pushed her dress further up to see. She tried to pull her dress back down, but he forced it further. When he persisted she swatted his hand away playfully.

"I can't wait," Mirabella said. "My favorite fighter is Mike Tyson. Fabiana and I had front row seats to watch him fight Larry Holmes. He knocked him out in the fourth round. We were on our feet screaming!"

He tried reaching between her thighs, but she captured his wrist and squeezed it with affection.

"Interesting. There are still things I don't know about my Bella." His gaze lifted to her face. "My Donna needs a pair of boxing gloves. If you want I can be your trainer."

"You got it, baby!" She threw a few shadow punches.

Giovanni tried to shift in his seat. The happier and more excitable she became, the harder it was to conceal his hard-on. He could act on his desire to have her, but the time was short. He checked his watch again. Decisions. Decisions.

"Can you imagine me down in the cellar training with you? If you become my trainer I don't have to wait to jump your bones when you come upstairs after working out? You are so damn sexy when you sweat," she grinned. "Yummy too. I have a sketch I did of you once. It's in my studio. It shows you're muscles and torso, with you throwing boxing punches. I keep it up there with me."

"You drew me and haven't shown me?" he chuckled.

"I look at it when you aren't home. I'll show you. I have to have you near me, Gio. You're my inspiration." She leaned over and kissed his jaw. "Gio?"

"Yes, Bella?"

"Is your dick hard?"

He chuckled.

"Are you kidding me?" she laughed.

Giovanni hit the intercom to the driver. The privacy divider in the limo kept their conversations from their escort. "Pull over, and then get out! Now!" he told the driver. They veered off the main artery of the road to another. The limo rolled to a stop, and so did the caravan of cars following them.

"What's going on?" she asked. She turned and looked back at the other cars following them. "Why are we stopping?"

Before Mirabella could counter his next move or understand his intentions, Giovanni was on her. And she felt nice.

Mirabella was taken by surprise. She struggled at first. He groaned and pulled her closer so she was pinned with her legs open and could feel the granite hard erection he had for her. Their eyes met. It was going to happen. She had no doubt about that. But the timing was terrible.

"Miss me?" he asked.

"So bad," she nodded and bit down on her bottom lip when he rubbed his erection into her pussy. His gaze lowered to her body. She could tell his only hesitation was regarding where he wanted to fuck her, with her on her back or on her stomach. The choice excited her so much she nearly voiced a request that he turn her over and enter her from behind. She was wetting the front of his silk trousers with her moist readiness. He brought his face in to run his tongue over her jugular. The heady fragrance of his aftershave overwhelmed her.

"Mmm, Gio, baby. You're killing me," she moaned.

He parted her thighs and sat back. Dazed she opened her eyes. He helped her sit upright. Had he changed his mind? She groaned in disappointment. But his next move revealed his true intentions. Her thighs were pushed further apart. Mirabella lifted her left leg and dropped it over his shoulder. She scooted her ass to the edge of the seat so her vagina was flush and on display. The first lick of his tongue, flattened, swiping over her sex, caused her to visibly quiver. Her left shoe dropped off her foot. God help her but there was no turning back now. If he didn't give her what she'd been craving for close to a week she'd scream.

She was his. She gripped the back of the seat to hold on. The sweet tangy scent of her pussy was edged with her natural spice. He loved the smell of his wife. He buried his head between her thighs and used his tongue to deliver soft strokes to coax her clit into his mouth. Her unique flavor rolled over his taste buds and became the sweetest nectar he'd tasted that day. He sucked hard with tugs on her clit until she climaxed. He eased his hands under her bottom to lift her pussy. It pulsed against his mouth and spilled her essence.

In an instant she lost her head. She scrambled to regain her senses. "Wait! Gio?" What just happened? Her mind couldn't comprehend. The only reason she got a brief reprieve was because he was trying to unbuckle his belt. She closed her thighs. At least her dress was up at her waist, and she was wetting the back of the seat. Of course he ignored her. He came for her again and she had to scoot to the door to escape him. He was so swift, and his hands so strong, he forced her to recline.

"Okay!" she said in a panic. "Okay, baby. Wait a second!" If she didn't think of something quick she'd miss the boxing match. She really wanted to make up with him. But she wanted them to have fun for the evening. Not exhaust themselves by fucking on the side of the road and then returning home to the drama. There had to be a compromise. He held her in his sights like a predator ready to pounce. She smiled for him. "A quickie, promise me." She put up a finger to warn him to obey. "And you can't come inside me. Use ah… oh shoot!" She reached for the towel under the ice bucket. Lucky for them the limo had one and plenty of napkins. "Promise me?"

He gave her a sly smile and nodded he'd behave. Mirabella pulled her dress over her head and tried to be careful of her hair. Giovanni unzipped himself.

"Take off your shirt, honey. I don't want you sweaty before we get to the fight."

He obeyed. He struggled with his diamond cufflinks so she assisted. They both did so with increasing hurry. She looked out the window and saw several of the men coming out of their cars to question the driver. Thank God the limousine tint prevented them from peering inside.

"This is crazy. This is crazy," she kept mumbling. Mirabella put Giovanni's diamond cufflinks she bought him last year for his birthday on top of her folded dress. Giovanni was kissing her stomach before sucking her nipples before she was ready. She tried to shift into a better position but it was useless. He wanted to pin her down where he could fuck her deep. He was too big of a man for his aggression. She figured if she gave in he'd not take too long. It was a costly mistake.

He cupped her vagina and she let out a shaky breath. All doubts were cast away. She gyrated against his hand while kissing him. There was nothing she wanted more than him inside of her. He eased up her.

"If you give me more time I can…" he began.

"Nice try," she chuckled. "You have ten minutes, Casanova."

He groaned. "I'm a man not a rabbit!"

Mirabella laughed. He dragged her underneath him. He stared into her eyes and her heart nearly exploded it was so filled with love for him. She grabbed his head and pulled it down to her. The kiss was scorching hot with intensity. And when he thrust into her, she was overwhelmed by his power and need. He pushed his hips forward and sank deeper. Mirabella bit his bottom lip. It felt so good.

She relaxed against the cool leather seat and wrapped her legs around his waist. He pumped into her—short, forceful thrusts that were uncomfortable. Mirabella tilted her hips up to help him deepen his thrusts. Giovanni grunted against her ear. Her bottom maneuvers were doing it for him. She could tell. Mirabella smiled and suffered a strange pang of guilt mixed in with her happiness. If she had allowed her man's touch in the past week, he wouldn't be so attention starved for her now. Giovanni liked to watch the way he went and in and out of her and curse in Sicilian as he did. It was such a turn on. She drifted on his gruff words and gave herself over to him.

"We need to leave," she tried to sex him into releasing. He looked at her again and then smiled. He dropped down on her and pinned her hips beneath him. At first Mirabella enjoyed it. And then his hurried passion indicated disaster. "Gio! Don't! Please don't!"

He grunted and released inside of her. Mirabella rolled her eyes and shook her head. He lifted his head and gave her a wolfish grin. "Sorry, Bella. I couldn't help myself."

"Get up. Get off me." She hit at his back. He lifted off her. Mirabella reached for the paper towel and did her best to clean them both. It was a disaster. Thankfully her dress and his pants didn't get the stains of their sex on them. But the back seat of the limo was wet from their passion. It took longer than she wished to dry up every trace. However, she managed the deed and they both dressed between kisses and smiles. He was happy. She was happy. They were back on track. She was forced to use her little compact mirror to reapply her makeup. It didn't give her a good view of her hair. Giovanni rolled down the window and gestured with his hand that the men should get rolling. They were back on the road.

"Are we late?" she asked.

"Of course," he smiled. He brought her hand up to his lips and kissed her knuckles. "I want to revisit our special place. Stay the night near the bay." He was talking about the apartment he owned that faced the bay of Napoli. They stayed there when she returned to Sorrento after being gone for two years. It was there they made up.

"Private?" she asked. "Sounds sweet."

He playfully growled in his throat. Mirabella laughed as if tickled. She leaned over and rubbed her nose against his cheek. "I've missed you, Gio. This week has been horrible."

"You have all night to make it up to me," he said.

"Me? I did nothing wrong!" she exclaimed.

He settled back with a pleased smile to his face.

"You're so spoiled, Gio," she laughed and snuggled against him for the rest of the ride.

—*B*—

"Cecilia, may I speak with you?" Marietta asked.

The young woman's head turned from the crib. She laid Gianni down. Gino was asleep in the crib next to Gianni. Eve sat in her bed, flipping the pages of her favorite book, with her dolls tucked in next to her. She playfully read the pages to her dolls.

"Yes of course, *signora*," Cecilia said. "Evie, time for sleep."

"Noooooo! I'm not done," Eve whined.

"*Scusami tanto*," Cecilia turned off the bedside lamp. "Please, princess, let's go to sleep now. No fussing."

The sun had set. It was the non-negotiable bedtime for the kids. Cecilia made sure the nightlight was on near the cribs. Though the kids could have separate rooms, Mirabella decided that the boys and Eve would share one for now.

Marietta observed Cecilia's duties as an *au pair* from the door. When Eve was nestled in her bed with her doll in her arms, Cecilia left the kids' side. Not before. She smiled sweetly at Marietta and pulled the door to the kids' room closed behind her. She had a baby monitor in her hand. They faced each other in the dark hall.

"What can I do for you?" Cecilia asked.

Marietta removed the gun from behind her back. She pointed it at Cecilia. "You're going to take me to my husband."

"I—" Cecilia dropped the monitor. It smashed on the floor and the batteries spilled out.

"Your car is here. We'll use it."

"But I can't. I have to see to the kids. I work tonight. I can't leave."

"We'll go to Zia and tell her you have an emergency. She'll check on the kids. Then you pull your car to the side of Melanzana near the wine cellar doors. I'll get in the back and—"

"*Signora,* please! I can't help. I don't know anything—"

"SHUT UP!" Marietta said through clenched teeth. "Don't lie to me. I heard Nico tell you he's with a whore named Maria."

Cecilia's eyes watered. She nodded and bit on her lip. Marietta held the gun on her. Cecilia stared at the weapon for a minute and then found her voice. "It's not a whore, it's a brothel. He may be staying in one of the rooms. Nico said he'd go back for him when he sobered. So he's going to bring him here."

"We're going! Move! Now!"

"But, *signora,* even if we get out of the gates we can't walk into Maria's. It's forbidden for women like yourself to be seen there." Cecilia pleaded. "That place is the devil's den, you're Lorenzo's wife. You have respect. They don't."

"I've waited all day for him to come home. You're taking me. Move!"

Cecilia nodded. She started to walk down the hall, nervously wringing her hands and crying. Marietta slipped the gun into her purse to keep it unseen.

Castel Sant'Elmo dated back to the 14th century. The medieval castle eventually evolved into a military fortress overlooking the gulf of Naples. It was so overwhelmingly massive her breath was caught in her lungs as they passed through the gates. There were plenty of street vendors and musicians entertaining the crowds. What if Ciro became the next 'knockout king' and fought his way up the ranks all the way to challenge Mike Tyson? Mirabella hadn't exaggerated when she told her husband she was about to explode with excitement. She first became interested in boxing when she was sixteen. She and her cousin Latoya sneaked away to a gym where they secretly watched young men train. One in particular was her favorite. He discovered them climbing the gate after his training session. Latoya got across and away. Mirabella didn't. She was certain he would turn her over to her grandfather. He was older than her, and everyone knew her grandparents. Instead Cedric took her into the gym and let her sit on the bench to watch him train. He got a kick out of her enthusiasm. Cedric became her first love and her worst nightmare. She didn't think of him often. She didn't think of Kei and their failed love affair often either. In her life she'd only had to kiss two frogs before finding her prince. The painful lessons were worth it.

Hand in hand she walked with Giovanni. Their arrival drew the open stares of many. He had at least thirty of his men with them for the evening. The men walked ahead and behind them down the long parapet. She felt like a prizefighter on the way to the ring. And the further they went down to the lower chambers, the larger the crowds they had to push through. She held tight to Giovanni's hand. A strangling feeling of claustrophobia descended on her. Those that could step out of their way did so. Others made an overzealous effort to greet them and were shoved aside.

It was a mix of people from all walks of life, but what struck her as surprising was the large number of Asians in attendance. All over the UK the Chinese boxer was taking down opponents. His fans had come in droves to the event.

"How did you get Ciro in the ring with Chao Lee?" Mirabella asked. Giovanni kept walking. He didn't answer. She should know better than to ask the 'how' about anything her husband dabbled in. Still Ciro had to leap over several higher ranked contenders to get a chance at this fight.

"Gio? Mirabella?" Dominic walked up and greeted them. Renaldo was with him. Domi wore a dark tailored suit, and looked a lot more distinguished and hardened than she ever envisioned him before. It was funny how differently all of the men appeared to her when they were in public. Very serious and very composed. He kissed Mirabella on both cheeks. "Come with me, we've reserved seats."

They were walked into the auditorium. At the center was a boxing ring and a fight was in progress. Mirabella could tell it wasn't the main event. That didn't subdue the audience. Men and women were yelling and shouting after every landed punch. She was rising on her toes to see over her husband's broad shoulders, and still couldn't. The Battaglias had reserved seating. She saw a few people with their cameras snapping her picture. She tried to be gracious and smile. She didn't want the attention. Just a night of fun and normalcy with the man she loved.

"Ringside seats," Mirabella said as she took her position next to her husband.

"Only the best for you." He winked.

The fighter threw another punch and the bell was sounded. The men were forced to their corners. Mirabella was on the edge of the seat bubbling with excitement.

—ℬ—

THE MOMENT SHE ARRIVED HE SAW HER. How could he not? She was the most strikingly beautiful woman in the arena. Kei reclined in his seat and watched as she walked with her husband to a less populated, designated area. Mirabella was the same: beautiful, young, and vibrant. When she passed the rows of spectators, the heads of every red blooded man turned. She wore a slimming dress that hugged tight to her body and curves. It appeared to be backless. Three children later she was shapelier in the hips, ass, and breasts. But she was still petite in the waist, arms, and slender legs. He absorbed every detail. She climbed a few steps to reach their elevated row. Her hair was pinned up away from her neck. He liked it that way. It revealed more of her beauty. In his heart he took that as a sign. She was ready for him.

"There they are," Santo said.

"I've changed plans." Kei spoke.

"You what—"

"In the fourth round Giovanni will receive my declaration of war." Kei's gaze slipped over to Santo. "You need to have her clear of here before the bell rings."

"He'll never let her go without two or three men," Santo said. "I think the ambush is the way to go."

Kei smirked. "Not my problem. It's yours. I'll warn you. If she's hurt in any way—"

"I won't hurt her," Santo assured him. He let go of an exasperated sigh. He stood and left. Kei stared at Giovanni and Mirabella. She smiled and whispered to her husband then pointed to the ring. Giovanni nodded and put his hand on Mirabella's thigh. Kei leaned forward. He saw the kid boxer enter the auditorium in his robe with the hood over his head and his fists taped up. The crowd of Italians and Sicilians gathered stood and cheered. This was the runt to challenge Chao Lee. Kei shook his head and chuckled. He looked forward to the show.

—ℬ—

"Is this the place?" Marietta asked.

Cecilia nodded. "I can't go in there, *signora*. I can't. I'm sorry."

"It's fine, don't worry about it. I won't tell anyone you brought me." She unhooked the seatbelt. She dug out the gun from her purse and checked the chamber for bullets.

"*Signora!*" Cecilia grabbed her arm. "What are you going to do with that gun?"

"I plan to get my husband. Who runs this place?" Marietta asked.

"The woman's name is Elsa. She used to work for your husband and for Tomosino. This was Lorenzo's place before Don Giovanni cut all ties with the prostitute brothels. They won't let you in to see him. He came here because they protect them. They aren't Italians. These women are thieves, harlots, dangerous. You can't trust them. They're beneath you, *signora*. Please. I beg you. Don't go in there."

"I'm going to get my husband." Marietta threw the door open.

The night was darkest on this street. Only the dull silver rays of a crescent moon cast any light. She had to walk up the narrow, cobblestone, one-way hill cramped by three story buildings. The front door of Maria's opened. A man stumbled out with a woman under his arm. She appeared to be the one to keep him standing. He was clearly intoxicated. Marietta kept the gun pointed down and close to her thigh. She dashed between parked cars and up the sidewalk to the door of the whorehouse. To her frustration she found it locked. Marietta looked back and saw that Cecilia hadn't left. The young woman sat in the car staring at her with troubled eyes.

Marietta banged on the door with her gun. She banged repeatedly.

The door opened. "*Che cosa!*" a very tall burly man with lots of facial hair yelled at her.

"Lorenzo Battaglia," Marietta said.

The man frowned. "Fuck off."

He turned to close the door and Marietta raised the gun. He must have caught sight of it from his peripheral vision because he froze. Good for him. She had her finger on the trigger with the intent to shoot it open.

"Let me in," she said.

"Who is it Gregieo?" a woman asked.

"Move out my fucking way, fat man. Now!" Marietta shouted.

The man stepped back with his chubby hands raised. Marietta climbed the steps and walked inside. She closed the door behind her. The stench of sex, fragrant candles, and cheap floral perfume made her stomach clench. The lighting inside was a dull red haze, and hard on the eyes. Two women, one older, came into the hall. They stopped at the sight of Marietta with a gun.

"I want to see my husband. Lorenzo Battaglia. Where is he?"

"I'm Elsa. You must be Marietta? *Buonasera*." The older woman smiled.

"Shut the fuck up with your fake greeting. Take me to him! Now!" Marietta fingered the trigger. *Is this the bitch that made it easy for Lorenzo to walk out on her? Maybe she should kill her first.* She leveled the gun directly at Elsa. The cool detachment in her voice, and steady aim, dimmed the confidence in the woman's smile. The tall fat man glanced to the older woman for instruction.

"*Va bene.* I'll take you to him." She tossed her dark hair. "It's okay, Gregieo. Make sure the girls stay in their rooms. Come with me, *Signora* Battaglia," said the Madam. Elsa had to be in her early sixties, but she had the body of a thirty year old. And her dark locks looked to be dyed black to cover the grey. It was the wrinkles and moles to her face that revealed her age. She was the only woman that Marietta passed as they walked down the hall that wore appropriate clothing. The working girls were topless and some even bottomless.

Marietta gripped the gun with both hands. She kept her eye on Gregieo when she passed him.

"I was at your party two years ago. The one you had in Bellagio," Elsa said.

"Were you? It figures that my husband would invite his whore to our wedding party," Marietta said.

Elsa looked back at her. She smiled. "I'm an ex-employee, not his whore. I was Tomosino's personal friend. If you're curious I can tell you our story."

"I don't give a fuck!" Marietta said.

Elsa chuckled. "When you return to Melanzana please tell Don Giovanni the girls miss him. Since he's been married we haven't seen him. Tell him I said hello."

"Where's Lorenzo?"

Elsa stopped. "I've worked for Tomosino Battaglia for many years, and then Lorenzo. I'm a friend to the family, not an enemy of yours. Please show me respect. I assure you I've shown you respect since he arrived here. We've been taking care of him. That's all the girls did."

"Bullshit! I'm not stupid!" Marietta shouted. "Get out of the way." She put the gun directly between Elsa's eyes. The woman stepped aside and bowed her head. Marietta stared at the door. All of a sudden she couldn't bring herself to enter. What if he was with another woman? What then? She had no plan for the disintegration of her marriage. Lorenzo was her life. She'd take his before she let him go. The heated stare of the old whore bore into her. Sure she was pleasant when she spoke, but the woman had the grace of a cobra. Cecilia was right. She was now in the devil's den. When she looked over to the gypsy she could have sworn she saw admiration in her smile.

"You're a tough one to come here. Alone," Elsa said. "Will you shoot him?"

"I'll fucking shoot you if you don't stop talking to me," Marietta pointed the gun at Elsa. And with a deep intake of breath she opened the door with her left hand. A brunette with deep olive skin and short brown hair sat up from the bed. She was topless. Her panty did little to cover her sex. She looked at Marietta and the gun. And then came the toilet flush. The woman slowly stood. Another door opened. Lorenzo walked out of what must have been the bathroom drying his hair. He was shirtless in dark slacks and bare feet. After a few steps into the room, his head lifted and he locked eyes with Marietta.

The tears came right before she pulled the trigger.

She hit the woman. She was certain by the way the girl dropped on the bed and screamed. There was blood. Marietta wanted to do more than hurt her. She fired again, and shattered the lamp a few inches from the woman. Terrified the woman dropped to the floor and scrambled to get under the bed, so Marietta fired at the bed before Lorenzo came for her. Marietta turned the gun on him and fired but it jammed. She un-cocked and released the bullet before she could be stopped.

He stopped in his tracks. He stood there frozen as she held the gun on him. She had meant to kill him. That was how bad the pain of his betrayal cut through her. Marietta wept, blinded by her rage. She shook her head in contempt. How could he hurt her so deeply? What had she ever done to deserve this? She'd never experienced so much misery at once. And under the roof of Octavio Leone she knew plenty of misery. Marietta gripped the gun tight with both her hands and shook all over. She'd make him pay. There was nothing left to them after this. And she knew she couldn't live without him.

Lorenzo raised his hands slowly. He shook his head to someone behind her, and Marietta turned in time to point the gun at Nico and another of his men. When they arrived she wasn't sure. Her head was spinning. Her chest hurt. She could barely catch her breath. And the damn tears would not stop long enough for her to have clear vision. She kept swinging the gun between Nico and Lorenzo. She felt like she was dying.

"Out. Get the fuck out!" she screamed at Nico until she went hoarse. "Now!"

"Vattene!" Lorenzo said to his men. The men looked at him with concern and then to Marietta. They were unsure of the order. "Leave us. I can handle her."

"Oh, you think so?" she swung the gun in Lorenzo's direction.

The two men stepped back. Lorenzo ignored his plight. "Angela, come out from under the bed," Lorenzo said. "Nico, make sure she gets medical attention."

The woman screamed and shouted in a language Marietta didn't understand.

"She comes out from under that bed and I'm going to kill her!" Marietta said.

Lorenzo smiled. He put his hand to his chest when he spoke. "This is between you and me, Marie. Let her go, *cara*."

"No! You fucking bastard, you made it between the three of us. Don't send her away now! I hate you!" she shouted.

"She'll bleed to death!" he said. "You don't want to kill anyone."

"I don't care!" Marietta screamed.

"Angela, come out. Now!" Lorenzo said.

The woman whimpered. She didn't move. Lorenzo took a step toward Marietta and she pulled the trigger. The bullet hit something and it ricocheted. It shattered the window behind him. She intended to miss.

"She's crazy!" The woman wept from under the bed.

"No, bitch, I'm quite sane! Come out and I'll prove it," Marietta wiped her tears with the back of her hand and kept the gun on Lorenzo.

To her surprise he went to the bed and shoved it aside to reveal the bleeding woman. Marietta had shot her in the arm. The woman scrambled for cover, but Lorenzo grabbed her up by the waist before she could scurry away. He forced her to stand upright. Marietta couldn't believe he'd help the whore in her face. He shoved the woman toward the door and the girl didn't stop. She ran for it. Marietta wanted to shoot her. She ached to do it. But how many bullets did she have left? She wanted to punish Lorenzo more, and then save one for herself.

"I don't understand why you would do this to me. Hurt me like this!" she shouted at him.

"Her name is Angela. She works here, Marie," Lorenzo said.

"I know what the fuck she is. What the fuck she does! I saw!"

"I didn't touch her," he said.

"You're lying! She was in the bed. Naked!"

"*Dio mio!* Half the women here are naked. I am not lying. That's you, the queen of lies!"

Marietta lowered the gun. She dropped her head and cried. He didn't say a word to comfort her. And she hurt too bad to fight off his verbal attacks. She felt lost and confused. For a minute she didn't even remember how she got there. The hysteria lessened. When she looked to him he stood there staring. His face was red and contorted with anger.

"I love you," she said. "I did. I really did love you."

He didn't answer.

She sniffed. "So this is it? You don't want to even try to fix our marriage? Ever?"

"How did you find me?" he asked.

"I hope that bitch gives you the mange and your dick falls off." She dropped the gun. She turned and started for the door.

"I didn't sleep with her," he called out to her. "I wouldn't do that to you, Marie."

"Why not?" she asked. She crossed her arms and faced the door. "Because you care? A husband that cares doesn't run out on his wife to a whorehouse for a week!"

"A wife that cares doesn't sterilize herself because she doesn't want to have her husband's child!"

She whirled on him. "Sterilization? Birth control pills are not sterilization."

"YES IT IS!" he shouted.

"I took them before I ever met you. Fuck you if you can't deal with it!"

"And you said you stopped after we were married. A lie!" he shouted her down.

"So what? You're the fucking king of lies! Who killed Tomosino? Huh? Care to tell the truth about that?"

He lunged at her. He grabbed her by the throat and pinned her to the door. He didn't squeeze her throat but he forced her to her toes from his strong grip. She looked him in the eye. "Who are you ever honest with when it doesn't serve you, Lorenzo? Name one person! You're a liar too! A liar!"

"You," he said and let her throat go. "You're only the person in my world that I never lie to. The only person who knows all my secrets. All my fears. You, Marie. And I can't fucking trust you! Do you know what that means for us?"

"I'm sorry!" She threw her hands up. "I'm sorry, okay?"

"It's not okay!" he yelled at her.

"Then what is?" she demanded. "I'll give you a baby, Lo. Just don't leave me. Please!"

"Which is it, Marie? One minute you hate me, the next you want me to stay!" he threw his hands up in the air. He walked over to the chair and dropped in it. "I don't know what we can do to fix it. A baby doesn't deserve to be born out of force, Marie!"

"I'll love the fucking kid. I will. I can learn to," Marietta said.

"Stop," Lorenzo said.

"I can do it!"

"*AMMAZZA!*" he shouted. "Stop. This is why I didn't come home. I don't want to hear this from you. Do this with you!"

"I'll kill myself," she said and picked up the gun.

He looked at her with alarm.

"I'll kill you. I'll kill everyone in here. Then I'll kill myself. Is that enough?"

"Marie, you're fucking out of your mind," he chuckled.

She walked over to him. "If you say you didn't sleep with that nasty woman then I'll believe you. I'll trust you again. Let's start over and we can trust each other. Okay? We'll just forget."

"You're out of your fucking mind, woman!"

"You make me crazy!" she shouted through her tears. "I can't do this! I can't go through this. I can't!"

He took the gun out of her hand. She released it to him. He looked at it. "You could have blown my fucking head off."

"I won't let you disrespect me. I don't care who she is, you don't disrespect me," she said softly.

He dropped back in the chair and sighed. She sat on his lap. She curled her legs up and rested her face on his chest. She ran her hand over his bare skin. He set the gun aside to the windowsill. When his arms came around to hold her she smiled. She closed her eyes and held on to him.

"Stop talking crazy, Marie. I married you. I'm not going anywhere. Okay?"

"You'll come home with me?" she asked.

He sighed. "I'll come home. We'll figure it out."

She hugged him and smiled to herself. The panic seizing her heart began to fade. Bad or not she wasn't going to let go of her marriage. Ever.

"Whose gun is it?" he asked and stroked her thigh.

"Mirabella's," she answered softly.

"How did you get here?" he asked.

"I walked," she said softly as she succumbed to her emotional exhaustion.

He chuckled.

"Lo?"

"Yes?" he answered.

"There is some good in the worst of us, and some evil in the best of us," she said. "That's my favorite quote. I learned it in elementary school. I didn't know why I liked it then. No, I'm lying. I know why I liked it then. A child wants to believe that even the cruelest act committed against them by a parent has to have meaning. I now know what it really means." She sat up. "I made a terrible mistake by lying to you. But I never once did it to hurt you. I love you. The worst of you and the best of you I love. I'd die for you."

He looked away. She turned his face around to look back into his eyes. "Forgive me. We're the same. Tell me you love me."

"I do, Marie."

"Are you sure?" she asked.

"I didn't betray you. I wanted to. I came here to hurt you. But I couldn't. There is some good in the worst of me, and some evil in the best of me," he smiled. "You make me strong, Marie. When you hurt me I don't know how to handle it. I see that now."

Marietta hugged his neck. Shae was right about her having a second chance at happiness. She had family now, and a husband she loved. She'd never lose sight of that again.

—*B*—

CIRO WENT DOWN. The crowd jumped to their feet. The referee entered the ring and stood over Ciro counting. Mirabella's breath caught in her chest. She clasped her hands together and said a silent prayer. Giovanni was standing too. They all waited. Ciro struggled. He wavered and then found the strength to rise. The ref grabbed him by the face and looked into his eyes. He nodded at the officials and Ciro was given another chance. Everyone in the clan cheered. Carlo was in the ring coaching his brother.

"He has skill, Gio, he's good," Mirabella said.

"I think you're right, Bella," Giovanni smiled.

They didn't think Ciro would win the fight. He had taken a beating. But he'd lasted three rounds. He landed some of the hardest hitting blows. For a rookie he was quite light on his feet.

"Gio," Santo shouted over the cheering. He scooted past Renaldo and then Dominic to reach them. Mirabella rolled her eyes and looked back to the ring.

"I got a page. Mirabella needs to call home. It's one of the kids."

"What? What did he say?" Mirabella asked.

"*Andiamo*," Giovanni said as he took her hand to stand.

"Boss! Wait," Santo said.

Giovanni frowned at Santo.

"The Donna just needs to call home. They said one of the kids is achy. They need to talk to her. Not an emergency. There's a phone in the ticket office. I can take her."

"Stay, honey," Mirabella said. "I'll go call and check in. If we need to leave we can."

Mirabella kissed Giovanni's cheek. She could see the objection in his furrowed brow. She had to use the bathroom as well. It was perfect timing for a break. Giovanni didn't immediately consent. He never let her out of his sight in public if he could help it. She didn't want him to shift into panic mode and end the evening. They were having so much fun. "It's probably Gianni and his ear infection. Cecilia has to give him his medicine. She has some questions possibly. I can handle it."

"Take three men with you," he told Santo. "No. Take six."

"Gio!" Mirabella laughed. "Three is fine, Santo. Please take me to the phone."

He bowed his head in respect. "She won't leave my sight."

Mirabella heard the bell ring and her heart sank. She glanced back to see Ciro step up and Chao Lee ready for the next round. If she hurried she'd possibly make it back before there was a knock out or official call. She crossed her fingers.

The men flanked her on the left and right. One walked behind her. Santo led the way. He glanced back at her twice when they breeched the crowd who couldn't return to their seats. They walked along chamber halls that curved in odd angles. He led them away from the people buying food and socializing. They turned a corner and then another. She found it odd that they kept walking. *How far was this ticket office with a phone?* She glanced over to Leonardo. He smiled at her with encouragement. She smiled in return and tried to ignore the knot of fear curling tighter in her gut.

These halls were dusty. She felt her nose itch and suppressed the urge to sneeze. With her head down she checked her purse for a tissue. It was then that Santo attacked. He grabbed her arm and yanked her forward, and then his arm went around her throat. Mirabella blinked in shock, not sure of what was happening. She believed at first he grabbed her to protect her, and possibly the men did so as well. All three froze and looked at Santo with confusion. In that split second he was an assassin. He drew his gun on them. Leonardo took a bullet between the eyes. The other two were both shot before Leonardo dropped. Mirabella screamed. She fought for release. Santo's arm snaked tighter around her neck. It cut off her breathing. She reached back and scratched at his eyes.

The bitch scratched him. Santo had to let her go. She ran as soon as she was released. She was screaming to the top of her lungs. With his face bleeding he ran her down before she got too far ahead, and she stopped and turned on him. She landed a punch to his face and a kick to his groin. The blows hurt him more than he thought possible. He stumbled back. She ran from him screaming for help. He ran after her again and grabbed her by the hair. Before she could use those razor sharp nails on him he threw her into the wall. She hit her head hard against the brick and dropped like a rag doll.

"Bitch! Damn it!" he yelled at her. He looked up. A confused couple was staring at them. He drew his gun and fired, killing the man but the woman got away. Santo had no time to deal with it. He had minutes to get out of the chamber to his car. Only minutes. He picked up an unconscious Mirabella and threw her over his shoulder. His heart was in his throat. If he didn't see it through he was a dead man.

— *B* —

CHAO LEE TOOK SEVERAL HARD PUNCHES to the face. Everyone jumped to their feet expecting this to be the take down. It looked as if Ciro had found his second wind. Chao hugged Ciro to stop his swing, and the ref was in the ring to make his customary attempt to separate the men. Giovanni checked his watch. His wife had been gone fifteen minutes. That was too long. He glanced to Dominic with a curious frown. It was in that split second he missed what precipitated murder.

When his gaze returned to the ring it felt as if it did so in slow motion. Chao delivered a jaw breaking punch to the referee and knocked him down. He then grabbed Ciro by the head. One hard twist and the kid's neck was broken. The crowd went silent. Even Carlo froze, not sure of what he saw. And slowly Ciro dropped dead to the center of the ring.

"Gio!" Renaldo yelled. Dominic was knocked back and Renaldo slammed into him. He was brought to the ground. Renaldo provided cover from the onslaught of bullets as panic spread through the auditorium. He could hear the projectile of gunfire zipping past him and his men. When Renaldo didn't move Giovanni pushed back and his top enforcer rolled down the bench seats. Renaldo's chest was covered in blood. The bullets meant Renaldo had been hit repeatedly. He wasn't sure if he was alive. There was no time to react. Amidst the chaos his wife was not at his side.

Giovanni's men returned fire. But at who? Who the fuck was shooting?

"Bella! Find her!" Giovanni shouted to the others. He was shoved to the exit. He glanced back to see one of his men's head explode by the ricochet of a bullet, and another two get dropped.

"Santo has her. Let's go!" Dominic said forcing him out of the arena.

"Renaldo?" Giovanni asked and then called the names of the countless other men who were down.

"Gio! Go!" Dominic shoved him. "We have to get you out of here."

Carlo was in the ring. Ciro was on the ground and the officials were charging in. It happened in a flash. In a blink of the eye his brother's life

372

was taken. And though he had a wall of men between him, the primal urge to avenge his brother gave him herculean strength. There were gunshots. He didn't care. Those that cowered and ran for safety gave him the advantage he needed. He reached Chao who was ready. Carlo took several hits to the head and throat before he brought the bastard out of his shield of protection. Men were on them. But Carlo was able to straddle Chao and his hands fit tightly around his throat. Men struggled to pull him off. He squeezed and squeezed with his hands until his arms shook and every vein in his face and throat bulged. Chao's tongue protruded and his eyes popped with the vacant sign of death. Chao was dead, and the auditorium was in pandemonium. Several of Carlo's attackers were shot. The others who were members of the Triad began to beat and kick Carlo. He didn't care. He wanted to die. And then the *Carabinieri* were inside the ring breaking up the fight. Carlo was freed; beaten and bleeding he crawled toward Ciro. His brother's neck was twisted, turned awkwardly to the left. Carlo dragged Ciro's lifeless body to him and wrapped him up in his arms. On his knees he hugged his dead brother to his chest.

"Maro'ch'aggio cumbinato!" he said through his tears. *"Maro'ch'aggio cumbinato!"*

"ARE YOU GOING TO STAY?" Marietta's head lifted from the pillow.

"I've been gone a week," Lorenzo said. He pulled down a fresh shirt. Marietta dropped on her pillow and closed her eyes. They barely spoke after leaving Maria's. When they returned home they went straight to bed. She tried to initiate sex. It was awkward for them both. He refused her. Lorenzo never refused sex. Instead he lay with her and held her until he thought she was sleep.

"I'll be back before morning," he said.

"Maybe you should sleep in a different room when you come home? Maybe that's what you prefer?"

Lorenzo walked around the bed. He sat down. He moved her hair from her face. "I don't need any more space from my wife. Stop with the crazy talk, Marie. You shot a woman and broke into a whorehouse. There are a few things I need to make sure are taken care of so no trouble comes to you."

She looked up at him. "You care?"

"Don't do this, Marie. We have problems but we can get past them."

"I need you to stay with me. I don't feel good, Lo."

He kissed her brow. "Sleep."

She bit down on her bottom lip and didn't respond. She'd never been so weak. Even with him in the heat of their worst arguments, she never broke. Something was different now. She was emotionally defeated. He kissed her cheek once more, and then her shoulder. He turned her chin and kissed her in the mouth. It was a sweet tease of a kiss. "Marie, when I come back we'll talk again. Whatever you want. *Ti amo.*"

"I'm tired." She rolled away.

"We'll talk again when I come back," he repeated.

Lorenzo headed for the door. He looked back at his wife. She had pulled the covers over her head and curled into a fetal position. He almost turned back to comfort her. There was love between them, he had no doubt. But something else had moved in to divide them. It was distrust. She shocked him. He'd never seen her so crazed and in so much pain. Maybe it was his fault. He took a lot of things for granted with Marie. He'd have to pay more attention to her now. Find a way to fix what's broken between them. He loved her deeply, and though her actions gutted him, he'd put a bullet in any man or person that tried to take her from him. They were the same on that score. When the door opened he saw Leo and Umberto headed toward him. He met them in the hall.

"Che cosa?" he asked.

"Got a call, boss. We have to get to Napoli," Leo said. "Nico is already gone."

"Perchè? Ciro lost the fight?" Lorenzo asked.

"Ciro is dead. The clans are headed to Venditto's. Someone took a shot at Giovanni."

Lorenzo ran down the hall for the door. The men were on his heels. "He has Mirabella with him. Umberto, stay here with the women. Leo, come with me."

CHAPTER THIRTEEN

The Dragon

GIOVANNI PACED WITH his hands to his head. The minutes ticked on in excruciating slowness. Several clans were mixed in with his. The bosses were all shouting at each other. A blatant attack on their turf was unheard of. He looked down at his hands. He could see them tremble as rage vibrated through every sinew, every muscle. It was the only proof that maddening fear gripped him. *Bella was missing! Bella was missing! Bella was missing!* He had to stay calm. He had to keep focused. Santo was with her. Santo would protect her. He reassured himself over and over. Giovanni clenched his hand into a fist to stop the shakes. Nothing worked.

Dominic was now in the room. He shoved his way through several of the underbosses and arrived to the back where Giovanni, Tacchi, Racchini, and Benicia waited. The men all stood. Giovanni continued to pace. Dominic threw Mirabella's purse on the table.

"Where is she?" Giovanni asked.

"Leonardo, Alexi, and Giulio are dead. The boys found her purse."

"Santo?" Giovanni asked.

"He's missing. He might have been ambushed. Renaldo and several of our men were hit. I don't know who's alive or who's dead. The *Carabinieri* and *polizia* are swarming the streets. Doors are closed to us right now."

Giovanni shuddered with rage. He tightened both his hands into fists. He spoke through clenched teeth to keep the emotion from his voice. Every man, including the clan bosses, understood the dangers of a kidnapping. They'd all been guilty at one time or another of ordering a hit. Rarely was the person who was kidnapped returned alive.

"Who? Who did this?" Giovanni stammered.

"Triad," Benicia spoke.

Don Tacchi frowned. "We don't know—"

"We know!" Don Benicia said. "The fucking place was infested with them, like cockroaches. It was the first thing I noticed when I arrived. It's them!" he slammed his fist into his hand.

"Boss, I shot a few myself, all of them Asian. Chao Lee turned on Ciro in the ring? It had to be a hit," said one of Tacchi's men.

"Which means they were after Mirabella. The fight, all of it was a cover. They were after Mirabella," Giovanni said. "And I fucking handed my wife over to them."

"How could they get to her? How could they know she'd be vulnerable?" Racchini asked.

"Santo, the *pentito*." Benicia said.

Giovanni fell forward with his fists slammed on the table and his head bowed. "FIND HIM! Bring him to me. NOW!" He shouted.

—*B*—

MIRABELLA OPENED HER EYES. The darkness surrounding her was impenetrable. She lay on her side with her hands and feet bound. A putrid rag was stuffed into her mouth, and then another was tied around her mouth to keep her silent. She blinked rapidly to confirm her eyes were open and she wasn't dreaming. The toxic stench of exhaust fumes and motor oil clogged her nostrils and polluted her lungs. She gagged. The side of her head hurt so badly, she kept battling against the urge to blank out once again. But she had to stay awake. She had to fight hard to stay alert.

In flashes she recalled the terror. It was Santo. He killed poor Leonardo and the men she considered family, right before her eyes. Mirabella began to cry for them and her self. She remembered trying to fight, to run, but the rest was a haze of being carried and thrown about. She closed her eyes and wept. She prayed. She waited. Whatever fate lie for her at the end of this car ride, she needed to be ready.

Santo switched the lights off on his car. He coasted along the marina with his foot barely pressed to the gas pedal. There was no one to be seen. Most of the boats docked were silent and unoccupied. And then he saw them. Kei Hyogo stood on the pier with Isabella. Why was she there? That wasn't the plan. Isabella was supposed to meet with Bonaduce and secure his protection while the Triad warred with *la Camorra*.

Kei took a step forward. He had changed into what looked like a long black silk shirt and trousers. The wind tussled his hair in his face. He stood with his hands clasped behind his back. This was it, the point of no return. Giovanni would have been told by now. He had to see it to the very end. Santo had been friends with Giovanni since they were kids. He'd loved him like a brother. Even when hatred festered in his heart he had regrets for what they had become. Santo opened the car door and stepped out into the night.

Kei's man stepped to him. Tall, with a shaven head of tattoos, he patted Santo down and removed the two guns he had on him.

"Do you have her?" Kei asked.

"She's in the trunk," Santo said.

The man looked back to Kei and nodded that he was clean. Santo waited as Kei Hyogo approached.

The car stopped. Mirabella blinked several times unable to focus. She heard the car door open. There were voices. She wanted to scream but the gag on her mouth was too tight. She struggled to get free. Maybe if she could release her hands she could find something to use as a weapon. And then she thought of her gun. Giovanni pleaded with her to keep it with her, and she had been foolish enough to actually believe she would never need it.

Mirabella felt hopeless.

Kei walked around to the back of the car. He waited for Santo to release the trunk and open it. The inner light flashed on. Mirabella lay still. Her eyes were closed. She had a gag in her mouth, and her hands and feet were bound.

He looked to Santo for an explanation of the blood on Mirabella's face. "Did you touch her?"

"She tried to get away. I only—"

Kei slammed his iron fist into Santo's face. Santo staggered and lost balance as his mouth poured blood. Kei stepped over him, flexing his iron fingers that had ripped flesh from the side of Santo's face. He spoke in Mandarin of his wishes to his men, who picked Santo up by the arms and dragged him away. The muffled cry behind him drew his attention. Mirabella was struggling against her restraints. He nodded to his men. The closest one to the car reached in and brought her out. Mirabella fought as best she could. Kei removed a blindfold from his pocket. He walked over. She hung upside down. He tied the blindfold over her eyes as she struggled harder. He then took her into his arms.

She froze. Did she recognize his touch or was it his imagination? She didn't resist. He kissed her cheek and she mumbled something under her gag. She turned her face away from him. Kei had no choice but to put her over his shoulder to carry her. He started for the boat.

"The marina," Dominic said.

The men looked up. Giovanni was now seated with the clan bosses. Unbeknownst to them he was too weak with grief and worry to stand. Trapped in his head were all the wild imaginings of what was happening to his wife, while he sat on his dick being fucking useless. There were raids going on now. The *polizia* were snatching his men off the streets. It made any plausible search impossible.

"They had to take her there. The only way to get her out would be the marina," said Dominic.

Giovanni nodded in agreement. "Send my men. Get them in the water," he managed to say. The other bosses looked at Giovanni and nodded in agreement that their men would join the search.

Mirabella was carried. She could smell the dank fishy water of the sea, and feel the bob and wave when they transferred her over to what she guessed to be a boat. She knew who had her and it only further confused and terrified her. The moment Kei spoke she recognized his voice. And when he spoke in Mandarin it was confirmed.

The only answer she could summon would be revenge. Giovanni told her Kei was connected to a crime syndicate. That he was not the man she fell in love with. It couldn't be him, her heart said, but her mind knew the truth. She was then set down on something plush. It felt like a sofa seat. Her captor untied the blindfold. She squinted at the harsh glare of light. It took only moments for her sight to focus. Shocked she stared up at him.

"Miss me?" Kei smiled.

—*B*—

THE WAIT WAS THE HARDEST. He couldn't return home. Not without his Bella. What would he tell his children? The ambush had divided the clans. Many were back in the streets raging war, slaughtering anyone who looked like they would be associated with the Triad. So many of his own men were in the wind, arrested, or dead.

Giovanni paced. No news came. The clan bosses kept glancing toward him. He knew what they were thinking. When was his mad obsession with his wife and family going to surface and break him? They waited for any sign of weakness, like vultures ready to pick at his bones. And he suffered, just not the way they hoped.

The door opened. Lorenzo stalked in. His gaze landed on Giovanni first. He nodded at him. "Let's talk, Gio," Lorenzo said.

The two left out of the side door. They entered the kitchen. Venditto's, a family owned and run restaurant, was closed. Alvo Venditto's mother was in the kitchen cooking for the men. She got out of bed when she heard the news of the attack against *la Camorra,* and the kidnapping of Mirabella. He stopped and greeted her. He kissed the old woman on both cheeks and hugged her. Lorenzo walked to the pantry. It was a large room where all the dry food items and pasta were stored.

"What do you know?" Giovanni asked.

"Nothing helpful. Carlo is in jail. They said he took a real fucking beating, but those cock-sucking bastards won't get him any medical attention. I think he murdered the boxer. Nico is in the streets, no word from him. Renaldo is alive. I think. He was taken to a hospital. One person tells me he's dead. Another said he's in surgery. And a fucking other person said he walked out with nothing but a bruise."

"No. He was hit. I saw him take the bullets to the chest and back. He saved my life."

Lorenzo sighed. "I don't know which hospital. The boys are hitting up each hospital to try to find our wounded and account for them. The others called from the marina. No sign of her. But they think they found Santo's car. Gio, there was blood near it and in the trunk,"

Giovanni closed his eyes to the news. "Continue."

"I'm sorry, brother. That's it. We have nothing else."

Giovanni shoved the shelf. It rocked back, almost pushing over. Several cans fell off. He gripped the shelves and dropped his head.

"You have to find her," he pleaded. "No matter the cost. I'll pay it. Whatever it takes. I'll do it. Do I have to fucking make myself any clearer? You have to find her for me, Lo."

"We're trying, Gio. Are we even sure it's the Triad? It could be Bonaduce? *N'drangheta*. We have to check everyone."

"There's no time! No fucking time!" Giovanni shouted at him. He put his hands to his hair. "Santo. He's the one. He's the fucking one! He set me up. That motherfucker! He set me up!"

"I'll put a bullet in him myself, Gio, but we can't jump to any conclusions. If we're rash it could cost Mirabella her life."

"I just handed her over to him. I'm a fucking idiot. You warned me. I didn't listen. I fucking handed my sweet Bella over to that MOTHERFUCKER!" Giovanni shouted.

Lorenzo grabbed him by the face. Giovanni breathed hard with his teeth clenched. He shuddered with anger. "Keep it together, Gio. Now is the time to keep it together. We will bring him to you. ALIVE. Do you hear me? Just fucking keep it together."

Giovanni shoved Lorenzo off and he was knocked into the shelf. This time it rattled and dropped cans and containers.

"Why did I let her go? I never fucking let her go! I was the one that suggested she come to the fucking fight. I did it on a whim. How did they know? How? It has to be Santo. No one kills him. You find him alive and you bring him to me," Giovanni said.

Lorenzo nodded. "Agreed."

"Don't you worry," he panted. His chest bulked with each deep intake of breath. "I'm not going mad. I'm far beyond that now."

He pushed of the double doors and stormed out.

—*B*—

Mirabella stared at Kei. She let her vision drink him in. He had changed so dramatically, she barely saw any semblance of the man she once loved. It appeared he had lost an eye. He wore a black eye patch and had a scar that traced across his cheek to the corner of his mouth. His dark hair was longer now. And his hand was in some gruesome looking iron glove. He moved his fingers like with robotic gestures. It dripped blood. He was muscular, not the tennis athletic body he once had. He was as muscular as Giovanni. His open black silk shirt revealed an extravagant tattoo that covered it. At first glance she thought it looked like a serpent.

She glanced around the boat and then to him. "Why?"

"Is that all you have to ask me? After two years? Why?" Kei asked.

Mirabella swallowed her fear. There was pain in her head. It was a throbbing ache. She felt a trickle of something to the side of her face. It dripped to her lap. Blood. She was bleeding. The boat engine gunned and they began to move. "Why am I here?"

"You're where you belong," he said. A man came in and handed him a small black case. Kei spoke to the man in Chinese. He gave a single nod and the man left. Mirabella noticed the man had a shaven head with tattoos that covered his neck and hands. She imagined his entire body was covered. These were gangsters. And their detached behavior scared her.

"What happened to you?" she asked.

"So now she cares," Kei said softly. He unzipped something with his back turned to her.

"You are a good man, Kei. I should know. I loved you for years. I wouldn't be who I am if it weren't for you. Why are you with these people? What are you trying to prove by doing this?" she asked. "Let me go and I won't tell Gio. I swear it."

He turned around with a syringe. Mirabella scooted on the sofa to get away from him. Due to her feet being bound she fell over on her side. He walked over to her.

"No! Don't! Don't do it!" she said. "Stay away from me!"

Kei turned her over on the sofa. Her hands were still bound behind her back but she bucked beneath him. He straddled her on the couch and pinned her down. She looked up into his face. The man who stared down at her had a hard and unforgiving, murderous glint to his eye.

"Please. Don't do this to me, Kei! I'm begging you!"

"It'll make you feel better," he gave her a sly smile.

Mirabella screamed as he turned her face and pressed his hand down hard on her jaw to keep her still. She squeezed her eyes tightly shut. The needle pierced her neck, and then eased in as he released the toxin. It was a hot burn. The blood in her neck sizzled. She opened her mouth in a silent cry of agony. Only seconds passed before the feeling of bliss followed. Her eyes rolled up in her head and she sighed with pleasure. All fear, anxiety, even thoughts of her babies slipped away. And then there was nothing.

Kei pulled the syringe out of her neck and sat back. She moaned for him. He missed the soft sounds of pleasure from her. He leaned over and laved her neck and then kissed it. Mirabella smiled. He eased off her.

"Bring him in," he said to his shadow who had returned. Santo was dragged inside with his bloody jaw and mouth.

"Isabella said you are still worth something alive. So I will give you back to Giovanni. Cast him a line of bait, and Giovanni will take to the hook. I want Eve," he said. "You will give him hope enough to bring her to me."

Santo spat blood. He was released and dropped on his hands and knees. He lifted his head and found it hard to talk. "I can't. They know it's me. He'll kill me on sight."

"Then you convince them it's not." Kei knelt and grabbed Santo by the throat. He slammed his iron fist into his face twice more until he was certain his jaw was broken. He dropped him. "I am not leaving without Eve."

Kei stood upright. "Take him as close to shore as you can then throw him over. Let him swim in."

Santo groaned. The men didn't wait for consent. They grabbed him as he struggled and dragged him out. Kei turned and looked at his love. She was moaning softly, lost in some deep sense of euphoria he wished he could join. He released the straps fastened to his right wrist and gently pulled at the fingers of the iron glove to take it off. He tossed it. There was some feeling in his hand. Enough for his crippled fingers to extend. Not enough to make it strong for use. However, he'd adjusted to his handicap and managed.

He unbuttoned his shirt and shrugged it off. In nothing but his trousers he walked over to the sofa seat.

"Gio?" Mirabella said softly. "Gio?"

He understood her confusion. There were many remedies for madness. Loving the wrong man was her madness. He'd cure her of it. When he was done healing her, his name would be the only one she'd whisper. He reached down and traced the side of her face with his finger. How many times had he taken her beauty for granted. Maybe if he told her he loved her more, showed her more, she would have never left him for Italy. If he had convinced her to marry then their lives would be different. He was her destiny. And she was his.

He turned her. He untied her hands. He untied her feet. She rolled over, lost in her dream. He scooped her up into his arms and she came willingly. She kissed his lips. He swept her tongue into his mouth and deepened the kiss.

"Gio," she smiled when the kiss ended. He kissed her again. He carried her to their room.

THE MEN WERE EATING. Giovanni sat in the corner. Every time a person entered the room his gaze lifted and his heart skipped a beat with hope.

"Eat, Gio," Mama Venditto said. He didn't respond. She went about her task to serve the other crime bosses and replenish their drinks.

"If the Triad did this it makes no sense." Benicia said as he forked food into his mouth. He was a sloppy eater with sauce dripping from his chin to his shirt. When he spoke his belly moved.

"Why not? They do kidnappings all the time." Tacchi answered. He smoked on his cigar at the table. He put up his hand to stop Mama Venditto from replenishing his plate.

"Yes. But they don't start wars unprovoked." Benicia pointed his fork at Tacchi. "Never. And if they do go to war, it's more territorial business, not random hits," Benicia said.

"To come here and strike at one of us in public sends a message to everyone. It feels personal." Tacchi looked over at Giovanni.

"Not personal. It's a power play. What the fuck do they care about his wife?" Benicia said and forked more food into his mouth.

"What did you say?" Giovanni sat upright.

Benicia stopped chewing. The other bosses stared. Benicia picked up his napkin and dabbed at his chin. "No disrespect, Gio, I only meant—"

Giovanni grabbed the bottle of wine closest to him and smashed it over Benicia's head. The glass exploded, and the man was thrown back in his chair.

Giovanni went over the table. He grabbed a fork, and he attacked. He stabbed Benicia in the face and throat. The other bosses were either too shocked or impressed with his viciousness to respond. However, Benicia's men were up to save their boss before the third strike of the fork gouged out Benicia's eye. They grabbed Giovanni's wrist and the fork dropped. It didn't matter. He broke free of their hold and used his fist. Each time he slammed his fist into Benicia's face he saw him. It was Kei. The Asian cockroach had stolen his Bella. He'd fucking kill him with his bare hands.

"Gio!" Dominic yelled. "Get him off!"

Men grabbed Giovanni but it may have been too late. His bloody hands were wrapped tighter than a vice around Benicia's fat throat, and he could feel the life being squeezed out of the pig as he gagged and bled over the insult.

"Get him off!" he heard yelling. It was possibly men in Benicia's clan too. He was dragged off, spewing curses like a mad dog. His taste for vengeance was not abated by the detainment. He'd draw his gun next. Dominic stepped in front of him.

"We're leaving."

—*B*—

Santo hacked and coughed up seawater. He dropped on the shore. The waves crashed over him but he was too weak to move. He swam in the dark with a dislocated shoulder, and what he prayed wasn't a broken jaw. He swam toward the lights of the city. It would prove ironic if after all that effort he were to drown in an inch of seawater. He pushed up with his hands and nearly collapsed. He pushed up once more and heaved himself forward. Santo crawled over the sand and flopped down and over to his back.

The stars were fading in the sky. What was left of them twinkled. Or so he thought as his consciousness slipped away.

"Stop the car," Lorenzo said.

Nico pulled the car over to the side of the road. An hour ago they joined together in the search. Lorenzo opened the car door. He stepped out into the morning breeze. The sun hadn't risen yet, but the darkness over the bay was slipping away. He could see the stretch of the beach.

"What is it?" Nico said.

"Looks like something washed ashore," Lorenzo said. Nico walked around the car. He stopped at Lorenzo's side.

"I don't fucking believe it," Nico said.

"C'mon," he went down the grass-topped embankment sideways, standing on the beach sand. Nico struggled with his large frame. Both men drew their guns. Lorenzo hurried. He had no cover on the beach and this could be an ambush.

The clans had united. Everyone had a common enemy. But no one understood the priority of finding Mirabella over annihilating the Triad. She was their Donna. And he loved her just as much as he loved all the women in the family. They had to find her. Alive. Lorenzo saw no point in kicking in doors and dragging random immigrants from their beds in search of information. The bastards had to have used the sea to escape.

The hunch paid off. He stopped and aimed the gun down at Santo. Lorenzo looked up to big Nico, who was panting and breathing hard. "Is he dead?" Nico wheezed.

"You really need to lose some weight," Lorenzo said. Nico dropped with his hands to his knees and wheezed in several deep breaths. Lorenzo knelt and turned Santo's face. The scarring was brutal. It was as if his face had been shredded with a cheese grater. He could see pink gum and flesh. He put his hand to his chest. The heartbeat he felt was faint.

"Well I'll be damn. He's alive." Lorenzo stood. He looked out to the ocean. "Fuck. If he came from the water they are long gone. Shit. They took her."

Nico glanced to the ocean. "What do we do now, boss?"

"He needs to live. He's the only one with answers. Take him. Let's get him back to Venditto's."

Nico reached down and grabbed Santo by the arm and belt. He threw him over his shoulder and started walking back up the beach. Lorenzo stuck his gun in the back of his pants and followed.

—*B*—

"Is BENICIA DEAD?" Giovanni paced. He held his bandaged hand. The doctor told him it was broken. Giovanni only accepted a pack of ice for the swelling. He had no time for them to set his knuckles. Dominic tried to convince him to leave. He refused.

"If he is we're fucked," Dominic said. He then pulled Giovanni to the side. "Why did you attack a clan boss in front of everyone? How does that help our cause, Gio? Mirabella needs us united. We need them!"

Giovanni didn't bother to explain himself. The answer was irrelevant. Everyone knew Giovanni was close to exploding. Sitting him with those men, while forcing him to wait for news of whether Mirabella was dead or alive, was too much to ask of a husband and father. It was also a deadly mistake for a mouthy crime boss like Benicia. Of course he would unload his anger. Something had to be on the immediate receiving end of that rage. They were upstairs in the Vendittos' home. Benicia was down the hall being cared for.

"They don't come back with her in a hour, I'm going out there to find her myself." Giovanni said. He glared at Dominic. "It's Kei. He took her."

"We still don't know—"

"I KNOW!" Giovanni shouted. "I feel it. Every minute that goes by I feel it. We have to find her, Domi. No matter the sacrifice. I'll do whatever it takes. Do you hear me?"

Dominic looked back at the closed door. He left several men outside of it so no one would be close enough to hear Giovanni's rants. He nodded. "I'd die for her, Gio. For our family, and every man under you would. But you have to be our leader. Every move you make will be watched and analyzed by friends and enemies. Take a breath and calm down."

"My Bella. My Bella is out there…" he panted and paced. "My sweet Bella. I'm her husband! She needs me!"

"She needs you strong, and clear headed. And she needs them, Gio. Half of our men are in jail cells. The other half are dead. We're crippled. We need the clans to unite with us. Now is not the time to divide us."

Giovanni sat. He looked at his busted hand. "I always tell her to carry her gun. I tell her to keep it with her. She's so fucking stubborn! She never listens!"

"What if we're wrong about Santo? He could very well have saved her life."

"My Bella won't give up. She'll fight them all," Giovanni said.

"And we'll find her. I promise," Dominic agreed.

Sunrise—

Mirabella turned over and gagged. She grabbed her throat and her lids flashed open. She was desperate to breathe. It hurt to swallow. She sat up and felt the sheet slip away. Nothing made sense. Her body was achy. It felt as if someone had taken a hammer and beat her across the head, chest, and legs with it.

"Gio?" she looked around. Her vision blurred and then cleared. It made seeing impossible, with flashes of images her brain couldn't discern. She put a hand to her forehead and squeezed her eyes shut. "Gio, where are you?" she asked in a shaky voice.

Nausea hit her and she nearly spewed in her lap. She raced from the bed to the open door. Thankfully it was the bathroom. She went to her knees and hacked up her stomach contents. She hacked so hard she thought she vomited a lung. With teary eyes she pressed the button to flush. Mirabella turned and sat on the cool hardwood floor. She put her face in her hands. And as soon as her breath regulated, her memory returned. Every terrifying moment, including the syringe going into her neck, returned with clarity. She struggled to stand. She grabbed the sink and pulled herself up. She hit the light switch on the wall and looked at herself. Her eyes were bloodshot. Her lips were dry and chapped. A small bandage covered the bruise on her forehead. She turned her neck and saw the bruise on her throat.

"Oh shit," she said.

She heard the door to the cabin open. Mirabella stepped back and realized she was naked. Naked? She panicked. She looked around and found a towel and covered herself. The door opened. Kei looked inside. He looked her over and then smiled. "Get dressed and come up for breakfast." He threw a kimono at her. He turned and closed the door.

"You bastard!" she screamed at the door. *Why was she naked?* What happened to her after he poisoned her? The heavy drugged feeling washed out all other emotions. Her body was weakened with trauma, but she didn't feel the familiar signs of sex. She grabbed some toilet tissue and wiped between her legs. She sniffed the tissue and smelled herself. There was no discharge. But she and Gio had had sex earlier in the limo. She couldn't tell if she was attacked. *Please, God. Please don't let him have raped me. Please!*

The boat stopped moving. She could feel it. She reached down to pick up the robe. When she held it out in front of her the towel dropped, as did her heart. The black kimono with the red dragon was exactly like the one that was given to her as a gift in Milano. "No. No!" she dropped her head and wept. "Oh my God. Help me please!"

CHAPTER FOURTEEN

The Return of the Dragon

MARIETTA WOKE. She turned over and found she was in bed alone. Lorenzo had failed to deliver on his promise. She wasn't surprised. Putting her hands to her head, she tried to soothe the ache she felt throbbing in her temples. Her mind refused to release her from her actions. *She shot someone.* She didn't know how badly the woman was hurt. She couldn't imagine that her rage would push her that far. What had she done?

There were times when she had suffered deep depressions where she fantasized about ending her life. But that was before she met Lorenzo. Before she found reasons to live. She was scared how far her anger and hurt pushed her. And the worst part of it, she didn't feel better.

A loud pounding on the door rattled her troubled thoughts. She frowned and sat up. Before she could grant permission for the person to enter, Catalina charged inside. Catalina looked grief stricken.

"What? What is it?" Marietta asked.

Catalina burst into tears. "Mirabella... she's missing!" she screamed.

—*B*—

"HOW LONG BEFORE HE WAKES?" Giovanni asked the doctor.

"I had to put him on a sedative to stitch him up." The doctor answered.

"What? I told you not to give him anything!" Giovanni shoved the doctor. Lorenzo put a hand on his shoulder to calm him. It wasn't enough. He felt his nostrils flare and knew his blood pressure skyrocketed. In fact the fever was in his blood. He was sweating and breathing hard. He hadn't been this sick with fear and anger since the Russians gunned his father down in the street. He couldn't save his father. He had to suffer days holding his mother and sister's hands as they waited for him to die.

"Don Giovanni, he has a concussion, maybe even a skull fracture. I don't think his jaw is broken, possibly dislocated, as his shoulder was. You won't know for sure until he wakes. Either way he needs a hospital. I've done the best I can. There could be internal injuries. I just don't know."

"I need him awake. I need information!" Giovanni hissed.

"How long before the sedative wears off?" Lorenzo asked.

The doctor wiped at his brow with his handkerchief. The man's hand shook. He looked away when he spoke. He was afraid of the answer. And Giovanni's stomach clenched with dread. Bella had been gone for over nine hours. She could be in China for all he knew.

"Two hours, maybe three. I'm sorry. When he wakes he will be in pain. If he doesn't get treated for his jaw, you risk problems of him bleeding to death."

Giovanni turned his gaze to Lorenzo. "I don't give a shit if he lives or dies, but you get answers out of him."

"You know I will," said Lorenzo.

"Gio, we need to talk," Domi began.

Giovanni threw up his hand in refusal. He turned his gaze back to the doctor. "Benicia? How is he?"

"He's lost several teeth and has deep cuts to his face and throat, several blood vessels burst in his eyes. He should be fine. He's asked for you," The doctor said. The man checked his watch. "I have to return to my clinic."

The doctor tried to step forward and Giovanni blocked him. "You are going nowhere. Stay with Santo and wait for him to wake. Do whatever you need to do to keep him conscious and giving us answers."

"I—" The doctor started to object. He looked from Giovanni to Lorenzo, and then to Dominic, and then thought better of leaving. *"Si, signor. Si."*

The doctor went back into the room. Giovanni closed his eyes and began to massage his temples.

"I've called home and told Catalina. She'll make sure no one leaves and no one visits," Dominic said.

"How is Renaldo?" Giovanni asked.

"We found him. He's alive. I'm sorry, Gio, but his injuries are severe. He made it through surgery. It's a waiting game for him. I made the call to Kyra and his mother. They are on their way to Napoli."

"How many dead?" Giovanni asked.

"So far the number is between sixteen and twenty-three. Could be more." Dominic answered. "Can't get any number on how many are in jail from our clan or the others. They're rounding our boys up. That new Chief Inspector is on a witch-hunt. The media is all over this."

"Bella? Does anyone know?" Giovanni asked.

"So far not a word of it from the press. But they are going through the footage. Her photo was taken so they will know she was there." Dominic advised.

"I don't want the *Carabinieri* involved. Those fuckers will get her killed. No one is to know that Bella was kidnapped," Giovanni paced.

"Good idea. We keep the hounds out of it and we buy more time," Lorenzo chimed in.

"China? Any way to know if any flights left for China? Out of the private airports in the *Campania*?" Giovanni asked.

"I've already put our people on it, Gio. It'll take time," Dominic said. "Manifestos are costly."

"If he took her by sea like Lorenzo said, then he's out there still," Giovanni said.

"Why stay?" Lorenzo asked. "If this is the Triad, the best defense is a good offense, Gio. He'd take her back to China."

"He wants more. He wants revenge. We need to know what Santo knows. That's how we'll find her." Giovanni sighed. "I'm going to see Benicia."

"Wait!" Dominic put his hand to his chest. "Let's not strain that relationship further. He's calm and so is his brother."

"I don't give a fuck about straining anything. I need everyone behind me. And whoever isn't needs to know the consequences." Giovanni walked down the hall to head to the room where Benicia was being kept. The Vendittos had closed their establishment for the day. The only people allowed in were *la Camorra*. And far as he was concerned he owned all of them.

"Do something," Dominic said to Lorenzo.

Lorenzo shrugged. "What am I to do? I agree with him. This is Mirabella we're talking about. If that fucking Chinese cocksucker has her we don't have much time to play nice. Either you stand with us or get the fuck out of the way."

Dominic wiped his hand down his face. "We have to talk about—" he looked up into Lorenzo's piercing stare. "If we don't find her or if she's dead, we have to prepare Gio."

"Don't say it." Lorenzo stepped forward. "Don't even fucking think it. We'll find her. And we'll protect him. We're his brothers."

With tears in his eyes Dominic nodded that he agreed. "I'm going to try to get those flight plans. I need to do something." He walked off. He glanced back to see Lorenzo staring. They wouldn't say it aloud again, but they both knew the bitter truth. If Mirabella dies then it'll destroy them all.

—*B*—

MIRABELLA STEPPED UP TO THE UPPER DECK. It was surrounded by tinted windows, which allowed for sunlight to be cooled before it poured in from every angle. She could see nothing but the ocean all around them. She held her kimono closed at the neck. Her dress was missing. She had no undergarments.

Kei looked up from his breakfast. He sat back in his chair. He reached for the glass of champagne with his iron glove. She convinced herself of what to say and do to survive this. But the moment their eyes met she wanted to attack. She actually looked at the knife next to the plate of food waiting for her, as a good choice of weapon.

"Join me," he ordered.

She walked over to the chair and pulled it out. She sat down.

"Hungry?" he asked.

"Kei—"

"You should eat. You need something on your stomach."

"Why are you doing this?" she asked.

Kei smiled. "Why? Again with the whys. You act as if you never knew this day would come."

"I didn't," she replied. "Tell me why you would come after me and do this? Drug me? Hurt me? Why?"

He glared at her. "For the past two years I've said that word over and over in my head. Why? Why did she betray me? Why did she leave me to die? Why wasn't my love enough for her? Why? Why? Why?"

"I loved you. You know that. We just… things happened."

"Things happened, Mirabella? Things?" he chuckled. He picked up his champagne and sipped.

"What happened to you?" she looked at him with genuine concern.

"Now this story I want to tell. Let's see. I was arrested…"

"Kei—"

He slammed his fist on the table, so hard the plates and dishes clinked. Mirabella flinched. She held back from speaking.

"As I was saying. I was arrested and thrown into a prison cell with criminals. And one day while lined up for the showers I was jumped. I think they used the sharpened edge of a spoon to cut my face and take out my eye. All the while they told me it was a gift for your husband's wedding day."

Mirabella lowered her gaze.

"The insult of my arrest reached the top of the mountain. My uncle Dao saved my life. And I was returned to China." He lifted his hand. "This was my welcome home present from the Triad."

"Your arrest and assault was wrong. I never meant for any of that to happen to you. I never blamed you. I never thought things between us would go this far. I begged for your life."

"Shhhh." He pressed an iron finger to his lips. He picked up the remote. "Let's see what you really thought." He pressed a button and a projector screen lowered. Mirabella frowned. The automatic shades for the windows around the upper deck were lowered. The sunlight was effectively blocked out.

He pressed play.

The screen flashed on with the image of her seated next to Giovanni. She glanced to Kei. He turned his head up so he could see with his good eye. "This right here is my favorite part!" he said and amped up the volume.

Mirabella squeezed Giovanni's hand. She knew this part of the interview would come. She had hoped it wouldn't happen so soon. "It was awful. What do you want me to say? My best friend died in a terrible accident. And the man I trusted, Kei Hyogo, he made me believe that disappearing from my life was the only way to cope with my trauma. The press has lied and exaggerated my story to sell magazines and papers. The truth is I fell in love with this man, and made a life for myself. A life I wouldn't trade for anyone or thing in the world."

"Wait for it… wait for it…" Kei grinned. The report continued with a flash of Kei Hyogo being escorted into court in an orange prison jumper. And then they replayed the footage of Mirabella standing in front of the Battaglia gates calling out Kei's crimes, and lauding her husband as her hero. The news reporter then gave commentary on Kei's exile back to China.

"Turn it off," Mirabella said as tears clouded her vision.

Kei grinned at the video footage of Mirabella smiling on screen.

"Turn it off!" Mirabella yelled.

He did as she asked. "So? You were saying?"

"Don't sit there and pretend you aren't responsible for this, Kei. You lied to me. You knew the entire time we were together that I was in love with him. You lied. You then sent a killer after my husband. He let you go and you sent a killer after him."

"Fabiana was dead. You barely survived a bomb attack. You begged me to be your hero, and then decided to take my daughter, and my heart away from me. And I am the monster?"

"She's not your daughter," Mirabella mumbled.

"How's my little rabbit doing," Kei tossed a strawberry into his mouth. "Is she still fond of Captain Hook?"

"What did you say?" Mirabella asked.

"Peter Pan. Her favorite book?"

"You've been spying on my children? Who told you? Santo! That bastard!"

Kei chuckled. "No. Santo didn't tell me. He brought me to her at the Diana. Left me with her. I told her that I was coming back for her and her mommy. She was happy to see me, Mirabella. Because she's mine."

"You're insane. Insane!"

"I was there when you first felt her kick. I was there when she was delivered. I held her when you wouldn't because you were too weak with guilt and grief over Fabiana. I am her father!"

Mirabella couldn't speak. Giovanni was right about Kei. She refused to believe it. Even after she knew about his lies, and his attempts to take Giovanni's life. There was madness in his eye. She didn't know him at all.

"Did you rape me?" she asked and her voice quivered at the end.

He didn't answer.

She looked up into his eyes. "Did you?"

"Am I a rapist? In the two years I longed for you, did everything to have you love me again, did I touch you?"

"That man is dead," she said. "I don't know who is before me now."

Kei smiled. "True."

"You drugged me. You undressed me. You had a video camera pointed at the bed."

Kei kicked out the chair to the side of him and put his feet in it. "Oh that? That was for your husband."

"He'll kill you, Kei, if you taunt him this way."

"And that makes you sad?" Kei asked.

"I am sad. I'm sad about who you are now. I'm sad that you had to rape me to make yourself feel important!"

He glared at her. "I didn't rape you. But I will have you. After I'm done with Giovanni, you and Eve will return home with me. And you will be mine, willingly. There are so many ways to make that true without me touching you," he winked.

—*B*—

"HAS ANYONE HEARD ANYTHING?" Marietta chewed on her fingernail.

Catalina walked into the parlor. She shook her head sadly. She sat down and Rocco put his arm around her. Marietta looked away. They agreed they wouldn't cry and scare the kids.

"Eve, how about some ice cream?" Marietta asked.

"Yay!" she said and stood up from the floor with her doll. Zia was rocking with Gianni in her arms. She glanced to Marietta who smiled.

"Let's give them some ice cream, and then we can get in the pool." She looked over to Cecilia who nodded that she understood. She took Eve by the hand. Marietta picked up Gino from the floor, and Zia was able to rise and follow. They all went to the kitchen. Marietta made sure the kids were settled in their chairs and smiling before she left and returned to the parlor. She now knew why Lorenzo was missing. She saw the video image of Carlo fighting with a mob in the boxing ring. He was missing too. It was a nightmare.

Catalina was now by the window staring out toward the gates. So many men had arrived. The place was guarded like a fortress. "I don't understand this. Domi wouldn't tell me how something like this could have happened."

"The news report says that Ciro was killed in the boxing fight. And the other fighter was killed in the chaos." Marietta said.

"And the shootings. Who was shot? Where is Gio?" Catalina wiped at her tears. "What the hell is going on?"

Marietta looked to Rocco. "Can you find out what happened? Anything, Zio Rocco. Please?"

He nodded and reached for his cane. He started using it over the past year. He walked out and Marietta went to Catalina. She hugged her. Marietta forced bravery to her voice when she spoke. "I paged Lorenzo several times. They'll call us."

"How can you be so calm?" Catalina wept. "I'm so scared."

Marietta cupped Catalina's face. "I'm her twin. I'd know if she was dead or hurt. I'd feel it."

"You sure about that?" Catalina asked. "Two years ago you didn't know she existed."

Marietta wavered in her confidence. How could she be sure? "Yes," she lied.

Catalina hugged her once more. "I just want her to come home. I want my brother."

"Me too, sweetie." Marietta said. She closed her eyes and prayed hard for her sister. Wherever she was he wanted her to have courage and strength. The same courage she gave Marietta the past week. There was no one sweeter than Mirabella. Without her they would all be lost.

"I'll page Lorenzo again. We'll get answers," Marietta assured Catalina. "I promise."

THE MEN ALL STOOD AROUND THE BED of their boss glaring. Giovanni looked Benicia in the eye. "Leave us," the clan boss said to his men.

"I won't leave your side, brother," Benicia's younger brother Mateo said. He was shorter than his brother, and much leaner.

"Get the fuck out. We have business to discuss." Don Benicia said.

Mateo glared at Giovanni. He nodded his respect and left. Giovanni found a chair and brought it over to the bed.

"Have they found her?" Benicia asked.

"They haven't." Giovanni answered dryly. He stared at the bruises and scarring all over Benicia's face. Both of the man's eyes were blackened and nearly swollen shut.

"I'm here to make an offer."

"I thought you were here to apologize," Benicia chuckled.

Giovanni did not.

"Gio, I meant no disrespect earlier. It was a slip of the tongue. My men are looking and will help to find—"

"You want more power. The money is in the export that's leaving out through Salerno."

"Drugs?" Benicia frowned.

"I know your interests," Giovanni said.

"But Racchini is working with Lorenzo. That pie has already been sliced," Benicia said.

Giovanni stood. "I'll cut you a piece, a larger piece."

"And what is asked of me in exchange?" Benicia asked.

"My wife. The boss who finds her unharmed and returns her to me gets forty percent of the business."

Benicia's eyes stretched, which was painful for him. He looked at Giovanni astounded. At most the clan bosses were able to negotiate fifteen percent with any business dealings with the Battaglias. "So you are going to expand from bringing it in, to distributing? We're getting in the business. Fully."

Giovanni nodded. "Think of what it means for you and your clan. Show me your loyalty and I'll be willing to give you the rewards."

"We'll find her," Benicia managed a crooked smile. "I'll make sure of it."

The clan boss extended his hand. Giovanni accepted the deal with a firm handshake. Giovanni turned and went to the door. He paused. He looked back. "I meant no disrespect to you, Benicia. But let's be clear, if she is harmed in any way, I'll show no mercy to any of those who failed me. That is the other side of the coin."

He opened the door and left.

—ℬ—

MIRABELLA SAT BEHIND A LOCKED DOOR in the cabin. She tried everything to pry it open. After an hour she gave up. All she could do was wait. The boat was moving fast. Where was he taking her now? The doorknob turned. She stood and waited with a fingernail file behind her back. She held it the way one would hold a dagger.

Kei entered. He looked at her and then to the bed where she tossed the hanger. "You haven't changed."

"I'm not putting that on. I want you to take me back," she said defiantly. "Now!"

"If you haven't figured it out by now, Mirabella, what you want no longer matters. I have other ways to convince you to accept what I want," Kei said. "You did so, so nicely last night."

"I know you. I've loved you. I grew up in our love. Built a company and reputation because of our love. This is not you!" she shouted through her tears. She turned the file on him. Held it out as a weapon to keep him back. "I'm warning you! I won't let you do this to me! I won't!"

"It's done," he reassured her.

"No!"

"Yes. You're in the middle of the ocean. My men are all over this boat. I get so much as a paper cut because of you, and they won't hesitate to throw you over. Remember how afraid you are of water."

"So that's why you brought me out here. Because of my fear of water? Are you so damn sadistic that you're enjoying this?" she asked.

"I'm the same man who loved you inside. Who will protect you. And when I strip you of everything that has poisoned you against me you'll see my sacrifices and honor me for it."

"I'm scared, for us both! You can't play games with Giovanni. I have tried to protect you, begged him to let you go. He did. But now, he'll kill you. Do you understand? There will be no place you can hide and he won't find you! Kei, stop it. Now! Let me go."

He walked over to her. She held out the nail file and stepped back. He grabbed her wrist and took the weapon with little effort. He tossed it. He kissed her hand and she snatched it away from his reach.

"Put the fucking dress on," he told her.

She looked to the garment splayed out on the bed. She wiped her tears and picked it up. The material was thin. The dress was familiar. She glanced over to him. "Where did you get this?"

"I had some of my things returned to me after I was exiled from the States. Funny they sent your things too. Remember when you wore that?"

"Kei—"

"The trip to Santorini. When we sailed to Mykonos. You were terrified of the water. But you wanted to look pretty for me. You made that dress for me. We fucked on top of the sea, and you told me you'd marry me. Only to change your mind by the time we arrived home."

"I never said that. You remember it wrong. You forced me to sail in Greece when you knew I was terrified. And you kept after me about marriage. I told you I would think about it. That's how it happened."

"Everything, Mirabella, has to be a challenge with you. Not because you can't make a decision, but because you can't trust yourself to believe in your decisions. You knew who I was, and who I wasn't. You always knew. And if Giovanni hadn't turned your head you would be my wife, having my children."

"Kei, that's not true."

"It is!" he shouted at her. "Put the dress on, and make me feel appreciated for my efforts. Or I'll help you relax." He removed a syringe from his pocket. Terror gripped her the moment she saw it. She sucked in a deep breath and exhaled slowly in an attempt to not show any fear on her face. There was no need for modesty. She was trapped with him. She opened her kimono. Kei stared at her body as he often did when she was with him. He would ask her to walk around their penthouse apartment in the nude. He had her painted in the nude. She'd wake sometimes in the night, and find him up with the sheets pulled down so he could stare at her naked body, run his hands over it. When she was in Switzerland with him, he staged several accidental run-ins on her by walking in the bathroom when she finished showering, or coming in her room while she was dressing. He even tried to convince her to make a sex tape with him and his new camcorder. She refused. But after plying her with wine one night, he videotaped them without her knowledge. She freaked out and he destroyed the tape. Or so she remembered. She ignored the lust in his eyes and put the dress on.

"Comb your hair. Put on makeup. And then meet topside."

She said nothing. He left. Mirabella looked over to the mirror at herself. The woman staring back at her was someone she didn't recognize. She touched the bandage on her forehead and then the bruise on her neck. She wondered what Giovanni was doing at that moment. Dread filled her as she thought of the lengths her husband would go to find her. The Calderone massacre had nearly brought down his kingdom and sent him to prison. A kidnapping like this? It would push Giovanni close to the edge. She knew it. She had to help herself. Find a way to escape. How?

—*B*—

THE PAIN TO THE LEFT SIDE of his face made him unable to move his head. He opened his eyes and tried to breathe. He could only do so through his nose. Santo blinked. Several stood before his bed staring. Before he was thrown in the ocean he could speak, now his jaw felt detached from his face.

Giovanni watched him curiously, with Lorenzo glaring at his side. Nico was in the room as well as Dominic. He was a dead man. Giovanni said something to Lorenzo. Santo tried to read his lips but his vision blurred and made it hard.

A doctor shined a light into his eyes. He leaned in closer to look at Santo. And when he touched his mouth Santo screamed in his head.

The doctor stepped back. "He's awake, Don Giovanni."

Giovanni stepped around the bed to stand over him. He held a gun in his hand. Santo could not stop staring at it. For all he had done, he should not have ended up where he started. Isabella had betrayed him. He was supposed to be under the protective care of the Bonaduces. That was the deal.

"You know what we do to *pentitos*?" Giovanni asked. Santo's gaze lifted to Giovanni's eyes. "You're going to tell me everything you know."

He tried to open his mouth to speak but couldn't. Either Giovanni understood this or he looked much worse than he knew. He glanced to Dominic. The young *consigliere* came over with a notepad and pen.

Giovanni tapped the notepad with his gun. "I ask the question, you write the answer."

He then put the gun against Santo's temple. He heard the safety release. "If you think you have a choice in this you don't. I intend to keep you alive until I find her. Every time you lie or fail to enlighten me, your wife, your children, your brother, your fucking cleaning lady, will feel my pain—tenfold," he said. "Are we understood?"

Santo nodded.

"Good. Let's begin."

—*B*—

KEI WAITED FOR MIRABELLA on the open deck to the back of the yacht. The image of her body brought forth so many decadent memories of the past. When he first saw her they were at a party. She entered the door with a red-haired woman. The only black woman in the place, and the most beautiful woman he'd seen in awhile. She shied away from the guests and spent most of the time by the door as her friend socialized. He brought her over a drink. She accepted and told him she was in fashion school and hoped to be a designer. Kei had money, influence, power that reached all the way back to China, he could have any woman of any color he wanted. What he didn't have was a young fashion designer, with doe eyes, and a voice so lovely it made his dick hard. From that moment on his obsession grew. And she teased him with her naiveté and inexperience in the big city. She teased him into believing her innocence. He has since sobered from that deception.

He stared out at the ocean. Surprisingly the wind had stopped whipping up the sea. The waters were calm. The sun blazed but the temperature was mild and comforting. He reclined in his chair and thought over his plans. Ordering Chao Lee to end his career by killing a boxer in front of thousands was a risky move. Even Bao questioned his sanity. And by now his uncle Dao was being told that he had brought the world's attention to the Triad. Interpol was making connections that would cost their empire dearly. And to make things even worse, Chao Lee was dead. The Triad would be furious. But if he brought the *Camorra* boss to his knees, and gave his uncle the spoils, he could be forgiven. The end justified the means. Isabella had better not fail him. Not only did Mirabella's life depend on it, but his as well.

Last Night –

Kei walked up the stairs to the upper deck. Isabella sat in a swivel chair sipping her wine. She glanced up when he entered. "How was she?"

The question stung. Kei had learned to weather many things that were unpleasant. From prison, to prison camps, he endured. The only thing that kept him alive and driven was Mirabella. He'd cut Isabella's throat when their business came to an end. For the moment she was a critical resource.

He dropped the VHS tape on the table. Isabella sat forward. She picked up the tape with her gloved hand and put it in an envelope.

"I'll make sure this is delivered," she said.

"I want the Battaglia boys dead. I want my daughter," he said.

"Yes. Yes. I know. And like I told you, it's one or the other. You can't have both."

Kei sat down. He glared at her. Isabella flashed him a pretty smile. "We stick to the plan. I have to flush the Battaglias out of Melanzana. They are prepared for war. But nothing can prepare them for the law. Let me use the new Chief Inspector's ambition against Giovanni. It'll put him on the move, and then Eve is mine for the taking. She will be delivered to you."

"This plan had better work," Kei said.

"It's bullet proof. Do you know why?" she smiled. "Because destroying Giovanni Battaglia isn't just about taking his wife and daughter, or murdering his sons. It's about wiping his family out completely. Remember his sons aren't the only ones close to him. He has a lovely sister who could be your sacrificial lamb as well. He has cousins who he considers brothers that we can break. He has his father's legacy that defines him. Take them all one by one and he's on his knees before you." She stood and picked up her purse. The boat had coasted far enough for her to debark and head back to the mainland. He could hear the men talking to the ones who followed them on a speedboat.

"You know you could leave and go to China. It's going to take several days, maybe even longer to get my hands on the kid."

"I'm not leaving until I have them both," Kei said.

Isabella smiled. "Is that so? A little birdie told me you won't leave because your uncle is not happy with you?"

"Careful, Isabella. I'm the monster. Remember?" Kei warned her.

"Right. You're the monster not me." she smiled. "But we need to do it my way. Santo will make it to the shore. When Giovanni finds him he'll have to confess to what he thinks he knows about our plans. You do as we agreed and everything will work out."

Kei nodded. He watched Isabella leave. After sipping tea he stood and returned to Mirabella. She lay under the covers nude. She moaned in her delirium. Kei opened his robe and shed it. Nude he rejoined her in bed. He took his time to study her body. It was as beautiful as he remembered. He ran his hand over her thigh, the curve of her hip. He turned her and traced the tip of his finger over her dark areola. He kissed her nipples. The moment he pulled the covers up, she said something and rolled over to him. She kissed his chest and neck. He felt his erection strengthen. Temptation was unbearable *when she lifted her lips to his mouth and kissed him.*

He wouldn't corrupt what they had shared this way. Not when she fantasized about making love to her husband. He stopped the kiss and brought her tight up against his chest. She stopped moaning and calling her husband's name. The drug took its final effect and she passed out. Kei relaxed. He slipped into the first blissful sleep he'd had in years.

—*B*—

"First question, and there is only one answer, who hired you to take my wife from me?" Giovanni asked.

Santo looked up at the gun and then into Giovanni's eyes. He wrote on the notepad and read the name. "Isabella? Who the fuck is Isabella?"

Lorenzo snatched the notepad. "It can't be."

"Do you know her?" Giovanni asked.

Lorenzo stared at the notepad. The day he read the name Isabella on the note Marietta had with the tapes, he felt he knew her. This could not be a coincidence. "No. I don't."

"Then you're fucking lying to me!" Giovanni raised the gun. Santo raised his hands in surrender. Giovanni threw the notepad at him and Santo picked it up. He scribbled again.

Dominic snatched the notepad. "It says Isabella hired him for Kei Hyogo."

"Find out who this bitch is." Giovanni told Dominic. "Next question. Where is she? Where did they take her?"

Santo looked up at him. He picked up the notepad and then the pen. Giovanni put the gun to Santo's skull. "No more second guesses. What you write down determines the life of everyone who has known you. Where is she?"

The scribbling was fast. Santo wrote the answer and handed the notepad over. Dominic read it out loud to the room. "The sea."

"No shit. Where are they going?"

"They threw him out in the ocean, Giovanni. He doesn't fucking know," Lorenzo said.

"Wait. Someone does," Dominic said. "Where can we find Isabella?" Dominic asked.

Santo looked to Giovanni and then the gun. He took the notepad and he wrote his answer. Dominic read it aloud. "29 Piazza Bagnoli."

Before Giovanni could respond the door kicked open. The *Carabinieri* rushed in shouting with their Uzis pointed at them. Giovanni, and all his men were forced to drop their weapons and get down on their knees. They had to put their hands up behind their heads. While he was being handcuffed Giovanni stared at Santo. When Santo held his stare Giovanni winked. No matter where this ended, he would pay Santo a visit personally for coming after his family. Giovanni was forced to his feet and marched out. Lorenzo and Dominic were handcuffed as well. All of them were walked out. The *Carabinieri* had been tipped off to where the *Camorra* bosses were gathered, by a woman. Or so he thought he heard one of the officers say. Each of them were put in the back of vans. In his criminal career he'd only been detained and questioned for as long as a few weeks. He'd never actually been formally charged.

"Don't say anything, Gio. I'll have us out soon," Dominic advised.

Giovanni stared out of the open doors to the van, and watched the men of different clans being forced to lay flat in the streets. His mind was blank. He had a new enemy and her name was Isabella. How many women had he known and been with in his lifetime under that same name? Lorenzo's mother was named Isabella. *Who the fuck was this bitch?*

He glanced to Lorenzo. His cousin's reaction to the name was curious. "Who is Isabella to you?" he asked him again.

"I don't know, Gio. But I swear to you I will help you find out." Giovanni narrowed his eyes on Lorenzo. Other men were shoved into the back of the van and Giovanni was forced to scoot down. Lorenzo never lowered his gaze. For some reason Giovanni didn't believe him.

THE KIDS WERE OUT IN THE POOL. Marietta stood by the terrace door watching. She sipped her wine with shaky hands. Her troubled heart had too many worries. Mirabella was kidnapped, being tortured for all they knew. Lorenzo was out in the streets and could be shot or arrested. Carlo was in jail suffering because of the death of his brother. The wine was the only thing that calmed her. She didn't want to be inebriated, but she had to remain calm. She heard someone enter from behind her. She turned. She saw a stricken look on Rocco's face. He was ghostly white.

"What? What is it?" Marietta asked and nearly dropped her glass. She set it on the counter. "Tell me!"

"Gio, the news report on the tele."

"News? What happened now?" she asked.

"The men have been arrested. Gio is in custody," Rocco said.

"And Lorenzo?" Marietta asked.

"Everyone." Rocco said. "I am going to call the attorneys."

"Rocco! What the hell is happening?" Marietta asked on the verge of tears.

Rocco shook his head. "I don't know."

He walked out on his cane. Marietta looked at the kids splashing around. Catalina was in the pool with them as well as Cecilia. Zia clapped her hands and fretted from the sidelines for the kids not to play so rough. Everything was falling apart. She went to the phone. She dialed and closed her eyes. She silently prayed as it rang. And then he answered.

"Oh God. Thank you for answering."

"Marietta?" he asked.

"Armando, you have to come. I don't know what to do! It's Mirabella, she's been taken."

"Slow down—"

"And now Lorenzo and Gio are in jail!" Marietta said.

"Where are you?"

"Here. Sorrento. Melanzana. Giovanni and the men have all been arrested. You said I could call you if I ever needed you. I need you. Our sister needs you."

"Of course," he replied.

"Then will you come?" she asked.

"I'll do everything I can. I'll fly into Sorrento before nightfall."

"Grazie, Armando."

"Don't worry, little sister, we'll bring her back."

—*B*—

WHEN SHE EMERGED FROM THE LOWER DECK she saw him seated in a lounge chair staring at the ocean. Mirabella sucked down a deep breath and scooped her hair behind her ears to keep it from flying in her face. When they were together her phobia of open bodies of water would leave her paralyzed. She knew it was no coincidence that he kidnapped her and kept her on a boat. Fear is what he would try to use against her.

But she had changed. Thanks to Giovanni she was stronger. She could swim. She could load and fire a gun. She learned how to be a fighter not a victim. And that's how she planned to return to her family. Fighting.

"Don't be afraid," Kei said. He must have sensed her standing behind him. He raised his hand. Mirabella walked to him and took his hand. He held it as she lowered to the deck chair.

"I don't want to be out here, Kei. Let's go inside," she said.

"It's a nice day. Relax," he said.

Mirabella rolled her eyes. She stared straight ahead.

Kei exhaled. "It's time I share my plans with you."

She looked over at him. His good eye was closed. He was shirtless. He wore very thin black linen trousers. His feet were crossed at the ankle. And on his chest was a serpent. A dragon.

"We are headed to Lipari. Ever heard of it?" he began.

"It's an island next to Sicily. I've heard of it."

"A very beautiful island." Kei looked over. "We'll have all the privacy we need."

"Why? Why there?"

"We're waiting," Kei said.

"For what?"

"Not what Mirabella, who. Eve," he said.

"Leave my daughter out of this." Mirabella sat up. "You want to play your sick game, then you play it with me."

"This is no game. In a few days I will have her. By then that fake gangster you call husband, and everything he's worked for, will be burned to the ground. Only a few more days. When Eve is brought to me we leave. And you will be ready." Kei sat upright. Anger coiled in her chest like a cobra ready to strike.

"My husband is the least of your worries, Kei. If you touch any of my children, I swear to God I'll kill you myself."

Kei smirked. "There she is."

Mirabella could swear the creep had lust in his eyes when he stared back.

"I miss that fire in you." He reached and touched her face. She turned it away.

Kei chuckled. "We have time, Mirabella. You'll be mine again. Willingly."

He stood and kissed the top of her head. She flinched and then he left. She looked at the ocean and fought to resist the urge to jump into it. She could swim, but how far was she from land? Mirabella stood. She used her hand as a shield against the glare of the sun. She looked east and west. There was no sign of land or any cruise ships that frequented the waters. Now was not the time to strike. She had to be patient, and she had to be observant. Somehow she'd find a way.

CHAPTER FIFTEEN

Isabella

"Signor Giovanni, we finally meet. I'm *Ispettore Capo* Donatello." A tall man who looked to be around Giovanni's age said.

"Chief Inspector?" Giovanni said. "What happened to Bonomo?"

Donatello glanced up from his notepad and looked Giovanni in the eye. "Oh, you weren't told? He retired two months ago. I was promoted to his chair."

Giovanni chuckled. *"Complimenti."*

"I have some questions for you." The Chief Inspector drawled.

"I've asked for a lawyer." Giovanni said.

"No need for one. You have some very powerful friends. I just left my office." The Inspector sat back and made a tent with his fingers. "I was on the phone with the Prime Minister. He's asked that you be released immediately. The prosecutor agrees. No charges are to be filed."

Giovanni arched a brow.

"I only have a few questions."

"Send them to my lawyer." Giovanni stood.

"Signor." The Inspector raised his voice. "I can't detain you. My power doesn't reach that high. But I can keep your men. All of your men. I have a slaughter on my hands, and two prizefighters are dead. On this rare occasion I don't believe *la Camorra* is at fault. If you work with me we can bring the people who made an attempt on your life to justice."

"Fuck you," Giovanni said.

The inspector narrowed his eyes on him. "Someone is going to answer for the slaughter brought to the *Campania. La Camorra* is a stain on the Republic. Men like you have an expiration date. I will not stop until you are all put down."

Giovanni nodded to the challenge. He turned and walked out. The officers glared at him, but no one said a word. He saw one of his attorneys waiting for him. Once they were outside and in the limo he spoke. "How soon can Domi and Lorenzo, and the rest of my men be released?"

"Don Giovanni, they are being detained for a tribunal. Santo is under police protection. No court date has been set. We are doing all we can."

"Do more!" Giovanni slammed his fist into the side of the door. "I need them with me."

The attorney nodded. Every man he trusted was locked away. Even the clan bosses were behind bars. He was on his own. And he knew in his gut that Mirabella wasn't in Italy anymore. He had to regroup. Come up with a better plan.

"Where to?" the attorney asked.

"Melanzana. I need to meet with my men."

THE PHONE RANG. Marietta jumped. Catalina looked up with questioning eyes. She picked it up. "*Pronto?*"

"Marietta? It's Kyra," a soft voice said.

"Oh thank God. Umberto told me he left the message for you to call me. How is he?"

Kyra began to cry. Marietta looked over to Catalina who was now standing. Tears pooled in Marietta's eyes but she kept the emotion down. "Kyra? Is he alive?"

"Yes. But these doctors keep telling me he lost too much blood. His heart stopped twice. I'm so scared," Kyra wept.

"Is anyone there with you?"

"Yes. Jamie is here. Renaldo's mother is here. We're here. What happened? Who would hurt him like this? Why?" Kyra wept into the phone. Marietta turned the phone over and put it on speakerphone so Catalina could stop kicking her.

"He's alive Kyra. He's strong. He'll come out of it. I wish I could be there for you," Marietta said.

"Kyra? It's Catalina. What do you need, honey? Anything? We can get the attorneys to find a good doctor. Okay?" Catalina said.

"Okay. Please. I think we need help. I don't know what to do. The doctors keep coming and going but they don't really explain anything to us. And he has all these tubes in him. He was shot seven times."

Marietta glanced up to Catalina who looked at her with equal horror. How is it possible that Renaldo was still alive? They felt weak with fear. "Okay, sweetheart. Tell me the hospital information and the surgeon's name. Everything," Catalina located a pen and pad from the desk.

Kyra began to share all she knew. Marietta had to stand and walk away. She put her hands to her head. She thought of telling Catalina that she called Armando but decided to keep that to herself for now. She didn't know if she did the right thing. But this was a nightmare. They needed help.

"Kyra, call us the moment anything changes," Catalina said.

"I will. Is the Donna there? Can I speak to her?" Kyra asked softly.

Catalina looked up at Marietta. She shook her head no to Catalina. They were told by Rocco not to share any details outside of the family. She'd already broken that rule with Armando.

"She's, ah, not right here at the moment. I'll have her call the hospital and check in. Okay?" Catalina asked. "You just be strong. Renaldo will make it. He will."

"Thanks. I'll call."

Kyra hung up. Catalina dropped back in the chair and cried. "Seven times? He was shot seven times!"

"I know," Marietta paced. "I heard that Leonardo was dead, Eduardo is dead, David is dead, Kaleb is dead…"

"Stop!" Catalina shouted. "Stop it!" she wept. "These men are my family. They raised me. They are family. Just shut the fuck up!" Catalina ran from the room. Marietta put her hands to her eyes and cried. She felt as if she was thrown in a wind tunnel and couldn't keep from spiraling to the darkness. She staggered over to the sofa and dropped on it. She lay on her side and cried.

The phone rang. It was the main phone to the house. Marietta looked up at it. She forced herself to stand on her shaky legs and picked it up. "Hello," she said.

"Marie? It's me."

"Lo! Oh thank God! Thank you God!" she wept.

"I don't have long. Is Rocco there?" he asked.

"He's in Villa Rosso with the attorneys. Are you okay? Is Carlo okay? Gio? What about Domi? Lo? What the hell is going on?" she pleaded.

"I'm okay. Tell Rocco we're being moved. We haven't seen Gio. He's probably being released. Tell him…"

"Lo?"

She heard men shouting. The phone line disconnected.

"Lo! Lo!" She tried to click over and back to recover the line. All she got was a dial tone. Her heart suffered several seizures of panic. She went to her knees. She held the phone to her chest and stared at the door. Tears kept streaming down her cheeks. She felt totally helpless.

THE OVERCROWDING IN THE JAILS forced the men to be moved. Lorenzo was escorted from the holding area, with Dominic and Nico down a dank hall. He had found a sympathizer among their jailers who let him use the phone. But the guard's superiors discovered this and shut him down. He seethed with rage. Marietta's terror added to his anxiety. She was fragile now. He needed to get back to her.

When they entered the next ward they were greeted with applause like celebrities. Many of the men cheered for them when they passed one unit and moved to the next. At the end of the corridor another guard opened the gate. Lorenzo glanced back to Dominic, who looked up to him and nodded. The cell was less crowded and Lorenzo soon noticed why. The men inside were all brothers of *la Camorra*. He smiled. He greeted and hugged several. They laughed and cheered at Dominic, Lorenzo, and Nico's inclusion.

Lorenzo noticed how Dominic scanned the top of the cell. There were cameras pointed from different angles. The jailers weren't that generous. They were being watched and listened to. He headed toward the back bench seat. It was there he found him.

Carlo sat with his head down and his shoulders slumped. He sat alone. Every man instinctively knew to give him room.

"Domi! Nico!" Lorenzo called out.

They all saw him. Lorenzo walked over and sat next to him. Nico told him what happened in the fourth round. How hard Ciro fought and was holding his own. And then the murderous attack launched by Chao Lee. The fucking cocksucker.

"Carlo," Lorenzo whispered.

Carlo didn't respond.

"We're all in. They raided Venditto's. Even Giovanni was picked up."

Carlo didn't respond. His head didn't lift. Lorenzo could see dark bruises over Carlo's arms and knuckles. He had no idea how bad his face must look.

"It was the Triad, Carlo. They kidnapped Mirabella. She's missing."

To this Carlo slowly lifted his head. He looked as if he had been kicked in the head repeatedly by a steel boot. Black, purple, red, and yellow bruises and swelling covered the lumps rising all over his face. He turned his head in a stiff motion to see out of his barely opened eyes. Lorenzo felt the urge to rage, weep for his broken brother. In fact his eyes teared up, and his throat clogged with emotion. "I'll fucking kill them all for you, brother. I swear it. I'm sorry for Ciro."

"Mirabella?" Carlo rasped.

"I don't know. We'll find her," Lorenzo said in a voice choked with emotion. "We'll get out of here, and find her, and you will get your revenge. I swear it on my life, brother."

Dominic sat down on the other side of Carlo. Lorenzo looked up. Men were now standing in a protective circle around them to block their conversation from the cameras.

"Domi? How long will they detain us?" Lorenzo asked.

"I don't know. I spoke to one of the guards. Bonomo has retired. They have a new Chief Inspector. They said Giovanni has been released."

"I thought so," Lorenzo let go a burdened sigh. "I got through to Melanzana. Sent a message to Rocco. He's already got the attorneys on it."

Dominic nodded in agreement.

Carlo sat back and leaned against the wall. Lorenzo frowned with concern. "Look at him. He needs medical attention. These fucking bastards have Santo in a hospital and Carlo in here? Where is the fucking justice?" Lorenzo got to his feet.

"Sit down!" Dominic warned.

Lorenzo glared at the cameras.

"Sit down!" Dominic repeated.

Lorenzo slowly sat.

"We keep it cool. Giovanni can handle it," Dominic said. They all sat and waited. And it was then the name surfaced in Lorenzo's mind.

—*B*—

THE *CARABINIERI* TAILED HIM FOR MILES. They had several hundred men in custody. He needed to think and regroup. The streets they travelled were quiet. Many store owners closed up their shops early. It was as if the entire *Campania* was in mourning. He knew that behind closed doors the Italians whispered about the kidnapping of his beloved. He knew many predicted his madness would return. Braced for it. Giovanni squeezed his eyes shut and endured.

The walk up the steps to Melanzana was the hardest. He vowed not to return without his Bella. The door was pulled open before he reached it. Catalina stood before him with Gino on her hip. His baby boy reached for him immediately. Giovanni froze.

"Gio! What is going on?" Catalina said with her face flushed from tears. "Where is Mirabella?"

He took the baby to keep him calm. He kissed his son who hugged his neck. Gino began to cry when Catalina started. His son never responded to his coming home with tears. It wrecked him.

Catalina paced in front of him, and prevented him from walking inside. Her hair was tangled from constantly pulling it and her eyes were red and swollen. "Where is she? Is she okay? Are you going to bring her home? When, Gio? When?"

"Catalina!" Marietta said. She marched toward them. "Take Gino and go find Zia. Now."

"No! I want to know about Mirabella!" Catalina shouted.

"Catalina? Look at Gino. You're scaring him," Marietta said.

Giovanni bounced Gino and smiled until the boy smiled back. Catalina looked at the toddler with understanding. She nodded. She took the baby from Gio. He kept crying as she walked down the hall.

"Can you tell me anything? If she's okay?" Marietta asked.

Giovanni lowered his gaze. "I'll be in Villa Rosso. Have my meals sent there."

"Wait!" She grabbed his arm. "There's something you need to know. I called Armando."

He turned and looked at her with genuine surprise. How could the woman make that leap? To tell the *Mafiosi* his business? His weakness?

"Before you get angry you need to understand, Gio. We had just found out you were arrested. We didn't know if you were coming home. I'm sorry, but I was afraid. You men have never told us what to do when something like this happens."

Instead of anger he felt another weight of sadness added to his already battered heart. He took Marietta into his arms and hugged her. The action soothed them both. He had never been a fan of hers. Especially recently. But the way she spoke and looked at him for understanding reminded him of his wife. He needed that reminder to calm his fears.

"If I lose her," Giovanni said, and his voice choked on emotion.

"We won't lose her, Gio. We'll figure it out," Marietta said.

He let her go. "I need you to help Catalina. Take care of the children. Keep her calm and away from me. I can't stand seeing her in pain," he said.

"I can do it. I can take care of them. I'll do it," Marietta said.

Giovanni wasn't sure he could trust her, but he had no choice. He forced a smile and his face barely had the strength to hold the action for long. "Send Rocco to Villa Rosso."

"He's there already. He's been there with a few of your men."

"Grazie."

"Gio?" she said as he walked away. "Do you know who took her?"

He nodded.

"Kill him. Make them pay," she said.

He vowed to make them all pay. As he left out of the back doors of Melanzana, and started toward Villa Rosso, several of his men began to follow him. By the time he reached the villa he had twenty of them wanting to offer support. Giovanni went inside and found Rocco seated on the sofa. His uncle used his cane to stand.

"Gio? We just received something," Rocco said.

The news stopped him. "Received what?"

Rocco nodded toward the open door of his office. Giovanni went inside. His eyes landed on an envelope waiting for him on his desk. Rocco closed the door on the men and joined him. "I sent the attorneys away to work on getting the boys out."

"When did it arrive?" Giovanni asked.

"The boys stopped a courier at the gate. A kid. He knew nothing. Said a woman gave him a hundred lira to bring it."

"Woman?" Giovanni asked.

"Yes." Rocco came closer on his cane. "Is that relevant?"

"Do you know a woman named Isabella?" Giovanni asked.

Rocco chuckled. It was a bitter dry chuckle. "I know a hundred women named Isabella."

"Yea. Me too." Giovanni picked up the envelope. There was a red lipstick kiss on the seal. His name was on the package. That was all. He opened it and removed a VHS tape. Curious, Giovanni turned it over. The words PLAY ME were written on the label.

"It's a video tape," Rocco stated the obvious.

"Open the cabinet," Giovanni said.

Rocco did as he was told. Giovanni stared at the tape for several minutes, unable to speak or move. If he played it and it was the death of his wife, he'd never recover. Nothing sent to a boss of his stature in the form of a videotape could be good.

"Do you want me to step out, Giovanni?"

"No." he snapped out of it. He walked over to the VCR and inserted the tape. He picked up the remote and pressed play.

The image of Kei Hyogo adjusting the video camera came into focus. He tilted the camera so it lifted and zoomed in on his face. Kei took a step back so he could be seen fully. He stared in the camera for a moment. Giovanni's jaw clenched.

"We meet again, Gio." Kei smiled. "Are you worried? Panicked? Are you afraid of who could pluck your rose from right under your nose? Blue right? You got a thing about blue roses," Kei smiled. "You should be. I expect you to run blindly in search of my ghost. I welcome it. As I've had to run blindly in search of this revenge. I've spent two years preparing for this. How long have you ignored your nagging feeling in your gut that I was coming for you? Did you really think I'd let you take her from me? When I am done with you, everything will be in ashes." Kei looked behind him. "I thought I'd send you this gift to mark this day. To make you a believer in the Dragon. I will record our reunion for you." Kei chuckled. "She's been begging for it all night."

Giovanni narrowed his eyes on the final statement. The camera was moved. It pointed to the bed. A woman lay with the covers around her waist and her back to the lens. Kei stepped to the bed. He removed his robe. He was nude.

"Turn it off, Gio," Rocco warned.

"Shut up, old man!" Giovanni said. Kei looked to the camera and smiled. He eased under the covers with Bella and she stirred. She turned into his arms and her body was revealed. Rocco lowered his gaze.

"Gio, turn it off. I beg you," Rocco said.

His uncle's advice was solid. He should listen. He knew he should but he couldn't look away. Kei kissed wife and she moaned with pleasure. He rolled on top of her and she parted her thighs for him. When his kisses traced from her cheek to her neck, Mirabella's head tilted back as if she enjoyed it. Kei lifted the remote and pointed it at the camera. The tape ended.

Giovanni staggered back. He stared at the static on the screen. "Give me a minute," he said to Rocco. When his uncle left he set the remote down on his desk. He went to his bar. He reached down to the bottom shelves and removed his aged Scotch. He didn't bother with a glass. Instead he walked over to the sofa and sat. He put the bottle down in front of him. He came close to losing his Bella twice. The first time he lost her, he turned to the bottle. He killed and avenged his broken heart until he was numb. The second time, when she nearly died in childbirth, he drank and sulked until everyone around him had to help him stand. And then he enjoyed the slaughter of the Mottolas.

He stared at the bottle.

His men were in jail. His children were scared and missing their mother. The enemy was at the front and back door. His empire rumbled with the threat of implosion. And all he had was the bottle before him. He could rage. His anger felt like lava pumping from his heart, soldering his bones into steel, preparing him for war. He had enough hate in him to burn on rage for the rest of his life. The only love he truly believed in was that of his wife. He put his head in his hands. He closed his eyes. If he prayed would God listen? Would he find him worthy this time? And then he knew the truth. This time he had to stand alone. He had to swallow his fears. He had to fight against his nature and keep a cool head.

He lifted his head from his hands and looked to the screen. He looked to the bottle. He felt his breathing shorten. In his head he screamed until he heard nothing. He picked up the bottle unscrewed the cap. Before he brought the bottle to his lips. The strong liquor aroma wafted under his nose. His throat went dry with the thirst. There was a knock at his door.

Giovanni paused. He set the bottle down.

"Come in," he said.

Rocco opened the door. Mateo Benicia, the younger brother of Don Benicia walked inside with another man.

"Giovanni," Mateo said with a respectful nod.

"Have a seat," Giovanni said. Mateo joined him. He sat across from Giovanni on the sofa chair. Rocco went to the bar on his cane and got a glass. When he placed it on the coffee table Giovanni poured Mateo a drink.

"My brother is in the hospital. They have the *polizia* in his room and won't let any of us in to see him."

"It's unfortunate Benicia and I argued. I regret it," Giovanni said swallowing a measure of pride.

"What's done is done, Gio," Mateo said.

He looked up into Mateo's eyes, and two seconds into the stare Mateo lowered his eyes first. "He told me we are to help you in any way we can. We've already started canvasing fishermen. We know Santo washed up from the sea."

"Forget Santo for a moment. Forget the raid at Venditto. We will deal with these things later." Giovanni said. He looked to the bottle of Scotch and then away. He reclined and crossed his legs. His face rested in the palm of his hand. "Do you know a woman by the name of Isabella?"

Mateo frowned. "My wife's name is Isabella, I have a sister as well."

"The fight was arranged by Santo. Ciro trained under Father Nicosia. I need one of your men to go with mine and find that priest. He has to be in Napoli somewhere. If he's returned to Bergamo then I want you to bring him back."

"I know the priest. You think he has answers?" Mateo asked.

"There's a woman by the name of Isabella who is working for the Triad. Someone has to have known or seen her. I need men to head to *Piazzia Bagnoli*. She's been spotted there. My guess is she's gone now. Still send them. And I want boats from here to Sicilia. Canvas the sea. As much as you can."

Mateo drank down what was left in the glass. "We can do all these things. But I am here to tell you that the deal you made with my brother needs to be sealed first."

"First?" Giovanni arched a brow.

"Half our men are either dead or in jail. The Benicias will assume a lot more risk than the Battaglias. We don't have your powerful friends, Giovanni. No disrespect. If we are to do this, the family wants guarantees on the distribution. The deal of a forty percent split."

"You want me to reward you before you fucking lift a finger to earn it?" Giovanni seethed.

"No. We want you to align with us. Give us a position in your family. And we will put our lives on the line for her. We'll give our lives for your Donna. I can't go to my men with the promise of a reward. I have to go to my men and tell them of a true alliance."

Giovanni looked over to Rocco. The old man shook his head no. He knew if he agreed he'd plunge the family deeper into drug trafficking and all his work to legitimize them would be for nothing. If it was the price to pay for the return of his wife he'd do it without question.

"Done. We are aligned." Giovanni said.

Mateo's eyes gleamed with triumph. He saw the hunger in the young man for power. A gleam of lust sparked in his eyes to remove Giovanni's power, and be crowned the boss of all bosses. He saw it and didn't care. All he cared about was his wife.

Mateo stood. "So it is the Triad?" he asked.

"It is. Bring me the priest and find out all you can on Isabella."

Mateo nodded and walked out. Rocco saw them to the door. He turned and looked at Giovanni who slumped down on the sofa.

"Gio? What have you done?" Rocco asked.

"Do you think he drugged her?" Giovanni asked.

"I don't understand? How could you agree to that deal, Gio? Benicia is not worthy of that kind of power!" Rocco shouted.

"Was she drunk? Confused?" Giovanni asked. He stared at the Scotch bottle. He saw his wife turn into the arms of his enemy. He saw her smile. She smiled for him the way she often smiled when he touched her.

"Of course he drugged her, Giovanni. You know your wife. She would never betray you."

"She has before," Giovanni said. He glanced up to Rocco. "She told me the time they were together in Switzerland that she never slept with him. Two years living with my Bella, and you're telling me he never tried what I just saw? She never let him in?"

"What does that matter now, Gio? She's in danger! Do you doubt that?"

He shook his head no.

"This is what he wants, Gio, to get in your head. Don't let him in," Rocco said. He reached for the bottle of Scotch. Giovanni didn't object when he screwed the cap on it and put it back on the bar. "You can't honor that deal with the Benicias. If you do it will spit on everything your father built. Drugs! We are not fucking drug dealers!" Rocco shouted.

"He hasn't left with her," Giovanni said. He ignored his uncle. The truth was he didn't hear him. He was too lost to his own hell. He wiped his hand down his face. "That video was to distract me. He's still here. Somewhere close. Why? Why taunt me? What is he after? He's after something."

"Everyone is looking for him, Gio. You have allies all through the *Campania*. They are all looking."

Giovanni scratched his brow. "I need to know what he's fucking after!"

"To destroy you," Rocco said.

"Maybe. But that's not it. You heard him. He's going to take back what's his. That's what he said." Giovanni glanced up to Rocco. "He has my Bella. What else does he think belongs to him?"

"Eve?" Rocco asked.

"Did you see his hand?" Giovanni stood. He went to the remote and picked it up. He rewound the tape. Giovanni hit play. Kei came on the camera and began to adjust the tilt. Giovanni paused the tape. "There! Look at his hand."

"What is that?" Rocco asked.

"Some kind of iron thing over his fingers." Giovanni went to the television and studied it. "It's like a glove." He hit play and Kei stepped back. He could see it clearly.

"Go get Eve." Giovanni said.

"What?" Rocco said.

"Bring her to me!"

"Why?" Rocco disagreed in his tone of voice.

"For days Zia and Bella have been complaining about Eve telling stories of the man with the hook hand. That the man was coming to take her and her mother to some fairytale place."

"He couldn't have possibly had access to Eve," Rocco said. "How could he?"

"HE HAS MY FUCKING BELLA! HE TOOK HER FROM UNDER MY NOSE! Nothing is a fucking coincidence, old man! Nothing! Santo comes out of jail and wants forgiveness, access to my family and my business.

What do I do? I put him in charge of security. FUCKING SECURITY! He's been with my children and my wife. And now Bella is gone. It's connected."

"Gio, let's wait until we get Domi and—"

"DON'T FUCKING QUESTION ME, OLD MAN! GET HER! NOW!" he stepped to Rocco. His uncle moved quickly on his cane. Giovanni sucked in a deep breath. He paced the floor. He turned to the television and pressed play. At first Bella was still. When Kei joined her in bed she turned over with her eyes closed. He watched the way she kissed and responded to his touch. He rewound that scene fifteen times and studied it. She never opened her eyes. Not once. It wasn't his wife. He knew her pleasures. Kei had barely touched her and she was moaning. Something was off. The bastard was drugging her. He couldn't imagine feeling an ounce of relief in his wife's suffering. But he believed his eyes. This was a violation of her and him. And it was then he was able to see her truly. The scar and dried blood on her forehead, the dark bruise on her neck. Giovanni found it hard to stand. The motherfucker was torturing his sweet Bella. *He wanted him dead!*

The wait for his daughter was excruciating. Rocco had returned and was seated with him in silence. He needed silence. He felt rational when no one was fucking talking and asking him stupid questions he couldn't answer.

There was a knock at the door. Marietta appeared. She had Eve by the hand. His daughter had two French braids with blue ribbons tied to the end. She wore blue overalls with a pink shirt underneath.

"Papa!" Eve ran over to him and he lifted her to his lap. "Papa, where have you been?" Eve asked. "Where is Mommy?"

"She's on a trip. She'll be back soon," Giovanni smiled. He looked up to Marietta who stared at him with confusion. "Papa needs your help. I want to show you someone. I need you to tell me if you've seen him before. Do you think you can do that?"

"Yes, Papa, I can do it." Eve said.

"Gio? What is this about?" Marietta asked with caution.

"No questions," Giovanni said. Marietta nodded that she'd obey. He picked up the remote. He pressed play and put it on mute. Kei adjusted the camera and then stepped into view. He hit pause.

"That's Poppy!" Eve said. She got down from her father's lap. "He's Captain Hook. He's going to take me and Mama to Neverland."

"When did you see Poppy, baby?" Marietta asked.

"In the room." Eve said.

"Eve," Giovanni said. "Who brought Poppy to you?"

"Zio Santo. He came in the room and told ChiChi to get lunch. And then he brought Poppy to see me. Gino cried and ran from him. Santo took Gino in another room. Me and Poppy played."

"At the hotel? During the fashion show? Cecilia was alone with them until Rocco came for them." Marietta added.

Giovanni closed his eyes to the news. His children were vulnerable. And he'd let his enemy walk in. Anything could have happened.

"Bring me Cecilia." Giovanni said. He reached for Eve's hand. She came over to him and he kissed her. He pulled her to him and hugged her so tight Marietta came over to separate them. Eve began to cry. Giovanni let her go. Marietta knelt in front of Eve and tried to calm her. The little girl pushed away from her aunt and returned to her father for comfort. He put her on his knee and kissed away her tears. He held her. "I'm sorry, Eve. Papa failed you. Papa will fix it."

"I want my Mommy. I want her now!" Eve said and began to wail loudly.

"Me too," Giovanni said. "Me too."

"Let me take her, Gio. You're scaring her," Marietta said. "Eve, mommy is coming home soon. How about we go upstairs and make her a picture. She'll like that."

Eve wiped at her tears. "I'll make you one too, Papa. A picture for you and Mommy."

He nodded and let her go. Marietta had to pick her up and carry her from the room.

"Wait, Marietta, Do you know a woman named Isabella?"

"Isabella?" Marietta paused.

"Have you heard that name before? It's important. Bella's life depends on it."

"Once, when I first came to Italy. I…" Marietta struggled with her explanation. Giovanni narrowed his eyes on her. Why was she conflicted? He sensed she was keeping things from him. "I got a note once. That told me the Battaglias knew what happened to my mother. A woman named Isabella signed it. I never knew who she was."

"Thank you for being honest," he said staring her in the eye. Marietta nodded and walked out carrying Eve.

"I let this happen," Giovanni said.

"You were supporting your wife. You did everything to support her."

"I knew the fucking fashion show was a bad idea. In my gut I knew we weren't ready. But I let her guilt me into agreeing!" he kicked the coffee table.

"So now it's her fault, Gio? Who are you going to blame next? Eve?" Rocco said.

"It's my fault. Every time I act against my nature I put this family at risk." Giovanni said.

"Which is why getting into the drug business with Benicia is a bad idea, son," Rocco reasoned.

"Fuck the drugs, old man! This is my life! My Bella! My children!" Giovanni shouted.

"Gio, you can't lock the family away from the world. You have to make the world afraid of your family. That's strength!" Rocco said. "Don't compromise now. Be who you are in all things!"

Giovanni put his face in his hands. "Go. Find Cecilia, bring her to me."

The phone rang at his desk. He stood and picked it up. "Gio speaking." he answered.

"It's Armando."

"What the fuck do you want?"

"Marietta called me. I'd like to offer my assistance," Armando began.

"Don't need it." He hung up the phone. Giovanni sat behind his desk. In less than ten minutes Cecilia was marched into his office. She looked terrified.

"Have a seat," he said through clenched teeth.

"Don Giovanni, I was told the Donna is missing. I'm so sorry," Cecilia said with tears in her eyes.

He leaned forward. "When did you leave my children alone?"

"I don't understand. I never leave the children. Never," she looked to Rocco for assistance.

"Gio, she's innocent in this." Rocco said.

"Shut the fuck up!" he said to Rocco. He pointed a finger at her. "In Milano, the day of the fashion show, you and the children were together. When did you leave them alone?"

"I-I-I-I dunno…"

"Think damn it!" he slammed his hand on the desk. "Or I'll bring someone in to make you think!"

Cecilia burst into tears. She dropped her head when she spoke. "Lunch. For lunch, *signor.* I… Santo come and say to go downstairs." She shook her head. "I went for lunch and the lady told me she had planned to send it up. I was confused. Santo said I was to bring it up." She lifted her gaze. "I come back upstairs with Leo and the door is locked. Santo comes to the door after a few minutes. He was alone with the children. That was the only time. I swear it. I swear."

"Calm down, it's okay," Rocco squeezed her shoulder. "Is there anything else you can remember?"

"I come in and Gino is upset. Santo said he was in the bathroom. Gino was scared of him. I could tell. He left. Eve told me she met Captain Hook. She showed me her book. That is all that I know."

"How the hell did he get to the floor past Nico and Renaldo?" Giovanni asked.

"The Diana is an old hotel, Gio. They have those servant entrances. I've used them before to get in and out of rooms. They lead everywhere. No way our men could have known one led to that floor."

"No way? There is always a way," Giovanni scoffed.

"Gio."

"Enough. Leave. Take her and go." When Rocco and Cecilia didn't move he glared at them both. "Now!"

Rocco helped Cecilia up and escorted her to the door. Giovanni rocked back in his chair. He picked up the remote and pressed play. The scene of Kei giving his performance came up on the screen. He rubbed his temples and tried to calm himself. He fell forward on his elbows to the desk. His hands covered his eyes. *How did he not know? Not suspect. How could he have not seen through Santo? Lorenzo had warned him. Countless times his cousin had warned him. And he did nothing!*

Giovanni tried to stand and stopped. He drew his gun. He held it in his left hand. The right had was fucking useless, broken and swollen. He lifted the gun and aimed it at the screen. He sucked in a deep breath, and before he could prevent it he broke. He unloaded his gun into the television. Sparks and smoke exploded from the contraption. Tears came with such force he dropped back in his chair. He dropped his gun and put his face in his hands. He was so angry, so frustrated, and another even more powerful emotion had a grip on him. Something he hadn't felt since his father told him what he expected of him on his deathbed. Giovanni was afraid.

—*B*—

LORENZO WAS LED INTO AN INTERROGATION ROOM with his hands cuffed. The men were given standard inmate uniforms to change into. He figured it was a ploy to add additional stress on them. He had no doubt that Giovanni would find a way to get them released and soon. A young inspector looked up from his folder when Lorenzo arrived. Another stood in the corner with his face covered by shadows.

"*Signor* Battaglia, have a seat please."

He sat in the only unoccupied chair before him. "I have nothing to say without an attorney."

"Your attorney has been notified. He will be meeting with you soon." The inspector smiled. "You've been a very bad boy in Italy, and Sicily, ah and in Paris too. I have here everything from assault to arson. You've been accused in six murders, all the cases were dropped."

"Innocent," Lorenzo grinned.

The inspector didn't smile. "You've been arrested a total of 32 times."

Lorenzo shrugged. "Misunderstood. Mistaken identity. It happens."

"You think this is funny?" The inspector asked.

Lorenzo arched a brow and held the officer's stare.

"I wasn't going to bother with you. I'm more interested in that goon you call a *capu* that killed a man in the boxing ring, or the young *consigliere* who has never been in a jail cell and has a clean record. Those two I can twist and get what I need."

"Then why the fuck am I here?" Lorenzo smirked.

"I received a call. A woman. She's been quite helpful. First she told me where to pick you and your clan boss up. And now she's given me more information. She said her name is Isabella. She told me I should look at you closely. She said, and I quote, 'Where there is sin there is audio'. Do you know what that means?"

Slowly Lorenzo's smile dimmed. It was a knife to the gut. Isabella's quote came from the deepest darkest fear he suppressed. The inspector studied his reaction. He didn't speak because he couldn't process a thought. David Capriccio told him Isabella was real. Marietta thought she was real. And he dismissed it. And then Santo says her name and he knows the truth. The bitch is out there. Who the fuck is she?

"*Signor* Battaglia, care to answer the question?" The inspector repeated.

"Are we done?" he asked.

The inspector smiled. "Where there is sin there is audio. I think that's a mystery worth solving. I'm going to get a warrant to search Melanzana. It will be the first time in several decades that the *polizia* were allowed to freely roam that place. I've already contacted the courts in Sorrento. We're done."

Lorenzo stood and clenched his fists. The guard led him out. Whoever the bitch was, she now had his attention.

—*B*—

Later –

GIOVANNI RECLINED IN HIS CHAIR. The sun had set. He hadn't bothered to turn on any of the lights in his office.

There was a knock at the door.

"Avanti," he said.

The door opened. Mateo Benicia walked inside. Giovanni pushed up from his chair. He went to his desk to turn on some light. "What news do you have?"

"The priest has returned to Bergamo. We think."

"You think?" Giovanni asked.

"We're looking. I've sent some men. A few of yours will join them. They are searching. It's Bonaduce territory. We have to be discreet."

"And?" Giovanni asked.

"Santo frequented a apartment in *Piazzia Bagnoli*. The owner said a woman was seen with him. Dark hair, she looked either Spanish or Sicilian. He believed her to be his wife. Santo called her Isabella." Mateo said.

"And she's gone?" he asked.

"No trace of her. We went door to door but no one saw anything."

"The fishermen? Did anyone see this boat Santo was thrown from?" Giovanni asked.

Mateo shook his head no. "And the patrols from the *polizia* around the bay have turned up nothing. They are in the water so we had to come out."

"You're useless. Get the fuck out. Don't return unless you have some news. Something useful."

The man left. It had been a full twenty-four hours. What was he to do next? He went to his bar. He gripped the edge of the bar and dropped his head. He wouldn't survive the wait.

—*B*—

"WHERE ARE YOU?" Marietta asked. She looked to the bed. Catalina was in Mirabella's bed with the kids. She insisted they all sleep with her. Everyone knew Giovanni would not enter this room until Mirabella was found. Catalina had Gianni in her arms. Eve and Gino were tucked under the covers. In times of extreme stress Catalina regressed. Without the family around her she became as needy and juvenile as the children. All she did was cry and beg for answers.

"Hello?" Marietta said.

"I'm in Sorrento," Armando said.

"Then why aren't you here? You said you would help. Lorenzo is in jail. They're all in jail. Gio is out in that damn office of his trying to figure out who some crazy woman named Isabella is. And it's Kei! He's Mirabella's ex-boyfriend. He's the one that kidnapped her."

"Slow down. Wait, Marietta, what did you say about Isabella?"

"Huh? I don't know. Gio was asking who she was. Do you know her? I think she has something to do with Mirabella's kidnapping."

Armando fell silent. Marietta's heart sank. There was one time when the name Isabella surfaced. It was the tapes. But that proved to be a lie from the Capriccios. Still Marietta shared what she could with Giovanni. She wouldn't hold back anything that could help save her sister, except the fact of what was on those tapes. To disclose that to Giovanni would sign her husband's death warrant. It made her sick with fear and regret. Could it be more than coincidence? Could there be someone in the Capriccio family responsible? Marietta considered telling Gio that, but it would put Lorenzo in the line of fire. She couldn't take that risk after lying to her husband. He'd never trust her again.

"You know her. Don't you? Did you have anything to do with this? Answer me!" she yelled.

Catalina sat up in bed. Marietta put her hand to her head. "Answer me!"

"I'll call Gio. I had nothing to do with this, but I think I can help."

The line disconnected. Marietta threw the phone.

"What is it?" Catalina asked. "*Mio Dio!* Is it Mirabella?"

"Catalina, stop. Okay? I can't do this with you acting like she's already dead. She isn't dead!"

"I know!" Catalina covered her mouth. Gianni began to cry. She rocked him. Gino and Eve didn't wake. Catalina scooted off the bed, keeping Gianni in her arms. "I know she isn't. I'm just so scared. You said Kei Hyogo has her. He's dangerous. He tried to kill Giovanni."

"Okay! Shhh… calm down. I'm sorry." She hugged her. Gianni pushed his aunts apart with his hands. Catalina laughed through her tears. Marietta smiled. "I'm getting Giovanni some help."

"How?" Catalina asked.

"Armando. I've asked him to come."

"That won't work. Gio will never ask him for help. Never," she said.

"Giovanni will do whatever he can to save Mirabella. And Armando may know something. We are out of options. No more crying, no more falling apart. Mirabella needs us to be strong. Let's try harder. I feel it now. She's in trouble and if we don't get to her soon it might be too late."

"Okay. Okay," Catalina agreed.

"Give me the baby. You've got two. I need someone to sleep with auntie tonight. Come here, sugar," Marietta took Gianni and kissed his lips. He wrapped his arms around her neck. She winked at Catalina. "We'll get the kids up and go see the horses tomorrow. Okay? Do something fun. Let the men bring our girl back."

"I love you, Marietta."

"I love you too, Catalina."

THE PHONE RANG. Giovanni sat up on the sofa where he slept with the unopened bottle of Scotch on his chest. He looked around the dark office. He set the bottle down and pushed himself up from the sofa. In the dark he found his desk and then the phone

"This is Gio," he answered.

"Don't hang up," came a response. "It's me. Armando."

Giovanni groaned. He was about to hang up when Armando spoke.

"Isabella."

"What did you say?" Giovanni asked.

"I know Isabella. We need to talk."

"Did Marietta call you? Drop a name and now you think you can use it to manipulate me?"

"Isabella Mancini Ricci is her full name. She's the bastard daughter of Flavio Ricci. Ask your uncle Rocco who she is. And then call me when you are ready to talk." The phone line went dead. Giovanni slumped down in his chair. Flavio's daughter? *What kind of bullshit was this?*

CHAPTER SIXTEEN

The Princess and the Dragon

Mirabella was helped from the jeep. She had no shoes. Kei didn't seem to care. They walked over stone steps toward the front of a medieval looking castle that had to be several hundred years old. In fact, in the dark she saw the crumbling remains of what looked like some ancient city. Kei held her hand. A man walked behind her. Several men walked ahead. They spoke in Chinese mostly. But there was one who all deferred to, and that man kept his eyes on her at all times. She glanced back. His gaze met hers with such evil cruelty she turned her head.

The castle, villa, or whatever it was, had little light. In fact the men used flashlights to guide the way. She stopped twice when her foot scraped a stone or something sharp. Kei would not give her a reprieve. He pulled on her hand and forced her to walk. She stumbled but kept up.

They sailed for an eternity. She mostly avoided Kei by staying in the cabin they shared. When he joined her in bed he didn't touch her, and she was grateful. She pretended to be sleep until exhaustion overcame her. And now she was here.

Kei stopped. He let go of her hand and took a lantern from one of his men. Another opened the large locked door for them, and he went inside. Mirabella followed. The draft that greeted them chilled her. The limestone walls were windowless. She saw steps that led up to another level.

"Welcome to your new home, princess. For now, at least until Eve joins us," Kei said.

"There is no way in hell you will get your hands on my daughter,"

Mirabella said under her breath. Kei heard her.

"I got my hands on you." Kei teased. "You have free reign of this place. There is a kitchen on this level. Rooms above. You'll share one with me on the third level."

"I'd rather not," Mirabella said.

Kei chuckled. "This place used to be a monastery. Then a home for orphaned boys and girls run by the Catholic Church. A friend owns it now. She keeps it cozy."

"I'm done with these games. I am not going to stay here as your prisoner!"

"You don't have a choice."

"I always have a choice! Always! Stay away from me!" Mirabella picked up the lantern he left on the table and glared at the men watching her. "All of you! Stay the hell away from me!" She went to the stairs. He said there were rooms above. She'd find one and lock him out of it. As she climbed the stairs she glanced back at Kei. Again he seemed unfazed. He was talking to the man who kept shadowing him. The man with the shaved head looked up as he listened to Kei and watched her. Mirabella hurried. She was on the second level and the empty hall was darker than the lower. The stone floor was cool under her feet. She tried several doors to find that they had no locks on them. Desperate she kept searching. And then she found a corner stairwell. She climbed the stairs and reached another door. This one was open. The room had a modern feel to it with a large sleigh bed, a balcony with furnishings, and a television set and chairs. It had to be the room he chose for them.

Mirabella tried the doorknob and found it had no lock. She went inside the room and closed the door anyway. She searched the room for a phone. She found none. She neared tears. Mirabella sat on the edge of the bed and put her face in her hands. She wanted to scream. When she lifted her head she saw the television through her tears. She walked over to the television and looked for a remote. She needed something to turn it on. The hour was late. Still she hoped she could find some news on what happened to her. Did Giovanni call the police?

The remote was in a chair facing the sofa. She picked it up and turned on the television. The first two channels were off the air. Nothing but color bars were seen. On the next channel she saw Ciro's picture. Mirabella turned up the volume. The news report replayed footage of the boxing match. To Mirabella's horror Chao Lee went for Ciro. He grabbed him by the head and snapped his neck. She dropped the remote and her hands went to her mouth. The crowd froze, and then all hell broke loose. Carlo and the trainers were in the ring throwing punches. Chao Lee's trainers were in the ring. The news reporter stated that both Ciro and Chao Lee were dead, and close to six hundred people were arrested. And then Giovanni's picture came on screen. He was detained. So were the clan bosses, all thrown in jail and questioned.

"No. No. No." Mirabella shook her head. This couldn't be happening. She didn't believe her own eyes. "God, please."

"Mirabella?"

She whirled on Kei. He glanced to the television and then to her.

"Did you do this?" she asked. "Did you kill Ciro?"

"Collateral damage." Kei shrugged. "It's regrettable. The kid actually had talent."

"You fucking evil bastard!" She picked up the remote and threw it at him. He ducked as it sailed past his head. When he came for her she ran. She went over the bed on hands and knees to get to the other side. He grabbed her ankle with that iron hand of his, and his steel pointed nails lacerated her skin. She turned and kicked with her free foot, hitting him in the face. That felt good. To fight back felt great. Kei got a hold of both of her feet and dragged her across the sheets. Her dress rolled up to her stomach and revealed she was bottomless. He got on top of her. He forced her thighs apart with his knees. She fought with all her might, but he captured her wrists and pinned them down above her head. She bucked her hips and kicked her legs. He had an erection. She screamed to the top of her lungs. She screamed as loud as she could. And when his tongue traced over her neck to reach her ear, she screamed some more. Nothing worked. She needed a weapon. A gun or something she could plunge into his black nasty heart.

"Let me go!" she moaned.

He kissed the side of her face. He lay on her. His body weight was equal to Giovanni's. She couldn't move. She could barely breathe. He began to roll his hips to grind his erection against her.

"Let me go, please!" she begged. She could feel his arousal. The more she struggled the more excited and insistent he became. Whatever held him back, she prayed it would continue to do so until she found a way to escape. "You're hurting me. I can't breathe. I won't run. I won't. I swear."

It felt as if he didn't hear her. He kept rolling his hips and grinding against her. His kisses were now on her breasts. He sucked her nipples through the front of her dress.

"You need something to help you sleep, make you feel relaxed?" he lifted his head and his voice was thick with desire.

"No. No. I don't, Kei. I am okay. I was in shock. I swear I just—" she bit down on her bottom lip and blinked several times to get rid of her tears. "I was shocked that's all. Please stop."

"Do you remember the first time we made love?" he asked.

"I don't want to talk about that," she said. If he didn't move soon she'd choke to death on her own vomit. The thought of him made her sick.

His gaze lowered to her heaving chest. He traced his iron-gloved hand down the front of her face. He used only one hand to hold her wrists. His fingers went to the front of her summer dress. The thin white material barely contained her breasts. He pulled down the front to reveal her left nipple. He lowered his mouth to her nipple and sucked.

Mirabella winced. She had to do something. Think of something to stop him. "Yes! I remember! I do!"

He stopped running his tongue over her nipple and looked up. "I remember," she smiled. She nodded. "We'd been dating two weeks and you came to Parsons to pick me up."

Kei studied her.

Mirabella kept fast-talking. "And… and… your driver was going to take us to dinner. We were in the back of your car. Remember? You kept touching my thigh, and, ah, you said you couldn't wait."

"You tried to resist me at first," he said.

She nodded. "Yes. But I wanted it, Kei. I wanted you. I was just afraid to do it with the driver in the car. You know how I was back then. Right?"

"We were on the streets of New York. You were on my lap. So sexy," he smiled.

Mirabella smiled. "We were so good together in the backseat of that car. I had never known a man like you, Kei. You were so handsome, and so different than me. I'd never met anyone like you. I still haven't."

"I loved you, Mirabella. From the moment I saw you, even down to the moment I lost you."

"I remember that too!" Mirabella's smile broadened. He let go of her wrist. She immediately covered her breast and tried to move from under him. He lay on his side and pulled her close to him. "I remember when we first met. Fabiana and I crashed that party. All those hedge fund investors and stockbrokers. She thought if we hooked up with one I could get some financial backing."

"Ahh… so you were a little minx."

She laughed. The laughter sounded fake, but he bought it. "You brought me a drink and asked me my name."

Kei smiled. He nodded his head.

"You didn't ask for my number. You talked to me a few minutes, complimented me, and then stared at me for the rest of the night from across the room. That was so sexy," Mirabella said. She eased down her dress and his eyes lowered to her sex. She tried to cover herself naturally so he wouldn't attack her again.

"I remember what you were wearing. A tight black skirt that made your ass bubble up," Kei chuckled.

"And the next day I was in my flat that I shared with Fabiana and two other girls. You sent me flowers. How did you find me?" Mirabella asked.

"I had my ways." He winked.

"You were always resourceful, powerful, caring. I was really intimidated and flattered that you chose me," she said.

"Why? You're all those things," Kei said.

"Only because you helped me evolve. Right?" Mirabella said.

Kei relaxed and smiled at her praising him.

"Let me go, Kei. I'm a mother now. My babies need me. Please." She reached over and touched his face. "I know I hurt you. I was wrong. I was angry over the lies you told, and then I told lies myself. I'm not innocent, I'm human. Can't you forgive me? Do you really want to hurt me like this?"

"Does he know?" Kei asked.

Mirabella lowered her hand.

"Does Giovanni know?" he asked.

"Know what?" she frowned.

"Why you choose men like us?" Kei asked. "Does he know about Cedric? Does he know why his wife always wants the darkness in a man?"

She closed her eyes as shame filled her. Cedric found her in New York. She never questioned how Kei dealt with Cedric. She ignored it and pretended Kei's reaction was normal, because Cedric was hateful and deserving of his wrath. And it was then she understood what the foundation of her relationship with Cedric was based on. In all the years she was with Kei, she was with him out of the need for protection and a nurturer. It's why she didn't marry Kei. She never loved him the way she loved Giovanni. She never loved Cedric that way. True love only came from the man who believed in her the way her husband did.

"You say I'm different, but you knew who I was when we met. Didn't you, Mirabella?" Kei asked.

"No," she shook her head.

"You used me to protect you from Cedric," he said.

"I didn't. I swear I didn't," Mirabella's eyes began to tear. "You pursued me. Cedric came to New York after we started our relationship. I had no idea he'd find me."

"You used me to protect you from Giovanni?"

"I was confused. A bomb had gone off in my face. My best friend was dead. I was scared and in so much pain. You were my friend. I didn't use you! I had no idea who you were!" she said.

"Somewhere deep down inside you knew what I was. Just as you knew what Cedric was when you wanted to turn against your grandfather, and who Giovanni is. Ask yourself, Mirabella. Why did you choose men like us? Why make us love you, and then punish us for being what is in our nature?"

"I don't. I don't."

"You do. You have. You always will, because that's the price of loving you." He kissed the side of her mouth, and then her lips. She rolled away from him and hugged herself. She forced his words from her head. He caressed her thigh. Spooned her from behind. Ran his hand over her body as he pleased.

"Let me go," She cringed.

He turned her to face him. He lifted her chin. "I want you to make love to me."

"I won't do it," she said.

"I want you to give in to me," Kei said.

"No!" she said.

"I will never let you go, and when Eve comes you will do whatever it takes to make us a family. To keep me happy. To keep Eve safe. Won't you?"

She opened her eyes and looked into his.

"Right, princess?"

He kissed her lips. Mirabella shoved him off. "Get the fuck off of me!" she slapped him. He chuckled and forced her into his embrace. "Shhh…" he said against her ear. "Too late for tears. You're mine again," he said and hugged her.

"Rocco, wake up." Giovanni said.

Zia reached for the lamp and turned it on. "What is it, Gio?"

"Rocco, come with me. Now! Join me downstairs, in the parlor," Giovanni said.

"It's okay, Zia. It's okay," Rocco said.

Giovanni walked out of the room. At first he wanted to dismiss Armando. He was vulnerable now, and time was precious. He couldn't waste a minute on chasing a lie. But the more the night dragged on, the harder it was to convince himself otherwise. He waited in the parlor for close to ten minutes before the old man shuffled inside. Giovanni couldn't sit. He hadn't eaten or taken a sip of alcohol. He was running on pure adrenaline.

"Who is Isabella Mancini Ricci?" Giovanni asked.

Rocco paused. He looked up at Giovanni with wide-eyed shock. "It couldn't be her," he said.

"Armando called. He shared news. He said Isabella was Flavio's daughter. How the hell did Flavio have a daughter by a Mancini and no one knew about it? And if you did know, why the fuck didn't you tell me this?"

"Giovanni that's a dead end. It's something that happened years ago. It's irrelevant."

"What are you keeping from me, old man?" Giovanni seethed.

"Leave it alone, Gio. It has nothing to do with this."

"I decide what is relevant! I decide!" he shouted. "Tell me. Tell me everything you know."

Rocco looked to have aged before him. The old man sat down and stared at the curved top of his cane. "My sister Isabella, your aunt."

"What? Zia Isabella has been dead for over twenty years." Giovanni said.

"She had a daughter, Lorenzo has a sister." Rocco said.

It was Giovanni's turn to be shocked. He tried to make sense of the news. Zia Isabella never spoke of a daughter. She was a bitter woman, and very controlling. In fact no one in the family ever mentioned a daughter. "How? Why weren't we told?"

"My sister was complicated," Rocco sighed. "She should have been born a man. She defied her brothers, our mother, anyone. When she was barely seventeen she took a lover."

"Mancini?" Giovanni asked.

"No." Rocco wiped his hand down his face. "It was Flavio."

Giovanni's brows lowered with concern. "Zia Isabella had an affair with Flavio?"

Rocco nodded. "Do you see why I say this is irrelevant?"

"It is very relevant! Secrets, Zio! Secrets destroy us. Does Lorenzo know?" Giovanni asked.

Rocco shook his head. "Tomosino didn't know the baby was Flavio's. Isabella and I were very close. She came to me in a panic. She told me about the baby. I forced her to confess to Tomosino. She refused to name the father. To spare her the shame, and Tomosino's wrath, Mancini stepped in. He offered up one of his men and labeled him the rapist who impregnated her. We murdered him. The baby was born. She was sent to an orphanage in Lipari, to give the child some hope of a life. Mancini was kind enough to give her his name."

"Kind? Don Mancini was kind? You want me to believe he sacrificed one of his men for Zia Isabella out of the kindness of his heart?" Giovanni scoffed.

"You're a godfather. You grant wishes all the time. The debts are to be paid later. Isn't it always this way, Gio?"

"What happened to her?" Giovanni asked.

"I know when she was older she was actually adopted by the Mancinis. Lived with Armando and his family until she ran off one day. After your zia Isabella died there was no curiosity as to who she became on my part. I forgot about her."

"You forgot? You made a deal with a Sicilian Don to save this child and my aunt, and then you just forgot?"

"It's the truth, Gio." Rocco mumbled.

"Did Zia Isabella ever see the child? Visit it? Anything?"

"Tomosino forced her to marry Lorenzo's father. She became even more resentful. She carried on the affair with Flavio for many years. Your father didn't know, but I did. Flavio loved her. I don't think Flavio ever knew the truth about his daughter. Those secrets are buried with the both of them."

"Could this be her?" Giovanni asked.

"Why? What is the motive, Gio?"

"Are you dense, old man? Revenge! She was thrown away like garbage. Her father..." Giovanni paused. He had Flavio killed for what happened to

Mirabella. That could explain revenge, and why Isabella would help to have his wife taken. "*Santo Maria!* Why wasn't I told this? Damn it!"

"She's in her forties. If she is alive she's either in the Catholic Church, or married with children. She couldn't possibly have the resources to do this.'"

"Flavio could," Giovanni said.

"Flavio is dead!" Rocco said.

"I know that! But he was a wealthy man. His wealth was spread out to his bastard children. She could have the resources. And more importantly she is Zia Isabella's daughter. You remember how resourceful and bitter your sister was. How she tortured Lorenzo for years until her death. What is her daughter capable of?"

Rocco stared in disbelief.

"In the morning I want the lawyers to get information for me on Flavio's will. Where his money was given, and then we find Isabella Mancini."

Rocco left him. He sat in the parlor staring at the floor. Giovanni wiped his hands down his face. It had been over twenty-four hours since he lost his wife. And the worry and stress had already broken heart. Now he hears news of the deception in his family, and he has to wonder if his sins, his father's sins, have finally caught up to him.

It took an extra surge of strength to stand. He hadn't taken a drink but he had a desert-like thirst drying his throat. He walked past the stairs. He paused. He looked up. Giovanni was drawn to the stairs. He climbed them and walked the halls of his home. With his men scattered, and his family hurting, the halls were empty. Every useable resource was dispatched in search of a clue to where his wife could be. Though he knew it would be painful, he returned to his room. He pushed open the door and peered inside. A woman lay in his bed.

For a startled moment his heart leapt. The shape of her, the way she held his son to her chest, and his daughter lay on the other side of her with the covers kicked off, were all reminiscent of how he'd find Mirabella. After a long trip, he'd come home to his family waiting for him. Giovanni stepped inside of the room. His heart sank to see it was Catalina sleeping in his bed. He held a faint smile to his face. He had to think that this was a good omen. His wife would never leave him. He knew she'd fight hard to survive. He had to believe this. He closed the door. Giovanni covered Eve and kissed her brow. His daughter rolled over to Catalina. He left the room and gently closed the door.

Unable to sleep, he walked down the hall aimlessly. When he reached the stairs he climbed them and headed to the third floor. Above were closed rooms and his wife's studio. Rarely did he venture up there. On a few nights when her insomnia took her from him, she went there to create. He'd find her sewing or sketching. He'd groan about needing her and she'd come back to bed with him. He smiled as those memories warmed his heart.

Giovanni went inside. The darkness engulfed him. He flipped up the wall switch and looked around. It was all Mirabella. In preparation for her big event in Milano, she had several dress Mannequins draped with garments she designed for the runway. Fabric rolls and cuts of material were spread over a table and two sewing machines.

He walked through the studio. He wiped his hand down his face. The further he went into the room the harder it became for him to breathe. The lungs in his chest shriveled. His heart rate accelerated. He nearly turned and ran for the door. Then he saw her sketchpad sitting on a chair near the window. Giovanni picked it up. He sat in the chair and flipped open the lid. The drawing was of a woman's legs and next to it were notes on measurements for something he didn't understand. He turned the page over and paused. The next sketch was of one of his sons. It was him seated on the floor with a truck in his hand. Giovanni smiled. He traced the image. When he turned the page again it was of Eve's face. Just her face. But the detail was uncanny. His wife had the kind of talent he often took for granted. He flipped the page once more. A smile slowly moved over his face. She'd drawn him, waist up, shirtless, with boxing gloves and a punch thrown mid air. Giovanni's hand was useless. Earlier Catalina or Marietta had sent for the doctor who confirmed it was broken and did his best to reset it. He used his numb fingers to trace the image. It was how she saw him. A fighter. No matter what, Giovanni vowed he'd never give up. He'd track them down to the end of the earth if he had too. He'd never let her go or give up.

Morning –

The morning rays warmed her face. She opened her eyes. The castle had no windows below their room. The tower she was in had several. She blinked awake and suffered blindness from the daylight. At some point he'd drawn the drapes open. Last night she had cried herself to sleep. Her head hurt as much as her heart did. She turned over. She sat up and looked out at Kei seated outside at a table sipping tea. The man who shadowed Kei was talking to him. She wished she could understand what they were saying. She never bothered to learn Kei's language. And he had often tried to teach her a few words.

Mirabella lay on her back flat. Kei didn't touch her. She was afraid all night with him in the bed with her. Several times she felt his hands in her hair. But he never went further than that. He said he loved her. He said he'd do anything to have her love him again. He was crazy with his obsession, and that madness could turn on her at any moment. She knew it.

"Morning, princess," Kei said.

Her gaze dropped over to the left. He was shirtless again. The dragon on his chest drew her eyes.

"Are you hungry?" he asked.

She swallowed. "Yes."

"Breakfast is ready. Join me." He tossed another satin robe at her. She'd love a bath and a toothbrush, but didn't bother to ask. She eased on the robe and slipped off the bed. She walked out to the balcony. The temperature was warm and beautiful, as was the view. And to her surprise she could see the beach and sea from her room. Along the coast were fishermen boats. Mirabella stared at them for a moment. This was a remote area, but there had to be people nearby.

"Sit."

She did as he asked. He did as he always did and fixed her plate. Kei's black hair was brushed from his face and then combed into a single braid down past his shoulder blades. With it so long and straight he looked more Native American than Asian.

"Are you the Dragon?" Mirabella asked.

"I'm many things."

"What does that mean?" she asked.

He didn't answer. He put food on her plate and then poured her coffee.

"You're a hypocrite," Mirabella said. Kei glanced up at the accusation. "How many times when were in Switzerland did you call Giovanni a thug, a murderer, dangerous, not worthy of me? How many times did you tell me to give Eve a better life rather than pine away for a criminal? Now you want to throw me and my daughter into your criminal life. Look at you, Kei!"

Kei smiled. "I was a different man then. You changed me," he smiled.

"No. This isn't all on me. You pretended to be different. This is who you really are. Isn't it?"

"And what does that make you? A lover of criminals? First Cedric, then me, and now the great Don Giovanni?"

"Is that what a Dragon is? A Don?" she asked.

"Don? Hmmm? I guess you can look at it that way. A Don is a boss, right? And your husband is the boss of all bosses." Kei chuckled. "Like *la Camorra* there are many bosses in the Triad. I am the Dragon and I am a descendant of the White Lotus Society. I come from a legacy of warriors. Our children will have royal blood in their veins that can be traced back to the Xia Dynasty."

Mirabella opened her mouth to tell him she couldn't have more children, and then thought better of it. She needed to feed his delusion to keep him calm. It was the best plan she could come up with until she found her escape.

Kei leaned forward. He looked into Mirabella's eyes and made sure he held her stare. "I am the head of the Dragon, but I have more legs than your husband. My family legacy goes back further than the Mafia."

"Do you love me?" she asked.

He sat back. "Yes."

"Why?" she asked.

The question must have surprised him. He stared at her for a moment with a sad smile. "Because I do. I know you."

"And if you know me, if you really love me, why do you think any of this will make me love you?" she tried to reason.

"Because I'm like your husband. I'm like Cedric. We all want what we don't deserve."

Mirabella had enough. There was no use in trying to reach the man she once knew. Kei was right. That man was gone. Instead she looked out to the sky and the sun. She thought of her husband and children waking to this day to find her gone. *Was Giovanni in jail? Were her children vulnerable? How did Kei plan to get past an army of men to snatch her baby girl and force them into his life? Why hadn't he bothered to mention her boys? Did he plan on kidnapping them too?*

"Eat, Mirabella," Kei said.

She picked up her fork and forced herself to do so. Kei sat back and watched.

— *B* —

GIOVANNI RETURNED TO HIS ROOM. He'd fallen asleep in the chair in Mirabella's studio. Catalina and the children hadn't woken. His gaze switched from the bed to the wedding photo on the night table. He walked around the bed and picked it up. Mirabella was in her veil. Blue rose petals were scattered around her feet. She smiled so beautifully into the camera.

"Giovanni?" Catalina said in a hoarse whisper.

He set the silver frame down. He glanced to Catalina. She rubbed her eyes and eased up to rest her back against the stack of pillows. "Mirabella? Any news?"

"Not yet. But I have a plan. I'll find her."

Catalina's eyes glistened with repressed tears. "Do you think she's okay? It's been over twenty-four hours. Gio, I know what they do to people they kidnap. If we don't find her in a couple of days—"

"She's strong, Catalina. Very. She knows I'm coming for her."

Catalina nodded. "They miss her," she said. She rubbed Gino's back. "They don't understand. Mirabella is never gone from them for too long."

"I'll find her. You have to help me. Keep the kids happy. Entertained."

"We spoke to Kyra. Renaldo is hurt really bad. The doctors say it doesn't look good. I spoke to a couple of other family members calling to ask for help. What are you going to do, Gio? What about Domi—"

"Stop asking questions, *piccoletta*."

Giovanni wiped his left hand down his face. He had little time to think of the fate of his men. Dominic was in jail. His *consigliere* had never ever been put behind bars. And then there was Carlo who was charged with the murder of Chao Lee. He had no clue as to what Lorenzo and Nico were doing behind bars. The news on Renaldo was dire and already shared with him. If he did come out of his coma, no one could predict if he would be the same man again. All of it weighed heavily on him, but he couldn't focus there. Finding Bella had to be his only priority.

"I need to shower," Giovanni said.

"You should eat. It's important to eat so you don't make yourself sick, Gio. Have you been drinking?" Catalina asked.

"Again with the fucking questions!" He was at his dresser looking for his things. He glanced back at her. She looked hurt by his outburst. He softened his tone. "You sound like Bella when you asked that."

"Have you?" Catalina asked.

"Feed me. I'm hungry," he winked. "I'm not drinking."

Catalina grinned. Giovanni went to the bathroom to shower. When he closed the door his smile had faded. He closed his eyes. By the end of the day he'd find Isabella and his wife. He swore it.

—*B*—

Mirabella roamed the halls of her prison. Kei had meant it when he said she would have free reign of the place. She visited every room on all three floors in search of a way out. There was none. She was reminded of Eve's books of the princess Rapunzel. After an hour of searching she gave up. She returned to her tower. She tried watching television but very little else was reported on the arrests.

The only solace she found was on the balcony. She walked out and looked at the ocean once more. There were fishermen with nets cast out on the shoreline. Mirabella thought to yell to them, but movement drew her gaze downward. Men were walking around in the forest between her prison and the sea. None of them looked up, but there were more than a few. She imagined they'd patrol and behave like Giovanni's men.

"Nǔshì," A man spoke.

Mirabella's head turned. The one who shadowed Kei stood there staring at her. He stepped out to the balcony.

"I am Bao Zei," he bowed his tattooed head. "May we speak?"

"Where's Kei?" she asked. The look Bao gave her was familiar. She knew that look. It was the way Santo used to look at her when Giovanni's back was turned.

"He has a visitor. This is the only time we can speak freely. If you want to see your family alive again you will listen to what I have to say."

Mirabella nodded.

"I am his brother. We were orphaned as kids and raised by our uncle Dao."

"Kei never said he had a brother." Mirabella frowned.

"Our mothers were the whores of Xing Yun. Since we were male children we were taken in by Hyogo until our father died. We are brothers, but there is no honor in saying so."

"Why are you telling me this?" Mirabella asked.

"Kei is uncle Dao's favorite. He is older. Smarter. He was sent to America to be successful. Uncle Dao was very angry when he shamed the family. And that was because of you."

Mirabella felt trapped. She couldn't jump from the balcony. She couldn't scream for help. She maintained his stare and kept her distance.

"Uncle Dao is dying," Bao Zei said. "When he dies Kei will be the Mountain Master. And I will be nothing more than his vanguard."

"And that upsets you?" Mirabella asked.

"No. It does not. What upsets me is you," Bao Zei said. "My brother is sick with obsession over you. It makes him vulnerable, and it makes the family weak. I want him to be his destiny. You are not his destiny."

Mirabella exhaled deeply. "If you hurt me he'll kill you. So don't come any closer."

Bao Zei smiled. "You are very perceptive. Yes. I do believe that Kei would take my life to save yours. In his madness to have you he will do anything. Even sacrifice our prizefighter Chao Lee, and let him die in disgrace. I cannot hurt you. If I did, I'd make you a martyr. The Triad will war with *la Camorra* for decades. My brother and your husband will spill the blood of many innocent men to avenge you. And then my brother would become consumed with grief and guilt. He is ten times weaker with you dead than alive."

"I don't understand what you want from me."

Bao Zei stepped forward. "I want you to open his eyes. We need to show him where your loyalties lie." He then glanced out to the ocean. "Those fishermen have been paid to ignore what they see and hear."

Mirabella looked out at the men along the coast.

"Do you see that purple boat?" Bao Zei asked.

She didn't speak. She was too scared to think. He was too close to her. "The man in the straw hat and rolled up green trouser pants, he's been paid by me. When the time is right a door will be opened for you. Run." He looked over to her. "Run to the man in the straw hat and purple boat."

Bao Zei turned and walked away. Not until he was gone from her sight did her breathing regulate. She sat down in the chair behind her. *Was it a trap, or her only hope?* She wasn't sure. She stared at the men by the sea. The man with a straw hat was the only one to turn his head and look back at the castle. He then hopped into his boat and used the little motor on the end to sail out to the blue waters.

If the opportunity came she'd run for it. She had no choice.

—*B*—

"WHY ARE YOU HERE? I told you I want Eve Battaglia, and you come empty handed?" Kei asked.

Isabella smiled. She sat across from him in the garden. "This is where I grew up. It was a monastery owned by the Catholic Church for orphaned children. My room was there." She pointed to a window at the top level. Kei glanced up. "I finally ran away at twelve to Sicilia with a boy from the village, to find my father, the great Don Mancini. Finding the truth changed my life."

"Answer the fucking question, you crazy bitch!" Kei seethed.

She glanced at him with a smile. "Giovanni keeps the children under guard. Even if you drove a tank into that compound you'd never get to them."

"So what is the plan?"

"I'm working on it. He needs to think Melanzana is no longer safe. If I can get the *Carabinieri* inside the gates he'll move the children."

"And then what?"

"And then, my handsome China man, he'll take them to the one place he thinks you won't know to look. Chianti. It's a little farm with olive groves and grapes as big as your thumb, a safety zone. I need to steer him there." Isabella grinned.

"How do you know it's a safety zone?" Kei asked.

"My father, Flavio, he told me many things over the years. The Battaglia family retreated to this farm when in crisis. Always. I'll snatch the brat, and execute the sweet little boys. Then you and your princess can live happily ever after."

Kei stared at her. "You have no remorse? Your lover Santo did."

"Do you?" she asked.

"I thought the Italians were all about family?" Kei asked.

"I'm Sicilian. We love our families. It's our enemies that need to be careful." She stood and picked up her purse. "By now my cousin knows who I am. I'm sure he'll look for me. Let him waste time. Wait for the raid. I should have your little rabbit to you soon."

CATALINA STARTED TOWARD THE STAIRS. The door opened to the front of the villa and she stopped. Armando Mancini was escorted inside. It was shocking to see him in their home. It was the first time he'd ever crossed through the gates. She stood there stunned for an awkward minute. Armando never lowered his gaze. He was as powerful as Giovanni. Marietta was right to call him. Maybe he could help her brother. Forcing herself, she walked to him. "You came?"

"You're surprised?" he asked.

"Yes. I am. Why are you here?"

"Your brother granted a meeting," Armando said. "I'm here to help."

"Do you think you can?" she asked, and her voice pitched high with desperation.

"And if I was to say yes. I can help. Would you trust me?" he asked.

"I'd trust the devil if it meant Mirabella would come home," she said.

He moved her hair from her shoulder and lifted her chin with his finger. "The devil would be flattered."

"Thank you so much for coming." Catalina threw her arms around him. She hugged his neck. Armando hugged her to his chest. He buried his face in her hair. There was something intimate about the way it felt to be held by him. Catalina saw the way the men frowned over their embrace and remembered the impropriety. She let him go.

He looked into her eyes. "We'll find her."

"Thank you," she said mindful of keeping her distance.

"Armando!" Marietta exclaimed. She hurried toward him with the kids running behind her. The twins ran for fun, and Eve because of fear. Marietta leapt at Armando and hugged him. The twins did the same, hugging Armando's legs. Catalina knew if Giovanni saw this celebrating it would anger him. She grabbed Gianni and put him on her hip, and pulled Gino away by the hand. Eve hid behind Catalina's legs.

Armando set Marietta down. "Thank God Giovanni called you. Maybe you can help."

"I'll try," he said. He knelt and smiled at Gino. *"Ciao piccoletto. Sono Zio Armando,"* he said to the little boy. Gino looked up to his aunt and she nodded that Armando was okay. Gino lifted his hand and waved at him. The little boy wouldn't come closer. Armando's gaze swiveled up to the other twin. The boy sucked his pacifier and stared at him with round blue eyes. He stood. Eve kept her distance as well. But he winked when he caught her peeking up at him.

"Don Mancini, come with us," Umberto said.

Marietta smiled and nodded goodbye to Armando. She and Catalina watched him walk away. He and his men were being marched to the back of their home to the terrace. From there they would go to Villa Rosso.

"You think he can help?" Catalina asked.

"Maybe. I'm not sure anymore," she sighed. "Catalina. I didn't want to bother your brother, but I've got to get to Napoli." Marietta said. She picked up a whiney Gino and put him on her hip. They started for the children's play room.

"Why? You know you can't," Catalina said.

"My husband is in jail. Domi is in jail. Finding Mirabella is a priority, but we have to help them. I can't just sit around here knowing they are locked away and do nothing."

"I don't know about this. We need to follow Gio's instruction."

"Gio asked about a woman that might be the cause of this. I need to talk to Lorenzo. I have to."

"What woman?"

"Never mind who she is. Lorenzo might be able to help and he can't if he's in jail."

"They won't let you in to see him." Catalina frowned. She put Gianni down. Gino was set down. The twins took each other's hands and went to play with their toys.

"This morning on the news they said Carlo would be charged with Chao Lee's murder. He has to face a tribunal." Marietta put her hands to her head. "How is this happening? How could we be so happy one day, and then at the lowest point of our lives the next?"

"I don't know. I keep thinking this is a bad dream I'm going to wake up from," Catalina said. Zia walked in. She hadn't spoken much since all of this began. She barely looked over at Catalina and Marietta. She went to the children. Eve took Zia's hand and went to her chair. She wanted to sit on her aunt's lap and read her book.

"You never said, but before this happened I saw Lorenzo had come home with you. Did you two make up? Before all of this I mean?" Catalina asked.

Marietta sighed. "I think so," she wiped her tears. "Lorenzo makes me so mad. But he makes me so happy too. We talked. I shot his whore and he came home with me."

"Wait? You did what? You shot someone?" Catalina gasped.

Marietta shrugged. "She'll live. But if something happens to him. I don't know what I'll do."

Catalina laughed. "Did you just say you shot someone?"

Zia glanced up and looked at them with concern.

"Damn right I did!" Marietta said and turned and walked out. Catalina hurried after her.

"Mio Dio!" Catalina grabbed her arm and stopped her. "Slow down. Let me think of something. Don't go doing one of your crazy stunts. Okay?"

Marietta stared at her unimpressed.

"Maybe with Armando here Gio will be reasonable? Or maybe we can get the attorneys to give us an update. Something," Catalina said.

Marietta shook her head. "If we don't find her soon something bad will happen. We have to get Lorenzo and Dominic out. Now."

"I agree."

—*B*—

GIOVANNI ATE AT HIS DESK, and Rocco sat with the portable phone. Without Dominic to run down the business, Rocco and Giovanni had to split the duties of a *consigliere*. That included trying to get a call in to their political contacts to free their men.

Armando entered the room. The others stayed out. Giovanni wiped his face. There was no better cooking for his heart than his Bella's, but the meal from Ana's kitchen gave him some nourishment.

"I came as soon I could. I have a gift for you." Armando said.

"Boss, he has a priest with him. Nicosia." Umberto said.

Giovanni's brows lowered. "You have Father Nicosia?"

"I picked him up in Bergamo. I thought he might be of use to you," Armando smiled. "I think we should keep him outside until we talk. Don't you?"

Rocco ended his call. He stood with the aid of his cane. "Armando," he said and extended his hand. Armando walked over and shook Rocco's hand. He unbuttoned his suit jacket and sat. Giovanni joined them. The Benicias were out searching for the priest and Isabella. Armando arriving with the priest was either suspicious or a good turn of luck.

"So? You have the answers. Fill me in," Giovanni said.

Armando looked at Rocco first. His gaze then slipped over to Giovanni. "Before my father died he called me to his room and gave me an assignment."

"And?" Giovanni asked.

"He wanted me to find Isabella and put a bullet in her skull," Armando said.

"Why?" Rocco asked.

"She was blackmailing him. She knew about his affair with Mirabella's mother. She was angry because she blamed you for her father's death. My father wanted to make the introduction to Mirabella his own way. She wanted to expose the ugly secrets of the past."

"Flavio?" Rocco said. "She wants to avenge Flavio?"

Armando nodded. "Papa thought she was a threat. He was convinced. I thought she died in the explosion that killed some of my men. Later I discovered she was still alive. I've been trying to find Isabella for close to two years. I lost track of her in China."

Giovanni leaned forward. "Flavio never mentioned a daughter. Not once."

"He apparently knew about my father and Tomosino keeping him from Isabella. How the two of them reconnected I'm not sure."

"Not true. Tomosino didn't know!" Rocco said. "He never knew. He would have killed Flavio if he discovered that he slept with Isabella."

"Then how did Flavio uncover the truth? Who kept the secret? Who told the secret?" Giovanni asked.

Rocco hesitated. Giovanni could see his conflict etched all over his face. He was about to force the issue when Rocco spoke. "I told Flavio about the baby, that the baby lived, over drinks one night after the grief of Isabella's suicide got to us both. He and I were the only ones that mourned her. Lorenzo was too screwed up in the head, and Tomosino was too focused on getting your mother back from Ireland. I couldn't keep it from him. By then," he looked over to Armando. "Mancini had already adopted her as your sister. Flavio was furious. But he understood the wisdom in not revealing who she was. I thought he got over it. Apparently he never did."

Giovanni glared at Rocco. "You let Flavio take a seat as my *consigliere* knowing that he loathed this family. It's why he sent Mirabella away. Revenge. And you never said a word."

"Gio—it wasn't an issue for Flavio," Rocco reasoned.

"Why would my father do this?" Armando asked.

Giovanni and Rocco both looked over at him curiously. Armando addressed Rocco. "My father wasn't a generous man. And he was distracted with his affairs in America. I don't understand why he would set up one of his men to take the fall for your sister."

Rocco's lips pressed together in a thin line. Giovanni's gaze then turned to his uncle. "The timeline. She's in her forties. That meant it wasn't Marsuvio who did this, who stepped in, it was his father, Don Peppino Mancini. Your grandfather."

"The why isn't important!" Rocco snapped. "The Mancinis stepped in and Marsuvio took her in as a daughter."

"What did you say? It's not important? My fucking wife is missing. That *puttana* has been planning this for years, and you want to tell me what is important?"

Rocco rubbed his brow. "What I mean, Gio, is some things happened in the past that don't concern any of this. And they should stay in the past. I told Flavio and he must have contacted Isabella. You have what you need. Let the rest of it stay buried."

"Get out, old man. Return to Chianti. In fact, don't let me see your face unless I request the meeting."

"Gio, I swear to you. There is nothing more I'm keeping from you. Nothing of importance. *Per favore*. I want to help."

"The fact that you think you know what is important makes you useless to me," Giovanni said. "This is the second time you have kept secrets from me. I want you out of my sight."

Rocco was stripped of his pride in front of Don Mancini, and Giovanni knew it hurt. His uncle looked away with shame. He used the cane to prop himself up and left. Armando observed and said nothing. There was more to the story of Isabella, and the Mancinis. However, Giovanni had no time to waste on that. He had what he needed.

"Will you bring in Nicosia?" Giovanni asked Armando.

"Before I do, I need your word that you will accept my help. I'm not here to be your errand boy. Mirabella is my sister. I want to be brought in to help find her."

"You had this information. A woman out there trying to kill my wife, your sister, and you didn't bother to warn me. I'm to believe that now you give a fuck?"

Armando smiled. "My feelings have changed toward my sisters. I only want to protect them now."

"Or the inheritance that is divided and lost if anything happens to them motivates you," Giovanni scoffed.

Armando chuckled. "Well, we all have our motives. Don't we?" he raised his glass to Giovanni and then swallowed the Scotch.

Giovanni dropped back. "Then let's deal in fact and not false sentiment.

Shall we? I will make the deal to sweeten your motivation. Mirabella comes home to me and she will hand over her inheritance to you for a fair price."

"What of Marietta's?" Armando asked.

"Not mine to give," Giovanni said.

"Bullshit!" Armando said.

"You and Lorenzo will come to terms. I suggest you help me free him so you can," Giovanni said.

Armando shook his head smiling. "Should I get this in writing?" he asked.

"My word is enough," Giovanni said.

Armando nodded. He stood, turned and walked out. Giovanni pushed up from his seat and went to the phone. He dialed his attorney who answered on the first ring.

"Gio, you were right. Flavio willed over twenty million to Isabella Ricci. She has a home in Rome, two in Sicily, a business, and an old monastery in Lipari. I'm trying to access more information on her expenses. I haven't gotten them yet."

"I already know where's she's been. Find out where she is."

"Gio, there's something else. You met him, Inspector Donatello. He's going to the courts to get a warrant to do a search and seizure of Melanzana."

"Let him try. The courts would not—"

"They might, Gio. There is a lot of demand for justice on this. I am fighting it. Because of the death of the boxers, most of our friends are refusing to get involved. I need Dominic. He has the relationships. I'm trying to get him released."

"Try harder. If the *polizia* come in through my gates I'll stop them before they reach the door," Giovanni said.

"You should consider moving the kids. The family. Somewhere safe."

"Try harder!" Giovanni slammed the phone down. No fucking way he'd suffer the humiliation of a raid in his own fucking home. He would find his wife and then hunt down every enemy for daring to cross him.

—*B*—

MIRABELLA WAS GIVEN CLOTHES, and when she checked the labels they were from her own line. He'd been withholding them to keep her in a state of undress. During their relationship Kei used to love to dress her. She thought it cute at first, like a competition for style. And then it became more controlling. As if he had to have a say in everything she did, including the way she dressed. At times in her marriage to Giovanni she considered him controlling. Now trapped with Kei on a remote island she had clarity. Giovanni was ruled by his fears, and his fears were now her reality. Her sweet husband wasn't controlling. He was aware. He knew what dangers they faced, and she was foolish enough to not believe.

Why hadn't she kept her gun on her?

She dressed in the purple strapless dress and slipped on the heels he left. She did her makeup as he requested. She even took time to make sure her hair was styled how he liked it. She didn't know if tonight was the night his brother gave her freedom. But she had to make sure Kei didn't suspect.

Kei slipped the disc into the CD player and pressed play. When he turned he was unprepared. Mirabella came down the stairs in the dress she'd chosen for him. Her hair covered the bruises over her brow, and the dress flattered her figure.

She looked at him and smiled. He applauded. She did a curtsy for him after coming off the bottom step.

He greeted her with a glass of wine. "You look beautiful."

"Thanks. It's a perfect fit," she said.

"I kept all your things. I have some of little rabbit's things too. Remember her favorite blanket? The yellow one with the bumblebee."

"I remember it," she replied.

"I kept it. Do you remember how she would cry if it wasn't in her hand when she went to sleep?" Kei sipped his wine and took her hand. "I have a photo. Lost it after my arrest. It's when she took her first steps. You took the photo. She walked to me."

"Kei, that's not true. You're twisting things to fit some warped fantasy. What happened to you? It's like you've changed our past to justify your rage. I'm sorry I hurt you, but…"

"I'm not psychotic, or delusional." He stopped in front of the table and pulled her chair out. She sat. "I'm not crazy. I love the kid. The same way you do."

Mirabella looked at him curiously. He knew she struggled with trusting him, but tonight he planned to convince her of his devotion, at any cost.

He sat down in his chair and set his glass of wine on the table. "What did I want when we were together, Mirabella?"

"Must we do this again?" she asked.

"Its not a game. It's a question. What did I want?"

"Marriage," she answered.

"And children," he reminded her. "I wanted you and a family."

"That was years ago. What do you want me to say? I was always honest. I fell in love with Giovanni—"

"You fell in love with me first!" he shouted her down.

She looked away. Unintentionally he ruined the mood. The CD switched to a different song and the timing was perfect. Mirabella's brows lifted. He smiled. "Hear that? Do you hear that? Does Giovanni know that's your favorite song?"

"Curtis Mayfield," she said in surprise.

"It's your favorite. Right?" he asked.

"Not really it was a song that—"

"You used to play it at night when you worked late. Every time I hear it I see you in your design studio cutting and sewing fabric."

"Do you know why I played that song? Why it was important to me?" she asked with a sad smile.

"You never told me," Kei said. "I don't think I ever asked."

"It's a gospel song. Not sure if you realized that," she said. "People get ready, there's a train coming…" she choked on emotion and lowered her gaze. "My grandfather, it was his favorite song. He'd play it on his record player and smoke his pipe. My granny would be sewing, cooking, or helping me with my homework. It was a song to comfort me. To remind me of who I was and where I came from," Mirabella smiled faintly and then looked away from his gaze. Kei left his chair. He went to her and extended his hand. She accepted it. He pulled her into his arms and held her close. She let him hold her. He listened to the lyrics. He never thought of the meaning behind the words. When he played it he only saw her. He remembered the nights he'd sit in her design studio and work while she sketched, cut, and sewed garments. She lifted her head from his shoulder. She looked into his eyes. "Let me go," she said to him again softly.

He kissed her. She tried to escape his kiss but he insisted. He kissed her deeply, and then kissed her neck as held tighter to her. He enjoyed how soft she felt with her body pressed to his.

"Kei?" his brother spoke.

He let her go. Mirabella stepped back and wiped her mouth.

"What is it?" Kei shouted.

"Uncle Dao. He insists on speaking with you. Now."

"He's on the phone?" Kei frowned.

Bao Zei nodded his head.

Kei looked to Mirabella. "I won't be long," he grunted.

She couldn't take much more of his touches and kisses. Her skin was crawling, her stomach twisted into a pretzel knot, and her face was frozen in pain from her fake smiles. She needed to get away from him. Bao Zei glanced back at her. When their eyes met he nodded his head in the direction behind her. She looked back and saw the door.

"Kei!" she said, a little too abruptly.

He stopped.

"I'll just go to the bathroom," she said.

He shrugged and left. What did he care about her stepping away? Kei believed she was completely trapped and blocked from escape. Mirabella backed toward the door and as soon as Kei turned the corner she ran for it. She opened the door and it led to a kitchen. She paused. She looked around. Was she sure he nodded toward this door? She put her hand to her forehead in panic. "Damn it! Damn it!"

She walked through the kitchen and saw the pantry door. She almost turned away from it. A draft blew it a few inches inward. She opened the door and discovered the pantry had yet another door. It was wide open. She didn't hesitate a moment longer. Once she was out the side door she took off her shoes. She ran for the forest. She didn't stop to think of direction. She didn't stop to think of the men she knew patrolled. He said to run to the beach and she'd have rescue. So she ran.

Chicago, America –

Shae laughed and sipped her drink. Sondra continued on with latest drama between her and her husband Chuck. Shae listened. Her gaze however switched to Tanisha. One of her best girls was on stage with three newbies, teaching them the latest dance moves. They had only three days for rehearsals before they were needed in L.A. for a video shoot. Her girls would be filmed as the background dancers to one of the top selling rap artists in the nation at a plush mansion. The gig promised to pay her close to a hundred and fifty grand. It could open doors with the record label to sign on for more of their artists.

"So? Are you and Chuck going to work it out?" she asked Sondra.

"Nah, I'm done with his lying ass. I just wanted to make sure he had something to remember me by," Tanisha said. She speared an olive at the bottom of her martini glass with her drink pick and plopped it into her mouth.

"Okay girl. Give it up," Tanisha said. She leaned forward on the table.

"Give what up?"

"You! Girl you were in Italy! With Mae! How was it? You haven't told us shit about those fancy parties and that big fashion show you went to," Tanisha smacked on her gum. "I am dying to know."

Shae shrugged. "It was fine. Nothing to tell."

"Bullshit!" Tanisha scoffed. "You ain't neva quiet. Did something happen?"

Before Shae could answer Tony, the owner of the club that her girls worked for at times approached. "Shae, yo baby, you got a call in my office."

"Thanks, Tony!" Shae smiled. She stood. Tanisha grabbed her arm.

"When you come back I want to know what is up! Shit! At least tell me you got to hang out with that fancy rich sister of Mae's."

Shae chuckled. She shook her head and walked to the back of the club. The music the girls rehearsed to finally muted when she closed Tony's office door. She sat behind the desk and found the phone waiting for her on the messy stack of litter that Tony kept covering it.

"This is Shae."

"Shae? It's me. Marietta!"

"Mae? Hi? What's up?" Shae asked.

"Have you been watching the news? Did you hear?" Marietta asked.

When Shae returned home she dove right back into work. She was burning the candle at both ends to keep from thinking of Carlo. "I've been really busy. Is something wrong?"

"Yes. I don't know if I should be calling you with this after the way things went down. It's just I thought you would want to know."

"What is it? Is it Carlo? Is he okay?" Shae's heart began to race. She put a hand to her chest. "Mae? What is it?"

"Ciro is dead. Something happened at the fight. The boxer killed him. Carlo saw it happen and he killed the boxer. He's in jail, Shae."

"Dead? Jail? Mae, that makes no sense!" Shae said.

"I know. Look there is a lot going on with my family now. My husband is in jail too. Long story. We're trying to get it all worked out."

"How the fuck did this happen? They were so excited about the fight. How did it happen?"

"Shae, I'm calling because... Well you were right. No one is ever looking out for Carlo. I know you care about him. He needs someone. If you could come back and help him. Be there for him."

"I can't," Shae put a hand to her brow. "I got so much going on right now. My girls... jobs... I can't." Shae swallowed down the emotion in her voice. "It's over between me and Carlo."

"I understand. I just had to call. Stay in touch okay?"

"Yeah, you too. And Mae?"

"Yes?" Marietta answered.

"Tell him... I hope you can help him," she said.

"I'll keep you posted," Marietta said. "Goodbye."

"Bye," Shae said. She hung up the phone. She put her hands to the side of her face and stared at the phone. None of it made any sense. How many times had she lay in bed with Carlo while he talked of his dreams of building a legitimate life for him and his brother? His plans to come to America and put Ciro in the boxing ring with Mike Tyson. He loved Ciro. Marietta was right. Without the kid Carlo had no one.

"Shae? The girls are taking a break. Wanna go get something to eat?" Tanisha said.

Shae wiped at her tears. "Ah, give me a second."

"Hey? What is it? What's wrong?" Tanisha asked. She came inside.

"Nothing, just some bad news. Let's go get something to eat. We need to wrap up early so we can all pack for L.A." Shae pushed up from the desk. She glanced at the phone once more. Her heart hurt. But she vowed after crying her heart out on her eleven-hour flight back to the States, to not look back.

Carlo wasn't an option. He was in love with Marietta. She should just forget him.

"Shae? You coming?"

Shae sighed. "Yeah, I'm coming."

Lipari, Sicilia—

The branches scratched and clawed at Mirabella's bare arms and legs. Several hit her in the face. She lost her shoes trying to fight her way through the brush. "God help me. Please, God, save me," she prayed. The harder she ran through the dark forest the more confused she became. She should have reached the beach by now. Mirabella stopped. She looked up at the stars in the sky. She listened for the ocean. She heard animal noises but not the rhythm of the sea. "Damn it!" she said. Her heart beat so fast in her chest she had a hard time breathing. She kept running. Her foot hit a stump or log. Mirabella went sailing forward and fell on her hands and knees. She cried out in pain. Her body then rolled down an embankment. She landed hard at the leafy bottom. Dazed and hurt she couldn't move. Her ankle felt funny. She forced herself to sit upright. She forced herself to not cry. She lay there looking up at the stars with her vision clouded by tears. She thought of her children. She thought of Giovanni and willed herself to be stronger And then she heard it. The crash of waves breaking over the shore was a soft whisper in her ear. Mirabella pulled herself up. She listened. She turned her head up and focused on the direction. She scrambled up the embankment. Her fingers sank into dirt and dug up clunks of moist soil. She winced when she tried to stand. She dropped to her knees again. She crawled. Her ankle was broken. Or at the very least it was a bad sprain. She couldn't run. When she made it past the trees she saw him. He was at the boat, sitting on it. He looked up. Mirabella tried to run to him but fell. She struggled in the sand.

"*Signora! Signora!* I help you! I help!" he said. He lifted her up and put her arm over his neck. With his help she managed to limp along. And they moved fast.

"We have to hurry. Please. Let's go. Please!" she begged him.

They were in the water now. It was knee deep. He nearly dropped her in the shallow waves when they reached his little boat. He lifted her and helped her inside. Mirabella wept with relief. "Thank you! Oh God, thank you!"

The man smiled. He removed a gun from the pocket of his pants and pointed it at her.

"What are you doing?" Mirabella asked.

"I'm sorry, *signora*," he said.

"No!" Mirabella threw up her hands in defense. A gunshot blasted off like a cannon. Mirabella screamed as the man's blood and fragments of his skull exploded all over her.

Confused she looked around in the dark. And then Kei and his men came across the sand. Mirabella tried to start the motor on the boat but there was no switch. She hopped from the boat. She fell to her knees. She was taken under by a very large wave. She swallowed seawater and sand. Dazed and panicked, she tried to swim out through the shallow waves. She was in too much pain, and trapped by her own fears after seeing a man murdered.

Men grabbed her. She screamed and fought them but she was dragged through the water to the shore. She was thrown on the beach not far from the dead fisherman.

Mirabella caught her breath. She looked up to Kei who stood right before her. He grabbed her by her hair and forced her to her knees. She swung at him but her reach wasn't long enough. Kei struck her. For the first time since they met he struck her. She landed on her side and nearly lost consciousness from the blow.

"So, my trying to appeal to the woman I thought you were doesn't work. Now it's time for me to teach the woman you are a lesson in obedience."

She blinked and forced her mind to stay awake.

Kei yelled something in Chinese. His brother was pushed, shoved, and forced to walk in the sand. One of the men hit Bao Zei to the back of his head, and he dropped to his knees. He looked up at Mirabella. In his eyes she saw nothing but raw hatred. She realized Bao Zei had set her up. He wasn't going to help her escape. He simply wanted her dead, shot and her body dropped out in the sea. Kei stepped over to his brother.

"We were born only months apart. Did he tell you that?" Kei asked.

Mirabella spit up seawater. She was able to sit upright on her knees.

"I love him." Kei pulled out a gun and shot his brother in the head. "But I love you more," he smirked. He turned and started to walk off. One of his men came over to her and picked her up. She hit the man and scratched his face. She was thrown over the man's shoulder. She screamed through her tears. When she lifted her head she saw the dead body of Bao Zei and closed her eyes. The nightmare continued.

CHAPTER SEVENTEEN

A Tale of Two Dons

IT DIDN'T TAKE LONG, but the wait was killing him. It was a physical pain. His chest was so tight with anxiety he had gone upstairs to the bathroom and located a pill bottle to take three painkillers. Nothing worked. The Benicias failed. The Tacchis and Racchinis were in prison. He had the *Mafiosi* at his door. Giovanni glanced up to the bottle of Scotch. It sat on the counter like a beacon of hope. He could dull the pain and clear his head if he took a sip. Just one.

He closed his eyes and swallowed his own saliva. The dry mouth and heart palpitations had him sweating across his brow and under his arms. He reached for the cool pitcher of lemonade brought to him by his sister, and poured another glass. He drank it down clean.

Father Nicosia entered his office. The priest carried himself with the same smug superiority he always did. Armando followed him in.

"Padre, join me," Giovanni said. He set down the glass and walked around the desk. The priest walked over and gave Giovanni a proper greeting. He kissed both his cheeks before taking a seat. Giovanni's gaze lifted to Armando, who stood by the door.

"Don Mancini tells me there is family trouble. I am shocked by what happened to young Ciro."

"Something to drink?" Giovanni asked.

"Scotch is looking good," The father answered.

Giovanni went to the bar and poured a drink.

"How can I help, Giovanni? I told Armando I know nothing about the madness. I wasn't part of the negotiations with Chao Lee."

Giovanni handed him the drink. He sat. Armando occupied the other seat. The priest gave a confident smile, but Giovanni noticed how his hand shook when he held the glass. He glanced to Armando who seemed to have seen the same thing.

"Before I agreed to sponsor Carlo's brother, you were working with him," Giovanni said.

"I have a popular gym. I work with all the talent that comes through the doors."

Giovanni nodded. "Yea, yea, I'm aware. But here's the thing, Nicosia. Carlo needed Ciro to raise his rank, to have the IBF notice him, and then Santo shows up with the sweet offer of being the middleman for a boxer who belongs to the Triad. Neither my money, nor my reputation could move a fight to Napoli. I'm not God."

"Neither am I, son," the priest smiled.

"But you have a direct line to him. Don't you?"

The priest chuckled. "I'm out of the church. I have friends, yes. But I'm not that powerful, Gio."

"Hmmm" Giovanni slumped back. "Then maybe it isn't the church alone that you have influence with. Maybe my enemies?"

"Gio…"

"Shut up," Giovanni warned. "Don't deny your ties to Bonaduce and the *Ndrangheta.*"

"I will not deny it. I never have, Gio. I am a strong supporter of peace between all of you. You know the man I am."

"I think you are a man who can walk away from the papacy, thumb his nose at the covenants of the church, and still dine with cardinals. A man who can sit between the *Mafiosi* and *Camorra* and still have respect. And a man who could make anything happen if he put his mind to it." Giovanni removed his gun from the back of his pants. He set it on his knee. "My wife was taken by the Triad. They can't move me into position to be so vulnerable. It would take an act of faith. Or maybe a fallen priest with a relationship to my enemies and a thirst for money. What did the Bonaduces offer you?"

"Gio… be reasonable, son."

He picked up his gun. "Armando, would you mind closing the blinds?"

The priest leapt to his feet. "Wait. Wait a second. Son, my sons, listen to me."

Giovanni pointed the gun. "Sit your ass down."

The priest sat. He looked to Armando who was closing the blinds.

"What was the offer?" Giovanni asked.

"Bonaduce wanted revenge. He lives for revenge against you, Giovanni. His son was murdered because of you. So he thinks. He and the *Ndrangheta* needed to weaken you. They can't move in to the *Campania* unless you are out. They handle the drugs in the triangle, and that has stopped since you started buying real estate and working with the officials. Now everyone has to go through you."

"What were you offered?" Giovanni asked.

"Territory in Rome. I can be of use to you, Giovanni. There's a woman. She's working with us. She is the reason your wife is gone. Her name is—"

"Too late." Giovanni pulled the trigger. The priest was hit in the chest and blown back several feet. He landed flat on his back. Blood pooled from beneath him. Armando dropped his drink. Giovanni stood. He walked past a confused Armando. He opened the door and Umberto walked in. "Get the boys to wrap this up and take a ride as far into Bonaduce territory as they can. Drop the body there."

"Yes, boss," Umberto said.

"Gio? Father Nicosia has friends in the church! He's connected!" Armando said.

"Not your problem. It's mine. Isn't it?" Giovanni said.

"I brought him here! This is blasphemous!" Armando shouted.

"I DON'T GIVE A FUCK! THEY CAME FOR MY WIFE. I WILL WALK INTO HELL TO GET HER BACK!"

"You will have to now!" Armando panted. He paced. He was visibly shaken. Two days ago Giovanni would have never done what he did. Even if he found out that the priest was conspiring against him, he would not have done so. He'd have sought revenge another way. All of his actions would need atonement. But not today.

Giovanni stuck the gun in the back of his pants. "Come with me." He walked to the door and paused. Armando was looking at Father Nicosia with disbelief.

"Andiamo!" Giovanni said.

Armando followed.

—ℬ—

"I CALLED THE JAIL. I asked how to schedule a visit. They said Lorenzo and Dominic could only be seen by their legal counsel." Marietta sat down. "I asked about Carlo."

"You did? How is he?"

Marietta shrugged. "No one would say. I asked if he had legal counsel, and I was directed to someone else who hung up on me."

"He's in deep trouble. I know Gio will have the men out, but Carlo, he's all over the news. They are calling him a murderer," Catalina said as she stared into her mug of tea. "Let's talk to Gio. To ask him what to do."

Before Marietta could answer they heard Giovanni's voice. The women got up from their seats and hurried out of the kitchen to the hall. To their surprise the Dons were walking side by side to Giovanni's office. Armando looked angry, and Giovanni looked angry.

"I wouldn't believe this if I hadn't seen it with my own eyes," Catalina said.

"Why? This is a crisis. All of our men are in jail. He's here to help," said Marietta.

"No, he isn't. They're enemies. They declared war on each other when they were kids, and they have hated each other every day since. Giovanni has to pay for Armando's help. I don't know the price, but I know if we rescue Mirabella because of the *Mafiosi,* there will be one."

Catalina walked away. Marietta dropped her head against the wall. She felt fear, deep in her heart. Lorenzo was gone. Her sister was missing. Carlo may be convicted and sent away to prison. And now Armando was here, and though she wanted to believe he came for the right reasons, she had her doubts. Could it be her fault? Could she be the reason the woman Isabella was after Mirabella? Did she bring this woman into their lives when she came to Italy in search of her family? Guilt and grief weighed on her emotions, and dragged her toward the dark space she retreated to whenever she was in pain. She had to fight against it. Be strong. It was hard.

—ℬ—

"YOU FUCKING BASTARD! I hate you! I hate you!" Mirabella screamed. She was thrown on the bed. She cried out in agony when her foot twisted awkwardly beneath her. She scooted across the bed, but her ankle burned. Kei paced at the foot of her bed. He was angrier than she'd ever seen him. Horrified by all she'd witnessed, and how close she'd come to being murdered, Mirabella scooted back to the headboard.

"You pushed me to this." Kei pointed a finger at her.

"You're crazy! You fucking psycho!" she shouted. "Do you think I would ever want you to touch me? Kiss me? I hate you! I hope my husband comes here and cuts your fucking black heart out of your chest. I hope he carves our names into it. Do you hear me? I hate you!" she screamed and wept.

He turned when someone walked into the door. He took the small black case and a folded pouch.

"Kei, wait. I'm sorry," she backpedaled. "I was scared. He said he was going to kill me. I was trying to get away. I'm not safe here."

"You're not safe anywhere once my uncle learns that Bao Zei is dead because of you."

"I didn't do anything wrong!" she said.

"You didn't trust me! You hate me still. That's your fucking crime. And my uncle knows I would never kill my brother unless I was driven to it." He came over to the bed and she tried to move away. He grabbed her hurt ankle with his iron hand and twisted it. Mirabella screamed with agony. She kicked and bucked on the sheets. It was of no use. The pain in her ankle stretched all the way up her leg and weakened her.

"You think I'm a monster. But you want to run away to another. How does that make you sane?" he shouted at her. "How am I different from Giovanni? Answer me!"

"Please! Please stop!" she wept.

"How?" he twisted her ankle harder.

Mirabella wept.

He let go of her ankle. He jumped on her on the bed and she fought him. She hit and scratched at his face. He overpowered her. He turned her face to the pillow. She bit down on her lip and drew blood to keep from screaming. She heard him open the case. She didn't care what he did to her at that point. The pain was her only focus. Then he let go of her face and moved off her. She dared to look up. She felt something cool and soothing on the cuts. Kei gently massaged in ointment. He then began to wrap her ankle tight.

"It's not broken. You got a good sprain," he said.

He was insane. And his kindness was scarier than his rage. She couldn't speak. She didn't know what to say other than how much she hated him and wished he were dead. She couldn't believe she ever felt anything for him. And to think she once thought Cedric was her biggest mistake. When he was done he put up the ointments and bandages.

"Take off the dress," he looked up at her.

She shook her head no. If he planned to hurt her she wouldn't let him do it easily. He closed the case.

"Then I'll take it off of you when I'm done."

Confused she stared at him. He removed a needle and something in a vial. Mirabella knew once he drugged her she'd never escape. "I promise, Kei, I won't run away anymore. I can't. Look at my ankle. I can't stand. I swear I won't try it again."

"I know you can't run. You were the one stupid enough to think you could."

"Then don't drug me." Mirabella pleaded.

Kei walked over to her with the needle.

She moved away from him on the bed. "No!"

He grabbed her ankle and foot. Mirabella screamed. He plunged the needle into the flesh between her toes. "I'm not doing this because you will run. I'm doing it because it's time to make you want to stay. I tried to convince you. Win back your love. Now I'm going to take it."

It was the last thing she heard before darkness descended on her mind and all the pain slipped away.

—*B*—

GIOVANNI HUNG UP THE PHONE. The lawyer confirmed that the Chief Inspector was pushing hard on his warrant. And now he had a dead body to get out of Melanzana. Armando paced the floor.

"We're out of time. The *Carabinieri* could arrive at my door any minute. My boys are fast but not that fast," Giovanni said.

"You shouldn't have killed him here," Armando said.

"Fuck the priest. I have here the places I know that Isabella frequents." He handed over the paper to Armando. "Do any of them sound like a good place to hide my Bella?"

Armando scanned the list. "If they left by sea and boat then it has to be

Lipari. The Asian wouldn't go into Sicily. It's too dangerous for him to head south."

Giovanni nodded. "I agree. It used to be an orphanage. It's isolated enough."

"I can have my men there in a few hours."

"I need to be there." He looked at his broken hand when Armando did. "We go in together. First I have to see a few old friends and call in some favors."

"What about the raid?"

"If I'm successful there won't be one. I think the raid is bullshit. Isabella is trying to flush my children out of Melanzana. She thinks I'll move them."

"Why would she give a fuck about your children?" Armando asked.

"Kei Hyogo hasn't left for China. He made many threats to me, but the one that I can't forget is his obsession with my daughter. He took a risk just to see her. He wants to take them both back. I feel it in my gut. Isabella has been being the puppeteer. She's playing us all against one another. Chaos. And the plan is to take my children. I'm a lot of things, Armando, but I'm not stupid."

"You should move them. You don't want to expose them to a search by the *Carabinieri*. They'll turn this place inside out."

"There will be no fucking raid." Giovanni paced away from his desk.

"Can I handle Carlo?" Armando asked.

Giovanni paused. "What did you say?"

"You can deal with the release of your men. I want to help Carlo. They are charging him with murder."

"How do you propose to help? They have his face all over the news as the one who killed Chao Lee."

"They have a mob fight in a boxing ring. I've seen the footage. They can't tell who did who. I have some favors of my own to call in. Let me do it."

"Then I'll ask a different question. Why do you want to?" Giovanni asked.

"I think it's time we fix past mistakes. Clean slate and all. To show you that I intend to make this right between us, I'm going to release you from any obligation of my help. I don't want the inheritance returned to me this way, Gio. We work out a deal that is strictly business, but not based on my sister's life. And I fix the thing that has been between us for years. I help Carlo."

"You do all of this, and I'm supposed to trust you?" Giovanni scoffed.

"I do all of this, and I can't see how you won't. Our fathers were friends.

Maybe one day the *Camorra* and *Mafiosi* will be beyond our truce?"

Giovanni looked him over. "Okay. Call your men. Get them ready. I'll get mine. We leave for Lipari in two hours."

Armando smiled. "We'll be ready."

—*B*—

DOMINIC LIFTED HIS HEAD FROM HIS PILLOW. The jailer opened his cell. He nodded at him to rise. He had been in lockup for close to forty-eight hours and not questioned. He figured it was his turn. He was walked out of his cell down several halls and then to an open door. When Dominic walked inside he saw the young hotshot Chief Inspector waited.

"Dominic Battaglia, please have a seat. Please." *Ispettore* Donatello gestured to the open chair. Dominic walked over and sat down. He waited while the inspector made a show of rifling through a file. "You by far are the most interesting of the Battaglias."

"I guess this is where I ask why?" Dominic said.

"Even Giovanni Battaglia has a record. You are the cleanest *consigliere* I've ever met. Not even a traffic citation."

"Yet I'm here," he said.

"You're here because you were in the room with a man who was being held at gunpoint."

Dominic smirked. "I wasn't holding the gun."

"No. Don Giovanni Battaglia was, but that apparently doesn't matter to my bosses. Do you know what I'm waiting for?" the inspector asked. He closed the folder.

"No. I'm sure you're going to tell me though."

"A warrant for a search of Melanzana. Never has one been served. After all the crimes your boss has done to terrorize the poor people of the *Campania,* no one has ever dared to search his home. All I need is one court, one judge, and I'm in those gates. What will I find?"

Dominic didn't answer.

The inspector stood. He started for the door and stopped. "Oh, by the way, I got a strange anonymous call. It said to look to Lorenzo for answers. The message was 'Where there is sin there is audio'. The caller said her name was Isabella. Does that mean anything?"

Dominic shrugged.

"I'll keep you posted."

Dominic glanced back over his shoulder. The inspector left. He frowned. Why did the name Isabella sound familiar to him?

—*B*—

CATALINA RINSED THE BOWL and put it on the drying rack. She picked up the towel and dried her hands. When she turned to wipe down the table she was startled.

"I didn't mean to scare you." Armando stepped into the kitchen.

"What are you doing in here?" she asked. She dried her hands on the dishrag.

"Looking for the bathroom," he replied. "Wrong turn."

"Liar. Where is my brother?" Catalina tossed the rag to the sink.

"Business. He will be back soon. We think we know where Mirabella is," Armando said.

"Really?" she took a step toward him. "Then why aren't you out there searching for her?" Catalina asked.

"We will. My men are already headed to Lipari."

"Lipari? Is that where she is?" Catalina asked.

Armando smiled. "I believe so."

"You found her, you helped her." Catalina stepped toward him, or he stepped toward her. She wasn't sure. In a blink they were closer.

"We haven't found her yet. Before we storm that island we need to be prepared."

"What do you want from us? For helping us? You must want something?" she asked.

"I don't. I told Giovanni he is released from any obligation. I meant it. Mirabella is my sister, I'm here for her."

"I don't believe you," Catalina said.

"It's okay not to believe me today. When I bring her home you'll have no choice but to believe me then." Armando smiled. His smile was so charming she had no choice but to believe.

Catalina threw her arms around his neck. He embraced her. It felt good to hear that her family may be saved. She clung to that hope, and for a brief moment his touch didn't feel wrong. She liked it.

"Are you okay?" he asked.

Catalina came out of her comfort and looked up into his dark eyes. "I am now. Thank you, Armando. For everything." She pushed at his arms to step back but he didn't let her go. He continued to stare at her. Catalina wasn't sure what to say. Her body was flush up against his. His face so irresistibly close, she saw every detail of his handsomeness.

"Can I share with you that I've had a crush for quite some time on your beauty?" he said.

"That's not appropriate," she answered.

"Maybe not. But I had to say it."

"Let me go. Now," she insisted. He did as she asked.

She stepped back, collected herself. She wasn't used to a man's touch affecting her. Ever. The only man's touch she ever craved was Dominic's.

"I need to go check on the kids. Excuse me," she tried to walk around him. He captured her hand. She glanced up at him. He kissed it.

"I'll make some calls to see how soon Dominic can be released. I know it's upsetting to be away from him for so long. Am I right?"

"Of course. Anything you can do to help Domi… thank you," Catalina pulled her hand away and walked out. She forced herself not to look back. She forced herself to not run away. Although she wanted to do both.

Later –

Giovanni stepped on the boat. Armando was right behind him. He checked his watch. Everything was set. His men should be freed by the time he returned. If his payments to his friends who were judges on the tribunal didn't work, then Melanzana would come under siege, and his children and family would be vulnerable. It was a risk. He had called in every favor he had. In doing so he had indebted himself to his enemies. But on the slim chance that he was right, and the raid was a trap to kidnap his daughter, he was willing to take the risk.

The Sicilian Don had kept his promise. At the shore, several small boats waited to carry them to the larger boat to take them to Lipari. And once on that boat a very impressive arsenal greeted him. Giovanni was a supplier of guns, he approved of the selection.

"I have some friends in the village. They said they've seen Asians near the beach. And there have been lights on at the old monastery. I really do think she's there," Armando said.

Giovanni picked up a gun with his left hand. The boat coasted to a high speed on its way to the island.

"Gio, let's speak," Armando said.

He put down the gun and followed Armando. They walked to the front of the boat. There were few gathered. And those near found somewhere else to socialize.

"We have to consider something," Armando began.

"That this is a trap?" he asked and looked down at his useless right hand.

"She has to know by now that you are on to her. And if so, that you would be searching the places she owns," Armando said. "I had a clue where to find her in Palermo. Almost caught her before a bomb was left for me and my men. Cost me two of my loyal *capus.*"

Giovanni rubbed his brow. "I've considered it. Whatever waits for me I am ready."

"Are you?" Armando looked to his hand. "I mean no disrespect. I understand this is your wife. But maybe you should let me and my men bring her out."

Giovanni smirked. "I'm going in."

"Do you think he's kept her alive?" Armando asked.

The question gutted him. The image of her on that video being violated by Kei played in his head constantly. He refused to think of her hurt, scared, or raped by that madman. If he stopped to even consider it he wouldn't have made it this far. He didn't bother to answer Armando. He turned his gaze to the dark sea they sailed through. They should reach the island in another hour. If God had any mercy left in his heart for his clan, he'd save her. It was his only prayer.

—*B*—

THE DOOR TO THE CELL OPENED. Dominic was marched to another room and given his clothes. He changed quickly. Afterwards he was taken to another holding cell. He found every man inside but Carlo. Lorenzo walked over to him and gave him a hug.

"We're being released," Lorenzo said.

"Giovanni?" Dominic asked. Their brother had come through. Typically a thirty-day hold was done on suspects. Afterwards the *polizia* would have to either charge them with a crime or release them. Apparently Giovanni got that lifted in just over forty-eight hours. The inspector was unable to get a court to sign off on his warrants. Many of their men were detained because of various charges, but Giovanni's top *capus* were all free and clear. Except for Carlo.

"I haven't seen Carlo since they took him away." Lorenzo said. "He needed medical attention. He could barely breathe through his lungs. I think he has a few broken ribs."

"As soon as we're out I'll handle it. And Santo too," Dominic clenched his fist.

"Santo is Giovanni's," Lorenzo said.

The wait was three hours long. And then the cell door opened. The men were walked. Dominic caught the scowl and hatred of the officers in their glares. He nodded to the inspector with a smile. And in true Battaglia style, Giovanni had sent cars for them. Over ten were lined up along the street. Several people were outside taking pictures, including the media. Dominic and Lorenzo didn't hesitate. They entered the first car available to them and closed out the world.

Umberto was the man inside waiting for them.

"Where is Giovanni? Any news on Mirabella?" Lorenzo asked.

"He has left with Don Mancini. They believe they knew where she is." Umberto said.

"Mancini?" Dominic asked.

"He's been at Melanzana with the boss. They left together. It's all I know," Umberto said.

Dominic and Lorenzo exchanged confused glances. Lorenzo was the first to speak. "Armando Mancini and Giovanni are together to bring home Mirabella. Where is she?"

Umberto kept driving. "The boss knew you wouldn't approve. He wants you and Nico to handle Santo. And he asked that I tell you, Domi, to speak with the prosecutor. He withdrew the charges, but Gio says there are expectations. He said you would understand."

"Where did Gio and Armando go?" Lorenzo demanded.

Umberto didn't answer.

He glanced back at Dominic. Dominic looked away. Whatever Giovanni planned he knew it meant taking risks. An alliance of any kind with the *Mafiosi* was dangerous and risky.

"Take us to Melanzana."

—*B*—

THEY SAILED TO THE END OF THE ISLAND where the beaches were isolated. Giovanni only had twelve men to bring. Armando had committed fifty of his men to the rescue. He was surrounded by some of the most ruthless criminals in the Sicilian mafia. He and his men showed no weakness or fear. But he smelled it on his boys. They stayed close and silent as Mancini's men laughed and talked up the night raid. Several looked to him for confidence. Giovanni hoped his presence was enough.

"I'm sending my men in first. If they have the monastery surrounded then we can…"

"No." Giovanni stood. "I go with them. And we go all in."

"We discussed this. It very well could be a trap," Armando said.

"And if it isn't he'll kill her before I can get in there. I won't take that risk." Giovanni ran his left hand back over his head. "If you don't want to see it through my way then say so. Me and my men can take it from here."

Armando stared at him in disbelief. What Giovanni proposed could be suicide. It was his call. He was going in guns blazing, and he was going to save his Bella. The men were all silent on the boat now. No one even dared breathe. Armando's gaze swept his men. He let go a deep frustrated sigh. He addressed the room. "Every man in *mio famiglia* will take the island and kill anyone who gets between us and the monastery. Anyone. Do you understand?"

The men said they did.

Armando extended his hand to Giovanni. He looked down at it for a moment. He then shook his hand. Armando smiled. "This should be interesting."

—*B*—

CATALINA LAUGHED. Zia shook her head smiling. It felt wrong to be making the children dance and laugh with Mirabella missing. But it was the only way she could keep sane. Eve was up holding the hands of Gianni, who rocked side to side to the music playing. She sang to Gianni in Italian. Marietta sat in a chair biting her nails. She stared at little Gino who played with his blocks. Catalina knew Marietta was lost in her own thoughts.

"*Signora* Catalina?" Cecilia said behind her.

"Yes? What is it?"

"I think the men are here. Or arriving?"

"What?" Marietta stood.

"I saw cars coming up the road from my window. I think they are—"

Dominic walked in first. Shocked Catalina screamed and ran to him. She nearly knocked him over. He hugged her tight to him. When she lifted her head from his shoulder she saw Marietta hadn't immediately rushed into Lorenzo's arms. She stood there staring at him. He stood there staring at her.

"We were so worried! I'm so glad you're home, Domi. Gio left with Armando," Catalina rushed out in a single sentence.

"I know." He kissed her brow. "I'm okay. We're okay."

Dominic let her go to bend down to pick up Eve. He kissed her face and neck. Eve giggled. The twins were running for Lorenzo. He stooped to pick up both of the boys. They hugged his neck with excitement.

Marietta found it hard to do or say anything. She couldn't sleep for worrying about him. But the moment he stood in front of her she could only remember their painful parting. Nothing felt resolved between them. She took a step toward him but Zia got ahead of her.

"*Ciao Zia,*" he kissed her brow. Zia hugged his waist as he held the boys. Lorenzo stared at Marietta and she couldn't help but look into his eyes. He nodded at her. She smiled for him.

"Why isn't Rocco here?" Dominic asked. "I was told he left for Chianti. Zia?"

Zia let go of Lorenzo and folded her shawl around her. She shook her head sadly and didn't answer.

"What is it, Zia?" Dominic insisted.

"Gio sent him away. They argued," Zia told them.

"I didn't know that," Marietta said.

"Me either." Catalina chimed in.

Lorenzo glanced to Dominic. They exchanged a look that made Catalina's stomach clench. How much trouble were they still in? "Do you know where Gio went?" Catalina asked Dominic. "Can you leave to help him?"

"It's too late. Let's just pray he knows what he's doing."

KEI SIPPED HIS WINE. Mirabella didn't move. She lay under the covers nude and unconscious. He stared at her and smiled. What he had done was the biggest crime any man could commit. He'd killed his brother. When his uncle told him to return to China, and not with her, he knew the fallout from Chao Lee's death would be severe. One look into Bao's eyes and he understood how his uncle would rid him of his obsession. If he had reached the beach a few seconds later his beloved would have been dead. He was angry. He was furious. And now he had signed their death warrant. There was no way he could take her into his world now. There was no way he could protect himself from his uncle's wrath. He had reached a dead end.

The last of his wine swirled over his tongue. He stood and untied his robe as he started toward the bed to join her again. And then he heard it. Gunfire. He glanced to the balcony. Mirabella didn't stir. He opened the balcony doors just as his men came charging inside.

"They're coming in from the beach!" One of his men yelled.

"Battaglias? How many?" he asked. He tied his robe and went for his pants.

"No way to tell," another man said.

Kei located his gun. He didn't bother with shoes. There was no time. If Giovanni Battaglia had found them he needed to welcome him properly. How had Giovanni found him? He considered Isabella betraying him and dismissed it. Maybe the Triad had revealed his location to extract him. He'd have to figure out the 'how' later.

Before he left he paused and glanced to the bed. Mirabella hadn't moved since he injected her. *Had he given her too much?* It didn't matter. If she overdosed, and he died in battle, it would be poetic justice. And if she didn't, her ankle and drugged state meant she was defenseless. He followed his men out.

Giovanni shot three men in the forest. The dark night was without the moon. The return of gunfire came from every direction. Without any thought to his own wellbeing he kept heading toward the monastery. A man ran past him firing into the trees. If Giovanni hadn't been crouched low he'd have been seen. He had to rely on his left hand. And that meant his aim was off. So most of the men he gunned down were either caught by surprise or had their backs turned.

There was yelling. Shouting in Chinese and Sicilian. His men were close to him. They had to not only shoot their way clear of their enemy, but also be mindful of the *Mafiosi* around them.

With his breath trapped in his lungs and adrenaline in his veins, Giovanni reloaded his gun and ran straight for the stone wall, which must have been the back of the old monastery. He didn't see any doors. It was a wrong move. Suddenly gunfire exploded all around him. He had no choice but to keep running. A few bullets passed so close he felt their trajectory split the air he breathed. He ran. He kept running.

How many men had Kei brought with him to the island? The darkness was his ally and his enemy. His only choice was to find a way inside.

Kei picked up an assault rifle and sprayed bullets into the forest from the second floor veranda. He could see and hear the death cries of many. He didn't care if he shot his men or theirs. No one would make it inside. He sacrificed his men at every entrance. Told them that if they retreated back inside he'd kill them himself. Once his magazine clip was emptied, he tossed the weapon and picked up two more of his guns. It was then he saw someone run for the building. And in spite of the shadowy darkness it wasn't just a figure. There was something about the man's fearlessness that gave him pause. Kei smiled. It couldn't be Giovanni. Could it?

He stormed off the veranda through the study, and out into the hall. He'd instructed the men to barricade all the doors they guarded. He had no doubt Giovanni would overcome every obstacle to find his way in.

Giovanni shot the door handle off. He tried to kick it in but something blocked it. Giovanni threw his weight against the door just as someone shot at him and missed. He turned and fired, killing the man. He again charged the door with his shoulder. After three consecutive body slams against the wood, the hinge broke and gave. It was forced to open a few inches. Giovanni pushed with his shoulder and forced it to open further. There was something barricading it from the inside. Instinct told him to go in low. He was saved because he obeyed his gut and ignored the panic in his heart. Someone must have heard him trying to get inside. The bullets zipped above his head. He returned fire but not with accuracy. He couldn't see. It was darker inside the monastery than out. He heard his men behind him. They were coming to join him. Giovanni had only one purpose, find Kei Hyogo. Kill Kei Hyogo.

The side entrance led to what looked like a kitchen. He kept low to avoid the shooter. When he tried to run past the counter, gunfire exploded to his left. Giovanni stood and blasted off several shots in the general direction of his assassin. Light flashed each time the trigger was pulled, and he saw his assassin drop. And then another who came running in took several bullets to his chest. The sulfuric stench of gun smoke made his eyes and throat burn. He ignored it and kept going. It was then he was met face to face with Kei Hyogo. Both men were startled at first to see each other. Giovanni was slow to react. Kei's gun clicked empty. Giovanni shot at him but his aim was off. The miss gave Kei a chance to attack. He charged Giovanni and several shots were released into the ceiling. The gun dropped. Kei delivered fast acting punches that hit Giovanni in his face, throat, and chest. If it weren't for pure adrenaline boiling in Giovanni's veins, he would have been dropped to his knees. Instead he wrestled Kei down by tackling him with a shoulder rush to Kei's gut. The man was tall but not as tall as Giovanni. He soon had the advantage, but it was short lived. In the struggle his broken hand was yanked, and another blow was delivered to Giovanni's head with Kei's iron fist. Giovanni was shoved off. He saw his gun. He needed Kei down and he had only minutes to react. He scrambled to his feet. Kei was up as well and coming for him. He swung his leg with a lighting strike of a karate kick to Giovanni's back. Giovanni went down again, but this time within reach of his gun. He grabbed it and rolled out of Kei's next kick. He fired.

The bullet hit Kei in the knee. He howled in agony. Giovanni stood. Taking down deep breaths he aimed at Kei.

"You're too late. Killing me won't change a thing. She'll never be with you and not think of me again!" Kei laughed.

Giovanni shot Kei in his other knee. He screamed in agony. Several men ran inside. Giovanni nearly shot them next. They froze. He recognized them as Mancini's men. Armando walked in. He was bleeding from the arm. He looked at Kei dragging himself across the floor.

"Keep him here for me," Giovanni spat blood from his bruised mouth.

"I'm going to get my wife." He panted.

Armando nodded. He stepped on Kei's leg and the man screamed again in agony. Giovanni realized he was bleeding in the chest, face, and the neck. Kei had used some iron glove to fight with that had shredded him. He didn't feel any of it. The blood didn't matter. Kei's words gutted him worse than his superficial wounds. He went for the stairs. It was pure instinct he was working on now.

"Bella!" he yelled.

There was no answer. He went left instead of right down the hall. He kicked open every door because his fucking hands were now useless. "Bella! Bella!" he yelled. He wanted to do the search on his own. He didn't know what he'd find. Kei's nasty words burned in his head. Each room was empty. Giovanni felt a surge of panic. *Was she dead? Is that what he meant? Was she hurt? No! No! She couldn't be dead. She was hidden somewhere. But why wasn't she answering him?* Giovanni arrived at another stairwell, a much narrower one that led to the unknown.

"Bella!" he cried out again.

There was only one door left to him. He pushed it open. The room was dark. The only light came from the open doors to the balcony. He walked toward the bed. Mirabella lay on her side under the covers. She was still.

"Bella?" Giovanni walked around the bed. Her hair was in her face. He could tell she was nude under the sheets. He went to his knees. He moved her hair from her face and found that she was damp, feverish with sweat. She wasn't fully unconscious, but she wasn't aware of him or where she was either. "It's me. It's Gio," he said softly. "I'm here, *mia amore.*"

Again she moaned and her lips moved wordlessly. Giovanni turned her. There was bruising to the side of her face and her throat. Some of it looked fresh. His rage surfaced again and paralyzed him. Giovanni swallowed the sob in his throat and blinked away his tears. He wrapped her up in the sheet and ignored the pain in his hand when he lifted her from the bed. Her head fell back and her arm swung in a listless motion. She felt light. It had only been seventy-two hours, and she felt as if she weighed nothing. He lifted her and pressed his ear to her breast. He heard her heart beat, and it was strong, but it had a very accelerated rhythm. He nearly wept with relief.

Kei had drugged her. Just as he suspected when he watched the video of them both. He refused to think of anything else he might have made his wife endure. He carried her out of the room and down two flights of stairs. Below, Armando and his men waited. Seven men out of the twelve Giovanni brought with him were waiting as well. To the middle of the floor were eight badly beaten Asian men on their knees with their hands behind their heads. Kei was before them seated, bleeding. He looked up first. His face covered in sweat, his eyes blazing with hatred. Giovanni did not take his eyes off him. Mancini's men held guns on them.

"Is she alive?" Armando approached.

Giovanni remembered who he was and answered with a stoic nod instead of the emotional breakdown he was on the verge of. Inside his head he screamed. "She's hurt. I need to bring her home."

"We can take her to the village doctor. There's a clinic not far from here," Armando said.

He looked at her for a moment, torn. He could never hand her over to anyone. He didn't trust them. He had to bring her home. "No. I'm taking her home."

"And them?" Armando said.

"Kill them all. But bring their leader on the boat, for me. I'll need a machete," Giovanni walked toward the door.

"Giovanni! Giovanni! We aren't done! We will never be done!" Kei shouted to his back as he walked out of the front door. The gunfire blasted behind him. The slaughter happened. He didn't bother to turn and witness it. He kissed Mirabella's feverish brow under the moonlight and carried his wife toward the beach.

Sorrento, Italy –

Lorenzo came in through their bedroom door. Mirabella stood. She had sat on the edge of the bed waiting. He glanced around the room and then to her. "You disappeared?" he asked.

"I was waiting for you," she answered. "How are you?"

"I'm better now." Lorenzo closed the door. He put his hands in his pockets. "I see they covered the holes in the walls. And the window is fixed."

Marietta nodded. "Looks like the way things used to be in here."

"Doesn't feel that way. Does it, Marie?" Lorenzo asked.

She bit back her tears. "I've done things I'm not proud of. Things I'm afraid to tell you. Because I don't want to lose you, Lo."

He sighed. "Me too."

The confession hurt. Neither asked for the other to explain the specifics. The truth was implied. He took a step toward her. "In jail I sobered up. Focused. I wish I had done so sooner."

She waited with baited breath. She feared what might come next. Maybe she didn't physically cheat on him, but she did emotionally. And she knew what end her lies would bring. All she wanted was a clean slate, a real chance for their marriage to work again.

"Can I touch you?" he asked.

Marietta nodded her head yes and tears of relief sprung to her eyes. Lorenzo towered over her as he often did. His rough hands felt gentle on her skin. One cupped the side of her face. "So beautiful. Marie, I'd give my life for you. I swear on it, *cara*, I did not take another woman into my bed. I tried. I failed. No matter how badly I hurt for you, I love you with all my heart. From the deepest most purest part of my heart. Say you believe me."

"I want to," she let tears fall. "When I think of what I did, how easy I lied to you, it's hard to believe you're not capable of the same."

"May I kiss my wife?" he asked.

Confused that he'd want to with her crying, she nodded her head yes. He lowered his face and brought his lips to hers. There was a soft gentle relief she felt when their lips met. She blinked up at him, surprised when their lips parted.

"We of all people should know how precious and rare it is to find our kind of love," Lorenzo said with a chuckle. "We can't let our fears defeat us, Marie. I won't lose you. Ever."

"You forgive me? Really?" she asked.

"I forgave you when you pulled the gun on me, my little gangster."

She threw her arms around his waist and laughed. He hugged her. Kept her close to his heart. He lifted her. Not that he had to, but he often did when he wanted to be the one to bring her to bed.

The feel of her lips on his face and neck soothed him. He ached for his wife the most when he was put away. He saw Carlo, saw Giovanni's pain, and wondered how he could jeopardize their happiness. How he of all people could forget the precious gift of love his wife gave him when she agreed to be his. Marie would be his. She'd give him sons, and he'd give her a family she could believe in.

Her thighs parted for him. He dragged his lips from her mouth to her neck. She let go a soft breath and closed her eyes. He tasted her left nipple. He coaxed what felt like a swollen berry on his tongue into his mouth, and then opened his mouth wider to swallow her areola. His hand rubbed down her stomach to the soft delta between her thighs. He stroked her pussy. He glanced up to see the pleasure twist and release the smile on her face. The long dark lashes that shadowed her amber brown, doe-like eyes, fluttered. Her breathing escaped her tiny nostrils. Lorenzo released her nipple to bury his face between her breasts. He didn't take his hands from the heated softness of her plump pussy. The softness of her pussy and breasts were such a comfort.

"I missed you, Marie," he groaned deep in his throat. He lifted his head and looked at her. She was now looking at him. "I love you."

Lorenzo took his time. But eventually lust and regret overwhelmed him. Her silent acceptance made his hunger for her insatiable. He eased up on her, with her beautifully stretched beneath him. He pressed into her, freed his dick. He moved the seat of her panty aside and glided straight inside her tightness, until his groin met with her sweet cunt. He pinned down her hips with both of his hands, and stared at her face as he moved in and out of her. Marie was beautiful to him. The most beautiful woman he's ever loved or seen. And when he fucked her, each time he fucked her, it felt like a privilege. The world outside was falling apart for them both. But this stolen moment between them was all they needed. He wouldn't let go.

Damn his dick hurt. It often did when he went past a week without this pleasure. It was swollen, and impossibly harder when she responded to him with a nice roll of her hips. Her tight pussy clamped down on his dick the deeper he tunneled, and then her inner muscles constricted even tighter. The lush sounds of his dick thrusting in and out of her slick channel, mixed with her shaky moans and the banging of the headboard. He fought hard against his nature to release.

"Lorenzo?" she gasped. The first words she spoke since he'd taken her. She gripped his shoulders and her nails dug into his biceps.

"Yes, baby," Lorenzo said working his hips to sink deeper after each thrust.

"Can't! Can't! Can't take it," she exhaled, warning of an impending release.

"Take me with you, Marie," he groaned. He sat back on his hunches and brought her with him. She was wrapped around him, seated on his dick. He grabbed the perfectly round globes of her ass cheeks, and parted them so he could open her even wider as she went up and down on his dick. "Mmm yes, Marie, yes!"

Marietta rocked, and pushed, and bounced on his cock. Together they found a rhythm that pleased them both. He crashed with her back on the bed. Her face was reddened, and her features were tight as she joined him in the ultimate climax. It felt pure between them.

He lay on her. He struggled to breathe. He rolled to his side and his dick slipped out of her. She came over into his arms. In his pursuit of happiness with his wife again, he'd forgotten to undress her and truly explore her body. Her dress was crumbled up at her waist and pulled down to the front to release her breasts. His dick lay limp against his thigh outside of his zipper. Marietta kissed his jaw and snuggled against his chest.

"Lo?" she asked.

"Hmmm?" he smiled.

"Isabella. She's back."

Lorenzo's eyes opened. "I know. I was told."

"Is it the same person? The one who came after us?" Marietta asked.

"I think so," he answered.

"What are you going to do?" she lifted her head. "If Giovanni can't find Mirabella, if this Isabella has killed her and we…"

"Marie," he cast his gaze over to her. "I'll take care of her. I swear it. And Giovanni will find your sister. He will bring her home."

She dropped her head and eased her arm around his waist. She put her thigh over his legs and held to him. Lorenzo closed his eyes. He would find Isabella, and before he snapped her neck, the bitch would hand over every tape she had of him betraying his family.

CHAPTER EIGHTEEN

Ospedale Cardarelli, Naples Italy —

"Santo?"

A soft voice whispered into his ear. Santo opened his eyes. He hurt all over. But his vision was clear. Isabella's face appeared. She presented the sweetest smile. Her fingers lightly grazed his cheek. "You're a survivor. Aren't you, sweetheart? A warrior," she said.

He blinked in response. He glanced around the hospital room. His jaw was wired shut. He remembered a team of doctors standing over him and explaining the extent of his injuries. The fracture was from chin to ear. They told him it would be months before he'd be able to speak, and even then he'd require more surgeries.

Isabella dropped her purse on his bed. She walked over to the door of his hospital room and locked it. "The *polizia* in Napoli are very helpful. Do you know that I told them that I was your wife, and they gave me a private escort up to your bedside?"

Santo frowned. *He was in the hospital under police protection?* It would explain why he was still alive. Isabella gave a very light laugh. She walked over to his window and his eyes followed her. "Giovanni will come for you," she glanced over to him once more. "I am sorry that there is nothing more that I can do to protect you."

A loud grunt escaped him. He grunted again in his throat to get her attention. That was not the plan. *She turned on him. Tricked him. The evil bitch had set him up.*

"I know! I know. You think you were used. That's not entirely true. Bonaduce hates everyone and everything with the stench of *la Camorra,* because of the death of his son. There was no way he would protect you and then put you in power. He wants to wipe southern Italy clean of *la Camorra.* You should have known better than to believe otherwise."

She walked over to him. He reached to grab her. He'd love to put his hand around her throat. But she effectively sidestepped the swipe of his arm.

"By now Giovanni knows who I am. I'm sure of it. Kei Hyogo was a madman. He even turned on his uncle to use the Triad here. A fool to be so fucking crazy over that mutt Gio is married to. But I saw that madness. I stroked it for two years. Until revenge consumed him with jealousy and brought him here. He actually believed I could steal the brat and bring her to him. Instead I left a few bread crumbs to put Giovanni on his scent." She checked her watch. "If I'm right, Gio's there now. Oh Santo!" she exclaimed, "You should have seen Giovanni begging all over the *Campania* for assistance. Indebting himself to his enemies, partnering with the *Mafiosi,* looking like a pathetic weakling to the other clan bosses because of his grief." She stepped closer. "That's how I will destroy him. Turning his madness in on him. The same way I turned Kei's madness inward. Oh the plans I have! I wish you could be around to see it!"

Santo frowned. He understood. Isabella helped return Mirabella back to Giovanni after letting Kei destroy her. And that was a far greater accomplishment than killing the bitch or his Don. Isabella stared at him with a triumphant smile that was pure evil.

"I will break him down piece by piece, until he is left with nothing. That's how you win the war. I am sorry, Santo. There is no payday for you. You know how this ends."

Santo's eyes stretched. She softened her smile and looked at him with pity. He lunged his hand out for her, but she again sidestepped his reach. "One night when that guard is asleep outside your door, someone will pay you a visit. Possibly Lorenzo. Maybe even Gio himself. They won't end it nicely for you. But when they do take your life, remember your contribution to justice. Your sacrifice will bring the most powerful man in our lives to his knees. Hopefully that will give you peace." She picked up her purse. She started for the door. She glanced back at him with a quizzical look.

"Do you think Giovanni will ever look at his wife the same after what we did to her?" Isabella grinned with excitement. "I don't think she's so precious anymore."

When Santo didn't respond Isabella shrugged.

Helpless and confused, Santo lay in his bed and watched as Isabella breezed out the door. He closed his eyes. He did want revenge. He betrayed every vow he ever made in the brotherhood. But he never took the time to consider that the revenge he sought was never his to have. Isabella had played him. He clenched his fist. He was a dead man. All he could do was wait to die.

—*B*—

GIOVANNI DROPPED THE MACHETE. *Kei's tortured screams ended over ten minutes ago. Still he kept hacking until there was nothing left of him. His hands and clothes were soaked in blood. Armando gave the signal to their men. Several began to toss body parts out into the sea. Others used a hose on the boat to wash down the stern.*

"How is she?" Armando asked Giovanni.

He glanced up to the moon fading in the sky. The sun was approaching. His rational mind returned. He could see and think past the black-layered rage that had consumed him earlier.

"There's a change of clothes below deck. Maybe you shouldn't let her wake to see you this way."

Giovanni looked at his blood soaked hands. He nodded. He turned and left them to it. All he wanted to do was find and heal his wife. And he feared Kei's dying words would prove true.

At sea he was left alone to care for her. She remained unresponsive to him. But he wiped her brow through her feverish deep sleep, and checked her bruises to make sure he didn't see any additional physical trauma. Her ankle gave him the most worry. The fact was, he was clueless as to what happened to her, and how she survived seventy-two hours with that bastard. It made him uneasy.

Armando didn't have any women's clothes. But Giovanni dressed her in a button down shirt, and then wrapped her again in the blanket. Her feverish moans pitched a few times. He thought he heard her say his name. He couldn't be sure. When they docked Giovanni transferred her from the boat at the pier to his waiting car. Inside he was told that Dominic, Nico, Lorenzo, and few more of his enforcers were free. It gave him a small measure of relief, but not much. If his Bella would open her eyes and speak to him, all would be right in the world.

The long ride to Melanzana from the coast dried his tears. When the gates parted he looked down at his wife and spoke. "Bella? We're home. You're home," he said.

He smiled.

He kissed her brow.

He didn't see her as she was now, but as he always saw her. His blue rose. Giovanni made sure the sheet wrapped around her was tightly done, so it could not slip. He needed help removing her from the car. When he passed her to his men and then eased out, he immediately took her back in his arms. To the front of Melanzana, under the morning sun, stood Marietta, Catalina, Zia, Lorenzo, Dominic, Nico, and what was left of his men. They all stared at Mirabella in stunned silence. He carried her up the stairs. Marietta approached first with tears in her eyes. She touched Mirabella's face and kissed her brow. It was more contact than he wanted to allow. He hurried to bring her to their room before the children woke and discovered her in such a state. He put her under the covers, and closed all doors and shutters on the windows. The darkness made the room very soothing. He turned on the lamp near their bed. Zia came in with her bible and chose a corner to sit and pray.

Giovanni wet a warm rag and wiped Mirabella's wounds. He removed the wrap on her ankle to find it darkly bruised and swollen. It had to be broken. The worst of it were the scratches to her ankle, leg, and thighs. A few were on her chest. He knew each were marks left by Kei. He picked up the phone and dialed downstairs. He told one of his men to send for the doctor, and to tell them that Bella had broken her ankle so to come prepared.

There was a knock at the door. Giovanni set the phone down and went to the door. *Why hadn't he thought of calling the doctor first thing?* He'd been too consumed with healing her on his own.

Dominic was at the door when he opened it. "We need the doctor. Bella's hurt."

"Can I come in, Gio?" Dominic asked.

He glanced back at Mirabella and then to Dominic. "I need to be with her," he said.

"Only for a moment. To talk," Dominic said.

"Wait a minute." Giovanni closed the door. He returned to the dresser to find something for Bella to wear. He glanced to Zia. She was of no threat. All the old woman did was hold her rosaries and pray. He covered Bella in her gown, the one she often wore when she was menstruating. He hated it. But she said it gave her comfort. He kissed her brow once more and pulled up the covers. When he knew she was okay he went to the door and opened it.

Dominic entered. He looked to the bed. "How is she?"

"I don't know. It's been hours. She hasn't woken. She's feverish. I felt her heart beat. It's strong. Whatever he did to her, she's survived it. I just don't know. Look at this." Giovanni walked over and pulled back the blanket. He had propped her ankle with a pillow. Dominic came closer. He touched it.

"Broken. To keep her from escaping?" Dominic asked.

"I killed him too quick. I should have prolonged it for days, weeks." Giovanni put his hand to his head.

"So he's dead?" Dominic asked.

"They're dead. All of them." Giovanni answered.

"Our men?" Dominic asked.

"I think five. I don't know. I left the bodies on Lipari." Giovanni replied. "When I found her I couldn't think straight."

"How did you know where to find her?" Dominic asked.

"I can't talk about that now. Get out." Giovanni went back to the bed and checked her pulse. "Make sure the doctor is on the way."

"Gio, I need to know what deals were made with Armando Mancini," Dominic said calmly. "What did we agree to?"

"Nothing. I offered. He refused. He said he wanted to help Bella. I think I believe him," Giovanni said.

"That's bullshit, Gio! He can't be trusted. And whether he accepted what you offered or not, he sent a message by being the one to help you. We have to deal with the ramifications. After we make sure Mirabella is okay we need to regroup, Gio."

"Don't you think I fucking know that!" he shouted. "Look at her. Look at what he did to my Bella! My fucking wife! Nothing is more important than her right now. Get the fuck out before I snap your neck!"

Dominic nodded and walked out. Giovanni took the chair near the desk. He brought it over to the bed and sat in it. He'd sit there for eternity until she woke.

—*B*—

"WHAT DID HE SAY?" Lorenzo asked Dominic when he entered Giovanni's office.

"Not much. We got a dead priest on our hands. Men in prison. Santo's alive. Renaldo isn't expected to live. And I suspect an alliance now with the *Mafiosi,* whether we want it or not," Dominic said.

"Shit. This Kei motherfucker did more damage than possible," Lorenzo grunted.

"Not Kei," Dominic said. "Isabella Ricci. I spoke to Rocco an hour ago."

"Ricci?" Lorenzo's stomach clenched. Isabella was real. The inspector confirmed it for him. But why had she attacked Mirabella? And did she really have anything to hang over his head still? "What did Rocco say? I don't remember an Isabella Ricci. Is she related to Flavio's people?"

"She was adopted into the Mancini family." The news landed hard between them. Dominic went on. "When she was young, and then she ran off a few years later. No one ever speaks of her. Turns out she's your sister."

Lorenzo turned and looked at Dominic and laughed. "Seriously? Who the fuck is she?"

Dominic sighed. "She's your sister."

"I don't have a fucking sister, you asshole."

"She was named after your mother," Dominic said.

"That doesn't make her my fucking sister!" Lorenzo shouted.

"Your mother had a child, a little girl. She had her with Flavio."

"This is bullshit! A lie!" Lorenzo collared Dominic. He threw him into the wall. Dominic shoved Lorenzo off him.

"I can't believe it either, but the story comes from Rocco, and Armando Mancini confirmed it. It fits. She's the one who has been working with Santo. Who helped the China man take Mirabella. She's been plotting and waiting since Flavio's death, to get revenge against Gio. It's true. And if you know anything about her, Lorenzo, anything, you need to tell me now. Because she is using our secrets and our love for our family against us." Dominic stepped forward. "Don't think for a moment she didn't set it all up. Even Mirabella's escape. She's been at this for awhile, and she's fucking winning."

Lorenzo stood there stunned. His brain couldn't process the news. He flashed back to the tapes and what David Capriccio told him. If it was his sister from that wicked woman who gave birth to him, then it would explain why she would have so much hate in her to plot against him. He lowered to a chair.

"Do you know this woman, Lorenzo? I need the truth," Dominic asked again.

"I don't know her. Madre never mentioned a bastard daughter. You know how she was. If it's true then I am just as clueless."

"The clan bosses will be freed soon. The prosecutor is dismantling his own case because they have Carlo. Giovanni could not bargain for his release. They are going to hang him for this. Do you understand?"

"Yeah," Lorenzo mumbled. "Give me a minute."

— *B* —

THERE WERE VOICES IN HER HEAD. She swallowed a metallic taste on her tongue, and her stomach clenched with nausea. Mirabella felt ill. She struggled to focus on the whispers. And then she heard one voice rise above the others and it gave her hope. The man sounded like her husband. She forced her lids to part. Giovanni stood at the foot of a bed with two men talking. It had to be a dream. She closed her eyes. The drug Kei gave her kept her numb and dreaming. She wanted more numbness. She wanted to escape, and the only way to do so was in her bed.

The whispers persisted. Confused by her inability to understand what was said, she opened her eyes again. This time one of the men looked directly at her. He said something. She saw his lips move and heard him, but her mind and thoughts were a haze. It was as if some part of her brain had been unplugged. Giovanni came forward. He sat on the edge of the bed and took her hand. He kissed it. He smiled. He hadn't shaved. There were scratches and bruises to his face. This was no dream. Mirabella tried to smile but she barely felt her lips move.

"Bella, you're okay now," he said. And this time she was able to do more than read his lips. She could hear him.

"Where is he? Where am I?"

"Shhh," he said. He kissed her brow. "You're home. Relax."

The joy she felt in that moment brought her to tears. "My children. Where are my children, Gio? Are they safe? Tell me please!"

Giovanni brought her up into his arms and he held her. He kept her in his arms until her tears lessened. *This was no dream!* How did she get there? When did she get home? She wanted to see her children. She tried to say so, but all she could do was cling to him and pray to God that this was no dream. She was so terrified she'd wake and Kei would be there. And the nightmares would start all over again.

"Kei?" she asked in fear. "Where is he?"

"He's dead."

"Oh my God! Thank you God!" she wept.

"He'll never hurt you again, Bella," Giovanni whispered in her ear. "I swear to you, he'll never hurt you again."

"Gio, I'm so sorry. It's my fault. I'm so sorry!" She said repeatedly.

"No. Bella, no, it's not. Bella? Look at me?" he held her face and looked into her eyes. "This is my fault. And I'm going to fix it. I'm going to make it up to you. I'm going to protect you. I promise. You'll never be hurt again. I promise," he said and his voice went hoarse with emotion. His eyes glazed over with tears. "I love you. From the bottom of my heart. From here to forever, Bella. I love you so much."

She was exhausted. She fought against the drug pulling down on her consciousness. Giovanni laid her back on the pillows and made sure she was comfortable. He smiled at her and then turned to stand. She grabbed his sleeve. "Don't leave me!" she whimpered. "Stay!"

"I'm not going anywhere." He assured her. He said something to the men gathered and she didn't care. She was resting on clouds. Her bed felt so good. She actually smiled as she turned over on her pillows and smelled his cologne and shampoo in the sheets. Giovanni eased into bed with her. His body curved around hers, and the warmth and love she felt in his embrace chased away the nightmare, for the moment.

"I'll bring the children in when you are stronger," he promised as he stroked her hair.

"Stay with me," she said softly. "Never leave me."

"Always," he said. He kissed the back of her head and held her. "Always, my sweet Bella."

— *B* —

"I HAVE TO TELL YOU SOMETHING," Lorenzo said. He took Marietta by the hand and pulled her from the room. They returned to theirs.

"I was waiting to see Mirabella," Marietta said. "He is she?"

"I'm not sure. The doctors told Giovanni they will have to send her blood to the lab to find out what he gave her. They couldn't give her anything until they know. She doesn't have any broken bones except her ankle."

"He was a fucking madman!" Marietta said.

"He's dead. He won't hurt her ever again."

Marietta walked away from Lorenzo. She felt like she'd been on a rollercoaster for seventy-two hours straight, and now she was forced to stand still. She was weak and dizzy with exhaustion. Making up with Lorenzo was only a small part of her relief. Their family was in trouble. Her sister was hurt. All of it scared her.

"Lorenzo, when you were in jail, Giovanni called me to his office. He… he asked me about Isabella," she said. "I told him that she contacted me once and said that you knew about my mother. It's all I said. I had to tell him something. Mirabella was missing."

Lorenzo nodded. "I'm not angry. I understand."

"Who is she?" Marietta asked.

"My sister." Lorenzo said. "That's what I brought you in here to tell you."

"Sister? You have a sister?" Marietta asked. "But that makes no sense."

"I guess my mother had her when she was young and they sent her away. She's angry because she thinks Giovanni killed her father."

"Who is her father?" Marietta asked.

Lorenzo sat on the edge of the bed. "Flavio. You remember what I told you about him. What he did to separate Giovanni and Mirabella."

"What are you going to do? If she's out there she has those tapes," Marietta said in a whisper.

"I'm going to find her before Giovanni does. And kill her." Lorenzo said.

"Are you sure? She's your sister!" Marietta said.

"And she tried to kill Mirabella, she tried to have me kill you. Or have you forgotten? When I find her I will put an end to it." Lorenzo said.

"That's not what I mean. If she's your sister you need to know why she never told you. Why she would do all of this. You need to understand her. Right?"

"I don't give a fuck. She's as rotten and dangerous as my mother was. Be grateful you never met her. And trust me, you'll never meet Isabella. Because when I do find her, I'll send her to hell with Mama."

Marietta walked over to Lorenz and combed her fingers through his hair. She pulled his face to her breasts and held him. "Tell me everything will be alright and I will believe you."

"Everything will be alright." He hugged her waist and kissed her belly.

She stroked his head. "Will you be okay? I have to leave. There's so much I have to do, I'm not sure when I will come back. I promise to come home as soon as I can."

"I'll pack you some things. Okay?" she asked.

He looked up at her. "Give me a kiss."

She leaned in and gave him a kiss. He pinched her on the butt and she laughed. He tickled her and tossed her on top of the bed. She laughed and bucked beneath him. He kept tickling her until she was slobbering with laughter. Lorenzo then held her on the bed. They lay there in silence.

Marietta summoned enough bravery to ask the question burning in her heart. "How is Carlo? When will they release him?"

"He's not well, Marie. I don't know what we can do to help."

"You have to try, Lorenzo. He has nobody but you to care," she said and buried her pains and regrets over Carlo's suffering.

"He's my brother, my best friend. I'm not giving up on him. I never do," Lorenzo said. Marietta sighed. She closed her eyes and said a silent prayer for them all.

Later –

Giovanni waited a full two hours before he left her side. She slept peacefully. Zia insisted on sitting in the room to watch her while he was gone. The business meeting could not be put off any longer. He showered, changed, and checked the wraps to his broken hand. When he returned to Villa Rosso he found Dominic and his men waiting. Only Dominic and Lorenzo joined him in his office.

"How is she, Gio?" Dominic asked.

"I don't know. She's still terrified of the bastard. It'll take time."

"I'm going to pay Santo a visit tonight," Lorenzo said.

"Not yet. The inspector knows we will make another attempt. Delay it. We'll strike when the time is right," said Giovanni. He stared at his cousin for a moment. "Have you heard? About this woman? Isabella?"

"My long lost sister? Yes. I heard. It's bullshit if you ask me."

"Rocco said it's true. I believe him," Dominic said.

"Rocco keeps secrets. Believing what he says now is stupid. We believe what we see and know. I've seen what this bitch can do, and I know why she is doing it. So yes, Lo, she's real. And we will find her," Giovanni said.

"Gio, we need to understand the state of things," Dominic said.

He nodded in agreement. "Some things are changing, I've made some deals. Some territory splits. Payments to officials. We have to keep a low profile for the next few months."

"How low?" Lorenzo asked.

"Invisible," Giovanni said.

"Our enemies will circle, we can't disappear. And we have unfinished business, Gio!" Lorenzo said. Giovanni didn't respond. He kept thinking of Bella. Wondering if he should return to her side.

"What about Carlo?" Lorenzo asked.

"He faces a tribunal. They will pin the murder on him. I had to agree to step aside," Giovanni told them. Dominic and Lorenzo exchanged looks.

"Agree? What does that mean, Gio?" Dominic asked.

"It means I had to make a choice. The inspector was going to raid Melanzana. You were going to be charged with conspiracy. Mirabella was missing. My enemy was at my side offering help. I had to act."

"By sacrificing Carlo? Gio! You can't make that deal! Carlo will get life in prison. He doesn't deserve that!"

"It's done!" Giovanni shouted.

Lorenzo glared and held his tongue. Dominic looked as if he didn't agree as well. Giovanni almost told them of Armando's bargain with him to assist. But another show of gratitude toward the *Mafiosi* would turn his men on him. He'd strained every relationship, including the ones in his own family.

"I finally spoke to Kyra," Dominic said. "She's distraught. No change for Renaldo. The doctors say it's not a good sign."

"What can we do?" Giovanni asked. He watched his cousin pace with caged rage. He could tell it was consuming him. Lorenzo would not heed his warning and be restrained. And he'd hate to have to take his cousin's balls to keep him in line. But he'd do it if necessary.

"I'm getting the doctors to tell us if we need to fly in more specialists. It's a waiting game for Renaldo to wake up now. He lost so much blood they aren't sure if it will mean brain damage."

"What is it you want us to do now, Giovanni?" Lorenzo asked. "Hold our dicks and wait for our throats to be slit? We need to do something now!"

"The only thing, the most important thing, for all of you, is to find Isabella Ricci and bring her to me." Giovanni told them. Dominic and Lorenzo agreed.

—*B*—

"MOMMY! MOMMY!"

Mirabella felt a tiny hand pushing at her face. She opened her eyes. Gino stared at her. His round blue eyes glistened with tears. "Mommy," he said.

"Gino?" Mirabella lifted her head from the pillow.

"I'm sorry, Mirabella." Zia came out of the bathroom. "I was going to change him. I only went to the bathroom for a minute."

"No! It's okay," Mirabella smiled. She reached for her son. He stretched his arms up to her. She kissed his brow as she brought him to her lap. Gino grinned. He touched the bruise on her neck. She still felt some tenderness there.

"You miss Mommy?" she asked.

He put his head to her breast. Zia came over and smiled. "How do you feel?"

"Better now. Stronger," Mirabella said.

"We were so scared. All of us."

"I'm sorry. I hate I put you through that," Mirabella said.

"No! It's not you. That animal who kidnapped you did this. May he burn in hell."

"Where's Giovanni?" she asked. She hoped Zia didn't hear the panic in her voice. Giovanni swore he'd stay close. He promised not to leave her.

"He's with the men meeting in his office. Here inside. He'll return soon." Zia said.

"He's going to be more protective of me. I need that. But I need my babies. Can you bring them? And my sister, and Catalina, bring them."

Zia nodded and left. Gino lifted his head from her breast and looked up at her. He spoke to her in his baby language, a long sentence that she tried to understand. "Is that so, baby? Mommy is so sorry she wasn't here to see it. Un huh, yes, Mommy understands. I missed you too." Mirabella laughed.

"Mirabella!" Catalina rushed inside. She looked up at a grinning Catalina who went to the bed and kissed and hugged her. The kids came in afterwards. Mirabella laughed through her tears as she hugged Gianni who started to cry the moment he saw her, and then Eve. She felt so much better seeing them all.

"How are you, sis?" Marietta asked. Mirabella looked up at her sister standing at the door. She nodded that she was okay. Marietta began to cry. She came over and hugged her neck. There were so many on the bed hugging and kissing her at once, Mirabella couldn't stop giggling with delight. One of the babies accidently fell on her ankle and she howled.

Everyone froze. The children looked at her terrified.

"It's okay. Mama just hurt her foot. She's okay," Mirabella said.

She hugged her babies. Catalina and Marietta told her so many stories at once of how they were. She was gone three days, but from the way they talked it was like she was gone for three years.

"What is going on in here?" Giovanni asked. He entered with concern. "Bella, you need your rest."

"No, Giovanni," Mirabella said. "I just need my family. I'm okay."

"Are you sure?" he asked.

She looked around at all the love surrounding her. She feared nothing with her family close. This is what she needed. "I'm positive."

Giovanni picked up Gino. He came around the bed and got on top. Marietta and Catalina sat on the edge of the bed talking at once. Eve found room to hold her mother's waist, while Mirabella held Gianni to her breast. She looked over to Giovanni and smiled. And her husband winked at her.

Napoli Italy –

Kyra sighed. She moaned as she slowly woke to the touch of a hand over hers. Her head lifted. Renaldo stared at her. Shocked she jumped to her feet.

"Renaldo! It's me! Baby! You're awake!"

"What is it?" Jamie asked. She sat up on the sofa with the sheet covering her. Kyra smiled at her fiancé. He stared at her, unable to speak. She kissed his brow.

"Go get the doctors, Jamie. Tell them Renaldo is awake."

Jamie did as she asked. Kyra couldn't tell if Renaldo heard her or understood her. The doctors said that there could be neurological damage. She didn't believe them. She would never give up on him. He was her life.

"I'm here, sweetheart. You're going to be okay. I swear it. You'll be fine."

The doctors and nurses came in. Kyra was pushed to the side. Jamie hugged her as they watched them un-tube Renaldo. It was harsh the way he gagged and coughed down air. She wanted to go to him, to comfort him. Jamie held her back.

"Wait, Kyra. Let them help him," Jamie whispered. Kyra nodded and tried to be strong. Renaldo always told her to be strong. He warned her that there would be a day when she would have to. She was so angry at him for risking his life. What about her? What about his son? What about their family? Would they ever be more important?

"*Signora,*" the doctor said. "We have to take him. For some tests."

"Can I come? He needs me." Kyra tried to look around the doctor. Renaldo's eyes were closed again. He hadn't spoken. "What's wrong with him?"

"Let us run some tests. Then we'll talk."

"No!" She pushed past him to Renaldo. She returned to his bed. He opened his eyes. When he gave her a faint smile she knew he recognized her. Kyra wept with relief. She kissed his chapped lips. She tried to hug him but the nurses pulled her away. "I love you!"

He nodded and mouthed the words back. The joy of that moment made up for the horrors of the past three days. She couldn't believe how good happiness and hope felt again.

They wheeled him out of the room.

"Did you see it, Jamie? Did you?" Kyra laughed.

"I did, baby doll. He's going to be okay! I saw it!"

Kyra hugged Jamie so tight. They were both crying and laughing. Maybe the nightmare was over.

That night –

Mirabella needed the use of crutches to walk to the bathroom. Giovanni had some brought in for her. She closed the door and vomited the contents of her dinner. Her body was racked with shivers. Her skin itched. She felt as if a million microscopic spiders crawled underneath. And the worst of it all was her stomach. The cramping. She endured it without alarming the family, but it was getting worse.

"Bella? You okay in there?"

"I'm fine, sweetheart!" she called out in a lighthearted way.

"You sure?" Giovanni asked.

"Yeah, check on the kids. I want to, uh, tuck them in. I'll be out in a minute!" she said.

"Okay," he said.

Mirabella closed her eyes. She held on to the crutches. When she lifted her face she got the first real glimpse of herself since her return home. What she saw shocked her. She lowered her eyes. The urge to vomit heaved up in her throat, and she dropped over the sink. Nothing came out. But the burning in her veins persisted. What had Kei given her?

Giovanni checked in on the twins. Eve was sleep in her bed. And then he heard it, a loud crash. He ran from the children's room back into his. He went to the bathroom. "Bella? Bella!"

He opened the door but couldn't move it. Mirabella's body blocked it. He pushed on the door and shoved harder. His wife was pushed aside.

"Bella! Bella!" he got to his knees and pulled her over to him. She had vomit all over her mouth and was unconscious. "Bella, wake up. What's wrong, sweetheart? What is it?"

She didn't respond. He had to get her help. He was desperate.

Three days later –

Mirabella sighed. She turned her head on her pillow and opened her eyes. It was then she saw the heart monitor, and the IV bag and line that dripped into her veins. She blinked at the sterilized white walls. Giovanni sat up. He leaned forward.

"Hi?" she said.

"Hi," he answered.

"What's going on?" she asked.

"What do you remember?" he asked.

"Bathroom, our house? Was it a dream? Was I there?" she asked.

"Yes." He took her hand and kissed it. "You were there. We're just in the hospital," he said.

"Why? What's wrong with me?"

Giovanni sighed. "I should have brought you here first. I'm so sorry,

Bella. I just wanted to protect you. Take you home."

"Gio, it's okay. I'm fine. Right?" she smiled.

Tears dropped. He lowered his gaze.

"I feel better. I'm fine!" she said.

"Bella, when you were with him, how many times did he inject you?" Giovanni asked.

"Why? Is it what Kei gave me that's made me sick?" she asked.

"The doctors, they said he put something in you, Bella. Your kidneys were shutting down. But they're better now. The doctors say you're improving."

"What did he give me?" she asked. "Tell me!"

Giovanni sighed. "It's some kind of drug. Derived from opium, more addictive than heroine. They don't know. They're sure it's a narcotic. When your organs started shutting down I was…" Giovanni swallowed the emotion clogging his throat. "I was scared. But you started to improve. They don't know why."

"I know why," she smiled for him. He looked so tired, so distraught. She touched his face. "I love you, Gio. I love our children. I'll never leave you. Never."

He leaned over and kissed her. "I'm just glad you're feeling better."

"The family? Our kids? How is everyone?" she asked.

"We're surviving. We just want our Donna home where she belongs."

"I'm fine, Gio. I'm going to be okay," she reassured him. But even she wasn't certain. Not anymore.

EPILOGUE

A month later –

"MIRABELLA? YOU DRESSED?" Mirabella turned from the mirror. She screwed the cap back down on her mascara and tossed it in with the rest of her makeup. Every window in her room was open. A balmy ocean breeze blew inside and reminded her of the beach. Marietta walked in. She wore a black dress that looked almost identical to hers. She smiled.

"Everyone ready?" Mirabella asked.

"The kids are in the car. Giovanni is on his way upstairs if you don't come on," Marietta said.

Mirabella nodded. She reached for her crutches and used them to balance her weight. Marietta looked as if she wanted to help. But Mirabella walked just fine. In another week or so the doctors said she'd come out of her plaster boot and be able to walk on her own. It wasn't as bad as her family made it out to be. She was able to get around now, and most days did so without the need of her crutches. The kids had drawn all over it with markers and crayons. She made it into a little game for them.

When she reached her sister she touched her hand. "Have you told Lorenzo?" she asked.

"No. We're staying behind. A chance for us to be together, you know. I want to tell him private. He's barely around lately. Constantly working or chasing something or the other," she said. They both knew what Lorenzo and the men were out doing. Hunting down a woman named Isabella, his long lost sister. Mirabella still couldn't wrap her head around the strange connection to

495

her kidnapping.

"Okay," Mirabella said. "Let's go."

She and Marietta walked out of the room. She balanced her steps with her crutch. It took her longer to come down the stairs, but she managed. Giovanni waited for her by the door. He was dressed conservatively in a dark suit, as were all of his men. The women and children were too. Mirabella smiled at her husband. He smiled back. It wasn't a happy day. A funeral in the family never was. And this death was even more bitterly felt. The men were solemn and remorseful. She took her husband's hand. Lorenzo escorted Marietta out.

"You okay, sweetheart?" she asked him as he led her to their car.

"I will be," he reassured her. She glanced to the Mercedes van where the children, Rocco and Zia rode. She then looked back at Villa Mare Blu. With a burdened sigh she eased inside the car. Why was the return to Sicily so bitterly felt, as it was for her last visit?

Once seated in the van the driver led the caravan out. Mirabella missed Renaldo's absence and the sadness of what happened to him squeezed her heart. He was typically Giovanni's driver and bodyguard. Today Umberto was the substitute. She glanced over to Giovanni. His eyes were hidden behind the dark lenses of his sunglasses. However, his profile revealed to her how fatigued with sadness they were. Giovanni felt guilty. They all did. She brought his hand up to her mouth and kissed it.

The Battaglias drove out of Mondello along the coastal highway. They made the long drive to Carini barely speaking. After the funeral they would host a dinner at Villa Mare Blu, and then return back to Sorrento the next day. She was going to miss the peace and tranquility of the beach side village. But she was ready to take her family home.

The car steered into the cemetery. The burial grounds were hundreds of years old. The ceremony would be done at the graveside. Mirabella was helped from the van. She glanced back for her children and found them all accounted for. The boys chirped happily as the men they considered uncles carried them. Eve held to her Zia a bit more, confused. It was Mirabella's duty to be at Giovanni's side to pay respects. But she wished they could have spared the kids this.

Catalina approached. She held Dominic's hand. "I think they are waiting on us," she said. Giovanni slipped his arm around Mirabella's waist. Together they made the walk to the gravesite. The first person Mirabella saw was Kyra. Her braids blew out behind her shoulders. Large black oval sunglasses concealed her eyes. She stared at the grave, lost in thought. And then she looked up. Their eyes met. Kyra gave Mirabella a faint smile. She'd only spoken to her on the phone. She never had a chance to really tell her how sorry she was that Renaldo was shot. She would that evening. And when Kyra turned to Renaldo and said something to him, he glanced in their direction as well. He nodded his head at Giovanni and Mirabella. They nodded in return. He was able to stand with the help of crutches similar to Mirabella's. He looked stronger.

"How is he?" Mirabella asked her husband.

"It'll take some time. He has recovery to do. I gave them a place in Napoli so they could be closer to the physical therapy."

"Sweet of you, Gio," Mirabella said.

"Come, Bella. They're waiting," Giovanni whispered.

The Battaglias were not the last to arrive. When Mirabella was helped to her seat she saw a long limousine drive in.

Giovanni glanced out across the tombstones to the arriving family. Carlo helped Ciro's mother from the vehicle. The woman looked broken with grief. It was hard to hear her wails and see her pain.

The Italian government only released Ciro's body a week ago. They kept the kid on ice for weeks while they built their case for murder. Giovanni made sure to cover all expenses to return the young man to Sicilia. His gaze turned to Armando Mancini. The Don stood with his men, observing. He considered Armando's request to not be named as the one to help free Carlo. But Giovanni didn't like sharing a secret, or favor, with him. Even now, after everything they've done together, their newfound friendliness made him uneasy.

The courts wanted to crucify Carlo. And then out of the blue a young man stepped forward and confessed to being the one to choke the life out of Chao Lee. At first the hotshot inspector scoffed. But when the tapes were rolled back it clearly showed the man jump into the mob fight in the boxing ring. Carlo went down with Chao Lee, so did several other men. Including the one who offered up his confession. The guy wasn't part of *la Camorra* or any other criminal enterprise. He was an ordinary spectator who had too much to drink and loved to fight. The prosecutor bought the story. The media bought the story. The Chief Inspector did not. And neither did Giovanni.

Armando Mancini had visited the man and his family. He made him an offer he could not refuse. Carlo was free and clear. And Carlo's freedom felt like justice.

When Carlo brought Ciro's mother to the grave the priest began to lead them in prayer.

Catalina listened. She prayed. And though she tried to focus on the sadness weighing down on her family, she could not. Often during the service she found it hard to keep from looking at Armando. Twice he met her stare, and dared her through his sly smile to hold the exchange inappropriately longer. She refused to return the gesture. She closed her eyes and tried to block any thoughts of his smile from her head.

"You okay?" Dominic asked.

"Huh?"

"Are you okay, sweetheart?" Dominic asked.

"No. Not really," she admitted. "This is hard."

Dominic put his arm around her and pulled her in closer. She trained her gaze straight ahead and kept it that way. Carlo stepped over to the open grave. He removed his father's pocket watch and tossed it inside. Ciro's mother wailed with tears. They had chosen to bury the young man next to Carmine. And when it was over, several grown men were concealing their teary eyes behind dark sunglasses. The day would be a long one of mourning.

After the service –

Carlo sat at his brother's graveside in a chair he pulled out from under the tent. He'd helped the gravediggers cover Ciro until his arms burned with exhaustion. Now it was done. His gaze volleyed between Ciro's and Carmine's graves. He put a hand to his face and wiped away the sweat. The sun was ruthless. It blazed and burned hotter than flames straight from hell. And he endured. Because hell is where he belonged. There were many regrets in his life, but this one, the death of his brothers; he knew their blood was on his hands. This was his curse. No matter his sin, he never suffered worse consequences than the people he loved.

A hand touched his shoulder. His sister had warned she would come after him if he stayed at the grave too long. He wasn't ready to let go. Not yet. "Go on, leave me," he said in Sicilian.

"Carlo?" a woman spoke. He turned his gaze and looked back over his shoulder. The sun temporarily blinded him. But her pink hair blew out in the wind, and she stepped between him and the harsh glare. Carlo stood. It was Shae.

"What are you doing here?" he asked.

She took another step toward him. He stared down at her in confused disbelief. She looked to Ciro's grave. She walked past him and put a white lily on the dirt mound. Carlo observed her, unable to speak. Her presence had not only surprised him, it rattled him. Shae leaving him the way she did hurt him more than he thought possible, considering their short time knowing each other.

"Marietta called me last week when you made the funeral arrangements. I had to come," she said softly.

"Why?" he asked.

"For you, Carlo." She looked at him again. She reached up and touched his face. "I'm so sorry about Ciro. He was a sweet kid. I liked him a lot. I'm so sorry for your pain."

"You said you didn't care." He turned his face away not wanting her touch.

Shae lowered her hand. "I lied. I care. Don't be angry. I didn't come all this way to upset you. Let me be here with you."

"Until you decide you don't want to be?" he asked.

"When will that be, Carlo? Before or after you finally see me, and not a replacement for Marietta?" she removed her sunglasses. "If you want to be loved, you've got to stop thinking you don't deserve to be." She stepped closer to him. "Be angry if you need to be. Go ahead. I can handle it."

"Leave, Shae," he turned away from her. She hurried and stepped around him. "I was wrong to up and leave you like that. I was a coward. But today isn't about me or us. Is it, Carlo? Ciro's dead. You barely escaped prison for murder. Let me be here, right now, and we'll worry about tomorrow, tomorrow."

Carlo put his hands to his head. He squeezed his eyes tightly shut. "I can't!" he groaned. "I can't do it anymore."

"I know," she said sadly.

Carlo felt weak in the gut and legs. He dropped to his knees in an instant. He grabbed Shae by the waist and pulled her to him. He put his face against her abdomen and held tight to her. "I can't go through this anymore!"

"Shhh… I know. I know, baby, I'm so sorry."

He couldn't cry. He didn't know how in that moment. He'd spent too many nights feeling his anger, to understand how to release it. But when he held Shae and she allowed him to, he began to understand why he needed her. Why he needed his brothers. And then the tears came. He brought her down before him. He held on to her. She wrapped her arms around his neck and held him. He cried.

"It's okay, Carlo. It'll be okay," she said. She kissed the side of his face and embraced him. "I'm here. I'm not leaving you. I swear it."

Two Weeks Later –

Mirabella walked up to the doors of Villa Rosso. The work crews were at it today. Finally Giovanni okayed the reconstruction of the villa. She wasn't told all that happened in there while she was gone. Something had. Giovanni switched his meetings to his office inside Melanzana. The carpet had to be pulled up. The floors scrubbed, and walls repainted. Which meant she could do some remodeling of her own.

The closer she came to the doors of the villa the weaker she felt. She wiped at her brow and shuddered. The medication they gave her often helped. But some days she felt nauseous, fatigued, and on other days she had a fever. The doctors said it was something in her blood. But even they couldn't quite explain what. For Mirabella it was a constant burn beneath her skin that made her worry as much as her husband.

"Donna, you shouldn't be here," Dreco said when she tried to enter the door.

She smiled and stepped back. "Oh hello, Dreco. I only wanted to make sure the painters do as I told them."

"Yes, but the boss doesn't want anyone inside. Even you. It's strict orders," Dreco said. He pleaded with her with his eyes. She relented. She turned to leave when a man came out carrying a bin of trash. He miscalculated a step and dropped it. The contents scattered.

The men started arguing over whose fault it was. Mirabella glanced down at the rubbish. One thing in particular drew her eyes. She knelt and picked up a smashed VHS tape. The label that said, 'Play Me' was caved inward. Mirabella remembered the video recorder next to the bed. She remembered Kei saying he recorded something for her husband. She and Giovanni never spoke of it. Not ever. And somehow she managed to suppress a lot of her memories. It was funny how the human mind found ways to recover from trauma. And even more frightening was how something as simple as a VHS tape dragged it all up to the surface of a person's memory.

And then there was something else. Since her return from the hospital and all through her recovery, Giovanni hadn't once tried to make love to her. At first they were both concerned about her health, and the doctors' inability to explain what Kei had used on her. The next major worry was for Carlo, and getting the family to Sicilia after his release for Ciro's funeral. Excuse after excuse came for why they were not behaving as husband and wife. Mirabella stared at the tape and began to tremble with cold dread. Her eyes welled with tears.

"Donna? Are you okay?" Dreco asked.

"I-I'm fine." She wiped her tears. She walked off with the tape. She went inside. She heard the kids' laughter nearby. Lorenzo and Marietta had stayed behind in Sicilia. Dominic and Giovanni were in a closed-door meeting in his office. She climbed the stairs with no problem now that her ankle was healed. She went in her room and closed the door. Giovanni constantly checked on her, and would return upstairs to check in on her soon. She set the broken VHS tape down next to her and waited for her husband.

—*B*—

"THAT'S NOT GOOD ENOUGH!" Giovanni shouted.

"There is no trace of her, Giovanni. We've looked everywhere. She's vanished," Dominic said. "I don't know how, but she has."

"She hasn't fucking vanished. She's retreated. She had this planned all along. And she used the *Ndrangheta* to help. That's where we need to strike. Flush her out."

"You said we had to lay low," Dominic reminded him.

"That time has passed. I'm not going to wait for her to come after this family again. We'll take it back to the triangle."

"Giovanni, after the Calderone war we have been advised to not spill any more blood there. Let me keep working my contacts."

With a burdened sigh he closed his eyes. His business was suffering, and so was his family. All he could think of now was finding Isabella and making her pay.

"What are the doctors saying, Gio?" Dominic asked.

"That's she's fine, physically. They have her on this anti-viral medication for the next ninety days. She's nauseous sometimes and runs a fever. But I don't see anything else wrong with her."

"He mixed heroine in that shit he gave her for what purpose, Gio? Why was he trying to make her sick?"

"I don't know. I need to find Isabella. I need to know what was done to my wife!" he said.

"No. Gio, look at me," Dominic said.

Giovanni lifted his gaze. Dominic stepped forward. "That's not how we get back on track. What we do is what you've always done. Remember when the Russians shot Patri? Remember the chaos, the uncertainty? We have an enemy. She is no different than all of the other enemies we have. We need to get strong. We need to rebuild our defenses. You have us spread thin with the clan bosses. Trafficking. Taking business deals from the *Mafiosi*. We need to focus on what makes us strongest—family."

The advice was solid. Part of him knew Isabella wanted him to chase her shadow. He had to find a way to build his family again, and then draw her back out. And this time he would be ready.

"When Lorenzo returns from Sicilia we refocus."

"I have some ideas, Gio. You've tried it Lorenzo's way. You've tried it your way. Now it's time you let me help. Try it my way."

Giovanni smiled at his little brother. "Okay, Domi. We'll try it your way. But there is some unfinished business. I've had time to think on it. I want you to be the one to finish it."

Dominic nodded. "Ask and I'll do it."

Villa Mare Blue, The Lagoon —

Marietta swam under the clear blue waters. Below her the sand had a crystalized sparkle from the sunrays, and above the waters rippled as she swam to the surface. She emerged at the mouth of the cave. Lorenzo waited for her. He had taken off his speedos and lay on his back, nude. His body was beautifully tanned a dark olive brown from sailing.

"Hi!" Marietta said.

"Hello, beautiful," he said.

"Shae and Carlo will be back soon. I should start dinner," she smiled. "You need to cover up, sweetie."

"Not yet. Stay longer." Lorenzo groaned. He closed his eyes. Marietta pulled herself up out of the water. She picked up a towel and dried herself. This was supposed to be her second honeymoon. Lorenzo had been gone. She had him all to herself for two beautiful weeks since the funeral, and every night she contemplated the right time to share the news. And every night her courage failed her. Marietta dropped her towel. She looked down at her small belly. The yellow bikini put the swell on display. Lorenzo lifted on his elbow and turned on his side. He smiled at her.

"You're getting fat, Marie. I like it," he chuckled.

She should have been insulted, but the way he stared at her hips she couldn't help but laugh. She shook her head. She had worked out the perfect way to reveal her pregnancy tonight. On the beach after dinner, but she'd waited long enough. After talking to Mirabella earlier that day she decided it was best to just say it.

"Come here," he said staring now at her tits. They were tender. The most painful part of sex was the way he handled her breasts.

"Lo, there's something I need to tell you—" she began.

"Lorenzo! Marietta!" Shae called out to them. Marietta looked out toward the canal that led into the lagoon. Carlo and Shae sped toward them in a small white boat. Lorenzo grabbed a towel and covered himself before they got closer. Shae waved and smiled. Marietta smiled and put on her cover-up as well. Her friend was in a strawberry pink bikini. The girl had killer curves on display. When she waved, her large breasts bounced, and the diamond bracelets on her wrists sparkled in the sun.

"What time were you two thinking of coming in?" Shae asked when they coasted in closer.

"Another hour or so. We'll walk back," Marietta answered.

Carlo stared at Marietta. They barely spoke to each other now. And though she was happy for him she missed their friendly banter. Either way it didn't matter. Her and Carlo would never dance so close to disaster again.

"They have several grottos," Shae said. "Carlo showed them to me. It's so beautiful out here!"

"I know. See you soon!" Marietta waved. Lorenzo waved. Carlo turned the speedboat in the lagoon and sped them back out toward the sea. She glanced to her husband who stood and tossed his towel. He stroked his dick with that smile of his that she knew meant trouble.

"Do you still want to be a father?" she asked.

He stopped in mid-stroke. He frowned at her. Marietta shed her cover-up. Her bellybutton piercing was a bit protruded. She ran her hand over her tummy. It drew his eyes to her stomach. She walked over.

"See anything different about me?" she asked.

"What are you telling me, Marie?" he asked.

"I've been trying to think of a way to tell you. I'm pregnant, Lo," she said.

"You're pregnant?" he asked with wide-eyed wonder.

She nodded slowly. "I am, you jerk. So I'm not fat!" she laughed.

"You're pregnant!" he went to her and touched her belly. "We're going to have *bambini?*"

"No, a b*ambino* or a *bambina*, not *bambini,*" she frowned.

"Twins!" he exclaimed.

"Lo? No! It's one baby!"

He swept her up in his arms and she squealed in fright. She held on to him. He kissed her deeply. Marietta laughed and kissed him back. "A baby, a son, our first. We made one the night you came home from jail, and we swore to start over again. Our baby."

"Our baby!" he laughed. "I love you, Marie!"

"I love you so much, Lo! So much!" she giggled and hugged his neck.

THE DOOR OPENED. Mirabella looked up from the floor. Giovanni walked inside and paused. "What is it, Bella? Are you not feeling well?"

Mirabella swore she wouldn't cry. She swore it. But one look at him and the urge to break down in tears overwhelmed her. She almost couldn't find her voice. "We need to talk," she managed to say.

He closed the door. "Talk? What is it? A headache? Another fever?"

"No damn it! No!" she stood and the tears did fall. She pointed at the tape. Giovanni looked at it confused at first. He then recognized it.

"What was on the tape?" she asked.

"Where did you get that?" he answered.

"What was on it, Gio!" she shouted.

"A threat, Bella. Kei sent me a threat." Giovanni stepped toward her.

"You're lying to me. Why? Because you don't want to tell me that he sent you a tape of him raping me?" she asked.

Giovanni stopped. He froze and the word rape forged a wall of emotion between them. Mirabella put her hands to her hair. "We never talk about it. Never! But it doesn't mean it didn't happen. When you found me, that night I almost escaped."

"Bella, don't be upset, let's talk about it later. First you need to calm—"

"I WANT TO TALK ABOUT IT NOW!" she screamed at him. She shook with heartache. "Now, Gio. Now!"

"Okay, okay *cara,* now," he said. "If you want to talk let's talk."

"I almost escaped. His brother set a trap for me. A man was to help me get out on a boat. But he pulled a gun on me. Kei got there. He killed the man, he killed his brother." Mirabella paced. The old pain in her ankle that was supposed to be healed surfaced, and she slipped into the memory. She began to limp, submerged in fear and anxiety. "He hit me. He dragged me back inside. He said he was going to make me want him. He injected me with the same stuff he injected me with when he made that tape. I didn't know if he raped me. He said he didn't. But I didn't know! I didn't know! I didn't know!"

"Bella, please don't do this," Giovanni stepped closer. She stepped back.

"What did he send you, Gio? Tell me!" she broke down in tears.

"He had a message for me. The video then showed you in bed. He kissed you. And then the tape ended. I swear on the lives of our children there was no rape. Just him threatening us." He told her.

"And when you found me? Did he rape me? Was I naked? Do you think he did?" she asked.

"No. No, Bella. You were clothed. You were not naked. I got there before anything happened. I stopped him, sweetheart. He didn't. Please, sweetheart. Believe me. You're okay."

"You're lying!" she said trembling. "Aren't you?"

"Look at me, Bella. Listen to me. I saved you. He didn't do it. He'd already injected you, but we got there in time."

"Then why, Gio?" she asked through her tears.

"Why what, Bella?"

"Why is it you can't touch me? Why is it you don't even try to kiss me? If Kei didn't rape me why is it you don't look at me like you used to?" she cried. "Why?"

He walked over to her. He pulled her into his arms and held her. She hugged him and cried against his chest. She loved him so much. Nothing for her had changed. She loved and wanted her husband today as much as she did the day before Kei brought the nightmare into their life. But did he still want her?

He lifted her chin. "I was afraid to push you. You had been through so much. Do you think I'm so selfish I would do anything to hurt you?"

"Making love to me is never hurting me. I need to feel loved by you. It's our way. I want to be your wife again. Don't you miss me?"

He kissed her tears away. His mouth brushed her quivering lips as an answer. Mirabella was so scared. The kiss was sweet, but awkward. She felt it. Was it her or him? She ran her hands over his chest. Flashes of Kei touching her and forcing her into sloppy kisses seared her brain. But she fought against the nightmare. She had to. She wouldn't let him win. Her tongue slipped into Giovanni's mouth and she rose on her toes. She trembled when his hands glided down her back to cup her backside. He squeezed her. He pulled her shirt out of her jeans. And when she dared to touch his dick, she found his erection coiled thickly behind his zipper. Her touch affected him. His kiss became swift and hard, but she didn't mind. He ripped her shirt open and the buttons popped and fell off. Mirabella chuckled through her tears. He smiled at her when their lips parted. He snatched the shirt down off her arms.

And then he went for it. Mirabella's mouth stretched and she deepened their kiss. Together they went to the bed, clawing at each other's clothes, wanting to feel their naked bodies pressed against each other. Giovanni unbuttoned her jeans. He snatched them off her legs. She helped by kicking them off. He took his time removing her panties and uncovering her sex. She kept her pubic hair mowed to a landing strip just the way he liked. He removed what was left of his clothes and joined her. She parted her thighs, and Giovanni placed them both on his shoulders.

The lips of her vagina spread for him. He slid his tongue deep between the folds. He used his fingers to fondle her the way she craved. And like his woman, she responded to his touch. He licked her again, teased her, before he dove from her clit to her pussy hole for a taste of her salty cream. Mirabella arched up off the bed. She gasped as her thighs fell off his shoulder to drop and spread wide for him. He put a hand on her stomach to press down, because she gyrated up against his mouth at an increasing speed.

He sucked her clit once more, and inserted two fingers. Her bottom lifted off the mattress. The taste of her, smell of her, all of her was pure heaven to him. She came for him. He made sure she did so in his mouth before pulling himself up over her. She was right. He had held back, laid in bed at night with blue balls and a clenched gut to keep from holding her as he wanted to. But he owed her peace. He wanted her well. He'd prove to her that nothing and no one could ever change his feelings for her.

Giovanni palmed both cheeks of her ass before he eased inside of her. She drew her legs up and bent her knees to hook them around his waist. He pushed deep and came down on top of her. The feel of her hands on his back, and her soft thighs pressed against his sides, was all he needed. He thrust into her with slow mounting eagerness. Their breathing was evenly matched. All he felt was wet pussy drawing him deeper and deeper. Nearly mindless, he thrust into her with full throttle. He missed her. He needed her. He worshiped her. He thrust harder and faster until the pressure of not having his wife for close to two months exploded in his balls and he released. Long after coming he continued to stroke in and out of her pussy with his face buried in her neck.

Dazed and confused he needed several long minutes to recover. Mirabella clung to him. When he lifted his face he found her crying. But she wasn't in pain as he first suspected. She looked up at him. "Don't ever leave me, Gio. Ever. You're everything to me."

"I'll never let you go, Bella. They'll never get to you again," he promised.

SANTO TOSSED THE REMOTE to his television aside. He rubbed his eyes. Day after day it was the same bullshit. He would go crazy soon, he feared. He glanced to the door. For weeks the *polizia* questioned him. And the moment he was well enough to be moved they took him into protective custody. He hadn't given them shit. But the fucking inspector wanted *la Camorra* to think he did. It was a mind-fuck and Santo was the bait.

After weeks of isolation he was moved again, under guard, in a small villa in a remote are of Napoli. No matter what the police offered, he would not live or die with the scornful tag of *pentito* by testifying against his clan. Giovanni would never appreciate his final act of loyalty. But his silence guaranteed his sons and ex-wife would not be sacrificed.

He needed to stretch his legs. He stood and bent his back. He walked out to the front of the villa. Two officers were seated in front, one sat by the door in a sofa chair with an Uzi propped up to the left of him. The other stretched out on the sofa. They were on constant rotation. After midnight another two arrived.

Santo went to the kitchen and then the fridge. He reached in and found a beer. He glanced to the television show and then looked away. Shaking his head he walked back inside the room and slammed the door. He sat on the edge of his bed. His gaze was fixed outside of the window. What man waited for death? He couldn't last much longer.

After a deep swallow Santo stood and walked over to the window. For the first time in days he saw a vehicle other than the one owned by the officers. It was parked on the street. He stared at the empty car and a plan began to form. He stared at it and waited to see if someone would come for it.

"I don't understand, Domi? Why don't we just go inside and kill him?" Umberto asked.

Dominic sat in the car with the young enforcer. He tapped his fingers on the side of the windowsill. He waited. "We don't go in because those two officers will have to be put down to get to him. And Giovanni wants this done clean. No attention can be cast toward our family now."

"And the car? Why leave the car sitting there?"

Dominic sighed. Must he explain everything? He glanced to Umberto who looked at him, eager to understand and learn. The men who worked for them were getting younger and younger. Dominic wasn't sure if that was such a good thing.

"Santo has been to prison twice. I was wrong about his loyalties to Gio. But I was right about his not wanting to be a *pentito*. He could have easily given us up by now. He hasn't. He's a prisoner again. What does a prisoner want more than anything?" Dominci asked.

"To escape?" Umberto asked.

"To escape. Bravo. We give him a chance to run, and Santo will run. When he does we will be there."

"So we wait?"

Dominic lowered his seat. He set this gun in his lap. Giovanni wanted his loyalty and a show of strength. Lorenzo said he didn't have the stomach for this work. Most times when a hit was pulled off, Dominic was summoned to be the cooler head, not the executioner. Franco was the first man he'd ever killed. He'd prove to his brothers how far he'd go to protect the family. And then find a way to dig them out of the drug trafficking shit they'd dragged their family into.

Palermo, Sicilia –

Ignazio accepted the package. He nodded to his man and started down the hall. It only had Armando's first name on it, and was delivered by a courier. He strolled down the hall to his boss's office. He knocked. Armando was on the phone. He signaled for him to come inside. He took a seat and waited. Armando ended his call. "What do you need?"

"Something came for you. Delivered by a hand courier." Ignazio tossed the package on the desk. Armando looked at it and frowned.

"You're my mailman now?" he asked.

"I need to talk to you. The boys are wondering when we plan to extend our business? Since we are now friends with *la Camorra*," Ignazio asked. "They are moving volume through the *Campania*. We should be in on this, Armando."

"So you think you know what's best for my business?"

"No. I think Giovanni owes *la cosa nostra* his gratitude. We should only remind him." Ignazio gave a sly smile.

"Leave me," Armando answered.

Ignazio stood and walked out. Armando reclined in his chair. He had not spoken to Giovanni since seeing him at the dinner after the boxer's funeral. He planned to give it time before reaching out. Of course he wanted his father's legacy under his control. And with Giovanni distracted he could have picked at the bones of his weakened men. Taken the spoils. Convinced him to sign over the inheritance. Be rid of Lorenzo's constant meddling into his affairs.

Armando glanced to the picture of his father in the silver frame on his desk. He made a tent of his fingers and stared into his Papa's dark eyes. The Mancinis were never rash. His father constantly beat into him the value of patience over his enemies and his friends. Armando would have his legacy restored. There, however, was a new prize he wanted. His gaze swiveled to the phone. He thought of Catalina in her tight black mini dress and high heels. She was fucking beautiful, the way the wind caressed her long brown hair, and the sun seemed to radiate off of her skin. She kept looking over at him. She thought he didn't notice. And when he caught her staring, he could sense her curiosity even though it was covered behind the dark lenses of his sunglasses. He smiled. He reached for the phone. Maybe he should call her and check in.

Armando lowered his hand. It would be foolish to push too hard on princess. Her uncles and brother, who she intended to marry, would not let him close. Not yet. Time. What was needed was a little more time.

He glanced to the envelope and picked it up. It felt hard. He frowned. He unsealed it and reached inside. A cassette recorder dropped out. Armando found that interesting. There was no note. He picked up the little cassette player. Laughter started the conversation. It sounded like two men. He listened and heard Lorenzo Battaglia and the Calderone runt talking. Armando reclined in his chair and soon understood the nature of the conversation. A deal was being made for the life of Tomosino Battaglia.

Napoli Italy –

Santo sat up in bed. He checked his watch. If he waited until after midnight his plan would be too risky. Still he had no idea how long the car would remain parked on the road. His watch said it was closer to ten. He turned on the bed and went to the window. The car he'd been watching from his window hadn't moved. He stared at it. Santo walked out of the room and to the kitchen. Both of the officers were there, but one was sleep and the other staring blankly at the television set. He got a beer from the fridge.

"Turning in for the night," he mumbled to the officer through his wired jaw.

The man didn't bother to look up at him. He walked back into the room and closed the door. He locked it. Santo set the beer aside and went to the dresser. He got his wallet and cigarettes. He then made his escape through the window. It wasn't the biggest of windows but he could get through. He dropped to his feet. He dusted his hands. There was no one on the street. The windows on the villa across from them were dark. The night was silent. He didn't run or try to look suspicious. He walked to the car and tried the door. He half expected to find it locked. To his surprise the door was open. He eased inside and closed the door softly. The plan was to head south to Portici. He'd catch a ferry out of Italy and try to reach Sicilia. He had cousins that could help him escape to Spain. Santo popped out the steering column panel and wired the car. The ignition started. He threw the car into gear and sped out on to the street.

The speed limit was ignored. At any moment the officer could check on him and all of the police officials in the *Campania* would swoop down on him. He dropped the visor and looked at his face. The scaring was severe. The wiring to his jaw and mouth connected and hooked around his ear. He looked like a monster. There was little hope he'd blend in.

Santo took the back roads. He drove out of the city and toward the rural area. He considered finding another car and leaving this one behind. But he was in Tacchi territory. He wouldn't risk it. When he turned off the next road he drove up to a traffic light. Santo reached for a cigarette. He lit it while he waited for the light to change. A car pulled up on his driver's side. He glanced over with the cigarette hanging from his lips. It only took a second for him to recognize the man behind the gun. Dominic pulled the trigger. Santo was dead before the light changed.

—B—

MIRABELLA TURNED OVER TO HER SIDE. She stared at her beloved husband. The sheets covered them, but his chest and arms were not. He was so handsome when he slept. He faced her, and lay on his side. She touched his face. When she did his eyes opened. "Sorry. I didn't mean to wake you," she said. She lied. She wanted to wake him. And be with him. Make love to him.

"Are you okay?" he asked.

She nodded. "Guess what?"

"Dica?" he answered.

"We're going to have another baby in the family," she smiled.

Giovanni's brows lowered with concern. She chuckled. "Not me. My sister. She should be telling Lorenzo tonight. He's going to be a father."

"That'll make my cousin very happy," Giovanni touched her hair. He traced his finger over her cheek. "Hopefully it will be a boy. The twins would love a cousin to play with."

"Or a girl, for Eve. She's so lonely sometimes," Mirabella smiled. "And we have a wedding in a month. Two! Kyra and Renaldo, Dominic and Catalina. So much to do. I'm excited," she smiled.

"Me too, Bella," he said.

She kissed him. "I learned a lot about myself, Gio. There are so many things I want to tell you. About my past."

"Whenever you're ready, Bella. Right now just let me love you," he said.

She came closer. She eased her arm around his waist. She pressed her face to his chest. "Yes. Love me, Gio. From now until forever."

"Always."

The End.

ABOUT SIENNA MYNX

Sienna Mynx was born in the beautiful city of Miami, Florida in 1971. The oldest of two children with a schoolteacher for a mother, she was taught the power of words and found countless adventures between the pages of a book. While other children her age shared an interest in music, sports, or even Girl Scouts, Sienna's interests never varied. Reading was her passion.

By the age of 13, she created a private collection of drawings and short stories based on heroines she could identify with, but who lived in imaginative worlds far removed from her suburban upbringing. She'd share them with anyone who cared to read.

Later she adapted to the changes in her life by journaling and continue to explore her writing. Entering the indie-publishing field in 2010 she has now published over 40 novels under two pennames. Sienna is employed as an IT Professional for a technology company and enjoys traveling, journaling, and the arts.

Social Media Links

Instagram

https://www.instagram.com/sienna_mynx

Website

https://thedivaspen.com/

Facebook Group

Sienna Mynx Lounge

https://www.facebook.com/groups/425298174168156

Facebook Fanpage:

Sienna Mynx Fan Hub

https://www.facebook.com/Sienna-Mynx-Fan-Hub-118212961533763

Twitter

https://twitter.com/SiennaMynx